The Deerslayer
or, The First War-Path

The Writings of
James Fenimore Cooper

JAMES FRANKLIN BEARD, Editor-in-Chief

JAMES P. ELLIOTT, Chief Textual Editor

LANCE SCHACHTERLE, Textual Editor

Sponsors

Series Sponsors

CLARK UNIVERSITY

AMERICAN ANTIQUARIAN SOCIETY

Volume Sponsors

CLARK UNIVERSITY

WORCESTER POLYTECHNIC INSTITUTE

NORTH CAROLINA STATE UNIVERSITY, RALEIGH

Editorial Board

JAMES FRANKLIN BEARD, Chairman

JAMES P. ELLIOTT

KAY SEYMOUR HOUSE

THOMAS L. PHILBRICK

DONALD A. RINGE

WARREN S. WALKER

Advisory Committee

ROBERT E. SPILLER, Chairman

CLIFTON WALLER BARRETT

LEONARD BERRY

HENRY S. F. COOPER, JR.

WILLIAM EASTMAN

MARCUS MC CORISON

The Deerslayer

or, The First War-Path

James Fenimore Cooper

Historical Introduction and Explanatory Notes

by James Franklin Beard

Text Established by Lance Schachterle,

Kent Ljungquist and James Kilby

— — —"What Terrors round him wait!
Amazement in his van, with Flight combined
And Sorrow's faded form, and Solitude behind."

Thomas Gray, *The Bard*, 11.60–62

State University of New York Press   Albany

The preparation of this volume was made possible (in part) by a grant from the Program for Editions of the National Endowment for the Humanities, an independent Federal Agency.

CENTER FOR
SCHOLARLY EDITIONS
AN APPROVED EDITION
MODERN LANGUAGE
ASSOCIATION OF AMERICA

The Center emblem means that one of a panel of textual experts serving the Center has reviewed the text and textual apparatus of the printer's copy by thorough and scrupulous sampling, and has approved them for sound and consistent editorial principles employed and maximum accuracy attained. The accuracy of the text has been guarded by careful and repeated proofreading according to standards set by the Center.

Published by
State University of New York Press, Albany

For information, address State University of New York Press, State University Plaza, Albany N.Y., 12246

Library of Congress Cataloging in Publication Data

Cooper, James Fenimore, 1789-1851.
The deerslayer, or, The first war-path.

(The writings of James Fenimore Cooper)
1. Delaware Indians--Fiction.   2. Iroquois Indians--Fiction.   3. United States--History--French and Indian War, 1755-1763--Fiction.   I. Beard, James Franklin, 1919-   II. Title.   III. Title: First war-path.
IV. Series: Cooper, James Fenimore, 1789-1851.   Works. 1980.
PS1406.A1   1987   813'.3   87-9928
ISBN 0-87395-361-4
ISBN 0-87395-790-3 (pbk.)

Contents

Acknowledgments

Like other volumes in the Cooper Edition, *The Deerslayer* is the product of the sustaining, collaborative efforts of many scholars, friends, students, and cooperating institutions. The editors are pleased to acknowledge here their appreciation of the support of the two sponsoring institutions, Clark University and the American Antiquarian Society; the volume sponsors, Clark University, Worcester Polytechnic Institute, and the North Carolina State University at Raleigh. We are grateful also for the continuing support of the Division of Research Programs of The National Endowment for the Humanities, which has made this book and this series possible. Additionally, the Editorial Board wishes to express its appreciation of the interest and encouragement of members of the Cooper family, especially the late Paul Fenimore Cooper and the late Dr. Henry S.F. Cooper and their sons Paul, Jr., and Henry, Jr.

Among the librarians who have graciously provided access to space and materials needed to establish the present text, the editors wish to extend thanks to all those at their own institutions; to Herbert Cahoon and Evelyn Semler of the Pierpont Morgan Library, who granted permission for our use of the manuscript; to Donald Gallup, formerly Curator of the Collection of American Literature at Yale's Beinecke Rare Book and Manuscript Library, and his successor, David Schoonover, who graciously assisted with Cooper materials at Yale; to Marcus McCorison, Frederic Bauer, and Nancy Burkett of the American Antiquarian Society, who made its superb collection of early Cooper editions available; to Roger E. Stoddard of the Houghton Library at Harvard; to Julius P. Barclay and Gloria M. Parks at Stanford; to Matt P. Lowman and J.S. Aubrey at the Newberry Library; to Clayton E. Rhodes, at the Enoch Pratt Free Library; to Frederick L. Arnold at Princeton; to Charles R. Andrews at Case Western Reserve University; to Helen W. Azhderian at the University of Southern California; to Lawrence E. Wikander at Williams College; to Leslie S. Clarke at the University of California, Berkeley; to John P. Harthan at the Victoria and Albert Museum; to Alan M. Cohn and Harold J. Rath at Southern Illinois University, Carbondale; to William Matheson, II, and Laura Kuelthau at Washington University; and to Frank Paluka, Keith A. Rageth, Richard M. Kolber, and Ann Ford at the University of Iowa.

The Editorial Board wishes to register its special appreciation to Dr. Kilby whose pioneering work on the text of *The Deerslayer* began long ago at the University of Iowa and was continued during the early stages of the study of the text at North Carolina State University at Raleigh, in part with assistance from the Faculty Research and Professional Development Fund at that institution. Dr. Kilby wishes, in turn, to thank Professor O.M. Brack, Jr., formerly Director of the Center of Textual Studies of the University of Iowa, for his advice and assistance in the early stages of the work. In short, Dr. Kilby established a firm bibliographical foundation for the edition before turning it over to Professors Schachterle and Ljungquist.

Working with the manuscript and materials supplied by Dr. Kilby, Professors Schachterle and Ljunquist edited the text, prepared the commentary and notes on the text, and established the textual apparatus. They also coordinated the successive phases of the proofreading. For help at various stages of their work, they wish to thank Joan Landry, Elizabeth Mendez, Patricia Bray, Harriet Zengos, and Helen Zengos. Carol Carofoli, Margaret Brodmerkle, and Pauline Vasil provided clerical assistance at Worcester Polytechnic Institute.

Though it is not possible to name here every individual who has had a part in the making of this book, some very special additional services and courtesies must be acknowledged:

The editors are grateful to the firm of Lea and Febiger in Philadelphia for providing a photocopy of the contract for the initial publication of *The Deerslayer* and for information about its initial printing and publication.

They are also grateful to Ms. Kathleen D. Stocking, Assistant Registrar at the New York State Historical Association, Cooperstown, for her kindness in supplying illustrations from the Association's collections of photographic negatives.

They also want to thank Ms. Lori Sklut of the Clark University Cartographic Laboratory for preparing the map of Lake Otsego, locating sites of familiar scenes in the romance.

And Mr. Scott H. Smith of West Georgia College, Carrollton, for sharing his researches on British reviews of Cooper's *The Deerslayer*.

And to the Committee on Scholarly Editions of the Modern Language Association and to Professor Douglas Emory Wilson, who performed the inspection of this volume, the Editorial Board expresses gratitude for a thorough, courteous and expeditious investigation of the text.

And, finally, since our list of contributors would be almost interminable, if it were not regrettably incomplete, we wish to thank each and every student, librarian, and colleague who has assisted along the way. They will, we hope, find some reward in the completion of the book.

Illustrations

Of all Cooper's romances, not excluding *The Pioneers, The Deerslayer* is most closely associated with the landscape and folklore of the Otsego Country. Place-names invented for purposes of the fiction have found their way into geodetic maps of the region and been accepted into the vocabulary of every resident. Boats on Lake Otsego still derive their names with fair regularity from *The Deerslayer* or others of the Leatherstocking Tales. While the physical outline of the lake and surrounding terrain has, fortunately, retained most of its original charm, inevitable change has eroded much of the fresh, rugged quality that intrigued Cooper as a boy and as an author. Fortunately, files of photographic negatives carefully preserved by the New York State Historical Association, particularly the late nineteen- and early twentieth-century plate glass negatives of the Smith-Telfer Collection, contain views of the lake and terrain which can help the reader visualize the scenes as Cooper saw and remembered them. It has seemed appropriate, therefore, to draw many of the illustrations for *The Deerslayer* (with the kind assistance of Ms. Kathleen D. Stocking and through the courtesy of the New York Historical Association) from these remarkable files. Other illustrations have been selected for their pertinence to the text or context. A scale map of Lake Otsego, with a Guide to sites important in the action, appears on pp. 18–19.

following page 63

PLATE I.　　　　Shadow Brook, near the point at which Deerslayer and Harry emerge from the "tangled labyrinth of a small swamp" in Chapter I. Courtesy of the New York State Historical Association.

PLATE II.   Hutter's "castle," as depicted on the title page of an 1842 French translation of *The Deerslayer*. Courtesy of the Library of Congress.

PLATE III.   The Susquehanna River near its source, where Deerslayer and Harry March find Hutter's Ark in Chapter II. Photograph courtesy of the New York State Historical Association.

PLATE IV.   "Northumberland on the Susquehanna." Steel engraving made from a drawing by the British illustrator William H. Bartlett, showing boats called "arks" of the kind Cooper evidently had in mind as models for Hutter's "Ark," reproduced here from N.P. Willis, *American Scenery: or, Land, Lake, and River: Illustrations of Transatlantic Nature* (London: George Virtue, 1840) II, opposite p. 62, and (New York: R. Martin & Co., 1840) opposite p. 248. Courtesy of the American Antiquarian Society.

following page 125

PLATE V.   Gravelly Point. Photograph of the presumed site of Deerslayer's first mortal combat, in which he kills the Indian called Lynx. Courtesy of New York State Historical Association.

PLATE VI.   "Death of the Indian." Engraving by B.J. Newman from a drawing by James Hamilton. Susan Fenimore Cooper, *Pages and Pictures* (New York: W.A. Townsend and Co., 1861), opposite page 322.

PLATE VII.   Death of the Red Man. Frontispiece engraving by James Smillie from a drawing by F.O.C. Darley, from the 1859–1861 Townsend-Darley edition of Cooper's fiction.

PLATE VIII.   Untitled watercolor adaptation of the preceding engraving, by R.W. Van

Boskieck, New York, 1879, as a mounting for a note from Cooper to Ned Myers, 3 April 1843. Courtesy of Paul Fenimore Cooper, Jr., Cooperstown.

HISTORICAL
INTRODUCTION

Historical Introduction

I

Unlike Henry James, whose explorations of motive and consciousness he anticipated in *The Deerslayer*, James Fenimore Cooper professed little interest in self-conscious literary criticism. "I question if there is a living writer who cares less for criticism than myself," he wrote to a curious inquirer in 1841. "I never had a thirst for criticism, but some twenty or thirty books have so hardened me, that I have some such dread of it, now, as certain individuals have of insolvency."[1] Cooper referred, of course, to criticism as he had known it, criticism founded more on popular taste than on principle, chiefly newspaper and periodical reviewing — parochial, biased, and impressionistic. Once discovered for literature, his own creativity abounded; and he preferred to be guided entirely by his own creative instincts, erratic as they sometimes were. He seldom confided in publishers while a work was in progress; and he could be reticent or evasive to the point of secretiveness about his intentions, sources, or literary practices. The more pointed the intrusion, the greater — in general — his reluctance to speak. In many if not most instances, the genesis of his works can be traced only through accidental, broken or inferential strands of evidence. Thus, though *The Deerslayer* is probably the book most deeply rooted in his total experience as man and artist, it has seemed to critics the most equivocal, elusive, and enigmatic. Available evidence suggests that it represents a convergence of several quite disparate levels of that experience, some of which Cooper and his daughter Susan — his chief interpreter after his death — preferred to pass over silently.

According to Susan Fenimore Cooper, the inspiration for the book came spontaneously one pleasant summer afternoon in 1840, as she and her father returned to Otsego Hall from his Chalet farm on the eastern slopes of Lake Otsego. They had stopped their cart about a mile and a half from the village of Cooperstown to give their pony a drink:

> Mr. Cooper was singing to himself, as he often did on that quiet woodland road, — it was generally some snatch of a song popular in his youth; — upon the afternoon in question it chanced to be an election song of the party with which he did *not* vote. Suddenly we came out of the wood, and a view of the lake opened before us, a familiar view, but more lovely than usual in the soft lights and shadows of that summer evening. There was a pause in the song. The pony indulged himself with a walk. The author's face was turned towards the lake, and the far-seeing look of inventive genius came into the clear gray eye. He was lost in thought for a moment, — figures and scenes foreign to the day and hour seemed to rise before him. Soon the vision passed away. Turning to his daughter with a smile he exclaimed, "I must write one more book, dearie, about our little lake!" Then the song was resumed, the whip cracked, the pony trotted on, and we went our way toward the village.[2]

The reader is led to infer that the "vision" recalled Cooper's boyhood experiences on and about the lake and expressed his profound, lifelong attachment to it and to the river, forests, and mountains of the Otsego Country.

Biographical information from these early years is regrettably scanty, but there can be no doubt that they were crucial to the germination of *The Deerslayer.* Placed as an infant in the midst of a magnificently picturesque country — in many respects analogous to Wordsworth's Cumberland and Westmorland — and given full freedom as a lad to roam and explore at his own pleasure, Cooper delighted, we know, in much the same activities that had engaged the older British poet — hiking, climbing, hunting, boating, and skating — cultivating his sensory faculties to the fullest extent and peopling his "mind with beauteous forms or grand."[3] Could he have read *The Prelude,* he would surely have found close parallels to his own experience. We know the strength of this boyhood attachment to Otsego partly from the threat of its loss. In a letter to the New Jersey historian Isaac Mickle, written from Cooperstown in 1844, the novelist tells how his father Judge William Cooper, elected in 1798 to his second term in the United States House of Representatives, established his wife and younger children in Burlington, New Jersey, while attending to his elective responsibilities in nearby Philadelphia:

> My mother was a Jersey-woman, and strongly attached to her native State. In 1798 her reluctance to return to this place was so strong that my father actually purchased a house in Burlington, with the intention of leaving my mother in it; but so great was the grief of my brother [William] and myself at the idea of giving up our lake and haunts at this place, that she abandoned her own wishes to ours, and consented to return. I am inclined to think that my father, whose interests in New York were very large, was afraid to go through the same risks again, for we returned to Burlington no more.[4]

While Mrs. Cooper and her younger children were in Burlington, their sister Hannah reported to her brother Isaac in Albany, "the Boys are well, Jim has grown almost as large as William . . . they are very wild and show plainly they have been bred in the Woods, they go to school and are learning Latin."[5]

Eight years — and even twenty-five years — later, James' attachment to the Otsego Country was undiminished, as he proclaimed in a little-known autobiographical sketch "The Eclipse," written in Paris in 1831. His only extended nonfictional account of a youthful experience in Otsego, it is an invaluable testament of affection, an illustration of his powers of sustained sensory recall, and a demonstration of his concept of Nature as cosmic process, encompassing moral and metaphysical as well as natural phenomena. The time was Monday, 16 June 1806; the occasion a total eclipse of the sun witnessed at mid-day while the sixteen-year-old Cooper, recently turned sailor, visited his family in Cooperstown. The narrative builds steadily and surely with a wealth of incremental detail, beginning with a casual early morning glance from the sailor's window:

> For a moment, my eye rested on the familiar view — the lim-
> pid lake, with its setting of luxuriant woods and farms, its
> graceful bay and varied points, the hills where every cliff and
> cave and glen had been trodden a thousand times by my
> boyish feet — all this was dear to me as the face of a
> friend. . . . There was one object in the landscape which a
> stranger would probably have overlooked, or might perhaps
> have called unsightly, but it was familiar to every eye in the
> village, and endowed by our people with the honors of an
> ancient landmark — the tall gray trunk of a dead and branch-
> less pine, which had been standing on the crest of the
> eastern hill, at the time of the foundation of the village, and
> which was still erect, though rocked since then by a thou-
> sand storms. To my childish fancy, it had seemed an
> imaginary flagstaff, or, in rustic parlance, the "liberty pole"
> of some former generation; but now, as I traced the familiar
> line of the tall trunk, in its peculiar shade of silvery gray, it
> became to the eye of the young sailor the mast of some
> phantom ship. I remember greeting it with a smile, as this
> was the first glance of recognition given to the old ruin of the
> forest since my return.[6]

Before the brightly illumined lake, hills, and buildings "of the little town" are "swallowed up in the darkness" of the eclipse,[7] the young sailor is taken by an acquaintance to the courthouse to gaze at an altogether different spectacle, the anguished countenance of a condemned murderer, tempo-rarily reprieved from execution, repentant, terrified, clinging to life. "I can see him now," Cooper wrote, twenty-five years after the event:

> standing at the window, pallid and emaciated by a year's
> confinement, stricken with grief, his cheeks furrowed with
> constant weeping, his whole frame attesting the deep and
> ravaging influences of conscious guilt and remorse. Here was
> a man drawn from the depths of human misery, to be im-
> mediately confronted with the grandest natural exhibition in
> which the Creator deigns to reveal his Omnipotence to our
> race. . . . He stood immovable as a statue, with uplifted and

manacled arms and clasped hands, the very image of impotent slavery and wretchedness.[8]

Restored shortly to his friends and family in the open air,
the narrator proceeds to the grander display, sketching and
interweaving at each stage in the progress of the eclipse the
changes observable in the watchers, their surroundings, and
the heavens. As the occultation begins, one of his brothers
shouts:

"The moon!" Quicker than thought, my eye turned eastward
again, and there floated the moon, distinctly apparent, to a
degree that was almost fearful. The spherical form, the
character, the dignity, the substance of the planet, were
clearly revealed as I have never beheld them before, or
since. It looked grand, dark, majestic, and mighty, as it thus
proved its power to rob us entirely of the sun's rays. We are
all but larger children. In daily life we judge of objects by
their outward aspect. We are accustomed to think of the sun,
and also of the moon, as sources of light, as ethereal, almost
spiritual, in their essence. But the positive material nature of
the moon was now revealed to our senses, with a force of
conviction, a clearness of perception, that changed all our
usual ideas in connection with the planet. This was no interposition of vapor, no deceptive play of shadow; but a vast
mass of obvious matter had interposed between the sun
above us and the earth on which we stood.[9]

Yet the climactic moment is not, as one might have
assumed, the three minutes of "all but absolute" darkness with
their sensation of "humiliation and awe," but the experience of
returning light:

It was not in the least like the gradual dawning of day, or
the actual rising of the sun. There was no gradation in the
change. It was sudden, amazing, like what the imagination
would teach us to expect of the advent of a heavenly vision.
I know that philosophically I am wrong; but to me, it
seemed that the rays might actually be seen flowing through
the darkness in torrents, till they had again illuminated the
forest, the mountain, the valley, and the lake with their
glowing, genial touch.[10]

Brief though it is — a random glance into an irrevocable album of youthful memories — "The Eclipse" defines special qualities of Cooper's imagination: the intensity of his lifelong absorption in a particular set of landscapes, his retentive capacity, and his ability to endow facets of the human situation with cosmic or mythopoetic dimension. Other witnesses of the same solar eclipse, Cooper noted, had *not* been "freely communicative" about their "individual feelings at the most solemn moment . . . . as if sensations were aroused too closely connected with the constitution of the spirit to be irreverently and familiarly discussed."[11] Yet in *his* sketch it is precisely *these* sensations the novelist seeks to capture and communicate. Much has been written, deservedly, about his use of the pictorial mode, too little about his incursions into the symbolic. For when sensory images engage the imagination with heightened, unexpected or inexplicable complexity, a frequent occurrence in *The Deerslayer*, the images translate as symbols, and the language registers a degree of specificity and resonance transcending overt description.

Cooper's own account of the origin of *The Deerslayer* in the Preface to the first edition asserts that the favorable reception of the four earlier books of the Leatherstocking series had

> created, in the mind of the author, at least, a sort of necessity
> for giving some account of the [hero's] younger days. In
> short, the pictures of his life, such as they are, were already
> so complete as to excite some little desire to see the "study,"
> from which they have all been drawn. (1840 Preface)*

The work Cooper proposed to himself at the outset would seem, then, to have been retrospective and nostalgic, the projection of an "essential" Natty Bumppo, a distillation of his salient qualities as they had presented themselves in his earlier incarnations — the Leatherstocking in *The Pioneers* (1823), Hawkeye in *The Last of the Mohicans* (1826), the Trapper in *The Prairie* (1827), and the Scout in *The Pathfinder* (1840). More specifically, he apparently intended to locate those distinctive qualities of mind and character at the critical moments of their

---

*Cross-references within the present edition are placed in parentheses.

early expression and with particular reference to *The Last of the Mohicans*, hitherto the earliest chapter in Natty's fictional biography.

Undoubtedly, the prospect held a double fascination for Cooper—the pleasures of reunion and rejuvenation. In the four earlier romances, his imaginative identification with Natty had become so close that the character was almost an alter ego. They spoke, at times, with a single voice. "Now my longing is for a wilderness—" Cooper wrote his nephew Richard from Paris on 25 May 1831, "Cooperstown is far too populous and artificial for me and it is my intention to plunge somewhere into the forest, for six months in the year, at my return."[12] In *The Prairie*, written five years earlier, the eighty-year-old Trapper mused over his long career in a manner that seems actually to anticipate *The Deerslayer*: " . . . if it was given me to choose my time and place again—as such things are not and ought not ever to be given to the will of man—though, if such a gift was to be given me, I would say, twenty and the wilderness!"[13] *Wilderness*, as Cooper and Natty employ the word here, does not, of course, connote license or lawlessness.* Rather, it presupposes a condition of untrammeled Nature, exemplifying the workings of the "laws of Nature and of Nature's God," universal laws, operative and observable in the heavens, on the ocean, or in the forests—evident also, less visibly but no less inexorably—in the governance of man, society, and human institutions. Insofar as they might be said to "regulate" human behavior, these "laws" (implicit in the inherited wisdom of the past) were presumably embodied in the "Higher Law" or "Natural Law," institutionalized in the Constitution of 1787 and its later Bill of Rights. Thus, though Natty is illiterate, unable to read the Bible, he is perfectly literate in its cultural counterpart, the all-important "Book of Nature." In recognition of this special form of literacy, Cooper causes one of the characters in *Home as Found* (1838) to recall Natty in his old haunts and to pair the old woodsman in unlikely combination with George Washington (and other Founding Fathers) as one of "the two only really great men of my time."[14]

---

*This is not to say that Cooper does not recognize and make significant use of obverse connotations of the word in *The Deerslayer*.

In presenting Natty of *The Deerslayer* as the "study" from which his earlier portraits had derived, Cooper was implying that the essential components of his hero's identity were moral; for in each of the earlier portrayals, as in this one, he is recognizably himself though he is sharply differentiated by age, thematic function, historical circumstances, and local detail. But if Natty appears in *The Deerslayer* in a setting redolent of the scenic splendors of the author's own youth—reflecting (by implication) his own early moral and political indoctrination—his situation in the novel also expresses, obliquely, Cooper's preoccupations at the time the book was written. It is not at all irrelevant, for example, that the setting most often evoked in the book, especially for scenes of violence, is the small projection on the western shore of the lake called by Cooper's time Myrtle Grove or Three Mile Point. Indeed, if the book is to be understood, as some critics have suggested, as Cooper's recension of a "myth of America" and Natty as a "mirror of the American conscience," it is to this moral and ethical dimension of its concern that one must turn.

During the 1830s Cooper had dedicated himself almost exclusively to his self-appointed mission of spurring the development of a distinctively American culture, society, and polity, fully enlightened and responsible, following a model he inherited from the generation of the Founders and refined through his own experience, observation, and associations at home and abroad. These efforts included publications of a remarkably varied and experimental kind: historical fiction set in Europe, with social and political implications (*The Bravo, The Heidenmauer,* and *The Headsman*); five European travel books, with elaborate cultural comparisons (the *Gleanings in Europe* series); a Swiftian political satire (*The Monikins*); letters to newspapers on various subjects, signed and unsigned; the first comprehensive *History of the Navy of the United States*; a text-book on American democracy (*The American Democrat*); and two novels of manners, with nautical, metropolitan, and provincial settings (*Homeward Bound* and *Home as Found*). Despite the energy and often brilliance displayed in these efforts, general readers—most of whom wanted merely to be entertained—were inclined to be unreceptive, petulant, and not infrequently dour. Reviewers were disposed to complain, and publishers were uniformly unhappy at the precipitous decline in sales.

The climax of Cooper's long estrangement from his public followed publication of *Home as Found* (1838), a novel in which he made the near-fatal miscalculation of borrowing circumstances (only superficially disguised) from a temporary but unpleasant squabble between himself and some Cooperstown residents over the use and ownership of Three Mile Point. In the three chapters concerned with this dispute, Cooper intended to illustrate the tendency of provincial Americans to be so saturated with liberty, that they become insensible to the finer feelings. In the book — as in real life — a group of villagers so long accustomed to using the Point as a place of public resort that they regard it as their own, damage the property and then resent fiercely the owner's (Cooper was merely the trustee) publishing a "No Trespass" notice. They hold a public protest meeting, pass resolutions denouncing the publisher of the notice, and even contest the ownership of the property. Almost as soon as Cooper grasped the tenor of local reaction, he published two extended letters in the Cooperstown *Freeman's Journal* explaining his action in detail.[15] Local resentment quickly subsided. Certain local editors chose to disregard the explanation, however, and published accounts subsequently determined to be libelous. Cooper demanded retractions and, after receiving defiant refusals, decided to sue. Before these cases could be tried, he wrote and published *Home as Found* which, with its caricature of the irresponsible newspaper editor Steadfast Dodge, so affronted journalistic pride that libelous attacks, now in the guise of reviews of *Home as Found*, were soon rampant in the Whig papers of New York State. Confident in their numbers and secure in their supposed immunity from prosecution, the editors now attacked the novelist in the press with extravagant ferocity, unsparing in their ridicule, utterly regardless of facts, and quite unmindful of their own public responsibilities.

Cooper was astonished and dismayed to find his satiric observations in *Home as Found* (directed against no specific editor) so overwhelmingly corroborated and so fully and promptly redounding upon himself. Nevertheless, with a sangfroid that seldom deserted him, he accepted the challenge and by 1841 had filed suits for libel against editors of New York State's most prominent Whig newspapers: James Watson Webb, William Leete Stone, Thurlow Weed, Park Benjamin, and Horace Greeley. His almost unqualified success in his first round of suits marked another turn of the screw, however; for the intensity of editorial violence escalated as the defendants found themselves obliged to report—and excuse—their own courtroom defeats. The press pleaded persecution, and Cooper was now charged with inhumanity. One editor complained that the novelist was "as destitute of the common feelings of humanity as the reddest of one of his own Indians," and another that when his counsel "appealed to Mr. Cooper's humanity . . .he might as well have appealed to the reddest of the Great Novelist's Indians, when the war-paint was on him, and the scalps of the palefaces hung reeking at his belt."[16] Both parties were losers in this Press War. Though Cooper won almost all his cases, the cost in time, trouble, and public relations was excessively heavy; and the editors discovered what they should have known already, that their freedom of expression was not absolute.

While the novelist and his daughter were careful—by their silence—to dissociate *The Deerslayer* from the Press War, Cooper and his lawyers were preparing confidently for the second round of confrontations as he wrote; and we may be reasonably certain that the rhetorical violence of the editors was echoed silently in the physical violence of the book. In her 1876 Introduction to *The Deerslayer*, Miss Cooper emphasized her father's strong emotional attachment to Three Mile Point, dwelling at length on his pleasure at presiding regularly at chowder parties on the spot. She described touchingly how three weeks before his death—an almost total invalid—he requested to be taken to the Point, where he tasted for the last time the delicious water from a spring near the lake that figures in the book. Though the last six pages of her Introduction stress the importance of the Point in her father's affections and in *The Deerslayer*, she refrains—intentionally it would seem—from any mention of the libel suits or their association with the Point.[17] Cooper's own silence, more demonstrably intentional, is confirmed by a cancellation in the manuscript that might have served as his retort to a particularly impudent and insulting letter published in Park Benjamin's *New World* on 5 October 1840, addressed "IRASIBLE SIR," and signed "YOUR MOST DEFENSIVE *Defendants*."[18] In Chapter XVII, shortly after Deerslayer has been captured by the enemy Hurons and insultingly harangued by an old squaw named Shebear, "famous for a pair of lungs that had been strengthened by long practice," Cooper wrote:

> Deerslayer <smiled as indifferently, on> ↑ looked upon ↓ these impotent attempts to arouse him, as ↑ indifferently as ↓ as a gentleman in our own state of society, regards the vituperative terms of a <ny> blackguard <who may happen to control> ↑ <a news scurrulous newspaper> ↓ <a press, the one party feeling> ↑ the one party feeling ↓ that the tongue of an old ↑ woman ↓ could never injure a warrior, and the other knowing that <scurrility> ↑ mendacity ↓ and <falsehood> ↑ vulgarity <in the end> ↓ can only ↑ permanently ↓ affect those who resort to their <youth, > ↑ use; but ↓ he* (293.31–37)

Fortunately, Cooper excised the references to the press at the points indicated in angle brackets, sublimating feelings that are infinitely richer in the expressive totality of the book.

II

Despite Miss Cooper's repeated assertion that the first pages of *The Deerslayer* were written "[w]ithin a few days" of its inception, the book almost surely remained in incubation for several months. In the autumn of 1840, the novelist was still at work on *Mercedes of Castile*, completing its composition, revising, and seeing the book through the press; attending to libel suits in progress; beginning to prepare for trials to come; completing the renovation of Otsego Hall; and purchasing Cooperstown real estate. Then, feeling the "desire for a little cruise . . . strong within" him, he spent much of October aboard the U.S.S. *Macedonian*, flagship of the West Indies fleet, with his friend Commodore William Branford Shubrick, first in New York harbor and later on a cruise to Norfolk, returning to Philadelphia on a Baltimore steamer — working intermittently all the while on the manuscript of *Mercedes*. At

---

* < . . . > Side-angle brackets denote cancellations
↑ . . . ↓ Arrows enclose superscript additions or substitutions.

last, on 10 November, on his way home after delivery of final copy of *Mercedes*, he wrote from New York to inform his British publisher Richard Bentley of his

> next book, which will be ready early in the spring.
> For this book, I now wish you to make proposals, without delay, It will contain the *early* life of Leatherstocking — a period that is only wanting to fill up his career. I think as good a book can be made, as Pathfinder out of it. I have to pay for some houses I have purchased, in the winter, and shall be nearly *à sec* — It would therefore, be an advantage to me, to have a right to draw, as the work advances — say £150 in sixty days — £150 thirty days later, and the balance on sending sheets and manuscript. Make your proposal full, if you please, and as soon as possible.[19]

Apparently Cooper did not discuss the new project with Lea and Blanchard, his American publishers. The reception of *Mercedes* was uncertain; and, in any event, he was not accustomed to receiving advances from American publishers.

Actual writing began, it would seem, in November, after the novelist was comfortably settled for the winter in the library of his newly refurbished Hall. A long, chatty letter to his son Paul, a freshman at Geneva (now Hobart) College, does not mention *The Deerslayer*, though it describes at length the novelist's cruise with Shubrick and speaks of his libel suits, woodchoppers, neighbors, friends, the election, the young turkeys outside his window, and even the fish in the lake. The one revelatory remark pertinent to *The Deerslayer* is his comment on the state of the times:

> Depend on it, my son, we live in bad times, and times that threaten a thousand serious consequences, through the growing corruption of the nation. If public virtue* be truly necessary to a republic, we cannot be one, but, unknown to ourselves, must be some thing else. The fact is, governments often profess to be one thing and practice another, and we are not what we profess to be.[20]

---

*Public virtue to Cooper meant private virtue in a public context.

Frequent and affectionate letters to Paul from his mother and four sisters are also silent about the progress of the new book. At the Hall, parlor conversation may have been freer; for Susan Cooper's 1876 Introduction includes a synoptic account of Natty's parentage and boyhood. But if Cooper ever considered a straightforward chronological or biographical narrative, he discarded it early for a highly structured, dramatic pattern, observing the Aristotelian unities of time and place and reaching out from the setting and central figure through the action and secondary characters to achieve the widest possible range of implication.

Unlikely as the suggestion may seem, the form actually adopted appears to derive from the pre-Scott pastoral romances with which Cooper had been conversant as a boy. According to Miss Cooper, her father (as a lad of eleven) and a playmate, son of the owner and publisher of *The Otsego Herald* (a Cooperstown weekly), were so much impressed by a romance in this tradition called *Don Belianis of Greece* (probably a derivation from the inveterate *Amadis of Gaul*) that they began an imitation and actually set several chapters from dictation in newspaper type. It was to have been, wrote Susan, "a great heroic romance, with knights, and squires, and horses, and ladies, and castles, and banners."[21] These romances, which had fascinated the young Cooper and his mother, flourished from medieval times to the seventeenth century and lingered long in popular memory; and we know that Cooper as a boy entertained his friends by improvising them. Customarily, they employed allegorical patterns of characterization and interwove separate but complementary strands of action to develop a single theme or a set of related ideas. They also employed exotic or distanced settings exhibiting characters in conceptually significant configurations; and, as Sir Philip Sidney suggested in his *Apology* and illustrated in his *Arcadia*, their allegorical patterning made them useful for disguised social and political commentary or protest. The potentialities of the form were inexhaustible, as the fiction of Hawthorne, Melville, and others was soon to demonstrate, far less limiting than the Scott formulae; and Cooper, who had recently protested his advertisement as "the American WALTER SCOTT," undoubtedly wished to demonstrate his independence in *The Deerslayer*.[22]

The setting and central symbol, "the pristine world of Glimmerglass," as D.H. Lawrence was to call it, is as multivalent as Cooper's expressive purpose required. Its loveliness ("lovelier," perhaps, said Lawrence, "than any place created in language: lovelier than Hardy or Turgenev, lovelier than the lands in ancient poetry or in Irish verse")[23] is conveyed less in the formal set-pieces or elaborate tableaux of Cooper's earlier fiction than in brief glimpses and snatches through the sensibility of the young Leatherstocking, who has never before seen a lake, and whose breathless enthusiasm creates simultaneously an effect of Edenic landscape and of a guileless participant. "[N]ever yet" having been "defaced or deformed" by the "hand of man" (36), the landscape can also be—and is—employed to etch by ironic contrast the darkest depths of human depravity. It would be a mistake, however, to assume with Lawrence and others that Cooper intended to celebrate Natty's sainthood or, in any readily intelligible sense, herald the birth of a new race, risen from the inscrutable consummation of two past races. Natty is never a Billy Budd or an Adam-before-the-Fall; and however magnificent the landscape may appear in his responses, its ambiance radiates from its own intrinsic qualities. Cooper's grasp of physical, moral, and psychological reality is, in short, quite firm; and the reader should not be surprised to find him exploring the possibilities of allegorical romance well before the longer fictions of Hawthorne and Melville.

The dramatic frame derived almost certainly from the Reverend John Heckewelder's description of the "vision quest," an initiation ritual in which Indian males, at puberty, were sent into the woods or mountains to seek their "guardian spirits," supposedly resident in Nature, or on other missions designed, as Heckewelder wrote, to place them "in a state of perturbation."[24] Tribal practices varied, but the rite was apparently a humane way to prepare youths for adult responsibilities without subjecting them to force or compulsion. "This was thought a good occasion for Chingachgook, a young chief who had never struck a foe, and myself," says Deerslayer, "to go on our first warpath in company" (73). Cooper's knowledge of this *rite de passage*, the exigencies in which he initially conceived his characters, his early reading and experimentation in allegorial forms, his concern about the quality of private and public morality in the Republic, his fascination with landscape (especially the landscape of his childhood), and his compulsive attraction to a character who symbolized all these concerns coalesced in *The Deerslayer* to produce, arguably, the first successful "initiation" fiction in American letters.

Though the book has frequently been denigrated as a "simple" adventure story, it becomes astonishingly complex if read as a work of serious fiction. Ludwig Lewisohn dismissed Cooper altogether because "invention in regard to pursuit and capture and physical combat are all that [he] has to offer";[25] and Yvor Winters, Donald Davie, George Dekker and others have complained, to borrow Davie's words, that the plot "does not hang together; it has no internal logic; one incident does not arise out of another. In short it lacks what Aristotle called 'unity of action.'"[26] While the action may not be Aristotelian, it has an essential cohesion. It is synchronous with Deerslayer's development as a character and with that of the subsidiary narrative strands interlacing and informing that development. Since Natty is not in this romance the relatively static figure he is in each of the earlier books of the series, the action is here focused on his developing moral consciousness and choreographed as a series of interlocking phases or movements. Since the unities of time and place are strictly observed, and the total action occupies less than one week, it is difficult to imagine a strictly linear movement that would not have been intolerably congested. The present recursive ordering, which points backward and outward as well as forward in meaning and reference, creates a desired effect of density, corroborating Cooper's remark in the first sentence of the book that a multiplicity of events enhances the impression of time passing.

At the center of this composite action is, of course, the young Leatherstocking, whose maturation the reader is invited to share in a performance testing the writer as well as the hero. Distinguished at first chiefly by his unaffected good will, simplicity, and humility, he is exposed progressively, like the knights of medieval romance, to situations of increasing stress testing both his physical prowess and his moral fortitude, while the sense of growth enabling the reader to accept his more strenuous feats is developed and confirmed in subsidiary actions. To this evolving image, the moral postures of the other characters are related in a manner that both elucidates and validates the qualities of the hero. Like romance writers of the European Renaissance, Cooper was fascinated by the variety and spectacle of human conduct, and the initiatory paradigm of *The Deerslayer* seems expressly designed to portray that spectacle in a uniquely American environment in a manner that explores and clarifies first principles of conduct.

If the reader is invited, as Marius Bewley urged, to attach a "maximum of meaning,"[27] to the care with which Cooper distinguishes between Natty and Henry March or "Hurry Harry" on their first appearance ("two men who had lost their way, and were searching in different directions for their path" [11]), the same injunction may be extended to distinctions or similarities between Natty and each of the other major characters, for they are all psychological archetypes with discrete "ways" or "paths," conceived — and sometimes fragmented — in a tightly interlocking pattern of parallels and contrasts. Sufficiently realistic to be acceptable as more than paradigms of conduct, their trajectories range over a wide and partially overlapping spectrum of motives. Natty himself — despite his initial inexperience — is endowed with a critical awareness that infers from the start the necessity for self-conscious choice and a promise of inner growth. Henry March, with whom he is throughout compared and contrasted, is a burly, fractious frontiersman, without fixed principles, a man whose reflexes are controlled by vanity, prejudice, whim, and the prospect of personal gain. Hutter, the ex-pirate, nicknamed the "Muskrat," who has assumed control of the lake and its accessories, is a man obsessed by greed, a penchant for self-protection, and a capacity for indiscriminate violence. His indeed is the "wilderness heart," of which he boasts with chilling irony. The Huron chief Rivenoak is no less a villain for having a civilized and ingratiating manner. Master of the arts of deception, he is an intriguing combination of Satanic purpose and almost benevolent demeanor. Hutter's stepdaughter Judith, a beautiful, sensitive, spirited, resourceful young woman, is flawed (like her Apocryphal counterpart) by an ineradicable strain of deceit or duplicity of which she, like Deerslayer, becomes only too conscious. Her sister Hetty, who associates herself with the Biblical Esther, is so vulnerable in her naive New Testament goodness that — despite certain similarities to Deerslayer — she lacks the prudence and discrimination to survive in a fallen world. Her innocence, in contrast to Deerslayer's, is primal. Parallels and contrasts in the moral constitutions of these and other characters, sustained throughout the action, enforce Cooper's meanings and emphases, providing what Seymour Katz has described, in another context, as a "cognitive model of experience, a hypothetical construction by means of which we come to know more about experience than experience alone can show."[28]

By conceiving Deerslayer's consciousness as the focal point of the action, Cooper was able simultaneously to suggest a model for a rational pattern of conduct and the apocalyptic consequences of the opposite course. Again and again, the action exposes the inadequacy of simplistic moral formulations: proverbs, maxims, precepts, aphorisms, even the Beatitudes. All are susceptible of parody and misapplication — a fact demonstrating a need for some more reliable guide in determining and judging human conduct. Lionel Trilling, writing of Captain Ahab and Natty Bumppo, attributes their mythic quality to the "rare fineness and abstractness of the ideas they represent."[29] Whether or not Cooper was familiar with Immanuel Kant's ethical teaching, he was an astute observer of conduct; and the nonempirical ethos that emerges through Deerslayer's consciousness is remarkably similar to that outlined in Kant's *Groundwork of the Metaphysic of Morals* (*Grundlegung zur Metaphysik der Sitten*, 1785).[30] Deerslayer was not, of course, capable of comprehending Kantian subtleties; yet much of the secret of his appeal is precisely the gyroscopic accuracy of his moral instincts and energies. His Kantianism is probably unconscious on Cooper's part; but it is clear that he, like Cooper, would have seen and understood the reciprocity implied in Kant's eloquent phrase "the starry heavens above me and the moral law within me."[31] The autonomy Deerslayer assumes includes an unlimited "good will," an intuitive understanding of the "Categorical Imperative," a disposition to respect it, and an insistence on treating people as ends and not means. Moral decisions, in short, are the function of a well-disposed and autonomous consciousness acting disinterestedly on the contingencies presented in specific situations.[32] To be sure, Deerslayer is not, to recall Cooper's prefatory disclaimer, "a moral monster," capable of conforming exactly to his code; but, as he confesses, "Whenever I've done wrong, I've gin'rally found 'twas owin' to some blindness of the mind, which hid the right view, and when sight has returned, then has come sorrow and repentance" (456).

Offsetting the Arcadian image with its intimation of exalted ethical possibilities in the American wilderness, Cooper subtended a stark and almost sordid image of actual frontier life with its unlimited freedoms, explosive violence, and physical and mental isolation. The significant subsidiary tension, interwoven with the stages of Deerslayer's initiation, develops between representatives of these two modes of life: Deerslayer, Chingachgook, Hist, and Hetty on the one hand, and Hutter, March, Rivenoak and his Hurons on the other. Deerslayer himself is not exempted from this polarity which Erik H. Erikson has called the "decisive influence" of the frontier in implanting "in the American identity the extreme polarization which characterizes it."[33] Torn between the Christian and humanitarian values of his Moravian childhood and his need to survive wilderness realities, he has acquired special skills in the employment of force, first as hunter and then as warrior, though inflicting suffering in any form contravenes his natural instincts and earns reproaches from Hetty, the apostle of nonviolence. Within the period of his initiation, however, Deerslayer is compelled to accommodate his reason and conscience to the employment of force when survival is in question, a point on which he is sustained more firmly by the Kantian than by the Christian ethos. Ultimately, Cooper seems to say, questions of right and wrong cannot be decided by formulae predicated in advance, but rather, must be decided by the autonomy of the individual consciousness; and the rightness or wrongness of choices inheres in the fineness of the individual consciousness acting disinterestedly upon an accurate perception of the specifics in a given situation. It is perhaps more than coincidence that the rejection of Judith is treated in a manner remarkably similar to final decisions of the heroes and heroines of Henry James.

III.

"We have had a very pleasant winter, and I have been at home since December," Cooper reported to Shubrick in a long, newsy letter on 28 February 1841, curiously though not uncharacteristically neglecting to mention that his writing had gone rapidly and that *The Deerslayer* was nearing completion.[34] It was apparently at about this time, as he recorded in the Preface to the first edition, that he became so discouraged that he was tempted "to burn his manuscript, and to turn to some other subject" (1840 Preface). He soon regained his confidence, however. By 5 May the book was in press; and the novelist, still captive to the nostalgia of his effort, was inviting boyhood friends like James Stevenson and Peter Gansevoort, Herman Melville's uncle, to visit him for a week at the Hall where, as he wrote Gansevoort, "[We] could all turn boys again. A few years hence, that exploit will be out of the question. Remember I put my foot down for this Concession, and about the beginning of July, you may expect to hear further on the subject."[35]

The discouragement to which Cooper referred in his Preface undoubtedly stemmed from the acute disadvantage in which his libel suits and declining sales had placed him in negotiations with publishers and also from a painful circumstance of which he complained privately: "the impatience of reputation which belongs to a democracy, and which induces the public to run eagerly, after every new name, and then to endeavor to destroy it as precipitately as it has been made."[36] Cooper's plight was widely known; it had, indeed, been sympathetically and constructively discussed in *The Knickerbocker Magazine* for January, 1841, in prefatory comments to a translation of Balzac's enthusiastic review of *The Pathfinder* from the *Revue Parisienne*:

> The name of COOPER now seldom appears in our journals, except for the purpose of censure or ridicule. His pro-

ductions, good or bad, are laid hold of as themes upon which the malignity of the press delights to dwell, and to pour forth its vials of wrath. In his case, the limits of criticism have been wantonly transgressed, in order to wound his pride, provoke his irascibility, and depreciate his writings. Even the unamiable attributes of his imaginary offspring have been identified with those supposed to exist in the breast of the author. Is this fair dealing? Ought a writer to be charged with the vices and follies of his literary progeny, and himself arraigned at the bar of criticism, to be tried, without a jury, for the delinquencies of beings necessarily created to advance the action and point the moral of his story? Had such a tribunal existed in the days of yore, alas for those culprits, SHAKESPEARE and MILTON! they could not have escaped condign punishment. . . . But is our literature so affluent in great names, that we can thus afford to impale the reputation of a writer whose genius has exalted the name and the fame of his country throughout the civilized world?[37]

For a time, evidently, the novelist feared that his long-established relations with his publishers were about to crumble. On 7 January, Richard Bentley, to whom the new project had been announced in a letter of 10 November, replied hesitantly: "With regard to the new work, I almost fear with whatever ability you may treat it, that it will be considered, like most *sequels*, not with the same favor as an original conception." Less tactfully, in the same letter, Bentley wrote that *Mercedes of Castile* had "been pronounced not equal to its predecessors," that it had been unprofitable to his firm, and that its predecessor, Cooper's *History of the Navy of the United States*, had left him a loser by £400. He therefore proposed to pay only £300 for *The Deerslayer*, £200 less than Cooper had proposed, and £200 less than he had been accustomed to receive for works in the same series.[38] Lea and Blanchard's report on the sale of *Mercedes* was even more threatening: "In a mercantile point of view the book has proved a total failure. . . . We would suggest to your consideration the remitting of the copy money on the 1000 copies not printed—Even then we shall have to work hard to get the money invested in the work returned to us."[39]

Whatever qualms he felt about continuing with *The Deerslayer*, Cooper proceeded pertinaciously, depending on the resilience and ingenuity that had sustained him through twenty years of multifarious dealings with publishers. Understanding his disadvantage as an American author, he had always maintained a self-consciously firm, if compliant stance in his negotiations with Bentley; and his reply to Bentley's first offer on 31 January was undoubtedly calculated to be persuasive. It recalled enticingly the popular appeal of the earlier Leatherstocking books; stressed the novelty of the present effort; and, above all, sought to convey a sense of his own imaginative involvement and excitement. Emphasizing the urgency of his need for the full £500, he proposed payment by notes in three installments: £150 on the completion of each of the two American volumes, and £200 on the delivery of the manuscript and the printed American sheets.[40] Then, presuming on Bentley's acceptance, he drew bills for the first installment in favor of Roskell, Ogden & Co., of New York and Liverpool, and sent them to his friend James De Peyster Ogden for collection, cautioning Ogden: "The letter must go with, or before the bills, or no pay — at least, it will be [an] act of grace, if there is."[41] The stratagem succeeded eventually, much as Cooper hoped, though not without persistence. Bentley accepted the first bill for £150 in a terse statement of 5 March before receiving Cooper's letter, but reiterated his original offer because: "Taken collectively all the later works including The Monikins[,] The Travels[,] Homeward Bound[,] Home as Found, The Pathfinder, & Mercedes have left me no profit; and this leaving out of the question altogether the great loss sustained by me in the publication of the Naval History of U States."[42] On the following day, after the delivery of Cooper's letter, Bentley repeated his complaint, regretfully reaffirmed his first offer, and suggested that "the new work" could be published "on joint account."[43] On 6 April, after the completion of the manuscript, Cooper drew for the £100 due under Bentley's stipulation, remarking "the other £200 will probably raise a serious difficulty as to future books."[44] In a further letter of 14 May, he played his final card:

> I send you this book, according to promise, but I do not accept your terms. Should you insist on them, the book will be yours, but there my connection with your house must cease. . . . This book you shall have, for it is promised you, and you will have paid £250 on it, but you are not to be hurt or surprised if I send the next work to another house, unless, I am authorized by the return packet to draw for the remaining £200.[45]

Two months later, after rereading Bentley's letters and deliberating on their long partnership, Cooper wrote again to state that, contrary to his original intention, he had drawn for the contested £200, at five months, requesting the publisher to withhold his decision against payment until he should be able to gauge the book's reception, and promising "to remit the money in season to take up [the] acceptance," should that become necessary.[46] No such necessity arose, however; for after the amicable display between the two men, Bentley accepted Cooper's draft and established an *ad valorum* price for his future productions: "if 1000 [copies], £300; if 1500, £500."[47]

Apparently Cooper's relations with Lea and Blanchard in Philadelphia were even more strained, partly from the harmful publicity attending the Press War and partly from the dismal reception of *Mercedes*, concerning which the publishers sent a painfully specific résumé on 9 February:

> . . . nothing that we have undertaken for years [has] more completely failed—We printed four thousand copies & of these the sales do not exceed 15 or 1800 copies in all. Every where we find, in place of being able to draw for the money, that the work is on hand. One house in Boston to whom we sent 80 copies returns us a sale of 10 copies & many others in nearly as bad a proportion—few have sold over half the quantity sent.
> In distributing a work, we expect, usually, the first distribution *to sell at once*, & then to receive orders for second supplies. In this case we have received no second orders.

Now under the circumstances of this state of the sale of the work & the fact that we stated to you our disappointment in the character of the work before publication[,] it being different from what you stated previously to finishing it, we would ask you if this heavy loss should fall entirely upon us. By our agreement we have no right to call upon you; but we think you will allow that the loss is to[o] much for us to take entirely.[48]

This letter may explain Cooper's motive for seeking insertion of an anonymous advance notice of *The Deerslayer* in the *Boston Notion*, an unprecedented measure for him. Writing to George Roberts, the editor and publisher of this elephantine sheet, about another matter on 13 February, Cooper noted:

If you want a paragraph, you can insert the following. It may serve a particular purpose of mine, and can do no harm. I do not wish it given, however, as coming directly from myself. My object is to draw the attention of a publisher to the fact.

"We learn that the Author of The Pioneers, Prairie, Mohicans and Pathfinder has nearly completed a fifth book, in which the Leatherstocking appears as a character. According to our information the work is not yet named, though Natty Bumppo is styled "Deerslayer," which may possibly turn out to be the title of the work. The scene is on one of the small New York lakes, and the date is in the early part of the eighteenth century. This book will represent the youth of Leatherstocking, with certain incidents connected with the love of Chingachgook the father of Uncas. The time occupies but three or four days."

You would oblige me by letting the above appear without any comment. My object is solely to call attention of a person at a distance to the fact, who will doubtless read the paragraph copied into some other paper.[49]

Roberts published the paragraph verbatim as a Literary Notice in the issue of the *Notion* for 27 February 1841, and Henry Lea and William Blanchard, the "person" or persons for whom it was obviously intended, would certainly have read it

there or in one of the papers into which it was copied. When
the book was completed in late March, Cooper proceeded to
Albany to wait for the first steamer to New York after the river
opened. Going down the Hudson with his friend Luther
Bradish on 27 March, he visited friends in New York, pursued
investigations at the Brooklyn Navy Yard, and proceeded to
Philadelphia on 30 March. Since the agreement for the
publication of *The Deerslayer* or "Natty Bumbo," as it was called
in the contract, was signed on 2 April, there can have been no
great difficulty in the negotiations, though the terms—in
which the right to print and publish the new work for a three-
year period was incorporated with Lea and Blanchard's similar
right to ten earlier books, including three other Leather-
stocking Tales—suggest a compromise. Payment for all
eleven was to be $2,500 "in Three notes at Twelve, Thirteen &
fourteen months" from the signing. In addition, the publishers
agreed to pay forty cents "per copy for all copies printed over
five Thousand of the new Romance . . . and to have a
period[?] of 9 mos from the time of publishing each edition
beyond the five thousand copies." They also agreed to give
Cooper a copy of each of their new publications during the
three years.[50] Though the amount was approximately half
what Carey and Lea had paid for a single new work a decade
earlier, the novelist confessed to Mrs. Cooper, "it is a great
relief to my mind."[51]

A coincidental source of gratification and a harbinger of
better times, as the novelist noted in the Preface to the first
edition (1840 Preface), was an anonymous letter from a young
English admirer dated simply "England—April" which probably arrived while he was reading proof in Philadelphia and
Cooperstown in May and June:

Sir
Having Read your most interesting novels, viz. The
Borderers, The Pathfinder, the Last of the Mohicans [,] The
Pioneers, and the Prairie; I beg leave to inform you that
they are universally esteemed, and that Hawk eye or the
Scout, together with the Mohicans, are very favourite
characters, and have created great interest. It would be
useless for me to attempt to point out, any *particular* inter-

esting part in them, as they are equally good all through, especially all relating to Indians and the Scout. <We> I therefore request, if agreable to yourself—that you will oblige *England* by writing some more novels of the same kind, about Indians, and the Scout, such as about various exploits alluded to by the Scout, and about his Prior Career, and about the Mohicans, in the times, when their tribe was in its best days. There are many People who are anxiously awaiting some more of your interesting Tales to appear, and it will be a great pleasure to my self and them to hear of your Tales being Published. <We> I therefore wish you success, and that you will continue to outstrip all your competitors in novel writing, who are nothing as authors compared with yourself—

I therefore subscribe myself
Yours obliged—

P.S) Any thing about Indians will be read with Pleasure.[52]

As the writer of this letter disclosed in a further letter, its object had been in part to deflect Cooper's attention from controversial historical and political subjects, a desire to which many of his American friends and admirers would have subscribed.

IV

Secretly, no doubt, the novelist's Whig detractors cherished the same desire: for some of them (Park Benjamin, for example) were resisting payment of verdicts for libel already obtained. When *The Deerslayer* was published in Philadelphia on 27 August, Cooper was in Philadelphia abridging his *History of the Navy* in one volume for general circulation, and watching somewhat anxiously for the novel's reception by the press.[53] "I hardly think it as good as Pathfinder," he had written to his wife on 22 June, "but sufficiently different—it has a strong moral, and some capital scenes—[Henry] Lea has read half, and likes it exceedingly. Thinks it quite equal to Pathfinder."[54] By 17 September, he could report, "Deerslayer is doing well, and I hope will still do better—The press says nothing about it."[55]

Actually, Park Benjamin, perhaps the most annoying of the Whig editors, had been following the novelist's career closely in his *New World*; and he had already begun to speak. The courts had dismissed as frivolous his plea against Cooper's verdict for libel; and he lost no opportunity to heckle. One of the first editors to reprint Cooper's paragraph from *The Boston Notion*, he announced on 3 July that *The Deerslayer* would be published in August, and he recounted his first impressions of the book on 4 September:

> THE DEERSLAYER — We have received Cooper's new novel with this title, and have, during the past week, been trying desperately hard to read it. After many severe struggles against drowsiness and the endurance of a tedium, that was really distressing, we have *tugged* through the first volume. We are now meditating an attack on the second, with but very faint hope of success. Should we survive the task, our readers shall be informed in due season. Meantime we implore their sympathy.[56]

On another page in the same issue, *The New World* carried a paragraph attributed to the *Louisville Advertiser* of 20 August, complaining that Cooper had found no new heroes "to give freshness and new life to his late works; so he drags his decrepid and bed-ridden heroes from their couches — even some from their graves, in which his former narratives left them. . . . It is bad, very bad, for an author to outlive his reputation — much worse, when, after attaining a bright reputation, he writes himself back into obscurity."

While the publication of *The Deerslayer* did not immediately silence the Whig editors, it provided no basis for further partisan attacks, demonstrated that Cooper had *not* written "himself back into obscurity," and so robbed them of the provocations they desired. The sense or senses in which the book was a reply to their attacks evidently escaped them completely. Thus, while a few Whig editors like Park Benjamin of the *New World*, Thurlow Weed of the *Albany Journal*, and James Watson Webb of the New York *Courier and Enquirer*, attempted for a time to maintain the so-called "Effingham Controversy" in their newspapers and to resist or forestall Cooper's verdicts in the courts, their own interest and readers' interest dwindled until the trouble and costs became prohibitive. In any case, the influence of these local partisan presses was negligible in comparison to the influence of magazines whose circulations were or were becoming national.

Although Chapter VI of *The Deerslayer* was excerpted for advance publication in *Brother Jonathan* in the issue of 14 August 1841, critical opinion did not begin to crystallize in print until October. A preview of the extremely favorable consensus to come appeared, however, in *The New-York Mirror* on 11 September:

> The book before us is certainly the best which has issued from his pen in many years. There is so much real merit in Mr. Cooper that it gives us great pleasure to praise him whenever he puts it in our power to do so, which, we regret to say, has not always been the case. He is the most original thinker of any of our American novelists; the manliest, most vigourous and independent spirit of them all, unrivalled in descriptive powers, and unapproached in the heartiness of his patriotic feelings . . . . Mr. Cooper could not have chosen a more popular hero . . . . The scene is laid on the borders of that beautiful lake near which the author himself resides. His descriptions of that fine sheet of water and the hills that encircle it are in his best style, that is, remarkably clear and minute, and exquisitely true to nature. We can almost fancy ourselves looking down on the unruffled surface of Otsego, and feel the night-breeze rising, damp and heavy with the odours of the forest . . . . [T]hroughout the work there is more knowledge of human nature and more successful delineation of character than Mr. Cooper has generally had credit for . . . . Let him go on and write a few more such works as the "Deerslayer," illustrating American history, scenery and manners, and identifying himself with his subject, and he cannot fail to reach a higher reputation than he has yet enjoyed. His own country will, of course, be the last to appreciate him, but, after his renown has been endorsed by England, France and Germany, it will begin to pass current here; and, it being proved already that he is a man of genius, it will go near to be thought so shortly.[57]

If Cooper had been nervous about his standing in the country at large, he should certainly have been reassured by the chorus of praise in the magazines for October. With almost no exception, they rejoiced in his return to the materials of his early successes, finding *The Deerslayer* equal if not superior to his earlier productions, his genius as "fresh and fervent as ever," and proclaiming the book "invincible against the ready censure of lynx-eyed and hostile critics."[58] *The Knickerbocker Magazine* praised his "close observation and fine powers of description," found his "pictures" "second to none of those vivid limnings by which he has won his reputation," and recorded "our high admiration of one of our author's finest creations, DEERSLAYER."[59] And *Graham's Magazine* called him so "skilful in the management of incident, or capable of whirling away the reader in the breathless interest of a story," that "no writer of the day, at least no American, can, at all, compare with Mr. Cooper."[60] *The Ladies Companion* rejoiced "that Mr. Cooper has given this novel to the public," found the characters "all touched with the pencil of a master," the "interest of the tale . . . intense, and the *denouement* most affecting."[61] *The United States Magazine and Democratic Review* marveled

> that without either characters or plot, deserving the name—excepting always the regular old staple, Leather-Stocking—by his admirable description and narrative talent, [Cooper] can keep the interest of his readers agreeably excited through a couple of volumes, recording the adventures and vicissitudes of not more than four or five days spent on the waters, and about the shore, of a little inland lake in the heart of the howling wilderness . . . . We are sorry Mr. Cooper has now exhausted our good old friend. We are almost tempted to wish that he might violate all the canons of dramatic criticism, and to the five acts of his life we already possess, add a sixth, with the introduction of Mr. and Mrs. Bumpo [sic], and the young Nathaniel in bib and tucker playing at hide-and-seek among the chairs of the nursery.[62]

Godey's Lady's Book was lukewarm in its praise, but it admired Cooper's "delineation of his hero" and his "descriptions of natural objects," predicting the book would "be extensively read and generally admired."[63] The only aggressively hostile review in American magazines appears to be that in the *Southern Literary Messenger*, which cast doubt on Cooper's prefatory account of the anonymous letter from England, singled out improbabilities, and labeled the book "beneath the dignity of a criticism" and "[a]ltogether . . . a 'poor thing.'"[64] The *New York Review* praised *The Deerslayer* above all Cooper's previous works, and *The Saturday Evening Post* for 28 October declared it completely successful in following "the borderer through every stage of his existence, from the young scout to the trapper on the western prairies," and concluded: "We repeat, no tale of the season equals 'The Deerslayer.' Every American especially should read this last work — the cope-stone of a series — by the first living novelist of his country."[65]

Curiously, since British copyright law required priority of publication, Richard Bentley delayed publication of *The Deerslayer* until 7 September, nine days after the American publication; but he had the good judgment to select Chapter VII for publication in his *Miscellany* in September. Almost all British reviewers dispensed generous praise of the new book and were, in general, even more enthusiastic than their American counterparts, selecting judiciously from a variety of passages for their quotations, welcoming "with hearty good will . . . our old friend Leatherstocking, . . . [as] we are led delighted through the vast solitude of the primæval forests, and made familiar with the lake, the mountain, and the wilderness."[66] *The Athenaeum*, in a long review of 11 September, attempted to dispel the author's anxiety, expressed in the original Preface, about the comparative merit of the work in the Leatherstocking series.[67] *The Literary Gazette and Journal of the Belles Lettres, Arts, Sciences, &c.*, in its issue of the same date, pronounced *The Deerslayer*

> more worthy of high reputation than any of [Cooper's] latter productions; it is, indeed, a stirring tale of the early history of America, full of startling incidents and thrilling descriptions; the characters, though few in number, are most ably drawn; and the locality (for there is no change of scene) admirably depicted. The heroine is quite a portrait; and the Deerslayer one of the fine borderers peculiar to Mr. Cooper's tales.[68]

The final scene between Deerslayer and Judith is then quoted almost in its entirety. *The Examiner*, also on 11 September, made much of historical values in the book:

> This tale is written in Mr. Cooper's best style: the style which won him his repute, and by which he will live. When nothing but a tradition of the magnificent race of the Red Indian shall be left to civilized Americans; when they have lost even such indifferent traces of the original White Hunter of the west, as their half civilized 'alligator' of Kentucky has been wont to furnish; — the Leather Stockings and Red Jackets, thanks to Mr. Cooper, will have lost nothing of their fame; nothing of their native wit; nothing of their hardy truth and rude generosity. Mr. Catlin's exhibition has been very well in its way, but it is nothing to a book of this kind. A good, faithful, life-like book, what can compare with it? There is the industrious and most able Mr. Stephens, stumbling over the gorgeous remains of Indian capitals and cities in Yucatan and so forth; but what if he had found an exact and vigorous descriptive tale, by the Cooper of that day? . . .
>
> The machinery of the tale is even more than ordinarily simple. The locality is confined . . . the actors are few; the incidents not many; and the time occupied extremely brief. But the book is full of fine description and vigorous character; no compromise is made with the wild and savage features of the time or of the scene: the town is not dragged headlong into the wilderness; there is some little love-talking, but there is much more scalp-hunting. The heroine of the tale is, perhaps, somewhat harshly dealt with; she has a sister, however, to whom the author is more kind; and to act against all defects, real or supposed, we have constantly at hand, and always doing us good, the touching simplicity, the quaint natural observation, the most manly truthfulness, of Deerslayer himself.[69]

The reviewer continues with a series of brief excerpts suggesting the pattern and structure of the book, concluding with the final experiences of Deerslayer in the hands of the Huron tribe:

The after sufferings of Deerslayer from this tribe are the
most powerful pieces of description in the book, but lively
feeling and local truth are found in every scene.[70]

A similar enthusiasm permeates the review in *The Court Journal*
for 11 September, in which the writer assures readers that the
hero

> never was more delightful; and that not even in the Last of
> the Mohicans can [readers] have felt a deeper interest in his fate
> than they will in these new volumes from Mr Cooper's able
> and fertile pen. The first, fresh impulses of youth, verging
> on manhood, in one depending solely on his own resources,
> placed in many situations of peril and danger, and even of
> responsibility, afford our author an excellent opportunity of
> drawing into play the early character of his hero. Never is
> the simplicity, the perfect freedom from guile, the noble
> heartedness of the primitive hunter, drawn out more for-
> cibly. We cannot hesitate in saying that it is certainly one of
> the best characters ever introduced into a novel. . . . We
> can only say that it is fully equal to his best efforts, and
> every reader of taste, who is an admirer of primitive nature
> and of primitive man, will be delighted with the work. . . .
> Not the least interesting portions of [the three volumes],
> —nay, indeed, we may almost say *the most* interesting—are
> the pictures of nature, the lovely descriptions of lake and
> forest scenery, of wild and savage encampment, of morning
> and even bursting on a spot almost uninhabited . . . . The
> wish which the reading of these tomes awakens within us, a
> wish which we are eager ever to gratify as we proceed, is to
> be transported to the spots which he describes, to revel in the
> luxuriant vegetation of a virgin American forest, and to look
> upon the face of Glimmerglass, the picture of which is to us
> as it were a miniature of the Swiss lakes, where so oft we
> have enjoyed scenery the most gorgeous in the world.[71]

The reviews in *The Metropolitan Magazine* and *The Monthly
Review* for October were briefer than reviews in the weeklies,
but not less enthusiastic. The reviewer for the *Metropolitan*
declared that even without Cooper's formidable reputation in
England, *The Deerslayer*

would immediately have challenged attention and secured admiration. There is a grandeur about its simplicity that belongs only to nature. There is but little of plot or intricate contrivance in the structure of the story, and it needed them not. It is a series, though not an extended one, of beautiful portraits after life, and a chronicle of startling adventure, in scenes novel to Englishmen, and a combination of situations more than dramatically fine. The action of the story, for the most part, takes place in the awful silence of the old forests, which seem coeval with the soil upon which they grow, or upon the torrent-impelled and desolate river, the isolated lake, or in the all but boundless wilderness. The Leatherstockings, the deerslayer, is a young hero, with but little of society's education, yet made most perfect for the vast and sublime theatre on which he is destined to act. Of course he is continually mixed up with both friendly and hostile red-men, and the adventures in which they involve him are of the most thrilling nature. It is this sort of wild life which arouses some of man's best and noblest energies, though it must be confessed that it too often awakens his worst passions. Unbridled by anything like human responsibility, his hand is too ready to do that which his heart dictates, and conscience is peculiarly torpid where there are none to accuse or to remonstrate. This reckless self-dependence no one ever portrayed better than Mr. Cooper, and thus his scenes of Indian life have not been equalled, and never will be surpassed.[72]

The Monthly Review, in one of the most perceptive of the British reviews, replied to Cooper's prefatory uneasiness about the relative merit of *The Deerslayer* in the Leatherstocking series by stating:

> in none of the other tales of the series have we found such manly simplicity, such shrewd wisdom, such quaint originality in the portraiture of the hero, as in the volumes before us. The white hunter of the border is sterling throughout, but here we find the foundations of his freshness, vigour, truth, prowess, and generosity.[73]

The excerpts reprinted in the review, including a landscape, were evidently selected to illustrate or explain Deerslayer's moral posture from various perspectives. The single exception, seemingly, to the overwhelmingly favorable reception of *The Deerslayer* in contemporaneous British periodicals appeared in *The New Monthly Belle Assemblé* for November, where the reviewer complained of its "excessive tediousness" and of the too frequent reappearance of "Mr. Cooper's perpetual hero, Hawkeye Leather-stocking." The review acknowledged the "well-earned reputation" of the author, however; and pronounced some parts of the book interesting and powerful.[74]

Though reviews of *The Deerslayer* were predominantly favorable in the United States as in England, Cooper was disappointed in the reception of the book at home, presumably because the newspapers, which had been among his strongest supporters earlier in his career, were now comparatively silent. The book "has not been licensed by the news-papers," he wrote to a young admirer,

> and it is a very bold American who presumes to wander from their dictation. The habit of being directed in their thoughts has got to be so strong in this country, that not one mind in a thousand can break it, and yet men fancy themselves free![75]

Although it is not clear how many reviews Cooper read, he wrote to Rufus Wilmot Griswold in 1845:

> Deerslayer was nearly as well recieved as Pathfinder. In some respects it is a better book; though I think not as a whole. Many excellent judges place it highest, however.[76]

Cooper's bittersweet response to the success of *The Deerslayer* is understandable; for his larger intention transcended any possible accomplishment by a work of fiction and included his hope of inspiring a reform of private and public morality in the United States, especially the morality of the press. In this larger sense, his purpose in the libel suits and in *The Deerslayer* was almost identical. One view of its extent is reflected in a congratulatory letter from the Rev. Joseph Ransom, who had supplied the pulpit at Christ Church, Cooperstown, and who had known Cooper well while the romance was in progress and may have been a confidant:

> On my journey home, the other day, from New York, I came to the knowledge, in a conversation about you & your excellent works, that you had beaten your miserable traducer Park Banjamin: & as your daughter, I heard, was returning to Cooperstown, I could not but avail myself of the opportunity of thus telling you how greatly I rejoiced at it; as well as at the same time of expressing my opinion, that the state of the public mind is, very obviously, I think, turning round in your favor. The fact is, you are accomplishing a most glorious achievement for your country: & this is beginning to be recognized by it, — except in those contemptible instances, where the mind, having become utterly vitiated, by an interested connexion with a villainous system, is no longer capable of entertaining any correct moral perceptions; nor can it be otherwise, I think, than that all sensible men, & especially those in publick capacities, will look to you with gratitude & reverence, as not only the champion of their liberties, but as the successful defender of every thing sacred & dear to them. — It may not, indeed, be yet, alas! that the country will be *able* to estimate *fully*, the true nature of the conquest wh[ich] you are making for it: — for such is the confused & disorganized state of things; & such, as a necessary consequence, the perverted medium through wh[ich] the judgment has to operate; that both your fearful position, & the work you are accomplishing, will, to a most serious extent, be inevitably overlooked. Yet to me, at least, who am not at all mixed up with the existing state of things, it appears that no mortal could occupy a more perilous station, than that into wh[ich], with so much courage & ability, you have thrown yourself: — for what is it, but to have entered the lists *alone*, against the powers by wh[ich] the country has been subjugated; & this, in defiance of all opposition whatsoever, to have succeeded, as you have done, in raising it from so degrading a predicament? My dear Sir, I cannot but regard this, as unquestionably the most glorious thing that you have done. By your works, indeed, you have been, & still are, at once the ornament & the light of your country; but in this matter you are truly a *Reformer*; & such a man I consider is, of all others, the greatest & most important to the world; inasmuch as his object is to bring men

back again to the truth of things, & consequently his work
must be, after a sort at best, *divine*. I pray that God may
still grant you success, & enable you to triumph over all
your enemies & this, indeed, I am compelled to do the more
earnestly, as I feel that, in a most important [sense?], you are
actually fighting *my own*, as well as every body else's
battles.[77]

The most frequent objection to *The Deerslayer*, one which
recurs again and again in the contemporaneous reviews and in
surviving correspondence with readers, is the treatment of
Judith, an objection broached in a characteristic manner in the
following paragraph from an anonymous letter postmarked
Boston, September 1841:

> A warm admirer of Mr. Cooper's genius, who has just read
> the Deerslayer, the third time, would modestly suggest a
> new edition of this wonderful tale. Cannot the author bestow
> upon Leatherstocking, the most winning hero of the imagi-
> nation since the tale of Hector, the glory of making a com-
> plete conversion of Judith, and call what is noble in her
> nature not into merely partial and transient, but into
> sovereign and enduring action by the nobleness of his? This
> would not be beyond the natural influence of a sentiment so
> awakened, and would leave the reader happy.[78]

Another young admirer, who described in great detail his
ecstatic experience in reading *The Deerslayer*, was so deeply
touched by Judith that, as he wrote, "I found my interest in the
principal actor in this play, completely absorbed and
swallowed up" by her predicament; and he enclosed a poem
entitled "Judith," which concluded with a meditation on her
life and fate:

> Oh who can pierce the gloom of years
> And tell what saddened hopes and fears
> What struggling with enwrapt despair
> Would crush her with its weight of care
> How that high Soul would spend her shame
> While soaring for a [jeweled?] fame

Tired with life would find release
But in the grave where all is peace.[79]

"Hetty," Cooper replied, "is my own favorite, and I think she is better done—requiring more finesse to execute, and a greater familiarity with human nature to conceive, but I find no one of my own way of thinking."[80] Apparently Cooper never detected the compositor's crucial misreading of the manuscript at page 525.20–21 where Judith's own "consciousness of undue erring" was transcribed as "consciousness of undeserving," an error that significantly altered authorial intention and one that has persisted through all 211 editions of the book previous to the present one. Cooper clearly intended to show Judith accepting at last the onus of her misconduct and thus exonerating Deerslayer.

When *The Deerslayer* was reissued in the slightly revised Putnam edition in October 1850, Cooper's quarrels with the press had, for the most part, faded into the past, though Duyckinck's *Literary World* regretted, in an aside, "to a new generation of readers," that their "great American countryman has been made known by the depreciation and misconception of an unfortunate series of newspaper abuse."[81] Of the hero, the reviewer for *The Literary World* wrote:

> The character of the Leather-Stocking, as entered upon in the Deerslayer, is one which will always interest the world, both from its essential ingredients, and the novel circumstances in which it exhibits itself. It is the author's ideal of a chivalresque [sic] manhood, of the grace which is the natural flower of purity and virtue; not the stoic, but the Christian of the woods, the man of honorable act and sentiment, of courage and truth. Leather-Stocking stands half way between savage and civilized life: he has the freshness of nature and the first fruits of Christianity, the seed dropped into this vigorous soil. These are the elements of one of the most original characters in fiction, in whom Mr. Cooper has transplanted all the chivalry ever feigned or practised in the middle ages, to the rivers, woods, and forests of the unbroken New World. In Deerslayer, which we are surprised to learn "has attracted very little notice," we have one of Mr. Cooper's purest compositions. There are passages of Saxon in the dialogues and speeches which would do honor to the

most admired pages of the romantic old Chroniclers. The language is as noble as the thought.[82]

On 26 September 1841, a few weeks after *The Deerslayer's* publication, Daniel D. Barnard, a prominent Whig friend, who thoroughly sympathized with the novelist in his battle with the Whig editors, had written:

> I have just read "The Deerslayer" — the only novel, with a single exception that I have looked at in many months. I like it hugely. Natty is now a full length — & he is immortal. He will never die.[83]

NOTES

1. *The Letters and Journals of James Fenimore Cooper*, Beard, James Franklin, ed. (Cambridge, Mass.: Belknap Press of Harvard University Press. 1960–1968), IV, 369–70 (cited hereafter as *Letters and Journals*).

2. Cooper, Susan Fenimore, Introduction to *The Deerslayer*, Household Edition (New York and Cambridge: Houghton Mifflin and Company, Hurt and Houghton, 1876), xxxiii (cited hereafter as SFC, Introduction).

3. Wordsworth, William *The Prelude* (1805), line 608, as quoted by Mary Moorman, *William Wordsworth: A Biography, The Early Years* (London: Oxford University Press, 1957), p. 40. Wordsworth was perhaps the British poet Cooper most wanted to meet when in London in 1828. After his friend Samuel Rogers arranged a dinner at which they were to be introduced, Cooper wrote, in *England* (SUNY edition, p. 166), "my old enemy the headache and a severe nervous attack, obliged me to send excuses, though I put them off as long as I could, and drank hot tea all the morning to get myself in trim. Mr. Rogers sent to press me to join them in the evening, but I was then in bed."

4. *Letters and Journals*, IV, 498.

5. Cooper, James Fenimore (grandson of the novelist), *The Legends and Traditions of a Northern County* (New York and London: G.P. Putnam's Sons, 1921), pp. 170–71.

6. Cooper, James Fenimore, "The Eclipse," Susan Fenimore Cooper, ed., *Putnam's Magazine*, n.s., IV (September, 1869), p. 353.

7. Ibid., p. 357.

8. Ibid., p. 356.

9. Ibid., p. 357.

10. Ibid., p. 358.

11. Ibid., p. 359.

12. *Letters and Journals*, II, 89.

13. *The Prairie* (SUNY Edition), p. 32.

14. *Home as Found* (New York: W.A. Townsend & Co., 1860), p. 229.

15. *Letters and Journals*, III. 276–82, 283–84.

16. Ibid., IV, 144–47.

17. SFC, Introduction, xxxvii-xi.

18. *Letters and Journals*, IV, 66–68.

19. Ibid., p. 102.

20. Ibid., p. 106.

21. Cooper, Susan Fenimore, *Pages and Pictures from the Writings of James Fenimore Cooper* (New York: W.A. Townsend and Company, 1861.), p. 20.

22. "Letter to the Editors of the Knickerbocker," *Knickerbocker Magazine*, XI (April, 1838), 380–86.

23. Lawrence, D.H., *The Symbolic Meaning: The Uncollected Versions of Studies in Classic American Literature*, Armin Arnold, ed. (New York: The Viking Press, 1964), p. 98.

24. Heckewelder, John, *An Account of the History, Manners and Customs of the Indian Nations* (Philadelphia: Abraham Small, 1819), p. 245. Chapter XXXIII, 245-48, is entitled "Initiation of Boys." "When a boy has thus been initiated, a name is given to him analogous to the visions he has seen, and to the destiny that is supposed to be prepared for him. The boy, imagining all that happened to him while under perturbation, to have been real, sets out in the world with lofty notions of himself, and animated with courage for the most desperate undertakings."

25. Lewisohn, Ludwig, *The Story of American Literature* (New York: Harper & Brothers, 1932), p. 55.

26. Davie, Donald, *The Heyday of Sir Walter Scott* (London: Routledge & Kegan Paul, 1961), pp. 125–26.

27. Bewley, Marius, *The Eccentric Design: Form in the Classic American Novel* (New York: Columbia University Press, 1959) p. 88.

28. Katz, Seymour, "'Culture' and Literature in American Studies," *American Quarterly*, XX (Summer Supplement), 1968, p. 323.

29. Trilling, Lionel, *The Liberal Imagination* (New York: The Viking Press, 1950), p. 262.

30. An extremely useful translation of and commentary on this work is provided in Brenden E.A. Liddell's *Kant on the Foundation of Morality: A Modern Version of the "Grundlegung"* (Bloomington and London: Indiana University Press, 1970).

31. Kant, Immanuel, *Critique of Practical Reason*, translated and edited with an Introduction by Lewis White Beck (Chicago: University of Chicago Press, 1949), p. 258.

32. One of the best explications of Kant's ethical position is contained in James Haden's translation of Ernst Cassirer's *Kant's Life and Thought* (New Haven and London: Yale University Press, 1981). See especially Chapter V, "The Growth and Structure of Critical Ethics."

33. Erikson, Erik H., *Childhood and Society* (New York: W.W. Norton & Company, 1963, Second Edition), p. 293.

34. *Letters and Journals*, IV 120-25.

35. Cooper to Peter Gansevoort, 5 May 1841, *Letters and Journals*, IV, 151-54.

36. Cooper to David H. Williams, 6 February 1841, *Letters and Journals*, IV, 115-16.

37. *Knickerbocker Magazine*, XVII (January, 1841) 72-73.

38. Richard Bentley to Cooper, London, 7 January 1841; MS: Collection of American Literature, Beinecke Rare Book and Manuscript Library, Yale University (cited hereafter as YCAL).

39. Lea and Blanchard to Cooper, Philadelphia, 9 February 1841; MS: YCAL.

40. Cooper to Richard Bentley, Cooperstown, 31 January 1841; *Letters and Journals*, IV, 111-13.

41. Cooper to James De Peyster Ogden, Cooperstown, 31 January 1841; *Letters and Journals*, IV, 113-14.

42. Bentley to Cooper, London, 5 March 1841; MS: YCAL.

43. Bentley to Cooper, London, 6 March 1841; MS: YCAL.

44. Cooper to Bentley, New York, 6 April 1841; *Letters and Journals*, IV, 147.

45. Cooper to Bentley, Cooperstown, 14 May 1841; *Letters and Journals*, IV, 153-54.

46. Cooper to Bentley, Cooperstown, 10 July 1841; *Letters and Journals*, IV, 163-64.

47. Bentley to Cooper, London, 14 August 1841; MS: YCAL.

48. Lea and Blanchard to Cooper, Philadelphia, 9 February 1841; MS: YCAL.

49. Cooper to George Roberts, Cooperstown, 13 February 1841; MS: unlocated, photograph furnished to the present writer.

50. Contract between Cooper and Lea and Blanchard for the publication of *The Deerslayer* and other literary works, negotiated on 2 April 1841. MS; Lea and Febiger, Philadelphia.

51. *Letters and Journals*, IV, 140.

52. Anonymous letter, dated "England—April" MS: YCAL.

53. Cooper to Mrs. Cooper, Philadelphia, 29 August 1841; *Letters and Journals*, IV, 167-68.

54. Cooper to Mrs. Cooper, Philadelphia, [22 June 1841]; *Letters and Journals*, IV, 159.

55. Cooper to Mrs. Cooper, Philadelphia, 17 September 1841; *Letters and Journals*, IV, 173-74.

56. *The New World*, III (4 September, 1841), 158.

57. *The New-York Mirror*, XIX (September 1841), 295.

58. *The Knickerbocker Magazine*, XVIII (October, 1841), 352.

59. Ibid., 349-52.

60. *Graham's Magazine*, XIX (October, 1841), 191.

61. *The Ladies' Companion*, XV (October, 1841), 310.

62. *United States Magazine and Democratic Review*, IX (October, 1841), 404-05.

63. *Godey's Lady's Book*, XIII (October, 1841), 189.
64. *Southern Literary Messenger*, VII (October, 1841), 742–43.
65. *The New York Review*, IX (October, 1841), 537–38 and *The Saturday Evening Post*, XXI (28 October 1841), 2 (column 8).
66. *The Athenaeum*, No. 724 (11 September 1841), 708.
67. Ibid., 708–11.
68. *The Literary Gazette and Journal of the Belles Lettres, Arts, Sciences, &c.*, No. 1286 (11 September 1841), 585–86.
69. *The Examiner*, No. 1754 (11 September 1841), 579.
70. Ibid., p. 580.
71. *The Court Journal*, No. 646 (11 September, 1841), 1493.
72. *The Metropolitan Magazine*, XXXII (October, 1841), 48–49.
73. *The Monthly Review*, s. 4, XI, No. 3 (October, 1841), 192–200.
74. *The New Monthly Belle Assemblee*, XV (November, 1841), 311.
75. Cooper to Thomas Warren Field, 17 August 1842; *Letters and Journals*, IV, 308–09.
76. *Letters and Journals*, IV, 345.
77. Joseph Ransom to Cooper, 15 October 1841; MS: YCAL. Published in *Correspondence of James Fenimore-Cooper*, Cooper, James Fenimore [grandson of the novelist], ed. (New Haven: Yale University Press, 1922), II, 451–53, MS: YCAL.
78. Anonymous letter to Cooper, postmarked Boston, September [1841?] MS: YCAL.
79. Thomas W. Field to Cooper, 15 August 1842; MS: YCAL.
80. Cooper to Thomas W. Field, 17 August 1842; *Letters and Journals*, IV, 308–09.
81. *The Literary World*, VII (5 October 1850), 271.
82. Ibid.
83. Daniel D. Barnard to Cooper, Albany, 26 September 1841; MS: YCAL.

THE DEERSLAYER

Preface.

[1841]

T his book has not been written, without many misgivings as to its probable reception. To carry one and the same character through five several works would seem to be a wilful over drawing on the good nature of the public, and many persons may very reasonably suppose it an act, of itself, that ought to invite a rebuke. To this natural objection, the author can only say that, if he has committed a grave fault on this occasion, his readers are in some measure answerable for it. The favorable manner in which the more advanced career, and the death of Leather Stocking were received, has created, in the mind of the author at least, a sort of necessity for giving some account of his younger days. In short the pictures, of his life, such as they are, were already so complete as to excite some little desire to see the 'study,' from which they have all been drawn.

"The Leather-Stocking Tales," form now something like a drama in five acts; complete as to material and design, though quite probably very incomplete as to execution. Such as they are, the reading world has them before it. Their author hopes, should it decide that this particular act, the last in execution, though the first in the order of perusal, is not the best of the series, it will also come to the conclusion that it is not absolutely the worst. More than once, he has been tempted to burn his manuscript, and to turn to some other subject, though he has met with an encouragement, in the course of his labors, of a character so singular, as to be worth mentioning. An anonymous letter from England, has reached him, written as he thinks by a lady, in which he is urged to do almost the very thing he had already more than half executed; a request that he has been willing enough to construe into a sign that his attempt will be partially forgiven, if not altogether commended.

Little need be said concerning the characters and scenery of this Tale. The former are fictitious, as a matter of course; but the latter is as true to nature, as an intimate knowledge of the present appearance of the region described, and such probable conjectures concerning its ancient state as could be furnished by the imagination, enabled the writer to render it. The lake, mountains, valley and forests, are all believed to be sufficiently exact, while the river, rock and shoal are faithful transcripts from nature. Even the points exist, a little altered by civilization, but so nearly answering to the descriptions, as to be easily recognised by all who are familiar with the scenery of the particular region in question.

As to the accuracy of the incidents, of this Tale, in whole or in part, it is the intention of the author to stand on his rights, and say no more than he deems to be necessary. In the great struggle for veracity, that is carrying on between History and Fiction, the latter has so often the best of it, that he is quite willing to refer the reader to his own researches, by way of settling this particular point. Should it appear on inquiry, that any professed historian, the public documents, or even the local traditions, contradict the statements of this book, the writer is ready to admit that the circumstance has entirely escaped his observation, and to confess his ignorance. On the other hand, should it be found that the annals of America do not contain a syllable, in opposition to what has been now laid before the world, as he firmly believes investigation will show to be the case, he shall claim for his legend just as much authority as it deserves.

There is a respectable class of novel-readers — respectable for numbers, quite as much as for every thing else — who have often been likened to the man that "sings when he reads, and reads when he sings." These persons are exceedingly imaginative in all matters of fact, and as literal as a school boy's translation, in every thing that relates to poetry. For the benefit of all such persons, it is explicitly stated, that Judith Hutter is Judith Hutter, and not Judith any one else; and, generally, that wherever a coincidence may occur in a christian name, or in the color of hair, nothing more is meant than can properly be inferred from a coincidence in a christian name, or in the color of hair. Long experience has taught the writer, that this portion of his readers is much the most difficult to please, and he would respectfully suggest, for the benefit of both parties, that they try the experiment of reading works of the imagination as if they were intended for matters of fact. Such a plan might possibly enable them to believe in the possibility of fiction.

There is another class of readers—less important certainly, in a republican country, inasmuch as it is materially in the minority—which is addicted to taking things as they are offered, and of understanding them as they are meant. These persons are advised to commence at chapter first, and to read consecutively, just as far as the occupation may prove agreeable to themselves, and not a page beyond it. Should any of this class reach the end of the book, and fancy the time spent in the perusal not entirely thrown away, the circumstance will afford its author sincere gratification.

Preface
to the
Leather-Stocking Tales.
[1850]

T HIS series of Stories, which has obtained the name of
"The Leather-Stocking Tales," has been written in a very
desultory and inartificial manner. The order in which the
several books appeared was essentially different from that in
which they would have been presented to the world, had the
regular course of their incidents been consulted. In "The Pioneers,"
the first of the series written, the Leather-Stocking is represented as already old, and driven from his early haunts in the
forest, by the sound of the axe, and the smoke of the settler.
"The Last of the Mohicans," the next book in the order of
publication, carried the readers back to a much earlier period
in the history of our hero, representing him as middle-aged,
and in the fullest vigor of manhood. In "The Prairie," his career
terminates, and he is laid in his grave. There, it was originally
the intention to leave him, in the expectation that, as in the
case of the human mass, he would soon be forgotten. But a latent
regard for this character induced the author to resuscitate him
in "The Pathfinder," a book that was not long after succeeded
by "The Deerslayer," thus completing the series as it now exists.

While the five books that have been written were originally
published in the order just mentioned, that of the incidents, in-
somuch as they are connected with the career of their principal
character, is, as has been stated, very different. Taking the life
of the Leather-Stocking as a guide, "The Deerslayer" should
have been the opening book, for in that work he is seen just
emerging into manhood; to be succeeded by "The Last of the
Mohicans," "The Pathfinder," "The Pioneers," and "The
Prairie." This arrangement embraces the order of events,

though far from being that in which the books at first appeared. "The Pioneers" was published in 1823; "The Deerslayer" in 1841; making the interval between them eighteen years. Whether these progressive years have had a tendency to lessen the value of the last-named book, by lessening the native fire of its author, or of adding somewhat in the way of improved taste and a more matured judgment, is for others to decide.

If anything from the pen of the writer of these romances is at all to outlive himself, it is, unquestionably, the series of "The Leather-Stocking Tales." To say this, is not to predict a very lasting reputation for the series itself, but simply to express the belief it will outlast any, or all, of the works from the same hand.

It is undeniable that the desultory manner in which "The Leather-Stocking Tales" were written, has, in a measure, impaired their harmony, and otherwise lessened their interest. This is proved by the fate of the two books last published, though probably the two most worthy an enlightened and cultivated reader's notice. If the facts could be ascertained, it is probable the result would show that of all those (in America, in particular) who have read the three first books of the series, not one in ten has a knowledge of the existence even of the two last. Several causes have tended to produce this result. The long interval of time between the appearance of "The Prairie" and that of "The Pathfinder," was itself a reason why the later books of the series should be overlooked. There was no longer novelty to attract attention, and the interest was materially impaired by the manner in which events were necessarily anticipated, in laying the last of the series first before the world. With the generation that is now coming on the stage this fault will be partially removed by the edition contained in the present work, in which the several tales will be arranged solely in reference to their connexion with each other.

The author has often been asked if he had any original in his mind, for the character of Leather-Stocking. In a physical sense, different individuals known to the writer in early life, certainly presented themselves as models, through his recollections; but in a moral sense this man of the forest is purely a creation. The idea of delineating a character that possessed little of civilization but its highest principles as they are exhibited in the uneducated, and all of savage life that is not incompatible with these great rules of conduct, is perhaps natural to the situation in which Natty was placed. He is too proud of his origin to sink into the condition of the wild Indian, and too much a man of the woods not to imbibe as much as was at all desirable, from his friends and companions. In a moral point of view it was the intention to illustrate the effect of seed scattered by the way side. To use his own language, his "gifts" were "white gifts," and he was not disposed to bring on them discredit. On the other hand, removed from nearly all the temptations of civilized life, placed in the best associations of that which is deemed savage, and favorably disposed by nature to improve such advantages, it appeared to the writer that his hero was a fit subject to represent the better qualities of both conditions, without pushing either to extremes.

There was no violent stretch of the imagination, perhaps, in supposing one of civilized associations in childhood, retaining many of his earliest lessons amid the scenes of the forest. Had these early impressions, however, not been sustained by continued, though casual connexion with men of his own color, if not of his own caste, all our information goes to show he would soon have lost every trace of his origin. It is believed that sufficient attention was paid to the particular circumstances in which this individual was placed, to justify the picture of his qualities that has been drawn. The Delawares early attracted the attention of the missionaries, and were a tribe unusually influenced by their precepts and example. In many instances they became Christians, and cases occurred in which their subsequent lives gave proof of the efficacy of the great moral changes that had taken place within them.

A leading character in a work of fiction has a fair right to the aid which can be obtained from a poetical view of the subject. It is in this view, rather than in one more strictly circumstantial, that Leather-Stocking has been drawn. The imagination has no great task in portraying to itself a being removed from the every-day inducements to err, which abound in civilized life, while he retains the best and simplest of his early impressions; who sees God in the forest; hears him in the winds; bows to him in the firmament that o'ercanopies all; submits to his sway in a humble belief of his justice and mercy; in a word, a being who finds the impress of the Deity in all the works of nature, without any of the blots produced by the expedients, and passion, and mistakes of man. This is the most that has been attempted in the character of Leather-Stocking. Had this been done without any of the drawbacks of humanity, the picture would have been, in all probability, more pleasing than just. In order to preserve the *vrai-semblable*, therefore, traits derived from the prejudices, tastes, and even the weaknesses of his youth, have been mixed up with these higher qualities and longings, in a way, it is hoped, to represent a reasonable picture of human nature, without offering to the spectator a "monster of goodness."

It has been objected to these books that they give a more favorable picture of the red man than he deserves. The writer apprehends that much of this objection arises from the habits of those who have made it. One of his critics, on the appearance of the first work in which Indian character was portrayed, objected that its "characters were Indians of the school of Heckewelder, rather than of the school of nature." These words quite probably contain the substance of the true answer to the objection. Heckewelder was an ardent, benevolent missionary, bent on the good of the red man, and seeing in him one who had the soul, reason, and characteristics of a fellow-being. The critic is understood to have been a very distinguished agent of the government, one very familiar with Indians, as they are seen at the councils to treat for the sale of their lands, where little or none of their domestic qualities come in play, and where, indeed, their evil passions are known to have the fullest scope. As just would it be to draw conclusions of the general state of American society from the scenes of the capital, as to suppose that the negotiating of one of these treaties is a fair picture of Indian life.

It is the privilege of all writers of fiction, more particularly when their works aspire to the elevation of romances, to present the *beau-idéal* of their characters to the reader. This it is which constitutes poetry, and to suppose that the red man is to be represented only in the squalid misery or in the degraded moral state that certainly more or less belongs to his condition, is, we apprehend, taking a very narrow view of an author's privileges. Such criticism would have deprived the world of even Homer.

Preface to Deerslayer.
[1850]

As has been stated in the preface to the series of the Leather-Stocking Tales, "The Deerslayer" is properly the first in the order of reading, though the last in that of publication. In this book the hero is represented as just arriving at manhood, with the freshness of feeling that belongs to that interesting period of life, and with the power to please that properly characterizes youth. As a consequence, he is loved; and, what denotes the real waywardness of humanity, more than it corresponds with theories and moral propositions, perhaps, he is loved by one full of art, vanity, and weakness, and loved principally for his sincerity, his modesty, and his unerring truth and probity. The preference he gives to the high qualities named, over beauty, delirious passion, and sin, it is hoped, will offer a lesson that can injure none. This portion of the book is intentionally kept down, though it is thought to be sufficiently distinct to convey its moral.

The intention has been to put the sisters in strong contrast; one admirable in person, clever, filled with the pride of beauty, erring, and fallen; the other, barely provided with sufficient capacity to know good from evil, instinct, notwithstanding, with the virtues of woman, reverencing and loving God, and yielding only to the weakness of her sex, in admiring personal attractions in one too coarse and unobservant to distinguish or to understand her quiet, gentle feeling in his favor.

As for the scene of this tale, it is intended for, and believed to be a close description of the Otsego, prior to the year 1760, when the first rude settlement was commenced on its banks, at that time only an insignificant clearing near the outlet, with a small hut of squared logs, for the temporary dwelling of the Deputy Superintendent of Indian affairs. The recollections of the writer carry him back distinctly to a time when nine tenths of the shores of this lake were in the virgin forest, a peculiarity that was owing to the circumstance of the roads running through the first range of valleys removed from the water side. The woods and the mountains have ever formed a principal source of beauty with this charming sheet of water, enough of the former remaining to this day to relieve the open grounds from monotony and tameness.

In most respects the descriptions of scenery in the tale are reasonably accurate. The rock appointed for the rendezvous between the Deerslayer and his friend the Delaware still remains, bearing the name of the Otsego Rock. The shoal on which Hutter is represented as having built his "castle" is a little misplaced, lying, in fact, nearer to the northern end of the lake, as well as to the eastern shore, than is stated in this book. Such a shoal, however, exists, surrounded on all sides by deep water. In the dryest seasons a few rocks are seen above the surface of the lake, and rushes, at most periods of the year, mark its locality. In a word, in all but precise position, even this feature of the book is accurate. The same is true of the several points introduced, of the bays, of the river, of the mountains, and all the other accessories of the place.

The legend is purely fiction, no authority existing for any of its facts, characters, or other peculiarities, beyond that which was thought necessary to secure the semblance of reality. Truth compels us to admit that the book has attracted very little notice, and that if its merits are to be computed by its popularity, the care that has been bestowed on this edition might as weil be spared. Such, at least, has been its fate in America; whether it has met with better success in any other country we have no means of knowing.

The Deerslayer

Chapter I.

"There is a pleasure in the pathless woods,
There is a rapture on the lonely shore,
There is society where none intrudes,
By the deep sea, and music in its roar:
I love not man the less, but nature more,
From these our interviews, in which I steal
From all I may be, or have been before,
To mingle with the universe, and feel
What I can ne'er express, yet cannot all conceal."
                    Byron, *Childe Harold's Pilgrimage*, IV.clxxviii.

On the human imagination, events produce the effects of time. Thus, he who has travelled far and seen much, is apt to fancy that he has lived long; and the history that most abounds in important incidents, soonest assumes the aspect of antiquity. In no other way can we account for the venerable air that is already gathering around American annals. When the mind reverts to the earliest days of colonial history, the period seems remote and obscure, the thousand changes that thicken along the links of recollections, throwing back the origin of the nation to a day so distant as seemingly to reach the mists of time; and yet four lives of ordinary duration would suffice to transmit, from mouth to mouth, in the form of tradition, all that civilized man has achieved within the limits of the republic. Although New-York, alone, possesses a population materially exceeding that of either of the four smallest kingdoms of Europe, or materially exceeding that of the entire Swiss Confederation, it is little more than two centuries since the Dutch commenced their settlement, rescuing the region from the savage state. Thus, what seems venerable by an accumulation of changes, is reduced to familiarity when we come seriously to consider it solely in connection with time.

This glance into the perspective of the past, will prepare the reader to look at the pictures we are about to sketch, with less surprise than he might otherwise feel, and a few additional explanations may carry him back in imagination, to the precise condition of society that we desire to delineate. It is matter of history that the settlements on the eastern shores of the Hudson, such as Claverack, Kinderhook, and even Poughkeepsie, were not regarded as safe from Indian incursions a century since, and there is still standing on the banks of the same river, and within musket shot of the wharves of Albany, a residence of a younger branch* of the van Rensselaers, that has loopholes constructed for defence against the same crafty enemy, although it dates from a period scarcely so distant. Other similar memorials of the infancy of the country are to be found, scattered through what is now deemed the very centre of American civilization, affording the plainest proofs that all we possess of security from invasion and hostile violence, is the growth of but little more than the time that is frequently filled by a single human life.

The incidents of this tale occurred between the years 1740 and 1745, when the settled portions of the Colony of New-York were confined to the four Atlantic counties, a narrow belt of country on each side of the Hudson, extending from its mouth to the falls near its head, and to a few advanced "neighborhoods" on the Mohawk and the Schoharie. Broad belts of the virgin wilderness, not only reached the shores of the first river, but they even crossed it, stretching away into New England, and affording forest cover to the noiseless moccasin of the native warrior, as he trod the secret and bloody war-path. A bird's eye view of the whole region east of the Mississippi, must then have offered one vast expanse of woods, relieved by a comparatively narrow fringe of cultivation along the sea, dotted by the glittering surfaces of lakes, and intersected by the waving lines of rivers. In such a vast picture of solemn solitude, the district of country we design to paint, sinks into insignificance, though we feel encouraged to proceed by the conviction that, with slight and immaterial distinctions, he who succeeds in giving an accurate idea of any portion of this wild region, must necessarily convey a tolerably correct notion of the whole.

Whatever may be the changes produced by man, the eternal round of the seasons is unbroken. Summer and winter, seed

---

* It is no more than justice to say that the Greenbush Van Rensselaers claim to be the oldest branch of that ancient and respectable family. [1850]

time and harvest, return in their stated order, with a sublime
precision, affording to man one of the noblest of all the occasions he enjoys of proving the high powers of his far reaching
mind, in compassing the laws that control their exact unifor-
mity, and in calculating their never ending revolutions. Centuries of summer suns had warmed the tops of the same noble
oaks and pines, sending their heats even to the tenacious roots,
when voices were heard calling to each other, in the depths of a
forest, of which the leafy surface lay bathed in the brilliant
light of a cloudless day in June, while the trunks of the trees
rose in gloomy grandeur in the shades beneath. The calls were
in different tones, evidently proceeding from two men who
had lost their way, and were searching in different directions
for their path. At length a shout proclaimed success, and
presently a man of gigantic mould broke out of the tangled
labyrinth of a small swamp, emerging into an opening that appeared to have been formed partly by the ravages of the wind,
and partly by those of fire. This little area, which afforded a
good view of the sky, although it was pretty well filled with
dead trees, lay on the side of one of the high hills, or low
mountains, into which nearly the whole surface of the adjacent
country was broken.

"Here is room to breathe in!" exclaimed the liberated
forester, as soon as he found himself under a clear sky, shaking
his huge frame like a mastiff that has just escaped from a snow
bank; "Hurrah! Deerslayer; here is day-light, at last, and
yonder is the lake, itself."

These words were scarcely uttered when the second forester
dashed aside the bushes of the swamp, and appeared in the
area. After making a hurried adjustment of his arms and
disordered dress, he joined his companion, who had already
begun his dispositions for a halt.

"Do you know this spot?" demanded the one called Deerslayer,
"or do you shout at the sight of the sun?"

"Both, lad, both; I know the spot, and am not sorry to see so
useful a friend as the sun. Now we have got the p'ints of the
compass in our minds, once more, and 'twill be our own faults
if we let any thing turn them topsy turvy, ag'in, as has just
happened. My name is not Hurry Harry, if this be not the
very spot where the land-hunters 'camped the last summer,

Guide to Important Sites

1. HYDE BAY.   Deerslayer and Harry March emerge here from the "tangled labyrinth of a small swamp" to their first clear view of the Glimmerglass.
2. PEGG'S POINT.   Here Deerslayer and Harry March first launch their canoe on Glimmerglass; and here Warley, his soldiers, and Judith depart for the Mohawk and Albany at the end.
3. MUSKRAT CASTLE.   Hutter's log stronghold, built on piles driven into a long narrow shoal near the middle of the lake.
4. 'RAT'S COVE.   The first Huron encampment, on or near Cooper's Fenimore Farm.
5. OTSEGO ROCK OR COUNCIL ROCK.   Deerslayer meets Chingachgook here at sunset on the second day.
6. SUSQUEHANNA RIVER.   Deerslayer and Harry find the Hutters and their Ark here.
7. THREEMILE POINT, SECOND HURON CAMP.   Site of Hist's rescue and Deerslayer's capture.
8. GRAVELLY POINT.   Deerslayer encounters the Huron named Lynx and receives the name Hawkeye after their mortal combat.
9. SIXMILE POINT, THIRD INDIAN CAMP.   Deerslayer delivers himself up for torture; also the site of the massacre.
10. HUTTER'S BURIAL GROUND.   Hetty, her mother, and Hutter receive watery interment here.
11. POINT JUDITH.   Here, in the epilogue, Hawkeye, Chingachgook, and Uncas discover the stranded and ruined Ark and a ribbon of Judith.

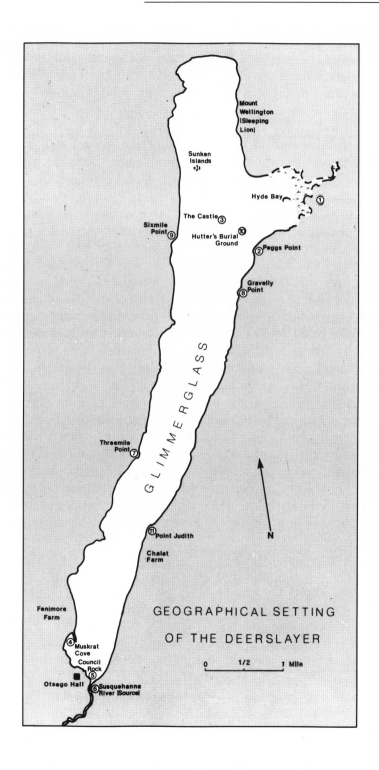

Mount
Wellington
(Sleeping
Lion)

Sunken
Islands

Hyde Bay ①

The Castle ③

Sixmile
Point ⑨

Hutter's Burial
Ground ⑩

② Peggs Point

Gravelly
Point ⑧

G L I M M E R G L A S S

Threemile
Point ⑦

⑪ Point Judith

Chalet
Farm

N

Fenimore
Farm

④ Muskrat
Cove

Council
Rock

⑤

Otsego Hall ⑥ Susquehanna
River (Source)

GEOGRAPHICAL SETTING

OF THE DEERSLAYER

0   1/2   1 Mile

and passed a week. See, yonder are the dead bushes of their bower, and here is the spring. Much as I like the sun, boy, I've no occasion for it to tell me it is noon; this stomach of mine is as good a timepiece as is to be found in the colony, and it already p'ints to half past twelve. So open the wallet, lad, and let us wind up for another six hours' run."

At this suggestion both set themselves about making the preparations necessary for their usual frugal, but hearty, meal. We will profit by this pause in the discourse to give the reader some idea of the appearance of the men, each of whom is destined to enact no insignificant part in our legend. It would not have been easy to find a more noble specimen of vigorous manhood, than was offered in the person of him who called himself Hurry Harry. His real name was Henry March, but the frontiermen having caught the practice of giving *sobriquets*, from the Indians, the appellation of Hurry was far oftener applied to him than his proper designation, and not unfrequently he was termed Hurry Skurry, a nick-name he had obtained from a dashing, reckless, off-hand manner, and a physical restlessness that kept him so constantly on the move, as to cause him to be known along the whole line of scattered habitations that lay between the province and the Canadas. The stature of Hurry Harry exceeded six feet four, and being unusually well proportioned, his strength fully realized the idea created by his gigantic frame. The face did no discredit to the rest of the man, for it was both good-humoured and handsome. His air was free, and though his manner necessarily partook of the rudeness of a border life, the grandeur that pervaded so noble a physique prevented it from becoming altogether vulgar.

Deerslayer, as Hurry called his companion, was a very different person in appearance, as well as in character. In stature, he stood about six feet in his moccasins, but his frame was comparatively light and slender, showing muscles, however, that promised unusual agility, if not unusual strength. His face would have had little to recommend it except youth, were it not for an expression that seldom failed to win upon those who had leisure to examine it, and to yield to the feeling of confidence it created. This expression was simply that of guileless truth, sustained by an earnestness of purpose, and a sincerity of feeling, that rendered it remarkable. At times this air of integrity seemed to be so simple as to awaken the suspicion of a want of the usual means to discriminate between artifice and truth, but few came in serious contact with the man, without losing this distrust in respect for his opinions and motives.

Both these frontiermen were still young, Hurry having reached the age of six or eight and twenty, while Deerslayer was several years his junior. Their attire needs no particular description, though it may be well to add that it was composed in no small degree of dressed deer skin, and had the usual signs of belonging to those who passed their time between the skirts of civilized society and the boundless forests. There was, notwithstanding, some attention to smartness and the picturesque in the arrangements of Deerslayer's dress, more particularly to the part connected with his arms and accoutrements. His rifle was in perfect condition, the handle of his hunting knife was neatly carved, his powder horn was ornamented with suitable devices lightly cut into the material, and his shot-pouch was decorated with wampum. On the other hand, Hurry Harry, either from constitutional recklessness, or from a secret consciousness how little his appearance required artificial aids, wore every thing in a careless, slovenly manner, as if he felt a noble scorn for the trifling accessories of dress and ornaments. Perhaps the peculiar effect of his fine form and great stature was increased, rather than lessened, by this unstudied and disdainful air of indifference.

"Come, Deerslayer, fall to, and prove that you have a Delaware stomach, as you say you have had a Delaware edication," cried Hurry, setting the example, by opening his mouth to receive a slice of cold venison steak, that would have made an entire meal for a European peasant. "Fall to, lad, and prove your manhood, on this poor devil of a doe, with your teeth, as you've already done with your rifle."

"Nay—nay, Hurry, there's little manhood in killing a doe, and that, too, out of season; though there might be some, in bringing down a painter, or a catamount," returned the other disposing himself to comply. "The Delawares have given me my name, not so much on account of a bold heart, as on account of a quick eye, and an act*y*ve foot. There may not be any coward*y*ce, in overcoming a deer, but sartain it is, there's no great valour."

"The Delawares, themselves, are no heroes," muttered Hurry through his teeth, the mouth being too full to permit it to be fairly opened, "or, they would never have allowed them loping vagabonds, the Mingos, to make them women."

"That matter is not rightly understood — has never been rightly explained," said Deerslayer earnestly, for he was as zealous a friend, as his companion was dangerous as an enemy. "The Mengwe fill the woods with their lies, and misconstruct words and treaties. I have now lived ten years with the Delawares, and know them to be as manful as any other nation, when the proper time to strike comes."

"Harkee, Master Deerslayer, since we are on the subject, we may as well open our minds to each other in a man to man way; answer me one question; you have had so much luck among the game as to have gotten a title, it would seem, but did you ever hit any thing human, or intelligible: did you ever pull trigger on an inimy that was capable of pulling one upon you?"

This question produced a singular collision between mortification and correct feeling, in the bosom of the youth, that was easily to be traced in the workings of his ingenuous countenance. The struggle was short, however, uprightness of heart soon getting the better of false pride, and frontier boastfulness.

"To own the truth, I never did," answered Deerslayer, "seeing that a fitting occasion never offered. The Delawares have been peaceable since my sojourn with 'em, and I hold it to be onlawful to take the life of man, except in open and ginerous warfare."

"What! — Did you never find a fellow thieving among your traps and skins, and do the law on him, with your own hands, by way of saving the magistrates trouble, in the settlements, and the rogue himself the costs of the suit?"

"I am no trapper, Hurry," returned the young man proudly. "I live by the rifle, a we'pon at which I will not turn my back on any man of my years, atween the Hudson and the St. Lawrence. I never offer a skin, that has not a hole in its head, besides them which natur' made to see with, or to breathe through."

"Ay—ay—this is all very well, in the animal way, though it makes but a poor figure along side of scalps and and-bushes. Shooting an Indian from an and-bush is acting up to his own principles, and now we have what you call a lawful war, on our hands, the sooner you wipe that disgrace off your character, the sounder will be your sleep; if it only come from knowing there is one inimy the less prowling in the woods. I shall not frequent your society long, friend Natty, unless you look higher than four footed beasts to practyse your rifle on."

"Our journey is nearly ended you say, Master March, and we can part to-night, if you see occasion. I have a fri'nd waiting for me, who will think it no disgrace to consart with a fellow creatur' that has never yet slain his kind."

"I wish I knew what has brought that skulking Delaware into this part of the country, so early in the season"—muttered Hurry to himself, in a way to show equally distrust, and a recklessness of its betrayal. "Where did you say, the young chief was to give you the meeting?"

"At a small round rock, near the foot of the lake, where they tell me the tribes are given to resorting to make their treaties, and to bury their hatchets. This rock have I often heard the Delawares mention, though lake and rock are equally strangers to me. The country is claimed by both Mingos and Mohicans, and is a sort of common territory to fish and hunt through, in times of peace, though what it may become in war-time, the Lord only knows!"

"Common territory!" exclaimed Hurry, laughing aloud. "I should like to know what Floating Tom Hutter would say to that? He claims the lake as his own property, in vartue of fifteen years' possession, and will not be likely to give it up to either Mingo or Delaware, without a battle for it."

"And what will the Colony say to such a quarrel—all this country must have some owner, the gentry pushing their cravings into the wilderness, even where they never dare to ventur' in their own parsons to look at the land they own."

"That may do in other quarters of the colony, Deerslayer, but it will not do here. Not a human being, the Lord excepted, owns a foot of s'ile, in this part of the country. Pen was never put to paper, consarning either hill or valley, hereaway, as I've heard old Tom say, time and ag'in, and so he claims the best right to it of any man breathing; and what Tom claims, he'll be very likely to maintain."

"By what I've heard you say, Hurry, this Floating Tom must be an oncommon mortal; neither Mingo, Delaware, nor Pale Face. His possession, too, has been long, by your tell, and altogether beyond frontier endurance. What's the man's history and human natur'?"

"Why as to old Tom's human natur' it is not much like other men's human natur', but more like a muskrat's human natur', seeing that he takes more to the ways of that animal than to the ways of any other fellow creatur'. Some think he was a free liver on the salt-water in his youth, and a companion of a sartain Kidd, who was hanged for piracy, long afore you and I were born, or acquainted, and that he came up into these regions, thinking that the King's cruisers could never cross the mountains, and that he might enjoy the plunder peaceably in the woods."

"There he was wrong, Hurry; very wrong. A man can enjoy plunder *peaceably* no where."

"That's much as his turn of mind may happen to be. I've known them that never could enjoy it at all, unless it was in the midst of a jollification, and them ag'in that enjoyed it best in a corner. Some men have no peace if they don't find plunder, and some if they do. Human natur' is crooked in these matters. Old Tom seems to belong to neither set, as he enjoys his, if plunder he has really got, with his darters, in a very quiet and comfortable way, and wishes for no more."

"Ay, he has darters, too; I've heard the Delawares, who've hunted this-a-way, tell their histories of these young women. Is there no mother, Hurry?"

"There was *once*, as in reason; but she has now been dead and sunk these two good years."

"Anan?" said Deerslayer, looking up at his companion in a little surprise.

"Dead and sunk, I say, and I hope that's good English. The old fellow lowered his wife into the lake, by way of seeing the last of her, as I can testify, being an eye-witness of the ceremony; but whether Tom did it to save digging, which is no easy job among roots, or out of a consait that water washes away sin sooner than 'arth, is more than I can say."

"Was the poor woman oncommon wicked, that her husband should take so much pains with her body?"

"Not onreasonable; though she had her faults. I consider Judith Hutter to have been as graceful, and about as likely to make a good ind, as any woman who had lived so long beyond the sound of church bells, and I conclude old Tom sunk her as much by way of *saving* pains, as by way of *taking* it. There was a little steel in her temper, it's true, and as old Hutter is pretty much flint, they struck out sparks once and awhile, but, on the whole, they might be said to live amicable like. When they did kindle, the listeners got some such insights into their past lives, as one gets into the darker parts of the woods, when a stray gleam of sunshine finds its way down to the roots of the trees. But Judith I shall always esteem, as it's recommend enough to one woman to be the mother of such a creatur' as her darter, Judith Hutter!"

"Ay, Judith was the name the Delawares mentioned, though it was pronounced after a fashion of their own. From their discourse I do not think the girl would much please my fancy."

"Thy fancy!" exclaimed March, taking fire equally at the indifference and at the presumption of his companion, "what the devil have you to do with a fancy, and that too consarning one like Judith? You are but a boy — a sapling that has scarce got root — Judith has had *men* among her suitors, ever since she was fifteen; which is now near five years; and will not be apt to cast even a look upon a half grown creatur' like you!"

"It is June, and there is not a cloud atween us and the sun, Hurry, so all this heat is not wanted," answered the other, altogether undisturbed; "any one may have a fancy, and a squirrel has a right to make up his mind touching a catamount."

"Ay, but it might not be wise, always, to let the catamount know it," growled March. "But you're young and thoughtless, and I'll overlook your ignorance. Come, Deerslayer," he added, with a good-natured laugh, after pausing a moment to reflect, "come, Deerslayer, we are sworn fri'nds, and will not quarrel about a light-minded, jilting jade, just because she happens to be handsome; more especially as you have never seen her.

Judith is only for a man whose teeth show the full marks, and it's foolish to be afeard of a boy. What *did* the Delawares say of the hussy; for, an Indian, after all, has his notions of womankind, as well as a white man?"

"They said she was fair to look on, and pleasant of speech; but over-given to admirers, and light-minded."

"They are devils incarnate! After all, what schoolmaster is a match for an Indian, in looking into natur'? Some people think they are only good on a trail, or the war-path, but I say that they are philosophers, and understand a man, as well as they understand a beaver, and a woman as well as they understand either. Now that's Judith's character to a riband! To own the truth to you, Deerslayer, I should have married the gal two years since, if it had not been for two particular things, one of which was this very light-mindedness."

"And what may have been the other?" demanded the hunter, who continued to eat like one that took very little interest in the subject.

"T' other was an insartainty about her having *me*. The hussy is handsome, and she knows it. Boy, not a tree that is growing in these hills is straighter, or waves in the wind with an easier bend, nor did you ever see the doe that bounded with a more nat'ral motion. If that was all, every tongue would sound her praises; but she has such failings that I find it hard to overlook them, and sometimes I swear I'll never visit the lake ag'in."

"Which is the reason that you always come back? Nothing is ever made more sure by swearing about it."

"Ah, Deerslayer, you are a novelty in these partic'lars; keeping as true to edication as if you had never left the settlements. With me the case is different, and I never want to clinch an idee, that I do not feel a wish to swear about it. If you know'd all that I know consarning Judith, you'd find a justification for a little cussing. Now, the officers sometimes stray over to the lake, from the forts on the Mohawk, to fish and hunt, and then the creatur' seems beside herself! You can see it in the manner in which she wears her finery, and the airs she gives herself with the gallants."

"That is unseemly in a poor man's darter," returned Deerslayer gravely, "the officers are all gentry, and can only look on such as Judith with evil intentions."

"There's the unsartainty, and the damper! I have my misgivings about a particular captain, and Jude has no one to blame but her own folly, if I'm wrong. On the whole, I wish to look upon her as modest and becoming, and yet the clouds that drive among these hills are not more unsartain. Not a dozen white men have ever laid eyes upon her, since she was a child, and yet her airs, with two or three of these officers, are extinguishers!"

"I would think no more of such a woman, but turn my mind altogether to the forest; *that* will not deceive you, being ordered and ruled by a hand that never wavers."

"If you know'd Judith, you would see how much easier it is to say this, than it would be to do it. Could I bring my mind to be easy about the officers, I would carry the gal off to the Mohawk by force, make her marry me in spite of her whiffling, and leave old Tom to the care of Hetty, his other child, who, if she be not as handsome, or as quick-witted as her sister, is much the most dutiful."

"Is there another bird in the same nest?" asked Deerslayer, raising his eyes with a species of half-awakened curiosity— "The Delawares spoke to me only of one."

"That's nat'ral enough, when Judith Hutter and Hetty Hutter are in question. Hetty is only comely, while her sister, I tell thee, boy, is such another as is not to be found atween this and the sea; Judith is as full of wit, and talk, and cunning, as an old Indian orator, while poor Hetty, is at the best but 'compass meant us.' "

"Anan?" inquired, again, the Deerslayer.

"Why, what the officers call, 'compass meant us,' which I understand to signify that she means always to go in the right direction, but sometimes does'nt know how. 'Compass' for the p'int, and 'meant us' for the intention. No, poor Hetty, is what I call on the varge of ignorance, and sometimes she stumbles on one side of the line, and sometimes on t'other."

"Them are beings that the Lord has in his 'special care," said Deerslayer, solemnly, "for he looks carefully to all who fall short of their proper share of reason. The Redskins honor and respect them who are so gifted, knowing that the Evil Spirit delights more to dwell in an artful body, than in one that has no cunning to work upon."

"I'll answer for it, then, that he will not remain long with poor Hetty—for the child is just 'compass meant us,' as I have told you. Old Tom has a feeling for the gal, and so has Judith, quick witted and glorious as she is herself; else would I not answer for her being altogether safe among the sort of men that sometimes meet on the lake shore."

"I thought this water an onknown and little frequented sheet," observed the Deerslayer, evidently uneasy at the idea of being too near the world.

"It's all that, lad, the eyes of twenty white men never having been laid on it; still, twenty true bred frontiermen—hunters, and trappers, and scouts, and the like,—can do a deal of mischief if they try. 'Twould be an awful thing to me, Deerslayer, did I find Judith married, after an absence of six months!"

"Have you the gal's faith, to incourage you to hope otherwise."

"Not at all. I know not how it is—I'm good-looking, boy; that much I can see in any spring on which the sun shines—and yet I could never get the hussy to a promise, or even a cordial willing smile, though she will laugh by the hour. If she *has* dared to marry in my absence, she'll be like to know the pleasures of widowhood, afore she is twenty!"

"You would not harm the man she had chosen, Hurry, simply because she found him more to her liking than yourself?"

"Why not? If an inimy crosses my path, will I not beat him out of it! Look at me—am I a man like to let any sneaking, crawling, skin-trader, get the better of me in a matter that touches me as near as the kindness of Judith Hutter? Besides, when we live beyond law, we must be our own judges and executioners. And if a man *should* be found dead in the woods, who is there to say who slew him, even admitting that the Colony took the matter in hand, and made a stir about it?"

"If that man should be Judith Hutter's husband, after what has passed, I might tell enough, at least, to put the Colony on the trail."

"You!—Half-grown, venison hunting bantling! You, dare to think of informing against Hurry-Harry in so much as a matter touching a mink, or a woodchuck!"

"I would dare to speak truth, Hurry, consarning you, or any man that ever lived."

March looked at his companion, for a moment, in silent amazement; then seizing him by the throat, with both hands, he shook his comparatively slight frame, with a violence that menaced the dislocation of some of the bones. Nor was this done jocularly, for anger flashed from the giant's eyes, and there were certain signs, that seemed to threaten much more earnestness than the occasion would appear to call for. Whatever might be the real intention of March, and it is probable there was none settled in his mind, it is certain that he was unusually aroused, and most men who found themselves throttled by one of a mould so gigantic, in such a mood, and in a solitude so deep and helpless, would have felt intimidated, and tempted to yield even the right. Not so, however, with Deerslayer. His countenance remained unmoved; his hand did not shake, and his answer was given in a voice that did not resort to the artifice of louder tones, even, by way of proving its owner's resolution.

"You may shake, Hurry, until you bring down the mountain," he said quietly, "but nothing beside truth will you shake from me. It is probable that Judith Hutter has no husband to slay, and you may never have a chance to way lay one, else would I tell her of your threat, in the first conversation I held with the gal."

March released his gripe, and sat regarding the other, in silent astonishment.

"I thought we had been friends," he at length added—"but you've got the last secret of mine, that will ever enter your ears."

"I want none, if they are to be like this. I know we live in the woods, Hurry, and are thought to be beyond human laws—and perhaps we are so, in fact, whatever it may be in right—but there is a law, and a law maker, that rule across the whole continent. He that flies in the face of either, need not call me fri'nd."

"Damme, Deerslayer, if I do not believe you are, at heart, a Moravian, and no fair minded, plain dealing hunter, as you've pretended to be!"

"Fair minded or not, Hurry, you will find me as plain-dealing in deeds, as I am in words. But this giving way to sudden anger is foolish, and proves how little you have sojourned with the red men. Judith Hutter no doubt is still single, and you spoke but as the tongue ran, and not as the heart felt. There's my hand, and we will say and think no more about it."

Hurry seemed more surprised than ever; then he burst forth in a loud good-natured laugh, which brought tears to his eyes. After this, he accepted the offered hand, and the parties became friends.

"'Twould have been foolish to quarrel about an idee," March cried, as he resumed his meal, "and more like lawyers in the towns, than like sensible men in the woods. They tell me, Deerslayer, much ill blood grows out of idees, among the people in the lower counties, and that they sometimes get to extremities upon them."

"That do they — that do they, and about other matters that might better be left to take care of themselves. I have heard the Moravians say that there are lands in which men quarrel even consarning their religion, and if they can get their tempers up on such a subject, Hurry, the Lord have marcy on 'em. Howsever, there is no occasion for our following their example, and more especially about a husband that this Judith Hutter may never see, or never wish to see. For my part, I feel more cur'osity about the feeble-witted sister, than about your beauty. There's something that comes close to a man's feelin's, when he meets with a fellow creatur' that has all the outward show of an accountable mortal, and who fails of being what he seems, only through a lack of reason. This is bad enough in a man, but when it comes to a woman, and she a young, and may-be a winning creatur', it touches all the pitiful thoughts his natur' has. God knows, Hurry, that such poor things be defenceless enough with all their wits about 'em; but it's a cruel fortun' when that great protector and guide fails 'em."

"Harkee, Deerslayer, you know what the hunters, and trappers, and peltry-men in general be, and their best friends will not deny that they are head-strong and given to having their own way without much bethinking 'em of other people's rights, or feelin's, and yet I don't think the man is to be found, in all this region, who would harm Hetty Hutter, if he could; no, not even a red skin."

"Therein, fri'nd Hurry, you do the Delawares at least, and all their allied tribes only justice, for a red skin looks upon a being thus struck by God's power, as especially under his care. I rejoice to hear what you say, howsever, I rejoice to hear it, but as the sun is beginning to turn towards the a'ternoon's sky, had we not better strike the trail ag'in, and make forward that we may get an opportunity of seeing these wonderful sisters."

Harry March giving a cheerful assent, the remnants of the meal were soon collected; then the travellers shouldered their packs, resumed their arms, and quitting the little area of light, they again plunged into the deep shadows of the forest.

Chapter II.

"Thou'rt passing from the lake's green side,
  And the hunter's hearth away;
For the time of flowers, for the summer's pride,
  Daughter! Thou canst not stay."
    Mrs. Hemans, "Edith. A Tale of the Woods," 11.191-94.

Our two adventurers had not far to go. Hurry knew the direction, as soon as he had found the open spot and the spring, and he now led on with the confident step of a man assured of his object. The forest was dark, as a matter of course, but it was no longer obstructed by under brush, and the footing was firm and dry. After proceeding near a mile, March stopped, and began to cast about him with an inquiring look, examining the different objects with care, and occasionally turning his eyes on the trunks of the fallen trees, with which the ground was well sprinkled, as is usually the case in an American wood, especially in those parts of the country where timber has not yet become valuable.

"*This* must be the place, Deerslayer," March at length observed—"Here is a beech by the side of a hemlock, with three pines at hand, and yonder is a white birch with a broken top; and yet I see no rock, nor any of the branches bent down, as I told you would be the case."

"Broken branches are onskilful land-marks, as the least exper'enced know that branches don't often break of themselves," returned the other, "and they also lead to suspicion and discoveries. The Delawares never trust to broken branches, unless it is in friendly times, and on an open trail. As for the beeches, and pines, and hemlocks, why, they are to be seen on all sides of us, not only by two and threes, but by forties, and fifties and hundreds."

"Very true, Deerslayer, but you never calcilate on positions? — Here is a beech and a hemlock—"

"Yes, and there is another beech and a hemlock, as loving as two brothers, or, for that matter, more loving than some brothers; and yonder are others, for neither tree is a rarity in these woods. I fear me, Hurry, you are better at trapping beaver and shooting bears, than at leading on a blindish sort of a trail—ha! There's what you wish to find, a'ter all!"

"Now, Deerslayer, this is one of your Delaware pretensions, for, hang me if I see any thing but these trees, which do seem to start up around us, in a most onaccountable and perplexing manner."

"Look this-a-way, Hurry—here in a line with the black oak—don't you see the crooked sapling that is hooked up in the branches of the bass-wood, near it?—now, that sapling was once snow-ridden and got the bend by its weight, but it never straightened itself, and fastened itself in among the bass-wood branches, in the way you see. The hand of man did that act of kindness for it."

"That hand was mine!" exclaimed Hurry. "I found the slender young thing bent to the airth, like an unfortunate creatur' borne down by misfortune, and stuck it up where you see it. After all, Deerslayer, I must allow you're getting to have an oncommon good eye for the woods!"

" 'Tis improving, Hurry—'tis improving, I will acknowledge, but 'tis still only a child's eye compared to some I know. There's Tamenund, now, though a man so old, that few remember when he was in his prime, Tamenund lets nothing escape his look, which is more like the scent of a hound, than the sight of an eye. Then Uncas,* the father of Chingachgook, and the lawful chief of the Mohicans, is another that it is almost hopeless to pass unseen. I'm improving, I will allow; I'm improving but far from being parfect, as yet."

"And who is this Chingachgook, of whom you talk so much, Deerslayer?" asked Hurry, as he moved off in the direction of the righted sapling—"a loping red skin, at the best, I make no question."

"Not so, Hurry, but the best of loping red-skins, as you call 'em. If he had his rights, he would be a great chief; but, as it is, he is only a brave and just minded Delaware; respected, and even obeyed in some things 'tis true, but of a fallen race, and

*Lest the similarity of the names should produce confusion, it may be well to say that the Uncas here mentioned is the grandfather of him who plays so conspicuous a part in the Last of the Mohicans. [1850]

belonging to a fallen people. Ah! Harry March, 'twould warm the heart within you, to sit in their lodges of a winter's night, and listen to the traditions of the ancient greatness and power of the Mohicans!"

"Harkee, fri'nd Nathaniel," said Hurry, stopping short to face his companion, in order that his words might carry greater weight with them, "if a man believed all that other people choose to say in their own favor, he might get an oversized opinion of them, and an undersized opinion of himself. These red-skins are notable boasters, and I set down more than half of their traditions, as pure talk."

"There is truth in what you say, Hurry; I'll not deny it, for I've seen it, and believe it. They *do* boast, but then that is a gift from natur', and it's sinful to withstand nat'ral gifts. See; this is the spot you come to find."

This remark cut short the discourse, and both the men now gave all their attention to the object immediately before them. Deerslayer pointed out to his companion the trunk of a huge linden, or bass-wood, as it is termed in the language of the country, which had filled its time, and fallen by its own weight. This tree, like so many millions of its brethren, lay where it had fallen, and was mouldering under the slow but certain influence of the seasons. The decay, however, had attacked its centre, even while it stood erect, in the pride of vegetation, hollowing out its heart, as disease sometimes destroys the vitals of animal life, even while a fair exterior is presented to the observer. As the trunk lay stretched for near a hundred feet along the earth, the quick eye of the hunter detected this peculiarity, and, from this, and other circumstances, he knew it to be the tree of which March was in search.

"Ay, here we have what we want," cried Hurry, looking in at the larger end of the linden; "every thing is as snug as if it had been left in an old woman's cupboard. Come, lend me a hand, Deerslayer, and we'll be afloat in half an hour."

At this call the hunter joined his companion, and the two went to work deliberately and regularly, like men accustomed to the sort of thing in which they were employed. In the first place, Hurry removed some pieces of bark that lay before the large opening in the tree, and which the other declared to be disposed in a way that would have been more likely to attract attention, than to conceal the cover, had any straggler passed that way. The two, then, drew out a bark canoe, containing its seats, paddles, and other appliances, even to fishing lines and rods. This vessel was by no means small, but such was its comparative lightness, and so gigantic was the strength of Hurry, that the latter shouldered it with seeming ease, declining all assistance even in the act of raising it to the awkward position in which he was obliged to hold it.

"Lead ahead, Deerslayer," said March, "and open the bushes; the rest I can do for myself."

The other obeyed, and the men left the spot, Deerslayer clearing the way for his companion, and inclining to the right, or to the left, as the latter directed. In about ten minutes, they both broke suddenly into the brilliant light of the sun, on a low gravelly point, that was washed by water, on quite half of its outline.

An exclamation of surprise broke from the lips of Deerslayer, an exclamation that was low and guardedly made, however, for his habits were much more thoughtful and regulated than those of the reckless Hurry, when on reaching the margin of the lake he beheld the view that unexpectedly met his gaze. It was, in truth, sufficiently striking to merit a brief description. On a level with the point lay a broad sheet of water, so placid and limpid, that it resembled a bed of the pure mountain atmosphere, compressed into a setting of hills and woods. Its length was about three leagues, while its breadth was irregular, expanding to half a league, or even more, opposite to the point, and contracting to less than half that distance more to the southward. Of course its margin was irregular, being indented by bays, and broken by many projecting, low, points. At its northern, or nearest end, it was bounded by an isolated mountain, lower land falling off, east and west, gracefully relieving the sweep of the outline. Still the character of the country was mountainous; high hills, or low mountains, rising abruptly from the water, on quite nine tenths of its circuit. The exceptions, indeed, only served a little to vary the scene, and even beyond the parts of the shore that were comparatively low, the back-ground was high, though more distant.

But the most striking peculiarities of this scene, were its solemn solitude, and sweet repose. On all sides, wherever the eye turned, nothing met it, but the mirror-like surface of the lake, the placid void of heaven, and the dense setting of wood. So rich and fleecy were the outlines of the forest, that scarce an opening could be seen, the whole visible earth, from the rounded mountain-top, to the water's edge, presenting one unvaried hue of unbroken verdure. As if vegetation were not satisfied with a triumph so complete, the trees overhung the lake, itself, shooting out towards the light, and there were miles along its eastern shore, where a boat might have pulled beneath the branches, of dark, Rembrandt-looking hem-locks, "quivering aspens," and melancholy pines. In a word, the hand of man had never yet defaced, or deformed any part of this native scene, which lay bathed in the sun-light, a glorious picture of affluent forest grandeur, softened by the balminess of June, and relieved by the beautiful variety afforded by the presence of so broad an expanse of water.

"This is grand! — 'Tis solemn! — 'Tis an edication of itself, to look upon!" exclaimed Deerslayer, as he stood leaning on his rifle, and gazing to the right and left, north and south, above and beneath, in whichever direction his eye could wander. "Not a tree disturbed, even by red skin hand, as I can discover, but every thing left in the ordering of the Lord, to live and die according to his own designs and laws! Hurry, your Judith ought to be a moral and well disposed young woman, if she has passed half the time you mention, in the centre of a spot so favored."

"That's a naked truth, and yet the gal has her vagaries. *All* her time has not been passed here, howsever, old Tom having the custom, afore I know'd him, of going to spend the winters, in the neighborhood of the settlers, or under the guns of the forts. No — no — Jude has caught more than is for her good, from the settlers, and especially from the gallantifying officers."

"If she has — if she has, Hurry, this is a school to set her mind right, ag'in. But what is this I see off here, abreast of us, that seems too small for an island, and too large for a boat, though it stands in the midst of the water."

"Why that is what these gallanting gentry from the forts, call Muskrat Castle, and old Tom, himself, will grin at the name, though it bears so hard on his own natur' and character. 'Tis the stationary house, there being two; this which never moves, and the other that floats, being sometimes in one part of the lake, and sometimes in another. The last goes by the name of the Ark, though what may be the meaning of the word, is more than I can tell you."

"It must come from the missionaries, Hurry, whom I have heard speak and read of such a thing. They say that the 'arth was once covered with water, and that Noah with his children, was saved from drowning by building a vessel called an Ark, in which he embarked in season. Some of the Delawares believe this tradition, and some deny it; but, it behoves you and me, as white men born, to put our faith in its truth. Do you see any thing of this ark?"

"'Tis down south, no doubt, or anchored in some of the bays. But the canoe is ready, and fifteen minutes will carry two such paddles as your'n and mine, to the castle."

At this suggestion, Deerslayer helped his companion to place the different articles in the canoe, which was already afloat. This was no sooner done, than the two frontiermen embarked, and by a vigorous push sent the light bark some eight or ten rods from the shore. Hurry now took the seat in the stern, while Deerslayer placed himself forward, and by leisurely but steady strokes of the paddles, the canoe glided across the placid sheet, towards the extraordinary looking structure, that the former had styled Muskrat Castle. Several times the men ceased paddling, and looked about them at the scene, as new glimpses opened from behind points, enabling them to see farther down the lake, or to get broader views of the wooded mountains. The only changes, however, were in the new forms of the hills, the varying curvature of the bays, and the wider reaches of the valley south, the whole earth apparently being clothed in a gala dress of leaves.

"This *is* a sight to warm the heart!" exclaimed Deerslayer, when they had thus stopped for the fourth or fifth time. "The lake seems made to let us get an insight into the noble forests; and land and water, alike, stand in the beauty of God's Providence! Do you say, Hurry, that there is no man who calls himself lawful owner of all these glories?"

"None but the King, lad. He may pretend to some right of that natur', but he is so far away that his claim will never trouble old Tom Hutter, who has got possession, and is like to keep it as long as his life lasts. Tom is no squatter, not being on land; I call him a floater."

"I in*vy* that man! — I know it's wrong, and I strive ag'in the feelin', but I in*vy* that man! Do'n't think, Hurry, that I'm consarting any plan to put myself in his moccasins, for such a thought does not harbor in my mind, but I can't help a little in*vy*. 'Tis a nat'ral feelin', and the best of us are but nat'ral, a'ter all, and give way to such feelin's, at times."

"You've only to marry Hetty to inherit half the estate," cried Hurry, laughing. "The gal is comely; nay, if it was n't for her sister's beauty, she would be even handsome; and then her wits are so small that you may easily convart her into one of your own way of thinking in all things. Do *you* take Hetty off the old fellow's hands, and *I'll* engage he'll give you an interest in every deer you can knock over, within five miles of his lake."

"Does game abound?" suddenly demanded the other, who paid but little attention to March's raillery.

"It has the country to itself. Scarce a trigger is pulled on it, and as for the trappers, this is not a region they greatly frequent. I ought not to be so much here, myself, but Jude pulls one way, while the beaver pulls another. More than a hundred Spanish dollars has that creatur' cost me, the two last seasons; and yet I could not forego the wish to look upon her face, once more."

"Do the red-men often visit this lake, Hurry?" continued Deerslayer, pursuing his own train of thought.

"Why, they come and go; sometimes in parties, and sometimes singly. The country seems to belong to no native tribe in particular, and so it has fallen into the hands of the Hutter tribe. The old man tells me that some sharp ones have been wheedling the Mohawks for an Indian deed, in order to git a title out of the Colony, but nothing has come of it, seeing that no one heavy enough for such a trade, has yet meddled with the matter. The hunters have a good life lease, still, of this wilderness."

"So much the better — so much the better, Hurry. If I was King of England the man that fell one of these trees without good occasion for the timber, should be banished to a desarted and forlorn region, in which no four footed animal ever trod.

Right glad am I that Chingachgook app'inted our meeting on this lake, for, hitherto, eye of mine never looked on such a glorious spectacle!"

"That's because you've kept so much among the Delawares, in whose country there are no lakes. Now, further north, and farther west, these bits of water abound, and you're young, and may yet live to see 'em. But, though there be other lakes, Deerslayer, there's no other Judith Hutter."

At this remark his companion smiled, and then he dropped his paddle into the water, as if, in consideration of a lover's haste. Both now pulled vigorously until they got within a hundred yards of the "castle," as Hurry familiarly called the house of Hutter, when they again ceased paddling, the admirer of Judith restraining his impatience the more readily, as he perceived that the building was untenanted, at the moment. This new pause was to enable Deerslayer to survey the singular edifice, which was of a construction so novel as to merit a particular description.

Muskrat Castle, as the house had been facetiously named by some waggish officer, stood in the open lake, at a distance of fully a quarter of a mile from the nearest shore. On every other side the water extended much farther, the precise position being distant about two miles from the northern end of the sheet, and near, if not quite a mile from its eastern shore. As there was not the smallest appearance of any island, but the house stood on piles with the water flowing beneath it, and Deerslayer had already discovered that the lake was of a great depth, he was fain to ask an explanation of this singular circumstance. Hurry solved the difficulty by telling him that on this spot alone, a long narrow shoal, which extended for a few hundred yards in a north and south direction, rose within six or eight feet of the surface of the lake, and that Hutter had driven piles into it, and placed his habitation on them, for the purpose of security.

"The old fellow was burnt out three times, atween the Indians and the hunters, and in one affray with the red skins he lost his only son; since which time he has taken to the water for safety. No one can attack him, here, without coming in a boat, and the plunder and scalps would scarce be worth the trouble of digging out canoes. Then, it's by no means sartain which would whip, in such a skrimmage, for, old Tom is well supplied with arms and ammunition, and the castle, as you may see, is a tight breast-work, ag'in light shot."

Deerslayer had some theoretical knowledge of frontier warfare, though he had never yet been called on to raise his hand, in anger, against a fellow creature. He saw that Hurry did not over-rate the strength of this position, in a military point of view, since it would not be easy to attack it, without exposing the assailants to the fire of the besieged. A good deal of art had also been manifested in the disposition of the timber, of which the building was constructed, and which afforded a protection much greater than was usual to the ordinary log cabins of the frontier. The sides and ends were composed of the trunks of large pines, cut about nine feet long, and placed upright, instead of being laid horizontally, as was the practice of the country. These logs were squared on three sides, and had large tennons on each end. Massive sills were secured on the heads of the piles, with suitable grooves dug out of their upper surfaces, which had been squared for the purpose, and the lower tennons of the upright pieces were placed in these grooves, giving them a secure fastening below. Plates had been laid on the upper ends of the upright logs, and were kept in their places, by a similar contrivance; the several corners of the structure being well fastened by scarfing and pinning the sills, and plates. The floors were made of smaller logs, similarly squared, and the roof was composed of light poles, firmly united, and well covered with bark. The effect of this ingenious arrangement was to give its owner a house that could be approached only by water, the sides of which were composed of logs, closely wedged together, which were two feet thick in their thinnest parts and which could be separated only by a deliberate and laborious use of human hands, or by the slow operation of time. The outer surface of the building was rude and uneven, the logs being of unequal sizes, but the squared surfaces within, gave both the sides and floors as uniform an appearance as was desired either for use, or show. The chimney was not the least singular portion of the castle, as Hurry made his companion observe, while he explained the process by which it had been made. The material was a stiff clay, properly worked, which had been put together in a mould of sticks, and suffered to harden a foot or two, at a time, commencing at the bottom. When the entire chimney had thus been raised, and had been properly bound in with outward props, a brisk fire was kindled, and kept going until it was burned to something like a brick red. This had not been an easy operation, nor had it succeeded entirely, but by dint of filling the cracks with fresh clay, a safe fire-place and chimney had been obtained in the end. This part of the work stood on the log floor, secured beneath by an extra pile. There were a few other peculiarities about this dwelling, which will better appear in the course of the narrative.

"Old Tom is full of contrivances," added Hurry, "and he set his heart on the success of his chimney, which threatened, more than once, to give out altogether, but parseverance will even overcome smoke; and now he has a comfortable cabin of it, though it did promise, at one time, to be a chinky sort of a flue to carry flames and fire."

"You seem to know the whole history of the castle, Hurry, chimney and sides," said Deerslayer, smiling. "Is love so overcoming that it causes a man to study the story of his sweetheart's habitation?"

"Partly that, lad, and partly eye sight," returned the good natured giant, laughing. "There was a large gang of us, in at the lake, the summer the old fellow built, and we helped him along with the job. I raised no small part of the weight of them uprights with my own shoulders, and the axes flew, I can inform you, Master Natty, while we were beeing it among the trees ashore. The old devil is no way stingy about food, and as we had often eat at his hearth, we thought we would just house him comfortably, afore we went in to Albany with our skins. Yes, many is the meal I've swallowed in Tom Hutter's cabins, and, Hetty, though so weak in the way of wits, has a wonderful particular way about a frying pan, or a grid-iron!"

While the parties were thus discoursing, the canoe had been gradually drawing nearer to the 'castle', and was now so close, as to require but a single stroke of a paddle to reach the landing. This was at a floored platform in front of the entrance, that might have been some twenty feet square.

"Old Tom calls this sort of a wharf, his door-yard," observed Hurry, as he fastened the canoe, after he and his companion had left it, "and the gallants from the forts have named it the 'castle court,' though what a 'court' can have to do here, is more than I can tell you, seeing that there is no law. 'Tis as I supposed; not a soul within, but the whole family is off on a v'y'ge of discovery!"

While Hurry was bustling about the 'door yard', examining the fishing spears, rods, nets and other similar appliances of a frontier cabin, Deerslayer, whose manner was altogether more rebuked and quiet, entered the building, with a curiosity that was not usually exhibited by one so long trained in Indian habits. The interior of the 'castle' was as faultlessly neat, as its exterior was novel. The entire space, some twenty feet by forty, was subdivided into several small sleeping rooms, the apartment into which he first entered serving equally for the ordinary uses of its inmates, and for a kitchen. The furniture was of the strange mixture that it is not uncommon to find in the remotely situated log tenements of the interior. Most of it was rude and to the last degree rustic, but there was a clock, with a handsome case of dark wood, in a corner, and two or three chairs, with a table and bureau, that had evidently come from some dwelling of more than usual pretension. The clock was industriously ticking, but its leaden-looking hands did no discredit to their dull aspect, for they pointed to the hour of eleven, though the sun plainly showed it was some time past the turn of the day. There was also a dark, massive chest. The kitchen utensils were of the simplest kind, and far from numerous, but every article was in its place, and showed the nicest care in its condition.

After Deerslayer had cast a look about him, in the outer room, he raised a wooden latch, and entered a narrow passage that divided the inner end of the house, into two equal parts. Frontier usages being no way scrupulous, and his curiosity being strongly excited, the young man now opened a door, and found himself in a bed-room. A single glance sufficed to show that the apartment belonged to females. The bed was of the feathers of wild geese, and filled nearly to overflowing, but it lay in a rude bunk, raised only a foot from the floor. On one side of it were arranged on pegs, various dresses of a quality much superior to what one would expect to meet in such a place, with ribbons and other similar articles to correspond.

Pretty shoes, with handsome silver buckles, such as were then worn by females in easy circumstances, were not wanting, and no less than six fans of gay colours, were placed, half open, in a way to catch the eye by their conceits and hues. Even the pillow on this side of the bed, was covered with finer linen than its companion, and it was ornamented with a small ruffle. A cap, coquettishly decorated with ribbons, hung above it, and a pair of long gloves, such as were rarely used in those days by persons of the laboring classes, were pinned ostentatiously to it, as if with an intention to exhibit them there, if they could not be shown on the owner's arms.

All this Deerslayer saw, and noted with a degree of minuteness that would have done credit to the habitual observation of his friends the Delawares. Nor did he fail to perceive the distinction that existed between the appearances on the different sides of the bed, the head of which stood against the wall. On that opposite to the one just described, every thing was homely, and uninviting except through its perfect neatness. The few garments that were hanging from the pegs, were of the coarsest materials, and of the commonest forms, while nothing seemed made for show. Of ribbons there was not one, nor was there either cap, or kerchief, beyond those which Hutter's daughters might be fairly entitled to wear.

It was now several years since Deerslayer had been in a spot especially devoted to the uses of females of his own colour and race. The sight brought back to his mind a rush of childish recollections, and he lingered in the room with a tenderness of feeling to which he had long been a stranger. He bethought him of his mother, whose homely vestments he remembered to have seen hanging on pegs, like those which he felt must belong to Hetty Hutter, and he bethought him of a sister whose incipient and native taste for finery had exhibited itself somewhat in the manner of that of Judith, though necessarily in a lesser degree. These little resemblances opened a long hidden vein of sensations, and as he quitted the room, it was with a saddened mien. He looked no farther, but returned slowly and thoughtfully towards the "door-yard."

"Old Tom has taken to a new calling, and has been trying his hand at the traps," cried Hurry, who had been coolly examining the borderer's implements. "If that is his humour, and you're disposed to remain in these parts, we can make an on-common comfortable season of it, for while the old man and I out-knowledge the beaver, you can fish and knock down the deer, to keep body and soul together. We always give the poorest hunters half a share, but one as actyve and sartain as yourself, might expect a full one."

"Thank'ee, Hurry; thank'ee, with all my heart, but I do a lit-tle beavering for myself, as occasions offer. 'Tis true the Delawares call me Deerslayer, but it's not so much because I'm pretty fatal with the venison, as because that while I kill so many bucks and does, I've never yet taken the life of a fellow creatur'. They say their traditions do not tell of another who had shed so much blood of animals, that had not shed the blood of man."

"I hope they don't account you chicken-hearted, lad? A faint-hearted man is like a no-tailed beaver."

"I don't believe, Hurry, that they account me as out-of-the-way timoursome, even though they may not account me as out-of-the-way brave. But I'm not quarrelsome, and that goes a great way towards keeping blood off the hands, among the hunters and red-skins, and then, Harry March, it keeps blood off the conscience, too."

"Well, for my part, I account game, a red skin, and a Frenchman, as pretty much the same thing; though I'm as on-quarrelsome a man, too, as there is in all the colonies. I despise a quarreller, as I do a cur dog, but one has no need to be over scrupulsome, when it's the right time to show the flint."

"I look upon him as the most of a man, who acts nearest the right, Hurry. But this is a glorious spot, and my eyes never aweary looking at it!"

" 'Tis your first acquaintance with a lake, and these idees come over us all, at such times. Lakes have a general character, as I say, being pretty much water, and land, and points, and bays."

As this definition by no means met the feelings that were up-permost in the mind of the young hunter, he made no im-mediate answer, but stood gazing at the dark hills and the glassy water, in silent enjoyment.

"Have the governor's, or the King's people given this lake a name?" he suddenly asked, as if struck with a new idea. "If

they've not begun to blaze their trees, and set up their com-
passes, and line off their maps, it's likely they've not bethought
them to disturb natur' with a name."

"They've not got to that yet, and the last time I went in with
skins, one of the king's surveyors was questioning me consarning all the region, hereabouts. He had heard that there was a
lake, in this quarter, and had got some general notions about
it, such as that there was water and hills, but how much of
either, he know'd no more than you know of the Mohawk
tongue. I did'nt open the trap any wider than was necessary,
giving him but poor encouragement in the way of farms and
clearings. In short, I left on his mind some such opinion of this
country, as a man gets of a spring of dirty water, with a path to
it that is so muddy that one mires afore he sets out. He told me
they had'n't got the spot down, yet, on their maps, though I
conclude that is a mistake, for he showed me his parchment,
and there is a lake down on it, where there is no lake in fact,
and which is about fifty miles from the place where it ought to
be, if they meant it for this. I don't think my account will encourage him to mark down another, by way of improvement."

Here Hurry laughed heartily, such tricks being particularly
grateful to a set of men who dreaded the approaches of civilization as a curtailment of their own lawless empire. The
egregious errors that existed in the maps of the day, all of
which were made in Europe, were, moreover, a standing topic
of ridicule among them, for, if they had not science enough to
make any better themselves, they had sufficient local information to detect the gross blunders contained in those that existed. Any one who will take the trouble to compare these
unanswerable evidences of the topographical skill of our
fathers a century since, with the more accurate sketches of our
own times, will at once perceive that the men of the woods had
sufficient justification for all their criticism on this branch of
the skill of the colonial governments, which did not at all
hesitate to place a river, or a lake, a degree or two out of the
way, even though they lay within a day's march of the in-
habited parts of the country.

"I'm glad it has no name," resumed Deerslayer, "or, at least,
no pale face name, for their christenings always foretel waste
and destruction. No doubt, howsever, the red skins have their

modes of knowing it, and the hunters and trappers, too, they are likely to call the place by something reasonable and resembling?"

"As for the tribes, each has its own tongue, and its own way of calling things, and they treat this part of the world just as they treat all the others. Among ourselves we've got to calling the place the 'Glimmerglass,' seeing that its whole basin is so often fringed with pines cast upward from its face, as if it would throw back the hills that hang over it."

"There is one outlet I know, for all lakes have outlets, and the rock at which I am to meet Chingachgook, stands near an outlet. Has *that* no Colony name, yet?"

"In that particular, they've got the advantage of us. Having one end, and that the biggest, in their own keeping, they've given it a name, which has found its way up to its source; names nat'rally working up stream. No doubt, Deerslayer, you've seen the Susquehannah, down in the Delaware country?"

"That have I, and hunted along its banks a hundred times."

"That and this are the same in fact, and I suppose the same in sound. I am glad they've been compelled to keep the red men's name, for it would be too hard to rob them of both land and names!"

Deerslayer made no answer, but he stood leaning on his rifle, gazing at the view which so much delighted him. The reader is not to suppose, however, that it was the picturesque alone, which so strongly attracted his attention. The spot was very lovely, of a truth, and it was then seen in one of its most favorable moments, the surface of the lake being as smooth as glass, and limpid as pure air, throwing back the mountains, clothed in dark pines, along the whole of its eastern boundary, the points thrusting forward their trees even to nearly horizontal lines, while the bays were seen glittering through an occasional arch beneath, left by a vault fretted with branches and leaves. It was the air of deep repose, the solitudes that spoke of scenes and forests untouched by the hands of man, the reign of nature, in a word, that gave so much pure delight to one of his habits and turn of mind. Still, he felt, though it was unconsciously, like a poet also. He found a pleasure in studying this large, and, to him, unusual opening into the mysteries and forms of the woods, as one is gratified in getting broader views of any subject that has long occupied his thoughts. He was not insensible to the innate loveliness of such a landscape, either, but felt a portion of that soothing of the spirit which is a common attendant of a scene so thoroughly pervaded by the holy calm of nature.

Chapter III.

"Come, shall we go and kill us venison?
And yet it irks me, the poor dappled fools, —
Being native burghers of this desert city, —
Should, in their own confines, with forked heads
Have their round haunches gored."

As You Like It, II.i.21–25.

Hurry Harry thought more of the beauties of Judith Hutter, than of those of the Glimmerglass, and its accompanying scenery. As soon as he had taken a sufficiently intimate survey of Floating Tom's implements, therefore, he summoned his companion to the canoe, that they might go down the lake in quest of the family. Previously to embarking, however, Hurry carefully examined the whole of the northern end of the water, with an indifferent ship's glass, that formed a part of Hutter's effects. In this scrutiny no part of the shore was overlooked, the bays and points, in particular, being subjected to a closer inquiry than the rest of the wooded boundary.

" 'Tis as I thought," said Hurry, laying aside the glass—"The old fellow is drifting about the south end, this fine weather, and has left the castle to defend itself. Well, now we know that he is not up this-a-way, 'twill be but a small matter to paddle down, and hunt him up in his hiding place."

"Does Master Hutter think it necessary to burrow on this lake?" inquired Deerslayer, as he followed his companion into the canoe. "To my eye, it is such a solitude as one might open his whole soul in, and fear no one to disarrange his thoughts, or his worship."

"You forget your friends the Mingos, and all the French savages. Is there a spot on 'arth, Deerslayer, to which them disquiet rogues don't go? Where is the lake, or even the deer lick, that the blackguards don't find out, and having found out, don't, sooner or later, discolour its water with blood."

"I hear no good character of 'em, sartainly, friend Hurry, though I've never been called on, yet, to meet them, or any other mortal, on the warpath. I dare to say that such a lovely spot as this, would not be likely to be overlooked by such plunderers, for, though I've not been in the way of quarrelling with them tribes myself, the Delawares give me such an account of 'em that I've pretty much set 'em down in my own mind, as thorough miscreants."

"You may do that with a safe conscience, or, for that matter, any other savage you may happen to meet."

Here Deerslayer protested, and as they went paddling down the lake, a hot discussion was maintained concerning the respective merits of the pale-faces and the redskins. Hurry had all the prejudices and antipathies of a white hunter, who generally regards the Indian as a sort of natural competitor, and not unfrequently as a natural enemy. As a matter of course, he was loud, clamorous, dogmatical and not very argumentative. Deerslayer, on the other hand, manifested a very different temper, proving by the moderation of his language, the fairness of his views, and the simplicity of his distinctions, that he possessed every disposition to hear reason, a strong, innate desire to do justice, and an ingenuousness that was singularly indisposed to have recourse to sophisms to maintain an argument, or to defend a prejudice. Still he was not altogether free from the influence of the latter feeling. This tyrant of the human mind, which rushes on its prey through a thousand avenues, almost as soon as men begin to think and feel, and which seldom relinquishes its iron sway until they cease to do either, had made some impression on even the just propensities of this individual, who probably offered in these particulars, a fair specimen of what absence from bad example, the want of temptation to go wrong, and native good feeling can render youth.

"You will allow, Deerslayer, that a Mingo is more than half devil," cried Hurry, following up the discussion with an animation that touched closely on ferocity, "though you want to overpersuade me that the Delaware tribe is pretty much made up of angels. Now, I gainsay that proposal consarning white men, even. All white men are not faultless, and therefore all Indians *ca'nt* be faultless. And so your argument is out at the elbow, in the start. But, this is what I call reason. Here's three colours on 'arth; white, black and red. White is the highest colour, and therefore the best man; black comes next, and is put to live in the neighborhood of the white man, as tolerable and fit to be made use of; and red comes last, which shows that those that made 'em never expected an Indian to be accounted as more than half human."

"God made all three, alike, Hurry—"

"Alike! Do you call a nigger like a white man, or me like an Indian?"

"You go off at half-cock, and do'n't hear me out. God made us all, white, black and red, and no doubt had his own wise intentions in colouring us differently. Still he made us, in the main, much the same in feelin's; though I'll not deny that he gave each race its gifts. A white man's gifts are christianized, while a red skin's are more for the wilderness. Thus it would be a great offence for a white man to scalp the dead, whereas it's a signal vartue in an Indian. Then, ag'in, a white man cannot amboosh women and children in war, while a red skin may. 'Tis *cruel* work I'll allow, but for them it's *lawful* work, while for *us* it would be a grievous sin."

"That depends on your inimy. As for scalping, or even skinning a savage, I look upon them, pretty much the same as cutting off the ears of wolves for the bounty, or stripping a bear of its hide. And, then, you're out significantly, as to taking the poll of a red skin in hand, seeing that the very Colony has offered a bounty for the job, all the same as it pays for wolves' ears, and crows' heads."

"Ay, and a bad business it is, Hurry. Even the Indians, themselves, cry shame on it, seeing it's ag'in a white man's gifts. I do not pretend that all that white men do is properly christianized and according to the lights given them; for then they would be what they *ought* to be, which we know they are not; but I will maintain that tradition, and use, and colour, and laws, make such a difference in races as to amount to gifts. I do not deny that there are tribes among the Indians that are nat'rally pervarse and wicked, as there are nations among the whites. Now, I account the Mingos as belonging to the first, and the Frenchers, in the Canadas, to the last. In a state of lawful warfare, such as we have lately got into, it is a duty to keep down all compassionate feelin's, so far as life goes, ag'in either; but when it comes to scalps, it's a very different matter."

"Just hearken to reason, if you please, Deerslayer, and tell me if the colony can make an onlawful law? Is'n't an onlawful law more ag'in natur', than scalpin' a savage? A law can no more be onlawful, than truth can be a lie."

"That *sounds* reasonable, but it has a most onreasonable bearing, Hurry. Laws don't all come from the same quarter. God has given us his'n, and some come from the colony, and other some from the King and parliament. When the colony's laws, or even the king's laws, run ag'in the laws of God, they get to be onlawful, and ought not to be obeyed. I hold to a white man's respecting white laws, so long as they do not cross the track of a law comin' from a higher authority, and for a red man to obey his own red-skin usages, under the same privilege. But, 'tis useless talking, as each man will think for himself, and have his say agreeable to his thoughts. Let us keep a good look-out for your friend, Floating Tom, lest we pass him, as he lies hidden under this bushy shore."

Deerslayer had not named the borders of the lake amiss. Along their whole length the smaller trees overhung the water, with their branches often dipping in the transparent element. The banks were steep, even from the narrow strand, and, as vegetation invariably struggles toward the light, the effect was precisely that at which the lover of the picturesque would have aimed, had the ordering of this glorious setting of forest been submitted to his control. The points, and bays, too, were sufficiently numerous to render the outline broken and diversified. As the canoe kept close along the western side of the lake, with a view, as Hurry had explained to his companion, of reconnoitring for enemies before he trusted himself too openly in sight, the expectations of the two adventurers were kept constantly on the stretch, as neither could foretel what the next turning of a point might reveal. Their progress was swift, the gigantic strength of Hurry enabling him to play with the light bark as if it had been a feather, while the skill of his companion almost equalized their usefulness, notwithstanding the disparity in natural means.

Each time the canoe passed a point, Hurry turned a look behind him, expecting to see the "Ark" anchored, or beached, in the bay. He was fated to be disappointed, however, and they had got within a mile of the southern end of the lake, or a distance of quite two leagues from the 'castle', which was now hidden from view by half a dozen intervening projections of the land, when he suddenly ceased paddling, as if uncertain in what direction next to steer.

"It is possible that the old chap has dropped into the river," said Hurry, often looking carefully along the whole of the eastern shore, which was about a mile distant, and open to his scrutiny for more than half its length; "for he has taken to trapping considerable of late, and, barring flood-wood, he might drop down it, a mile or so, though he would have a most scratching time in getting back again!"

"Where is this outlet?" asked Deerslayer. "I see no opening in the banks, or the trees, that looks as if it would let a river like the Susquehannah run through it."

"Ay, Deerslayer, rivers are like human mortals; having small beginnings, and ending with broad shoulders, and wide mouths. You don't see the outlet, because it passes atween high steep banks, and the pines, and hemlocks, and basswoods hang over it, as a roof hangs over a house. If old Tom is not in the "Rat's Cove', he must have burrowed in the river; we'll look for him first in the Cove, and then we'll cross to the outlet."

As they proceeded Hurry explained that there was a shallow bay, formed by a long low point, that had gotten the name of the "'Rat's Cove" from the circumstance of its being a favorite haunt of the muskrat, and which offered so complete a cover for the 'ark' that its owner was fond of lying in it, whenever he found it convenient.

"As a man never knows who may be his visiters, in this part of the country," continued Hurry, "it's a great advantage to get a good look at 'em, before they come too near. Now, it's war, such caution is more than commonly useful, since a Canada man, or a Mingo might get into his hut afore he invited 'em. But, Hutter is a first rate look-outer, and can pretty much scent danger, as a hound scents the deer."

"I should think the castle so open, that it would be sartain to draw inimies, if any happened to find the lake, a thing onlikely enough I will allow, as it's off the trail of the forts and settlements."

"Why, Deerslayer, I've got to believe that a man meets with inimies easier than he meets with fri'nds. It's skearful to think for how many causes one gets to be your inimy, and for how few your fri'nd. Some take up the hatchet because you do n't think just as they think, other some because you run ahead of 'em in the same idees, and I once know'd a vagabond that quarrelled with a fri'nd because he did n't think him handsome. Now, you're no monument in the way of beauty, yourself, Deerslayer, and yet you would n't be so onreasonable as to become my inimy for just saying so."

"I'm as the Lord made me, and I wish to be accounted no better, nor any worse. Good looks I may not have, that is to say to a degree that the light minded and vain crave, but I hope I'm not altogether without some ricommend in the way of good conduct. There's few nobler looking men to be seen than yourself, Hurry, and I know that I am not to expect any to turn their eyes on me, when such a one as you can be gazed on; but I do not know that a hunter is less expart with the rifle, or less to be relied on for food, because he does'n't wish to stop at every shining spring he may meet to study his own countenance in the water."

Here Hurry burst into a fit of loud laughter, for, while he was too reckless to care much about his own manifest physical superiority, he was well aware of it, and, like most men who derive an advantage from the accidents of birth or nature, he was apt to think complacently on the subject whenever it happened to cross his mind.

"No—no—Deerslayer, you're no beauty, as you will own yourself if you'll look over the side of the canoe," he cried. "Jude will say *that* to your face, if you start her, for a parter tongue is not to be found in any gal's head, in or out of the settlements, if you provoke her to use it. My advice to you, is never to aggravate Judith; though you may tell any thing to Hetty, and she'll take it as meek as a lamb. No, Jude will be just as like as not to tell you her opinion consarning your looks."

"And if she does, Hurry, she will tell me no more than you have said already"—

"You're not thick'ning up about a small remark, I hope, Deerslayer, when no harm is meant. You are *not* a beauty, as you must know, and why should'n't fri'nds tell each other these little trifles? If you *was* handsome, or ever like to be, I'd be one of the first to tell you of it, and that ought to content you. Now, if Jude was to tell me that I'm as ugly as a sinner, I'd take it as a sort of obligation, and try not to believe her."

"It's easy for them that natur' has favored, to jest about such matters, Hurry, though it is sometimes hard for others. I'll not deny but I've had my cravings towards good looks; yes I have; but then I've always been able to get them down by considering how many I've known with fair outsides, who have had nothing to boast of inwardly. I'll not deny, Hurry, that I often wish I'd been created more comely to the eye, and more like such a one as yourself, in them particulars, but then I get the feelin' under by remembering how much better off I am in a great many respects, than some fellow mortals. I might have been born lame, and onfit even for a squirrel hunt; or, blind, which would have made me a burthen on myself, as well as on my fri'nds, or, without hearing, which would have totally onqualified me for ever campaigning, or scouting, which I look forward to, as part of a man's duty in troublesome times. Yes—yes; it's not pleasant, I will allow, to see them that's more comely, and more sought a'ter, and honored than yourself; but it may all be borne, if a man looks the evil in the face, and don't mistake his gifts and his obligations."

Hurry, in the main, was a good hearted, as well as good-natured fellow, and the self abasement of his companion completely got the better of the passing feeling of personal vanity. He regretted the allusion he had made to the other's appearance, and endeavored to express as much, though it was done in the uncouth manner that belonged to the habits and opinions of the frontier.

"I meant no harm, Deerslayer," he answered in a deprecating manner, "and hope you'll forget what I've said. If you're not downright handsome, you've a sartain look that says plainer than any words, that all's right within. Then you set no valie by looks, and so will the sooner forgive any little slight to your appearance. I will not say that Jude will greatly admire you, for that might be to raise hopes that would only breed disapp'intment, but there's Hetty, now, would be just as likely to find satisfaction in looking at *you*, as in looking at any other man. Then you're altogether too grave and considerate like, to care much about Judith — for, though the gal *is* oncommon, she is so general in her admiration that a man need not be exalted because she happens to smile. I sometimes think the hussy loves herself better than she does any thing else breathin'!"

"If she did, Hurry, she'd do no more, I'm afeard, than most queens on their thrones, and ladies in the towns," answered Deerslayer, smiling, and turning back towards his companion, with every trace of feeling banished from his honest-looking and frank countenance. "I never yet know'd even a Delaware of whom you might not say that much. But here is the end of the long p'int, you mentioned, and the 'Rat's Cove, can't be far off."

This point, instead of thrusting itself forward, like all the others, ran in a line with the main shore of the lake, which here swept within it, in a deep and retired bay, circling round south, again, at the distance of a quarter of a mile, and crossed the valley, forming the southern termination of the water. In this bay, Hurry felt almost certain of finding the Ark, since, anchored behind the trees that covered the narrow strip of the point, it might have lain concealed from prying eyes an entire summer. So complete, indeed, was the cover, in this spot, that a boat hauled close to the beach within the point, and near the bottom of the bay, could by possibility be seen from only one direction, and that was from a densely wooded shore, within the sweep of the water, where strangers would be little apt to go.

"We shall soon see the Ark," said Hurry, as the canoe glided round the extremity of the point, where the water was so deep as actually to appear black; "he loves to burrow up among the rushes, and we shall be in his nest, in five minutes, although the old fellow may be off among the traps himself."

March proved a false prophet. The canoe completely doubled the point, so as to enable the two travellers to command a view of the whole cove, or bay, for it was more properly the last, and no object, but those that nature had placed there, became visible. The placid water swept round in a graceful curve, the rushes bent gently towards its surface, and the trees over-hung it as usual, but all lay in the soothing and sublime solitude of a wilderness. The scene was such as a poet, or an artist would have delighted in, but it had no charm for Hurry Harry, who was burning with impatience to get a sight of his light-minded beauty.

The motion of the canoe had been attended with little, or no noise, the frontier-men from habit getting accustomed to caution in most of their movements, and it now lay on the glassy water, appearing to float in air, partaking of the breathing stillness that seemed to pervade the entire scene. At this instant, a dry stick was heard cracking on the narrow strip of land that concealed the bay from the open lake. Both the adventurers started, and each extended a hand towards his rifle, the weapon never being out of reach of the arm.

"'Twas too heavy, for any light creatur'," whispered Hurry, "and it sounded like the tread of a man!"

"Not so — not so —" returned Deerslayer — "'twas, as you say, too heavy for one, but it was too light for the other. Put your paddle in the water, and send the canoe in to that log; I'll land and cut off the creatur's retreat up the p'int, be it a Mingo, or be it only a muskrat."

As Hurry complied, Deerslayer was soon on the shore, advancing into the thicket with a moccasined foot, and a caution that prevented the least noise. In a minute he was in the centre of the narrow strip of land, and moving slowly down towards its end, the bushes rendering extreme watchfulness necessary. Just as he reached the centre of the thicket, the dried twigs cracked again, and the noise was repeated, at short intervals, as if some creature having life, walked slowly towards the point. Hurry heard these sounds also, and pushing the canoe off into the bay, he seized his rifle to watch the result. A breathless minute succeeded, after which a noble buck walked out of the thicket, proceeded with a stately step to the sandy extremity of the point, and began to slake his thirst from the water of the lake. Hurry hesitated an instant, and then raising his rifle hastily to his shoulder, he took sight and fired. The effect of this sudden interruption of the solemn stillness of such a scene, was not its least striking peculiarity. The report of the weapon, had the usual sharp, short sound of the rifle, but, when a few moments of silence had succeeded the sudden crack, during which the noise was floating in air across the water, it reached the rocks of the opposite mountain, where the vibrations accumulated, and were rolled from cavity to cavity, for miles along the hills, seeming to awaken the sleeping thunders of the woods. The buck merely shook his head at the report of the rifle and the whistling of the bullet, for never before had he come in contact with man; but the echoes of the hills awakened his distrust, and leaping forward, with his four legs drawn under his body, he fell at once into deep water, and began to swim towards the foot of the lake. Hurry shouted and dashed forward in chase, and for one or two minutes the water foamed around the pursuer and the pursued. The former was dashing past the point, when Deerslayer appeared on the sand and signed to him to return.

" 'Twas inconsiderate to pull a trigger, afore we had reconn'itred the shore, and made sartain that no inimies harbored near it," said the latter, as his companion slowly and reluctantly complied. "This much I have l'arned from the Delawares, in the way of schooling and traditions, even though I've never yet been on a war-path. And, moreover, venison can hardly be called in season now, and we do not want for food. They call me Deerslayer, I'll own, and perhaps I desarve the name, in the way of understanding the creatur's habits, as well as for some sartainty in the aim, but they can't accuse me of killing an animal when there is no occasion for the meat, or the skin. I may be a slayer, it's true, but I'm no slaughterer."

" 'Twas an awful mistake to miss that buck!" exclaimed Hurry, doffing his cap and running his fingers through his handsome but matted curls, as if he would loosen his tangled ideas by the process. "I've not done so onhandy a thing since I was fifteen."

"Never lament it, as the creatur's death could have done neither of us any good, and might have done us harm. Them echoes are more awful in my ears, than your mistake, Hurry, for they sound like the voice of natur' calling out ag'in a wasteful and onthinking action."

"You'll hear plenty of such calls, if you tarry long in this quarter of the world, lad," returned the other laughing. "The echoes repeat pretty much all that is said or done on the Glimmerglass, in this calm summer weather. If a paddle falls you hear of it sometimes, ag'in and ag'in, as if the hills were mocking your clumsiness, and a laugh, or a whistle, comes out of them pines, when they're in the humour to speak, in a way to make you believe they can r'ally convarse."

"So much the more reason for being prudent and silent. I do not think the inimy can have found their way into these hills yet, for I do'nt know what they are to gain by it, but all the Delawares tell me that, as courage is a warrior's first vartue, so is prudence his second. One such call from the mountains, is enough to let a whole tribe into the secret of our arrival."

"If it does no other good, it will warn old Tom to put the pot over, and let him know visiters are at hand. Come, lad; get into the canoe, and we will hunt the ark up, while there is yet day."

Deerslayer complied, and the canoe left the spot. Its head was turned diagonally across the lake, pointing towards the south-eastern curvature of the sheet. In that direction, the distance to the shore, or to the termination of the lake, on the course the two were now steering, was not quite a mile, and, their progress being always swift, it was fast lessening under the skilful, but easy sweeps of the paddles. When about half way across, a slight noise drew the eyes of the men towards the nearest land, and they saw that the buck was just emerging from the lake and wading towards the beach. In a minute, the noble animal shook the water from his flanks, gazed upward at the covering of trees, and, bounding against the bank, plunged into the forest.

"That creatur' goes off with gratitude in his heart," said Deerslayer, "for natur' tells him he has escaped a great danger. You ought to have some of the same feelin's, Hurry, to think your eye was'n't true, or that your hand was onsteady, when no good could come of a shot that was intended onmeaningly rather than in reason."

"I deny the eye and the hand," cried March with some heat. "You've got a little character, down among the Delawares, there, for quickness and sartainty, at a deer, but I should like to see you behind one of them pines, and a full painted Mingo behind another, each with a cock'd rifle and astriving for the chance! Them's the situations, Nathaniel, to try the sight and the hand, for they begin with trying the narves. I never look upon killing a creatur' as an explite, but killing a savage is.

The time will come to try your hand, now we've got to blows ag'in, and we shall soon know what a ven'son repitation can do in the field. I deny that either hand or eye was onsteady; it was all a miscaculation on the buck, which stood still when he ought to have kept in motion, and so I shot ahead of him."

"Have it your own way, Hurry; all I contend for is, that it's lucky. I dare say I shall not pull upon a human mortal, as steadily, or with as light a heart, as I pull upon a deer — "

"Who's talking of mortals, or of human beings at all, Deer-slayer? I put the matter to you on the suppersition of an Injin. I dare say any man would have his feelin's when it got to be life, or death, ag'in another human mortal, but there would be no such scruples in regard to an Injin, nothing but the chance of his hitting you, or the chance of you hitting him."

"I look upon the red men to be quite as human as we are ourselves, Hurry. They have their gifts, and their religion, it's true, but that makes no difference in the end, when each will be judged according to his deeds, and not according to his skin."

"That's downright missionary, and will find little favor, up in this part of the country where the Moravians don't con-gergate. Now, skin makes the man. This is reason; else how are people to judge of each other. The skin is put on, over all, in order that when a creatur', or a mortal, is fairly seen, you may know at once what to make of him. You know a bear from a hog by his skin, and a grey squirrel from a black."

"True, Hurry," said the other looking back and smiling, "nevertheless they are both squirrels."

"Who denies it? — But you'll not say that a red man and a white man are both Injins?"

"No; but I *do* say they are both men. Men of different races and colours, and having different gifts and traditions, but, in the main, with the same natur's. Both have souls and both will be held accountable for their deeds in this life."

Hurry was one of those theorists who believed in the in-feriority of all of the human race, who were not white. His no-tions on the subject were not very clear, nor were his defini-tions at all well settled, but his opinions were none the less dogmatical, or fierce. His conscience accused him of sundry lawless acts against the Indians, and he had found it an exceedingly easy mode of quieting it, by putting the whole family of red men, incontinently, without the category of human rights. Nothing angered him sooner, than to deny his proposition, more especially if the denial were accompanied by a show of plausible argument, and he did not listen to his companion's remarks, with much composure, of either manner, or feeling.

"You're a boy, Deerslayer, mislead and misconsaited by Delaware arts, and Missionary ignorance," he exclaimed, with his usual indifference to the forms of speech, when excited. "*You* may account yourself as a red skin's brother, but *I* hold 'em all to be animals, with nothing human about 'em but cunning. *That* they have, I'll allow; but so has a fox, or even a bear. I'm older than you, and have lived longer in the woods — or, for that matter, have lived always there, — and am not to be told what an Injin is, or what he is not. If you wish to be considered a savage you've only to say so, and I'll name you as such to Judith and the old man, and then we'll see how you'll like your welcome."

Here, Hurry's imagination did his temper some service, since, by conjuring up the reception his semi aquatic acquaintance would be likely to bestow on one thus introduced, he burst into a hearty fit of laughter. Deerslayer too well knew the uselessness of attempting to convince such a being of any thing against his prejudices, to feel a desire to undertake the task, and he was not sorry that the approach of the canoe to the south eastern curve of the lake, gave a new direction to his ideas. They were now, indeed, quite near to the place that March had pointed out for the position of the outlet, and both began to look for it, with a curiosity that was increased by the expectation of finding the Ark.

It may strike the reader as a little singular that the place where a stream of any size passed through banks that had an elevation of some twenty feet, should be a matter of doubt with men, who could not now have been more than two hundred yards distant from the precise spot. It will be recollected, however, that the trees and bushes, here as elsewhere, fairly overhung the water, making such a fringe to the lake, as to conceal any little variations from its general outline.

"I've not been down at this end of the lake, these two summers," said Hurry, standing up in the canoe the better to look about him. — "Ay — There's the rock, showing its chin above the water, and I know that the river begins in its neighborhood."

The men now plied the paddles, again, and they were presently within a few yards of the rock, floating towards it, though their efforts were suspended. This rock was not large, being merely some five or six feet high, only half of which elevation rose above the lake. The incessant washing of the water, for centuries, had so rounded its summit, that it resembled a large bee-hive in shape, its form being more than usually regular and even. Hurry remarked as they floated slowly past, that this rock was well known to all the Indians in that part of the country, and that they were in the practice of using it as a mark to designate their place of meeting, when separated by their hunts and marches.

"And here is the river, Deerslayer," he continued, "though so shut in by trees and bushes, as to look more like an andbush, than the outlet of such a sheet as the Glimmerglass."

Hurry had not badly described the place, which did truly seem to be a stream lying in ambush. The high banks might have been a hundred feet asunder, but on the western side a small bit of low land, extended so far forward, as to diminish the breadth of the stream to half that width. As the bushes hung in the water beneath, and pines that had the stature of church steeples, rose in tall columns above, all inclining towards the light until their branches intermingled, the eye, at a little distance, could not easily detect any opening in the shore to mark the egress of the water. In the forest above, no traces of this outlet were to be seen from the lake, the whole presenting the same connected and seemingly interminable carpet of leaves. As the canoe slowly advanced, sucked in by the current, it entered beneath an arch of trees, through which the light from the heavens struggled, by casual openings, faintly relieving the gloom beneath.

"This is a nat'ral and-bush," half-whispered Hurry, as if he felt that the place was devoted to secrecy and watchfulness, "and, depend on it, old Tom has burrowed with the Ark, somewhere in this quarter. We will drop down with the current, a short distance, and ferret him out."

"This seems no place for a vessel of any size," returned the other, "and it appears to me that we shall have hardly room enough for the canoe."

Hurry laughed at this suggestion, and, as it soon appeared with reason, for the fringe of bushes immediately on the shore of the lake was no sooner passed, than the adventurers found themselves in a narrow stream, of a sufficient depth of limpid water, with a strong current, and a canopy of leaves, upheld by arches composed of the limbs of hoary trees. Bushes lined the shores, as usual, but they left sufficient space between them to admit the passage of any thing that did not exceed twenty feet in width, and to allow of a perspective ahead of eight or ten times that distance.

Neither of our two adventurers used his paddle except to keep the light bark in the centre of the current, but both watched each turning of the stream, of which there were two or three within the first hundred yards, with jealous vigilance. Turn after turn, however, was passed, and the canoe had dropped down with the current some little distance, when Hurry caught a bush, and arrested its movement, so suddenly and silently as to denote some unusual motive for the act. Deerslayer laid his hand on the stock of his rifle, as soon as he noted this proceeding, but it was quite as much with a hunter's habit, as from any feeling of alarm.

"There the old fellow is!" whispered Hurry, pointing with a finger, and laughing heartily, though he carefully avoided making a noise. "'Ratting it away, just as I supposed, up to his knees in the mud and water, looking to the traps and the bait. But, for the life of me, I can see nothing of the Ark, though I'll bet every skin I take this season, Jude is'n't trusting her pretty little feet in the neighborhood of that black mud. The gal's more likely to be braiding her hair, by the side of some spring, where she can see her own good looks, and collect scornful feelings ag'in us men."

"You over-judge young women, yes you do, Hurry, who as often bethink them of their failings as they do of their perfections. I dare to say, this Judith now, is no such admirer of herself, and no such scorner of our sex, as you seem to think; and that she is quite as likely to be sarving her father in the house, wherever that may be, as he is to be sarving her among the traps."

"It's a pleasure to hear truth from a man's tongue, if it be only once in a girl's life," cried a pleasant, rich, and yet soft female voice so near the canoe, as to make both the listeners start. "As for you, Master Hurry, fair words are so apt to choak you, that I no longer expect to hear them from your mouth, the last you uttered sticking in your throat and coming near to death. But I'm glad to see you keep better society than formerly, and that they who know how to esteem and treat women, are not ashamed to journey in your company."

As this was said, a singularly handsome and youthful female face was thrust through an opening in the leaves, within reach of Deerslayer's paddle. Its owner smiled graciously on the young man, and the frown that she then cast on Hurry, though simulated and pettish, had the effect to render her beauty more striking, by exhibiting the play of an expressive but capricious countenance; one that seemed to change from the soft to the severe, the mirthful to the reproving, with facility and indifference.

A second look explained the nature of the surprise. Unwittingly the men had dropped along side of the Ark, which had been purposely concealed in bushes, cut and arranged for the purpose, and Judith Hutter had merely pushed aside the leaves that lay before a window, in order to show her face, and speak to them.

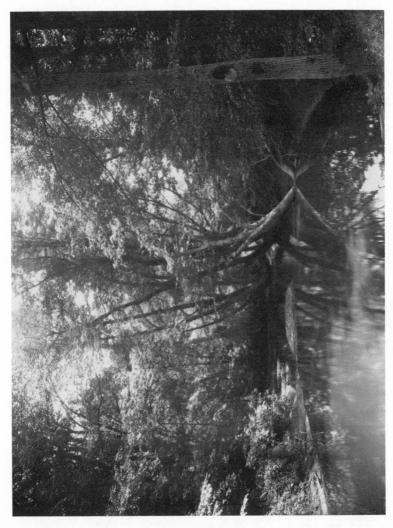

1. Shadow Brook, near the pit at which Deerslayer and Hutter emerge from the "tangled labyrinth of a small swamp"

J. F. COOPER

TRADUCTION

par Defauconpret,

LE TUEUR DE DAIMS.

Paris,
FURNE & Cie CH. GOSSELIN
Éditeurs.
1842.

II. Artist's conception of Muskrat Castle, from an early French edition of *The Deerslayer*

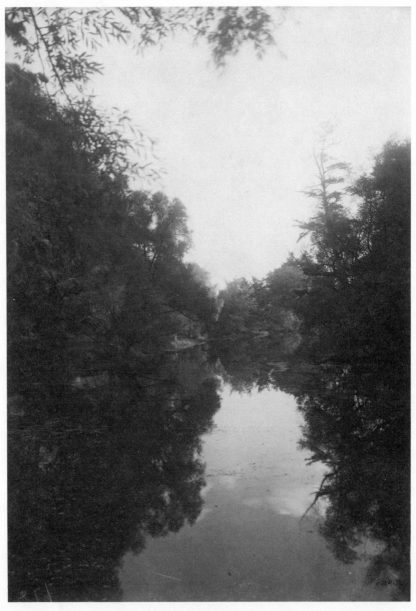

III. The Susquehanna River near its source, where Deerslayer and Harry find the Hutters and their Ark in Chapter II

IV.   Northumberland on the Susquehanna, engraving from a drawing by William H. Bartlett, showing types of the barges that suggested Hutter's Ark

Chapter IV.

"And that timid fawn starts not with fear
When I steal to her secret bower,
And that young May violet to me is dear,
And I visit the silent streamlet near,
To look on the lovely flower."

Bryant, "An Indian Story," 11.ıı-ı5.

T H E Ark, as the floating habitation of the Hutters was generally called, was a very simple contrivance. A large flat, or scow, composed the buoyant part of the vessel, and, in its centre, occupying the whole of its breadth and about two thirds of its length, stood a low fabric, resembling the castle in construction, though made of materials so light as barely to be bullet-proof. As the sides of the scow were a little higher than usual, and the interior of the cabin had no more elevation than was necessary for comfort, this unusual addition had neither a very clumsy, nor a very obtrusive appearance. It was, in short, little more than a modern canal boat, though more rudely constructed, of greater breadth than common, and bearing about it the signs of the wilderness, in its bark-covered posts and roof. The scow, however, had been put together with some skill, being comparatively light, for its strength, and sufficiently manageable. The cabin was divided into two apartments, one of which served for a parlor, and the sleeping-room of the father, and the other was appropriated to the uses of the daughters. A very simple arrangement sufficed for the kitchen, which was in one end of the scow, and removed from the cabin, standing in the open air; the Ark being altogether a summer habitation.

The 'and-bush', as Hurry in his ignorance of English termed it, is quite as easily explained. In many parts of the lake and river, where the banks were steep and high, the smaller trees, and larger bushes, as has been already mentioned, fairly overhung the stream, their branches not unfrequently dipping into the water. In some instances they grew out in nearly horizontal lines, for thirty or forty feet. The water being uniformly deepest near the shores, where the banks were highest and the nearest to a perpendicular, Hutter had found no difficulty in letting the Ark drop under one of these covers, where it had been anchored with a view to conceal its position, security requiring some such precautions, in his view of the case. Once beneath the trees and bushes, a few stones fastened to the ends of the branches had caused them to bend sufficiently to dip into the river, and a few severed bushes, properly disposed, did the rest. The reader has seen that this cover was so complete, as to deceive two men accustomed to the woods, and who were actually in search of those it concealed, a circumstance that will be easily understood by those who are familiar with the matted and wild luxuriance of a virgin American forest, more especially in a rich soil.

The discovery of the Ark produced very different effects on our two adventurers. As soon as the canoe could be got round to the proper opening, Hurry leaped on board, and in a minute was closely engaged in a gay, and a sort of recriminating discourse with Judith, apparently forgetful of the existence of all the rest of the world. Not so with Deerslayer. He entered the Ark with a slow, cautious step, examining every arrangement of the cover, with curious and scrutinizing eyes. It is true, he cast one admiring glance at Judith, which was extorted by her brilliant and singular beauty, but even this could detain him but a single instant from the indulgence of his interest in Hutter's contrivances. Step by step did he look into the construction of the singular abode, investigate its fastenings and strength, ascertain its means of defence, and make every inquiry that would be likely to occur to one whose thoughts dwelt principally on such expedients. Nor was the cover neglected. Of this he examined the whole minutely, his commendation escaping him more than once in audible comments. Frontier usages admitting of this familiarity, he passed through the rooms, as he had previously done at the 'Castle', and opening a door issued into the end of the scow opposite to that where he had left Hurry and Judith. Here he found the other sister, employed at some coarse needle-work, seated beneath the leafy canopy of the cover.

As Deerslayer's examination was by this time ended, he dropped the butt of his rifle, and, leaning on the barrel, with both hands, he turned towards the girl with an interest the singular beauty of her sister had not awakened. He had gathered from Hurry's remarks that Hetty was considered to have less intellect than ordinarily falls to the share of human beings, and his education among Indians had taught him to treat those who were thus afflicted by Providence, with more than common tenderness. Nor was there any thing in Hetty Hutter's appearance, as so often happens, to weaken the interest her situation excited. An idiot she could not properly be termed, her mind being just enough enfeebled to lose most of those traits that are connected with the more artful qualities, and to retain its ingenuousness and love of truth. It had often been remarked of this girl, by the few who had seen her, and who possessed sufficient knowledge to discriminate, that her perception of the right seemed almost intuitive, while her aversion to the wrong formed so distinctive a feature of her mind, as to surround her with an atmosphere of pure morality; peculiarities that are not infrequent with persons who are termed feeble-minded; as if God had forbidden the evil spirits to invade a precinct so defenceless, with the benign purpose of extending a direct protection to those, who had been left without the usual aids of humanity. Her person, too, was agreeable, having a strong resemblance to that of her sister's, of which it was a subdued and humble copy. If it had none of the brilliancy of Judith's, the calm, quiet, almost holy expression of her meek countenance, seldom failed to win on the observer, and few noted it long, that did not begin to feel a deep and lasting interest in the girl. She had no colour, in common, nor was her simple mind apt to present images that caused her cheek to brighten, though she retained a modesty so innate, that it almost raised her to the unsuspecting purity of a being superior to human infirmities. Guileless, innocent, and without distrust, equally by nature and from her mode of life, providence had, nevertheless, shielded her from harm, by a halo of moral light, as it is said 'to temper the wind to the shorn lamb.'

"You are Hetty Hutter," said Deerslayer, in the way one puts a question, unconsciously to himself assuming a kindness of tone and manner that were singularly adapted to win the confidence of her he addressed. "Hurry Harry has told me of you, and I know you must be the child?"

"Yes, I'm Hetty Hutter," returned the girl in a low, sweet voice, which nature, aided by some education, had preserved from vulgarity of tone and utterance—"I'm Hetty; Judith Hutter's sister; and Thomas Hutter's youngest daughter."

"I know your history, then, for Hurry Harry talks considerable, and he is free of speech when he can find other people's consarns to dwell on. You pass most of your life on the lake, Hetty."

"Certainly. Mother is dead; father is gone a-trapping, and Judith and I stay at home. What's *your* name?"

"That's a question more easily asked than it is answered, young woman, seeing that I'm so young, and yet have borne more names than some of the greatest chiefs in all America."

"But you've *got* a name—you don't throw away one name, before you come honestly by another?"

"I hope not, gal—I hope not. My names have come nat'rally, and I suppose the one I bear now, will be of no great lasting, since the Delawares seldom settle on a man's ra'al title, until such time as he has an opportunity of showing his true natur', in the council, or on the warpath; which has never behappened me; seeing firstly, because I'm not born a red skin and have no right to sit in *their* councillings, and am much too humble to be called on for opinions from the great of my own colour; and, secondly, because this is the first war that has befallen in my time, and no inimy has yet inroaded far enough into the colony, to be reached by an arm even longer than mine."

"Tell me your names," added Hetty, looking up at him, artlessly, "and maybe I'll tell you your character."

"There is some truth in that, I'll not deny, though it often fails. Men are deceived in other men's characters, and frequently give 'em names they by no means desarve. You can see the truth of this in the Mingo names, which in their own tongue signify the same things as the Delaware names—at least, so they tell me, for I know little of that tribe unless it be by report,—and no one can say they are as honest, or as upright a nation. I put no great dependence, therefore, on names."

"Tell me *all* your names," repeated the girl, earnestly, for her mind was too simple to separate things from professions, and she *did* attach importance to a name; "I want to know what to think of you."

"Well, sartain; I've no objection, and you shall hear them all. In the first place, then, I'm christian, and white born, like yourself, and my parents had a name that came down from father to son, as is a part of their gifts. My father was called Bumppo, and I was named after him, of course, the given name being Nathaniel, or, Natty, as most people saw fit to tarm it. —"

"Yes—yes—Natty—and Hetty—" interrupted the girl quickly, and looking up from her work, again, with a smile—"You are Natty, and I'm Hetty—though you are Bumppo and I'm Hutter. Bumppo is'n't as pretty as Hutter, is it?"

"Why that's as people fancy. Bumppo has no lofty sound, I admit, and yet men have bumped through the world with it. I did not go by this name, howsever, very long, for the Delawares soon found out, or thought they found out, that I was not given to lying, and they called me, firstly, Straight-tongue."

"That's a *good* name," interrupted Hetty, again, earnestly and in a positive manner. "Do'n't tell me there's no virtue in names!"

"I do not say *that*, for, perhaps, I desarved to be so called, lies being no favorites with me, as they are with some. After a while they found out that I was quick of foot, and then they called me 'The Pigeon,' which you know has a swift wing, and flies in a direct line."

"*That* was a *pretty* name!" exclaimed Hetty: "pigeons are pretty birds!"

"Most things that God has created are pretty in their way, my good gal, though they get to be deformed by mankind, so as to change their natur's, as well as their appearances. From carrying messages, and striking blind trails, I got at last to following the hunters, when it was thought I was quicker and surer at finding the game than most lads, and then they called me the 'Lap-ear,' as they said I partook of the sagacity of a hound."

"That's not so pretty—" answered Hetty. "I hope you did'n't keep *that* name long."

"Not after I was rich enough to buy a rifle," returned the

other, betraying a little pride through his usually quiet and subdued manner. "*Then* it was seen I could keep a wigwam in ven'son, and, in time, I got the name of 'Deerslayer,' which is that I now bear; homely as some will think it, who set more valie on the scalp of a fellow mortal, than on the horns of a buck."

"Well, Deerslayer, I'm not one of them," answered Hetty, simply. "Judith likes soldiers, and flaring coats, and fine feathers, but they're all nought to me. *She* says the officers are great, and gay, and of soft speech, but they make me shudder, for their business is to kill their fellow creatures. I like your calling better, and your last name is a very good one — better than Natty Bumppo."

"This is nat'ral in one of your turn of mind, Hetty, and much as I should have expected. They tell me your sister is handsome — oncommon, for a mortal, and beauty is apt to seek admiration."

"Did you never see Judith?" demanded the girl, with quick earnestness. "If you never have, go, at once, and look at her. Even Hurry Harry is'n't more pleasant to look at, though *she* is a woman and *he* is a man."

Deerslayer regarded the girl, for a moment, with concern. Her pale face had flushed a little, and her eye usually so mild and serene, brightened as she spoke, in the way to betray the inward impulses.

"Ay, Hurry Harry," he muttered to himself, as he walked through the cabin towards the other end of the boat, "this comes of good looks, if a light tongue has had no consarn in it. It's easy to see which way that poor creatur's feelin's are leanin', whatever may be the case with your Jude's."

But an interruption was put to the gallantry of Hurry, the coquetry of his mistress, the thoughts of Deerslayer and the gentle feelings of Hetty, by the sudden appearance of the canoe of the Ark's owner, in the narrow opening among the bushes, that served as a sort of moat to his position. It would seem that Hutter, or Floating Tom, as he was familiarly called by all the hunters who knew his habits, recognised the canoe of Hurry, for he expressed no surprise at finding him in the scow. On the contrary, his reception was such as to denote not only gratification, but a pleasure mingled with a little disappointment at his not having made his appearance some days sooner.

"I look'd for you last week," he said, in a half grumbling, half welcoming manner, "and was disappointed uncommonly, that you did'n't arrive. There came a runner through to warn all the trappers and hunters that the Colony and the Canadas were again in trouble, and I felt lonesome up in these mountains, with three scalps to see to, and only one pair of hands to protect them."

"That's reasonable," returned March, "and 't'was feelin' like a parent. No doubt if I had two such darters as Judith and Hetty, my exper'ence would tell the same story, though in gin'ral I am just as well satisfied with having the nearest neighbor fifty miles off, as when he is within call."

"Notwithstanding, you did'n't choose to come into the wilderness alone, now you knew that the Canada savages are likely to be stirring—" returned Hutter, giving a sort of distrustful and, at the same time, enquiring glance at Deerslayer.

"Why should I— They say a bad companion on a journey helps to shorten the path, and this young man I account to be a reasonably good one. This is Deerslayer, old Tom, a noted hunter among the Delawares, and christian born, and christian edicated too, like you and me. The lad is not parfect, perhaps, but there's worse men in the country that he came from, and it's likely he'll find some that's no better, in this part of the world. Should we have occasion to defend our traps and the territory, he'll be useful in feeding us all, for he's a reg'lar dealer in ven'son."

"Young man, you are welcome," growled Tom, thrusting a hard bony hand towards the youth, as a pledge of his sincerity; "in such times a white face is a friend's, and I count on you as a support. Children sometimes make a stout heart feeble, and these two daughters of mine give me more concern than all my traps, and skins, and rights in the country."

"That's nat'ral!" cried Hurry. "Yes, Deerslayer, you and I do'n't know it yet by exper'ence, but, on the whole, I consider that as nat'ral. If we *had* darters, it's more than probable we should have some such feelin's, and I honor the man that owns 'em. As for Judith, old man, I enlist, at once, as her soldier, and here is Deerslayer to help you to take care of Hetty."

"Many thanks to you, Master March," returned the beauty, in a full rich voice, and with an accuracy of intonation and utterance, that she shared in common with her sister, and which showed that she had been better taught than her father's life and appearence would give reason to expect; "many thanks to you; but Judith Hutter has the spirit and the experience that will make her depend more on herself, than on good-looking rovers like you. Should there be need to face the savages, do you land with my father, instead of burrowing in the huts, under the show of defending us females, and—"

"Girl—girl—" interrupted the father, "quiet that glib tongue of thine, and hear the truth. There are savages on the lake shore, already, and no man can say how near to us they may be at this very moment, or when we may hear more from them!"

"If this be true, Master Hutter," said Hurry, whose change of countenance denoted how serious he deemed the information, though it did not denote any unmanly alarm— "if this be true, your Ark is in a most misfortinate position for, though the cover did deceive Deerslayer and myself, it would hardly be overlooked by a full-blooded Injin, who was out seriously, in s'arch of scalps!"

"I think as you do, Hurry, and wish, with all my heart, we lay any where else, at this moment, than in this narrow, crooked, stream, which has many advantages to hide in, but which is almost fatal, to them that are discovered. The savages are near us, moreover, and the difficulty is, to get out of the river, without being shot down like deer standing at a 'lick.' "

"Are you sartain, Master Hutter, that the red skins you dread are ra'al Canadas?" asked Deerslayer, in a modest, but earnest manner. "Have you seen any, and can you describe their paint?"

"I have fallen in with the signs of their being in the neighborhood, but have seen none of 'em. I was down stream, a mile or so, looking to my traps, when I struck a fresh trail, crossing the corner of a swamp, and moving northward. The man had not passed an hour, and I know'd it for an Indian footstep by the size of the foot, and the in-toe, even before I found a worn moccasin, which its owner had dropped as useless. For that matter, I found the spot, where he halted to make a new one, which was only a few yards from the place where he had dropped the old one."

"That does'n't look much like a red skin on the war path!" returned the other shaking his head. "An exper'enced warrior, at least, would have burned, or buried, or sunk in the river, such signs of his passage, and your trail is, quite likely, a peaceable trail. But the moccasin may greatly relieve my mind, if you bethought you of bringing it off. I've come here to meet a young chief, myself, and his course would be much in the direction you've mentioned. The trail may have been his'n."

"Hurry Harry, you're well acquainted with this young man, I hope, who has meetings with savages in a part of the country where he has never been before?" demanded Hutter, in a tone, and in a manner, that sufficiently indicated the motive of the question; these rude beings seldom hesitating, on the score of delicacy, to betray their feelings. "Treachery is an Indian virtue, and the whites that live much in their tribes, soon catch their ways and practices."

"True, — true as the gospel, Old Tom, but not personable to Deerslayer, who's a young man of truth, if he has no other riccommend. I'll answer for his *honesty*, whatever I may do for his valor in battle."

"I should like to know his errand in this strange quarter of the country?"

"That is soon told, Master Hutter," said the young man, with the composure of one who kept a clean conscience; "I think, moreover, you've a *right* to ask it. The father of two such darters, who occupies a lake, after your fashion, has just the same right to inquire into a stranger's business in his neighborhood, as the Colony would have to demand the reason why the Frenchers put more rijiments than common, along the lines. No — no — I'll not deny your right to know why a stranger comes into your habitation, or country, in times as serious as these."

"If such is your way of thinking, friend, let me hear your story, without more words."

"'Tis soon told, as I said afore, and shall be honestly told. I'm a young man, and as yet have never been on a war path, but, no sooner did the news come among the Delawares, that wampum and a hatchet was about to be sent in to the tribe, than they wished me to go out among the people of my own colour, and get the exact state of things for 'em. This I did, and, after delivering my talk to the chiefs, on my return, I met an officer of the crown, on the Schoharie, who had messages to send to some of the fri'ndly tribes that live farther west. This was thought a good occasion for Chingachgook, a young chief who has never struck a foe, and myself, to go on our first war path in company, and an app'intment was made for us, by an old Delaware, to meet at the rock near the foot of this lake. I'll not deny that Chingachgook has *another* object in view, but it has no consarn with any here, and is his secret and not mine; therefore I'll say no more about it. — "

"'Tis something about a young woman," interrupted Judith hastily, then laughing at her own impetuosity, and even having the grace to colour a little, at the manner in which she had betrayed her readiness to impute such a motive. "If 'tis neither war, nor a hunt, it must be love."

"Ay, it comes easy for the young and handsome, who hear so much of them feelin's, to suppose that they lie at the bottom of most proceedin's; but, on that head, I say nothin'. Chingachgook is to meet me at the rock, an hour afore sunset to-morrow evening, after which we shall go our way together, molesting none but the king's inimies, who are lawfully our own. Knowing Hurry of old, who once trapped in our hunting grounds, and falling in with him on the Schoharie, just as he was on the p'int of starting for his summer ha'nts, we agreed to journey in company; not so much from fear of the Mingos, as from good fellowship, and, as he says, to shorten a long road."

"And you think the trail I saw may have been that of your friend, ahead of his time?" said Hutter.

"That's my idee, which may be wrong, but which may be right. If I saw the moccasin, howsever, I could tell, in a minute, whether it is made in the Delaware fashion, or not."

"Here it is, then," said the quick witted Judith, who had already gone to the canoe in quest of it. "Tell us what it says; friend or enemy. You look honest, and *I* believe all you say, whatever father may think."

"That's the way with you, Jude; forever finding out friends, where I distrust foes," grumbled Tom: "but, speak out, young man, and tell us what you think of the moccasin."

"That's not Delaware made," returned Deerslayer, examining the worn and rejected covering for the foot, with a cautious eye. "I'm too young on a war-path to be positive, but I should say that moccasin has a northern look, and comes from beyond the Great Lakes."

"If such is the case, we ought not to lie here, a minute longer than is necessary," said Hutter, glancing through the leaves of his cover, as if he already distrusted the presence of an enemy, on the opposite shore of the narrow and sinuous stream. "It wants but an hour, or so, of night, and to move in the dark, will be impossible, without making a noise that would betray us. Did you hear the echo of a piece, in the mountains, half an hour since?"

"Yes, old man, and heard the piece itself," answered Hurry, who now felt the indiscretion of which he had been guilty, "for the last was fired from my own shoulder."

"I feared it came from the French Indians; still, it may put them on the look-out, and be a means of discovering us. You did wrong to fire, in war-time, unless there was good occasion."

"So I begin to think myself, uncle Tom; and, yet, if a man can't trust himself to let off his rifle in a wilderness that is a thousand miles square, lest some inimy should hear it, where's the use in carrying one!"

Hutter now held a long consultation with his two guests, in which the parties came to a true understanding of their situation. He explained the difficulty that would exist in attempting to get the Ark out of so swift, and narrow a stream in the dark, without making a noise that could not fail to attract Indian ears. Any strollers in their vicinity, would keep near the river, or the lake, but the former had swampy shores, in many places, and was both so crooked, and so fringed with bushes, that it was quite possible to move by day-light without incurring much danger of being seen. More was to be apprehended, perhaps, from the ear than from the eye, especially as long as they were in the short, straitened, and canopied reaches of the stream.

"I never drop down into this cover, which is handy to my traps, and safer than the lake from curious eyes, without providing the means of getting out ag'in," continued this singular being, "and that is easier done by a pull than a push. My anchor is now lying above the suction, in the open lake, and here is a line, you see, to haul us up to it. Without some such help, a single pair of hands would make heavy work, in forcing a scow, like this, up stream. I have a sort of a crab too, that lightens the pull on occasion. Jude can use the oar astern, as well as myself, and when we fear no enimy, to get out of the river gives us but little trouble."

"What should we gain, Master Hutter, by changing the position?" asked Deerslayer, with a good deal of earnestness. "This is a safe cover, and a stout defence might be made from the inside of this cabin. I've never fou't, unless in the way of traditions, but it seems to me, we might beat off twenty Mingos, with palisades like these afore us."

"Ay — ay; you've never fought, except in traditions, that's plain enough, young man! Did you ever see as broad a sheet of water as this above us, before you came in upon it, with Hurry?"

"I can't say that I ever did," Deerslayer answered, modestly. "Youth is the time to l'arn, and I'm far from wishing to raise my voice in council, afore it is justified by exper'ence."

"Well, then, I'll teach you the disadvantage of fighting in this position, and the advantage of taking to the open lake. Here, you may see, the savages will know where to aim every shot, and it would be too much to hope that *some* would not find their way through the crevices of the logs. Now, on the other hand, *we* should have nothing but a forest to aim at. Then we are not safe from fire, here, the bark of this roof being little better than so much kindling wood. The Castle, too, might be entered and ransacked, in my absence, and all my possessions overrun and destroyed. Once in the lake, we can be attacked only in boats, or on rafts, shall have a fair chance with the enemy, and can protect the Castle with the Ark. Do you understand this reasoning, youngster?"

"It sounds well — yes, it has a rational sound, and I'll not gainsay it."

"Well, old Tom," cried Hurry, "if we are to move, the sooner we make a beginning, the sooner we shall know whether we are to have our scalps for night-caps, or not."

As this proposition was self-evident, no one denied its justice. The three men, after a short preliminary explanation, now set about their preparations to move the Ark in earnest. The slight fastenings were quickly loosened, and by hauling on the line, the heavy craft slowly emerged from the covers. It was no sooner free from the incumbrance of the branches, than it swung into the stream, sheering quite close to the western shore by the force of the current. Not a soul on board, heard the rustling of the branches as the cabin came against the bushes and trees of the western bank, without a feeling of uneasiness, for no one knew at what moment, or in what place, a secret and murderous enemy might unmask himself. Perhaps the gloomy light, that still struggled through the impending canopy of leaves, or found its way through the narrow, riband-like opening which seemed to mark, in the air above, the course of the river that flowed beneath, aided in augmenting the appearance of the danger, for it was little more than sufficient to render objects visible, without giving up all their outlines at a glance. Although the sun had not absolutely set, it had withdrawn its direct rays from the valley, and the hues of evening were beginning to gather around objects that stood uncovered, rendering those within the shadows of the woods, still more sombre and gloomy.

No interruption followed the movement, however, and, as the men continued to haul on the line, the Ark passed steadily ahead, the great breadth of the scow preventing its sinking into the water, and from offering much resistance to the progress of the swift element beneath its bottom. Hutter, too, had adopted a precaution, suggested by experience, which might have done credit to a seaman, and which completely prevented any of the annoyances and obstacles which, otherwise, would have attended the short turns of the river. As the Ark descended, heavy stones, attached to the line, were dropped in the centre of the stream, forming local anchors, each of which was kept from dragging by the assistance of those above it, until the uppermost of all was reached, which got its 'backing' from the anchor, or grapnel, that lay well out in the lake. In consequence of this expedient, the Ark floated clear of the incumbrances of the shore, against which it would otherwise have been unavoidably hauled at every turn, producing embarrassments that

Hutter, single-handed, would have found it very difficult to overcome.

Favored by this foresight, and stimulated by the apprehensions of discovery, Floating Tom and his two athletic companions hauled the Ark ahead, with quite as much rapidity as comported with the strength of the line. At every turn in the stream a stone was raised from the bottom, when the direction of the scow changed to one that pointed towards the stone that lay above. In this manner, with the channel buoyed out for him, as a sailor might term it, did Hutter move forward, occasionally urging his friends in a low and guarded voice, to increase their exertions, and, then, as occasions offered, warning them against efforts that might, at particular moments, endanger all by too much zeal. In spite of their long familiarity with the woods, the gloomy character of the shaded river added to the uneasiness that each felt, and when the Ark reached the first bend in the Susquehannah, and the eye caught a glimpse of the broader expanse of the lake, all felt a relief, that perhaps none would have been willing to confess. Here the last stone was raised from the bottom, and the line led directly towards the grapnel, which, as Hutter had explained, was dropped above the suction of the current.

"Thank God!" ejaculated Hurry, "*there* is day-light, and we shall soon have a chance of *seeing* our inimies, if we are to *feel* 'em."

"That is more than you, or any man can say," growled Hutter. "There is no spot so likely to harbor a party, as the shore around the outlet, and the moment we clear these trees, and get into open water will be the most trying time, since it will leave the enemy a cover, while it puts us out of one. Judith, girl; do you and Hetty leave the oar to take care of itself, and go within the cabin, and be mindful not to show your faces at a window, for they who will look at them, won't stop to praise their beauty. And, now Hurry, we'll step into this outer room, ourselves, and haul through the door, where we shall all be safe from a surprise at least. Friend Deerslayer, as the current is lighter, and the line has all the strain on it that is prudent, do you keep moving from window to window, taking care not to let your head be seen, if you set any value on your life. No one knows, when or where, we shall hear from our neighbors."

Deerslayer complied, with a sensation that had nothing in common with fear, but which had all the interest of a perfectly novel and a most exciting situation. For the first time in his life, he was in the vicinity of enemies, or had good reason to think so, and that too, under all the thrilling circumstances of Indian surprises, and Indian artifices. As he took his stand at a window, the Ark was just passing through the narrowest part of the stream, a point where the water first entered what was properly termed the river, and where the trees fairly interlocked over-head, causing the current to rush into an arch of verdure, a feature as appropriate and peculiar to the country, perhaps, as that of Switzerland, where the rivers come rushing literally from chambers of ice.

The Ark was in the act of passing the last curve of this leafy entrance, as Deerslayer, having examined all that could be seen of the eastern bank of the river, crossed the room to look from the opposite window at the western. His arrival at this aperture was most opportune, for he had no sooner placed his eye at a crack, than a sight met his gaze that might well have alarmed a sentinel so young and inexperienced. A sapling overhung the water, in nearly half a circle, having first grown towards the light, and then been pressed down into this form by the weight of the snows; a circumstance of common occurrence in the American woods. On this tree no less than six Indians had already appeared, others standing ready to follow them as they left room, each evidently bent on running out on the trunk, and dropping on the roof of the Ark, as it passed beneath. This would have been an exploit of no great difficulty, the inclination of the tree admitting of an easy passage, the adjoining branches offering ample support for the hands, and the fall being too trifling to be apprehended. When Deerslayer first saw this party, it was just unmasking itself, by ascending the part of the tree nearest to the earth, or that which was much the most difficult to overcome, and his knowledge of Indian habits told him, at once, that they were all in their war paint, and belonged to a hostile tribe.

"Pull, Hurry," he cried; "pull for your life, and as you love Judith Hutter. Pull, man, pull!"

This call was made to one that the young man knew had the strength of a giant. It was so earnest and solemn, that both

Hutter and March felt it was not idly given, and they applied all their force to the line simultaneously, and at a most critical moment. The scow redoubled its motion, and seemed to glide from under the tree, as if conscious of the danger that was impending over head. Perceiving that they were discovered, the Indians uttered the fearful war-whoop, and running forward on the tree leaped desperately towards their fancied prize. There were six on the tree and each made the effort. All but their leader fell into the river, more or less distant from the Ark, as they came sooner or later to the leaping place. The chief who had taken the dangerous post in advance, having an earlier opportunity than the others, struck the scow just within the stern. The fall proving so much greater than he had anticipated, he was slightly stunned, and for a moment he remained half bent and unconscious of his situation. At this instant, Judith rushed from her cabin, her beauty heightened by the excitement that produced the bold act, which flushed her cheek to crimson, and throwing all her strength into the effort, she pushed the intruder over the edge of the scow, headlong into the river. This decided feat was no sooner accomplished than the woman resumed her sway; Judith looked over the stern to ascertain what had become of the man, and the expression of her eyes softened to concern; next, her cheek crimsoned between shame and surprise at her own temerity, and then she laughed in her own merry and sweet manner. All this occupied less than a minute, when the arm of Deerslayer was thrown around her waist, and she was dragged swiftly within the protection of the cabin. This retreat was not effected too soon. Scarcely were the two in safety, when the forest was filled with yells, and bullets began to patter against the logs.

The Ark being in swift motion, all this while, it was beyond the danger of pursuit by the time these little events had occurred, and the savages, as soon as the first burst of their anger had subsided, ceased firing, with the consciousness that they were expending their ammunition in vain. When the scow came up over her grapnel, Hutter tripped the latter in a way not to impede the motion, and being now beyond the influence of the current, the vessel continued to drift ahead, until fairly in the open lake, though still near enough to the land to render exposure to a rifle-bullet dangerous. Hutter and March got out two small sweeps, and covered by the cabin, they soon urged the Ark far enough from the shore, to leave no inducement to their enemies to make any further attempt to injure them.

Chapter V.

"Why, let the strucken deer go weep,
　The hart ungalled play:
For some must watch, while some must sleep;
　Thus runs the world away."

Hamlet, III. ii 271-74.

ANOTHER consultation took place, in the forward part of the scow, at which both Judith and Hetty were present. As no danger could now approach unseen, immediate uneasiness had given place to the concern which attended the conviction that enemies were, in considerable force, on the shores of the lake, and that they might be sure no practicable means of accomplishing their own destruction would be neglected. As a matter of course, Hutter felt these truths the deepest, his daughters having an habitual reliance on his resources, and knowing too little to appreciate fully all the risks they ran, while his male companions were at liberty to quit him at any moment they saw fit. His first remark showed that he had an eye to the latter circumstance, and might have betrayed to a keen observer, the apprehension that was, just then, uppermost.

"We've a great advantage over the Iroquois, or the enemy, whoever they are, in being afloat," he said. "There's not a canoe on the lake, that I do'n't know where it's hid, and now yours is here, Hurry, there are but three more on the land, and they're so snug in hollow logs, that I do'n't believe the Indians could find them, let them try ever so long."

"There's no telling that—no one can say that," put in Deerslayer. "A hound is not more sartain on the scent, than a redskin when he expects to get any thing by it. Let this party see scalps afore 'em, or plunder, or honor, accordin' to their idees of what honor is, and 't'will be a tight log that hides a canoe from their eyes."

"You're right, Deerslayer," cried Harry March; "you're downright gospel in this matter, and I rej'ice that my bunch of bark is safe enough, here, within reach of my arm. I calcilate they'll be at all the rest of the canoes, afore to-morrow night, if they are in ra'al 'arnest to smoke you out, old Tom, and we may as well overhaul our paddles for a pull."

Hutter made no immediate reply. He looked about him in silence for quite a minute, examining the sky, the lake, and the belt of forest which enclosed it, as it might be hermetically, like one consulting their signs. Nor did he find any alarming symptoms. The boundless woods were sleeping in the deep repose of nature, the heavens were placid, but still luminous with the light of the retreating sun, while the lake looked more lovely and calm than it had before done that day. It was a scene altogether soothing, and of a character to lull the passions into a species of holy calm. How far this effect was produced, however, on the party in the Ark must appear in the progress of our narrative.

"Judith," called out the father, when he had taken this close but short survey of the omens, "night is at hand; find our friends food; a long march gives a sharp appetite."

"We're not starving, Master Hutter," March observed, "for we filled up just as we reached the lake, and for one, I prefar the company of Jude, even to her supper. This quiet evening is very agreeable to sit by her side."

"Natur' is natur'," objected Hutter, "and must be fed. Judith, see to the meal, and take your sister to help you. I've a little discourse to hold with you, friends," he continued, as soon as his daughters were out of hearing, "and wish the girls away. You see my situation, and I should like to hear your opinions concerning what is best to be done. Three times have I been burnt out, already, but that was on the shore, and I've considered myself as pretty safe, ever since I got the castle built, and the Ark afloat. My other accidents, however, happened in peaceable times, being nothing more than such flurries as a man must meet with, in the woods; but this matter looks serious, and your ideas would greatly relieve my mind."

"It's my notion, old Tom, that you, and your huts, and your traps, and your whole possessions, hereaway, are in desperate j'iparday," returned the matter-of-fact Hurry, who saw no use in concealment; "accordin' to my idees of valie, they're altogether not worth half as much to-day, as they was yesterday, nor would I give more for 'em, taking the pay in skins."

"Then I've children! — " continued the father, making the allusion in a way that it might have puzzled even an indifferent observer to say was intended as a bait, or as an exclamation of paternal concern. "Daughters, as you know, Hurry, and good girls too, I may say, though I *am* their father."

"A man may say any thing, Master Hutter, particularily when pressed by time and circumstances. You've darters, as you say, and one of them has'n't her equal on the frontiers, for good-looks, whatever she may have for good behaviour. As for poor Hetty, she's Hetty Hutter, and that's as much as one can say about the poor thing. Give me Jude, if her conduct was only equal to her looks."

"I see, Harry March, I can only count on you as a fair weather friend, and I suppose that your companion will be of the same way of thinking — " returned the other, with a slight show of pride, that was not altogether without dignity, "well; I must depend on Providence, which will not turn a deaf ear, perhaps, to a father's prayers."

"If you've understood Hurry, here, to mean that he intends to desart you," said Deerslayer, with an earnest simplicity that gave double assurance of its truth, "I *think* you do him injustice, as I *know* you do me in supposing I would follow him, was he so ontrue-hearted as to leave a family of his own colour in such a strait as this. I've come on this lake, Master Hutter, to rende'vous a fri'nd, and I only wish he was here, himself, as I make no doubt he will be, at sunset to-morrow, when you'd have another rifle to aid you — an inexper'enced one, I'll allow, like my own, but one that has proved true so often ag'in the game, big and little, that I'll answer for its sarvice ag'in mortals."

"May I depend on *you* to stand by me and my daughters, then, Deerslayer?" demanded the old man with a father's anxiety in his countenance.

"That may you, Floating Tom, if that's your name, and as a brother would stand by a sister, a husband his wife, or a suitor his sweetheart. In this strait, you may count on me, through all advarsities, and I think Hurry does discredit to his natur', and wishes, if you can't count on him."

"Not he," cried Judith thrusting her handsome face out of the door, "his nature is hurry, as well as his name, and he'll hurry off, as soon as he thinks his fine figure in danger. Neither 'old Tom,' nor his 'gals', will depend much on Master March, now they know him, but *you* they will rely on, Deerslayer; for your honest face, and as honest heart, tell us that what you promise you will perform."

This was said as much, perhaps, in affected scorn for Hurry as in sincerity; still it was not said without feeling. The fine face of Judith sufficiently proved the latter circumstance; and if the conscious March fancied that he had never seen in it, a stronger display of contempt — a feeling in which the beauty was apt to indulge — than while she was looking at him, it certainly seldom exhibited more of womanly softness and sensibility than when her speaking blue eyes were turned on his travelling companion.

"Leave us, Judith," Hutter ordered sternly, before either of the young men could reply. "Leave us, and do not return until you come with the venison and fish. The girl has been spoilt by the flattery of the officers who sometimes find their way up here, Master March, and you'll not think any harm of her silly words."

"You never said truer syllable, old Tom," retorted Hurry, who smarted under Judith's observations — "The devil-tongued youngsters of the garrisons, have proved her undoing! I scarce know Jude any longer, and shall soon take to admiring her sister, who is getting to be much more to my fancy."

"I'm glad to hear this, Harry, and look upon it as a sign that you're coming to your right senses. Hetty would make a much safer and more rational companion than Jude, and would be much the most likely to listen to your suit, as the officers have, I greatly fear, unsettled her sister's mind."

"No man need a safer wife than Hetty," said Hurry, laughing, "though I'll not answer for her being of the most rational. But, no matter; Deerslayer has not misconceived me when he told you I should be found at my post. I'll not quit *you*, uncle Tom, just now, whatever may be my feelin's and intentions respecting your eldest darter."

Hurry had a respectable reputation for prowess among his associates, and Hutter heard this pledge with a satisfaction that was not concealed. Even the great personal strength of such an aid, became of moment in moving the Ark, as well as in the species of hand to hand conflicts that were not unfrequent in the woods, and no commander, who was hard pressed, could feel more joy at hearing of the arrival of reinforcements, than this borderer experienced at being told this important auxiliary was not about to quit him. A minute before, Hutter would have been well content to compromise his danger, by entering into a compact to act only on the defensive, but no sooner did he feel some security on this point, than the restlessness of man induced him to think of the means of carrying the war into the enemy's country.

"High prices are offered for scalps on both sides," he observed with a grim smile, as if he felt the force of the inducement, at the very time he wished to affect a superiority to earning money by means that the ordinary feelings of those who aspire to be civilized men repudiated, even while they were adopted. "It is'nt right, perhaps, to take gold for human blood, and yet when mankind is busy in killing one another, there can be no great harm in adding a little bit of skin to the plunder. What's your sentiments, Hurry, touching these p'ints."

"That you've made a vast mistake, old man, in calling savage blood, human blood, at all. I think no more of a red skin's scalp, than I do of a pair of wolf's ears; and would just as lief finger money for the one, as for the other. With *white* people 'tis different, for they've a nat'ral avarsion to being scalped, whereas your Indian shaves his head in readiness for the knife, and leaves a lock of hair, by way of braggadocia, that one can lay hold of, in the bargain."

"That's manly, however, and I felt, from the first, that we had only to get you on our side, to have you heart and hand," returned Tom, losing all his reserve, as he gained a renewed confidence in the dispositions of his companions. "Something more may turn up from this inroad of the red skins, than they have bargained for. Deerslayer, I conclude you're of Hurry's way of thinking, and look upon money 'arned in this way, as being as likely to pass, as money 'arned in trapping, or hunting."

"I've no such feelin', nor any wish to harbor it, not I," returned the other. "My gifts are not scalper's gifts, but such as belong to my religion and colour. I'll stand by you, old man, in the Ark, or in the castle, the canoe, or the woods, but I'll not unhumanize my natur' by falling into ways that God intended for another race. If you and Hurry have got any thoughts that lean towards the colony's gold, go by yourselves in s'arch of it, and leave the females to my care. Much as I must differ from you both, on all gifts that do not properly belong to a white man, we shall agree that it is the duty of the strong to take care of the weak, especially when the last belong to them that natur' intended man to protect and console by his gentleness and strength."

"Hurry Harry, that is a lesson you might learn and practise on to some advantage," said the sweet but spirited voice of Judith, from the cabin, a proof that she had overheard all that had hitherto been said.

"No more of this, Jude!" called out the father angrily. "Move further off; we are about to talk of matters unfit for a woman to listen to."

Hutter did not take any steps, however, to ascertain whether he was obeyed or not, but, dropping his voice a little, he pursued the discourse.

"The young man is right, Hurry," he said, "and we can leave the children in his care. Now, my idea is just this, and I think you'll agree that it is rational and correct. There's a large party of these savages on the shore, and, though I did'n't tell it before the girls, for they're womanish and apt to be troublesome when any thing like real work is to be done, there's women among 'em. This I know from moccasin prints, and 'tis likely they are hunters, after all, who have been out so long that they know nothing of the war, or of the bounties—"

"In which case, old Tom, why was their first salute an attempt to cut all our throats?"

"We do'n't know that their design was so bloody. It's natural and easy for an Indian to fall into ambushes and surprises, and no doubt they wished to get on board the Ark first, and to make their conditions afterwards. That a disapp'inted savage should fire at us, is in rule, and I think nothing of that. Besides, how often have they burned me out, and robbed my traps—ay, and pulled trigger on me,—in the most peaceful times?"

"The blackguards will do such things, I must allow, and we pay 'em off pretty much in their own c'ine. Women would not be on the war-path, sartainly, and so far there's reason in your idee."

"Nor would a hunter be in his war-paint," returned Deerslayer. "I saw the Mingos, and *know* that they are out on the trail of mortal men, and not for beaver, or deer."

"There you have it ag'in, old fellow," said Hurry. "In the way of an eye, now, I'd as soon trust this young man as trust the oldest settler in the colony; and if he says paint, why paint it was."

"Then a hunting party and a war-party have met, for women must have been with 'em. It's only a few days since the runner went through with the tidings of the troubles, and it may be that warriors have come out to call in their women and children, and to get an early blow."

"That would stand the courts and is just the truth," cried Hurry. "You've got it now, old Tom, and I should like to hear what you mean to make out of it?"

"The bounty—" returned the other, looking up at his attentive companion, in a cool, sullen, manner, in which, however, heartless cupidity, and indifference to the means, were far more conspicuous than any feelings of animosity, or revenge. "If there's women, there's children, and big and little have scalps; the Colony pays for all alike."

"More shame to it, that it should do so," interrupted Deerslayer; "more shame to it that it do'n't understand its gifts, and pay greater attention to the will of God."

"Hearken to reason, lad, and do'n't cry out afore you understand a case," returned the unmoved Hurry. "The savages scalp—your fr'inds the Delawares, or Mohicans, whichever they may be, among the rest—and why should'n't we scalp? I will own it would be ag'in right for you and I, now, to go into the settlements and bring out scalps, but it's a very different matter as consarns Indians. A man should'n't take scalps, if he is'n't ready to be scalped, himself, on fitting occasions. One good turn desarves another, all the world over. That's reason, and I believe it to be good religion."

"Ay, Master Hurry," again interrupted the rich voice of Judith—"is it religion to say that one *bad* turn deserves another."

"I'll never reason ag'in you, Judy, for you beat me with beauty, if you can'n't with sense. Here's the Canadas paying their Injins for scalps, and why not we pay—"

"*Our* Indians!" exclaimed the girl, laughing with a sort of melancholy merriment. "Father—Father!—Think no more of this, and listen to the advice of Deerslayer, who *has* a conscience, which is more than I can say, or think, of Harry March."

Hutter now rose, and entering the cabin, he compelled his daughters to go into the adjoining room, when he secured both the doors and returned. Then he and Hurry pursued the subject, but, as the purport of all that was material in this discourse will appear in the narrative, it need not be related here, in detail. The reader, however, can have no difficulty in comprehending the morality that presided over their conference. It was in truth that, which, in some form or other, rules most of the acts of men, and in which the controlling principle is that one wrong will justify another. Their enemies paid for scalps, and this was sufficient to justify the colony for retaliating. It is true, the French used the same argument, a circumstance, as Hurry took occasion to observe in answer to one of Deerslayer's objections, that proved its truth, as mortal enemies would not be likely to have recourse to the same reason, unless it were a good one. But, neither Hutter, nor Hurry was a man likely to stick at trifles, in matters connected with the rights of the aborigines, since it is one of the consequences of aggression that it hardens the conscience, as the only means of quieting it. In the most peaceable state of the country, a species of warfare was carried on between the Indians, especially those of the Canadas, and men of their caste, and the moment an actual and recognised warfare existed, it was regarded as the means of lawfully revenging a thousand wrongs, real and imaginary. Then, again, there was some truth, and a good deal of expediency in the principle of retaliation, of which they both availed themselves, in particular to answer the objections of their juster minded and more scrupulous companion.

"You must fight a man with his own we'pons, Deerslayer," cried Hurry, in his uncouth dialect, and in his dogmatical manner of disposing of all moral propositions—"If he's f'erce, you must be f'ercer; if he's stout of heart, you must be stouter. This is the way to get the better of christian, or savage; by keepin' up to this trail, you'll get soonest to the ind of your journey."

"That's not Moravian doctrine, which teaches that all are to be judged according to their talents, or l'arning; the Injin like an Injin, and the white-man like a white-man. Some of their teachers say that if you're struck on the cheek, it's a duty to turn the other side of the face, and take another blow, instead of seeking revenge, whereby I understand—"

"That's enough!" shouted Hurry. "That's all I want to prove a man's doctrine! How long would it take to kick a man through the colony—in at one ind, and out at the other—on that principle?"

"Do'n't mistake me, March," returned the young hunter, with dignity. "I do'n't understand by this any more than that it's *best* to do this, if *possible*. Revenge is an Injin gift, and forgiveness a white-man's. That's all. Overlook all you *can*, is what's meant, and not *revenge* all you can. As for kicking, Master Hurry—" Deerslayer's sun burnt cheek flushed, as he continued— "into the colony, or out of the colony, that's neither here nor there, seeing no one proposes it, and no one would be likely to put up with it. What I wish to say is that a red skin's scalping, do'n't justify a pale face's scalping."

"Do as you're done by, Deerslayer; that's even the christian parsons' doctrine."

"No, Hurry, I've asked the Moravians consarning that, and it's altogether different. 'Do as you *would* be done by,' they tell me is the *true* saying, while men practyse the *false*. They think all the colonies wrong that offer bounties for scalps, and believe no blessing will follow the measures. Above all things they forbid revenge."

"*That* for your Moravians!" cried March, snapping his fingers. "They're the next thing to quakers, and if you'd believe all they tell you, not even a 'rat would be skinned, out of marcy. Who ever heard of marcy on a muskrat!"

The disdainful manner of Hurry prevented a reply, and he and the old man resumed the discussion of their plans in a more quiet and confidential manner. This conference lasted until Judith appeared, bearing the simple but savory supper.

March observed, with a little surprise, that she placed the choicest bits before Deerslayer, and that in the little nameless attentions it was in her power to bestow, she quite obviously manifested a desire to let it be seen that she deemed him the honored guest. Accustomed, however, to the waywardness and coquetry of the beauty, this discovery gave him little concern, and he ate with an appetite that was in no degree disturbed by any moral causes. The easily digested food of the forests offering the fewest possible obstacles to the gratification of this great animal indulgence, Deerslayer, notwithstanding the hearty meal both had taken in the woods, was in no manner behind his companions in doing justice to the viands.

An hour later the scene had greatly changed. The lake was still placid and glassy, but the gloom of the hour had succeeded to the soft twilight of a summer evening, and all within the dark setting of the woods lay in the quiet repose of night. The forests gave up no song, or cry, or even murmur, but looked down from the hills on the lovely basin they encircled in solemn stillness, and the only sound that was audible was the regular dip of the sweeps, at which Hurry and Deerslayer lazily pushed, impelling the Ark towards the Castle. Hutter had withdrawn to the stern of the scow, in order to steer, but finding that the young men kept even strokes, and held the desired course by their own skill, he had permitted the oar to drag in the water, taken a seat on the end of the vessel and lighted his pipe. He had not been thus placed many minutes, ere Hetty came stealthily out of the cabin, or house, as they usually termed that part of the Ark, and placed herself at his feet, on a little bench that she had brought with her. As this movement was by no means unusual in his feeble minded child, the old man paid no other attention to it, than to lay his hand kindly on her head, in an affectionate and approving manner, an act of grace that the girl received in meek silence.

After a pause of several minutes, Hetty began to sing. Her voice was low and tremulous, but it was earnest and solemn. The words and the tune were of the simplest form, the first being a hymn that she had been taught by her mother, and the last one of those natural melodies that find favor with all classes, in every age, coming from, and being addressed to, the feelings. Hutter never listened to this simple strain without finding his heart and manner softened, facts that his daughter well knew, and by which she had often profited, through the sort of holy instinct that enlightens the weak of mind, more especially in their aims toward good.

Hetty's low, sweet, tones had not been raised many moments, when the dip of the oars ceased, and the holy strain arose singly, on the breathing silence of that wilderness. As if she gathered courage with her theme, her powers appeared to increase as she proceeded, and, though nothing vulgar or noisy mingled in her melody, its strength and melancholy tenderness grew on the ear, until the air was filled with this simple homage of a soul that seemed almost spotless. That the men forward were not indifferent to this touching interruption was proved by their inaction, nor did their oars again dip until the last of the sweet sounds had actually died among the remarkable echoes, which, at that witching hour would waft, even the lowest modulations of the human voice, more than a mile. Hutter was much affected, for, rude as he was by early habits, and even ruthless as he had got to be by long exposure to the practices of the wilderness, his nature was of that fearful mixture of good and evil, that so generally enters into the moral composition of man.

"You are sad to-night, child," said the father, whose manner and language usually assumed some of the gentleness and elevation of the civilized life he had led in youth, when he thus communed with this particular child. "We have just escaped from enemies, and ought rather to rejoice."

"You can never do it, father!" said Hetty, in a low remonstrating manner, taking his hard knotty hand into both her own— "You have talked long with Harry March, but neither of you have the heart to do it!"

"This is going beyond your means, foolish child; you must have been naughty enough to have listened, or you could know nothing of our talk."

"Why should you and Hurry kill people—especially women and children?"

"Peace, girl, peace. We are at war, and must do to our enemies as our enemies would do to us."

"That's not it, father!—I heard Deerslayer say how it was. You must do to your enemies, as you *wish* your enemies would do to you. No one wishes his enemies to kill him."

"We kill our enemies in war, girl, lest they should kill us. One side or the other must begin, and them that begin first are most apt to get the victory. You know nothing about these things, poor Hetty, and had best say nothing."

"*Judith* says it is wrong, father; and Judith has sense, though I have none."

"Jude understands better than to talk to me of these matters, for she has sense, as you say, and knows I'll not bear it. Which would you prefer, Hetty; to have your own scalp taken and sold to the French, or that we should kill our enemies, and keep them from harming us?"

"That's not it, father! Do'n't kill them, nor let them kill us. Sell your skins, and get more if you can, but do'n't sell human blood."

"Come, come, child; let us talk of matters you understand. Are you glad to see our old friend March back, again?—You like Hurry, and must know that one day he may be your brother—if not something nearer."

"That ca'n't be, father—" returned the girl, after a considerable pause. "Hurry has had one father and one mother, and people never have two."

"So much for your weak mind, Hetty. When Jude marries, her husband's father will be her father, and her husband's sister, her sister. If she should marry Hurry, then he will be your brother."

"Judith will never have Hurry," returned the girl mildly; but positively. "Judith do'n't like Hurry."

"That's more than you can know, Hetty. Harry March is the handsomest, and the strongest, and the boldest young man that ever visits the lake, and as Jude is the greatest beauty, I do'n't see why they should'n't come together. He has as much as promised that he will enter into this job with me, on condition that I'll consent."

Hetty began to move her body back and forth, and otherwise to express mental agitation, but she made no answer for more than a minute. Her father, accustomed to her manner, and suspecting no immediate cause of concern, continued to smoke with the apparent phlegm which would seem to belong to that particular species of enjoyment.

"Hurry *is* handsome, father—" said Hetty with a simple emphasis that she might have hesitated about using had her mind been more alive to the inferences of others.

"I told you so, child," muttered old Hutter, without removing the pipe from between his teeth. "He's the likeliest youth in these parts, and Jude is the likeliest young woman I've met with since her poor mother was in her best days."

"Is it wicked to be ugly, father?"

"One might be guilty of worse things—but you're by no means ugly, though not as comely as Jude."

"Is Judith any happier for being so handsome?"

"She may be, child; and she may not be. But talk of other matters now, for you hardly understand these, poor Hetty. How do you like our new acquaintance, Deerslayer?"

"He is'n't handsome, father. Hurry is far handsomer than Deerslayer."

"That's true, but they say he is a noted hunter. His fame had reached me before I ever saw him, and I did hope he would prove to be as stout a warrior, as he is dexterous with the deer. All men are not alike, howsever, child, and it takes time, as I know by experience, to give a man a true wilderness heart."

"Have I got a wilderness heart, father?—and, Hurry, is *his* heart true wilderness?"

"You sometimes ask queer questions, Hetty! Your heart is good, child, and fitter for the settlements than for the woods, while your reason is fitter for the woods than for the settlements."

"Why has Judith more reason than I, father?"

"Heaven help thee, child!—This is more than I can answer. God gives sense, and appearance, and all these things, and he grants them as he seeth fit. Dost thou wish for more sense?"

"Not I. The little I have troubles me, for when I think the hardest, then I feel the unhappiest. I do'n't believe thinking is good for me, though I *do* wish I was as handsome as Judith!"

"Why so, poor child?—Thy sister's beauty may cause her trouble, as it caused her mother before her. It's no advantage, Hetty, to be so marked for any thing, as to become an object of envy, or to be sought after more than others".

"Mother was good, if she *was* handsome," returned the girl, the tears starting to her eyes, as usually happened when she adverted to her deceased parent.

Old Hutter, if not equally affected, was moody and silent at this allusion to his wife. He continued smoking, without appearing disposed to make any answer, until his simple-minded daughter repeated her remark in a way to show that she felt uneasiness, lest he might be inclined to deny her assertion. Then he knocked the ashes out of his pipe, and laying his hand in a sort of rough kindness on the girl's head, he made her a reply.

"Thy mother was too good for this world," he said, "though others might not think so. Her good looks did not befriend her, and you have no occasion to mourn that you are not as much like her as your sister. Think less of beauty, child, and more of your duty, and you'll be as happy on this lake, as you could be in the King's palace."

"I know it, father; but Hurry says beauty is every thing in a young woman."

Hutter made an ejaculation expressive of dissatisfaction, and went forward, passing through the house in order to do so. Hetty's simple betrayal of her weakness in behalf of March gave him uneasiness on a subject concerning which he had never felt before, and he determined to come to an explanation at once with his visiter, for directness of speech, and decision in conduct, were two of the best qualities of this rude being, in whom the seeds of a better education seemed to be constantly struggling upward, to be choked by the fruits of a life, in which his hard struggles for subsistence and security, had steeled his feelings and indurated his nature. When he reached the forward end of the scow, he manifested an intention to relieve Deerslayer at the oar, directing the latter to take his own place aft. By these changes, the old man and Hurry were again left alone, while the young hunter was transferred to the other end of the Ark.

Hetty had disappeared when Deerslayer reached his new post, and for some little time he directed the course of the slow-moving craft by himself. It was not long, however, before Judith came out of the cabins, as if disposed to do the honors of the place to a stranger engaged in the service of her family.

The star-light was sufficient to permit objects to be plainly distinguished, when near at hand, and the bright eyes of the girl had an expression of kindness in them, when they met those of the youth, that the latter was easily enabled to discern. Her rich hair shaded her spirited and yet soft countenance, even at that hour rendering it the more beautiful, as the rose is loveliest when reposing amid the shadows and contrasts of its native foliage. Little ceremony is used in the intercourse, of the woods, and Judith had acquired a readiness of address, by the admiration, that she so generally excited, which, if it did not amount to forwardness, certainly in no degree lent to her charms the aid of that retiring modesty on which poets love to dwell.

"I thought I should have killed myself with laughing, Deerslayer," the beauty abruptly, but coquettishly commenced, "when I saw that Indian dive into the river! He was a good-looking savage, too—" the girl always dwelt on personal beauty as a sort of merit—"And yet one coul'n't stop to consider whether his paint would stand water!"

"And I thought they would have killed you with their we'pons, Judith," returned Deerslayer, "for it was an awful risk for a female to run, in the face of a dozen Mingos!"

"Did *that* make *you* come out of the cabin, in spite of their rifles too?" asked the girl, with more real interest than she would have cared to betray, though with an indifference of manner that was the result of a good deal of practice, united to native readiness.

"Men are'n't apt to see females in danger, and not come to their assistance. Even a Mingo knows that."

This sentiment was uttered with as much simplicity of manner as of feeling, and Judith rewarded it, with a smile so sweet that even Deerslayer, who had imbibed a prejudice against the girl, in consequence of Hurry's suspicions of her levity, felt its charm, notwithstanding half its winning influence was lost in the feeble light. It at once created a sort of confidence between them, and the discourse was continued on the part of the hunter without the lively consciousness of the character of this coquette of the wilderness, with which it had certainly commenced.

"You are a man of deeds and not of words, I see plainly,

Deerslayer," continued the beauty, taking her seat near the spot where the other stood, "and I foresee we shall be very good friends. Hurry-Harry has a tongue, and giant as he is, he talks more than he performs."

"March is your fri'nd, Judith; and fri'nds should be tender of each other, when apart."

"We all know what Hurry's friendship comes to. Let him have his own way in every thing, and he's the best fellow in the colony; but, 'head him off', as you say of the deer, and he is master of every thing near him, but himself. Hurry is no favorite of mine, Deerslayer, and I dare say, if the truth was known, and his conversation about me repeated, it would be found that he thinks no better of me, than I own I do of him."

The latter part of this speech was uttered not without uneasiness. Had the girl's companion been more sophisticated, he might have observed the averted face, the manner in which the pretty little foot was agitated, and other signs that, for some reason unexplained, the opinions of March were not quite as much matter of indifference to her as she thought fit to pretend. Whether this was no more than the ordinary working of female vanity, feeling keenly even where it affected not to feel at all, or whether it proceeded from that deeply seated consciousness of right and wrong, which God himself has implanted in our breasts that we may know good from evil, will be made more apparent to the reader, as we proceed in the tale. Deerslayer felt embarrassed. He well remembered the cruel imputations left by March's distrust, and, while he did not wish to injure his associate's suit by exciting resentment against him, his tongue was one that literally knew no guile. To answer without saying more or less than he wished, was consequently a delicate duty.

"March has his say of all things in natur', whether of fri'nd, or foe," slowly and cautiously rejoined the hunter. "He's one of them that speak as they feel, while the tongue's a-going, and that's sometimes different from what they'd speak if they took time to consider. Give me a Delaware, Judith, for one that reflects and rumernates on his idees. Inmity has made 'em thoughtful, and a loose tongue is no riccommend at their Council Fires."

"I dare say March's tongue goes free enough when it gets on

the subject of Judith Hutter and her sister," said the girl, rousing herself as if in careless disdain. "Young women's good names are a pleasant matter of discourse with some that would'n't dare to be so open mouthed, if there was a brother in the way. Master March may find it pleasant to traduce us, but, sooner or later, he'll repent!"

"Nay, Judith, this is taking the matter up too much in 'arnest. Hurry has never whispered a syllable ag'in the good-name of Hetty, to begin with—"

"I see how it is—I see how it is—" impetuously interrupted Judith. "*I* am the one he sees fit to scorch with his withering tongue!—Hetty, indeed!—Poor Hetty—" she continued, her voice sinking into low husky tones, that seemed nearly to stifle her in the utterance—"*She* is beyond and above his slanderous malice! Poor Hetty! If God has created her feeble-minded, the weakness lies altogether on the side of errors which she seems to know nothing about. The earth never held a purer being than Hetty Hutter, Deerslayer!"

"I can believe it—yes I can believe *that*, Judith, and I hope 'arnestly that the same can be said of her handsome sister."

There was a soothing sincerity in the voice of Deerslayer, which touched the girl's feelings, nor did the allusion to her beauty lessen the effect with one who only knew too well the power of her personal charms. Nevertheless, the still, small voice of conscience was not hushed, and it prompted the answer which she made, after giving herself time to reflect.

"I dare say Hurry had some of his vile hints about the people of the garrisons—" she added. "He knows they are gentlemen, and can never forgive any one for being what he feels he can never become himself."

"Not in the sense of a King's officer, Judith, sartainly, for March has no turn that-a-way, but in the sense of reality, why may not a beaver-hunter be as respectable as a governor. Since you speak of it, yourself, I'll not deny that he *did* complain of one as humble as you, being so much in the company of scarlet coats and silken sashes. But 'twas jealousy that brought it out of him, and I do think that he mourned over his own thoughts, as a mother would have mourned over her child."

Perhaps Deerslayer was not aware of the full meaning that his earnest language conveyed. It is certain he did not see the colour that crimsoned the whole of Judith's fine face, nor detect the uncontrollable distress that, immediately after, changed its hue to a deadly paleness. A minute or two elapsed in profound stillness, the splash of the water seeming to occupy all the avenues of sound, and then Judith arose, and grasped the hand of the hunter, almost convulsively, with one of her own.

"Deerslayer," she said hurriedly—"I'm glad the ice is broke between us. They say that sudden friendships lead to long enmities, but I do not believe it will turn out so with us. I know not how it is—but, you are the first man I ever met, who did not seem to wish to flatter—to wish my ruin—to be an enemy in disguise—never mind; say nothing to Hurry, and another time we'll talk together, again."

As the girl released her grasp, she vanished in the house leaving the astonished young man standing at the steering-oar, as motionless as one of the pines on the hills. So abstracted indeed had his thoughts become, that he was hailed by Hutter to keep the scow's head in the right direction, before he remembered his actual situation.

Chapter VI.

"So spake th' apostate Angel, though in pain,
Vaunting aloud, but racked with deep despair:"
Paradise Lost, I.125–26.

S H O R T L Y after the disappearance of Judith, a light southerly air arose, and Hutter set a large square sail, that had once been the flying top-sail of an Albany sloop, but which, having become threadbare in catching the breezes of Tappan, had been condemned and sold. He had a light tough spar of tamarack that he could raise on occasion, and with a little contrivance, his duck was spread to the wind in a sufficiently professional manner. The effect on the Ark was such as to supersede the necessity of rowing, and, in about two hours, the Castle was seen, in the darkness, rising out of the black water, at the distance of a hundred yards. The sail was then lowered, and by slow degrees the scow drifted up to the building, and was secured.

No one had visited the house, since Hurry and his companion left it. The place was found in the quiet of midnight, a sort of type of the solitude of a wilderness. As an enemy was known to be near, Hutter directed his daughters to abstain from the use of lights, luxuries in which they seldom indulged during the warm months, lest they might prove beacons to direct their foes where they might be found.

"In open day-light, I should'n't fear a host of savages, behind these stout logs, and they without any cover to skulk into," added Hutter, when he had explained to his guests the reason why he forbade the use of lights, "for I've three or four trusty weapons always loaded, and Killdeer, in particular, is a piece that never misses. But it's a different thing at night. A canoe might get upon us unseen, in the dark, and the savages have so many cunning ways of attacking, that I look upon it as bad enough to deal with 'em, under a bright sun. I built this dwelling, in order to have 'em at arm's length, in case we should ever get to blows, again. Some people think it's too open and exposed, but I'm for anchoring out here, clear of underbrush and thickets, as the surest means of making a safe berth."

"You was once a sailor, they tell me, old Tom?" said Hurry, in his abrupt manner, struck by one or two expressions that the other had just used; "and some people believe you could give us strange accounts of inimies and ship wrecks, if you'd a mind to come out with all you know?"

"There are people in this world, Hurry," returned the other evasively, "who live on other men's thoughts, and some such often find their way into the woods. What I've been, or what I've seen in youth, is of less matter now, than what the savages are. It's of more account to find out what will happen in the next twenty four hours, than to talk over what happened twenty four years since."

"That's judgment, Deerslayer; yes, that's sound judgment. Here's Judith and Hetty to take care on, to say nothing of our own top-knots; and for my part I can sleep as well in the dark, as I could under a noon day sun. To me it's no great matter whether there is light, or not, to see to shut my eyes by."

As Deerslayer seldom thought it necessary to answer his companion's peculiar vein of humour, and Hutter was evidently indisposed to dwell longer on the subject, its discussion ceased with this remark. The latter had something more on his mind, however, than recollections. His daughters had no sooner left them, with an expressed intention of going to bed, than he invited his two companions to follow him again into the scow. Here the old man opened his project, keeping back the portions that he had reserved for execution by Hurry and himself.

"The great object for people posted like ourselves, is to command the water," he commenced. "So long as there is no other craft on the lake, a bark canoe is as good as a man-of-war, since the castle will not be easily taken by swimming. Now, there are but five canoes remaining in these parts, two of which are mine, and one is Hurry's. These three we have with us, here, one being fastened in the canoe-dock beneath the house, and the other two being along side the scow. The other canoes are housed on the shore, in hollow logs, and the savages, who are such venomous enemies, will leave no likely place unexamined in the morning, if they're serious in s'arch of bounties"—

"Now, friend Hutter," interrupted Hurry, "the Indian do'n't live that can find a canoe that is suitably wintered. I've done something at this business before now, and Deerslayer, here, knows that I am one that can hide a craft in such a way that I can't find it myself."

"Very true, Hurry," put in the person to whom the appeal had been made, "but you overlook the sarcumstance that if you couldn't see the trail of the man who did the job, *I could.* I'm of Master Hutter's mind that it's far wiser to mistrust a savage's ingenuerty, than to build any great expectations on his want of eye-sight. If these two canoes can be got off to the castle, therefore, the sooner it's done the better."

"Will you be of the party that's to do it?" demanded Hutter, in a way to show that the proposal both surprised and pleased him.

"Sartain. I'm ready to enlist in any interprise that's not ag'in a white man's lawful gifts. Natur' orders us to defend our lives, and the lives of others too, when there's occasion and opper-tunity. I'll follow you, Floating Tom, into the Mingo camp on such an ar'n'd, and will strive to do my duty, should we come to blows, though, never having been tried in battle, I do'n't like to promise more than I may be able to perform. We all know our wishes, but none know their might 'till put to the proof."

"That's modest and suitable, lad," exclaimed Hurry. "You've never yet heard the crack of an angry rifle, and let me tell you, 'tis as different from the persuasion of one of your ven-ison speeches, as the laugh of Judith Hutter, in her best humour, is from the scolding of a Dutch housekeeper on the Mohawk. I do'n't expect you'll prove much of a warrior, Deerslayer, though your equal with the bucks, and the does, do'n't exist in all these parts. As for the ra'al sarvice, howsever, you'll turn out rather rearward, according to my consait."

"We'll see, Hurry, we'll see," returned the other meekly, and so far as human eye could discover not at all disturbed by these expressed doubts concerning his conduct on a point on which men are uniformly sensitive, precisely in the degree that they feel the consciousness of demerit,—"having never been tried, I'll wait to know, before I form any opinion myself, and then there'll be sartainty instead of bragging. I've heard of them that was valiant afore the fight, who did little in it, and of them that waited to know their own tempers, and found that they were'n't as bad as some expected, when put to the proof."

"At any rate we know you can use a paddle, young man," said Hutter, "and that's all we shall ask of you to-night. Let us waste no more time, but get into the canoe, and *do* in place of talking."

As Hutter led the way in the execution of his project, the boat was soon ready, with Hurry and Deerslayer at the paddles. Before the old man embarked himself, however, he held a conference of several minutes with Judith, entering the house for that purpose; then, returning, he took his place in the canoe, which left the side of the Ark at the next instant.

Had there been a temple reared to God, in that solitary wilderness, its clock would have told the hour of midnight as the party set forth on their expedition. The darkness had increased, though the night was still clear, and the light of the stars sufficed for all the purposes of the adventurers. Hutter alone knew the places where the canoes were hid, and he directed the course, while his two athletic companions raised and dipped their paddles with proper caution, lest the sound should be carried to the ears of their enemies, across that sheet of placid water, in the stillness of deep night. But the bark was too light to require any extraordinary efforts, and, skill supplying the place of strength, in about half an hour, they were approaching the shore, at a point near a league from the Castle.

"Lay on your paddles, men," said Hutter, in a low voice; "and let us look about us for a moment. We must now be all eyes and ears, for these vermin have noses like blood hounds."

The shores of the lake were examined closely, in order to discover any glimmering of light that might have been left in a camp, and the men strained their eyes, in the obscurity, to see if some thread of smoke was not still stealing along the mountain-side, as it arose from the dying embers of a fire. Nothing unusual could be traced, and as the position was at some distance from the outlet, or the spot where the savages had been met, it was thought safe to land. The paddles were plied, again, and the bows of the canoe ground up on the gravelly beach, with a gentle motion, and a sound barely audible. Hutter and Hurry immediately landed, the former carrying his own and his friend's rifle, leaving Deerslayer in charge of the canoe.

The hollow log lay at a little distance up the side of the mountain, and the old man led the way towards it, using so much caution as to stop at every third or fourth step to listen if any tread betrayed the presence of a foe. The same death like stillness, however, reigned on the midnight scene, and the desired place was reached without an occurrence to induce alarm.

"This is it," whispered Hutter, laying a foot on the trunk of a fallen linden—"hand me the paddles first, and draw the boat out with care, for the wretches may have left it for a bait, after all."

"Keep my rifle handy, butt towards me, old fellow," answered March—"If they attack me loaded, I shall want to unload the piece at 'em, at least. And feel if the pan is full."

"All's right—" muttered the other. "Move slow when you get your load, and let me lead the way."

The canoe was drawn out of the log with the utmost care, raised by Hurry to his shoulder, and the two began to return to the shore, moving but a step at a time, lest they should tumble down the steep declivity. The distance was not great, but the descent was extremely difficult, and towards the end of their little journey, Deerslayer was obliged to land and meet them, in order to aid in lifting the canoe through the bushes. With his assistance, the task was successfully accomplished, and the light craft soon floated by the side of the other canoe. This was no sooner done, than all three turned anxiously toward the forest and the mountain, as if expecting an enemy to break out of the one, or to come rushing down the other. Still the silence was unbroken, and they all embarked with the caution that had been used in coming ashore.

Hutter now steered broad off towards the centre of the lake. Having got a sufficient distance from the shore, he cast his prize loose, knowing that it would drift slowly up the lake, before the light southerly air, and intending to find it on his return. Thus relieved of his tow, the old man held his way down the lake, steering towards the very point, where Hurry had made his fruitless attempt on the life of the deer. As the distance from this point to the outlet was less than a mile, it was like entering an enemy's country, and redoubled caution became necessary. They reached the extremity of the point, however, and landed in safety, on the little gravelly beach already mentioned. Unlike the last place at which they had gone ashore, here was no acclivity to ascend, the mountains looming up in the darkness quite a quarter of a mile further west, leaving a margin of level ground between them and the strand. The point itself, though long, and covered with tall trees, was nearly flat, and, for some distance, only a few yards in width. Hutter and Hurry landed as before, leaving their companion in charge of the boat.

In this instance the dead tree that contained the canoe of which they had come in quest, lay about half way between the extremity of this narrow slip of land, and the place where it joined the main shore; and, knowing that there was water so near him on his left, the old man led the way along the eastern side of the belt, with some confidence, walking boldly though still with caution. He had landed at the point expressly to get a glimpse into the bay, and to make certain that the coast was clear; otherwise he would have come ashore directly abreast of the hollow tree. There was no difficulty in finding the latter, from which the canoe was drawn as before, and, instead of carrying it down to the place where Deerslayer lay, it was launched at the nearest favorable spot. As soon as it was in the water, Hurry entered it, and paddled down to the point, whither Hutter also proceeded following the beach. As the three men had now in their possession all the boats on the lake, their confidence was greatly increased, and there was no longer the same feverish desire to quit the shore, or the same necessity for extreme caution. Their position on the extremity of the long, narrow bit of land added to the feeling of security, as it permitted an enemy to approach in only one direction, that in their front, and under circumstances that would render discovery, with their habitual vigilance, almost certain. The three now landed together, and stood grouped in consultation on the gravelly point.

"We've fairly tree'd the scamps," said Hurry, chuckling at

their success, "and if they wish to visit the castle, let 'em wade or swim! Old Tom, that idee of your'n, in burrowing out in the lake was high proof, and carries a fine bead. There be men who would think the land safer than the water, but after all reason shows it is'n't; the beavers, and 'rats, and other l'arned creatur's, taking to the last, when hard pressed. I call our position, now, entrenched, and set the Canadas at defiance."

"Let us paddle along this south shore," said Hutter, "and see if there's no signs of an encampment — but, first, let me have a better look into the bay, for no one has been far enough round the inner shore of the point, to make sure of that quarter, yet."

As Hutter ceased speaking all three moved in the direction he had named. Scarce had they fairly opened the bottom of the bay, when a general start proved that their eyes had lighted on a common object, at the same instant. It was no more than a dying brand, giving out its flickering and failing light, but at that hour, and in that place, it was at once as conspicuous as "a good deed in a naughty world." There was not a shadow of doubt that this fire had been kindled at an encampment of the Indians. The situation, sheltered from observation on all sides but one, and even on that except for a very short distance, proved that more care had been taken to conceal the spot, than would be used for ordinary purposes, and Hutter, who knew that a spring was near at hand, as well as one of the best fishing stations on the lake, immediately inferred that this encampment contained the women and children of the party.

"That's not a warrior's encampment," he growled to Hurry, "and there's a bounty enough sleeping round that fire to make a heavy division of head-money. Send the lad to the canoes, for there'll come no good of him in such an onset, and let us take the matter in hand, at once, like men."

"There's judgment in your notion, old Tom, and I like it to the back-bone. Deerslayer, do you get into the canoe, lad, and paddle off into the lake, with the spare one, and set it adrift, as we did with the other; after which you can float along shore, as near as you can get to the head of the bay, keeping outside the point, howsever, and outside the rushes too. You can hear us when we want you, and if there's any delay I'll call like a loon — yes, that'll do it — the call of a loon shall be the signal. If you hear rifles, and feel like sogering, why you may close in, and see if you can make the same hand with the savages that you do with the deer."

"If my wishes could be followed, this matter would not be undertaken, Hurry—"

"Quite true—no body denies it, boy; but your wishes *ca'n't* be followed, and that inds the matter. So just canoe yourself off into the middle of the lake, and by the time you get back, there'll be movements in that camp!"

The young man set about complying with great reluctance and a heavy heart. He knew the prejudices of the frontier men too well, however, to attempt a remonstrance. The latter, indeed, under the circumstances, might prove dangerous, as it would certainly prove useless. He paddled the canoes, therefore, silently and with the former caution to a spot near the centre of the placid sheet of water, and set the boat just recovered adrift, to float towards the castle, before the light southerly air. This expedient had been adopted, in both cases, under the certainty that the drift could not carry the light barks more than a league or two before the return of light, when they might easily be overtaken. In order to prevent any wandering savage from using them, by swimming off and getting possession, a possible but scarcely a probable event, all the paddles were retained.

No sooner had he set the recovered canoe adrift, than Deerslayer turned the bows of his own towards the point on the shore that had been indicated by Hurry. So light was the movement of the little craft, and so steady the sweep of its master's arm, that ten minutes had not elapsed ere it was again approaching the land, having in that brief time passed over fully half a mile of distance. As soon as Deerslayer's eye caught a glimpse of the rushes, of which there were many growing in the water a hundred feet from the shore, he arrested the motion of the canoe, and anchored his boat by holding fast to the delicate but tenacious stem of one of the drooping plants. Here he remained, awaiting with an intensity of suspense that can be easily imagined, the result of the hazardous enterprise.

It would be difficult to convey to the minds of those who have never witnessed it, the sublimity that characterizes the silence of a solitude as deep as that which now reigned over the

Glimmerglass. In the present instance, this sublimity was increased by the gloom of night, which threw its shadowy and fantastic forms around the lake, the forest, and the hills. It is not easy, indeed, to conceive of any place more favorable to heighten these natural impressions than that Deerslayer now occupied. The size of the lake brought all within the reach of human senses, while it displayed so much of the imposing scene at a single view, giving up, as it might be, at a glance, a sufficiency to produce the deepest impressions. As has been said, this was the first lake Deerslayer had ever seen. Hitherto his experience had been limited to the courses of rivers and smaller streams, and never before had he seen so much of that wilderness, which he so well loved, spread before his gaze. Accustomed to the forest, however, his mind was capable of portraying all its hidden mysteries, as he looked upon its leafy surface. This was also the first time he had been on a trail, when human lives depended on the issue. His ears had often drunk in the traditions of frontier warfare, but he had never yet been confronted with an enemy.

The reader will readily understand, therefore, how intense must have been the expectation of the young man, as he sat in his solitary canoe, endeavoring to catch the smallest sound that might denote the course of things on the shore. His training had been perfect, so far as theory could go, and his self-possession, notwithstanding the high excitement that was the fruit of novelty, would have done credit to a veteran. The visible evidences of the existence of the camp, or of the fire, could not be detected from the spot where the canoe lay, and he was compelled to depend on the sense of hearing alone. He did not feel impatient, for the lessons he had heard, taught him the virtue of patience, and most of all inculcated the necessity of wariness in conducting any covert assault on the Indians. Once he thought he heard the cracking of a dried twig, but expectation was so intense it might mislead him. In this manner, minute after minute passed, until the whole time since he left his companions was extended to quite an hour. Deerslayer knew not whether to rejoice in, or to mourn over this cautious delay, for if it augured security to his associates, it foretold destruction to the feeble and innocent.

It might have been an hour and a half after his companions

and he had parted, when Deerslayer was aroused by a sound that filled him equally with concern and surprise. The quavering call of a loon arose from the opposite side of the lake; evidently at no great distance from its outlet. There was no mistaking the note of this bird, which is so familiar to all who know the sounds of the American lakes. Shrill, tremulous, loud and sufficiently prolonged, it seems the very cry of warning. It is often raised also, at night, an exception to the habits of most of the other feathered inmates of the wilderness, a circumstance which had induced Hurry to select it as his own signal. There had been sufficient time certainly for the two adventurers to make their way by land, from the point where they had been left, to that whence the call had come, but it was not probable that they would adopt such a course. Had the camp been deserted, they would have summoned Deerslayer to the shore, and did it prove to be peopled, there could be no sufficient motive for circling it, in order to re-embark at so great a distance. Should he obey the signal, and be drawn away from the landing, the lives of those who depended on him might be the forfeit, and should he neglect the call, on the supposition that it had been really made, the consequences might be equally disastrous, though from a different cause. In this indecision, he waited, trusting that the call, whether feigned or natural, would be speedily renewed. Nor was he mistaken. A very few minutes elapsed before the same shrill, warning cry was repeated, and from the same part of the lake. This time, being on the alert, his senses were not deceived. Although he had often heard admirable imitations of this bird, and was no mean adept himself in raising its notes, he felt satisfied that Hurry, to whose efforts in that way he had attended, could never so completely and closely follow nature. He determined, therefore, to disregard that cry, and to wait for one less perfect, and nearer at hand.

Deerslayer had hardly come to this determination, when the profound stillness of night and solitude was broken by a cry so startling, as to drive all recollection of the more melancholy call of the loon, from the listener's mind. It was a shriek of agony, that came either from one of the female sex, or from a boy so young as not yet to have attained a manly voice. This appeal could not be mistaken. Heart rending terror — if not writhing agony—was in the sounds, and the anguish that had awakened them was as sudden as it was fearful. The young man released his hold of the rush, and dashed his paddle into the water; to do, he knew not what—to steer, he know not whither. A very few moments, however, removed his indecision. The breaking of branches, the cracking of dried sticks, and the fall of feet were distinctly audible, the sounds appearing to approach the water, though in a direction that led diagonally towards the shore, and a little farther north than the spot that Deerslayer had been ordered to keep near. Following this clue, the young man urged the canoe ahead, paying but little attention to the manner in which he might betray its presence. He had reached a part of the shore, where its immediate bank was tolerably high and quite steep. Men were evidently threshing through the bushes and trees, on the summit of this bank, following the line of the shore, as if those who fled sought a favorable place for descending. Just at this instant, five or six rifles flashed, and the opposite hills gave back, as usual, the sharp reports, in prolonged, rolling echoes. One or two shrieks, like those which escape the bravest when suddenly overcome by unexpected anguish and alarm, followed, and then the threshing among the bushes was renewed, in a way to show that man was grappling with man.

"Slippery devil!" shouted Hurry, with the fury of disappointment, "his skin's greased! I sha'n't grapple!—Take *that* for your cunning!"

The words were followed by the fall of some heavy object among the smaller trees that fringed the bank, appearing to Deerslayer as if his gigantic associate had hurled an enemy from him, in this unceremonious manner. Again the flight and pursuit were renewed, and then the young man saw a human form break down the hill, and rush several yards into the water. At this critical moment the canoe was just near enough to the spot to allow this movement, which was accompanied by no little noise, to be seen, and feeling that there he must take in his companions, if anywhere, Deerslayer urged the canoe forward, to the rescue. His paddle had not been raised twice, when the voice of Hurry was heard filling the air with imprecations, and he rolled on the narrow beach, literally loaded down with enemies. While prostrate, and almost smothered with his foes, the athletic frontier-man gave his loon-call, in a manner that would have excited laughter, under circumstances less terrific. The figure in the water seemed suddenly to repent his own flight, and rushed to the shore to aid his companion, but was met and immediately overpowered, by half a dozen fresh pursuers who, just then, came leaping down the bank.

"Let up—you painted riptyles—let up!" cried Hurry, too hard pressed to be particular about the terms he used—"is'n't it enough that I'm withed like a saw-log, that ye must choke, too?"

This speech satisfied Deerslayer that his friends were prisoners, and that to land would be to share their fate. He was already within a hundred feet of the shore, when a few timely strokes of the paddle, not only arrested his advance, but forced him off to six or eight times that distance from his enemies. Luckily for him, all of the Indians had dropped their rifles in the pursuit, or this retreat might not have been effected with impunity; though no one had noted the canoe in the first confusion of the *mêlée*.

"Keep off the land, lad," called out Hutter—"The girls depend only on you, now; you will want all your caution to escape these savages. Keep off, and God prosper you, as you aid my children!"

There was little sympathy in general, between Hutter and the young man, but the bodily and mental anguish with which this appeal was made, served at the moment, to conceal from the latter all the former's faults. He saw only the father in his sufferings, and resolved at once to give a pledge of fidelity to his interests, and to be faithful to his word.

"Put your heart at ease, Master Hutter," he called out; —"The gals shall be look'd to, as well as the castle. The inimy has got the shore, 'tis no use to deny, but he has'n't got the water. Providence has the charge of all, and no one can say what will come of it; but, if good will can sarve you and your'n, depend on that much. My exper'ence is small, but my will is good."

"Ay—ay, Deerslayer—" returned Hurry, in his stentorian voice, which was losing some of its heartiness, notwithstanding—"Ay—ay—Deerslayer, you *mean* well enough, but what can you *do*. You're no great matter in the best of times, and such a person is not likely to turn out a miracle in the worst. If there's one savage on this lake shore, there's forty, and that's an army you a'nt the man to overcome. The best way, in my judgment, will be to make a straight course to the castle, get the gals into the canoe, with a few eatables, then strike off for the corner of the lake where we came in, and take the best trail for the Mohawk. These devils won't know where to look for you, for some hours, and if they did, and went off hot in the pursuit, they must turn either the foot, or the head, of the lake to get at you. That's my judgment in the matter, and if old Tom, here, wishes to make his last will and testament in a manner favorable to his darters he'll say the same."

"Twill never do, young man," rejoined Hutter. "The enemy has scouts out, at this moment, looking for canoes, and you'll be seen and taken. Trust to the castle, and above all things, keep clear of the land. Hold out a week, and parties from the garrisons will drive the savages off."

"T'won't be four and twenty hours, old fellow, afore these foxes will be rafting off, to storm your castle," interrupted Hurry, with more of the heat of argument, than might be expected from a man who was bound and a captive, and about whom nothing could be called free but his opinions and his tongue. "Your advice has a stout sound, but it will have a fatal tarmination. If you, or I, was in the house, we might hold out a few days, but remember that this lad has never seen an inimy afore to-night, and is what you yourself called settlement-conscienced; though, for my part I think the consciences in the settlements pretty much the same as they are out here in the woods. These savages are making signs, Deerslayer, for me to incourage you to come ashore with the canoe, but that I'll never do, as it's ag'in reason and natur'. As for old Tom and myself, whether they'll scalp us to-night, keep us for the torture by fire, or carry us to Canada, is more than any one knows, but the Devil that advises them how to act. I've such a big and bushy head, that it's quite likely they'll indivor to get two scalps off it, for this bounty is a tempting thing, or old Tom and I would'n't be in this scrape. Ay — there they go with their signs ag'in, but if I advise you to land, may they eat me as well as roast me. No—no—Deerslayer, do you keep off where you are, and after day-light, on no account, come within two hundred yards—"

This injunction of Hurry's was stopped by a hand's being rudely slapped against his mouth, the certain sign that some one in the party understood English sufficiently, to have at length detected the drift of his discourse. Immediately after the whole group entered the forest, Hutter and Hurry apparently making no resistance to the movement. Just as the sounds of the cracking bushes were ceasing, however, the voice of the father was again heard.

"As you're true to my children, God prosper you, young man!" were the words that reached Deerslayer's ears; after which he found himself left to follow the dictates of his own discretion.

Several minutes elapsed, in death-like stillness, after the party on the shore had disappeared in the woods. Owing to the distance, rather more than two hundred yards, and the obscurity, Deerslayer had been able barely to distinguish the group, and to see it retiring, but even this dim connection with human forms, gave an animation to the scene, that was strongly in contrast to the absolute solitude that remained. Although the young man leaned forward to listen, holding his breath and condensing every faculty in the single sense of hearing, not another sound reached his ears, to denote the vicinity of human beings. It seemed as if a silence that had never been broken, reigned on the spot again, and, for an instant, even that piercing shriek which had so lately broken the stillness of the forest, or the execrations of March, would have been a relief to the feeling of desertion, to which it gave rise.

This paralysis of mind and body, however, could not last long in one constituted mentally and physically, like Deerslayer. Dropping his paddle into the water, he turned the head of the canoe, and proceeded slowly, as one walks who thinks intently, towards the centre of the lake. When he believed himself to have reached a point in a line with that where he had set the last canoe adrift, he changed his direction northward, keeping the light air as nearly on his back as possible. After paddling a quarter of a mile in this direction, a dark object became visible on the lake, a little to the right, and turning on one side for the purpose, he had soon secured his last prize to his own boat. Deerslayer now examined the heavens, the course of the air, and the position of the two canoes. Finding nothing in either to induce a change of plan, he lay down and prepared to catch a few hours' sleep, that the morrow might find him equal to its exigencies.

Although the hardy and the tired sleep profoundly, even in scenes of danger, it was some time before Deerslayer lost his recollection. His mind dwelt on what had passed, and his half conscious faculties kept figuring the events of the night, in a sort of waking dream. Suddenly he was up and alert, for he fancied he heard the preconcerted signal of Hurry, summoning him to the shore. But all was still as the grave, again. The canoes were slowly drifting northward, the 'thoughtful stars' were glimmering in their mild glory, over his head, and the forest bound sheet of water, lay embedded between its mountains, as calm and melancholy, as if never troubled by the winds, or brightened by a noon-day sun. Once more the loon raised his tremulous cry, near the foot of the lake, and the mystery of the alarm was explained. Deerslayer adjusted his hard pillow, stretched his form in the bottom of the canoe, and slept.

Chapter VII.

"Clear, placid Leman! Thy contrasted lake
With the wild world I dwelt in, is a thing
Which warns me, with its stillness, to forsake
Earth's troubled waters for a purer spring.
This quiet sail is as a noiseless wing
To waft me from distraction: once I lov'd
Torn ocean's roar, but thy soft murmuring
Sounds sweet as if a sister's voice reproved,
That I with stern delights should ere have been so mov'd."
Byron, *Childe Harold's Pilgrimage,* III.LXXXV.

D A Y had fairly dawned, before the young man, whom we have left in the situation described in the last chapter, again opened his eyes. This was no sooner done, than he started up, and looked about him with the eagerness of one who suddenly felt the importance of accurately ascertaining his precise position. His rest had been deep and undisturbed, and when he awoke it was with a clearness of intellect, and a readiness of resources that were much needed at that particular moment. The sun had not risen, it is true, but the vault of heaven was rich with the winning softness that 'brings and shuts the day', while the whole air was filled with the carols of birds, the hymns of the feathered tribe. These sounds first told Deerslayer the risks he run. The air, for wind it could scarce be called, was still light it is true, but it had increased a little in the course of the night, and, as the canoes were mere feathers on the water, they had drifted twice the expected distance, and what was still more dangerous, had approached so near the base of the mountain that here rose precipitously from the eastern shore, as to render the carols of the birds plainly audible. This was not the worst. The third canoe had taken the same direction, and was slowly drifting towards a point where it must inevitably touch, unless turned aside by a shift of wind, or human hands. In other respects, nothing presented itself to attract attention, or to awaken alarm. The Castle stood on its shoal, nearly abreast of the canoes, for the drift had amounted to miles, in the course of the night, and the Ark lay fastened to its piles, as both had been left so many hours before.

As a matter of course, Deerslayer's attention was first given to the canoe ahead. It was already quite near the point, and a very few strokes of the paddle sufficed to tell him that it must touch before he could possibly overtake it. Just at this moment, too, the wind inopportunely freshened, rendering the drift of the light craft much more rapid and certain. Feeling the impossibility of preventing a contact with the land, the young man wisely determined not to heat himself with unnecessary exertions, but, first looking to the priming of his piece, he proceeded slowly and warily towards the point, taking care to make a little circuit, that he might be exposed on only one side, as he approached.

The canoe adrift, being directed by no such intelligence, pursued its proper way, and grounded on a small sunken rock, at the distance of three or four yards from the shore. Just at that moment, Deerslayer had got abreast of the point, and turned the bows of his own boat to the land; first casting loose his tow, that his movements might be unencumbered. The canoe hung an instant on the rock, then it rose a hair's breadth on an almost imperceptible swell of the water, swung round, floated clear, and reached the strand. All this the young man noted, but it neither quickened his pulses, nor hastened his hand. If any one had been lying in wait for the arrival of the waif, he must be seen, and the utmost caution in approaching the shore became indispensable. If no one was in ambush, hurry was unnecessary. The point being nearly diagonally opposite to the Indian encampment, he hoped the last, though the former was not only possible, but probable; for the savages were prompt in adopting all the expedients of their particular modes of warfare, and quite likely had many scouts searching the shores for craft to carry them off to the castle. As a glance at the lake from any height, or projection, would expose the smallest object on its surface, there was little hope that either of the canoes could pass unseen, and Indian sagacity needed no instruction to tell which way a boat, or a log, would drift, when the direction of the wind was known.

As Deerslayer drew nearer and nearer to the land, the stroke of his paddle grew slower, his eye became more watchful, and

his ears and nostrils almost dilated with the effort to detect any
lurking danger. 'Twas a trying moment for a novice, nor was
there the encouragement which even the timid sometimes feel,
when conscious of being observed and commended. He was
entirely alone, thrown on his own resources, and was cheered
by no friendly eye, emboldened by no encouraging voice. Notwithstanding all these circumstances, the most experienced
veteran in forest warfare could not have behaved better.
Equally free from recklessness and hesitation, his advance was
marked by a sort of philosophical prudence, that appeared to
render him superior to all motions but those which were best
calculated to effect his purpose. Such was the commencement
of a career in forest exploits, that afterwards rendered this
man, in his way, and under the limits of his habits and opportunities, as renowned as many a hero whose name has adorned
the pages of works more celebrated than legends simple as ours
can ever become.

When about a hundred yards from the shore, Deerslayer
rose in the canoe, gave three or four vigorous strokes with the
paddle, sufficient of themselves to impel the bark to land, and
then quickly laying aside the instrument of labor, he seized
that of war. He was in the very act of raising the rifle, when a
sharp report, was followed by the buzz of a bullet that passed
so near his body, as to cause him involuntarily to start. The
next instant Deerslayer staggered, and fell his whole length in
the bottom of the canoe. A yell—it came from a single
voice—followed, and an Indian leaped from the bushes, upon
the open area of the point, bounding towards the canoe. This
was the moment the young man desired. He rose on the instant, and levelled his own rifle, at his uncovered foe; but his
finger hesitated about pulling the trigger on one whom he held
at such a disadvantage. This little delay, probably saved the
life of the Indian, who bounded back into the cover, as swiftly
as he had broken out of it. In the mean time Deerslayer had
been swiftly approaching the land, and his own canoe reached
the point just as his enemy disappeared. As its movements had
not been directed, it touched the shore a few yards from the
other boat, and though the rifle of his foe had to be loaded,
there was not time to secure his prize, and to carry it beyond
danger, before he would be exposed to another shot. Under

the circumstances, therefore, he did not pause an instant, but dashed into the woods and sought a cover.

On the immediate point there was a small open area, partly in native grass, and partly beach, but a dense fringe of bushes lined its upper side. This narrow belt of dwarf vegetation passed, one issued immediately into the high, and gloomy vaults of the forest. The land was tolerably level for a few hundred feet, and then it rose precipitously in a mountain side. The trees were tall, large, and so free from underbrush, that they resembled vast columns, irregularly scattered, upholding a dome of leaves. Although they stood tolerably close together, for their ages and size, the eye could penetrate to considerable distances, and bodies of men, even, might have engaged beneath their cover, with concert and intelligence.

Deerslayer knew that his adversary must be employed in reloading, unless he had fled. The former proved to be the case, for the young man had no sooner placed himself behind a tree, than he caught a glimpse of the arm of the Indian, his body being concealed by an oak, in the very act of forcing the leathered bullet home. Nothing would have been easier than to spring forward and decide the affair by a close assault on his unprepared foe, but every feeling of Deerslayer revolted at such a step, although his own life had just been attempted from a cover. He was as yet unpractised in the ruthless expedients of savage warfare, of which he knew nothing except by tradition and theory, and it struck him as an unfair advantage to assail an unarmed foe. His colour had heightened, his eye frowned, his lips were compressed, and all his energies were collected and ready, but, instead of advancing to fire, he dropped his rifle to the usual position of a sportsman in readiness to catch his aim, and muttered to himself, unconscious that he was speaking—

"No—no—that may be red-skin warfare, but it's not a christian's gifts. Let the miscreant charge, and then we'll take it out like men; for the canoe he *must* not and *shall* not have. No—no; let him have time to load, and then God will take care of the right!"

All this time the Indian had been so intent on his own movements, that he was even ignorant that his enemy was in the wood. His only apprehension was that the canoe would be recovered and carried away, before he might be in readiness to prevent it. He had sought the cover from habit, but was within a few feet of the fringe of bushes, and could be at the margin of the forest, in readiness to fire in a moment. The distance between him and his enemy was about fifty yards, and the trees were so arranged by nature that the line of sight was not interrupted, except by the particular tree behind which each party stood.

His rifle was no sooner loaded, than the savage glanced around him, and advanced, incautiously as regarded the real, but stealthily as respected the fancied position of his enemy, until he was fairly exposed. Then Deerslayer stepped from behind his own cover, and hailed him.

"This-a-way, red-skin; this-a-way, if you're looking for me," he called out. "I'm young in war, but not so young as to stand on an open beach to be shot down like an owl by day-light. It rests on yourself whether it's peace, or war, atween us, for my gifts are white gifts, and I'm not one of them that thinks it valiant to slay human mortals singly, in the woods."

The savage was a good deal startled by this sudden discovery of the danger he run. He had a little knowledge of English, however, and caught the drift of the other's meaning. He was also too well schooled to betray alarm, but dropping the butt of his rifle to the earth, with an air of confidence, he made a gesture of lofty courtesy. All this was done with the ease and self possession of one accustomed to consider no man his superior. In the midst of this consummate acting, however, the volcano that raged within, caused his eyes to glare, and his nostrils to dilate, like those of some wild beast, that is suddenly prevented from taking the fatal leap.

"Two canoe," he said, in the deep guttural tones of his race, holding up the number of fingers he mentioned, by way of preventing mistakes—"one for you—one for me."

"No—no—Mingo, that will never do. You own neither; and neither shall you have, as long as I can prevent it. I know it's war atween your people and mine, but that's no reason why human mortals should slay each other, like savage creatur's, that meet in the woods; go your way then, and leave me to go mine. The world is large enough for us both, and when we meet fairly in battle, why the Lord will order the fate of each of us."

"Good!" exclaimed the Indian—"My brother, missionary—great talk; all about Manitou."

"Not so—not so, warrior. I'm not good enough for the Moravians, and am too good for most of the other vagabonds that preach about in the woods. No—no—I'm only a hunter as yet, though afore the peace is made, 'tis like enough there'll be occasion to strike a blow at some of your people. Still I wish it to be done in fair fight, and not in a quarrel about the ownership of a miserable canoe."

"Good! My brother very young—but, he very wise. Little warrior, great talker. Chief, sometime, in council."

"I do'n't know this, nor do I say it, Injin," returned Deerslayer, colouring a little at the ill concealed sarcasm of the other's manner. "I look forward to a life in the woods, and I only hope it may be a peaceable one. All young men must go on the war path when there's occasion, but war is'n't needfully massacre. I've seen enough of the last, this very night, to know that providence frowns on it, and I now invite you to go your own way, while I go mine; and hope that we may part fri'nds."

"Good! My brother has two scalp—gray hair under t' other. Old wisdom, young tongue."

Here the savage advanced with confidence, his hand extended, his face smiling, and his whole bearing denoting amity and respect. Deerslayer met his offered friendship in a proper spirit, and they shook hands cordially, each endeavoring to assure the other of his sincerity and desire to be at peace.

"All have his own," said the Indian—"my canoe, mine; your canoe, your'n. Go look; if your'n, you keep; if mine, my keep."

"That's just, red-skin, though you must be wrong in thinking the canoe your property. Howsever, seein' is believin', and we'll go down to the shore, where you may look with your own eyes, for it's likely you'll object to trustin' altogether to mine."

The Indian uttered his favorite exclamation of "good!" and then they walked, side by side, towards the shore. There was no apparent distrust in the manner of either, the Indian moving in advance, as if he wished to show his companion that he did not fear turning his back to him. As they reached the open ground, the former pointed towards Deerslayer's boat, and said emphatically —

"No mine — Pale face canoe — *this* red man's. No want other man's canoe — want his own."

"You're wrong, red-skin, you're altogether wrong. This canoe was left in old Hutter's keeping, and is his'n according to all law, red or white, 'till its owner comes to claim it. Here's the seats and the stitching of the bark to speak for themselves — no man ever know'd an Injin to turn off such work."

"Good — my brother little ole, big wisdom. Injin no make him. White man's work."

"I'm glad you think so, for holding out to the contrary might have made ill blood atween us. Every one having a right to take possession of his own, I'll just shove the canoe out of reach of dispute, at once, as the quickest way of settling difficulties."

While Deerslayer was speaking he put a foot against the end of the light boat, and giving a vigorous shove, he sent it out into the lake, a hundred feet or more, where, taking the true current, it would necessarily float past the point, and be in no further danger of coming ashore. The savage started at this ready and decided expedient, and his companion saw that he cast a hurried and fierce glance at his own canoe, or that which contained the paddles. The change of manner, however, was but momentary, and then the Iroquois resumed his air of friendliness, and a smile of satisfaction.

"Good," he repeated with stronger emphasis than ever. "Young head, old mind. Know how to settle quarrel. Farewell, brother. He go to house in water — muskrat house — Injin go to camp; tell chief no find canoe."

Deerslayer was not sorry to hear this proposal, for he felt anxious to join the females, and he took the offered hand of the Indian very willingly. The parting words were friendly, and while the red man walked calmly towards the wood, with his rifle in the hollow of his arm, without once looking back in uneasiness or distrust, the white man moved towards the remaining canoe, carrying his piece in the same pacific manner it is true, but keeping his eyes fastened on the movements of the other. This distrust, however, seemed to be altogether uncalled for, and, as if ashamed to have entertained it, the young man averted his look, and stepped carelessly up to his boat.

Here he began to push the canoe from the shore, and to make his other preparations for departing. He might have been thus employed a minute, when happening to turn his face towards the land, his quick and certain eye told him at a glance, the imminent jeopardy in which his life was placed. The black, ferocious eyes of the savage were glaring on him, like those of the crouching tiger, through a small opening in the bushes, and the muzzle of his rifle seemed already to be opening in a line with his own body.

Then, indeed, the long practice of Deerslayer as a hunter, did him good service. Accustomed to fire with the deer on the bound, and often when the precise position of the animal's body, had in a manner to be guessed at, he used the same expedients here. To cock and poise his rifle were the acts of a single moment, and a single motion; then, aiming almost without sighting, he fired into the bushes where he knew a body ought to be, in order to sustain the appalling countenance which alone was visible. There was not time to raise the piece any higher, or to take a more deliberate aim. So rapid were his movements that both parties discharged their pieces at the same instant, the concussions mingling in one report. The mountains, indeed, gave back but a single echo. Deerslayer dropped his piece, and stood, with head erect, steady as one of the pines in the calm of a June morning, watching the result; while the savage gave the yell that has become historical for its appalling influence, leaped through the bushes, and came bounding across the open ground, flourishing a tomahawk. Still, Deerslayer moved not, but stood with his unloaded rifle fallen against his shoulder, while with a hunter's habits, his hands were mechanically feeling for the powder horn and charger. When about forty feet from his enemy, the savage hurled his keen weapon, but it was with an eye so vacant, and a hand so unsteady and feeble, that the young man caught it by the handle, as it was flying past him. At that instant, the Indian staggered and fell, his whole length on the ground.

"I know'd it — I knowed it!" exclaimed Deerslayer, who was already preparing to force a fresh bullet into his rifle — "I know'd it must come to this, as soon as I had got the range from the creatur's eyes. A man sights suddenly, and fires quick, when his own life's in danger; yes, I know'd it would come to this. I was about the hundredth part of a second too quick for him, or it might have been bad for me! The riptyle's bullet has just grazed my side, but say what you will, for or ag'in 'em, a red-skin is by no means as sartain with powder and ball, as a white man. Their gifts do'n't seem to lie that-a-way. Even Chingach-gook, great as he is in other matters, is not downright deadly with the rifle."

By this time the piece was reloaded, and Deerslayer, after tossing the tomahawk into the canoe, advanced to his victim, and stood over him, leaning on his rifle, in melancholy atten-tion. It was the first instance in which he had seen a man fall in battle, it was the first fellow creature against whom he had ever seriously raised his own hand. The sensations were novel; and regret, with the freshness of our better feelings, mingled with his triumph. The Indian was not dead, though shot directly through the body. He lay on his back motionless, but his eyes, now full of consciousness, watched each action of his victor, as the fallen bird regards the fowler, jealous of every movement. The man probably expected the fatal blow, which was to precede the loss of his scalp; or, perhaps he anticipated that this latter act of cruelty would precede his death. Deerslayer read his thoughts, and he found a melancholy satisfaction in relieving the apprehensions of the helpless savage.

"No—no—red-skin," he said. "You've nothing more to fear from me. I am of a christian stock, and scalping is not of my gifts—I'll just make sartain of your rifle, and then come back and do you what sarvice I can. Though here I can't stay much longer, as the crack of three rifles will be apt to bring more of your devils upon me."

The close of this was said in a sort of a soliloquy, as the young man went in quest of the fallen rifle. The piece was found where its owner had dropped it, and was immediately put into the canoe. Laying his own rifle at its side, Deerslayer then returned and stood over the Indian, again.

"All inmity atween you and me's at an ind, red-skin," he said, "and you may set your heart at rest, on the score of the scalp, or any further injury. My gifts are white, as I've told you, and I hope my conduct will be white also."

Could looks have conveyed all they meant, it is probable Deerslayer's innocent vanity on the subject of colour, would have been rebuked a little, but he comprehended the gratitude that was expressed in the eyes of the dying savage, without, in the least, detecting the bitter sarcasm that struggled with the better feeling.

"Water—" ejaculated the thirsty and unfortunate creature— "give poor Injin water—"

"Ay, water you shall have, if you drink the lake dry. I'll just carry you down to it, that you may take your fill. This is the way, they tell me, with all wounded people—water is their greatest comfort and delight."

So saying, Deerslayer raised the Indian in his arms and carried him to the lake. Here he first helped him to take an attitude in which he could appease his burning thirst; after which he seated himself on a stone, and took the head of his wounded adversary in his own lap, and endeavored to soothe his anguish, in the best manner he could.

"It would be sinful in me to tell you your time had'n't come, warrior," he commenced, "and, therefore, I'll not say it. You're passed the middle age, already, and considerin' the sort of lives ye lead, your days have been pretty well filled. The principal thing now, is to look forward to what comes next. Neither red skin nor pale face, on the whole, calculates much on sleepin' forever, but both expect to live in another world. Each has his gifts, and will be judged by 'em, and I suppose you've thought these matters over enough, not to stand in need of sarmons when the trial comes. You'll find your happy hunting grounds, if you've been a just Injin, and if an onjust, you'll meet your desarts in another way. I've my own idees about these things, but you're too old and exper'enced to need any explanations from one as young as I."

"Good!" ejaculated the Indian, whose voice retained its depth, even as life ebbed away. "Young head—ole wisdom."

"It's sometimes a consolation when the ind comes to know that them we've harmed, or *tried* to harm, forgive us. I suppose natur' seeks this relief, by way of getting a pardon on 'arth, as we never can know whether *He* pardons, who is all in all, 'till judgment itself comes. It's soothing to know that *any* pardon, at such times, and that I conclude is the secret. Now, as for myself, I overlook altogether your designs ag'in my life; first, because no harm came of 'em; next, because it's your gifts, and natur' and trainin', and I ought not to have trusted you, at all; and, finally and chiefly, because I can bear no ill will to a dying man, whether heathen or christian. So put your heart at ease, so far as I'm consarned; you know best what other matters ought to trouble you, or what ought to give you satisfaction in so trying a moment."

It is probable that the Indian had some of the fearful glimpses of the unknown state of being, which God, in mercy, seems, at times, to afford to all the human race, but they were necessarily in conformity with his habits and prejudices. Like most of his people, and like too many of our own, he thought more of dying in a way to gain applause among those he left, than to secure a better state of existence, hereafter. While Deerslayer was speaking, his mind was a little bewildered, though he felt that the intention was good; and when he had done, a regret passed over his spirit that none of his own tribe were present to witness his stoicism, under extreme bodily suffering, and the firmness with which he met his end. With the high, innate courtesy that so often distinguishes the Indian warrior, before he becomes corrupted by too much intercourse with the worst class of the white men, he endeavored to express his thankfulness for the other's good intentions, and to let him understand that they were appreciated.

"Good!" he repeated, for this was an English word much used by savages — "good — young head; young *heart*, too. *Old* heart tough; no shed tear. Hear Indian when he die, and no want to lie — what he call him?"

"Deerslayer is the name I bear now, though the Delawares have said that when I get back from this war-path, I shall bear a more manly title, provided I can 'arn one."

"That good name for boy — poor name for warrior. Get better quick. No fear *there* —" the savage had strength sufficient, under the strong excitement he felt, to raise a hand and tap the young man on his breast — "eye, sartain — finger, lightening — aim, death. Great warrior, soon — No Deerslayer — Hawkeye — Hawkeye — Hawkeye — Shake hand."

Deerslayer — or Hawkeye as the youth was then first named, for in after years he bore the appellation throughout all that region — Deerslayer took the hand of the savage, whose last breath was drawn in that attitude, gazing in admiration at the countenance of a stranger, who had shewn so much readiness, skill and firmness, in a scene that was equally trying and novel. When the reader remembers it is the highest gratification an Indian can receive to see his enemy betray weakness, he will be better able to appreciate the conduct which had extorted so great a concession, at such a moment.

"His spirit has fled!" said Deerslayer, in a suppressed, melancholy, voice. "Ah's, me! — Well, to this we must all come, sooner or later; and he is happiest, let his skin be of what colour it may, who is best fitted to meet it. Here lies the body of, no doubt, a brave warrior, and the soul is already flying towards its heaven, or hell, whether that be a happy hunting ground, or a place scant of game, regions of glory according to Moravian doctrine, or flames of fire! So it happens, too, as regards other matters! Here have old Hutter and Hurry Harry got themselves into difficulty, if they have'n't got themselves into torment and death, and all for a bounty that luck offers to me in what many would think a lawful and suitable manner. But not a farthing of such money shall cross my hand. White I was born, and white will I die; clinging to colour to the last, even though the King's Majesty, his governors, and all his councils, both at home and in the colonies, forget from what they come, and where they hope to go, and all for a little advantage in warfare. No — no — warrior; hand of mine shall never molest your scalp, and so your soul may rest in peace on the p'int of making a decent appearance, when the body comes to join it, in your own land of spirits."

Deerslayer arose as soon as he had spoken. Then he placed the body of the dead man, in a sitting posture, with its back against the little rock, taking the necessary care to prevent it from falling, or in any way settling into an attitude that might be thought unseemly by the sensitive, though wild, notions of a savage. When this duty was performed, the young man stood gazing at the grim countenance of his fallen foe, in a sort of melancholy abstraction. As was his practice, however, a

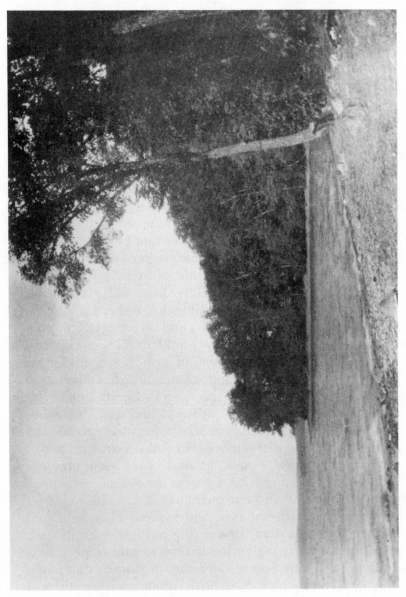

v.   Gravelly Point, the presumed site of Deerslayer's first mortal combat in Chapter VII

VI. "Death of the Indian," engraving by B.J. Newman of a drawing by James Hamilton

VII. "Death of the Red Man," Frontispiece, engraving by James Smillie of a drawing by F.O.C. Darley

VIII.   Untitled watercolor adaptation of the preceding Darley illustration by R.W. Van Boskieck, employed as background for the mounting of a Cooper letter to Ned Myers.

habit gained by living so much alone in the forest, he then began, to give utterance to his thoughts, and feelings aloud.

"I did'n't wish your life, red-skin," he said, "but you left me no choice atween killing, or being killed. Each party acted according to his gifts, I suppose, and blame can light on neither. You were treacherous, according to your natur' in war, and I was a little oversightful, as I'm apt to be in trusting others. Well, this is my first battle with a human mortal, though it's not likely to be the last. I have fou't most of the creatur's of the forest, such as bears, wolves, painters and catamounts, but this is the beginning with red-skins. If I was Injin born, now, I might tell of this, or carry in the scalp, and boast of the expl'ite afore the whole tribe; or, if my inimy had only been even a bear, 'twould have been nat'ral and proper to let every body know what had happened; but I do'n't well see how I'm to let even Chingachgook into this secret, so long as it can be done only by boasting with a white tongue. And why should I wish to boast of it, a'ter all? It's slaying a human, although he was a savage; and how do I know that he was a just Injin; and that he has not been taken away suddenly, to any thing but happy hunting grounds. When it's onsartain whether good, or evil, has been done, the wisest way is not to be boastful — still, I *should* like Chingachgook to know that I have'n't discredited the Delawares, or my training!"

Part of this was uttered aloud, while part was merely muttered between the speaker's teeth; his more confident opinions enjoying the first advantage, while his doubts were expressed in the latter mode. Soliloquy and reflections received a startling interruption, however, by the sudden appearance of a second Indian on the lake shore, a few hundred yards from the point. This man, evidently another scout, who had probably been drawn to the place by the reports of the rifles, broke out of the forest with so little caution that Deerslayer caught a view of his person, before he was himself discovered. When the latter event did occur, as was the case a moment later, the savage gave a loud yell, which was answered by a dozen voices from different parts of the mountain-side. There was no longer any time for delay, and, in another minute the boat was quitting the shore under long and steady sweeps of the paddle.

As soon as Deerslayer believed himself to be at a safe distance, he ceased his efforts, permitting the little bark to drift, while he leisurely took a survey of the state of things. The canoe first sent adrift was floating before the air, quite a quarter of a mile above him, and a little nearer to the shore than he wished, now that he knew more of the savages were so near at hand. The canoe shoved from the point was within a few yards of him, he having directed his own course towards it, on quitting the land. The dead Indian lay in grim quiet, where he had left him, the warrior who had shown himself from the forest had already vanished, and the woods themselves were as silent, and seemingly as deserted, as the day they came fresh from the hands of their great creator. This profound stillness, however, lasted but a moment. When time had been given to the scouts of the enemy to reconnoitre, they burst out of the thicket, upon the naked point, filling the air with yells of fury, at discovering the death of their companion. These cries were immediately succeeded by shouts of delight, when they reached the body, and clustered eagerly around it. Deerslayer was a sufficient adept in the usages of the natives, to understand the reason of the change. The yell was the customary lamentation at the loss of a warrior, the shout a sign of rejoicing that the conqueror had not been able to secure the scalp; the trophy, without which a victory was never considered complete. The distance at which the canoes lay, probably prevented any attempts to injure the conqueror, the American Indian, like the panther of his own woods, seldom making any effort against his foe, unless tolerably certain it is under circumstances that may be expected to prove effective.

As the young man had no longer any motive to remain near the point, he prepared to collect his canoes, in order to tow them off to the castle. That nearest was soon in tow, when he proceeded in quest of the other, which was, all this time, floating up the lake. The eye of Deerslayer was no sooner fastened on this last boat, than it struck him that it was nearer to the shore than it would have been, had it merely followed the course of the gentle current of air. He began to suspect the influence of some unseen current in the water, and he quickened his exertions, in order to regain possession of it, before it could drift in to a dangerous proximity to the woods. On getting nearer, he thought that the canoe had a perceptible motion through the water, and, as it lay broadside to the air, that this motion was taking it towards the land. A few vigorous strokes of the paddle carried him still nearer, when the mystery was explained. Something was evidently in motion on the off side of the canoe, or that which was furthest from himself, and closer scrutiny, showed that it was a naked human arm. An Indian was lying in the bottom of the canoe, and was propelling it slowly, but certainly, to the shore, using his hand as a paddle. Deerslayer understood the whole artifice at a glance. A savage had swam off to the boat, while he was occupied with his enemy on the point, got possession, and was using these means to urge it to the shore.

Satisfied that the man in the canoe could have no arms, Deerslayer did not hesitate to dash close along side of the retiring boat, without deeming it necessary to raise his own rifle. As soon as the wash of the water, which he made in approaching, became audible to the prostrate savage, the latter sprang to his feet, and uttered an exclamation that proved how completely he was taken by surprise.

"If you've enj'yed yourself enough in that canoe, red-skin," Deerslayer coolly observed, stopping his own career in sufficient time to prevent an absolute collision between the two boats — "if you've enj'yed yourself enough in that canoe, you'll do a prudent act by taking to the lake ag'in. I'm reasonable in these matters, and do'n't crave your blood, though there's them about, that would look upon you more as a due-bill for the bounty, than a human mortal. Take to the lake, this minute, afore we get to hot words."

The savage was one of those who did not understand a word of English, and he was indebted to the gestures of Deerslayer, and to the expression of an eye that did not often deceive, for an imperfect comprehension of his meaning. Perhaps, too, the sight of the rifle that lay so near the hand of the white man quickened his decision. At all events, he crouched like a tiger about to take his leap, uttered a yell, and the next instant his naked body disappeared in the water. When he rose to take breath, it was at a distance of several yards from the canoe, and the hasty glance he threw behind him, denoted how much he feared the arrival of a fatal messenger from the rifle of his foe. But the young man made no indication of any hostile intention. Deliberately securing the canoe to the others, he began to paddle from the shore, and by the time the Indian reached the land, and had shaken himself, like a spaniel on quitting the water, his dreaded enemy was already beyond rifle shot, on his way to the castle. As was so much his practice, Deerslayer did not fail to soliloquize on what had just occurred while steadily pursuing his course, towards the point of destination.

"Well — well — " he commenced, "'twould have been wrong to kill a human mortal without an object. Scalps are of no account with me, and life is sweet, and ought not to be taken marcilessly, by them that have white gifts. The savage was a Mingo, it's true, and I make no doubt he is, and will be, as long as he lives, a ra'al riptyle and vagabond, but that's no reason I should forget my gifts and colour. No — no — let him go; if ever we meet ag'in, rifle in hand, why then t'will be seen which has the stoutest heart and the quickest eye. — Hawkeye! That's not a bad name for a warrior, sounding much more manful and valiant than Deerslayer! 'Twould'n't be a bad title to begin with, and it has been fairly 'arned. If 'twas Chingachgook, now, he might go home and boast of his deeds, and the chiefs would name him Hawkeye, in a minute, but it do'n't become white blood to brag and 'tis'n't easy to see how the matter can be known, unless I do. Well — well — every thing is in the hands of Providence; this affair as well as another; and I'll trust to that for getting my desarts in all things."

Having thus betrayed what might be termed his weak spot, the young man continued to paddle in silence, making his way diligently, and as fast as his tows would allow him, towards the castle. By this time the sun had not only risen, but it had appeared over the eastern mountains, and was shedding a flood of glorious light on this, as yet, unchristened sheet of water. The whole scene was radiant with beauty, and no one unaccustomed to the ordinary history of the woods, would fancy it had so lately witnessed incidents so ruthless and barbarous. As he approached the building of old Hutter, Deerslayer thought, or rather *felt*, that its appearance was in singular harmony with all the rest of the scene. Although nothing had been consulted but strength and security, the rude massive logs, covered with their rough bark, the projecting roof, and the form would contribute to render the building picturesque in almost any situation, while its actual position added novelty and piquancy to its other points of interest.

When Deerslayer drew nearer to the castle, however, objects of interest presented themselves, that at once eclipsed any beauties that might have distinguished the scenery of the lake, and the site of the singular edifice. Judith and Hetty stood on the platform, awaiting his approach with manifest anxiety, the former, from time to time, taking a survey of his person and of the canoes, through the old ship's spy glass that has been already mentioned. Never probably did this girl seem more brilliantly beautiful than at that moment; the flush of anxiety and alarm increasing her colour to its richest tints, while the softness of her eyes, a charm that even poor Hetty shared with her, was deepened by intense concern. Such at least, without pausing, or pretending, to analyze motives, or to draw any other very nice distinctions between cause and effect, were the opinions of the young man as his canoes reached the side of the Ark, where he carefully fastened all three, before he put his foot on the platform.

Chapter VIII.

"His words are bonds, his oaths are oracles;
His love sincere, his thoughts immaculate;
His tears pure messengers sent from his heart;
His heart as far from fraud, as heaven from earth."
Two Gentlemen of Verona, II.vii.75–78.

NEITHER of the girls spoke, as Deerslayer stood before them alone, his countenance betraying all the apprehension he felt on account of the two absent members of their party.

"Father!" Judith at length exclaimed, succeeding in uttering the word, as it might be, by a desperate effort.

"He's met with misfortune, and there's no use in concealing it," answered Deerslayer, in his direct and simple-minded manner. "He and Hurry are in Mingo hands, and Heaven only knows what's to be the tarmination. I've got all the canoes safe, and that's a consolation, since the vagabonds will have to swim for it, or raft off, to come near this place. At sunset we'll be reinforced by Chingachgook, if I can manage to get him into a canoe, and then, I think, we two can answer for the ark and the castle, 'till some of the officers in the garrisons, hear of this war-path, which sooner or later must be the case, when we may look for succour, from that quarter, if from no other."

"The officers!" exclaimed Judith, impatiently, her colour deepening, and her eye expressing a lively but passing emotion. "Who thinks, or speaks of the heartless gallants, now? — We are sufficient of ourselves, to defend the castle; — but what of my father — and of poor Hurry Harry?"

" 'Tis natural you should feel this consarn for your own parent, Judith, and I suppose it's equally so that you should feel it for Hurry Harry too."

Deerslayer, then, commenced a succinct but clear narrative of all that occurred during the night, in no manner concealing what had befallen his two companions, or his own opinion of what might prove to be the consequences. The girls listened with profound attention, but neither betrayed that feminine apprehension and concern, which would have followed such a communication, when made to those who were less accustomed to the hazards and incidents of a frontier life. To the surprise of Deerslayer, Judith seemed the most distressed, Hetty listening eagerly, but appearing to brood over the facts in melancholy silence, rather than betraying any outward signs of feeling. The former's agitation, the young man did not fail to attribute to the interest she felt in Hurry, quite as much as to her filial love, while Hetty's apparent indifference was ascribed to that mental darkness which, in a measure, obscured her intellect, and which possibly prevented her from foreseeing all the consequences. Little was said, however, by either, Judith and her sister busying themselves in making their preparations for the morning meal, as they who habitually attend to such matters, toil on mechanically even in the midst of suffering and sorrow. The plain but nutritious breakfast was taken by all three, in sombre silence. The girls ate little, but Deerslayer gave proof of possessing one material requisite of a good soldier, that of preserving his appetite in the midst of the most alarming and embarrassing circumstances. The meal was nearly ended before a syllable was uttered; then, however, Judith spoke in the convulsive and hurried manner in which feeling breaks through restraint, after the latter has become more painful than even the betrayal of emotions.

"Father would have relished this fish!" she exclaimed; "he says the salmon of the lakes is almost as good as the salmon of the sea."

"Your father has been acquainted with the sea, they tell me, Judith," returned the young man, who could not forbear throwing a glance of inquiry at the girl, for, in common with all who knew Hutter he had some curiosity on the subject of his early history. "Hurry Harry tells he was once a sailor."

Judith first looked perplexed; then influenced by feelings that were novel to her, in more ways than one, she became suddenly communicative, and seemingly much interested in the discourse.

"If Hurry knows any thing of father's history, I would he had told it to me!" she cried. "Sometimes I think too, he was once a sailor, and then again I think he was not. If that chest were open, or if it could speak, it might let us into his whole history. But its fastenings are too strong to be broken like pack-thread."

Deerslayer turned to the chest in question, and for the first time examined it closely. Although discolored, and bearing proofs of having received much ill treatment, he saw that it was of materials and workmanship altogether superior to any thing of the same sort he had ever before beheld. The wood was dark, rich, and had once been highly polished, though the treatment it had received left little gloss on its surface, and various scratches and indentations proved the rough collisions that it had encountered with substances still harder than itself. The corners were firmly bound with steel, elaborately and richly wrought, while the locks, of which it had no less than three, and the hinges were of a fashion and workmanship that would have attracted attention even in a warehouse of curious furniture. This chest was quite large, and when Deerslayer arose, and endeavored to raise an end by its massive handle, he found that the weight fully corresponded with the external appearance.

"Did you never see that chest opened, Judith," the young man demanded with frontier freedom, for delicacy on such subjects was little felt among the people on the verge of civilization, in that age, even if it be to-day.

"Never. Father has never opened it in my presence, if he ever opens it at all. No one here, has ever seen its lid raised, unless it be father; nor do I even know that he has ever seen it."

"Now, you're wrong, Judith," Hetty quietly answered. "Father *has* raised the lid, and *I've* seen him do it."

A feeling of manliness kept the mouth of Deerslayer shut, for, while he would not have hesitated about going far beyond what would be thought the bounds of propriety, in questioning the elder sister, he had just scruples about taking what might be thought, an advantage of the feeble intellect of the younger. Judith, being under no such restraint, however turned quickly to the last speaker, and continued the discourse.

"When and where did you ever see that chest opened, Hetty?"

"Here, and, again and again. Father often opens it, when *you* are away, though he do'n't in the least mind my being by, and seeing all he does, as well as hearing all he says."

"And what is it that he does, and what does he say?"

"That I cannot tell *you*, Judith—" returned the other in a low, but resolute voice—"*Father's* secrets, are not *my* secrets."

"Secrets! — This is stranger still, Deerslayer; that father should tell them to Hetty, and not tell them to me!"

"There's good reason for that, Judith, though you're not to know it. Father's not here to answer for himself, and I'll say no more about it."

Judith and Deerslayer looked surprised, and, for a minute, the first seemed pained. But, suddenly recollecting herself, she turned away from her sister, as if in pity for her weakness, and addressed the young man.

"You've told but half your story," she said, "breaking off at the place where you went to sleep in the canoe — or, rather, where you rose to listen to the cry of the loon. We heard the call of the loons too, and thought their cries might bring a storm, though we are little used to tempests on this lake, at this season of the year."

"The winds blow, and the tempests howl as God pleases; sometimes at one season, and sometimes at another," answered Deerslayer; "and the loons speak accordin' to their natur'. Better would it be, if men were as honest and frank. After I rose to listen to the birds, finding it could not be Hurry's signal, I lay down and slept. When the day dawned, I was up and stirring as usual, and then I went in chase of the two canoes, lest the Mingos should lay hands on 'em."

"You have not told us all, Deerslayer," said Judith, earnestly — "We heard rifles, under the eastern mountain; the echoes were full and long, and came so soon after the reports that the pieces must have been fired on, or quite near to the shore. Our ears are used to these signs, and are not to be deceived."

"They've done their duty, gal, this time; yes, they've done their duty. Rifles have been sighted, this morning, ay, and triggers pulled too, though not as often as they might have been. One warrior has gone to his happy hunting grounds, and that's the whole of it. A man of white blood, and white gifts, is not to be expected to boast of his expl'ites, and to flourish scalps."

Judith listened almost breathlessly, and, when Deerslayer, in his quiet, modest, manner, seemed disposed to quit the subject, she rose, and, crossing the room, took a seat by his side.

The manner of the girl had nothing forward about it, though it betrayed the quick instinct of a female's affection, and the sympathizing kindness of a woman's heart. She even took the hard hand of the hunter, and pressed it in both her own, unconsciously to herself perhaps, while she looked earnestly and even reproachfully into his sun burned face.

"You have been fighting the savages, Deerslayer, singly and by yourself!" she said. "In your wish to take care of us — of Hetty — of me, perhaps — you've fought the enemy bravely, with no eye to encourage your deeds, or to witness your fall, had it pleased Providence to suffer so great a calamity!"

"I've fou't, Judith; yes I *have* fou't the inimy, and that, too, for the first time in my life. These things must be, and they bring with 'em a mix'd feelin' of sorrow and triumph. Human natur' is a fightin' natur', I suppose, as all nations and colours kill in battle, and we must be true to our rights and gifts. What has yet been done is no great matter, but, should Chingachgook come to the rock this evening, as is agreed atween us, and I get him off it, onbeknown to the savages, or if known to them, ag'in their wishes and designs, then may we all look to something like warfare, afore the Mingos shall get possession of either the castle, or the Ark, or yourselves."

"Who is this Chingachgook; from what place does he come, and *why* does he come *here*?"

"The questions are nat'ral, and right, I suppose, though the youth has a great name, already, in his own part of the country. Chingachgook is a Mohican by blood, consorting with the Delawares by usage, as is the case with most of his tribe; which has long been broken up by the increase of our colour. He is of the family of the great chiefs; Uncas, his father, having been the considerablest warrior and counsellor of his people. Even old Tamenund honors Chingachgook, though he is thought to be yet too young to lead in war; and then the nation is so disparsed and diminished, that chieftainship among 'em has got to be little more than a name. Well, this war having commenced in 'arnest, the Delaware and I rendezvous'd an app'intment to meet this evening, at sunset, on the rendezvous-rock, at the foot of this very lake, intending to come out on our first hostile expedition ag'in the Mingos. *Why* we come exactly this-a-way, is our own secret, but thoughtful young men, on a war-path, as you may suppose, do nothing without a calculation, and a design."

"A Delaware can have no unfriendly intentions towards us," said Judith, after a moment's hesitation, "and we know you to be friendly."

"Treachery is the last crime I hope to be accused of," returned Deerslayer, hurt at the gleam of distrust that had shot through Judith's mind; "and, least of all, treachery to my own colour."

"No one suspects *you*, Deerslayer," the girl impetuously cried — "No — no — your honest countenance would be a sufficient surety, for the truth of a thousand hearts! If all men had as honest tongues, and no more promised what they did not mean to perform, there would be less wrong done in the world, and fine feathers and scarlet cloaks would not be thought excuses for baseness and deception!"

The girl spoke with strong, nay even with convulsed feeling, and her fine eyes, usually so soft and alluring, flashed fire as she concluded. Deerslayer could not but observe this extraordinary emotion, but, with the tact of a courtier, he avoided not only any allusion to the circumstance, but succeeded in concealing the effect of his discovery on himself. Judith gradually grew calm, again, and, as she was obviously anxious to appear to advantage in the eyes of the young man, she was soon able to renew the conversation as composedly as if nothing had occurred to disturb her.

"I have no right to look into your secrets, or the secrets of your friends, Deerslayer," she continued, "and am ready to take all you say on trust. If we can really get another male ally to join us, at this trying moment, it will aid us much, and I am not without hopes that when the savages find we are able to keep the lake, they will offer to give up their prisoners in exchange for skins, or at least for the keg of powder that we have in the house."

The young man had the words "scalps" and "bounty" on his lips, but a reluctance to alarm the feelings of the daughters, prevented him from making the allusion he had intended to the probable fate of their father. Still, so little was he practised in the arts of deception, that his expressive countenance was, of itself, understood by the quick witted Judith, whose intelligence had been sharpened by the risks and habits of her forest life.

"I understand what you mean," she continued, hurriedly, "and what you would say, but for the fear of hurting me — *us* — I mean; for Hetty loves her father quite as well as I do. But this is not as we think of Indians. They never scalp an unhurt prisoner, but would rather take him away alive; unless, indeed, the fierce wish for torturing should get the mastery of them. I fear nothing for my father's scalp, and little for his life. Could they steal on us, in the night, we should all probably suffer in this way, but men taken in open strife are seldom injured; not, at least, until the time of torture comes."

"That's tradition I'll allow, and it's accordin' to practise — but, Judith, do you know the ar'n'd on which your father and Hurry went ag'in the savages?"

"I do; and a cruel errand it was! But, what will you have? Men will be men, and some even that flaunt in their gold and silver, and carry the king's commission in their pockets, are not guiltless of equal cruelty — " Judith's eye again flashed, but, by a desperate struggle, she resumed her composure. "I get warm, when I think of all the wrong that men do," she added, affecting to smile, an effort in which she only succeeded indifferently well — "All this is silly. What is done, is done, and it cannot be mended by complaints. But the Indians think so little of the shedding of blood, and value men so much for the boldness of their undertakings, that did they know the business on which their prisoners came, they would be more likely to honor, than to injure them for it."

"For a time, Judith; yes, I allow *that* for a time. But, when that feelin' dies away, then will come the love of revenge. We must indivour, Chingachgook and I, we must indivour to see what we can do to get Hurry and your father, free; for the Mingos will no doubt, hover about this lake some days, in order to make the most of their success."

"You think this Delaware can be depended on, Deerslayer?" demanded the girl, thoughtfully.

"As much as I can myself. You say you do not suspect *me*, Judith?"

"*You!*" taking his hand again, and pressing it between her own with a warmth that might have awakened the vanity of one less simple-minded, and more disposed to dwell on his own good qualities, "I would as soon suspect a brother! I have known you but a day, Deerslayer, but it has awakened the confidence of a year. Your name, however, is not unknown to me, for the gallants of the garrisons frequently speak of the lessons you have given them in hunting, and all proclaim your honesty."

"Do they ever talk of the shooting, gal? — " inquired the other eagerly, after, however, laughing, in a silent but heart-felt manner — "Do they ever talk of the shooting? I want to hear nothing about my own, for, if that is'n't sartified to, by this time, in all these parts, there's little use in being skilful and sure; but what do the officers say of their own — yes, what do they say of their own! Arms, as they call it, is their trade, and yet there's some among 'em that know very little how to use 'em!"

"Such, I hope, will not be the case with your friend Chingachgook, as you call him — what is the English of his Indian name?"

"Big Sarpent. — So called for his wisdom and cunning. Uncas is his ra'al name — all his family being called Uncas; until they get a title that has been 'arned by deeds."

"If he has all this wisdom, we may expect a useful friend in him, unless his own business, in this part of the country, should prevent him from serving us?"

"I see no great harm in telling you his ar'n'd, a'ter all, and, as you may find means to help us, I will let you and Hetty into the whole matter, trusting that you'll keep the secret as if it was your own. You must know that Chingachgook is a comely Injin, and is much look'd upon and admired by the young women of his tribe, both on account of his family, and on account of himself. Now, there is a chief that has a darter called Wah-ta!-Wah, which is intarpreted into Hist-oh!-Hist, in the English tongue; the rarest gal among the Delawares, and the one most sought a'ter and craved for a wife, by all the young warriors of the nation. Well, Chingachgook, among others took a fancy to Wah-ta!-Wah, and Wah-ta!-Wah took a fancy to him." Here Deerslayer paused an instant, for, as he got thus far in his tale, Hetty Hutter arose, approached, and stood attentive, at his knee, as a child draws near to listen to the legends of its mother. "Yes, he fancied *her*, and she fancied *him*," resumed Deerslayer, casting a friendly and approving glance at the innocent and interested girl, "and when that is the case, and all the elders are agreed, it does not often happen that the young couple keep apart. Chingachgook could'n't well carry off such a prize without making inimies among them that wanted her as much as he did himself. A sartain Briarthorn, as we call him in English, or Yocommon as he is tarmed in Injin, took it most to heart, and we mistrust him of having a hand in all that followed. Wah-ta!-Wah went with her father and mother, two moons ago, to fish for salmon, on the western streams, where, it is agreed by all in these parts, that fish most abounds, and while thus empl'y'd the gal vanished. For several weeks we could get no tidings of her, but, here, ten days since, a runner that came through the Delaware country brought us a message, by which we l'arn that Wah-ta!-Wah was stolen from her people — we think, but do not know it, by Briarthorn's sarcumventions — and that she was now with the inimy, who had adopted her, and who wanted her to marry a young Mingo chief. The message said, that the party intended to hunt and forage through this region, for a month or two, afore it went back into the Canadas, and that if we could contrive to get on a scout in this quarter, something might turn up, that would lead to our getting the maiden off."

"And how does that concern *you*, Deerslayer?" demanded Judith, a little anxiously.

"It consarns me, as all things that touches a fri'nd consarn a fri'nd. I'm here as Chingachgook's aid and helper, and if we can get the young maiden he likes back ag'in, it will give me almost as much pleasure, as if I'd got back my own sweetheart."

"And where, then, *is your* sweet-heart, Deerslayer?"

"She's in the forest, Judith — hanging from the boughs of the trees, in a soft rain — in the dew on the open grass — the clouds that float about in the blue heavens — the birds that sing in the woods — the sweet springs where I slake my thirst — and in all the other glorious gifts that come from God's Providence."

"You mean that — as yet — you've never loved one of my sex, but love best your haunts, and your own manner of life."

"That's it — that's just it. I am white — have a white heart, and can't, in reason, love a red skinned maiden, who must have a red-skin heart and feelin's. No—no—I'm sound enough, in them partic'lars, and hope to remain so; at least, 'till this war is over. I find my time too much taken up with Chingachgook's affair, to wish to have one of my own, on my hands, afore that is settled."

"The girl that finally wins you, Deerslayer, will at least, win an *honest* heart; one without treachery or guile, and that will be a victory, that most of her sex ought to envy."

As Judith uttered this, her beautiful face had a resentful frown on it, while a bitter smile lingered around a mouth that no derangement of the muscles could render any thing but handsome. Her companion observed the change, and, though little skilled in the workings of the female heart, he had sufficient native delicacy to understand that it might be well to drop the subject.

As the hour when Chingachgook was expected, still remained distant, Deerslayer had time enough to examine into the state of the defences, and to make such additional arrangements as were in his power, and the exigency of the moment seemed to require. The experience and foresight of Hutter had left little to be done, in these particulars; still several precautions suggested themselves to the young man, who may be said to have studied the art of frontier warfare, through the traditions and legends of the people among whom he had so long lived. The distance between the castle and the nearest point on the shore, prevented any apprehensions on the subject of rifle bullets thrown from the land. The house was within musket shot, in one sense, it was true, but aim was entirely out of the question, and even Judith professed a perfect disregard of any danger from that source. So long then as the party remained in possession of the fortress, they were safe; unless their assailants could find the means to come off and carry it, by fire, or storm; or, by some of the devices of Indian cunning and Indian treachery. Against the first source of danger Hutter had made ample provision, and the building itself, the bark roof excepted, was not very combustible. The floor was scuttled in several places, and buckets provided with ropes, were in daily use, in readiness for any such emergency. One of the girls could easily extinguish any fire that might be lighted, provided it had not time to make much headway. Judith, who appeared to understand all her father's schemes of defence, and who had the spirit to take no unimportant share in the execution of them, explained all these details to the young man, who was thus saved much time and labor in making his investigations.

Little was to be apprehended during the day. In possession of the canoes, and of the Ark, no other vessel was to be found on the lake. Nevertheless, Deerslayer well knew that a raft was soon made, and as dead trees were to be found in abundance, near the water, did the savages seriously contemplate the risks of an assault, it would not be a very difficult matter to find the necessary means. The celebrated American axe, a tool that is quite unrivalled in its way, was then not very extensively known, and the savages were far from expert in the use of its hatchet-like substitute; still, they had sufficient practice in crossing streams by this mode, to render it certain they would construct a raft, should they deem it expedient to expose themselves to the risks of an assault. The death of their warrior might prove a sufficient incentive, or it might act as a caution, but Deerslayer thought it more than possible that the succeeding night would bring matters to a crisis, and in this precise way. This impression caused him to wish ardently for the presence and succour of his Mohican friend, and to look forward to the approach of sunset with an increasing anxiety.

As the day advanced, the party in the castle matured their plans, and made their preparations. Judith was active, and seemed to find a pleasure in consulting and advising with her new acquaintance, whose indifference to danger, manly devotion to herself and sister, guilelessness of manner and truth of feeling had won rapidly on both her imagination and her affections. Although the hours appeared long in some respects to Deerslayer, Judith did not find them so, and when the sun began to descend towards the pine-clad summits of the western hills, she felt and expressed her surprise that the day should so soon be drawing to a close. On the other hand, Hetty was moody and silent. She was never loquacious, or if she occasionally became communicative, it was under the influence of some temporary excitement, that served to arouse her unsophisticated mind; but, for hours at a time, in the course of this all-important day, she seemed to have absolutely lost the use of her tongue. Nor did apprehension on account of their father, materially affect the manner of either sister. Neither appeared seriously to dread any evil greater than captivity, and, once or twice, when Hetty did speak, she intimated the expectation that Hutter would find the means to liberate himself. Although Judith was less sanguine on this head, she too betrayed the hope that propositions for a ransom would come, when the Indians discovered that the castle set their expedients and artifices at defiance. Deerslayer, however, treated these passing suggestions, as the ill digested fancies of girls, making his own arrangements as steadily, and brooding over the future as seriously, as if they had never fallen from their lips.

At length the hour arrived, when it became necessary to proceed to the place of rendezvous appointed with the Mohican; or Delaware, as Chingachgook was more commonly called. As the plan had been matured by Deerslayer, and fully communicated to his companions, all three set about its execution, in concert, and intelligently. Hetty passed into the ark, and fastening two of the canoes together, she entered one, and paddled up to a sort of gate-way in the palisadoes that surrounded the building, through which she carried both; securing them beneath the house by chains that were fastened within the building. These palisadoes were trunks of trees, driven firmly into the mud, and served the double purpose of a small enclosure that was intended to be used in this very manner, and to keep any enemy that might approach in boats at arm's length. Canoes thus *docked* were, in a measure, hid from sight, and as the gate was properly barred and fastened, it would not be an easy task to remove them, even in the event of their being seen. Previously however to closing the gate, Judith also entered within the enclosure with the third canoe, leaving Deerslayer busy in securing the door and windows, inside the building, over her head. As every thing was massive and strong, and small saplings were used as bars, it would have been the work of an hour or two, to break into the building, when Deerslayer had ended his task, even allowing the assailants the use of any tools but the axe, and to be unresisted. This attention to security, arose from Hutter's having been robbed, once or twice, by the lawless whites of the frontiers, during some of his many absences from home.

As soon as all was fast, in the inside of the dwelling, Deerslayer appeared at a trap, from which he descended into the canoe of Judith. When this was done, he fastened the door, with a massive staple, and stout padlock. Hetty was then received in the canoe, which was shoved outside of the palisadoes. The next precaution was to fasten the gate, and the keys were carried into the Ark. The three were now fastened out of the dwelling, which could only be entered by violence, or by following the course taken by the young man in quitting it.

The glass had been brought outside, as a preliminary step, and Deerslayer next took a careful survey of the entire shore of the lake, as far as his own position would allow. Not a living thing was visible, a few birds excepted, and even the last fluttered about in the shade of the trees, as if unwilling to encounter the heat of a sultry afternoon. All the nearest points, in particular, were subjected to a severe scrutiny, in order to make certain that no raft was in preparation, the result every where giving the same picture of calm solitude. A few words will explain the greatest embarrassment belonging to the situation of our party. Exposed themselves, to the observation of any watchful eyes, the movements of their enemies were concealed by the drapery of a dense forest. While the imagination would be very apt to people the latter, with more warriors than it really contained, their own weakness must be too apparent to all who might choose to cast a glance in their direction.

"Nothing is stirring, howsever," exclaimed Deerslayer, as he finally lowered the glass, and prepared to enter the Ark, "If the vagabonds do harbor mischief in their minds, they are too cunning to let it be seen; it's true, a raft may be in preparation in the woods, but it has not yet been brought down to the lake. They can't guess that we are about to quit the castle, and, if they did, they've no means of knowing where we intend to go."

"This is so true, Deerslayer," returned Judith, "that now all is ready, we may proceed, at once, boldly, and without the fear of being followed. Else we shall be behind our time."

"No—no—the matter needs management—for, though the savages are in the dark as to Chingachgook and the rock, they've eyes and legs, and will see in what direction we steer, and will be sartain to follow us. I shall strive to baffle 'em, hows'ever, by heading the scow in all manner of ways, first in one quarter, and then in another, until they get to be a-leg-weary, and well tired of tramping a'ter us."

So far as it was in his power, Deerslayer was as good as his word. In less than five minutes after this speech was made, the whole party was in the Ark, and in motion. There was a gentle breeze from the north, and boldly hoisting the sail, the young man laid the head of the unwieldy craft in such a direction as, after making a liberal but necessary allowance for lee-way, would have brought it ashore a couple of miles down the lake, and on its eastern side. The sailing of the Ark was never very swift, though; floating as it did on the surface, it was not difficult to get it in motion, or to urge it along, over the water, at the rate of some three or four miles in the hour. The distance between the Castle and the Rock was a little more than two leagues. Knowing the punctuality of an Indian, Deerslayer had made his calculations closely, and had given himself a little more time than was necessary to reach the place of rendez-vous, with a view to delay, or to press his arrival, as might prove most expedient. When he hoisted the sail, the sun lay above the western hills, at an elevation that promised rather more than two hours of day, and a few minutes satisfied him that the progress of the scow was such as to equal his expectations.

It was a glorious June afternoon, and never did that solitary sheet of water seem less like an arena of strife and bloodshed. The light air scarce descended as low as the bed of the lake, hovering over it, as if unwilling to disturb its deep tranquility, or to ruffle its mirror-like surface. Even the forests appeared to be slumbering in the sun, and a few piles of fleecy clouds had lain for hours along the northern horizon, like fixtures in the atmosphere, placed there purely to embellish the scene. A few aquatic fowls occasionally skimmed along the water, and a single raven was visible, sailing high above the trees, and keeping a watchful eye on the forest beneath him, in order to detect any thing having life that the mysterious woods might offer as prey.

The reader will probably have observed, that, amidst the frankness and abruptness of manner, which marked the frontier habits of Judith, her language was superior to that used by her male companions, her own father included. This difference extended as well to pronunciation, as to the choice of words and phrases. Perhaps nothing so soon betrays the education and association as the modes of speech, and few accomplishments so much aid the charm of female beauty as a graceful and even utterance, while nothing so soon produces the disenchantment that necessarily follows a discrepancy between appearance and manner, as a mean intonation of voice, or a vulgar use of words. Judith and her sister were marked exceptions to all the girls of their class, along that whole frontier, the officers of the nearest garrison having often flattered the former with the belief that few ladies of the towns acquitted themselves better than herself, in this important particular. This was far from being literally true, but it was sufficiently near the fact to give birth to the compliment. The girls were indebted to their mother for this proficiency, having acquired from her, in childhood, an advantage that no subsequent study or labor can give without a drawback, if neglected beyond the earlier periods of life. Who that mother was, or, rather, had been, no one but Hutter knew. She had now been dead two summers, and, as was stated by Hurry, she had been buried in the lake, whether in indulgence of a prejudice, or from a reluctance to take the trouble to dig her grave, had frequently been a matter of discussion between the rude beings of that region. Judith had never visited the spot, but Hetty was present at the interment, and she often paddled a canoe, about sunset, or by the light of the moon, to the place, and gazed down into the limpid water, in the hope of being able to catch a glimpse of a form that she had so tenderly loved, from infancy to the sad hour of their parting.

"Must we reach the rock, exactly at the moment the sun sets?" Judith demanded of the young man, as they stood near each other, Deerslayer holding the steering-oar, and she working with a needle at some ornament of dress, that much exceeded her station in life, and was altogether a novelty in the woods. "Will a few minutes, sooner or later, alter the matter; it will be very hazardous to remain long as near the shore as that Rock!"

"That's it—Judith;—that's the very difficulty! The Rock's within p'int blank for a shot-gun, and 'twill never do to hover about it too close, and too long. When you have to deal with

an Injin, you must calculate and manage, for a red natur'
dearly likes sarcumvention. Now, you see, Judith, that I do
not steer towards the rock at all, but here to the eastward of it,
whereby the savages will be tramping off in that direction, and
get their legs awearied, and all for no advantage!"

"You think, then, they see us, and watch our movements,
Deerslayer? I was in hopes they might have fallen back into the
woods, and left us to ourselves, for a few hours."

"That's altogether a woman's consait. There's no let-up in an
Injin's watchfulness when he's fairly on a war path, and eyes are
on us at this minute, 'though the lake presarves us. We must
draw near the rock on a calculation, and indivour to get the
miscreants on a false scent. The Mingos have good noses, they
tell me, but a white man's reason ought always to equalize
their instinct."

Judith now entered into a desultory discourse with Deerslayer, in which the girl betrayed her growing interest in
the young man; an interest that his simplicity of mind, and her
decision of character, sustained as it was by the consciousness
awakened by the consideration her personal charms so universally produced, rendered her less anxious to conceal than
might otherwise have been the case. She was scarcely forward
in her manner, though there was sometimes a freedom in her
glances, that it required all the aids of her exceeding beauty to
prevent from awakening suspicions unfavorable to her discretion, if not to her morals. With Deerslayer, however, these
glances were rendered less obnoxious to so unpleasant a construction, for she seldom looked at him, without discovering
much of the sincerity and nature that accompany the purest
emotions of woman. It was a little remarkable that, as his captivity lengthened neither of the girls manifested any great concern for her father, but, as has been said already, their habits
gave them confidence, and they looked forward to his liberation, by means of a ransom, with a confidence that might, in a
great degree, account for their apparent indifference. Once
before Hutter had been in the hands of the Iroquois, and a few
skins had readily effected his release. This event, however,
unknown to the sisters, had occurred in a time of peace between England and France, and when the savages were

restrained, instead of being encouraged to commit their excesses, by the policy of the different colonial governments.

While Judith was loquacious and caressing in her manner,
Hetty remained thoughtful and silent. Once, indeed, she drew
near to Deerslayer, and questioned him a little closely, as to
his intentions, as well as concerning the mode of effecting his
purpose, but her wish to converse went no farther. As soon as
her simple queries were answered—and answered they all
were, in the fullest and kindest manner—she withdrew to her
seat, and continued to work on a coarse garment that she was
making for her father, sometimes humming a low melancholy
air, and frequently sighing.

In this manner the time passed away, and when the sun was
beginning to glow behind the fringe of pines that bounded the
western hill, or about twenty minutes before it actually set, the
Ark was nearly as low as the point where Hutter and Hurry
had been made prisoners. By sheering first to one side of the
lake, and then to the other, Deerslayer managed to create an
uncertainty as to his object, and, doubtless, the savages, who
were unquestionably watching his movements, were led to
believe that his aim was to communicate with them, at or near
this spot, and would hasten in that direction, in order to be in
readiness to profit by circumstances. This artifice was well
managed, since the sweep of the bay, the curvature of the lake,
and the low marshy land that intervened would probably allow
the Ark to reach the rock, before its pursuers, if really collected near the point, could have time to make the circuit
that would be required to get there by land. With a view to aid
this deception, Deerslayer stood as near the western shore, as
was at all prudent, and, then, causing Judith and Hetty to
enter the house, or cabin, and crouching himself so as to conceal his person by the frame of the scow, he suddenly threw the
head of the latter round, and began to make the best of his way
towards the outlet. Favored by an increase in the wind, the
progress of the Ark was such as to promise the complete success of this plan, though the crab-like movement of the craft
compelled the helmsman to keep its head looking in a direction
very different from that in which it was actually moving.

Chapter IX.

"Yet art thou prodigal of smiles—
Smiles, sweeter than thy frowns are stern:
Earth sends from all her thousand isles,
    A shout at thy return.
The glory that comes down from thee
Bathes, in deep joy, the land and sea."
                    Bryant, "The Firmament," ll.19-24.

I T may assist the reader in understanding the events we are about to record, if he has a rapidly sketched picture of the scene, placed before his eyes at a single view. It will be remembered that the lake was an irregularly shaped basin, of an outline that, in the main, was oval, but with bays and points to relieve its formality and ornament its shores. The surface of this beautiful sheet of water was now glittering like a gem, in the last rays of the evening sun, and the setting of the whole, hills clothed in the richest forest verdure, was lighted up with a sort of radiant smile, that is best described in the beautiful lines we have placed at the head of this chapter. As the banks, with few exceptions, rose abruptly from the water, even where the mountain did not immediately bound the view, there was a nearly unbroken fringe of leaves overhanging the placid lake, the trees starting out of the acclivities, inclining to the light, until, in many instances they extended their long limbs and straight trunks some forty or fifty feet beyond the line of the perpendicular. In these cases we allude only to the giants of the forest, pines of a hundred or a hundred and fifty feet in height, for of the smaller growth, very many inclined so far as to steep their lower branches in the water.

In the position in which the Ark had now got, the castle was concealed from view by the projection of a point, as indeed was the northern extremity of the lake itself. A respectable mountain, forest clad, and rounded, like all the rest, limited the view in that direction, stretching immediately across the whole of the fair scene, with the exception of a deep bay that passed its western end, lengthening the basin, for more than a mile.

The manner in which the water flowed out of the lake, beneath the leafy arches of the trees that lined the sides of the stream, has already been mentioned, and it has also been said that the rock, which was a favorite place of rendezvous throughout all that region, and where Deerslayer now expected to meet his friend, stood near this outlet, and at no great distance from the shore. It was a large, isolated stone that rested on the bottom of the lake, apparently left there when the waters tore away the earth from around it, in forcing for themselves a passage down the river, and which had obtained its shape from the action of the elements, during the slow progress of centuries. The height of this rock could scarcely equal six feet, and, as has been said, its shape was not unlike that which is usually given to bee-hives, or to a hay-cock. The latter, indeed, gives the best idea not only of its form, but of its dimensions. It stood, and still stands, for we are writing of real scenes, within fifty feet of the bank, and in water that was only two feet in depth, though there were seasons in which its rounded apex, if such a term can properly be used, was covered by the lake. Many of the trees stretched so far forward, as almost to blend the rock with the shore, when seen from a little distance, and one tall pine in particular overhung it in a way to form a noble and appropriate canopy to a seat that had held many a forest chieftain, during the long succession of unknown ages, in which America, and all it contained, had existed apart, in mysterious solitude, a world by itself; equally without a familiar history, and without an origin that the annals of man can reach.

When distant some two or three hundred feet from the shore, Deerslayer took in his sail. He dropped his grapnel, as soon as he found the Ark had drifted in a line that was directly to windward of the rock. The motion of the scow was then checked, when it was brought head to wind, by the action of the breeze. As soon as this was done, Deerslayer "paid out line," and suffered the vessel to "set down" upon the rock, as fast as the light air could force it to leeward. Floating entirely on the surface, this was soon effected, and the young man checked the drift when he was told that the stern of the scow was within fifteen or eighteen feet of the desired spot.

In executing this manoeuvre, Deerslayer had proceeded promptly, for, while he did not in the least doubt that he was both watched and followed by the foe, he believed he had distracted their movements, by the apparent uncertainty of his own, and he knew they could have no means of ascertaining that the rock was his aim, unless indeed one of their prisoners had betrayed him; a chance so improbable in itself, as to give him no concern. Notwithstanding the celerity and decision of his movements, he did not, however, venture so near the shore without taking due precautions to effect a retreat, in the event of its becoming necessary. He held the line in his hand, and Judith was stationed at a loop, on the side of the cabin next the shore, where she could watch the beach and the rock, and give timely notice of the approach of either friend or foe. Hetty was also placed on watch, but it was to keep the trees over head in view, lest some enemy might ascend one, and, by completely commanding the interior of the scow render the defences of the hut, or cabin, useless.

The sun had disappeared from the lake and valley, when Deerslayer checked the Ark, in the manner mentioned. Still it wanted a few minutes to the true sun-set, and he knew Indian punctuality too well to anticipate any unmanly haste in his friend. The great question was, whether, surrounded by enemies as he was known to be, he had escaped their toils. The occurrences of the last twenty-four hours must be a secret to him, and like himself, Chingachgook was yet young on a war-path. It was true, he came prepared to encounter the party that withheld his promised bride, but he had no means of ascertaining the extent of the danger he run, or the precise positions occupied by either friends, or foes. In a word, the trained sagacity, and untiring caution of an Indian were all he had to rely on, amid the critical risks he unavoidably ran.

"Is the rock empty, Judith?" enquired Deerslayer, as soon as he had checked the drift of the Ark, deeming it imprudent to venture unnecessarily near the shore. "Is any thing to be seen of the Delaware chief?"

"Nothing, Deerslayer. Neither rock, shore, trees, nor lake, seems to have ever held a human form."

"Keep close, Judith — keep close, Hetty — a rifle has a prying eye, a nimble foot, and a desperate fatal tongue. Keep close then, but keep up actyve looks, and be on the alert. 'T would grieve me to the heart, did any harm befal either of you."

"And *you*, Deerslayer—" exclaimed Judith, turning her handsome face from the loop, to bestow a gracious and grateful look on the young man—"do *you* 'keep close', and have a proper care that the savages do not catch a glimpse of you! A bullet might be as fatal to *you*, as to one of us; and the blow that you felt, would be felt by us all."

"No fear of me, Judith—no fear of me, my good gal. Do not look this-a-way, although you look so pleasant and comely, but keep your eyes on the rock, and the shore, and the—"

Deerslayer was interrupted by a slight exclamation from the girl, who, in obedience to his hurried gestures, as much as in obedience to his words, had immediately bent her looks again, in the opposite direction.

"What is't?—What is't, Judith?" he hastily demanded—"Is any thing to be seen?"

"There is a man on the rock!—An Indian warrior, in his paint—and armed!"

"Where does he wear his hawk's feather?" eagerly added Deerslayer, relaxing his hold of the line, in readiness to drift nearer to the place of rendezvous. "Is it fast to the war-lock, or does he carry it above the left ear?"

" 'Tis as you say, above the left ear; he smiles, too, and mutters the word 'Mohican.' "

"God be praised, 'tis the Sarpent, at last!" exclaimed the young man, suffering the line to slip through his hands, until hearing a light bound, in the other end of the craft, he instantly checked the rope, and began to haul it in, again, under the assurance that his object was effected.

At that moment the door of the cabin was opened hastily, and, a warrior, darting through the little room, stood at Deerslayer's side, simply uttering the exclamation "hughh!" At the next instant, Judith and Hetty shrieked, and the air was filled with the yell of twenty savages, who came leaping through the branches, down the bank, some actually falling headlong into the water, in their haste.

"Pull, Deerslayer," cried Judith, hastily barring the door, in order to prevent an inroad by the passage through which the Delaware had just entered; "pull, for life and death—the lake is full of savages, wading after us!"

The young men—for Chingachgook immediately came to

his friend's assistance — needed no second bidding, but they applied themselves to their task in a way that showed how urgent they deemed the occasion. The great difficulty was in suddenly overcoming the *vis inertia* of so large a mass, for, once in motion, it was easy to cause the scow to skim the water, with all the necessary speed.

"Pull, Deerslayer, for Heaven's sake!" cried Judith, again at the loop — "These wretches rush into the water like hounds following their prey! Ah — the scow moves! and now, the water deepens, to the arm-pits of the foremost, but they reach forward, and will seize the Ark!"

A slight scream, and then a joyous laugh followed from the girl; the first produced by a desperate effort of their pursuers, and the last by its failure; the scow, which had now got fairly in motion gliding ahead into deep water, with a velocity that set the designs of their enemies at nought. As the two men were prevented by the position of the cabin, from seeing what passed astern, they were compelled to enquire of the girls, into the state of the chase.

"What now, Judith? — What next? — Do the Mingos still follow, or are we quit of 'em, for the present," demanded Deerslayer, when he felt the rope yielding as if the scow was going fast ahead, and heard the scream and the laugh of the girl, almost in the same breath.

"They have vanished! — One — the last — is just burying himself in the bushes of the bank — There, he has disappeared in the shadows of the trees! You have got your friend, and we are all safe!"

The two men now made another great effort, pulled the Ark up swiftly to the grapnel, tripped it, and when the scow had shot some distance, and lost its way, they let the anchor drop again. Then, for the first time since their meeting, they ceased their efforts. As the floating house now lay several hundred feet from the shore, and offered a complete protection against bullets, there was no longer any danger, or any motive for immediate exertion.

The manner in which the two friends now recognised each other, was highly characteristic. Chingachgook, a noble, tall, handsome and athletic young Indian warrior, first examined his rifle, with care, opening the pan to make sure that the priming was not wet, and, assured of this important fact, he next cast furtive but observant glances around him, at the strange habitation, and at the two girls. Still he spoke not, and most of all, did he avoid the betrayal of a womanish curiosity, by asking questions.

"Judith and Hetty—" said Deerslayer, with an untaught, natural courtesy—"this is the Mohican chief of whom you've heard me speak; Chingachgook as he is called; which signifies Big Sarpent; so named for his wisdom and prudence, and cunning, and my 'arliest and latest fri'nd. I know'd it must be he, by the hawk's feather, over the left ear, most other warriors wearing 'em on the war-lock."

As Deerslayer ceased speaking, he laughed heartily, excited more perhaps by the delight of having got his friend safe at his side, under circumstances so trying, than by any conceit that happened to cross his fancy, and exhibiting this outbreaking of feeling in a manner that was a little remarkable, since his merriment was not accompanied by any noise. Although Chingachgook both understood and spoke English, he was unwilling to communicate his thoughts in it, like most Indians, and when he had met Judith's cordial shake of the hand, and Hetty's milder salute, in the courteous manner that became a chief, he turned away, apparently to await the moment when it might suit his friend to enter into an explanation of his future intentions, and to give a narrative of what had passed since their separation. The other understood his meaning, and discovered his own mode of reasoning in the matter, by addressing the girls.

"This wind will soon die away altogether, now the sun is down," he said, "and there is no need for rowing ag'in it. In half an hour, or so, it will either be a flat calm, or the air will come off from the south shore, when we will begin our journey back ag'in to the castle; in the mean while, the Delaware and I will talk over matters, and get correct idees of each other's notions, consarning the course we ought to take."

No one opposed this proposition, and the girls withdrew into the cabin to prepare the evening meal, while the two young men took their seats on the head of the scow and began to converse. The dialogue was in the language of the Delawares. As that dialect, however, is but little understood, even by the learned, we shall, not only on this, but on all subsequent occasions, render such parts, as it may be necessary to give closely, into liberal English; preserving, as far as possible, the idioms and peculiarities of the respective speakers, by way of presenting the pictures in the most graphic forms to the minds of the readers.

It is unnecessary to enter into the details first related by Deerslayer, who gave a brief narrative of the facts that are already familiar to those who have read our pages. In relating these events, however, it may be well to say that the speaker touched only on the outlines, more particularly abstaining from saying any thing about his encounter with, and victory over the Iroquois, as well as to his own exertions in behalf of the two deserted young women. When Deerslayer ended, the Delaware took up the narrative, in turn, speaking sententiously and with grave dignity. His account was both clear and short, nor was it embellished by any incidents that did not directly concern the history of his departure from the villages of his people, and his arrival in the valley of the Susquehannah. On reaching the latter, which was at a point only half a mile south of the outlet, he had soon struck a trail, which gave him notice of the probable vicinity of enemies. Being prepared for such an occurrence, the object of the expedition calling him directly into the neighborhood of the party of Iroquois that was known to be out, he considered the discovery as fortunate, rather than the reverse, and took the usual precautions to turn it to account. First following the river to its source, and ascertaining the position of the rock, he met another trail, and had actually been hovering for hours on the flanks of his enemies, watching equally for an opportunity to meet his mistress, and to take a scalp; and it may be questioned which he most ardently desired. He kept near the lake, and occasionally he ventured to some spot, where he could get a view of what was passing on its surface. The Ark had been seen and watched, from the moment it hove in sight, though the young chief was necessarily ignorant that it was to be the instrument of his effecting the desired junction with his friend. The uncertainty of its movements, and the fact that it was unquestionably managed by white men, soon led him to conjecture the truth, however, and he held himself in readiness to get on board whenever a suitable occasion might offer. As the sun drew near the horizon he repaired to the rock, where, on emerging from the forest, he was gratified in finding the Ark lying, apparently in readiness to receive him. The manner of his appearance, and of his entrance into the craft is known.

Although Chingachgook had been closely watching his enemies for hours, their sudden and close pursuit, as he reached the scow, was as much a matter of surprise to himself, as it had been to his friend. He could only account for it, by the fact of their being more numerous than he had at first supposed, and by their having out parties of the existence of which he was ignorant. Their regular, and permanent encampment, if the word permanent can be applied to the residence of a party that intended to remain out, in all probability, but a few weeks, was not far from the spot where Hutter and Hurry had fallen into their hands, and, as a matter of course, near a spring.

"Well, Sarpent," asked Deerslayer, when the other had ended his brief but spirited narrative, speaking always in the Delaware tongue, which for the reader's convenience only we render into the peculiar vernacular of the speaker — "Well, Sarpent, as you've been scouting around these Mingos, have you any thing to tell us of their captyves, the father of these young women, and of another, who, I somewhat conclude, is the lovyer of one of 'em."

"Chingachgook has seen them. An old man, and a young warrior — the falling hemlock and the tall pine."

"You're not so much out, Delaware; you're not so much out. Old Hutter is decaying, of a sartainty, though many solid blocks might be hewn out of his trunk yet, and, as for Hurry Harry, so far as heighth, and strength and comliness go, he may be called the pride of the human forest. Were the men bound, or, in any manner, suffering torture? I ask on account of the young women, who, I dare to say, would be glad to know."

"It is not so, Deerslayer. The Mingos are too many to cage their game. Some watch; some sleep; some scout; some hunt. The pale faces are treated like brothers to-day; to-morrow they will lose their scalps."

"Yes, that's red natur', and must be submitted to! Judith and Hetty, here's comforting tidings for you, the Delaware telling me that neither your father nor Hurry Harry is in suffering, but, bating the loss of liberty, as well off, as we are ourselves. Of course they are kept in the camp; otherwise they do much as they please."

"I rejoice to hear this, Deerslayer," returned Judith, "and now we are joined by your friend, I make no manner of question that we shall find an opportunity to ransom the prisoners. If there are any women in the camp, I have articles of dress that will catch their eyes, and, should the worst come to the worst, we can open the great chest, which, I think will be found to hold things that may tempt the chiefs."

"Judith," said the young man, looking up at her, with a smile, and an expression of earnest curiosity, that, spite of the growing obscurity did not escape the watchful looks of the girl, "can you find it in your heart, to part with your own finery, to release prisoners; even though one be your own father, and the other is your sworn suitor and lovyer?"

The flush on the face of the girl arose in part from resentment, but more perhaps from a gentler and a novel feeling, that, with the capricious waywardness of taste, had been rapidly rendering her more sensitive to the good opinion of the youth who questioned her, than to that of any other person. Suppressing the angry sensation, with instinctive quickness, she answered with a readiness and truth, that caused her sister to draw near to listen, though the obtuse intellect of the latter was far from comprehending the workings of a heart as treacherous, as uncertain, and as impetuous in its feelings, as that of the spoiled and flattered beauty.

"Deerslayer," answered Judith, after a moment's pause, "I shall be honest with *you*. I confess, that the time *has* been when what you call finery, was to me the dearest thing on earth; but I begin to feel differently. Though Hurry Harry is nought to me nor ever can be, I would give all I own to set him free. If I would do this, for blustering, bullying, talking Hurry, who has nothing but good looks to recommend him, you may judge what I would do for my own father."

"This sounds well, and is according to woman's gifts. Ah's, me! The same feelin's is to be found among the young women of the Delawares. I've known 'em, often and often, sacrifice their vanity to their hearts. 'Tis as it should be — 'tis as it should be I suppose, in both colours. Woman was created for the feelin's, and is pretty much ruled by feelin'."

"Would the savages let father go, if Judith and I give them all our best things?" demanded Hetty, in her innocent, mild, manner.

"Their women might interfere, good Hetty; yes, their women might interfere with such an ind in view. But, tell me, Sarpent, how is it as to squaws among the knaves; have they many of their own women in the camp?"

The Delaware heard, and understood all that passed, though with Indian gravity and finesse he had sat, with averted face, seemingly inattentive to a discourse in which he had no direct concern. Thus appealed to, however, he answered his friend in his ordinary sententious manner.

"Six—" he said, holding up all the fingers of one hand, and the thumb of the other, "beside *this*." The last number denoted his betrothed, whom, with the poetry and truth of nature, he described by laying his hand on his own heart.

"Did you see her, chief—did you get a glimpse of her pleasant countenance, or come close enough to her ear, to sing in it the song she loves to hear?"

"No, Deerslayer—the trees were too many, and leaves covered their boughs like clouds hiding the heavens, in a storm. But"—and the young warrior turned his dark face towards his friend, with a smile on it that illuminated its fierce-looking paint, and naturally stern lineaments, with a bright gleam of human feeling, "Chingachgook heard the laugh of Wah-ta!-Wah, and knew it from the laugh of the women of the Iroquois. It sounded in his ears, like the chirp of the wren."

"Ay, trust a lovyer's ear for that, and a Delaware's ear for all sounds that are ever heard in the woods. I know not why it is so, Judith, but when young men—and I dares to say it may be all the same with young women, too—but when they get to have kind feelin's towards each other, it's wonderful how pleasant the laugh, or the speech becomes, to the other person. I've seen grim warriors listening to the chattering and the laughing of young gals, as if it was church music, such as is heard in the old Dutch church that stands in the great street of Albany, where I've been, more than once, with peltry and game."

"And *you*, Deerslayer," said Judith quickly, and with more

sensibility than marked her usually light and thoughtless manner, — "have *you* never felt how pleasant it is to listen to the laugh of the girl you love?"

"Lord bless you gal! — Why I've never lived enough among my own colour to drop into them sort of feelin's, — no never! I dares to say, they are nat'ral and right, but to me there's no music so sweet as the sighing of the wind in the tree tops, and the rippling of a stream from a full, sparkling, nat*y*ve fountain of pure forest water — unless, indeed," he continued, dropping his head for an instant in a thoughtful manner — "unless indeed it be the open mouth of a sartain hound, when I'm on the track of a fat buck — As for unsartain dogs, I care little for their cries, seein' they are as likely to speak when the deer is not in sight, as when it is."

Judith walked slowly and pensively away, nor was there any of her ordinary calculating coquetry, in the light tremulous sigh, that, unconsciously to herself, arose to her lips. On the other hand Hetty listened with guileless attention, though it struck her simple mind as singular that the young man should prefer the melody of the woods, to the songs of girls, or even to the laugh of innocence and joy. Accustomed, however, to defer, in most things, to her sister, she soon followed Judith into the cabin, where she took a seat, and remained pondering intensely over some occurrence, or resolution, or opinion — which was a secret to all but herself. Left alone, Deerslayer and his friend resumed their discourse.

"Has the young pale-face hunter been long on this lake?" demanded the Delaware, after courteously waiting for the other to speak first.

"Only since yesterday noon, Sarpent, though that has been long enough to see and do much."

The gaze that the Indian fastened on his companion was so keen it seemed to mock the gathering darkness of the night. As the other furtively returned his look, he saw the two black eyes glistening on him, like the balls of the panther, or those of the penned wolf. He understood the meaning of this glowing gaze, and answered evasively, as he fancied would best become the modesty of a white man's gifts.

"'Tis as you suspect, Sarpent; yes, 'tis somewhat that-a-way.

I *have* fell in with the inimy, and I suppose it may be said I've fou't them, too."

An exclamation of delight and exultation escaped the Indian, and then laying his hand eagerly on the arm of his friend, he asked if there were any scalps taken.

"That I *will* maintain in the face of all the Delaware tribe, old Tamenund, and your own father, the great Uncas, as well as the rest, is ag'in white gifts! *My* scalp is on my head, as you can see, Sarpent, and that was the only scalp that was in danger, when one side was altogether Christian and white."

"Did no warrior fall? — Deerslayer did not get his name, by being slow of sight, or clumsy with the rifle!"

"In that particular, chief, you're nearer reason, and therefore nearer being right. I may say one Mingo fell."

"A chief!" demanded the other with startling vehemence.

"Nay, that's more than I know, or can say. He was artful, and treacherous, and stout-hearted, and may well have gained popularity enough with his people to be named to that rank. The man fou't well, though his eye was'n't quick enough for one who had had his schooling in your company, Delaware."

"My brother and friend struck the body?"

"That was uncalled for, seeing that the Mingo died in my arms. The truth may as well be said, at once; he fou't like a man of red gifts, and I fou't like a man with gifts of my own colour. God gave me the victory; I coul'n't fly in the face of his Providence by forgetting my birth and natur'. White he made me, and white I shall live and die."

"Good! Deerslayer is a pale face, and has pale-face hands. A Delaware will look for the scalp, and hang it on a pole, and sing a song in his honour, when we go back to our people. The glory belongs to the tribe; it must not be lost."

"This is easy talking, but 'twill not be as easy doing. The Mingo's body is in the hands of his fri'nds, and, no doubt, is hid in some hole, where Delaware cunning will never be able to get at the scalp."

The young man then gave his friend a succinct, but clear account, of the event of the morning, concealing nothing of any moment, and yet touching on every thing modestly and with a careful attention to avoid the Indian habit of boasting.

Chingachgook again expressed his satisfaction at the honour won by his friend, and then both arose, the hour having arrived when it became prudent to move the Ark further from the land.

It was now quite dark, the heavens having become clouded, and the stars hid. The north wind had ceased, as was usual with the setting of the sun, and a light air arose from the south. This change favoring the design of Deerslayer, he lifted his grapnel, and the scow immediately and quite perceptibly began to drift more into the lake. The sail was set, when the motion of the craft increased to a rate not much less than two miles in the hour. As this superseded the necessity of rowing, an occupation that an Indian would not be likely to desire, Deerslayer, Chingachgook and Judith seated themselves in the stern of the scow, where they first governed its movements by holding the oar. Here they discoursed on their future movements, and on the means that ought to be used in order to effect the liberation of their friends.

In this dialogue Judith held a material part, the Delaware readily understanding all she said, while his own replies and remarks, both of which were few and pithy, were occasionally rendered into English by his friend. Judith rose greatly in the estimation of her companions, in the half hour that followed. Prompt of resolution and firm of purpose, her suggestions and expedients partook of her spirit and sagacity, both of which were of a character to find favor with men of the frontier. The events that had occurred since their meeting, as well as her isolated and dependant situation, induced the girl to feel towards Deerslayer like the friend of a year instead of an acquaintance of a day, and so completely had she been won by his guileless truth of character and of feeling, pure novelties in our sex, as respected her own experience, that his peculiarities excited her curiosity, and created a confidence that had never been awakened by any other man. Hitherto she had been compelled to stand on the defensive, in her intercourse with men, with what success was best known to herself, but here had she been suddenly thrown into the society, and under the protection of a youth, who evidently as little contemplated evil towards herself, as if he had been her brother. The freshness of his integrity, the poetry and truth of his feelings, and even the quaintness of his forms of speech, all had their influence, and aided in awakening an interest that she found as pure as it was sudden and deep. Hurry's fine face and manly form had never compensated for his boisterous and vulgar tone, and her inter-course with the officers had prepared her to make comparisons under which even his great natural advantages suffered. But this very intercourse with the officers who occasionally came upon the lake to fish and hunt, had an effect in producing her present sentiments towards the young stranger. With them, while her vanity had been gratified, and her self-love strongly awakened, she had many causes deeply to regret the acquain-tance — if not to mourn over it, in secret sorrow — for it was im-possible for one of her quick intellect not to perceive how hollow was the association between superior and inferior, and that she was regarded as the play thing of an idle hour, rather than as an equal and a friend, by even the best intentioned and least designing of her scarlet-clad admirers. Deerslayer, on the other hand, had a window in his breast, through which the light of his honesty was ever shining; and even his indifference to charms that so rarely failed to produce a sensation, piqued the pride of the girl, and gave him an interest that another, seemingly more favored by nature, might have failed to excite.

In this manner half an hour passed, during which time the Ark had been slowly stealing over the water, the darkness thickening around it; though it was easy to see that the gloom of the forest at the southern end of the lake, was getting to be distant, while the mountains that lined the sides of the beautiful basin were overshadowing it, nearly from side to side. There was, indeed, a narrow stripe of water, in the centre of the lake where the dim light that was still shed from the heavens, fell upon its surface in a line extending north and south; and along this faint track, a sort of inverted milky way, in which the obscurity was not quite as dense as in other places, the scow held her course, he who steered well knowing that it led in the direction he wished to go. The reader is not to suppose, however, that any difficulty could exist as to the course. This would have been determined by that of the air, had it not been possible to distinguish the mountains, as well as by the dim opening to the south, which marked the position of the valley in that quarter, above the plain of tall trees, by a sort of lessened obscurity; the difference between the darkness of the forest, and that of the night, as seen only in the air. The peculiarities at length caught the attention of Judith and the Deerslayer, and the conversation ceased, to allow each to gaze at the solemn stillness and deep repose of nature.

"Tis a gloomy night—" observed the girl, after a pause of several minutes—"I hope we may be able to find the castle."

"Little fear of our missing *that*, if we keep this path, in the middle of the lake," returned the young man. "Natur' has made us a road here, and, dim as it is, there'll be little difficulty in following it."

"Do you hear nothing, Deerslayer?—It seemed as if the water was stirring quite near us!"

"Sartainly something *did* move the water, oncommon like; it must have been a fish. Them creatur's prey upon each other like men, and animals on the land; one has leaped into the air, and fallen hard, back into his own element. 'Tis of little use, Judith, for any to strive to get out of their elements, since it's natur' to stay in 'em, and natur' will have its way. Ha! *That* sounds like a paddle, used with more than common caution!"

At this moment the Delaware bent forward, and pointed significantly into the boundary of gloom, as if some object had suddenly caught his eye. Both Deerslayer and Judith followed the direction of his gesture, and each got a view of a canoe at the same instant. The glimpse of this startling neighbor was dim, and to eyes less practised, it might have been uncertain; though to those in the Ark, the object was evidently a canoe, with a single individual in it; the latter, standing erect, and paddling. How many lay concealed in its bottom, of course could not be known. Flight, by means of oars, from a bark canoe impelled by vigorous and skilful hands, was utterly impracticable, and each of the men seized his rifle, in expectation of a conflict.

"I can easily bring down the paddler," whispered Deerslayer, "but we'll first hail him, and ask his ar'n'd." Then raising his voice, he continued in a solemn manner—"hold! If ye come nearer, I must fire, though contrary to my wishes, and then sartain death will follow. Stop paddling, and answer."

"Fire, and slay a poor, defenceless, girl," returned a soft tremulous female voice. "And God will never forgive you! Go your way, Deerslayer, and let me go mine."

"Hetty!" exclaimed the young man and Judith in a breath; and the former sprang instantly to the spot where he had left the canoe they had been towing. It was gone, and he understood the whole affair. As for the fugitive, frightened at the menace, she ceased paddling, and remained dimly visible, resembling a spectral outline of a human form, standing on the water. At the next moment, the sail was lowered, to prevent the Ark from passing the spot where the canoe lay. This last expedient, however, was not taken in time, for the momentum of so heavy a craft, and the impulsion of the air, soon set her by, bringing Hetty directly to windward, though still visible, as the change in the positions of the two boats, now placed her in that species of milky way which has been mentioned.

"What can this mean, Judith?" demanded Deerslayer—"Why has your sister taken the canoe, and left us?"

"You know she is feeble-minded, poor girl!—and she has her own ideas of what ought to be done. She loves her father more than most children love their parents—and—then—"

"Then, what, gal?—This is a trying moment; one in which truth must be spoken!"

Judith felt a generous and womanly regret at betraying her sister, and she hesitated ere she spoke again. But once more urged by Deerslayer, and conscious herself of all the risks the whole party was running by the indiscretion of Hetty, she could refrain no longer.

"Then, I fear, poor, weak-minded, Hetty has not been altogether able to see all the vanity, and rudeness and folly, that lie hid behind the handsome face and fine form of Hurry Harry. She talks of him, in her sleep, and sometimes betrays the inclination, in her waking moments."

"You think, Judith, that your sister is now bent on some mad scheme to serve her father and Hurry, which will, in all likelihood, give them riptyles the Mingos, the mastership of a canoe?"

"Such, I fear, will turn out to be the fact, Deerslayer: Poor Hetty has hardly sufficient cunning to outwit a savage."

All this while, the canoe, with the form of Hetty, erect in one end of it, was dimly perceptible, though the greater drift of the Ark, rendered it, at each instant, less and less distinct. It was evident no time was to be lost, lest it should altogether disappear. The rifles were now laid aside, as useless, the two men seizing the oars, and sweeping the head of the scow round, in the direction of the canoe. Judith, accustomed to the office, flew to the other end of the Ark, and placed herself at what might be called the helm. Hetty took the alarm, at these preparations, which could not be made without noise, and started off like a bird, that had been suddenly put up by the approach of unexpected danger.

As Deerslayer and his companion rowed with the energy of those who felt the necessity of straining every nerve, and Hetty's strength was impaired by a nervous desire to escape, the chase would have quickly terminated in the capture of the fugitive, had not the girl made several short and unlooked-for deviations in her course. These turnings gave her time, and they had also the effect of gradually bringing both canoe and Ark within the deeper gloom, cast by the shadows from the hills. They also gradually increased the distance between the fugitive and her pursuers, until Judith called out to her companions to cease rowing, for she had completely lost sight of the canoe.

When this mortifying announcement was made, Hetty was actually so near as to understand every syllable her sister uttered, though the latter had used the precaution of speaking as low as circumstances would allow her to do, and to make herself heard. Hetty stopped paddling at the same moment, and waited the result with an impatience that was breathless, equally from her late exertions, and her desire to land. A dead silence immediately fell on the lake, during which the three in the Ark were using their senses differently, in order to detect the position of the canoe. Judith bent forward to listen, in the hope of catching some sound that might betray the direction in which her sister was stealing away, while her two companions brought their eyes, as near as possible, to a level with the water, in order to detect any object that might be floating on its surface. All was vain, however, for neither sound, nor sight, rewarded their efforts. All this time Hetty, who had not the cunning to sink into the canoe, stood erect, a finger pressed on her lips, gazing in the direction in which the voices had last been heard, resembling a statue of profound and timid attention. Her ingenuity had barely sufficed to enable her to seize the canoe and to quit the Ark, in the noiseless manner related, and then it appeared to be momentarily exhausted. Even the doublings of the canoe had been as much the consequence of an uncertain hand, and of nervous agitation, as of any craftiness, or calculation.

The pause continued several minutes, during which Deerslayer and the Delaware conferred together, in the language of the latter. Then the oars dipped, again, and the Ark moved away, rowing with as little noise as possible. It steered westward, a little southerly, or in the direction of the encampment of the enemy. Having reached a point, at no great distance from the shore, and where the obscurity was intense, on account of the proximity of the land, it lay there near an hour, in waiting for the expected approach of Hetty, who, it was thought, would make the best of her way, to that spot, as soon as she believed herself released from the danger of pursuit. No success rewarded this little blockade, however, neither appearance nor sound denoting the passage of the canoe. Disappointed at this failure, and conscious of the importance of getting possession of the fortress, before it could be seized by the enemy, Deerslayer now took his way towards the castle, with the apprehension that all his foresight in securing the canoes would be defeated, by this unguarded and alarming movement on the part of the feeble minded Hetty.

Chapter X.

"— But who in this wild wood
May credit give to either eye, or ear?
From rocky precipice or hollow cave,
'Midst the confused sound of rustling leaves,
And creaking boughs, and cries of nightly birds,
Returning seeming answer!"
Joanna Baillie, *Rayner: A Tragedy*, II.i.3-4, 6-9.

FEAR, as much as calculation, had induced Hetty to cease paddling, when she found that her pursuers did not know in which direction to proceed. She remained stationary until the Ark had pulled in near the encampment, as has been related in the preceding chapter, when she resumed the paddle, and with cautious strokes made the best of her way towards the western shore. In order to avoid her pursuers, however, who, she rightly suspected, would soon be rowing along that shore themselves, the head of the canoe was pointed so far north, as to bring her to land on a point that thrust itself into the lake, at the distance of near a league from the outlet. Nor was this altogether the result of a desire to escape, for, feeble minded as she was, Hetty Hutter had a good deal of that instinctive caution which so often keeps those whom God has thus visited from harm. She was perfectly aware of the importance of keeping the canoes from falling into the hands of the Iroquois, and long familiarity with the lake had suggested one of the simplest expedients, by which this great object could be rendered compatible with her own purpose.

The point in question, was the first projection that offered on that side of the lake, where a canoe, if set adrift with a southerly air would float clear of the land, and where it would be no great violation of probabilities to suppose it might even hit the castle; the latter lying above it, almost in a direct line with the wind. Such then was Hetty's intention, and she landed on the extremity of the gravelly point, beneath an overhanging oak, with the express intention of shoving the canoe off from the shore, in order that it might drift up towards her father's insulated abode. She knew, too, from the logs that occasionally floated about the lake, that did it miss the castle, and its appendages, the wind would be likely to change before the canoe could reach the northern extremity of the lake, and that Deerslayer might have an opportunity of regaining it, in the morning, when no doubt he would be earnestly sweeping the surface of the water, and the whole of its wooded shores, with the glass. In all this, too, Hetty was less governed by any chain of reasoning, than by her habits, the latter often supplying the defects of mind, in human beings, as they perform the same office for animals of the inferior classes.

The girl was quite an hour finding her way to the point, the distance and the obscurity equally detaining her, but she was no sooner on the gravelly beach, than she prepared to set the canoe adrift, in the manner mentioned. While in the act of pushing it from her, she heard low voices, that seemed to come from among the trees behind her. Startled at this unexpected danger, Hetty was on the point of springing into the canoe again, in order to seek safety in flight, when she thought she recognised the tones of Judith's melodious voice. Bending forward, so as to catch the sounds more directly, they evidently came from the water, and then she understood that the Ark was approaching from the south, and so close in with the western shore, as necessarily to cause it to pass the point, within twenty yards of the spot where she stood. Here, then, was all she could desire; the canoe was shoved off into the lake, leaving its late occupant alone on the narrow strand.

When this act of self-devotion was performed, Hetty did not retire. The foliage of the overhanging trees and bushes would have almost concealed her person, had there been light, but in that obscurity, it was utterly impossible to discover any object thus shaded, at the distance of a few feet. Flight, too, was perfectly easy, as twenty steps would effectually bury her in the forest. She remained, therefore, watching with intense anxiety the result of her expedient, intending to call the attention of the others to the canoe, with her voice, should they appear to pass without observing it. The Ark approached under its sail, again, Deerslayer standing in its bow, with Judith near him, and the Delaware at the helm. It would seem that, in the bay below, it had got too close to the shore, in the lingering hope of intercepting Hetty, for, as it came nearer, the latter distinctly heard the directions that the young man forward, gave to his companion aft, in order to clear the point.

"Lay her head more off the shore, Delaware," said Deerslayer for the third time, speaking in English that his fair companion might understand his words—"Lay her head well off shore. We have got embayed here, and needs keep the mast clear of the trees. Judith, there's a canoe!"

The last words were uttered with great earnestness, and Deerslayer's hand was on his rifle, ere they were fairly out of his mouth. But the truth flashed on the mind of the quickwitted girl, and she instantly told her companion that the boat *must* be that in which her sister had fled.

"Keep the scow straight, Delaware; steer as straight as your bullet flies when sent ag'in a buck—There,—I have it."

The canoe was seized, and immediately secured again to the side of the Ark. At the next moment the sail was lowered, and the motion of the Ark arrested, by means of the oars.

"Hetty!" called out Judith, concern, even affection betraying itself in her tones. "Are you within hearing, sister—for God's sake answer, and let me hear the sound of your voice, again! Hetty!—dear Hetty."

"I'm here, Judith—here on the shore, where it will be useless to follow me, as I will hide in the woods."

"Oh! Hetty what is't you do! Remember 'tis drawing near midnight, and that the woods are filled with savages and wild beasts!"

"Neither will harm a poor half-witted girl, Judith. God is as much with me, here, as he would be in the Ark or in the hut. I am going to help my father, and poor Hurry Harry, who will be tortured and slain, unless some one cares for them."

"We all care for them, and intend to-morrow to send them a flag of truce, to buy their ransom. Come back then, sister; trust to us, who have better heads than you, and who will do all we can for father."

"I know your head is better than mine, Judith, for mine is very weak, to be sure; but, I must go to father and poor Hurry. Do you and Deerslayer keep the castle, sister; leave me in the hands of God."

"God is with us all, Hetty—in the castle, or on the shore—father as well as ourselves, and it is sinful not to trust to his goodness. You can do nothing in the dark; will lose your way in the forest, and perish for want of food."

"God will not let that happen to a poor child that goes to serve her father, sister. I must try and find the savages."

"Come back for this night only; in the morning, we will put you ashore, and leave you to do as you may think right."

"You *say* so, Judith, and you *think* so; but you would not. Your heart would soften, and you'd see tomahawks and scalping knives, in the air. Besides, I've got a thing to tell the Indian chief that will answer all our wishes, and I'm afraid I may forget it, if I do'n't tell it to him at once. You'll see that he will let father go, as soon as he hears it!"

"Poor Hetty! What can *you* say to a ferocious savage that will be likely to change his bloody purpose!"

"That which will frighten him, and make him let father go—" returned the simple minded girl, positively. "You'll see, sister; you'll see, how soon it will bring him to, like a gentle child!"

"Will you tell *me*, Hetty, what you intend to say?" asked Deerslayer. "I know the savages well, and can form some idee how far fair words will be likely, or not, to work on their bloody natur's. If it's not suited to the gifts of a red skin, twill be of no use; for reason goes by gifts, as well as conduct."

"Well, then," answered Hetty, dropping her voice to a low, confidential, tone, for the stillness of the night, and the nearness of the Ark, permitted her to do this, and still to be heard—"Well, then, Deerslayer, as you seem a good and honest young man I will tell *you*. I mean not to say a word to any of the savages until I get face to face with their head chief, let them plague me with as many questions as they please— no—I'll answer none of them, unless it be to tell them to lead me to their wisest man—Then, Deerslayer, I'll tell him that God will not forgive murder, and thefts; and that if father and Hurry did go after the scalps of the Iroquois, he must return good for evil, for so the bible commands, else he will go into everlasting punishment. When he hears this, and feels it to be true, as feel it he must, how long will it be before he sends father, and Hurry, and me to the shore, opposite the castle, telling us all three to go our way in peace?"

The last questionwas put in a triumphant manner, and then the simple minded girl laughed at the impression she never doubted that her project had made on her auditors. Deerslayer was dumb-founded at this proof of guileless feebleness of mind, but Judith had suddenly bethought her of a means of counteracting this wild project, by acting on the very feelings that had given it birth. Without adverting to the closing question, or the laugh, therefore, she hurriedly called to her sister by name, as one suddenly impressed with the importance of what she had to say. But no answer was given to the call.

By the snapping of twigs, and the rustling of leaves, Hetty had evidently quitted the shore, and was already burying herself in the forest. To follow would have been bootless, since the darkness, as well as the dense cover that the woods every where offered, would have rendered her capture next to impossible, and there was also the never ceasing danger of falling into the hands of their enemies. After a short and melancholy discussion, therefore, the sail was again set, and the Ark pursued its course towards its habitual moorings, Deerslayer silently felicitating himself on the recovery of the canoe, and brooding over his plans for the morrow. The wind rose as the party quitted the point, and in less than an hour they reached the castle. Here all was found, as it had been left, and the reverse of the ceremonies had to be taken, in entering the building, that had been used on quitting it. Judith occupied a solitary bed that night, bedewing the pillow with her tears, as she thought of the innocent and hitherto neglected creature, who had been her companion, from childhood, and bitter regrets came over her mind, from more causes than one, as the weary hours passed away, making it nearly morning before she lost her recollection in sleep. Deerslayer and the Delaware took their rest in the Ark, where we shall leave them enjoying the deep sleep of the honest, the healthful and fearless, to return to the girl we have last seen in the midst of the forest.

When Hetty left the shore, she took her way unhesitatingly into the woods, with a nervous apprehension of being followed. Luckily, this course was the best she could have hit on to effect her own purpose, since it was the only one that led her from

the point. The night was so intensely dark, beneath the branches of the trees, that her progress was very slow, and the
direction she went altogether a matter of chance, after the first
few yards. The formation of the ground, however, did not permit her to deviate far from the line in which she desired to proceed. On one hand it was soon bounded by the acclivity of the
hill, while the lake, on the other, served as a guide. For two
hours did this single-hearted and simple-minded girl toil
through the mazes of the forest, sometimes finding herself on
the brow of the bank that bounded the water, and at others
struggling up an ascent that warned her to go no farther in that
direction, since it necessarily ran at right angles to the course
on which she wished to proceed. Her feet often slid from
beneath her, and she got many falls, though none to do her injury; but, by the end of the period mentioned, she had become
so weary as to want strength to go any farther. Rest was indispensable, and she set about preparing a bed, with the
readiness and coolness of one to whom the wilderness
presented no unnecessary terrors. She knew that wild beasts
roamed through all the adjacent forest, but animals that
preyed on the human species were rare, and of dangerous
serpents there were literally none. These facts had been taught
her by her father, and whatever her feeble mind received at all,
it received so confidingly as to leave her no uneasiness from
any doubts, or scepticism. To her the sublimity of the solitude
in which she was placed, was soothing, rather than appalling,
and she gathered a bed of leaves, with as much indifference to
the circumstances that would have driven the thoughts of sleep
entirely from the minds of most of her sex, as if she had been
preparing her place of nightly rest, beneath the paternal roof.

As soon as Hetty had collected a sufficient number of the
dried leaves to protect her person from the damps of the
ground, she kneeled beside the humble pile, clasped her raised
hands in an attitude of deep devotion, and in a soft, low, but
audible voice repeated the Lord's Prayer. This was followed
by those simple and devout verses, so familiar to children, in
which she recommended her soul to God, should it be called
away to another state of existence, ere the return of morning.
This duty done, she lay down and disposed herself to sleep.
The attire of the girl, though suited to the season, was suffi-

ciently warm for all ordinary purposes, but the forest is ever cool, and the nights of that elevated region of country, have always a freshness about them, that renders clothing more necessary than is commonly the case in the summers of a low latitude. This had been foreseen by Hetty, who had brought with her, a coarse heavy mantle, which, when laid over her body, answered all the useful purposes of a blanket. Thus protected, she dropped asleep, in a few minutes, as tranquilly as if watched over by the guardian care of that mother, who had so recently been taken from her forever, affording in this particular, a most striking contrast between her own humble couch, and the sleepless pillow of her sister.

Hour passed after hour, in a tranquility as undisturbed and a rest as sweet, as if angels, expressly commissioned for that object, watched around the bed of Hetty Hutter. Not once did her soft eyes open, until the grey of the dawn came struggling through the tops of the trees, falling on their lids, and, united to the freshness of a summer's morning, giving the usual summons to awake. Ordinarily, Hetty was up ere the rays of the sun tipped the summits of the mountains, but on this occasion her fatigue had been so great, and her rest was so profound, that the customary warnings failed of their effect. The girl murmured in her sleep, threw an arm forward, smiled as gently as an infant in its cradle, but still slumbered. In making this unconscious gesture, her hand fell on some object that was warm, and in the half unconscious state in which she lay, she connected the circumstance with her habits. At the next moment, a rude attack was made on her side, as if a rooting animal were thrusting its snout beneath, with a desire to force her position, and then, uttering the name of "Judith" she awoke. As the startled girl arose to a sitting attitude she perceived that some dark object sprang from her, scattering the leaves and snaping the fallen twigs in its haste. Opening her eyes, and recovering from the first confusion and astonishment of her situation, Hetty perceived a cub, of the common American brown bear, balancing itself on its hinder legs, and still looking towards her, as if doubtful whether it would be safe to trust itself near her person again. The first impulse of Hetty, who had been mistress of several of these cubs, was to run and seize the little creature as a prize, but a loud growl warned her of the danger of such a procedure. Recoiling a few steps, the girl looked hurriedly round, and perceived the dam, watching her movements, with fiery eyes, at no great distance. A hollow tree, that had once been the home of bees, having recently fallen, the mother with two more cubs, was feasting on the dainty food that this accident had placed within her reach; while the first kept a jealous eye on the situation of its truant and reckless young.

It would exceed all the means of human knowledge to pretend to analyze the influences that govern the acts of the lower animals. On this occasion, the dam, though proverbially fierce when its young is thought to be in danger, manifested no intention to attack the girl. It quitted the honey, and advanced to a place within twenty feet of her, where it raised itself on its hind legs, and balanced its body in a sort of angry, growling discontent, but approached no nearer. Happily, Hetty did not fly. On the contrary, though not without terror, she knelt with her face towards the animal, and with clasped hands and uplifted eyes, repeated the prayer of the previous night. This act of devotion was not the result of alarm, but it was a duty she never neglected to perform ere she slept, and when the return of consciousness awoke her to the business of the day. As the girl arose from her knees, the bear dropped on its feet again, and collecting its cubs around her, permitted them to draw their natural sustenance. Hetty was delighted with this proof of tenderness in an animal that has but a very indifferent reputation for the gentler feelings, and as a cub would quit its mother to frisk and leap about in wantonness, she felt a strong desire again to catch it up in her arms, and play with it. But admonished by the growl, she had self command sufficient not to put this dangerous project in execution, and recollecting her errand among the hills, she tore herself away from the group, and proceeded on her course, along the margin of the lake, of which she now caught glimpses again through the trees. To her surprise, though not to her alarm, the family of bears arose and followed her steps, keeping a short distance behind her; apparently watching every movement as if they had a near interest in all she did.

In this manner, escorted by the dam and cubs, the girl proceeded nearly a mile, thrice the distance she had been able to achieve in the darkness, during the same period of time. She then reached a brook that had dug a channel for itself into the earth, and went brawling into the lake, between steep and high banks, covered with trees. Here, Hetty performed her ablutions; then drinking of the pure mountain water, she went her way, refreshed and lighter of heart, still attended by her singular companions. Her course now lay along a broad and nearly level terrace, which stretched from the top of the bank that bounded the water, to a low acclivity that rose to a second and irregular platform above. This was at a part of the valley where the mountains ran obliquely, forming the commencement of a plain that spread between the hills, southward of the sheet of water. Hetty knew, by this circumstance, that she was getting near to the encampment, and had she not, the bears would have given her warning of the vicinity of human beings. Snuffing the air, the dam refused to follow any further, though the girl looked back and invited her to come by childish signs, and even by direct appeals made in her own sweet voice. It was while making her way slowly through some bushes, in this manner, with averted face and eyes riveted on the immovable animals, that the girl suddenly found her steps arrested by a human hand, that was laid lightly on her shoulder.

"Where go? — " said a soft female voice, speaking hurriedly, and in concern. "Indian — red-man — savage — wicked warrior — thataway."

This unexpected salutation alarmed the girl no more than the presence of the fierce inhabitants of the woods. It took her a little by surprise, it is true, but she was in a measure prepared for some such meeting, and the creature who stopped her, was as little likely to excite terror as any who ever appeared in the guise of an Indian. It was a girl, not much older than herself, whose smile was sunny as Judith's in her brightest moments, whose voice was melody itself, and whose accents and manner had all the rebuked gentleness that characterizes the sex among a people, who habitually treat their women as the attendants and servitors of the warriors. Beauty among the women of the aboriginal Americans, before they have become exposed to the hardships of wives and mothers, is by no means uncommon. In this particular, the original owners of the country were not unlike their more civilized successors, *nature* ap-

pearing to have bestowed that delicacy of mien and outline
that forms so great a charm in the youthful female, but of
which they are so early deprived; and that, too, as much by the
habits of domestic life, as from any other cause.

The girl who had so suddenly arrested the steps of Hetty was
dressed in a calico mantle that effectually protected all the upper part of her person, while a short petticoat of blue cloth edged
with gold lace, that fell no lower than her knees, leggings of the
same, and moccasins of deer-skin, completed her attire. Her
hair fell in long dark braids down her shoulders and back, and
was parted above a low smooth forehead, in a way to soften the
expression of eyes that were full of archness and natural feeling. Her face was oval, with delicate features, the teeth were
even and white, while the mouth expressed a melancholy
tenderness, as if it wore this peculiar meaning in intuitive
perception of the fate of a being who was doomed from birth to
endure a woman's sufferings, relieved by a woman's affections.
Her voice, as has been already intimated, was soft as the
sighing of the night air, a characteristic of the females of her
race, but which was so conspicuous in herself as to have produced for her the name of Wah-ta!-Wah; which rendered into
English means Hist-oh!-Hist.

In a word, this was the betrothed of Chingachgook, who
having succeeded in lulling their suspicions, was permitted to
wander around the encampment of her captors. This indulgence was in accordance with the general policy of the red
man, who well knew, moreover, that her trail could have been
easily followed in the event of flight. It will also be
remembered that the Iroquois, or Hurons, as it would be better to call them, were entirely ignorant of the proximity of her
lover, a fact, indeed, that she did not know herself.

It is not easy to say which manifested the most self-
possession at this unexpected meeting; the pale face, or the
red-girl. But, though a little surprised, Wah-ta!-Wah was the
most willing to speak, and far the readier in foreseeing consequences, as well as in devising means to avert them. Her
father, during her childhood, had been much employed as a
warrior by the authorities of the Colony, and dwelling for
several years near the forts, she had caught a knowledge of the
English tongue, which she spoke in the usual, abbreviated

manner of an Indian, but fluently, and without any of the ordinary reluctance of her people.

"Where go? —" repeated Wah-ta!-Wah, returning the smile of Hetty, in her own gentle, winning, manner —"*wicked* warrior that-a-way —*good* warrior, far off."

"What's your name?" asked Hetty, with the simplicity of a child.

"Wah-ta!-Wah. I no Mingo—good Delaware—Yengeese friend. Mingo cruel, and love scalp, for blood—Delaware love him, for honor. Come here, where no eyes."

Wah-ta!-Wah now led her companion towards the lake, descending the bank so as to place its overhanging trees and bushes between them, and any probable observers. Nor did she stop until they were both seated, side by side, on a fallen log, one end of which actually lay buried in the water.

"*Why* you come for?" the young Indian eagerly inquired—"*Where* you come for?"

Hetty told her tale in her own simple and truth-loving manner. She explained the situation of her father, and stated her desire to serve him, and if possible to procure his release.

"Why your fader come to Mingo 'camp in night?" asked the Indian girl, with a directness, which if not borrowed from the other, partook largely of its sincerity. "He know it war-time, and he no boy—he no want beard—no want to be told Iroquois carry tomahawk, and knife, and rifle. Why he come night time, seize *me* by hair, and try to scalp, Delaware girl?"

"You!" said Hetty, almost sickening with horror—"Did he seize *you*—did he try to scalp *you*?"

"Why no? Delaware scalp sell for much as Mingo scalp. Governor no tell difference. Wicked t'ing for pale face to scalp. No his gifts, as the good Deerslayer alway tell me."

"And do *you* know the Deerslayer?" said Hetty, coloring with delight and surprise; forgetting her regrets, at the moment, in the influence of this new feeling. "I know him, too. He is now in the Ark, with Judith and a Delaware who is called the Big Serpent. A bold and handsome warrior is this Serpent, too!"

Spite of the rich deep colour that nature had bestowed on the Indian beauty, the tell-tale blood deepened on her cheeks, until the blush gave new animation and intelligence to her jet-black eyes. Raising a finger in an attitude of warning, she dropped her voice, already so soft and sweet, nearly to a whisper, as she continued the discourse.

"Chingachgook!" returned the Delaware girl, sighing out the harsh name, in sounds so softly guttural, as to cause it to reach the ear in melody — "His father, Uncas — great chief of the Mahicanni — next to old Tamenund! — More as warrior, not so much gray hair, and less at Council Fire. *You* know Serpent?"

"He joined us last evening, and was in the Ark with me, for two or three hours before I left it. I'm afraid, Hist —" Hetty could not pronounce the Indian name of her new friend, but having heard Deerslayer give her this familiar appellation, she used it without any of the ceremony of civilized life — "I'm afraid Hist, he has come after scalps, as well as my poor father and Hurry Harry."

"Why he should'n't — ha? Chingachgook red warrior — very red — scalp make his honor — Be sure he take him."

"Then," said Hetty, earnestly, "he will be as wicked as any other. God will not pardon in a red-man, what he will not pardon in a white man."

"No true —" returned the Delaware girl, with a warmth, that nearly amounted to passion. "No true, I tell you! The Manitou smile and pleased when he see young warrior come back from the war path, with two, ten, hundred scalp on a pole! Chingachgook father take scalp — grandfather take scalp — all old chief take scalp, and Chingachgook take as many scalp as he can carry, himself!"

"Then, Hist, his sleep, of nights, must be terrible to think of! No one can be cruel, and hope to be forgiven."

"No cruel — plenty forgiven —" returned Wah-ta!-Wah, stamping her little foot on the stony strand, and shaking her head in a way to show how completely feminine feeling, in one of its aspects, had gotten the better of feminine feeling in another. "I tell you, Serpent brave; he go home, this time, with four, — yes — *two* scalp."

"And is that his errand, here? — Did he really come all this distance, across mountain, and valley, rivers and lakes, to torment his fellow creatures, and do so wicked a thing?"

This question at once appeased the growing ire of the half-offended Indian beauty. It completely got the better of the prejudices of education, and turned all her thoughts to a gentler and more feminine channel. At first, she looked around her, suspiciously, as if distrusting eaves-droppers; then she gazed wistfully into the face of her attentive companion; after which this exhibition of girlish coquetry and womanly feeling, terminated by her covering her face with both her hands, and laughing in a strain that might well be termed the melody of the woods. Dread of discovery, however, soon put a stop to this *naïve* exhibition of feeling, and removing her hands, this creature of impulses, gazed again wistfully into the face of her companion, as if inquiring how far she might trust a stranger with her secret. Although Hetty had no claims to her sister's extraordinary beauty, many thought her countenance the most winning of the two. It expressed all the undisguised sincerity of her character, and it was totally free from any of the unpleasant physical accompaniments, that so frequently attend mental imbecility. It is true that one accustomed to closer observations than common, might have detected the proofs of her feebleness of intellect in the language of her sometimes vacant eyes, but they were signs that attracted sympathy by their total want of guile, rather than by any other feeling. The effect on Hist, to use the English and more familiar translation of the name, was favorable, and yielding to an impulse of tenderness, she threw her arms around Hetty, and embraced her with an outpouring emotion, so natural that it was only equalled by its warmth.

"*You* good—" whispered the young Indian—"you good, I know; it so long since Wah-ta!-Wah have a friend—a sister—any body to speak her heart to! You Hist friend; do'n't I say trut'?"

"I never had a friend," answered Hetty, returning the warm embrace with unfeigned earnestness. "I've a sister, but no friend. Judith loves me, and I love Judith; but that's natural, and as we are taught in the bible—but I *should* like to have a *friend!* I'll be your friend, with all my heart, for I like your voice and your smile, and your way of thinking in every thing, except about the scalps—"

"No t'ink more of him—no say more of scalp—" interrupted Hist, soothingly—"You pale face, I red skin; we bring up different fashion. Deerslayer and Chingachgook great friend, and no the same colour, Hist and — what your name, pretty pale face?"

"I am called Hetty, though when they spell the name in the bible, they always spell it, Esther."

"What that make? — no good, no harm. No need to spell name at all — Moravian try to make Wah-ta!-Wah spell, but no won't let him. No good for Delaware girl to know too much — know more than warrior some time; that great shame. My name Wah-ta!-Wah — that say Hist in your tongue; you call him, Hist — I call him, Hetty."

These preliminaries settled to their mutual satisfaction, the two girls began to discourse of their several hopes and projects. Hetty made her new friend more fully acquainted with her intentions in behalf of her father, and, to one in the least addicted to prying into the affairs, Hist would have betrayed her own feelings and expectations in connection with the young warrior of her own tribe. Enough was revealed on both sides, however, to let each party get a tolerable insight into the views of the other, though enough still remained in mental reservation, to give rise to the following questions and answers, with which the interview in effect closed. As the quickest witted, Hist was the first with her interrogatories. Folding an arm about the waist of Hetty, she bent her head so as to look up playfully into the face of the other, and, laughing, as if her meaning were to be extracted from her looks, she spoke more plainly.

"Hetty got broder, as well as fader? — " she said — "Why no talk of broder, as well as fader?"

"I have no brother, Hist. I had one once, they say, but he is dead many a year, and lies buried in the lake, by the side of my mother."

"No got broder — got a young warrior — Love him, almost as much as fader, eh? Very handsome, and brave-looking; fit to be chief, if he *good* as he *seem* to be."

"It's wicked to love any man as well as I love my father, and so I strive not to do it, Hist," returned the conscientious Hetty, who knew not how to conceal an emotion, by an approach to an untruth as venial as an evasion, though powerfully tempted by female shame to err, "though I sometimes think wickedness will get the better of me, if Hurry comes so often to the lake. I *must* tell you the truth, dear Hist, because you ask me, but I should fall down and die in the woods, if he knew it!"

"Why he no ask you, himself? — Brave looking — why not bold speaking? Young warrior ought to ask young girl, no make young girl speak first. Mingo girls too shame for *that*."

This was said indignantly, and with the generous warmth a young female of spirit would be apt to feel, at what she deemed an invasion of her sex's most valued privilege. It had little influence on the simple-minded, but also just-minded Hetty, who, though inherently feminine in all her impulses, was much more alive to the workings of her own heart, than to any of the usages with which convention has protected the sensitiveness of her sex.

"Ask me *what?*" the startled girl demanded, with a suddenness that proved how completely her fears had been aroused. "Ask me, if I like him as well as I do my own father! Oh! I hope he will never put such a question to *me*, for I should have to answer, and that would *kill* me!"

"No — no — no kill, *quite* — almost," returned the other, laughing in spite of herself. "Make blush come — make shame come, too: but he no stay great while; then feel happier than ever. Young warrior must tell young girl he want to make wife, else never can live in his wigwam."

"Hurry do'n't want to marry me — No body will ever want to marry me, Hist."

"How you can know? P'raps every body want to marry you, and by-and-bye, tongue say what heart feel. Why nobody want to marry you?"

"I am not full witted, they say. Father often tells me this; and so does Judith, sometimes, when she is vexed; but I should'n't so much mind them, as I did mother. *She* said so *once*; and then she cried as if her heart would break; and, so, I *know* I'm not full witted."

Hist gazed at the gentle, simple, girl, for quite a minute without speaking, and then the truth appeared to flash all at once on the mind of the young Indian maid. Pity, reverence and tenderness seemed struggling together in her breast, and then rising, suddenly, she indicated a wish to her companion that she would accompany her to the camp, which was situated at no great distance. This unexpected change from the precautions that Hist had previously manifested a desire to use, in order to prevent being seen, to an open exposure of the person of her friend, arose from the perfect conviction that no Indian would harm a being whom the Great Spirit had disarmed, by depriving it of its strongest defence, reason. In this respect, nearly all unsophisticated nations resemble each other, appearing to offer spontaneously, by a feeling creditable to human nature, that protection by their own forbearance, which has been withheld by the inscrutable wisdom of Providence. Wah-ta!-Wah, indeed, knew that, in many tribes, the mentally imbecile and the mad, were held in a species of religious reverence, receiving from these untutored inhabitants of the forest respect and honors, instead of the contumely and neglect that it is their fortune to meet with, among the more pretending and sophisticated.

Hetty accompanied her new friend without apprehension, or reluctance. It was her wish to reach the camp, and, sustained by her motives, she felt no more concern for the consequences, than did her companion herself, now the latter was apprized of the character of the protection that the pale face maiden carried with her. Still, as they proceeded slowly along a shore that was tangled with overhanging bushes, Hetty continued the discourse, assuming the office of interrogating, which the other had instantly dropped, as soon as she ascertained the character of the mind to which her questions had been addressed.

"But *you* are not half-witted," said Hetty, and there's no reason why the Serpent should not marry *you*."

"Hist prisoner, and Mingo got big ear. No speak of Chingachgook when they by. Promise Hist that, good Hetty."

"I know — I know — " returned Hetty, half-whispering, in her eagerness to let the other see she understood the necessity of caution. "I know — Deerslayer and the Serpent mean to get you away from the Iroquois, and you wish me not to tell the secret."

"How you know?" said Hist, hastily, vexed at the moment, that the other was not even more feeble minded than was actually the case. "How you know? Better not talk of any but fader and Hurry — Mingo understand *dat*; he no understand *t'udder*. Promise you no talk about what you no understand."

"But I *do* understand this, Hist, and so I *must* talk about it. Deerslayer as good as told father all about it, in my presence, and as nobody told me not to listen, I overheard it all, as I did Hurry and father's discourse about the scalps."

"Very bad for pale faces to talk about scalps, and very bad for young woman to hear! Now you love Hist, I know, Hetty, and so, among Injins, when love hardest never talk most."

"That's not the way among white people, who talk most about them they love best. I suppose it's because I'm only half-witted that I do'n't see the reason why it should be so different among red people."

"That what Deerslayer call gift. One gift to talk; t'udder gift to hold tongue. Hold tongue your gift, among Mingos. If Sarpent want to see Hist, so Hetty want to see Hurry. Good girl never tell secret of friend."

Hetty understood this appeal, and she promised the Delaware girl not to make any allusion to the presence of Chingachgook, or to the motive of his visit to the lake.

"Maybe he get off Hurry and fader, as well as Hist, if let him have his way," whispered Wah-ta!-Wah to her companion, in a confiding flattering way, just as they got near enough to the encampment to hear the voices of several of their own sex, who were apparently occupied in the usual toils of women of their class. "T'ink of dat, Hetty, and put two, twenty finger on mouth. No get friend free without Sarpent do it."

A better expedient could not have been adopted, to secure the silence and discretion of Hetty, than that which was now presented to her mind. As the liberation of her father and the young frontier man was the great object of her adventure, she felt the connection between it and the services of the Delaware, and with an innocent laugh, she nodded her head, and in the same suppressed manner, promised a due attention to the wishes of her friend. Thus assured, Hist tarried no longer, but immediately and openly led the way into the encampment of her captors.

Chapter XI.

—"The great King of Kings
Hath in the table of his law commanded,
That thou shalt do no murder.
Take heed; for he holds vengeance in his hand,
To hurl upon their heads that break his law."
Richard III, I.iv.195-97; 199-200.

THAT the party to which Hist compulsorily belonged was not one that was regularly on the war path, was evident by the presence of females. It was a small fragment of a tribe that had been hunting and fishing within the English limits, where it was found by the commencement of hostilities, and, after passing the winter and spring by living on what was strictly the property of its enemies, it chose to strike a hostile blow before it finally retired. There was also deep Indian sagacity in the manoeuvre which had led them so far into the territory of their foes. When the runner arrived who announced the breaking out of hostilities between the English and French—a struggle that was certain to carry with it all the tribes that dwelt within the influence of the respective belligerents—this particular party of the Iroquois were posted on the shores of the Oneida, a lake that lies some fifty miles nearer to their own frontier than that which is the scene of our tale. To have fled in a direct line for the Canadas would have exposed them to the dangers of a direct pursuit, and the chiefs had determined to adopt the expedient of penetrating deeper into a region that had now become dangerous, in the hope of being able to retire in the rear of their pursuers, instead of having them on their trail. The presence of the women had induced the attempt at this *ruse*, the strength of these feebler members of the party being unequal to the effort of escaping from the pursuit of warriors. When the reader remembers the vast extent of the American wilderness, at that early day, he will perceive that it was possible for even a tribe to remain months undiscovered in particular portions of it; nor was the danger of encountering a foe, the usual precautions being observed, as great in the woods, as it is on the high seas, in a time of active warfare.

The encampment being temporary, it offered to the eye no more than the rude protection of a bivouac, relieved in some slight degree by the ingenious expedients which suggested themselves to the readiness of those who passed their lives amid similar scenes. One fire, that had been kindled against the roots of a living oak, sufficed for the whole party; the weather being too mild to require it for any purpose but cooking. Scattered around this centre of attraction, were some fifteen or twenty low huts, or perhaps kennels would be a better word, into which their different owners crept at night, and which were also intended to meet the exigencies of a storm. These little huts were made of the branches of trees, put together with some ingenuity, and they were uniformly topped with bark that had been stripped from fallen trees; of which every virgin forest possesses hundreds, in all stages of decay. Of furniture they had next to none. Cooking utensils of the simplest sort were lying near the fire, a few articles of clothing were to be seen in, or around the huts, rifles, horns, and pouches leaned against the trees, or were suspended from the lower branches, and the carcases of two or three deer were stretched to view on the same natural shambles.

As the encampment was in the midst of a dense wood, the eye could not take in its *tout ensemble* at a glance, but hut after hut started out of the gloomy picture, as one gazed about him in quest of objects. There was no centre, unless the fire might be so considered, no open area where the possessors of this rude village might congregate, but all was dark, covert and cunning, like its owners. A few children strayed, from hut to hut, giving the spot a little of the air of domestic life, and the suppressed laugh, and low voices of the women occasionally broke in upon the deep stillness of the sombre forest. As for the men, they either ate, slept, or examined their arms. They conversed but little, and then usually apart, or in groups withdrawn from the females, whilst an air of untiring, innate, watchfulness and apprehension of danger seemed to be blended even with their slumbers.

As the two girls came near the encampment, Hetty uttered a slight exclamation, on catching a view of the person of her father. He was seated on the ground, with his back to a tree, and Hurry stood near him, indolently whittling a twig. Apparently they were as much at liberty as any others in, or about the camp, and one unaccustomed to Indian usages would have mistaken them for visiters, instead of supposing them to be captives. Wah-ta!-Wah led her new friend quite near them, and then modestly withdrew, that her own presence might be no restraint on her feelings. But Hetty was not sufficiently familiar with caresses, or outward demonstrations of fondness, to indulge in any outbreaking of feeling. She merely approached and stood at her father's side without speaking, resembling a silent statue of filial affection. The old man expressed neither alarm, nor surprise, at her sudden appearance. In these particulars, he had caught the stoicism of the Indians, well knowing that there was no more certain mode of securing their respect than by imitating their self-command. Nor did the savages themselves betray the least sign of surprise at this sudden appearance of a stranger among them. In a word, this arrival produced much less visible sensation, though occurring under circumstances so peculiar, than would be seen in a village of higher pretensions to civilization, did an ordinary traveller drive up to the door of its principal inn. Still a few warriors collected, and it was evident by the manner in which they glanced at Hetty as they conversed together, that she was the subject of their discourse, and probable that the reasons of her unlooked-for appearance were matters of discussion. This phlegm of manner is characteristic of the North American Indian — some say of his white successor also — but, in this case much should be attributed to the peculiar situation in which the party was placed. The force in the Ark, the presence of Chingachgook excepted, was well known, no tribe or body of troops was believed to be near, and vigilant eyes were posted round the entire lake, watching, day and night, the slightest movement of those whom it would not be exaggerated now to term the besieged.

Hutter was inwardly much moved by the conduct of Hetty, though he affected so much indifference of manner. He recollected her gentle appeal to him, before he left the Ark, and misfortune rendered that of weight, which might have been forgotten amid the triumph of success. Then he knew the simple, single-hearted fidelity of his child, and understood why she had come, and the total disregard of self that reigned in all her acts.

"This is not well, Hetty," he said, deprecating the consequences to the girl herself, more than any other evil. "These are fierce Iroquois, and are as little apt to forget an injury, as a favor."

"Tell me, father—" returned the girl, looking furtively about her, as if fearful of being overheard, "did God let you do the cruel errand on which you came? I want much to know this, that I may speak to the Indians plainly, if he did not."

"You should not have come hither, Hetty; these brutes will not understand your nature, or your intentions!"

"How was it, father; neither you, nor Hurry, seems to have any thing that looks like scalps."

"If that will set your mind at peace, child, I can answer you, no. I had caught the young creatur' who came here with you, but her screeches soon brought down upon me a troop of the wild cats, that was too much for any single christian to withstand. If that will do you any good, we are as innocent of having taken a scalp, this time, as I make no doubt we shall also be innocent of receiving the bounty."

"Thank god for that, father! Now I can speak boldly to the Iroquois, and with an easy conscience. I hope Hurry, too, has not been able to harm any of the Indians?"

"Why, as to that matter, Hetty," returned the individual in question, "you've put it pretty much in the natyve character of the religious truth. Hurry has not been *able*, and that is the long and short of it. I've seen many squalls, old fellow, both on land and on the water, but never did I feel one as lively and as snappish as that which come down upon us, night afore last, in the shape of an Indian hurrah-boys! Why, Hetty, you're no great matter at a reason, or an idee that lies a little deeper than common, but you're human, and have some human notions— now, I'll just ask you to look at them circumstances. Here was old Tom, your father, and myself, bent on a legal operation, as is to be seen in the words of the law and the proclomation; thinking no harm; when we were set upon by critturs that were more like a pack of hungry wolves, than mortal savages even, and there they had us tethered like two sheep, in less time than it has taken me to tell you the story."

"You are free, now, Hurry," returned Hetty, glancing timidly at the fine unfettered limbs of the young giant—"You have no cords, or withes, to pain your arms, or legs, now."

"Not I, Hetty. Natur' is natur', and freedom is natur', too. My limbs have a free look, but that's pretty much the amount of it, sin' I can't use them in the way I should like. Even these trees have eyes; ay, and tongues too; for was the old man, here, or I, to start one single rod beyond our gaol limits, sarvice would be put on the bail afore we could 'gird up our loins' for a race, and, like as not, four or five rifle bullets would be travelling arter us, carrying so many invitations to curb our impatience. There is'n't a gaol in the colony as tight as this, we are now in; for I've tried the vartues of two or three on 'em, and I know the mater'als they are made of, as well as the men that made 'em; takin' down being the next step in schoolin', to puttin' up, in all such fabrications."

Lest the reader should get an exaggerated opinion of Hurry's demerits, from this boastful and indiscreet revelation, it may be well to say that his offences were confined to assaults and batteries, for several of which he had been imprisoned, when, as he has just said, he often escaped by demonstrating the flimsiness of the constructions in which he was confined, by opening for himself doors, in spots where the architects had neglected to place them. But Hetty had no knowledge of gaols, and little of the nature of crimes, beyond what her unadulterated and almost instinctive perceptions of right and wrong taught her, and this sally of the rude being who had spoken, was lost upon her. She understood his general meaning, however, and answered in reference to that alone.

"It's so best, Hurry," she said. "It is best father and you should be quiet and peaceable, 'till I have spoken to the Iroquois, when all will be well and happy. I do'n't wish either of you to follow, but leave me to myself. As soon as all is settled, and you are at liberty to go back to the castle, I will come and let you know it."

Hetty spoke with so much simple earnestness, seemed so confident of success, and wore so high an air of moral feeling and truth, that both the listeners felt more disposed to attach an importance to her mediation, than might otherwise have happened. When she manifested an intention to quit them, therefore, they offered no obstacle, though they saw she was about to join the group of chiefs who were consulting apart, seemingly on the manner and motive of her own sudden appearance.

When Hist—for so we love best, to call her—quitted her companion, she strayed near one or two of the elder warriors, who had shown her most kindness in her captivity, the principal man of whom, had even offered to adopt her as his child, if she would consent to become a Huron. In taking this direction, the shrewd girl did so to invite inquiry. She was too well trained in the habits of her people, to obtrude the opinions of one of her sex and years on men and warriors, but nature had furnished a tact and ingenuity that enabled her to attract the attention she desired, without wounding the pride of those to whom it was her duty to defer, and respect. Even her affected indifference stimulated curiosity, and Hetty had hardly reached the side of her father, before the Delaware girl was brought within the circle of the warriors, by a secret but significant gesture. Here she was questioned as to the person of her companion, and the motives that had brought her to the camp. This was all that Hist desired. She explained the manner in which she had detected the weakness of Hetty's reason, rather exaggerating than lessening the deficiency in her intellect, and then she related, in general terms, the object of the girl in venturing among her enemies. The effect was all that the speaker expected, her account investing the person and character of their visiter with a sacredness and respect, that she well knew would prove her protection. As soon as her own purpose was attained, Hist withdrew to a distance, where, with female consideration, and a sisterly tenderness she set about the preparation of a meal, to be offered to her new friend, as soon as the latter might be at liberty to partake of it. While thus occupied, however, the ready girl in no degree relaxed in her watchfulness, noting every change of countenance among the chiefs, every movement of Hetty's, and the smallest occurrence that could be likely to affect her own interests, or that of her new friend.

As Hetty approached the chiefs, they opened their little circle, with an ease and deference of manner, that would have done credit to men of more courtly origin. A fallen tree lay near, and the oldest of the warriors made a quiet sign for the girl to be seated on it, taking his place at her side, with the gentleness of a father. The others arranged themselves around the two, with grave dignity, and then the girl, who had sufficient observation to perceive that such a course was expected of her, began to reveal the object of her visit. The moment she opened her mouth to speak, however, the old chief gave a gentle sign for her to forbear, said a few words to one of his juniors, and then waited in silent patience until the latter had summoned Hist to the party. This interruption proceeded from the chief's having discovered that there existed a necessity for an interpreter, few of the Hurons present understanding the English language, and they but imperfectly.

Wah-ta!-Wah was not sorry to be called upon to be present at the interview, and least of all in the character in which she was now wanted. She was aware of the hazards she run in attempting to deceive one or two of the party, but was none the less resolved to use every means that offered, and to practice every artifice that an Indian education could supply, to conceal the facts of the vicinity of her betrothed, and of the errand on which he had come. One unpractised in the expedients and opinions of savage life, would not have suspected the readiness of invention, the wariness of action, the high resolution, the noble impulses, the deep self-devotion, and the feminine disregard of self when the affections were concerned, that lay concealed beneath the demure looks, the mild eyes, and the sunny smiles of this young Indian beauty. As she approached them, the grim old warriors regarded her with pleasure, for they had a secret pride in the hope of engrafting so rare a scion on the stock of their own nation; adoption being as regularly practised, and as distinctly recognized among the tribes of America, as it ever had been among those nations that submit to the sway of the Civil Law.

As soon as Hist was seated by the side of Hetty, the old chief desired her to ask "the fair young pale-face" what had brought her among the Iroquois, and what they could do to serve her.

"Tell them, Hist, who I am — Thomas Hutter's youngest

daughter; Thomas Hutter, the oldest of their two prisoners; he who owns the castle and the Ark, and who has the best right to be thought the owner of these hills, and that lake, since he has dwelt so long, and trapped so long, and fished so long, among them — They'll know whom you mean by Thomas Hutter, if you tell them, *that*. And then tell them that I've come here to convince them they ought not to harm father, and Hurry, but let them go, in peace, and to treat them as brethren, rather than as enemies. Now tell them all this plainly, Hist, and fear nothing for yourself, or me. God will protect us."

Wah-ta!-Wah did as the other desired, taking care to render the words of her friend as literally as possible into the Iroquois tongue, a language she used with a readiness almost equal to that with which she spoke her own. The chiefs heard this opening explanation, with grave decorum, the two who had a little knowledge of English, intimating their satisfaction with the interpreter, by furtive but significant glances of the eyes.

"And, now, Hist," continued Hetty, as soon as it was intimated to her that she might proceed, "and, now, Hist, I wish you to tell these red men, word for word, what I am about to say. Tell them first, that father and Hurry came here with an intention to take as many scalps as they could, for the wicked governor and the province have offered money for scalps, whether of warriors, or women, men or children, and the love of gold was too strong for their hearts to withstand it. Tell them this, dear Hist, just as you have heard it from me, word for word."

Wah-ta!-Wah hesitated about rendering this speech as literally as had been desired, but detecting the intelligence of those who understood English, and apprehending even a greater knowledge than they actually possessed she found herself compelled to comply. Contrary to what a civilized man would have expected, the admission of the motives and of the errands of their prisoners, produced no visible effect, on either the countenances or the feelings of the listeners. They probably considered the act meritorious, and that which neither of them would have hesitated to perform in his own person, he would not be apt to censure in another.

"And, now, Hist," resumed Hetty, as soon as she perceived

that her first speeches were understood by the chiefs, "you can tell them more. They know that father and Hurry did not succeed, and therefore they can bear them no grudge for any harm that has been done. If they had slain their children and wives, it would not alter the matter, and I'm not certain that what I am about to tell them would not have more weight had there been mischief done. But ask them first, Hist, if they know there is a God, who reigns over the whole earth, and is ruler and chief of all who live, let them be red, or white, or what color they may?"

Wah-ta!-Wah looked a little surprised at this question, for the idea of the Great Spirit is seldom long absent from the mind of an Indian girl. She put the question, as literally as possible, however, and received a grave answer in the affirmative.

"This is right," continued Hetty, "and my duty will now be light. This Great Spirit, as you call our God, has caused a book to be written, that we call a bible, and in this book have been set down all his commandments, and his holy will and pleasure, and the rules by which all men are to live, and directions how to govern the thoughts even, and the wishes, and the will. Here, this is one of these holy books, and you must tell the chiefs what I am about to read to them, from its sacred pages."

As Hetty concluded, she reverently unrolled a small English bible from its envelope of coarse calico, treating the volume with the sort of external respect that a Romanist would be apt to show to a religious relic. As she slowly proceeded in her task the grim warriors watched each movement with riveted eyes, and when they saw the little volume appear a slight expression of surprise escaped one or two of them. But Hetty held it out towards them, in triumph as if she expected the sight would produce a visible miracle, and then, without betraying either surprise or mortification at the Stoicism of the Indian, she turned eagerly to her new friend, in order to renew the discourse.

"This is the sacred volume, Hist," she said—"and these words, and lines, and verses, and chapters, all came from God."

"Why Great Spirit no send book to Injin, too?" demanded Hist, with the directness of a mind that was totally unsophisticated.

"Why?" answered Hetty, a little bewildered by a question so unexpected. "Why? — Ah! you know the Indians do'n't know how to read."

If Hist was not satisfied with this explanation, she did not deem the point of sufficient importance to be pressed. Simply bending her body, in a gentle admission of the truth of what she heard, she sat patiently awaiting the further arguments of the pale-face enthusiast.

"You can tell these chiefs that throughout this book, men are ordered to forgive their enemies; to treat them as they would brethren; and never to injure their fellow creatures, more especially on account of revenge, or any evil passions. Do you think you can tell them this, so that they will understand it, Hist?"

"Tell him well enough, but he no very easy to understand."

Hist then conveyed the ideas of Hetty, in the best manner she could, to the attentive Indians, who heard her words, with some such surprise as an American of our own times would be apt to betray at a suggestion that the great modern, but vacillating ruler of things human, public opinion, might be wrong. One or two of their number, however, having met with missionaries, said a few words in explanation, and then the group gave all its attention to the communications that were to follow. Before Hetty resumed she enquired earnestly of Hist if the chiefs had understood her, and receiving an evasive answer, was fain to be satisfied.

"I will now read to the warriors some of the verses that it is good for them to know," continued the girl, whose manner grew more solemn and earnest as she proceeded — "and they will remember that they are the very words of the Great Spirit. First, then, ye are commanded to '*love thy neighbor as thyself.*' Tell them *that*, dear Hist."

"Neighbor, for Injin, no mean pale face," answered the Delaware girl, with more decision than she had hitherto thought it necessary to use. "Neighbor mean Iroquois for Iroquois, Mohican for Mohican, Pale face for pale face. No need tell chief any thing else."

"You forget, Hist, these are the words of the Great Spirit, and the chiefs must obey them as well as others. Here is another commandment—'*Whosoever shall smite thee on the right cheek, turn to him the other also.*'"

"What that mean?" demanded Hist, with the quickness of lightning.

Hetty explained that it was an order not to resent injuries, but rather to submit to receive fresh wrongs from the offender.

"And hear this, too, Hist," she added. "'*Love your enemies, bless them that curse you, do good to them that hate you, and pray for them which despitefully use you and persecute you.*'"

By this time Hetty had become excited; her eye gleamed with the earnestness of her feelings, her cheeks flushed, and her voice, usually so low and modulated, became stronger and more impressive. With the bible she had been early made familiar by her mother, and she now turned from passage to passage, with surprising rapidity, taking care to cull such verses as taught the sublime lessons of christian charity and christian forgiveness. To translate half she said, in her pious earnestness, Wah-ta!-Wah would have found impracticable, had she made the effort, but wonder held her tongue tied, equally with the chiefs, and the young, simple-minded enthusiast had fairly become exhausted with her own efforts, before the other opened her mouth, again, to utter a syllable. Then, indeed, the Delaware girl gave a brief translation of the substance of what had been both read and said, confining herself to one or two of the more striking of the verses, those that had struck her own imagination as the most paradoxical, and which certainly would have been the most applicable to the case, could the uninstructed minds of the listeners embrace the great moral truths they conveyed.

It will be scarcely necessary to tell the reader the effect that such novel duties would be likely to produce among a group of Indian warriors, with whom it was a species of religious principle never to forget a benefit, or to forgive an injury. Fortunately, the previous explanations of Hist had prepared the minds of the Hurons for something extravagant, and most of that which to them seemed inconsistent and paradoxical, was accounted for by the fact that the speaker possessed a mind that was constituted differently from those of most of the human race. Still there were one or two old men who had heard similar doctrines from the missionaries, and these felt a desire to occupy an idle moment by pursuing a subject that they found so curious.

"This is the Good Book of the pale faces," observed one of these chiefs, taking the volume from the unresisting hands of Hetty, who gazed anxiously at his face, while he turned the leaves, as if she expected to witness some visible results from the circumstance. "This is the law by which my white brethren professes to live?"

Hist, to whom this question was addressed, if it might be considered as addressed to any one, in particular, answered simply in the affirmative; adding that both the French of the Canadas, and the Yengeese of the British provinces equally admitted its authority, and affected to revere its principles.

"Tell my young sister," said the Huron, looking directly at Hist, "that I will open my mouth and say a few words."

"The Iroquois chief go to speak — My pale face friend listen," said Hist.

"I rejoice to hear it!" exclaimed Hetty. "God has touched his heart, and he will now let father and Hurry go."

"This is the pale face law," resumed the chief. "It tells him to do good to them, that hurt him, and when his brother asks him for his rifle to give him the powder horn, too. Such is the pale face law?"

"Not so — not so —" answered Hetty earnestly, when these words had been interpreted — "There is not a word about rifles in the whole book, and powder and bullets give offence to the Great Spirit."

"Why then does the pale face use them? If he is ordered to *give* double to him that asks only for one thing, why does he *take* double from the poor Indian who ask for *no* thing. He comes from beyond the rising sun, with this book in his hand, and he teaches the red man to read it, but why does he forget himself all it says? When the Indian gives, he is never satisfied; and now he offers gold for the scalps of our women and children, though he calls us beasts if we take the scalp of a warrior killed in open war. My name is Rivenoak."

When Hetty had got this formidable question fairly presented to her mind in the translation, and Hist did her duty with more than usual readiness on this occasion, it scarcely need be said that she was sorely perplexed. Abler heads than that of this poor girl have frequently been puzzled by questions of a similar drift, and it is not surprising that with all her own earnestness and sincerity she did not know what answer to make.

"What shall I tell them, Hist," she asked imploringly — "I *know* that all I have read from the book is true, and yet it would'n't seem so, would it, by the conduct of those to whom the book was given?"

"Give 'em pale-face reason," returned Hist, ironically — "that always good for one side; though he bad for t'other."

"No — no — Hist there can't be two sides to truth — and yet it does seem strange! I'm certain I have read the verses right, and no one would be so wicked as to print the word of God wrong. *That* can never be, Hist."

"Well, to poor Injin girl, it seem every thing *can* be to pale faces," returned the other, coolly. "One time 'ey say white, and one time 'ey say black. Why *never can be?*"

Hetty was more and more embarrassed, until overcome with the apprehension that she had failed in her object, and that the lives of her father and Hurry would be the forfeit of some blunder of her own, she burst into tears. From that moment the manner of Hist lost all its irony and cool indifference, and she became the fond caressing friend, again. Throwing her arms around the afflicted girl, she attempted to soothe her sorrows, by the scarcely ever failing remedy of female sympathy.

"Stop cry — no cry — " she said, wiping the tears from the face of Hetty, as she would have performed the same office for a child, and stopping to press her occasionally to her own warm bosom with the affection of a sister. "Why you so trouble? You no make he book, if he be wrong, and you no make he pale face if he wicked. There wicked red man, and wicked white man — no colour all good — no colour all wicked. Chiefs know *that* well enough."

Hetty soon recovered from this sudden burst of grief, and then her mind reverted to the purpose of her visit, with all its single-hearted earnestness. Perceiving that the grim looking chiefs were still standing around her in grave attention, she hoped that another effort to convince them of the right might be successful.

"Listen, Hist," she said, struggling to suppress her sobs, and to speak distinctly — "Tell the chiefs that it matters not what the wicked do — right is right — The words of The Great Spirit are the words of The Great Spirit — and no one can go harmless for doing an evil act, because another has done it before him. '*Render good for evil*,' says this book, and that is the law for the red man as well as for the white man."

"Never hear such law among Delaware, or among Iroquois —" answered Hist soothingly. "No good to tell chiefs any such laws as *dat*. Tell 'em somet'ing they believe."

Hist was about to proceed, notwithstanding, when a tap on the shoulder, from the finger of the oldest chief caused her to look up. She then perceived that one of the warriors had left the group, and was already returning to it with Hutter and Hurry. Understanding that the two last were to become parties in the inquiry, she became mute, with the unhesitating obedience of an Indian woman. In a few seconds the prisoners stood face to face with the principal men of the captors.

"Daughter," said the senior chief to the young Delaware, "ask this grey beard why he came into our camp?"

The question was put by Hist, in her own imperfect English, but in a way that was easy to be understood. Hutter was too stern and obdurate by nature, to shrink from the consequences of any of his acts, and he was also too familiar with the opinions of the savages not to understand that nothing was to be gained by equivocation or an unmanly dread of their anger. Without hesitating, therefore, he avowed the purpose with which he had landed, merely justifying it by the fact that the government of the province had bid high for scalps. This frank avowal was received by the Iroquois, with evident satisfaction, not so much, however, on account of the advantage it gave them in a moral point of view, as by its proving that they had captured a man worthy of occupying their thoughts and of becoming a subject of their revenge. Hurry, when interrogated, confessed the truth, though he would have been more disposed to concealment than his sterner companion, did the circumstances very well admit of its adoption. But he had tact enough to discover that equivocation would be useless, at that moment, and he made a merit of necessity by imitating a frankness, which, in the case of Hutter, was the offspring of habits of indifference acting on a disposition that was always ruthless, and reckless of personal consequences.

As soon as the chiefs had received the answers to their questions, they walked away, in silence, like men who deemed the matter disposed of, all Hetty's dogmas being thrown away on beings trained in violence, from infancy to manhood. Hetty and Hist were now left alone with Hutter and Hurry, no visible restraint being placed on the movements of either; though all four, in fact, were vigilantly and unceasingly watched. As respects the men, care was had to prevent them from getting possession of any of the rifles, that lay scattered about, their own included; and there all open manifestations of watchfulness ceased. But they, who were so experienced in Indian practices, knew too well how great was the distance between appearances and reality, to become the dupes of this seeming carelessness. Although both thought incessantly of the means of escape, and this without concert, each was aware of the uselessness of attempting any project of the sort that was not deeply laid, and promptly executed. They had been long enough in the encampment, and were sufficiently observant to have ascertained that Hist, also, was a sort of captive, and, presuming on the circumstance, Hutter spoke in her presence, more openly than he might otherwise have thought it prudent to do; inducing Hurry to be equally unguarded by his example.

"I'll not blame you, Hetty, for coming on this errand, which was well meant if not very wisely planned," commenced the father, seating himself by the side of his daughter, and taking her hand; a sign of affection that this rude being was accustomed to manifest to this particular child. "But preaching, and the bible, are not the means to turn an Indian from his ways. Has Deerslayer sent any message; or has he any scheme by which he thinks to get us free?"

"Ay, that's the substance of it!" put in Hurry. "If you can help us, gal, to half a mile of freedom, or even a good start of a short quarter, I'll answer for the rest. Perhaps the old man may want a little more, but for one of my height and years *that* will meet all objections."

Hetty looked distressed, turning her eyes from one to the other, but she had no answer to give to the question of the reckless Hurry.

"Father," she said, "neither Deerslayer, nor Judith knew of my coming, until I had left the Ark. They are afraid the Iroquois will make a raft, and try to get off to the hut, and think more of defending *that*, than of coming to aid you."

"No — no — no —" said Hist hurriedly, though in a low voice, and with her face bent towards the earth, in order to conceal from those whom she knew to be watching them the fact of her speaking at all. "No — no — no — Deerslayer different man. He no t'ink of defending 'self, with friend in danger. Help one another, and all get to hut."

"This sounds well, old Tom," said Hurry, winking and laughing, though he too used the precaution to speak low — "Give me a ready witted squaw for a fri'nd, and though I'll not downright defy an Iroquois, I think I would defy the devil."

"No talk loud," said Hist. "Some Iroquois got Yengeese tongue, and all got Yengeese ear."

"Have we a friend in you, young woman?" enquired Hutter with an increasing interest in the conference. "If so, you may calculate on a solid reward, and nothing will be easier than to send you to your own tribe, if we can once fairly get you off with us to the castle. Give us the Ark and the canoes, and we can command the lake, spite of all the savages in the Canadas. Nothing but artillery could drive us out of the castle, if we can get back to it."

"'S'pose 'ey come ashore to take scalp?" retorted Hist, with cool irony, at which the girl appeared to be more expert than is common for her sex.

"Ay — ay — that was a mistake; but there is little use in lamentations, and less still, young woman, in flings."

"Father," said Hetty, "Judith thinks of breaking open the big chest, in hopes of finding something in *that* which may buy your freedom of the savages."

A dark look came over Hutter at the announcement of this fact, and he muttered his dissatisfaction in a way to render it intelligible enough.

"What for no break open chest?" put in Hist. "Life sweeter than old chest—scalp sweeter than old chest. If no tell darter to break him open, Wah-ta!-Wah no help him to run away."

"Ye know not what ye ask—ye are but silly girls, and the wisest way for ye both is to speak of what ye understand and to speak of nothing else. I little like this cold neglect of the savages, Hurry; it's a proof that they think of something serious, and if we are to do any thing, we must do it soon. Can we count on this young woman, think you?"

"Listen—" said Hist quickly, and with an earnestness that proved how much her feelings were concerned—"Wah-ta!-Wah no Iroquois—All over Delaware—got Delaware heart—Delaware feeling. She prisoner, too. One prisoner help t'udder prisoner. No good to talk more, now. Darter stay with fader—Wah-ta!-Wah come and see friend—all look right—*Then* tell what he do."

This was said in a low voice, but distinctly, and in a manner to make an impression. As soon as it was uttered the girl arose, and left the group, walking composedly towards the hut she occupied, as if she had no further interest in what might pass between the pale-faces.

Chapter XII.

"She speaks much of her father; says she hears,
There's tricks i' the world; and hems, and beats her breast;
Spurns enviously at straws; speaks things in doubt,
That carry but half sense; her speech is nothing,
Yet the unshaped use of it doth move
The hearers to collection; — "

Hamlet, IV.v.4–9.

Wᴇ left the occupants of the castle and the ark, buried in sleep. Once, or twice, in the course of the night, it is true, Deerslayer, or the Delaware, arose and looked out upon the tranquil lake; when, finding all safe, each returned to his pallet, and slept like a man who was not easily deprived of his natural rest. At the first signs of the dawn, the former arose, however, and made his personal arrangements for the day; though his companion, whose nights had not been tranquil, or without disturbances, of late, continued on his blanket, until the sun had fairly risen. Judith too, was later than common, that morning, for the earlier hours of the night had brought her little of either refreshment, or sleep. But ere the sun had shown himself over the eastern hills, these too were up and afoot, even the tardy in that region seldom remaining on their pallets, after the appearance of the great luminary.

Chingachgook was in the act of arranging his forest toilet, when Deerslayer entered the cabin of the Ark and threw him a few coarse but light summer vestments that belonged to Hutter. "Judith hath given me them for your use, chief," said the latter, as he cast the jacket and trousers at the feet of the Indian, "for it's ag'in all prudence and caution to be seen in your war dress and paint. Wash off all them fiery streaks from your cheeks, put on these garments, and here is a hat, such as it is, that will give you an awful oncivilized sort of civilization, as the missionaries call it. Remember that Hist is at hand, and what we do for the maiden, must be done while we are doing for others. I know it's ag'in your gifts and your natur' to wear clothes, unless they are cut and carried in a red man's fashion, but make a vartue of necessity, and put these on, at once, even if they do rise a little in your throat."

Chingachgook, or the Serpent, eyed the vestments with strong disgust; but he saw the usefulness of the disguise, if not its absolute necessity. Should the Iroquois discover a red-man, in or about the Castle, it might, indeed, place them more on their guard, and give their suspicions a direction towards their female captive. Any thing was better than a failure as it regarded his betrothed, and, after turning the different garments round and round, examining them with a species of grave irony, affecting to draw them on in a way that defeated itself, and otherwise manifesting the reluctance of a young savage to confine his limbs in the usual appliances of civilized life, the chief submitted to the directions of his companion, and finally stood forth, so far as the eye could detect, a red man in colour alone. Little was to be apprehended from this last peculiarity, however, the distance from the shore, and the want of glasses preventing any very close scrutiny, and Deerslayer, himself, though of a brighter and fresher tint, had a countenance that was burnt by the sun to a hue scarcely less red than that of his Mohican companion. The awkwardness of the Delaware in his new attire, caused his friend to smile, more than once that day, but he carefully abstained from the use of any of those jokes, which would have been bandied among white men on such an occasion, the habits of a chief, the dignity of a warrior on his first path, and the gravity of the circumstances in which they were placed, uniting to render so much levity out of season.

The meeting at the morning meal of the three islanders, if we may use the term, was silent, grave and thoughtful. Judith showed by her looks that she had passed an unquiet night, while the two men had the future before them, with its unseen and unknown events. A few words of courtesy passed between Deerslayer and the girl, in the course of the breakfast, but no allusion was made to their situation. At length Judith, whose heart was full, and whose novel feelings disposed her to entertain sentiments more gentle and tender than common, introduced the subject, and this in a way to show how much of her thoughts it had occupied, in the course of the last sleepless night.

"It would be dreadful, Deerslayer," the girl abruptly exclaimed, "should any thing serious befall my father and Hetty! We cannot remain quietly here, and leave them in the hands of the Iroquois, without bethinking us of some means of serving them."

"I'm ready, Judith, to sarve them, and all others who are in trouble, could the way to do it be p'inted out. It's no trifling matter to fall into red-skin hands, when men set out on an ar'n'd like that which took Hutter and Hurry ashore; that I know as well as another, and I would'n't wish my worst inimy in such a strait, much less them with whom I've journeyed, and eat, and slept. Have you any scheme, that you would like to have the Sarpent and me, indivour to carry out?"

"I know of no other means to release the prisoners, than by bribing the Iroquois. They are not proof against presents, and we might offer enough, perhaps, to make them think it better to carry away what to them will be rich gifts, than to carry away poor prisoners; if, indeed, they should carry them away at all!"

"This is well enough, Judith; yes, it's well enough, if the inimy is to be bought, and we can find articles to make the purchase with. Your father has a convenient lodge, and it is most cunningly placed, though it does'n't seem overstock'd with riches that will be likely to buy his ransom. There's the piece he calls Killdeer, might count for something, and I understand there's a keg of powder about, which might be a make weight, sartain; and yet two able bodied men are not to be bought off for a trifle—besides—"

"Besides what?" demanded Judith impatiently, observing that the other hesitated to proceed, probably from a reluctance to distress her.

"Why, Judith, the Frenchers offer bounties as well as our own side, and the price of two scalps would purchase a keg of powder, and a rifle; though I'll not say one of the latter altogether as good as Killdeer, there, which your father va'nts as oncommon, and onequalled, like. But fair powder, and a pretty sartain rifle; then the red men are not the expartest in fire arms, and do'n't always know the difference atwixt that which is ra'al, and that which is seeming."

"This is horrible!" muttered the girl, struck by the homely manner in which her companion was accustomed to state his facts. "But you overlook my own clothes, Deerslayer, and they, I think, might go far with the women of the Iroquois."

"No doubt they would; no doubt they would, Judith," returned the other, looking at her keenly, as if he would ascertain whether she were really capable of making such a sacrifice. "But, are you sartain, gal, you could find it in your heart, to part with your own finery for such a purpose? Many is the man who has thought he was valiant 'till danger stared him in the face; I've known them, too, that consaited they were kind and ready to give away all they had to the poor, when they've been listening to other people's hard heartedness; but whose fists have clench'd as tight as the riven hickory when it came to downright offerings of their own. Besides, Judith, you're handsome—oncommon in that way, one might obsarve and do no harm to the truth—and they that have beauty, like to have that which will adorn it. Are you sartain you could find it in your heart to part with your own finery?"

The soothing allusion to the personal charms of the girl, was well timed, to counteract the effect produced by the distrust that the young man expressed of Judith's devotion to her filial duties. Had another said as much as Deerslayer, the compliment would most probably have been overlooked in the indignation awakened by the doubts, but even the unpolished sincerity, that so often made this simple minded hunter bare his thoughts, had a charm for the girl; and, while she colored, and, for an instant her eyes flashed fire, she could not find it in her heart to be really angry with one whose very soul seemed truth and manly kindness. Look her reproaches she did, but conquering the desire to retort, she succeeded in answering in a mild and friendly manner.

"You must keep all your favorable opinions, for the Delaware girls, Deerslayer, if you seriously think thus of those of your own colour," she said, affecting to laugh. "But, *try* me; if you find that I regret either ribband or feather, silk or muslin, then may you think what you please of my heart, and say what you think."

"That's justice!—The rarest thing to find on 'arth, is a truly just man. So says Tamenund, the wisest prophet of the Delawares, and so all must think, that have occasion to see, and talk and act among mankind. I love a just man, Sarpent. His eyes are never covered with darkness towards his inimies, while they are all sunshine and brightness towards his fri'nds. He uses the reason that God has given him, and he uses it with a feelin' of his being ordered to look at, and to consider things as they *are*, and not as he *wants* them to be. It's easy enough to find men who *call* themselves just, but it's wonderful oncommon to find them that are the very thing, in fact. How often have I seen Indians, gal, who believed they were lookin' into a matter agreeable to the will of the Great Spirit, when, in truth, they were only striving to act up to their own will and pleasure, and this, half the time, with a temptation to go wrong that could no more be seen by themselves, than the stream that runs in the next valley, can be seen by us through yonder mountain; though any looker on might have discovered it, as plainly as we can discover the parch that are swimming around this hut!"

"Very true, Deerslayer," rejoined Judith, losing every trace of displeasure in a bright smile—"very true, and I hope to see you act on this love of justice, in all matters in which I am concerned. Above all, I hope you will judge for yourself, and not believe every evil story that a prating idler, like Hurry Harry, may have to tell, that goes to touch the good name of any young woman, who may not happen to have the same opinion of his face and person that the blustering gallant has of himself."

"Hurry Harry's ideas do not pass for gospel with me, Judith; but even worse than he may have eyes and ears," returned the other gravely.

"Enough of this!" exclaimed Judith, with flashing eye and a flush that mounted to her temples, "and more of my father and his ransom. 'Tis as you say, Deerslayer; the Indians will not be likely to give up their prisoners, without a heavier bribe than my clothes can offer, and father's rifle and powder. There is the chest—"

"Ay, there is the chist, as you say, Judith, and when the question gets to be between a secret and a scalp, I should think most men would prefar keeping the last. Did your father ever give you any downright commands consarning that chist?"

"Never. He has always appeared to think its locks, and its steel bands, and its strength, its best protection."

" 'Tis a rare chist, and altogether of curious build," returned Deerslayer, rising and approaching the thing in question, on which he seated himself, with a view to examine it with greater ease. "Chingachgook, this is no wood that comes of any forest that you or I have ever trailed through! 'Tis'n't the black walnut, and yet it's quite as comely, if not more so, did the smoke and the treatment give it fair play."

The Delaware drew near, felt of the wood, examined its grain, endeavored to indent the surface with a nail, and passed his hand curiously over the steel bands, the heavy padlocks, and the other novel peculiarities of the massive box.

"No—nothing like this grows in these regions—" resumed Deerslayer. "I've seen all the oaks, both the maples, the elms, the bass woods, all the walnuts, the butternuts, and every tree that has a substance and colour, wrought into some form or other, but never have I before seen such a wood as this! Judith, the chist itself, would buy your father's freedom, or Iroquois cur'osity is'n't as strong as red skin cur'osity, in general; especially in the matter of woods."

"The purchase might be cheaper made, perhaps, Deerslayer. The chest is full, and it would be better to part with half than to part with the whole. Besides, father—I know not why—but, father values that chest highly."

"He would seem to prize what it holds more than the chist, itself, judging by the manner in which he treats the outside, and secures the inside. Here are three locks, Judith; is there no key?"

"I've never seen one; and yet key there must be, since Hetty told us, *she* had often seen the chest opened."

"Keys no more lie in the air, or float on the water, than humans, gal; if there is a key, there must be a place in which it is kept."

"That is true, and it might not be difficult to find it, did we dare to search!"

"This is for you, Judith; it is altogether for you. The chist is your'n, or your father's; and Hutter is your father, not mine. Cur'osity is a woman's, and not a man's failing, and there you have got all the reasons before you. If the chist has articles for ransom, it seems to me they would be wisely used in redeeming their owner's life, or even in saving his scalp; but that is a matter for your judgment, and not for ourn. When the lawful owner of a trap, or a buck, or a canoe, is'n't present, his next of kin becomes his riprisent*y*ve by all the laws of the woods. We therefore leave you to say whether the chist shall, or shall not be opened."

"I hope you do not believe I can hesitate, when my father's life's in danger, Deerslayer!"

"Why, it's pretty much putting a scolding ag'in tears and mourning. It's not onreasonable to foretell that old Tom may find fault with what you've done, when he sees himself, once more, in his hut, here, but there's nothing unusual in men's falling out with what has been done for their own good; I dare to say that even the moon would seem a different thing from what it now does, could we look at it from the other side."

"Deerslayer, if we can find the key, I will authorize you to open the chest, and to take such things from it, as you may think will buy father's ransom."

"First find the key, gal; we'll talk of the rest a'terwards. Sarpent, you've eyes like a fly, and a judgment that's seldom out; can you help us, in calculating where Floating Tom would be apt to keep the key of a chist that he holds to be as private as this."

The Delaware had taken no part in the discourse, until he was thus directly appealed to, when he quitted the chest, which had continued to attract his attention, and cast about him for the place in which a key would be likely to be concealed, under such circumstances. As Judith and Deerslayer were not idle, the while, the whole three were soon engaged in an anxious and spirited search. As it was certain that the desired key was not to be found in any of the common drawers, or closets, of which there were several in the building, none looked there, but all turned their enquiries to those places that struck them as ingenious hiding places, and more likely to be used for such a purpose. In this manner the outer room was thoroughly but fruitlessly examined, when they entered the sleeping apartment of Hutter. This part of the rude building was better furnished than the rest of the structure, containing several articles that had been especially devoted to the service of the deceased wife, of its owner, but as Judith had all the rest of the keys, it was soon rummaged, without bringing to light the particular key desired.

They now entered the bed room of the daughters. Chingachgook was immediately struck with the contrast between the articles, and the arrangement, of that side of the room that might be called Judith's and that which more properly belonged to Hetty. A slight exclamation escaped him, and pointing in each direction he alluded to the fact in a low voice, speaking to his friend in the Delaware tongue.

"Tis as you think, Sarpent," answered Deerslayer, whose remarks we always translate into English, preserving as much as possible of the peculiar phraseology and manner of the man, "'Tis just so, as any one may see, and 'tis all founded in natur'. One sister loves finery, some say overmuch; while t'other is as meek and lowly as God ever created goodness and truth. Yet, after all, I dare say that Judith has her vartues, and Hetty has her failin's."

"And the 'Feeble-Mind' has seen the chist opened?" inquired Chingachgook, with curiosity in his glance.

"Sartain; that much I've heard from her own lips; and, for that matter, so have you. It seems her father does'n't misgive *her* discretion, though he does that of his eldest darter."

"Then, the key is hid only from the 'Wild Rose'?" for so Chingachgook had begun gallantly to term Judith, in his private discourse with his friend.

"That's it! That's just it! One he trusts, and the other he does'n't. There's red and white in that, Sarpent, all tribes and nations agreeing in trusting some, and refusing to trust other some. It depends on character and judgment."

"Where could a key be put, so little likely to be found by the Wild Rose, as among coarse clothes?"

Deerslayer started, and turning to his friend, with admiration expressed in every lineament of his face, he fairly laughed, in his silent but hearty manner, at the ingenuity and readiness of the conjecture.

"Your name's well bestowed, Sarpent—yes, 'tis well bestowed! Sure enough, where would a lover of finery be so little likely to s'arch, as among garments as coarse and onseemly as these of poor Hetty's. I dares to say, Judith's delicate fingers have'n't touched a bit of cloth as rough and oncomely as that petticoat, now, since she first made acquaintance with the officers! Yet, who knows? The key may be as likely to be on the same peg, as in any other place. Take down the garment, Delaware, and let us see if you are ra'ally a prophet."

Chingachgook did as desired, but no key was found. A coarse pocket, apparently empty, hung on the adjoining peg, and this was next examined. By this time, the attention of Judith was called in that direction, and she spoke hurriedly and like one who wished to save unnecessary trouble.

"Those are only the clothes of poor Hetty, dear simple girl!" she said, "nothing we seek, would be likely to be there."

The words were hardly out of the handsome mouth of the speaker, when Chingachgook drew the desired key from the pocket. Judith was too quick of apprehension, not to understand the reason a hiding place so simple and exposed, had been used. The blood rushed to her face, as much with resentment perhaps, as with shame, and she bit her lip, though she continued silent. Deerslayer and his friend now discovered the delicacy of men of native refinement, neither smiling or even by a glance betraying how completely he understood the motives and ingenuity of this clever artifice. The former, who had taken the key from the Indian, led the way into the adjoining room, and applying it to a lock ascertained that the right instrument had actually been found. There were three padlocks, each of which however was easily opened by this single key. Deerslayer removed them all, loosened the hasps, raised the lid a little to make certain it was loose, and then he drew back from the chest, several feet, signing to his friend to follow.

"This is a family chist, Judith," he said, "and 'tis like to hold family secrets. The Sarpent and I will go into the Ark, and look to the canoes, and paddles, and oars, while you can examine it by yourself, and find out whether any thing that will be a make weight in a ransom, is, or is not, among the articles. When you've got through, give us a call, and we'll all sit in council, together, touching the valie of the articles."

"Stop, Deerslayer," exclaimed the girl, as he was about to withdraw. "Not a single thing will I touch—I will not even raise the lid—unless you are present. Father and Hetty have seen fit to keep the inside of this chest a secret from me, and I am much too proud to pry into their hidden treasures, unless it were for their own good. But, on no account, will I open the chest alone. Stay with me, then; I want witnesses of what I do."

"I rather think, Sarpent, that the gal is right! Confidence and reliance beget security, but suspicion is like to make us all wary. Judith has a right to ask us to be present, and should the chist hold any of Master Hutter's secrets, they will fall into the keeping of two as close mouthed young men as are to be found. We *will* stay with you, Judith—but, first let us take a look at the lake and the shore, for this chist will not be emptied in a minute."

The two men now went out on the platform, and Deerslayer swept the shore with the glass, while the Indian gravely turned his eye on the water and the woods, in quest of any sign that might betray the machinations of their enemies. Nothing was visible, and assured of their temporary security, the three collected around the chest, again, with the avowed object of opening it.

Judith had held this chest, and its unknown contents, in a species of reverence as long as she could remember. Neither her father, nor her mother, ever mentioned it, in her presence, and there appeared to be a silent convention, that in naming the different objects that occasionally stood near it, or even lay on its lid, care should be had to avoid any allusion to the chest itself. Habit had rendered this so easy, and so much a matter of course, that it was only quite recently the girl had began even to muse on the singularity of the circumstance. But there had never been sufficient intimacy between Hutter and his eldest daughter to invite confidence. At times he was kind, but in general, with her more especially, he was stern and morose. Least of all had his authority been exercised in a way to embolden his child to venture on the liberty she was about to take, without many misgivings of the consequences, although the liberty proceeded from a desire to serve himself. Then Judith was not altogether free from a little superstition, on the subject of this chest, which had stood a sort of tabooed relic before her eyes, from childhood to the present hour. Nevertheless the time had come when it would seem that this mystery was to be explained, and that under circumstances, too, which left her very little choice in the matter.

Finding that both her companions were watching her movements, in grave silence, Judith placed a hand on the lid, and endeavored to raise it. Her strength, however, was insufficient, and it appeared to the girl, who was fully aware that all the fastenings were removed, that she was resisted in an unhallowed attempt by some supernatural power.

"I cannot raise the lid, Deerslayer!" she said—"Had we not better give up the attempt, and find some other means of releasing the prisoners?"

"Not so—Judith; not so, gal. No means are as sartain and easy, as a good bribe," answered the other. "As for the lid, 'tis held by nothing but its own weight, which is prodigious for so small a piece of wood, loaded with iron as it is."

As Deerslayer spoke, he applied his own strength to the effort, and succeeded in raising the lid against the timbers of the house, where he took care to secure it, by a sufficient prop. Judith fairly trembled, as she cast her first glance at the interior, and she felt a temporary relief in discovering that a piece of canvass, that was carefully tucked in, around the edges, effectually concealed all beneath it. The chest was apparently well stored, however, the canvass lying within an inch of the lid.

"Here's a full cargo," said Deerslayer, eyeing the arrangement, "and we had needs go to work leisurely, and at our ease. Sarpent, bring some stools, while I spread this blanket on the floor, and then we'll begin work orderly, and in comfort."

The Delaware complied, Deerslayer civilly placed a stool for Judith, took one himself, and commenced the removal of the canvas covering. This was done deliberately, and in as cautious a manner, as if it were believed that fabrics of a delicate construction lay hidden beneath. When the canvass was removed, the first articles that came in view were some of the habiliments of the male sex. They were of fine materials, and, according to the fashions of the age, were gay in colours, and rich in ornaments. One coat in particular was of scarlet, and had button holes worked in gold thread. Still it was not military, but was part of the attire of a civilian of condition, at a period when social rank was rigidly respected in dress. Chingachgook could not refrain from an exclamation of pleasure, as soon as Deerslayer opened this coat, and held it up to view, for, notwithstanding all his trained self-command, the splendor of the vestment was too much for the philosophy of an Indian. Deerslayer turned quickly, and he regarded his friend with momentary displeasure, as this burst of weakness escaped him, and then he soliloquized as was his practice, whenever any strong feeling suddenly got the ascendant.

"'Tis his gift! — yes, 'tis the gift of a redskin to love finery, and he is not to be blamed. This is an extr'ornary garment, too, and extr'ornary things get up extr'ornary feelin's. I think this will do, Judith, for the Indian heart is hardly to be found in all America, that can withstand, colours like these, and glitter like that. If this coat was ever made for your father, you've come honestly by the taste for finery, you have."

"That coat was never made for father," answered the girl, quickly — "it is much too long, while father is short and square."

"Cloth was plenty if it was, and glitter cheap," answered Deerslayer, with his silent, joyous laugh. "Sarpent, this garment was made for a man of your size, and I should like to see it on your shoulders."

Chingachgook, nothing loth, submitted to the trial, throwing aside the coarse and thread bare jacket of Hutter, to deck his person in a coat that was originally intended for a gentleman. The transformation was ludicrous, but as men are seldom struck with incongruities in their own appearance, any more than in their own conduct, the Delaware studied this change in a common glass, by which Hutter was in the habit of shaving, with grave interest. At that moment he thought of Hist, and we owe it to truth, to say, though it may militate a little against the stern character of a warrior to avow it, that he wished he could be seen by her, in his present improved aspect.

"Off with it, Sarpent — off with it," resumed the inflexible Deerslayer. "Such garments as little become you, as they would become me. Your gifts are for paint, and hawk's feathers, and blankets, and wampum, and mine are for doublets of skins, tough leggings, and sarviceable moccasins. I say moccasins, Judith, for though white, living as I do in the woods, it's necessary to take to some of the prac*ty*ces of the woods, for comfort's sake, and cheapness."

"I see no reason, Deerslayer, why one man may not wear a scarlet coat, as well as another," returned the girl. "I wish I could see *you* in this handsome garment."

"See me in a coat fit for a Lord! — Well, Judith, if you wait till that day, you'll wait until you see me beyond reason and memory. No — no — gal, my gifts are my gifts, and I'll live and die in 'em, though I never bring down another deer, or spear another salmon. What have I done that you should wish to see *me* in such a flaunting coat, Judith."

"Because I think, Deerslayer, that the false-tongued and false-hearted young gallants of the garrisons, ought not alone to appear in fine feathers, but that truth and honesty have *their* claims to be honored and exalted."

"And what exaltification — " the reader will have remarked that Deerslayer had not very critically studied his dictionary — "and what exaltification would it be to me, Judith, to be bedizzened and bescarleted like a Mingo chief that has just got his presents up from Quebec? No — no — I'm well as I am; and if not, I can be no better. Lay the coat down on the blanket, Sarpent, and let us look farther into the chist."

The tempting garment, one surely that was never intended for Hutter, was laid aside, and the examination proceeded. The male attire, all of which corresponded with the coat in quality, was soon exhausted, and then succeeded female. A beautiful dress of brocade, a little the worse from negligent treatment, followed, and this time open exclamations of delight escaped the lips of Judith. Much as the girl had been addicted to dress, and favorable as had been her opportunities of seeing some little pretension in that way, among the wives of the different commandants, and other ladies of the forts, never before had she beheld a tissue, or tints, to equal those that were now so unexpectedly placed before her eyes. Her rapture was almost childish, nor would she allow the enquiry to proceed, until she had attired her person in a robe so unsuited to her habits and her abode. With this end, she withdrew into her own room, where with hands practised in such offices, she soon got rid of her own neat gown of linen, and stood forth in the gay tints of the brocade. The dress happened to fit the fine, full, person of Judith, and certainly it had never adorned a being, better qualified by natural gifts, to do credit to its really rich hues and fine texture. When she returned, both Deerslayer and Chingachgook, who had passed the brief time of her absence, in taking a second look at the male garments, arose in surprise, each permitting exclamations of wonder and pleasure to escape him, in a way so unequivocal as to add new lustre to the eyes of Judith, by flushing her cheeks with a glow of triumph. Affecting, however, not to notice the impression she had made, the girl seated herself with the stateliness of a queen, desiring that the chest might be looked into, further.

"I do'n't know a better way to treat with the Mingos, gal," cried Deerslayer, "than to send you ashore, as you be, and to tell 'em that a queen has arrived among 'em! They'll give up old Hutter, and Hurry, and Hetty, too, at such a spectacle!"

"I thought your tongue too honest to flatter, Deerslayer," returned the girl, gratified at this admiration more than she would have cared to own. "One of the chief reasons of my respect for you, was your love for truth."

"And 'tis truth, and solemn truth, Judith, and nothing else. Never did eyes of mine gaze on as glorious a lookin' creatur', as you be yourself, at this very moment! I've seen beauties in my time too; both white and red; and them that was renowed and talk'd of, far and near; but never have I beheld one that could hold any comparison with what you are at this blessed instant, Judith; never."

The glance of delight which the girl bestowed on the frank-speaking hunter, in no degree lessened the effect of her charms, and as the humid eyes blended with it a look of sensibility, perhaps Judith never appeared more truly lovely, than at what the young man had called that "blessed instant." He shook his head, held it suspended a moment over the open chest, like one in doubt, and then proceeded with the examination.

Several of the minor articles of female dress came next, all of a quality to correspond with the gown. These were laid at Judith's feet, in silence, as if she had a natural claim to their possession. One or two, such as gloves, and lace, the girl caught up, and appended to her already rich attire in affected playfulness, but with the real design of decorating her person as far as circumstances would allow. When these two remarkable suits, male and female they might be termed, were removed, another canvass covering separated the remainder of the articles from the part of the chest which they had occupied. As soon as Deerslayer perceived this arrangement, he paused, doubtful of the propriety of proceeding any further.

"Every man has his secrets, I suppose," he said, "and all men have a right to their enj'yment. We've got low enough in this chist, in my judgment to answer our wants, and it seems to me we should do well by going no farther; and by letting Master Hutter have to himself, and his own feelin's, all that's beneath this cover."

"Do you mean, Deerslayer, to offer these clothes to the Iroquois, as ransom?" demanded Judith, quickly.

"Sartain. What are we prying into another man's chist for, but to sarve its owner, in the best way we can. This coat, alone, would be very apt to gain over the head chief of the riptyles, and if his wife or darter should happen to be out with him, that there gownd would soften the heart of any woman that is to be found atween Albany and Montreal. I do not see that we want a larger stock in trade than them two articles."

"To you it may seem so, Deerslayer," returned the disappointed girl, "but of what use could a dress like this be to any Indian woman? She could not wear it among the branches of the trees, the dirt and smoke of the wigwam would soon soil it, and how would a pair of red arms appear, thrust through these short, laced sleeves!"

"All very true, gal, and you might go on and say, it is altogether out of time, and place and season, in this region at all. What is it to us how the finery is treated, so long as it answers our wishes? I do not see that your father can make any use of such clothes, and it's lucky he has things that are of no valie to himself, that will bear a high price with others. We can make no better trade for him, than to offer these duds for his liberty. We'll throw in the light frivol'ties, and get Hurry off in the bargain."

"Then you think, Deerslayer, that Thomas Hutter has no one in his family—no child—no daughter, to whom this dress may be thought becoming, and whom you could wish to see in it, once and awhile, even though it should be at long intervals, and only in playfulness?"

"I understand you, Judith—yes, I now understand your meaning, and I think I can say, your wishes. That you are as glorious, in that dress, as the sun when it rises, or sets, in a soft October day, I'm ready to allow, and that you greatly become it, is a good deal more sartain than that it becomes you. There's gifts in clothes, as well as in other things. Now I do not think that a warrior on his first path, ought to lay on the same awful paints as a chief that has had his virtue tried, and knows from exper'ence he will not disgrace his pretensions. So it is with all of us, red or white. You are Thomas Hutter's darter, and that gownd was made for the child of some governor, or a lady of high station, and it was intended to be worn among fine furniture, and in rich company. In my eyes, Judith, a modest maiden never looks more becoming, than when becomingly clad, and nothing is suitable that is out of character. Besides, gal, if there's a creatur' in the colony that can afford to do without finery, and to trust to her own good looks, and sweet countenance, it's yourself."

"I'll take off the rubbish this instant, Deerslayer," cried the girl, springing up to leave the room, "and never do I wish to see it on any human being, again."

"So it is with 'em, all, Sarpent," said the other, turning to his friend and laughing, as soon as the beauty had disappeared. "They like finery, but they like their nat*y*ve charms most of all. I'm glad the gal has consented to lay aside her furbelows, howsever, for it's ag'in reason for one of her class to wear 'em; and then she *is* handsome enough, as I call it, to go alone. Hist would show oncommon likely, too, in such a gownd, Delaware!"

"Wah-ta!-Wah is a red skin girl, Deerslayer," returned the Indian, "like the young of the pigeon, she is to be known by her own feathers. I should pass by without knowing her, were she dressed in such a skin. It's wisest always to be so clad that our friends need not ask us for our names. The 'Wild Rose' is very pleasant, but she is no sweeter for so many colours."

"That's it!—that's natur', and the true foundation for love and protection. When a man stoops to pick a wild strawberry, he does not expect to find a melon; and when he wishes to gather a melon, he's disapp'inted if it proves to be a squash;

though squashes *be* often brighter to the eye than melons. That's it, and it means, stick to your gifts, and your gifts will stick to you."

The two men had now a little discussion together, touching the propriety of penetrating any farther into the chest of Hutter, when Judith re-appeared, divested of her robes, and in her own simple, linen frock again.

"Thank you, Judith," said Deerslayer, taking her kindly by the hand—"for I know it went a little ag'in the nat'ral cravings of woman, to lay aside so much finery, as it might be in a lump. But you're more pleasing to the eye as you stand, you be, than if you had a crown on your head, and jewels dangling from your hair. The question now is, whether to lift this covering, to see what will be ra'ally the best bargain we can make for Master Hutter, for we must do as we think *he* would be willing to do, did he stand here in our places."

Judith looked very happy. Accustomed as she was to adulation, the homely homage of Deerslayer had given her more true satisfaction, than she had ever yet received from the tongue of man. It was not the terms in which this admiration had been expressed, for *they* were simple enough, that produced so strong an impression; nor yet their novelty, or their warmth of manner, nor any of those peculiarties that usually give value to praise; but the unflinching truth of the speaker, that carried his words so directly to the heart of the listener. This is one of the great advantages of plain dealing and frankness. The habitual and wily flatterer may succeed until his practises recoil on himself, and like other sweets his aliment cloys by its excess; but he who deals honestly, though he often necessarily offends, possesses a power of praising that no quality but sincerity can bestow, since his words go directly to the heart, finding their support in the understanding. Thus it was with Deerslayer and Judith. So soon and so deeply did this simple hunter impress those who knew him, with a conviction of his unbending honesty, that all he uttered in commendation was as certain to please, as all he uttered in the way of rebuke was as certain to rankle and excite enmity, where his character had not awakened a respect and affection, that in another sense rendered it painful. In after life, when the career of this untutored being brought him in contact with officers of rank, and others entrusted with the care of the interests of the state, this same influence was exerted on a wider field, even generals listening to his commendations with a glow of pleasure, that it was not always in the power of their official superiors to awaken. Perhaps Judith was the first individual of his own colour, who fairly submitted to this natural consequence of truth and fair-dealing, on the part of Deerslayer. She had actually pined for his praise, and she had now received it, and that in the form which was most agreeable to her weaknesses and habits of thought. The result will appear in the course of the narrative.

"If we knew all that chest holds, Deerslayer," returned the girl, when she had a little recovered from the immediate effect produced by his commendations of her personal appearance, "we could better determine on the course we ought to take."

"That's not onreasonable, gal, though it's more a pale-face than a red-skin gift to be prying into other people's secrets."

"Curiosity is natural, and it is expected that all human beings, should have human failings. Whenever I've been at the garrisons, I've found that most, in and about them, had a longing to learn their neighbor's secrets."

"Yes, and sometimes to fancy them, when they could'n't find 'em out! That's the difference atween an Indian gentleman, and a white gentleman. The Sarpent, here, would turn his head aside, if he found himself onknowingly lookin' into another chief's wigwam, whereas, in the settlements while all pretend to be great people, most prove they've got betters, by the manner in which they talk of their consarns. I'll be bound, Judith, you would'n't get the Sarpent, there, to confess there was another in the tribe so much greater than himself, as to become the subject of his idees, and to empl'y his tongue in conversations about his movements, and ways, and food, and all the other little matters that occupy a man when he's not empl'y'd in his greater duties. He who does this, is but little better than a blackguard, in the grain, and them that encourages him, is pretty much of the same kidney, let them wear coats as fine as they may, or of what dye they please."

"But this is not another man's wigwam; it belongs to my father, these are his things, and they are wanted in his service."

"That's true, gal; that's true, and it carries weight with it.

Well, when all is before us, we may, indeed, best judge, which to offer for the ransom, and which to withhold."

Judith was not altogether as disinterested in her feelings, as she affected to be. She remembered that the curiosity of Hetty had been indulged, in connection with this chest, while her own had been disregarded, and she was not sorry to possess an opportunity of being placed on a level with her less gifted sister, in this one particular. It appearing to be admitted all round, that the enquiry into the contents of the chest ought to be renewed, Deerslayer proceeded to remove the second covering of canvass.

The articles that lay uppermost, when the curtain was again raised on the secrets of the chest, were a pair of pistols, curiously inlaid with silver. Their value would have been considerable, in one of the towns, though as weapons, in the woods, they were a species of arms seldom employed; never, indeed, unless it might be by some officer from Europe, who visited the colonies, as many were then wont to do, so much impressed with the superiority of the usages of London, as to fancy they were not to be laid aside on the frontiers of America. What occurred on the discovery of these weapons, will appear, in the succeeding chapter.

Chapter XIII.

"An oaken, broken, elbow-chair;
A caudle-cup without an ear;
A battered, shattered ash bedstead;
A box of deal without a lid;
A pair of tongs, but out of joint;
A back-sword poker, without point;
A dish which might good meat afford once;
An Ovid, and an old Concordance."
Thomas Sheridan, "A True and Faithful Inventory of the
Goods belonging to Dr. Swift," ll.1–6, 13–14.

N o sooner did Deerslayer raise the pistols, than he turned
to the Delaware and held them up, for his admiration.

"Child gun," said the Serpent, smiling, while he handled one
of the instruments as if it had been a toy.

"Not it, Sarpent; not it—t'was made for a man and would
satisfy a giant, if rightly used. But stop; white men are
remarkable for their carelessness in putting away fire arms, in
chists and corners. Let me look if care has been given to these."

As Deerslayer spoke, he took the weapon from the hand of
his friend, and opened the pan. The last was filled with priming, caked like a bit of cinder, by time, moisture and compression. An application of the ramrod showed that both the pistols
were charged, although Judith could testify that they had probably lain for years in the chest. It is not easy to portray the surprise of the Indian, at this discovery, for he was in the practice
of renewing his priming daily, and of looking to the contents of
his piece, at other short intervals.

"This is white neglect," said Deerslayer, shaking his head,
"and scarce a season goes by, that some one, in the settlements
does n't suffer from it. It's extr'ornary too, Judith—yes, it's
downright extr'ornary that the owner shall fire his piece at a
deer, or some other game, or perhaps at an inimy, and twice
out of three times he'll miss; but let him catch an accident with
one of these forgotten charges, and he makes it sartain death to

a child, or a brother, or a fri'nd! Well, we shall do a good turn
to the owner if we fire these pistols for him, and as they're
novelties to you and me, Sarpent, we'll try our hands at a
mark. Freshen that priming, and I'll do the same with this,
and then we'll see who is the best man with a pistol; as for the
rifle, that's long been settled atween us."

Deerslayer laughed heartily, at his own conceit, and, in a
minute or two, they were both standing on the platform,
selecting some object in the Ark for their target. Judith was led
by curiosity to their side.

"Stand back, gal, stand a little back; these we'pons have
been long loaded," said Deerslayer, "and some accident may
happen in the discharge."

"Then *you* shall not fire them! Give them both to the
Delaware; or it would be better to unload them, without
firing."

"That's ag'in usage—and some people say, ag'in manhood;
though I hold to no such silly doctrine. We must fire 'em,
Judith; yes, we must fire 'em; though I foresee that neither will
have any great reason to boast of his skill."

Judith, in the main, was a girl of great personal spirit, and
her habits prevented her from feeling any of the terror that is
apt to come over her sex, at the report of fire arms. She had
discharged many a rifle, and had even been known to kill a
deer, under circumstances that were favorable to the effort.
She submitted therefore, falling a little back by the side of
Deerslayer, giving the Indian the front of the platform to
himself. Chingachgook raised the weapon several times, endeavored to steady it by using both hands, changed his attitude, from one that was awkward, to another still more so,
and finally drew the trigger with a sort of desperate indifference, without having, in reality, secured any aim at all. The
consequence was, that instead of hitting the knot which had
been selected for the mark, he missed the ark altogether; the
bullet skipping along the water, like a stone that was thrown
by hand.

"Well done—Sarpent—well done—" cried Deerslayer
laughing, with his noiseless glee, "you've hit the lake, and
that's an expl'ite for some men! I know'd it, and as much as
said it, here, to Judith; for your short we'pons do'n't belong to

red skin gifts. You've hit the lake, and that's better than only
hitting the air! Now, stand back and let us see what white gifts
can do with a white we'pon. A pistol is'n't a rifle, but colour is
colour."

The aim of Deerslayer was both quick and steady, and the
report followed almost as soon as the weapon rose. Still the
pistol hung fire, as it is termed, and fragments of it flew in
a dozen directions, some falling on the roof of the castle, others
in the Ark, and one in the water. Judith screamed, and when
the two men turned anxiously towards the girl, she was as pale
as death, trembling in every limb.

"She's wownded—yes, the poor gal's wownded—Sarpent,
though one could'n't foresee it, standing where she did. We'll
lead her in to a seat, and we must do the best for her, that our
knowledge and skill can afford."

Judith allowed herself to be supported to a seat, swallowed a
mouthful of the water that the Delaware offered her in a
gourd, and, after a violent fit of trembling, that seemed ready
to shake her fine frame to dissolution, she burst into tears.

"The pain must be borne, poor Judith—yes, it must be
borne," said Deerslayer, soothingly, "though I am far from
wishing you not to weep; for weeping often lightens galish
feelin's. Where can she be hurt, Sarpent?—I see no signs of
blood, nor any rent of skin, or garments?"

"I am uninjured, Deerslayer—" stammered the girl, through
her tears. "It's fright—nothing more, I do assure you, and,
God be praised! no one, I find, has been harmed by the accident."

"This is extr'ornary!" exclaimed the unsuspecting and simple
minded hunter—"I thought, Judith, you'd been above settlement weaknesses, and that you was a gal not to be frightened
by the sound of a bursting we'pon—No—I didn't think you so
skeary! *Hetty* might well have been startled; but you've too
much judgment and reason to be frightened when the danger's
all over. They're pleasant to the eye, chief, and changeful, but
very unsartin in their feelin's!"

Shame kept Judith silent. There had been no acting in her
agitation, but all had fairly proceeded from sudden and uncontrollable alarm—an alarm that she found almost as inexplicable to herself, as it proved to be to her companions. Wip-

ing away the traces of tears, however, she smiled again, and was soon able to join in the laugh at her own folly.

"And you, Deerslayer," she at length succeeded in saying—"are you, indeed, altogether unhurt? It seems almost miraculous that a pistol should have burst in your hand, and you escape without the loss of a limb, if not of life!"

"Such wonders ar'n't oncommon, at all, among worn out arms. The first rifle they gave me play'd the same trick, and yet I liv'd through it, though not as onharmless as I've got out of this affair. Thomas Hutter is master of one pistol less than he was this morning, but, as it happened in trying to sarve him, there's no ground of complaint. Now, draw near, and let us look farther into the inside of the chist."

Judith, by this time, had so far gotten the better of her agitation as to resume her seat, and the examination went on. The next article that offered was enveloped in cloth, and on opening it, it proved to be one of the mathematical instruments that were then in use among seamen, possessing the usual ornaments and fastenings in brass. Deerslayer and Chingachgook expressed their admiration and surprise at the appearance of the unknown instrument, which was bright and glittering, having apparently been well cared for.

"This goes beyond the surveyors, Judith!" Deerslayer exclaimed, after turning the instrument several times in his hands. "I've seen all their tools often, and wicked and heartless enough are they, for they never come into the forest but to lead the way to waste and destruction; but none of them have as designing a look as this! I fear me, after all, that Thomas Hutter has journeyed into the wilderness with no fair intentions towards its happiness. Did you ever see any of the cravings of a surveyor about your father, gal?"

"He is no surveyor, Deerslayer, nor does he know the use of that instrument, though he seems to own it. Do you suppose that Thomas Hutter ever wore that coat? It is as much too large for him, as this instrument is beyond his learning."

"That's it—that must be it, Sarpent, and the old fellow, by some onknown means, has fallen heir to another man's goods! They say he has been a mariner, and no doubt this chist, and all it holds—ha! What have we here?—This far out does the brass and black wood of the tool!"

Deerslayer had opened a small bag, from which he was taking, one by one, the pieces of a set of chess-men. They were of ivory, much larger than common, and exquisitely wrought. Each piece represented the character, or thing after which it is named; the knights being mounted, the castles stood on elephants, and even the pawns possessed the heads and busts of men. The set was not complete, and a few fractures betrayed bad usage; but all that was left had been carefully put away and preserved. Even Judith expressed wonder, as these novel objects were placed before her eyes, and Chingachgook fairly forgot his Indian dignity in admiration and delight. The latter took up each piece, and examined it with never tiring satisfaction, pointing out to the girl, the more ingenious and striking portions of the workmanship. But the elephants gave him the greatest pleasure. The "Hugh's!" that he uttered, as he passed his fingers over their trunks, and ears, and tails, were very distinct, nor did he fail to note the pawns, which were armed as archers. This exhibition lasted several minutes, during which time Judith and the Indian had all the rapture to themselves. Deerslayer sate silent, thoughtful, and even gloomy, though his eyes followed each movement of the two principal actors, noting every new peculiarity about the pieces as they were held up to view. Not an exclamation of pleasure, nor a word of condemnation passed his lips. At length his companions observed his silence, and, then, for the first time since the chess men had been discovered, did he speak.

"Judith," he asked earnestly, but with a concern that amounted almost to tenderness of manner, "did your parents ever talk to you of religion?"

The girl coloured, and the flashes of crimson that passed over her beautiful countenance were like the wayward tints of a Neapolitan sky in November. Deerslayer had given her so strong a taste for truth, however, that she did not waver in her answer, replying simply and with sincerity.

"My *mother* did often," she said, "my father *never*. I thought it made my mother sorrowful to speak of our prayers and duties, but my father has never opened his mouth on such matters, before or since her death."

"That I can believe—that I can believe. He has no God—no such God as it becomes a man of white skin to worship, or even a red-skin. Them things are idols!"

Judith started, and for a moment she seemed seriously hurt.

Then she reflected, and in the end she laughed. "And you think, Deerslayer, that these ivory toys are my father's Gods? I have heard of idols, and know what they are."

"Them are idols!" repeated the other, positively. "Why should your father keep 'em, if he does'n't worship 'em."

"Would he keep his gods in a bag, and locked up in a chest? No—no—Deerslayer; my poor father carries his God with him, wherever he goes, and that is in his own cravings. These things may really be idols—I think they are myself, from what I have heard and read of idolatry, but they have come from some distant country, and like all the other articles, have fallen into Thomas Hutter's hands, when he was a sailor."

"I'm glad of it—I am downright glad to hear it, Judith, for I do not think I could have mustered the resolution to strive to help a white idolater out of his difficulties! The old man is of my colour and nation and I wish to sarve him, but as one who denied all his gifts, in the way of religion, it would have come hard to do so. That animal seems to give you great satisfaction, Sarpent, though it's an idolatrous beast at the best."

"It is an elephant," interrupted Judith. "I've often seen pictures of such animals, at the garrisons, and mother had a book in which there was a printed account of the creature. Father burnt that with all the other books, for he said Mother loved reading too well. This was not long before mother died, and I've sometimes thought that the loss hastened her end."

This was said equally without levity and without any very deep feeling. It was said without levity, for Judith was saddened by her recollections, and yet she had been too much accustomed to live for self, and for the indulgence of her own vanities, to feel her mother's wrongs very keenly. It required extraordinary circumstances to awaken a proper sense of her situation, and to stimulate the better feelings of this beautiful, but misguided girl, and those circumstances had not yet occurred in her brief existence.

"Elephant, or no elephant, t'is an idol," returned the hunter, "and not fit to remain in christian keeping."

"Good for Iroquois!" said Chingachgook, parting with one of the castles with reluctance, as his friend took it from him to replace it in the bag—"Elephon buy whole tribe—Buy Delaware, almost!"

"Ay, that it would, as any one who comperhends red-skin natur' must know," answered Deerslayer, "but the man that passes false money, Sarpent, is as bad as he who makes it. Did you ever know a just Injin that would'n't scorn to sell a 'coon skin, for the true marten, or to pass off a mink for a beaver. I know that a few of these idols, perhaps *one* of them elephants, would go far towards buying Thomas Hutter's liberty, but it goes ag'in conscience to pass such counterfeit money. Perhaps no Injin tribe, hereaway, is downright idolators but there's some that come so near it, that white gifts ought to be particular about encouraging them in their mistake."

"If idolatry is a *gift*, Deerslayer, and *gifts* are what you seem to think them, idolatry in such people can hardly be a sin," said Judith with more smartness than discrimination.

"God grants no such gifts to any of his creatur's, Judith," returned the hunter, seriously. "*He* must be adored, under some name or other, and not creatur's of brass or ivory. It matters not whether the Father of All is called God, or Manitou, Deity or Great Spirit, he is none the less our common maker and master; nor does it count for much whether the souls of the just go to Paradise, or Happy Hunting Grounds, since He may send each his own way, as suits his own pleasure and wisdom; but it curdles my blood, when I find human mortals so bound up in darkness and consait, as to fashion the 'arth, or wood, or bones, things made by their own hands, into motionless, senseless iffigies, and then fall down afore them, and worship 'em as a Deity!"

"After all, Deerslayer, these pieces of ivory may not be idols, at all. I remember, now, to have seen one of the officers, at the garrison, with a set of fox and geese made in some such a design as these, and here is something hard, wrapped in cloth, that may belong to your idols."

Deerslayer took the bundle the girl gave him, and unrolling it, he found the board within. Like the pieces it was large, rich, and inlaid with ebony and ivory. Putting the whole in conjunction, the hunter, though not without many misgivings, slowly came over to Judith's opinion, and finally admitted that the fancied idols must be merely the curiously carved men of some unknown game. Judith had the tact to use her victory with great moderation, nor did she once, even in the most indirect manner, allude to the ludicrous mistake of her companion.

This discovery of the uses of the extraordinary-looking little images, settled the affair of the proposed ransom. It was agreed generally, and all understood the weaknesses and tastes of Indians, that nothing could be more likely to tempt the cupidity of the Iroquois, than the elephants, in particular. Luckily the whole of the castles were among the pieces, and these four tower-bearing animals it was finally determined should be the ransom offered. The remainder of the men, and, indeed, all the rest of the articles in the chest, were to be kept out of view, and to be resorted to only as a last appeal. As soon as these preliminaries were settled, every thing but those intended for the bribe was carefully replaced in the chest, all the covers were 'tucked in', as they had been found, and it was quite possible, could Hutter have been put in possession of the castle again, that he might have passed the remainder of his days in it, without even suspecting the invasion that had been made on the privacy of the chest. The rent pistol would have been the most likely to reveal the secret, but this was placed by the side of its fellow, and all were pressed down as before, some half a dozen packages in the bottom of the chest not having been opened at all. When this was done, the lid was lowered, the padlocks replaced, and the key turned. The latter was then replaced in the pocket from which it had been taken.

More than an hour was consumed in settling the course proper to be pursued, and in returning every thing to its place. The pauses to converse were frequent, and Judith, who experienced a lively pleasure in the open, undisguised admiration, with which Deerslayer's honest eyes gazed at her handsome face, found the means to prolong the interview, with a dexterity that seems to be innate in female coquetry. Deerslayer, indeed, appeared to be the first who was conscious of the time that had been thus wasted, and to call the attention of his companions to the necessity of doing something towards putting the plan of ransoming into execution. Chingachgook had remained in Hutter's bed room, where the elephants were laid, to feast his eyes with the images of animals so wonderful, and so novel. Perhaps an instinct told him that his presence would not be as acceptable to his companions, as this holding himself aloof, for Judith had not much reserve in the manifestations of her preferences, and the Delaware had not got so far as one betrothed without acquiring some knowledge of the symptoms of the master passion.

"Well, Judith," said Deerslayer, rising, after the interview had lasted much longer than even he himself suspected, "t'is pleasant conversing with you, and settling all these matters, but duty calls us another way. All this time, Hurry and your father, not to say Hetty—"

The word was cut short in the speaker's mouth, for, at that critical moment, a light step was heard on the platform, or 'court-yard', a human figure darkened the door-way, and the person last mentioned stood before him. The low exclamation that escaped Deerslayer and the slight scream of Judith were hardly uttered, when an Indian youth, between the ages of fifteen and seventeen, stood beside her. These two entrances had been made with moccasined feet, and consequently almost without noise, but, unexpected and stealthy as they were, they had not the effect to disturb Deerslayer's self possession. His first measure was to speak rapidly in Delaware to his friend, cautioning him to keep out of sight, while he stood on his guard; the second was to step to the door to ascertain the extent of the danger. No one else, however, had come, and a simple contrivance, in the shape of a raft, that lay floating at the side of the Ark, at once explained the means that had been used in bringing Hetty off. Two dead and dry, and consequently buoyant, logs of pine were bound together with pins and withes and a little platform of riven chestnut had been rudely placed on their surfaces. Here Hetty had been seated, on a billet of wood, while the young Iroquois had rowed the primitive, and slow-moving, but perfectly safe, craft, from the shore. As soon as Deerslayer had taken a close survey of this raft, and satisfied himself nothing else was near, he shook his head, and muttered in his soliloquizing way—

"This comes of prying into another man's chist! Had we been watchful, and keen eyed, such a surprise could never have happened, and, getting this much from a boy, teaches us what we may expect when the old warriors set themselves fairly about their sarcumventions. It opens the way, howsever, to a treaty for the ransom, and I will hear what Hetty has to say."

Judith, as soon as her surprise and alarm had a little abated, discovered a proper share of affectionate joy, at the return of her sister. She folded her to her bosom, and kissed her, as had been her wont in the days of their childhood and innocence. Hetty herself was less affected, for to her there was no surprise, and her nerves were sustained by the purity and holiness of her purpose. At her sister's request she took a seat, and entered into an account of her adventures since they had parted. Her tale commenced just as Deerslayer returned, and he also became an attentive listener, while the young Iroquois stood near the door, seemingly as indifferent to what was passing, as one of its posts.

The narrative of the girl was sufficiently clear, until she reached the time where we left her in the camp, after the interview with the chiefs, and, at the moment when Hist quitted her, in the abrupt manner already related. The sequel of the story may be told in her own language.

"When I read the texts to the chiefs, Judith, you could not have seen that they made any changes on their minds," she said, "but if seed is planted, it *will* grow. God planted the seeds of all these trees—"

"Ay that did he—that did he—" muttered Deerslayer—"and a goodly harvest has followed."

"God planted the seeds of all these trees," continued Hetty, after a moment's pause, "and you see to what a height and shade they have grown! So it is with the bible. You may read a verse this year, and forget it, and it will come back to you a year hence, when you least expect to remember it."

"And did you find any thing of this, among the savages, poor Hetty."

"Yes, Judith, and sooner, and more fully than I had even hoped. I did not stay long with father and Hurry, but went to get my breakfast with Hist. As soon as we had done, the chiefs came to us, and *then* we found the fruits of the seed that had been planted. They said what I had read from the good book was right—it *must* be right—it sounded *right*; like a sweet bird singing in their ears; and they told me to come back and say as much to the great warrior who had slain one of their braves; and to tell it to you, and to say how happy they should be to come to church here, in the castle, or to come out in the sun, and hear me read more of the sacred volume—and to tell you that they wish you would lend them some canoes that they can bring father and Hurry, and their women to the castle, that we might all sit on the platform there, and listen to the singing of the Pale Face Manitou. There, Judith; did you ever know of any thing that so plainly shows the power of the bible, as *that!*"

"If it were true 't would be a miracle, indeed, Hetty. But all this is no more than Indian cunning and Indian treachery, striving to get the better of us by management, when they find it is not to be done by force."

"Do you doubt the bible, sister, that you judge the savages so harshly!"

"I do not doubt the bible, poor Hetty, but I much doubt an Indian and an Iroquois. What do you say to this visit, Deerslayer?"

"First let me talk a little with Hetty," returned the party appealed to; "Was the raft made a'ter you had got your breakfast, gal, and did you walk from the camp to the shore opposite to us, here?"

"Oh! no, Deerslayer. The raft was ready made and in the water—could that have been by a miracle, Judith!"

"Yes—yes—an Indian miracle—" rejoined the hunter—"They're expart enough in them sort of miracles. And you found the raft ready made to your hands, and in the water, and in waiting like for its cargo?"

"It was all as you say. The raft was near the camp, and the Indians put me on it, and had ropes of bark, and they dragged me to the place opposite to the castle, and then they told that young man to row me off, here."

"And the woods are full of the vagabonds, waiting to know what is to be the upshot of the miracle. We comperhend this affair, now, Judith, but I'll first get rid of this young Canada blood sucker, and then we'll settle our own course. Do you and Hetty leave us together, first bringing me the elephants, which the Sarpent is admiring, for 'twill never do to let this loping deer be alone a minute, or he'll borrow a canoe without asking."

Judith did as desired, first bringing the pieces, and retiring with her sister into their own room. Deerslayer had acquired some knowledge of most of the Indian dialects of that region, and he knew enough of the Iroquois to hold a dialogue in the language. Beckoning to the lad, therefore, he caused him to take a seat on the chest, when he placed two of the castles suddenly before him. Up to that moment, this youthful savage had not expressed a single intelligible emotion, or fancy. There were many things, in and about the place, that were novelties to him, but he had maintained his self-command with philosophical composure. It is true, Deerslayer had detected his dark eye scanning the defences and the arms, but the scrutiny had been made with such an air of innocence, in such a gaping, indolent, boyish manner, that no one but a man who had himself been taught in a similar school, would have even suspected his object. The instant, however, the eyes of the savage fell upon the wrought ivory, and the images of the wonderful, unknown, beasts, surprise and admiration got the mastery of him. The manner in which the natives of the South Sea Islands first beheld the toys of civilized life has been often described, but the reader is not to confound it with the manner of an American Indian, under similar circumstances. In this particular case, the young Iroquois or Huron, permitted an exclamation of rapture to escape him, and then he checked himself like one who had been guilty of an indecorum. After this, his eyes ceased to wander, but became riveted on the elephants, one of which, after a short hesitation, he even presumed to handle. Deerslayer did not interrupt him for quite ten minutes, knowing that the lad was taking such note of the curiosities, as would enable him to give the most minute and accurate description of their appearance, to his seniors, on his return. When he thought sufficient time had been allowed to produce the desired effect, the hunter laid a finger on the naked knee of the youth and drew his attention to himself.

"Listen—" he said—"I want to talk with my young friend from the Canadas. Let him forget that wonder for a minute."

"Where t'other pale brother?" demanded the boy, looking up and letting the idea that had been most prominent in his mind, previously to the introduction of the chess men, escape him involuntarily.

"He sleeps,—or if he is'n't fairly asleep, he is in the room, where the men do sleep—" returned Deerslayer. "How did my young friend know there was another?"

"See him from the shore. Iroquois have got long eyes—see beyond the clouds—see the bottom of the Great Spring!"

"Well, the Iroquois are welcome. Two pale faces are prisoners in the camp of your fathers, boy."

The lad nodded, treating the circumstance with great apparent indifference; though a moment after, he laughed as if exulting in the superior address of his own tribe.

"Can you tell me, boy, what your chiefs intend to do with these captyves, or have'n't they yet made up their minds?"

The lad looked, a moment, at the hunter with a little surprise. Then he coolly put the end of his fore finger on his own head, just above the left ear, and passed it round his crown with an accuracy and readiness that showed how well he had been drilled in the peculiar art of his race.

"When—" demanded Deerslayer, whose gorge rose at this cool demonstration of indifference to human life. "And why not take them to your wigwams?"

"Road too long, and full of pale faces. Wigwam full, and scalps sell high. Small scalp, much gold."

"Well that explains it—yes, that does explain it. There's no need of being any plainer. Now, you know, lad, that the oldest of your prisoners, is the father of these two young women, and the other is the suitor of one of them. The gals nat'rally wish to save the scalps of such fri'nds, and they will give them two ivory creatur's, as ransom. One for each scalp. Go back and tell this to your chiefs, and bring me the answer before the sun sets."

The boy entered zealously into this project, and with a sincerity that left no doubt of his executing his commission with intelligence and promptitude. For a moment he forgot his love of honor, and all his clannish hostility to the British and their Indians, in his wish to have such a treasure in his tribe, and Deerslayer was satisfied with the impression he had made. It is true the lad proposed to carry one of the elephants with him, as a specimen of the other, but to this his brother negotiator was too sagacious to consent; well knowing that it might never reach its destination if confided to such hands. This little difficulty was soon arranged, and the boy prepared to depart. As he stood on the platform, ready to step aboard of the raft, he hesitated, and turned short with a proposal to borrow a canoe, as the means most likely to shorten the negotiations. Deerslayer quietly refused the request, and, after lingering a little longer, the boy rowed slowly away from the castle, taking the direction of a thicket on the shore, that lay less than half a mile distant. Deerslayer seated himself on a stool, and watched the progress of the ambassador, sometimes closely scanning the whole line of shore, as far as eye could reach, and then placing an elbow on a knee, he remained a long time with his chin resting on the hand.

During the interview between Deerslayer and the lad, a different scene took place in the adjoining room. Hetty had enquired for the Delaware, and being told why and where he remained concealed, she joined him. The reception which Chingachgook gave his visiter was respectful and gentle. He understood her character, and, no doubt, his disposition to be kind to such a being was increased by the hope of learning some tidings of his betrothed. As soon as the girl entered, she took a seat, and invited the Indian to place himself near her; then she continued silent, as if she thought it decorous for him to question her, before she consented to speak on the subject she had on her mind. But, as Chingachgook did not understand this feeling, he remained respectfully attentive to any thing she might be pleased to tell him.

"You are Chingachgook, — the Great Serpent of the Delawares, ar'n't you?" the girl at length commenced, in her own simple way losing her self-command in the desire to proceed, but anxious first to make sure of the individual.

"Chingachgook," returned the Delaware with grave dignity. "That say Great Sarpent, in Deerslayer tongue."

"Well, that is my tongue. Deerslayer, and father, and Judith, and I, and poor Hurry Harry — do you know Henry March, Great Serpent? I know you do'n't, however, or *he* would have spoken of *you*, too."

"Did any tongue name Chingachgook, Drooping-Lily"? for so the chief had named poor Hetty. "Was his name sung by a little bird among Iroquois?"

Hetty did not answer at first, but, with that indescribable feeling that awakens sympathy and intelligence among the youthful and unpractised of her sex, she hung her head, and the blood suffused her cheek ere she found her tongue. It would have exceeded her stock of intelligence to explain this embarrassment, but, though poor Hetty could not reason, on every emergency, she could always feel. The colour slowly receded from her cheeks, and the girl looked up archly at the Indian, smiling with the innocence of a child, mingled with the interest of a woman.

"My sister, the Drooping Lily hear such bird!" Chingachgook added, and this with a gentleness of tone and manner that would have astonished those who sometimes heard the discordant cries that often came from the same throat; these transitions from the harsh and guttural, to the soft and melodious not being infrequent in ordinary Indian dialogues. "My sister's ears were open—has she lost her tongue?"

"You *are* Chingachgook—you *must* be; for there is no other red man here, and she thought Chingachgook would come."

"Chin—gach—gook—" pronouncing the name slowly, and dwelling on each syllable—"Great Sarpent, Yengeese* tongue."

"Chin—gach—gook—" repeated Hetty, in the same deliberate manner. "Yes, so Hist called it, and you *must* be the chief."

"Wah—ta!—Wah—" added the Delaware.

"Wah—ta!—Wah, or Hist—oh!—Hist. I think Hist prettier than Wah, and so I call her Hist."

"Wah! very sweet in Delaware ears!"

"You make it sound differently from me. But, never mind; I *did* hear the bird you speak of sing, Great Serpent."

"Will my sister say words of song. What she sing most—how she look—often she laugh?"

"She sang Chin—gach—gook oftener than any thing else;

---

*It is singular there should be any question concerning the origin of the well known *sobriquet* of "Yankees." Nearly all the old writers, who speak of the Indians first known to the Colonists, make them pronounce the word "English," as "Yengeese." Even at this day, it is a provincialism of New England to say "*E*nglish" instead of "*I*nglish" and there is a close conformity of sound between "*E*nglish" and "Yengeese," more especially if the latter word, as was probably the case, be pronounced short. The transition from "Yengeese," thus pronounced, to "Yankees" is quite easy. If the former is pronounced "Yangis" it is almost identical with "Yankees," and Indian words have seldom been spelt as they are pronounced. Thus the scene of this tale is spelt "Ot*s*ego," and is properly pronounced "Ot*s*ago." The liquids of the Indians would easily convert "En" into "Yen." [1841]

and she laughed heartily, when I told how the Iroquois waded into the water after us, and could'n't catch us. I hope these logs have'n't ears, Serpent!"

"No fear logs; fear sister next room — No fear Iroquois; Deerslayer stuff his eyes and ears, with strange beast."

"I understand you, Serpent, and I understood Hist. Sometimes I think I'm not half as feeble minded as they say I am. Now, do you look up at the roof, and I'll tell you all. But you frighten me you look so eager, when I speak of Hist."

The Indian controlled his looks, and affected to comply with the simple request of the girl.

"Hist told me to say, in a very low voice, that you must'n't trust the Iroquois in any thing. They are more artful than any Indians she knows. Then she says that there is a large bright star that comes over the hill, about an hour after dark, — (Hist had pointed out the planet Jupiter, without knowing it) — and just as that star comes in sight, she will be on the point, where I landed last night, and that you must come for her, in a canoe."

"Good — Chingachgook understand well enough, now; but he understand better if my sister sing him, ag'in."

Hetty repeated her words, more fully explaining what star was meant, and mentioning the part of the point where he was to venture ashore. She now proceeded in her own unsophisticated way to relate her intercourse with the Indian maid, and to repeat several of her expressions and opinions that gave great delight to the heart of her betrothed. She particularly renewed her injunctions to be on their guard against treachery, a warning that was scarcely needed, however, as addressed to men as wary as those to whom it was sent. She also explained, with sufficient clearness, for on all such subjects the mind of the girl seldom failed her, the present state of the enemy, and the movements they had made since morning. Hist had been on the raft with her, until it quitted the shore, and was now somewhere in the woods, opposite to the castle, and did not intend to return to the camp, until night approached; when she hoped to be able to slip away from her companions, as they followed the shore on their way home, and conceal herself on the point. No one appeared to suspect the presence of Chingachgook, though it was necessarily known that an Indian had entered the Ark, the previous night, and it was suspected that he had since appeared in, and about the castle, in the dress of a pale-face. Still some little doubt existed on the latter point, for, as this was the season when white men might be expected to arrive, there was some fear that the garrison of the castle was increasing by these ordinary means. All this had Hist communicated to Hetty while the Indians were dragging them along shore, the distance, which exceeded six miles, affording abundance of time.

"Hist do'n't know, herself, whether they suspect her, or not; or, whether they suspect *you*, but she hopes neither is the case. And now, Serpent, since I have told you so much from your betrothed," continued Hetty, unconsciously taking one of the Indian's hands, and playing with the fingers, as a child is often seen to play with those of a parent, "you must let me tell you something from myself. When you marry Hist, you must be kind to her, and smile on her, as you do now on me, and not look cross as some of the chiefs do at their squaws. Will you promise this?"

"Alway good to Wah! — too tender to twist hard; else she break."

"Yes, and smile, too; you do'n't know how much a girl craves smiles from them she loves. Father scarce smiled on me once, while I was with him — and, Hurry — yes — Hurry talked loud and laughed, but I do'n't think *he* smiled once either. You know the difference between a smile and a laugh?"

"Laugh, best. Hear Wah! laugh, think bird sing!"

"I know that; her laugh *is* pleasant, but *you* must smile. And then, Serpent, you must'n't make her carry burthens and hoe corn, as so many Indians do; but treat her more as the pale faces treat their wives."

"Wah-ta!-Wah no pale face — got red skin; red heart, red feelin's. All red; no pale. *Must* carry papoose."

"Every woman is willing to carry her child," said Hetty smiling, "and there is no harm in *that*. But you must love Hist, and be gentle, and good to her; for she is gentle and good herself."

Chingachgook gravely bowed, and then he seemed to think this part of the subject might be dismissed. Before there was time for Hetty to resume her communications, the voice of Deerslayer was heard calling on his friend, in the outer room. At this summons the Serpent arose to obey, and Hetty joined her sister.

Chapter XIV.

" 'A stranger animal,' cries one,
'Sure never liv'd beneath the sun;
A lizard's body lean and long,
A fish's head, a serpent's tongue,
Its foot, with triple claw disjoined;
And what a length of tail behind!' "
James Merrick, "The Chameleon," ll.21-26.

THE first act of the Delaware, on rejoining his friend, was to proceed gravely to disencumber himself of his civilized attire, and to stand forth an Indian warrior again. The protest of Deerslayer was met by his communicating the fact that the presence of an Indian in the hut, was known to the Iroquois, and that maintaining the disguise would be more likely to direct suspicions to his real object, than if he came out openly as a member of a hostile tribe. When the latter understood the truth, and was told that he had been deceived in supposing the chief had succeeded in entering the Ark undiscovered, he cheerfully consented to the change, since further attempt at concealment was useless. A gentler feeling than the one avowed, however, lay at the bottom of the Indian's desire to appear as a son of the forest. He had been told that Hist was on the opposite shore, and nature so far triumphed over all distinctions of habit, and tribes and people, as to reduce this young savage warrior to the level of a feeling which would have been found in the most refined inhabitant of a town, under similar circumstances. There was a mild satisfaction in believing that she he loved could see him, and as he walked out on the platform in his scanty, native attire, an Apollo of the wilderness, a hundred of the tender fancies that fleet through lovers' brains, beset his imagination and softened his heart.

All this was lost on Deerslayer, who was no great adept in the mysteries of Cupid, but whose mind was far more occupied with the concerns that forced themselves on his attention, than with any of the truant fancies of love. He soon recalled his companion, therefore, to a sense of their actual condition, by summoning him to a sort of council of war, in which they were to settle their future course. In the dialogue that followed, the parties mutually made each other acquainted with what had passed in their several interviews. Chingachgook was told the history of the treaty about the ransom, and Deerslayer heard the whole of Hetty's communications. The latter listened with generous interest to his friend's hopes, and promised cheerfully all the assistance he could lend.

"'Tis our main ar'n'd, Sarpent, as you know, this battling for the castle and old Hutter's darters, coming in as a sort of accident. Yes—yes—I'll be actyve in helping little Hist, who's not only one of the best and handsomest maidens of the tribe, but the *very* best and handsomest. I've always encouraged you, chief, in that liking, and it's proper, too, that a great and ancient race like your'n shouldn't come to an end. If a woman of red skin and red gifts could get to be near enough to me to wish her for a wife, I'd s'arch for just such another, but that can *never* be; no, that can *never* be. I'm glad Hetty has met with Hist, howsever, for though the first is a little short of wit and understanding, the last has enough for both. Yes, Sarpent—" laughing heartily—"put 'em together, and two smarter gals is'n't to be found in all York Colony!"

"I will go to the Iroquois camp," returned the Delaware, gravely. "No one knows Chingachgook but Wah!, and a treaty for lives and scalps should be made by a chief! Give me the strange beasts, and let me take a canoe."

Deerslayer dropped his head, and played with the end of a fish-pole in the water, as he sate dangling his legs over the edge of the platform, like a man who was lost in thought, by the sudden occurrence of a novel idea. Instead of directly answering the proposal of his friend, he began to soliloquize, a circumstance however that in no manner rendered his words more true, as he was remarkable for saying what he thought, whether the remarks were addressed to himself, or to any one else.

"Yes—yes—" he said— "this must be what they call love! I've heard say that it sometimes upsets reason altogether, leaving a young man as helpless, as to calculation and caution, as a brute beast. To think that the Sarpent should be so lost to reason, and cunning, and wisdom! We must, sartainly, manage to get Hist off, and have 'em married as soon as we get back to the tribe, or this war will be of no more use to the chief, than a hunt a little oncommon extr'ornary. Yes — yes — he'll never be the man he was, till this matter is off his mind, and he comes to his senses like all the rest of mankind. Sarpent, you can't be in airnest, and therefore I shall say but little to your offer. But you're a chief, and will soon be sent out on the warpath at head of the parties, and I'll just ask if you'd think of putting your forces into the inimy's hands, afore the battle is fou't?"

"Wah!" ejaculated the Indian.

"Ay — Wah! — I know well enough it's Wah!, and altogether Wah! — Ra'ally, Sarpent, I'm consarned and mortified about you! I never heard so weak an idee come from a chief, and he, too, one that's already got a name for being wise, young and inexper'enced as he is. Canoe you sha'n't have, so long as the v'ice of fri'ndship and warning can count for any thing."

"My pale-face friend is right. A cloud came over the face of Chingachgook, and weakness got into his mind, while his eyes were dim. My brother has a good memory for good deeds, and a weak memory for bad. He will forget."

"Yes, that's easy enough. Say no more about it chief, but if another of them clouds blow near you, do your endivours to get out of its way. Clouds are bad enough in the weather, but when they come to the reason, it gets to be serious. Now, sit down by me here, and let us calculate our movements a little, for we shall soon either have a truce and a peace, or we shall come to an ac*ty*ve, and bloody war. You see the vagabonds can make logs sarve their turn, as well as the best raftsmen on the rivers, and it would be no great expl'ite for them to invade us in a body. I've been thinking of the wisdom of putting all old Tom's stores into the Ark, of barring and locking up the Castle, and of taking to the Ark, altogether. That is moveable, and by keeping the sail up, and shifting places, we might worry through a great many nights, without them Canada wolves finding a way into our sheep fold!"

Chingachgook listened to this plan, with approbation. Did the negotiation fail, there was now little hope that the night would pass without an assault, and the enemy had sagacity enough to understand that, in carrying the castle, they would probably become masters of all it contained, the offered ransom included, and still retain the advantages they had hitherto gained. Some precaution of the sort appeared to be absolutely necessary, for now the numbers of the Iroquois were known, a night attack could scarcely be successfully met. It would be impossible to prevent the enemy from getting possession of the canoes and the Ark, and the latter itself would be a hold in which the assailants would be as effectually protected against bullets as were those in the building. For a few minutes, both the men thought of sinking the Ark, in the shallow water, of bringing the canoes into the house, and of depending altogether on the castle for protection. But reflection satisfied them that, in the end, this expedient would fail. It was so easy to collect logs on the shore, and to construct a raft of almost any size, that it was certain the Iroquois, now they had turned their attention to such means, would resort to them seriously, so long as there was the certainty of success by perseverance. After deliberating maturely, and placing all the considerations fairly before them, the two young beginners in the art of forest warfare, settled down into the opinion that the Ark offered the only available means of security. This decision was no sooner come to, than it was communicated to Judith. The girl had no serious objection to make, and all four set about the measures necessary to carrying the plan into execution.

The reader will readily understand that Floating Tom's worldly goods were of no great amount. A couple of beds, some wearing apparel, the arms and ammunition, a few cooking utensils, with the mysterious and but half examined chest formed the principal items. These were all soon removed, the Ark having been hauled on the eastern side of the building, so that the transfer could be made without being seen from the shore. It was thought unnecessary to disturb the heavier and coarser articles of furniture, as they were not required in the Ark, and were of but little value in themselves. As great caution was necessary in removing the different objects, most of which were passed out of a window with a view to conceal what was going on, it required two or three hours before all could be effected. By the expiration of that time, the raft made its appearance, moving from the shore. Deerslayer immediately had recourse to the glass, by the aid of which he perceived that two warriors were on it, though they appeared to be unarmed. The progress of the raft was slow, a circumstance that formed one of the great advantages that would be possessed by the scow, in any future collision between them, the movements of the latter being comparatively swift and light. As there was time to make the dispositions for the reception of the two dangerous visiters, every thing was prepared for them, long before they had got near enough to be hailed. The Serpent, and the girls retired into the building, where the former stood near the door, well provided with rifles, while Judith watched the proceedings without through a loop. As for Deerslayer, he had brought a stool to the edge of the platform, at the point towards which the raft was advancing, and taken his seat with his rifle leaning carelessly between his legs.

As the raft drew nearer, every means possessed by the party in the castle was resorted to, in order to ascertain if their visiters had any fire arms. Neither Deerslayer nor Chingachgook could discover any, but Judith, unwilling to trust to simple eye-sight, thrust the glass through the loop, and directed it towards the hemlock boughs that lay between the two logs of the raft, forming a sort of flooring, as well as a seat for the use of the rowers. When the heavy moving craft was within fifty feet of him, Deerslayer hailed the Hurons, directing them to cease rowing, it not being his intention to permit them to land. Compliance, of course, was necessary, and the two grim-looking warriors instantly quitted their seats, though the raft continued slowly to approach, until it had driven in much nearer to the platform.

"Are ye chiefs?" demanded Deerslayer with dignity—"Are ye chiefs?—Or have the Mingos sent me warriors without names, on such an ar'n'd? If so, the sooner ye go back, the sooner them will be likely to come that a warrior can talk with."

"Hugh!" exclaimed the elder of the two on the raft, rolling his glowing eyes over the different objects that were visible in and about the Castle, with a keenness that showed how little escaped him. "My brother is very proud, but Rivenoak (we use the literal translation of the term, writing as we do in English) is a name to make a Delaware turn pale."

"That's true, or it's a lie, Rivenoak, as it may be; but I am not likely to turn pale, seeing that I was born pale. What's your ar'n'd, and why do you come among light bark canoes, on logs that are not even dug out?"

"The Iroquois are not ducks, to walk on water! Let the pale faces give them a canoe, and they'll come in a canoe."

"That's more rational, than likely to come to pass. We have but four canoes, and being four persons that's only one for each of us. We thank you for the offer, howsever, though we ask leave not to accept it. You are welcome, Iroquois, on your logs."

"Thanks—My young pale face warrior—he has got a name—how do the chiefs call him?"

Deerslayer hesitated a moment, and a gleam of pride and human weakness came over him. He smiled, muttered between his teeth, and then looking up proudly, he said—

"Mingo, like all who are young and actyve, I've been known by different names, at different times. One of your warriors whose spirit started for the Happy Grounds of your people, as lately as yesterday morning, thought I desarved to be known by the name of Hawkeye, and this because my sight happened to be quicker than his own, when it got to be life or death, atween us."

Chingachgook, who was attentively listening to all that passed, heard and understood this proof of passing weakness in his friend, and on a future occasion he questioned him more closely concerning the transaction on the point, where Deerslayer had first taken human life. When he had got the whole truth, he did not fail to communicate it to the tribe, from which time the young hunter was universally known among the Delawares, by an appellation so honorably earned. As this, however, was a period posterior to all the incidents of this tale, we shall continue to call the young hunter by the name under which he has been first introduced to the reader. Nor was the Iroquois less struck with the vaunt of the white man. He knew of the death of his comrade, and had no difficulty in understanding the allusion, the intercourse between the conqueror and his victim on that occasion, having been seen by several savages on the shore of the lake, who had been stationed at different points just within the margin of bushes to watch the drifting canoes, and who had not time to reach the scene of action, ere the victor had retired. The effect on this rude being of the forest, was an exclamation of surprise; then such a smile of courtesy, and wave of the hand, succeeded, as would have done credit to Asiatic diplomacy. The two Iroquois spoke to each other, in low tones, and both drew near the end of the raft that was closest to the platform.

"My brother, Hawkeye, has sent a message to the Hurons," resumed Rivenoak, "and it has made their hearts very glad. They hear he has images of beasts with two tails! Will he show them to his friends."

"Inimies would be truer," returned Deerslayer, "but sound is n't sense, and does little harm. Here is one of the images; I toss it to you under faith of treaties. If it's not returned, the rifle will settle the p'int atween us."

The Iroquois seemed to acquiesce in the conditions, and Deerslayer arose and prepared to toss one of the elephants to the raft, both parties using all the precaution that was necessary to prevent its loss. As practice renders men expert in such things, the little piece of ivory was soon successfully transferred from one hand to the other, and then followed another scene on the raft, in which astonishment and delight got the mastery of Indian stoicism. These two grim old warriors manifested even more feeling, as they examined the curiously wrought chess-man, than had been betrayed by the boy; for, in the case of the latter, recent schooling had interposed its influence; while the men, like all who are sustained by well established characters, were not ashamed to let some of their emotions be discovered. For a few minutes they apparently lost the consciousness of their situation, in the intense scrutiny they bestowed on a material so fine, work so highly wrought, and an animal so extraordinary. The lip of the moose is, perhaps, the nearest approach to the trunk of the elephant that is to be found in the American forest, but this resemblance was far from being sufficiently striking to bring the new creature within the range of their habits and ideas, and the more they studied the image, the greater was their astonishment. Nor did these children of the forest mistake the structure on the back of the elephant for a part of the animal. They were familiar with horses and oxen, and had seen towers in the Canadas, and found nothing surprising in creatures of burthen. Still, by a very natural association, they supposed the carving meant to represent, that the animal they saw, was of a strength sufficient to carry a fort on its back; a circumstance that, in no degree, lessened their wonder.

"Has my pale face brother any more such beasts?" at last the senior of the Iroquois asked, in a sort of petitioning manner.

"There's more where them came from, Mingo," was the answer; "one is enough, howsever, to buy off fifty scalps."

"One of my prisoners is a great warrior—tall as a pine—strong as the moose—active as a deer—fierce as the panther! Some day he'll be a great chief, and lead the army of King George!"

"Tut—tut—Mingo; Hurry Harry is Hurry Harry, and you'll never make more than a corporal of him, if you do that. He's tall enough, of a sartainty; but that's of no use, as he only hits his head ag'in the branches as he goes through the forest. He's strong too, but a strong body is'n't a strong head, and the king's generals are not chosen for their sinews; he's swift, if you will, but a rifle bullet is swifter; and as for f'erceness, it's no great ricommend to a soldier; they that think they feel the stoutest, often givin' out at the pinch. No—no—you'll niver make Hurry's scalp pass for more than a good head of curly hair, and a rattle pate beneath it!"

"My old prisoner very wise—king of the lake—great warrior, wise counsellor!"

"Well, there's them that might gainsay all this, too, Mingo. A very wise man would'n't be apt to be taken in so foolish a manner as befel Master Hutter, and if he gives good counsel, he must have listened to very bad, in that affair. There's only one king of this lake, and he's a long way off, and is'n't likely ever to see it. Floating Tom is some such king of this region, as the wolf that prowls through the woods, is king of the forest. A beast with two tails is well worth two such scalps!"

"But my brother has another beast?—He will give two—" holding up as many fingers—"for old father?"

"Floating Tom is no father of mine, but he'll fare none the worse for that. As for giving two beasts for his scalp, and each

IX. Engraving by William Charles of a scene on the "Frontiers as practiced by the Humane British and their Worthy Allies."

x. Otsego Rock or Council Rock, where Deerslayer meets Chingachgook in Chapter IX.

XI. "Three Mile Point," a painting by Louis Ramy Mignot and Julius Collman

XII. Chingachgook examines one of the ivory elephant "castles" found in Hutter's trunk beast with two tails, it is quite beyond reason. Think yourself well off, Mingo, if you make a much worse trade."

By this time the self-command of Rivenoak had got the better of his wonder, and he began to fall back on his usual habits of cunning, in order to drive the best bargain he could. It would be useless to relate more than the substance of the desultory dialogue that followed, in which the Indian manifested no little management, in endeavoring to recover the ground lost under the influence of surprise. He even affected to doubt whether any original for the image of the beast existed, and asserted that the oldest Indian had never heard a tradition of any such animal. Little did either of them imagine, at the time, that long ere a century elapsed, the progress of civilization would bring even much more extraordinary and rare animals into that region, as curiosities to be gazed at by the curious, and that the particular beast, about which the disputants contended, would be seen laving its sides, and swimming in the very sheet of water, on which they had met.* As is not uncommon on such occasions, one of the parties got a little warm, in the course of the discussion, for Deerslayer met all the arguments and prevarication of his subtle opponent, with his own cool directness of manner, and unmoved love of truth. What an elephant was he knew little better than the savage, but he perfectly understood that the carved pieces of ivory must have some such value in the eyes of an Iroquois, as a bag of gold, or a package of beaver skins would in those of a trader. Under the circumstances, therefore, he felt it to be prudent not to concede too much at first, since there existed a nearly unconquerable obstacle to making the transfers, even after the contracting parties had actually agreed upon the terms. Keeping this difficulty in view, he held the extra chessmen in reserve, as a means of smoothing any difficulty in the moment of need.

At length the savage pretended that further negotiation was useless, since he could not be so unjust to his tribe as to part with the honor and emoluments of two excellent, full grown,

---

*The Otsego is a favorite place for the caravan keepers to let their elephants bathe. The writer has seen two at a time, since the publication of this book, swimming about in company. [1850]

male, scalps for a consideration so trifling as a toy like that he had seen, and he prepared to take his departure. Both parties now felt as men are wont to feel, when a bargain that each is anxious to conclude, is on the eve of being broken off, in consequence of too much pertinacity in the way of management. The effect of the disappointment was very different, however, on the respective individuals. Deerslayer was mortified, and filled with regret, for he not only felt for the prisoners, but he also felt deeply for the two girls. The conclusion of the treaty, therefore, left him melancholy and full of regret. With the savage, his defeat produced the desire of revenge. In a moment of excitement, he had loudly announced his intention to say no more, and he felt equally enraged with himself and with his cool opponent, that he had permitted a pale face to manifest more indifference and self-command than an Indian chief. When he began to urge his raft away from the platform, his countenance lowered, and his eye glowed, even while he affected a smile of amity and a gesture of courtesy, at parting.

It took some little time to overcome the *vis inertiæ* of the logs, and while this was being done by the silent Indian, Rivenoak stalked over the hemlock boughs that lay between the logs, in sullen ferocity, eyeing keenly the while, the hut, the platform, and the person of his late disputant. Once he spoke in low, quick tones to his companion, and he stirred the boughs with his feet, like an animal that is restive. At that moment, the watchfulness of Deerslayer had a little abated, for he sat musing on the means of renewing the negotiation without giving too much advantage to the other side. It was perhaps fortunate for him that the keen and bright eyes of Judith were as vigilant as ever. At the instant when the young man was least on his guard, and his enemy was the most on the alert, she called out, in a warning voice, to the former, most opportunely, giving the alarm.

"Be on your guard, Deerslayer," the girl cried—"I see rifles with the glass, beneath the hemlock brush, and the Iroquois is loosening them with his feet!"

It would seem that the enemy had carried their artifices so far as to employ an agent who understood English. The previous dialogue had taken place in his own language, but it was evident, by the sudden manner in which his feet ceased their treacherous occupation, and in which the countenance of Rivenoak changed from sullen ferocity to a smile of courtesy, that the call of the girl was understood. Signing to his companion to cease his efforts to set the logs in motion, he advanced to the end of the raft which was nearest to the platform, and spoke.

"Why should Rivenoak and his brother leave any cloud between them," he said. "They are both wise, both brave, and both generous; they ought to part friends. One beast shall be the price of one prisoner."

"And, Mingo," answered the other, delighted to renew the negotiations on almost any terms, and determined to clinch the bargain if possible by a little extra liberality, "you'll see that a pale face knows how to pay a full price, when he trades with an open heart, and an open hand. Keep the beast that you had forgotten to give back to me, as you was about to start, and which I forgot to ask for, on account of consarn at parting in anger. Show it to your chiefs. When you bring us our fri'nds, two more shall be added to it—and—" hesitating a moment in distrust of the expediency of so great a concession; then, deciding in its favor—"and, if we see them afore the sun sets, we may find a fourth to make up an even number."

This settled the matter. Every gleam of discontent vanished from the dark countenance of the Iroquois, and he smiled as graciously, if not as sweetly, as Judith Hutter, herself. The piece already in his possession was again examined, and an ejaculation of pleasure, showed how much he was pleased with this unexpected termination of the affair. In point of fact, both he and Deerslayer had momentarily forgotten what had become of the subject of their discussion, in the warmth of their feelings, but such had not been the case with Rivenoak's companion. This man retained the piece, and had fully made up his mind, were it claimed under such circumstances as to render its return necessary, to drop it in the lake, trusting to his being able to find it, again, at some future day. This desperate expedient, however, was no longer necessary, and after repeating the terms of agreement, and professing to understand them, the two Indians finally took their departure, moving slowly towards the shore.

"Can any faith be put in such wretches?" asked Judith, when

she and Hetty had come out on the platform, and were standing at the side of Deerslayer, watching the dull movement of the logs. "Will they not rather keep the toy they have, and send us off some bloody proofs of their getting the better of us in cunning, by way of boasting? I've heard of acts as bad as this."

"No doubt—Judith; no manner of doubt, if it was'n't for Indian natur'. But I'm no judge of a red skin, if that two tail'd beast does'n't set the whole tribe in some such stir, as a stick raises in a beehive! Now, there's the Sarpent; a man with narves like flint, and no more cur'osity in every day consarns, than is befitting prudence; why he was so overcome with the sight of the creatur', carved as it is in bone, that I felt ashamed for him! That's just their gifts, howsever, and one can't well quarrel with a man for his gifts, when they are lawful. Chingachgook will soon get over his weakness, and remember that he's a chief, and that he comes of a great stock, and has a renowned name to support and uphold; but, as for yonder scamps, there'll be no peace among 'em, until they think they've got possession of every thing of the natur' of that bit of carved bone, that's to be found among Thomas Hutter's stores!"

"They only know of the elephants, and can have no hopes about the other things."

"That's true, Judith; still, covetousness is a craving feelin'! They'll say, if the pale faces have these cur'ous beasts with two tails, who knows but they've got some with three, or, for that matter, with four! That's what the schoolmasters call nat'ral arithmetic, and t'will be sartain to beset the feelin's of savages. They'll never be easy, till the truth is known."

"Do you think, Deerslayer," inquired Hetty, in her simple and innocent manner, "that the Iroquois wo'n't let father and Hurry go?—I read to them several of the very best verses in the whole bible, and you see what they have done, already."

The hunter, as he always did, listened kindly and even affectionately to Hetty's remarks; then he mused a moment in silence. There was something like a flush on his cheek, as he answered, after quite a minute had passed.

"I do'n't know whether a white man ought to be ashamed, or not, to own he can't read, but such is my case, Judith. You are skilful, I find, in all such matters, while I have only studied the hand of God, as it is seen in the hills and the valleys, the mountain-tops, the streams, the forests and the springs. Much l'arning may be got in this way, as well as out of books; and, yet, I sometimes think it is a white man's gift to read! When I hear from the mouths of the Moravians, the words of which Hetty speaks, they raise a longing in my mind, and I then think I *will* know how to read 'em myself; but the game in summer, and the traditions, and lessons in war, and other matters, have always kept me behind hand."

"Shall I teach you, Deerslayer?" asked Hetty, earnestly. "I'm weak-minded, they say, but I can read as well as Judith. It might save your life to know how to read the bible to the savages, and it will certainly save your soul; for mother told me *that*, again and again!"

"Thankee, Hetty—yes, thankee, with all my heart. These are like to be too stirring times for much idleness, but, after it's peace, and I come to see you ag'in on this lake, then I'll give myself up to it, as if 'twas pleasure and profit, in a single business. Perhaps I ought to be ashamed, Judith, that 'tis so; but truth is truth. As for these Iroquois, tis'n't very likely they'll forget a beast with two tails, on account of a varse or two from the bible. I rather expect they'll give up the prisoners, and trust to some sarcumvention, or other, to get 'em back, ag'in, with us and all in the castle and the Ark, in the bargain. Howsever, we must humour the vagabonds, first to get your father and Hurry out of their hands, and next to keep the peace atween us, until such time as the Sarpent there, can make out to get off his betrothed wife. If there's any sudden outbreakin' of anger and ferocity, the Indians will send off all their women and children to the camp, at once, whereas, by keeping 'em calm and trustful, we may manage to meet Hist, at the spot she has mentioned. Rather than have the bargain fall through, now, I'd throw in half a dozen of them effigy bow-and-arrow men, such as we've in plenty in the chist."

Judith cheerfully assented, for she would have resigned even the flowered brocade, rather than not redeem her father and please Deerslayer.

The prospects of success were now so encouraging, as to raise the spirits of all in the castle, though a due watchfulness, of the movements of the enemy was maintained. Hour passed

after hour, notwithstanding, and the sun had once more begun
to fall towards the summits of the western hills, and yet no
signs were seen of the return of the raft. By dint of sweeping
the shore with the glass, Deerslayer at length discovered a
place in the dense and dark woods, where, he entertained no
doubt, the Iroquois were assembled in considerable numbers.
It was near the thicket whence the raft had issued, and a little
rill that trickled into the lake, announced the vicinity of a spring.
Here, then, the savages were probably holding their consultation, and the decision was to be made that went to settle the
question of life or death for the prisoners. There was one
ground for hope in spite of the delay, however, that Deerslayer
did not fail to place before his anxious companions. It was far
more probable that the Indians had left their prisoners in the
camp, than that they had encumbered themselves by causing
them to follow through the woods, a party that was out on a
merely temporary excursion. If such was the fact, it required
considerable time to send a messenger the necessary distance,
and to bring the two white men to the spot where they were to
embark. Encouraged by these reflections, a new stock of patience was gathered, and the declension of the sun was viewed
with less alarm.

The result justified Deerslayer's conjecture. Not long before
the sun had finally disappeared, the two logs were seen coming
out of the thicket, again, and, as it drew near, Judith announced
that her father and Hurry, both of them pinioned, lay on the
bushes in the centre. As before, the two Indians were rowing.
The latter seemed to be conscious that the lateness of the hour
demanded unusual exertions, and contrary to the habits of
their people, who are ever averse to toil, they labored hard at
the rude substitutes for oars. In consequence of this diligence,
the raft occupied its old station, in about half the time that had
been taken in the previous visits.

Even after the conditions were so well understood, and matters had proceeded so far, the actual transfer of the prisoners
was not a duty to be executed without difficulty. The Iroquois
were compelled to place great reliance on the good faith of
their foes, though it was reluctantly given; and was yielded to
necessity rather than to confidence. As soon as Hutter and
Hurry should be released, the party in the castle numbered

two to one, as opposed to those on the raft, and escape by flight was out of the question, as the former had three bark canoes, to say nothing of the defences of the house and the Ark. All this was understood by both parties, and it is probable the arrangement never could have been completed, had not the honest countenance and manner of Deerslayer wrought their usual effect on Rivenoak.

"My brother knows I put faith in *him*—" said the latter, as he advanced with Hutter, whose legs had been released to enable the old man to ascend to the platform. "One scalp—one more beast."

"Stop—Mingo—" interrupted the hunter— "keep your prisoner a moment. I have to go and seek the means of payment."

This excuse, however, though true in part, was principally a fetch. Deerslayer left the platform, and entering the house, he directed Judith to collect all the arms, and to conceal them in her own room. He then spoke earnestly to the Delaware, who stood on guard as before, near the entrance of the building, put the three remaining castles in his pocket, and returned.

"You are welcome back, to your old abode, Master Hutter," said Deerslayer, as he helped the other up on the platform, slily passing into the hand of Rivenoak, at the same time, another of the castles. "You'll find your darters right glad to see you, and here's Hetty come herself, to say as much in her own behalf."

Here the hunter stopped speaking and broke out into a hearty fit of his silent and peculiar laughter. Hurry's legs were just released, and he had been placed on his feet. So tightly had the ligatures been drawn, that the use of his limbs was not immediately recovered, and the young giant presented, in good sooth, a very helpless and a somewhat ludicrous picture. It was this unusual spectacle, particularly the bewildered countenance, that excited the merriment of Deerslayer.

"You look like a girdled pine in a clearin', Hurry Harry, that is rocking in a gale," said Deerslayer, checking his unseasonable mirth, more from delicacy to the others, than from any respect to the liberated captive. "I'm glad, howsever, to see that you have'n't had your hair dressed by any of the Iroquois barbers, in your late visit to their camp."

"Harkee, Deerslayer," returned the other a little fiercely, "it will be prudent for you to deal less in mirth, and more in friendship, on this occasion. Act like a christian, for once, and not like a laughing gal, in a country school, when the master's back is turned, and just tell me whether there's any feet, or not, at the end of these legs of mine. I think I can see them, but as for feelin' they might as well be down on the banks of the Mohawk, as be where they seem to be."

"You've come off whole, Hurry, and that's not a little," answered the other, secretly passing to the Indian the remainder of the stipulated ransom, and making an earnest sign, at the same moment, for him to commence his retreat. "You've come off whole, feet and all, and are only a little numb, from a tight fit of the withes. Natur'll soon set the blood in motion, and then you may begin to dance, to celebrate what I call a most wonderful and onexpected deliverance from a den of wolves."

Deerslayer released the arms of his friends, as each landed, and the two were now stamping and limping about on the platform, growling and uttering denunciations, as they endeavored to help the returning circulation. They had been tethered too long, however, to regain the use of their limbs in a moment, and the Indians being quite as diligent on their return, as on their advance, the raft was fully a hundred yards from the castle, when Hurry, turning accidentally in that direction, discovered how fast it was getting beyond the reach of his vengeance. By this time, he could move with tolerable facility, though still numb and awkward. Without considering his own situation, however, he seized the rifle that leaned against the shoulder of Deerslayer, and attempted to cock and present it. The young hunter was too quick for him. Seizing the piece he wrenched it from the hands of the giant, not, however, until it had gone off in the struggle, when pointed directly upward. It is probable that Deerslayer could have prevailed in such a contest, on account of the condition of Hurry's limbs, but the instant the gun went off, the latter yielded, and stumped towards the house, raising his legs at each step, quite a foot from the ground, from an uncertainty of the actual position of his feet. But he had been anticipated by Judith. The whole stock of Hutter's arms, which had been left in the building, as a resource in the event of a sudden outbreaking of hostilities, had been removed, and were already secreted, agreeably to Deerslayer's directions. In consequence of this precaution, no means offered by which March could put his designs in execution.

Disappointed in his vengeance, Hurry seated himself, and like Hutter, for half an hour, he was too much occupied in endeavoring to restore the circulation, and in regaining the use of his limbs, to indulge in any other reflections. By the end of this time the raft had disappeared, and night was beginning to throw her shadows once more over the whole silvan scene. Before darkness had completely set in, and while the girls were preparing the evening meal, Deerslayer related to Hutter an outline of events that had taken place, and gave him a history of the means he had adopted for the security of his children and property.

Chapter XV.

"As long as Edwarde rules thys lande,
Ne quiet you wylle know;
Your sonnes and husbandes shall be slayne,
And brookes with blowde shall flowe.

You leave youre goode and lawfulle kynge
Whenne ynne aduersitye
Like mee, untoe the true cause stycke,
And for the true cause dye."
                          Chatterton, "Bristowe Tragedie," ll.357–64.

THE calm of evening was again in singular contrast to, while its gathering gloom was in as singular unison with, the passions of men. The sun was set, and the rays of the retiring luminary ceased to gild the edges of the few clouds that had sufficient openings to admit the passage of its fading light. The canopy overhead was heavy and dense, promising another night of darkness, but the surface of the lake was scarcely disturbed by a ripple. There was a little air, though it scarce deserved to be termed wind. Still, being damp and heavy it had a certain force. The party in the castle were as gloomy and silent as the scene. The two ransomed prisoners felt humbled and dishonored, but their humility partook of the rancor of revenge. They were far more disposed to remember the indignity with which they had been treated during the last few hours of their captivity, than to feel grateful for the previous indulgence. Then that keensighted monitor conscience, by reminding them of the retributive justice of all they had endured, goaded them, rather to turn the tables on their enemies, than to accuse themselves. As for the others, they were thoughtful equally from regret and joy. Deerslayer and Judith felt most of the former sensation, though from very different causes, while Hetty for the moment was perfectly happy. The Delaware had also lively pictures of felicity in the prospect of so soon regaining his betrothed. Under such circumstances, and in this mood, all were taking the evening meal.

"Old Tom!" cried Hurry, bursting into a fit of boisterous laughter, "you look'd amazin'ly like a tethered bear, as you was stretched on them hemlock boughs, and I only wonder you did n't growl, more. Well, it's over, and syth's and lamentations won't mend the matter! There's the blackguard Rivenoak, he that brought us off, has an oncommon scalp, and I'd give as much for it myself, as the colony. Yes, I feel as rich as the governor, in these matters now, and will lay down with 'em, doubloon for doubloon. Judith, darling, did you mourn for me much, when I was in the hands of the Philipsteins."

The last were a family of German descent on the Mohawk, to whom Hurry had a great antipathy, and whom he had confounded with the enemies of Judea.

"Our tears have raised the lake, Harry March, as you might have seen by the shore!" returned Judith, with a feigned levity she was far from feeling. "That Hetty and I should have grieved for father was to be expected, but we fairly rained tears for you."

"We *were* sorry for poor Hurry, as well as for father, Judith!" put in her innocent and unconscious sister.

"True, girl, true; but we feel sorrow for every body that's in trouble, you know," returned the other in a quick, admonitory manner and a low tone. "Nevertheless, we are glad to see you, Master March, and out of the hands of the Philipsteins, too."

"Yes, they're a bad set, and so is the other brood of 'em, down on the river. It's a wonderment to me, how you got us off, Deerslayer, and I forgive you the interference that prevented my doin' justice on that vagabond, for this small sarvice. Let us into the secret, that we may do you the same good turn, at need. Was it by lying, or by coaxing?"

"By neither, Hurry, but by buying. We paid a ransom for you both, and that, too, at a price so high, you had well be on your guard ag'in another cap*ty*vement, lest our stock of goods should'n't hold out."

"A ransom! — Old Tom has paid the fiddler, then, for nothing of mine would have bought off the hair, much less the skin. I did'n't think men as keen set as them vagabonds, would let a fellow up so easy, when they had him fairly at a close hug, and floored. But money is money and somehow it's unnat'ral hard to withstand. Injin or White man, 'tis pretty much the same. It must be owned, Judith, there's a considerable of human natur' in mankind ginirally, arter all!"

Hutter now rose, and signing to Deerslayer, he led him to an inner room, where, in answer to his questions he first learned the price that had been paid for his release. The old man expressed neither resentment nor surprise at the inroad that had been made on his chest, though he did manifest some curiosity to know how far the investigation of its contents had been carried. He also inquired where the key had been found. The habitual frankness of Deerslayer prevented any prevarication, and the conference soon terminated by the return of the two to the outer room, or that which served for the double purpose of parlor and kitchen.

"I wonder if it's peace or war, between us and the savages!" exclaimed Hurry, just as Deerslayer, who had paused for a single instant, listened attentively, and was passing through the outer door without stopping. "This givin' up captives has a friendly look, and when men have traded together, on a fair and honorable footing, they ought to part fri'nds, for that occasion, at least. Come back, Deerslayer, and let us have your judgment, for I'm beginnin' to think more of you, since your late behaviour, than I used to do."

"There's an answer to your question, Hurry, since you're in such haste to come, ag'in, to blows."

As Deerslayer spoke, he threw on the table, on which the other was reclining with one elbow, a sort of miniature faggot, composed of a dozen sticks bound tightly together with a deerskin thong. March seized it eagerly, and holding it close to a blazing knot of pine that lay on the hearth, and which gave out all the light there was in the room, ascertained that the ends of the several sticks had been dipped in blood.

"If this is'n't plain English," said the reckless frontier man, "it's plain Injin! Here's what they call a dicliration of war, down at York, Judith. How did you come by this defiance, Deerslayer?"

"Fairly enough. It lay, not a minut' since, in what you call Floatin' Tom's door yard."

"How came it there? It never fell from the clouds, Judith, as little toads sometimes do, and then it don't rain. You must prove where it come from, Deerslayer, or we shall suspect some design to skear them that would have lost their wits long ago, if fear could drive 'em away."

Deerslayer had approached a window, and cast a glance out of it, on the dark aspect of the lake. As if satisfied with what he beheld, he drew near Hurry, and took the bundle of sticks into his own hand, examining it attentively.

"Yes, this is an Indian dicliration of war, sure enough," he said, "and it's a proof how little you're suited to be on the path it has travelled, Harry March, that it has got here, and you never the wiser, as to the means. The savages may have left the scalp on your head, but they must have taken off the *ears*; else you'd have heard the stirring of the water made by the lad as he come off, ag'in, on his two logs. His ar'n'd was to throw these sticks at our door, as much as to say, we've struck the war post, since the trade, and the next thing will be to strike *you*."

"The prowling wolves! But hand me that rifle Judith, and I'll send an answer back to the vagabonds, through their messenger."

"Not while I stand by, Master March," coolly put in Deerslayer, motioning for the other to forbear. "Faith is faith, whether given to a redskin, or to a christian. The lad lighted a knot, and came off fairly, under its blaze, to give us this warning, and no man, here, should harm him, while empl'yed on such an ar'n'd. There's no use in words, for the lad is too cunning to leave the knot burning, now his business is done, and the night is already too dark for a rifle to have any sartainty."

"That may be true enough, as to a gun, but there's virtue still in a canoe," answered Hurry passing towards the door, with enormous strides, carrying a rifle in his hands. "The being doesn't live that shall stop me from following, and bringing back that riptyle's scalp. The more on 'em, that you crush in the egg, the fewer they'll be to dart at you in the woods!"

Judith trembled like the aspen, she scarce knew why herself, though there was the prospect of a scene of violence; for, if Hurry was fierce and overbearing in the consciousness of his vast strength, Deerslayer had about him the calm determination that promises greater perseverance, and a resolution more likely to effect its object. It was the stern, resolute eye of the latter, rather than the noisy vehemence of the first, that excited her apprehensions. Hurry soon reached the spot where the canoe was fastened, but not before Deerslayer had spoken in a quick, earnest voice to the Serpent in Delaware. The latter had been the first, in truth, to hear the sounds of the oars, and he had gone upon the platform, in jealous watchfulness. The light satisfied him that a message was coming, and when the boy cast his bundle of sticks at his feet, it neither moved his anger, nor induced surprise. He merely stood at watch, rifle in hand, to make certain that no treachery lay behind the defiance. As Deerslayer now called to him, he stepped into the canoe, and quick as thought removed the paddles. Hurry was furious when he found that he was deprived of the means of proceeding. He first approached the Indian with loud menaces, and even Deerslayer stood aghast at the probable consequences. March shook his sledge-hammer fists, and flourished his arms, as he drew near the Indian, and all expected he would attempt to fell the Delaware to the earth; one of them, at least, was well aware that such an experiment would be followed by immediate bloodshed. But even Hurry was awed by the stern composure of the chief, and he, too, knew that such a man was not to be outraged with impunity; he, therefore, turned to vent his rage on Deerslayer, where he foresaw no consequences so terrible. What might have been the result of this second demonstration if completed, is unknown, since it was never made.

"Hurry," said a gentle, soothing voice at his elbow—"it's wicked to be so angry, and God will not overlook it. The Iroquois treated you well, and they did n't take *your* scalp, though you and father wanted to take *theirs*."

The influence of mildness on passion is well known. Hetty, too, had earned a sort of consideration, that had never before been enjoyed by her, through the self-devotion and decision of her recent conduct. Perhaps her established mental imbecility, by removing all distrust of a wish to control, aided her influence. Let the cause be as questionable as it might, the effect was sufficiently certain. Instead of throttling his old fellow traveller, Hurry turned to the girl, and poured out a portion of his discontent, if none of his anger, on her attentive ears.

" 'Tis too bad, Hetty!" he exclaimed; "as bad as a county gaol, or a lack of beaver, to get a creatur' into your very trap, and then to see it get off. As much as six first quality skins, in valie, has paddled off on them clumsy logs, when twenty strokes of a well turned paddle, would overtake 'em. I say in valie, for as to the boy in the way of natur', he is only a boy, and is worth neither more nor less than one. Deerslayer, you've been ontrue to your fri'nds in letting such a chance slip through my fingers, as well as your own."

The answer was given quietly, but with a voice as steady as a fearless nature, and the consciousness of rectitude could make it.

"I should have been ontrue to the right, had I done otherwise—" returned the Deerslayer, steadily, "and neither you, nor any other man has authority to demand that much of me. The lad came on a lawful business, and the meanest red-skin that roams the woods, would be ashamed of not respecting his ar'n'd. But he's now far beyond your reach, Master March, and there's little use in talking, like a couple of women, of what can no longer be helped."

So saying, Deerslayer turned away, like one resolved to waste no more words on the subject, while Hutter pulled Hurry by the sleeve, and led him into the Ark. There they sat long, in private conference. In the mean time, the Indian and his friend, had their secret consultation, for, though it wanted some three or four hours to the rising of the star, the former could not abstain from canvassing his scheme, and from opening his heart to the other. Judith, too, yielded to her softer feelings, and listened to the whole of Hetty's artless narrative of what occurred after she had landed. The woods had few terrors for either of these girls, educated as they had been, and accustomed as they were to look out daily at their rich expanse, or to wander beneath their dark shades, but the elder sister felt that she would have hesitated about thus venturing alone into an Iroquois camp. Concerning Hist, Hetty was not very communicative. She spoke of her kindness, and gentleness and of the meeting in the forest, but the secret of Chingachgook was guarded with a shrewdness and fidelity, that many a sharper witted girl might have failed to display.

At length the several conferences were broken up by the reappearance of Hutter on the platform. Here he assembled the whole party, and communicated as much of his intentions as he deemed expedient. Of the arrangement made by Deerslayer, to abandon the castle during the night, and to take refuge in the Ark he entirely approved. It struck him, as it had the others, as the only effectual means of escaping destruction. Now that the savages had turned their attention to the construction of rafts, no doubt could exist of their at least making an attempt to carry the building, and the message of the bloody sticks sufficiently showed their confidence in their own success. In short, the old man viewed the night as critical, and he called on all to get ready as soon as possible, in order to abandon the dwelling, temporarily, at least, if not forever.

These communications made, every thing proceeded promptly and with intelligence. The castle was secured in the manner already described, the canoes were withdrawn from the dock, and fastened to the Ark, by the side of the other, the few necessaries that had been left in the house, were transferred to the cabin, the fire was extinguished, and all embarked.

The vicinity of the hills, with their drapery of pines, had the effect to render nights that were obscure, darker than common, on the lake. As usual, however, a belt of comparative light was stretched through the centre of the sheet, while it was within the shadows of the mountains that the gloom rested most heavily on the water. The island, or castle, stood in this belt of comparative light, but still the night was so dark, as to cover the departure of the Ark. At the distance of an observer on the shore, her movements could not be seen at all, more particularly as a back ground of dark hillside filled up the perspective of every view that was taken diagonally, or directly across the water. The prevalent winds on the lakes of that region are west, but owing to the avenues formed by the mountains, it is frequently impossible to tell the true direction of the currents, as they often vary, within short distances, and brief differences of time. This is truer in light, fluctuating puffs of air, than in steady breezes, though the squalls of even the latter, are familiarly known to be uncertain and baffling in all mountainous regions and narrow waters. On the present occasion, Hutter himself, as he shoved the Ark from her berth, at the side of the platform, was at a loss to pronounce which way the wind blew. In common, this difficulty was solved by the clouds, which, floating high above the hill tops, as a matter of course obeyed the true currents, but now the whole vault of heaven seemed a mass of gloomy wall. Not an opening of any sort was visible, and Chingachgook was already trembling lest the non-appearance of the star might prevent his betrothed from being punctual to her appointment. Under these circumstances, Hutter hoisted his sail, seemingly with the sole intention of getting away from the castle, as it might be dangerous to remain much longer in its vicinity. The air soon filled the cloth; and when the scow was got under command, and the sail was properly trimmed, it was found that the direction was southerly, inclining towards the eastern shore. No better course offering for the purposes of the party, the singular craft was suffered to skim the surface of the water in this direction for more than an hour, when a change in the currents of the air drove them over towards the camp.

Deerslayer watched all the movements of Hutter and Hurry, with jealous attention. At first, he did not know whether to ascribe the course they held to accident, or to design, but he now began to suspect the latter. Familiar as Hutter was with the lake, it was easy to deceive one who had little practice on the water, and let his intentions be what they might, it was evident, ere two hours had elapsed, that the Ark had got over sufficient space to be within a hundred rods of the shore, directly abreast of the known position of the camp. For a considerable time previously to reaching this point, Hurry, who had some knowledge of the Algonquin languages, had been in close conference with the Indian, and the result was now announced by the latter to Deerslayer, who had been a cold, not to say distrusted, looker-on of all that passed.

"My old father, and my young brother, the Big Pine, —" for so the Delaware had named March, "want to see Huron scalps at their belts," said Chingachgook to his friend. "There is room for some on the girdle of the Serpent, and his people will look for them when he goes back to his village. Their eyes must not be left long in a fog, but they must see what they look for. I know that my brother has a white hand; he will not strike even the dead. He will wait for us; when we come back he will not hide his face from shame for his friend. The Great Serpent of the Mohicans, must be worthy to go on the warpath with Hawkeye."

"Ay — ay — Sarpent, I see how it is; that name's to stick, and in time, I shall get to be known by it," returned Deerslayer. "Well, if such honors will come, the humblest of us all must be willing to abide by 'em. As for you looking for scalps, it belongs to your gifts, and I see no harm in it. Be marciful, Sarpent, howsever; be marciful, I beseech of you. It surely can do no harm to a red skin's honor to show a little marcy. As for the old man, the father of two young women who might ripen better feelin's in his heart, and Harry March, here, who, pine as he is, might better bear the fruit of a more christianized tree, as for *them* two, I leave 'em in the hands of the white man's god. Was'n't it for the bloody sticks no man should go ag'in the Mingos this night, seein' that it would dishonor our faith and characters; but them that crave blood, can't complain if blood is shed at their call. Still, Sarpent, you can be *marciful*. Do'n't begin your career with the wails of women, and the cries of children. Bear yourself so that Hist will smile, and not weep, when she meets you. Go, then; and the Manitou presarve you."

"My brother will stay here with the scow. Wah! will soon be standing on the shore waiting, and Chingachgook must hasten."

The Indian then joined his two coadventurers, and first lowering the sail, they all three entered a canoe, and left the side of the Ark. Neither Hutter nor March spoke to Deerslayer concerning their object, or the probable length of their absence. All this had been confided to the Indian, who had acquitted himself of the trust with characteristic brevity. As soon as the canoe was out of sight, and that occurred ere the paddles had given a dozen strokes, Deerslayer made the best dispositions he could to keep the Ark as nearly stationary as possible, and then he sat down in the end of the scow, to chew the cud of his own bitter reflections. It was not long, however, before he was joined by Judith, who now sought every occasion to be near him, managing her attack on his affections, with the address that was suggested by native coquetry aided by no little practice, but which received much of its most dangerous power, from the touch of feeling that threw around her manner, voice, accents, thoughts and acts the indescribable witchery of natural tenderness. Leaving the young hunter exposed to these dangerous assailants, it has become our more immediate business to follow the party in the canoe, to the shore.

The controlling influence that led Hutter and Hurry to repeat their experiment against the camp was precisely that which had induced the first attempt, a little heightened, perhaps, by the desire of revenge. But, neither of these two rude beings, so ruthless in all things that touched the rights and interests of the red man, though possessing veins of human feeling on other matters, was much actuated by any other desire than a heartless longing for profit. Hurry had felt angered at his sufferings, when first liberated, it is true, but that emotion soon disappeared in the habitual love of gold, which he sought with the reckless avidity of a needy spendthrift, rather than with the ceaseless longings of a miser. In short, the motive that urged them both so soon to go against the Hurons was an habitual contempt of their enemy, acting on the unceasing cupidity of prodigality. The additional chances of success, however, had their place in the formation of the second enterprise. It was known that a large portion of the warriors — perhaps all — were encamped for the night, abreast of the castle, and it was hoped that the scalps of helpless victims would be the consequence. To confess the truth, Hutter in particular — he who had just left two daughters behind him — expected to find few besides women and children in the camp. This fact had been but slightly alluded to, in his communications with Hurry, and with Chingachgook it had been kept entirely out of view. If the Indian thought of it at all, it was known only to himself.

Hutter steered the canoe; Hurry had manfully taken his post in the bows, and Chingachgook stood in the centre. We say stood, for all three were so skilled in the management of that species of frail bark, as to be able to keep erect positions, in the midst of the darkness. The approach to the shore was made with great caution, and the landing effected in safety. The three now prepared their arms, and began their tiger-like approach upon the camp. The Indian was on the lead, his two companions treading in his footsteps, with a stealthy cautiousness of manner, that rendered their progress almost literally noiseless. Occasionally a dried twig snapped under the heavy weight of the gigantic Hurry, or the blundering clumsiness of the old man, but, had the Indian walked on air his step could not have seemed lighter. The great object was first to discover the position of the fire, which was known to be the centre of the whole encampment. At length the keen eye of Chingachgook caught a glimpse of this important guide. It was glimmering at a distance, among the trunks of trees. There was no blaze, but merely a single smouldering brand, as suited the hour; the savages usually retiring and rising with the revolutions of the sun.

As soon as a view was obtained of this beacon, the progress of the adventurers became swifter and more certain. In a few minutes they got to the edge of the circle of little huts. Here they stopped to survey their ground, and to concert their movements. The darkness was so deep, as to render it difficult to distinguish any thing but the glowing brand, the trunks of the nearest trees, and the endless canopy of leaves that veiled the clouded heaven. It was ascertained, however, that a hut was quite near, and Chingachgook attempted to reconnoitre its interior. The manner in which the Indian approached the place that was supposed to contain enemies, resembled the wily advances of the cat on the bird. As he drew near he stooped to his hands and knees, for the entrance was so low as to require this attitude, even as a convenience. Before trusting his head inside, however, he listened long to catch the breathings of sleepers. No sound was audible, and this human Serpent thrust his head in at the door, or opening, as another serpent would have peered in at the nest. Nothing rewarded the hazardous experiment, for, after feeling cautiously with a hand, the place was found to be empty.

The Delaware proceeded in the same guarded manner to one or two more of the huts, finding all in the same situation. He then returned to his companions, and informed them, that the Hurons had deserted their camp. A little further enquiry corroborated this fact, and it only remained to return to the canoe. The different manner in which the adventurers bore the disappointment, is worthy of a passing remark. The chief, who had landed solely with the hope of acquiring renown, stood stationary, leaning against a tree waiting the pleasure of his companions. He was mortified, and a little surprised it is true, but he bore all with dignity, falling back for support on the sweeter expectations that still lay in reserve for that evening. It was true, he could not now hope to meet his mistress with the proofs of his daring and skill on his person, but he might still hope to meet her; and the warrior, who was zealous in the search, might always hope to be honored. On the other hand, Hutter and Hurry, who had chiefly been instigated by the basest of all human motives, the thirst of gain, could scarce control their feelings. They went prowling among the huts, as if they expected to find some forgotten child, or careless sleeper, and, again and again, did they vent their spite on the insensible huts, several of which were actually torn to pieces, and scattered about the place. Nay, they even quarrelled with each other, and fierce reproaches passed between them. It is possible some serious consequences might have occurred, had not the Delaware interfered to remind them of the danger of being so unguarded, and of the necessity of returning to the Ark. This checked the dispute, and in a few minutes they were paddling sullenly back to the spot where they hoped to find that vessel.

It has been said that Judith took her place at the side of Deerslayer, soon after the adventurers departed. For a short time the girl was silent, and the hunter was ignorant which of the sisters had approached him; but he soon recognised the rich full spirited voice of the elder, as her feelings escaped in words.

"This is a terrible life for women, Deerslayer!" she exclaimed. "Would to Heaven, I could see an end of it!"

"The life is well enough, Judith," was the answer, "being pretty much as it is used, or abused. What would you wish to see in its place?"

"I should be a thousand times happier to live nearer to civilized beings—where there are farms and churches, and houses built as it might be by christian hands; and where my sleep at night would be sweet and tranquil! A dwelling near one of the forts, would be far better than this dreary place where we live!"

"Nay, Judith, I can't agree too lightly in the truth of all this. If forts are good to keep off inimies, they sometimes hold inimies of their own. I do'n't think twould be for your good, or the good of Hetty to live near one, and if I *must* say what I think, I'm afeard you are a little too near, as it is." Deerslayer went on, in his own steady, earnest, manner, for the darkness concealed the tints that coloured the cheeks of the girl almost to the brightness of crimson, while her own great efforts suppressed the sounds of the breathing that nearly choked her — "As for farms, they have their uses, and there's them that like to pass their lives on 'em, but what comfort can a man look for in a clearin', that he can't find in double quantities in the forest? If air, and room, and light are a little craved, the wind-rows, and the streams will furnish 'em, or here are the lakes for such as have bigger longings in that way; but where are you to find your shades, and laughing springs, and leaping brooks, and vinerable trees, a thousand years old, in a clearin'? You do'n't find *them*, but you find their disabled trunks, marking the 'arth like head-stones in a grave yard. It seems to me that the people who live in such places, must be always thinkin' of their own inds, and of univarsal decay; and that, too, not of the decay that is brought about by time and natur', but the decay that follows waste and violence. Then as to churches, they are good, I suppose, else would'n't good men uphold 'em. But they are not altogether necessary. They call 'em the temples of the Lord, but, Judith, the whole 'arth is a temple of the Lord's, to such as have the right minds. Neither forts nor churches make people happier of themselves. Moreover, all is contradiction in the settlements, while all is concord in the woods. Forts and churches almost always go together, and yet they're downright contradictions; churches being for peace, and forts for war. No — no — give me the strong places of the wilderness, which is the trees, and the churches, too, which are arbors raised by the hand of natur'."

"Woman is not made for scenes like these, Deerslayer; scenes of which we shall have no end, as long as this war lasts."

"If you mean women of white colour, I rather think you're not far from the truth, gal; but as for the females of the red men, such visitations are quite in character. Nothing would make Hist, now, the bargained wife of yonder Delaware, happier than to know that he is at this moment prowling around his nat'ral inimies, striving after a scalp."

"Surely, surely, Deerslayer, she cannot be a woman, and not feel concern when she thinks the man she loves is in danger!"

"She does'n't think of the danger, Judith, but of the honor, and when the heart is desperately set on such feelin's, why there is little room to crowd in fear. Hist is a kind, gentle, laughin', pleasant creatur', but she loves honor, as well as any Delaware gal I ever know'd. She's to meet the Sarpent an hour hence, on the p'int where Hetty landed, and no doubt she has her anxiety about it, like any other woman; but she'd be all the happier did she know that her lovyer was at this moment way-laying a Mingo for his scalp."

"If you really believe this, Deerslayer, no wonder you lay so much stress on gifts. Certain am I, that no white girl could feel any thing but misery while she believed her betrothed in danger of his life! Nor do I suppose, even you, unmoved and calm as you ever seem to be, could be at peace, if you believed *your* Hist, in danger."

"That's a different matter — tis altogether a different matter, Judith. Woman is too weak and gentle to be intended to run such risks, and man *must* feel for her. Yes, I rather think that's as much red natur', as it's white. But I have no Hist, nor am I like to have, for I hold it wrong to mix colours, any way except in friendship, and sarvices."

"In that you act and feel as a white man should! As for Hurry Harry, I do think it would be all the same to him, whether his wife were a squaw, or a governor's daughter, pro-vided she was a little comely, and could help to keep his crav-ing stomach full!"

"You do March injustice, Judith; yes, you do. The poor fellow dotes on *you*, and when a man has ra'ally set his heart on such a creatur', it is'n't a Mingo, or even a Delaware gal, that'll be likely to unsettle his mind. You may laugh at such men as Hurry, and I, for we're rough, and unteached in the way of books and other knowledge, but we've our good p'ints, as well as our bad ones. An honest heart is not to be despised, gal, even though it be not varsed in all the niceties that please a female fancy."

"*You*, Deerslayer! — And *do* you — *can* you, for an instant, suppose I place *you*, by the side of Harry March? No — no. I am not as far gone in dulness as that. No one — man or woman, could think of naming your honest heart, manly nature, and simple truth, with the boisterous selfishness, greedy avarice, and overbearing ferocity of Henry March.

The very best that can be said of him, is to be found in his name of Hurry Skurry, which if it means no great harm, means no great good. Even my father, following his feelings with the other, as he is doing, at this moment, well knows the difference between you. This I *know*, for he has said as much to me, in plain language."

Judith was a girl of quick sensibilities, and of impetuous feelings, and, being under few of the restraints that curtail the manifestations of maiden emotions, among those who are educated in the habits of civilized life, she sometimes betrayed the latter with a freedom that was so purely natural, as to place it as far above the wiles of coquetry, as it was superior to its heartlessness. She had now even taken one of the hard hands of the hunter, and pressed it between both her own, with a warmth and earnestness that proved how sincere was her language. It was perhaps, fortunate that she was checked by the very excess of her feelings since the same power might have urged her on to avow *all* that her father had said, the old man not having been satisfied with making a comparison favorable to Deerslayer, as between the hunter and Hurry, but having actually, in his blunt rough way, briefly advised his daughter to cast off the latter entirely, and to think of the former as a husband. Judith would not willingly have said this to any other man, but there was so much confidence awakened by the guileless simplicity of Deerslayer, that one of her nature found it a constant temptation to overstep the bounds of habit. She went no farther, however, immediately relinquishing the hand, and falling back on a reserve that was more suited to her sex, and, indeed, to her natural modesty.

"Thankee, Judith, thank'ee, with all my heart," returned the hunter, whose humility prevented him from placing any flattering interpretation on either the conduct, or the language of the girl. "Thankee, as much as if it all was true. Harry's sightly — yes, he's as sightly as the tallest pine of these mountains, and the Sarpent has named him accordingly; howsever, some fancy good looks, and some fancy good conduct, only. Hurry has one advantage, and it depends on himself whether, he'll have the t'other or — Hark! That's your father's voice, gal, and he speaks like a man who's riled, at something."

"God save us from any more of these horrible scenes!" exclaimed Judith, bending her face to her knees, and endeavoring to exclude the discordant sounds, by applying her hands to her ears. "I sometimes wish I had no father!"

This was bitterly said, and the repinings which extorted the words, were bitterly felt. It is impossible to say what might next have escaped her, had not a gentle, low, voice, spoken at her elbow.

"Judith, I ought to have read a chapter to father and Hurry!" said the innocent, but terrified speaker, "and *that* would have kept them from going again on such an errand. Do you call to them, Deerslayer, and tell them I want them, and that it will be good for them both, if they'll return, and hearken to my words."

"Ahs! me—poor Hetty, you little know the cravin's for gold and revenge, if you believe they are so easily turned aside from their longin's! But this is an oncommon business, in more ways than one, Judith! I hear your father and Hurry, growling like bears, and yet no noise comes from the mouth of the young chief. There's an ind of secrecy, and yet his whoop, which ought to ring in the mountains, accordin' to rule, in such sarcumstances, is silent!"

"Justice may have alighted on him, and his death have saved the lives of the innocent!"

"Not it—not it—the Sarpent is not the one to suffer, if *that's* to be the law. Sartainly there has been no onset, and 'tis most likely that the camp's deserted, and the men are coming back disapp'inted. That accounts for the growls of Hurry and the silence of the Sarpent."

Just at this instant a fall of a paddle was heard in the canoe, for vexation had made March reckless, and Deerslayer felt convinced that his conjecture was true. The sail being down, the Ark had not drifted far, and ere many minutes, he heard Chingachgook, in a low quiet tone directing Hutter how to steer, in order to reach it. In less time than it takes to tell the fact, the canoe touched the scow, and the adventurers entered the latter. Neither Hutter nor Hurry spoke of what had occurred. But the Delaware in passing his friend merely uttered the words "fires out," which if not literally true, sufficiently explained the truth to his listener.

It was now a question as to the course to be steered. A short surly conference was held, when Hutter decided that the wisest way would be to keep in motion, as the means most likely to defeat any attempt at a surprise, announcing his own and March's intention to requite themselves for the loss of sleep, during their captivity, by lying down. As the air still baffled and continued light, it was finally determined to sail before it, let it come in what direction it might, so long as it did not blow the Ark upon the strand. This point settled, the released prisoners helped to hoist the sail, and then they threw themselves on two of the pallets, leaving Deerslayer and his friend to look after the movements of the craft. As neither of the latter was disposed to sleep, on account of the appointment with Hist, this arrangement was acceptable to all parties. That Judith and Hetty remained up also, in no manner impaired the agreeable features of this change.

For some time the scow rather drifted than sailed along the western shore, following a light southerly current of the air. The progress was slow, not exceeding a couple of miles in the hour, but the two men perceived that it was not only carrying them towards the point they desired to reach, but at a rate that was quite as fast as the hour yet rendered necessary. But little was said the while, even by the girls, and that little had more reference to the rescue of Hist, than to any other subject. The Indian was calm, to the eye, but as minute after minute passed, his feelings became more and more excited, until they reached a state that might have satisfied the demands of even the most exacting mistress. Deerslayer kept the craft, as much in the bays as was prudent, for the double purpose of sailing within the shadows of the woods, and of detecting any signs of an encampment they might pass on the shore. In this manner they doubled one low point, and were already in the bay that was terminated north, by the goal at which they aimed. The latter was still a quarter of a mile distant, when Chingachgook came silently to the side of his friend and pointed to a place directly ahead. A small fire was glimmering just within the verge of the bushes that lined the shore, on the southern side of the point, leaving no doubt that the Indians had suddenly removed their camp to the very place, or at least to the very projection of land, where Hist had given them the rendezvous!

Chapter XVI.

"I hear thee babbling to the vale
Of sunshine and of flowers,
But unto me thou bring'st a tale
Of visionary hours."
                    Wordsworth, "To the Cuckoo," ll.9–12.

THE discovery mentioned at the close of the preceding chapter, was of great moment in the eyes of Deerslayer and his friend. In the first place, there was the danger, almost the certainty, that Hutter and Hurry would make a fresh attempt on this camp should they awake and ascertain its position. Then there was the increased risk of landing to bring off Hist, and there were the general uncertainty and additional hazards that must follow from the circumstance that their enemies had begun to change their position. As the Delaware was aware that the hour was near when he ought to repair to the rendezvous, he no longer thought of trophies torn from his foes, and one of the first things arranged between him and his associate, was to permit the two others to sleep on, lest they should disturb the execution of their plans, by substituting some of their own. The Ark moved slowly, and it would have taken fully a quarter of an hour to reach the point, at the rate at which they were going, thus affording time for a little forethought. The Indians, in the wish to conceal their fire from those who were thought to be still in the Castle, had placed it so near the southern side of the point, as to render it extremely difficult to shut it in by the bushes, though Deerslayer varied the direction of the scow, both to the right and to the left, in the hope of being able to effect that object.

"There's one advantage, Judith, in finding that fire so near the water," he said, while executing these little manoeuvres, "since it shows the Mingos believe we are in the hut, and our coming on 'em, from this quarter, will be an onlooked for event. But 'tis lucky Harry March and your father are asleep, else we should have 'em prowling after scalps ag'in. Ha! There—

The bushes are beginning to shut in the fire — and now it can't be seen at all!"

Deerslayer waited a little to make certain that he had at last gained the desired position, when he gave the signal agreed on, and Chingachgook let go the grapnel, and lowered the sail.

The situation in which the Ark now lay had its advantages, and its disadvantages. The fire had been hid by sheering towards the shore, and the latter was nearer perhaps than was desirable. Still, the water was known to be very deep further off in the lake, and anchoring in deep water, under the circumstances in which the party was placed, was to be avoided if possible. It was also believed no raft could be within miles, and, though the trees in the darkness appeared almost to overhang the scow, it would not be easy to get off to her, without using a boat. The intense darkness that prevailed so close in with the forest, too, served as an effectual screen, and so long as care was had not to make a noise, there was little, or no danger of being detected. All these things Deerslayer pointed out to Judith, instructing her as to the course she was to follow in the event of an alarm, for it was thought to the last degree inexpedient to arouse the sleepers, unless it might be in the greatest emergency.

"And now, Judith, as we understand one another, it is time the Sarpent and I had taken to the canoe," the hunter concluded. "The star has not risen yet, it's true; but it soon must, though none of us are likely to be any the wiser for it, to-night, on account of the clouds. Howsiver, Hist has a ready mind, and she's one of them that does'n't always need to have a thing afore her, to see it. I'll warrant you she'll not be either two minutes, or two feet out of the way, unless them jealous vagabonds, the Mingos, have taken the alarm, and put her as a stool pigeon to catch us; or have hid her away, in order to prepare her mind for a Huron instead of a Mohican husband."

"Deerslayer—" interrupted the girl earnestly—"This is a most dangerous service; why do *you* go on it, at all!"

"Anan! — Why you know, gal, we go to bring off Hist, the Sarpent's betrothed — The maid he means to marry, as soon as we get back to the tribe."

"That is all right for the Indian — but *you* do not mean to marry Hist; — *you* are not betrothed, and why should *two* risk their lives and liberties, to do that which one can just as well perform?"

"Ah!—now I understand you, Judith—yes, now I begin to take the idee. You think as Hist is the Sarpent's betrothed, as they call it, and not mine, it's altogether his affair; and as one man can paddle a canoe, he ought to be left to go after his gal alone! But you forget this is our ar'n'd here, on the lake, and it would not tell well to forget an ar'n'd just at the pinch. Then, if love does count for so much with some people, particularly with young women, fri'ndship counts for something, too, with other some. I dares to say, the Delaware can paddle a canoe by himself, and can bring off Hist, by himself, and perhaps he would like that quite as well, as to have me with him, but he could'n't sarcumvent sarcumventions, or stir up an ambushment, or fight with the savages and get his sweetheart off at the same time, as well by himself as if he had a fri'nd with him to depend on, even if that fri'nd is no better than myself. No—no—Judith, you would'n't desart one that counted on *you*, at such a moment, and you can't, in reason, expect me to do it."

"I fear—I believe you are right, Deerslayer, yet I wish you were not to go! Promise me one thing, at least, and that is not to trust yourself among the savages, or to do anything more than to save the girl. That will be enough for once, and with that you ought to be satisfied."

"Lord bless you! gal; one would think it was Hetty that's talking, and not the quick witted, and wonderful Judith Hutter! But fright makes the wise, silly, and the strong, weak. Yes, I've seen proofs of that, time and ag'in! Well, it's kind, and soft hearted in you, Judith, to feel this consarn for a fellow creatur', and I shall always say that you are kind and of true feelin's, let them that inv*y* your good looks, tell as many idle stories of you as they may."

"Deerslayer!" hastily said the girl, interrupting him, though nearly choked by her emotions—"do you believe all you hear about a poor, motherless, girl? Is the foul tongue of Hurry Harry to blast my life!"

"Not it, Judith—not it. I've told Hurry it was'n't manful to backbite them he could'n't win by fair means, and that even an Indian is always tender, touching a young woman's good name."

"If I had a brother, he would'n't dare to do it!" exclaimed Judith, with eyes flashing fire. "But, finding me without any protector but an old man, whose ears are getting to be as dull as his feelings, he has his way as he pleases!"

"Not exactly that, Judith; no, not exactly that, neither! *No* man, brother or stranger, would stand by and see as fair a gal as yourself hunted down, without saying a word in her behalf. Hurry's in 'arnest in wanting to make you his wife, and the little he does let out, ag'in you, comes more from jealousy, like, than from any thing else. Smile on him when he awakes, and squeeze his hand only half as hard as you squeezed mine a bit ago, and my life on it, the poor fellow will forget every thing but your comeliness. Hot words do'n't always come from the heart, but oftener from the stomach, than any where else. Try him, Judith, when he wakes, and see the vartue of a smile."

Deerslayer laughed, in his own manner, as he concluded, and then he intimated to the patient looking, but really impatient Chingachgook, his readiness to proceed. As the young man entered the canoe, the girl stood immovable as stone, lost in the musings that the language and manner of the other were likely to produce. The simplicity of the hunter had completely put her at fault, for, in her narrow sphere, Judith was an expert manager of the other sex, though in the present instance she was far more actuated by impulses, in all she had said and done, than by calculation. We shall not deny that some of Judith's reflections were bitter, though the sequel of the tale must be referred to, in order to explain how merited, or how keen were her sufferings.

Chingachgook, and his pale face friend set forth on their hazardous and delicate enterprise, with a coolness and method that would have done credit to men who were on their twentieth, instead of being on their first war-path. As suited his relation to the pretty fugitive in whose service they were engaged, the Indian took his place in the head of the canoe, while Deerslayer guided its movements in the stern. By this arrangement the former would be the first to land, and of course the first to meet his mistress. The latter had taken his post, without comment, but in secret influenced by the reflection that one who had so much at stake as the Indian, might not possibly guide the canoe with the same steadiness and intelligence, as another who had more command of his feelings. From the instant they left the side of the Ark, the movements of the two adventurers were like the manoeuvres of highly drilled soldiers, who for the first time were called on to meet the enemy in the field. As yet, Chingachgook had never fired a shot in anger, and the *debût* of his companion in warfare is known to the reader. It is true the Indian had been hanging about his enemy's camp for a few hours, on his first arrival, and he had even once entered it, as related in the last chapter, but no consequences had followed either experiment. Now, it was certain that an important result was to be effected, or a mortifying failure was to ensue. The rescue, or the continued captivity of Hist depended on their enterprise. In a word, it was virtually the maiden expedition of these two ambitious young forest soldiers, and while one of them set forth, impelled by sentiments that usually carry men so far, both had all their feelings of pride and manhood enlisted in their success.

Instead of steering in a direct line to the point, then distant from the Ark less than a quarter of a mile, Deerslayer laid the head of his canoe diagonally towards the centre of the lake, with a view to obtain a position, from which he might approach the shore, having his enemies in his front only. The spot where Hetty had landed, and where Hist had promised to meet them, moreover, was on the upper side of the projection rather than on the lower, and to reach it, would have required the adventurers to double nearly the whole point, close in with the shore, had not this preliminary step been taken. So well was the necessity for this measure understood, that Chingachgook quietly paddled on, although it was adopted without consulting him, and apparently was taking him in a direction nearly opposite to that one might think he most wished to go. A few minutes sufficed, however, to carry the canoe the necessary distance, when both the young men ceased paddling as it were by instinctive consent, and the boat became stationary.

The darkness increased rather than diminished, but it was still possible, from the place where the adventurers lay, to distinguish the outlines of the mountains. In vain did the Delaware turn his head eastward, to catch a glimpse of the promised star; for, notwithstanding the clouds broke a little, near the horizon, in that quarter of the heavens, the curtain continued so far drawn as effectually to conceal all behind it. In front, as was known by the formation of land above and behind it, lay the point, at a distance of about a thousand feet. No signs of the castle could be seen, nor could any movement in that quarter of the lake reach the ear. The latter circumstance might have been equally owing to the distance, which was several miles, or to the fact that nothing was in motion. As for the Ark, though scarcely farther from the canoe than the point, it lay so completely buried in the shadows of the shore, that it would not have been visible even had there been many degrees more of light than actually existed.

The adventurers now held a conference in low voices, consulting together as to the probable time. Deerslayer thought it wanted yet some minutes to the rising of the star, while the impatience of the chief caused him to fancy the night further advanced, and to believe that his betrothed was already waiting his appearance on the shore. As might have been expected, the opinion of the latter prevailed, and his friend disposed himself to steer for the place of rendezvous. The utmost skill and precaution now became necessary in the management of the canoe. The paddles were lifted, and returned to the water in a noiseless manner, and when within a hundred yards of the beach, Chingachgook took in his, altogether, laying his hand on his rifle in its stead. As they got still more within the belt of darkness that girded the woods, it was seen that they were steering too far north, and the course was altered accordingly. The canoe now seemed to move by instinct, so cautious and deliberate were all its motions. Still it continued to advance, until its bows grated on the gravel of the beach, at the precise spot where Hetty had landed, and whence her voice had issued, the previous night, as the Ark was passing. There was, as usual, a narrow strand, but bushes fringed the woods, and in most places overhung the water.

Chingachgook stepped upon the beach, and cautiously examined it, for some distance, on each side of the canoe. In order to do this, he was often obliged to wade to his knees in the lake, but no Hist rewarded his search. When he returned he found his friend, also on the shore. They now conferred in whispers, the Indian apprehending that they must have mistaken the place of rendezvous. But Deerslayer thought it more probable they had mistaken the hour. While he was yet speaking, he grasped the arm of the Delaware, caused him to turn his head in the direction of the lake, and pointed towards the summits of the eastern mountains. The clouds had broken a little, apparently behind rather than above the hills, and the selected star was glittering among the branches of a pine. This was every way a flattering omen, and the young men leaned on their rifles, listening intently for the sound of approaching footsteps. Voices they often heard, and mingled with them were the suppressed cries of children, and the low but sweet laugh of Indian women. As the native Americans are habitually cautious, and seldom break out in loud conversation, the adventurers knew by these facts, that they must be very near the encampment. It was easy to perceive that there was a fire within the woods, by the manner in which some of the upper branches of the trees were illuminated, but it was not possible, where they stood, to ascertain exactly how near it was to themselves. Once or twice, it seemed as if stragglers from around the fire, were approaching the place of rendezvous, but these sounds were either altogether illusion, or those who had drawn near, returned again without coming to the shore. A quarter of an hour was passed in this state of intense expectation and anxiety, when Deerslayer proposed that they should circle the point in the canoe, and by getting a position close in, where the camp could be seen, reconnoitre the Indians, and thus enable themselves to form some plausible conjectures for the non-appearance of Hist. The Delaware, however, resolutely refused to quit the spot, plausibly enough offering as a reason, the disappointment of the girl, should she arrive in his absence. Deerslayer felt for his friend's concern, and offered to make the circuit of the point, by himself, leaving the latter concealed in the bushes to await the occurrence of any fortunate event that might favor his views. With this understanding, then, the parties separated.

As soon as Deerslayer was at his post again, in the stern of the canoe, he left the shore with the same precautions, and in the same noiseless manner, as he had approached it. On this occasion he did not go far from the land, the bushes affording a sufficient cover, by keeping as close in as possible. Indeed, it would not have been easy to devise any means more favorable to reconnoitring round an Indian camp, than those afforded by the actual state of things. The formation of the point permitted the place to be circled on three of its sides, and the progress of the boat was so noiseless, as to remove any apprehensions from an alarm through sound. The most practised and guarded foot might stir a bunch of leaves, or snap a dried stick, in the dark, but a bark canoe could be made to float over the surface of smooth water, almost with the instinctive readiness, and certainly with the noiseless movements of an aquatic bird.

Deerslayer had got nearly in a line between the camp and the Ark, before he caught a glimpse of the fire. This came upon him suddenly, and a little unexpectedly, at first causing an alarm, lest he had incautiously ventured within the circle of light it cast. But, perceiving at a second glance, that he was certainly safe from detection, so long as the Indians kept near the centre of the illumination, he brought the canoe to a state of rest, in the most favorable position he could find, and commenced his observations.

We have written much, but in vain, concerning this extraordinary being, if the reader require now to be told, that, untutored as he was in the learning of the world, and simple as he ever showed himself to be in all matters touching the subtleties of conventional taste, he was a man of strong, native, poetical feeling. He loved the woods for their freshness, their sublime solitudes, their vastness, and the impress that they every where bore of the divine hand of their creator. He rarely moved through them, without pausing to dwell on some peculiar beauty that gave him pleasure, though seldom attempting to investigate the causes, and never did a day pass without his communing in spirit, and this too without the aid of forms, or language, with the infinite source of all he saw, felt, and beheld. Thus constituted in a moral sense, and of a steadiness that no danger could appal, or any crisis disturb, it is not surprising that the hunter felt a pleasure at looking on the scene he now beheld, that momentarily caused him to forget the object of his visit. This will more fully appear when we describe it.

The canoe lay in front of a natural vista, not only through the bushes that lined the shore, but of the trees also, that afforded a clear view of the camp. It was by means of this same opening that the light had been first seen from the Ark. In consequence of their recent change of ground, the Indians had not yet retired to their huts, but had been delayed by their preparations, which included lodging as well as food. A large fire had been made, as much to answer the purpose of torches, as for the uses of their simple cookery, and at this precise moment it was blazing high and bright, having recently received a large supply of dried brush. The effect was to illuminate the arches of the forest, and to render the whole area occupied by the camp as light as if hundreds of tapers were burning. Most of the toil had ceased and even the hungriest child had satisfied its appetite. In a word, the time was that moment of relaxation, and general indolence which is apt to succeed a hearty meal, and when the labors of the day have ended. The hunters and the fishermen had been equally successful, and food, that one great requisite of savage life, being abundant, every other care appeared to have subsided in the sense of enjoyment dependant on this all important fact.

Deerslayer saw at a glance that many of the warriors were absent. His acquaintance Rivenoak, however, was present, being seated in the foreground of a picture that Salvator Rosa would have delighted to draw, his swarthy features illuminated as much by pleasure, as by the torch-like flame, while he showed another of the tribe, one of the elephants that had caused so much sensation among his people. A boy was looking over his shoulder, in dull curiosity, completing the group. More in the back-ground eight or ten warriors lay half recumbent on the ground, or sat with their backs inclining against trees, so many types of indolent repose. Their arms were near them, sometimes leaning against the same trees as themselves, or were lying across their bodies in careless preparation. But the group that most attracted the attention of Deerslayer was that composed of the women and children. All the females appeared to be collected together, and, almost as a matter of course, their young were near them. The former laughed and chatted, in their rebuked and quiet manner, though one who knew the habits of the people might have detected that every thing was not going on in its usual train. Most of the young women seemed to be light hearted enough; but one old hag was seated apart, with a watchful, soured aspect, which the hunter at once knew betokened that some duty of an unpleasant character had been assigned her by the chiefs. What that duty was he had no means of knowing, but he felt satisfied it must be, in some measure, connected with her own sex, the aged among the women generally being chosen for such offices, and for no other.

As a matter of course, Deerslayer looked eagerly and anxiously for the form of Hist. She was nowhere visible, though the light penetrated to considerable distances, in all directions around the fire. Once, or twice, he started, as he thought he recognised her laugh, but his ears were deceived by the soft melody that is so common to the Indian female voice. At length the old woman spoke loud and angrily, and then he caught a glimpse of one or two dark figures, in the back ground of trees, which turned as if obedient to the rebuke, and walked more within the circle of the light. A young warrior's form first came fairly into view; then followed two youthful females, one of whom proved to be the Delaware girl. Deerslayer now comprehended it all. Hist was watched, possibly by her young companion, certainly by the old woman. The youth was probably some suitor of either hers, or her companion's, but even his discretion was distrusted under the influence of his admiration. The known vicinity of those who might be supposed to be her friends, and the arrival of a strange red-man on the lake, had induced more than the usual care, and the girl had not been able to slip away from those who watched her, in order to keep her appointment. Deerslayer traced her uneasiness, by her attempting, once or twice, to look up through the branches of the trees, as if endeavoring to get glimpses of the star she had herself named, as the sign for meeting. All was vain, however, and after strolling about the camp, a little longer, in affected indifference, the two girls quitted their male escort, and took seats among their own sex. As soon as this was done, the old sentinel changed her place to one more agreeable to herself, a certain proof that she had hitherto been exclusively on watch.

Deerslayer now felt greatly at a loss how to proceed. He well knew that Chingachgook could never be persuaded to return to the Ark, without making some desperate effort for the recovery of his mistress, and his own generous feelings well disposed him to aid in such an undertaking. He thought he saw the signs of an intention among the females to retire for the night, and should he remain, and the fire continue to give out its light, he might discover the particular hut, or arbor under which Hist reposed; a circumstance that would be of infinite use, in their future proceedings. Should he remain however, much longer where he was, there was great danger that the impatience of his friend, would drive him into some act of imprudence. At each instant, indeed, he expected to see the swarthy form of the Delaware, appearing in the background, like the tiger prowling around the fold. Taking all things into consideration, therefore, he came to the conclusion it would be better to rejoin his friend, and endeavor to temper his impetuosity by some of his own coolness and discretion. It required but a minute or two to put this plan in execution, the canoe returning to the strand some ten or fifteen minutes after it had left it.

Contrary to his expectations, perhaps, Deerslayer found the Indian at his post, from which he had not stirred, fearful that his betrothed might arrive during his absence. A conference followed, in which Chingachgook was made acquainted with the state of things in the camp. When Hist named the point as the place of meeting, it was with the expectation of making her escape from the old position, and of repairing to a spot that she expected to find without any occupants, but the sudden change of localities had disconcerted all her plans. A much greater degree of vigilance than had been previously required, was now necessary, and the circumstance that an aged woman was on watch, also denoted some special grounds of alarm. All these considerations, and many more that will readily suggest themselves to the reader, were briefly discussed, before the young men came to any decision. The occasion, however, being one that required acts instead of words, the course to be pursued was soon chosen.

Disposing of the canoe in such a manner that Hist must see it, should she come to the place of meeting, previously to their return, the young men looked to their arms, and prepared to enter the wood. The whole projection into the lake contained about two acres of land, and the part that formed the point, and on which the camp was placed, did not compose a surface of more than half that size. It was principally covered with oaks, which, as is usual in the American forests, grew to a great height without throwing out a branch, and then arched in a dense and rich foliage. Beneath, except the fringe of thick bushes along the shore, there was very little underbrush; though, in consequence of their shape, the trees were closer together than is common in regions where the axe has been freely used, resembling tall, straight, rustic columns, upholding the usual canopy of leaves. The surface of the land was tolerably even, but it had a small rise near its centre, which divided it into a northern and southern half. On the latter the Hurons had built their fire, profiting by the formation to conceal it from their enemies, who it will be remembered were supposed to be in the castle, which bore northerly. A brook also came brawling down the sides of the adjacent hills, and found its way into the lake on the southern side of the point. It had cut for itself a deep passage through some of the higher portions of the ground, and, in later days, when this spot has become subjected to the uses of civilization, by its windings and shaded banks, it has become no mean accessory in contributing to the beauty of the place. This brook lay west of the encampment, and its waters found their way into the great reservoir of that region on the same side, and quite near to the spot chosen for the fire. All these peculiarities, so far as circumstances allowed, had been noted by Deerslayer, and explained to his friend.

The reader will understand that the little rise in the ground, that lay behind the Indian encampment, greatly favored the secret advance of the two adventurers. It prevented the light of the fire diffusing itself on the ground directly in the rear, although the land fell away towards the water so as to leave what might be termed the left, or eastern flank of the position, unprotected by this covering. We have said 'unprotected,' though that is not properly the word, since the knoll behind the huts and the fire, offered a cover for those who were now stealthily approaching, rather than any protection to the Indians. Deerslayer did not break through the fringe of bushes immediately abreast of the canoe, which might have brought him too suddenly within the influence of the light, since the hillock did not extend to the water, but he followed the beach northerly until he had got nearly on the opposite side of the tongue of land, which brought him under the shelter of the low acclivity, and consequently more in shadow.

As soon as the friends emerged from the bushes, they stopped to reconnoitre. The fire was still blazing, behind the little ridge, casting its light upward, into the tops of the trees, producing an effect that was more pleasing than advantageous. Still the glare had its uses, for, while the back ground was in obscurity, the fore-ground was in strong light; exposing the savages and concealing their foes. Profiting by the latter circumstance, the young men advanced cautiously towards the ridge, Deerslayer in front, for he insisted on this arrangement, lest the Delaware should be led by his feelings into some indiscretion. It required but a moment to reach the foot of the little ascent, and then commenced the most critical part of the enterprise. Moving with exceeding caution, and trailing his rifle, both to keep its barrel out of view and in readiness for service, the hunter put foot before foot, until he had got sufficiently high to overlook the summit, his own head being alone brought into the light. Chingachgook was at his side, and both paused to take another close examination of the camp. In order, however, to protect themselves against any straggler in the rear, they placed their bodies against the trunk of an oak, standing on the side next the fire.

The view that Deerslayer now obtained of the camp, was exactly the reverse of that he had perceived from the water. The dim figures which he had formerly discovered must have been on the summit of the ridge, a few feet in advance of the spot where he was now posted. The fire was still blazing brightly, and around it were seated on logs, thirteen warriors, which accounted for all whom he had seen from the canoe. They were conversing, with much earnestness among themselves, the image of the elephant passing from hand to hand. The first burst of savage wonder had abated, and the question now under discussion, was the probable existence, the history and habits of so extraordinary an animal. We have not leisure to record the opinions of these rude men on a subject so peculiar to their lives and experience, but little is hazarded in saying that they were quite as plausible, and far more ingenious, than half the conjectures that precede the demonstrations of science. However much they may have been at fault as to their conclusions and inferences, it is certain that they discussed the questions with a zealous and most undivided attention. For the time being, all else was forgotten, and our adventurers could not have approached at a more fortunate instant.

The females were collected near each other, much as Deerslayer had last seen them, nearly in a line between the place where he now stood and the fire. The distance from the oak against which the young men leaned, and the warriors, was about thirty yards; the women may have been half that number of yards nigher. The latter, indeed, were so near as to make the utmost circumspection, as to motion and noise, indispensable. Although they conversed in their low, soft, voices, it was possible, in the profound stillness of the woods, even to catch passages of the discourse, and the light hearted laugh that escaped the girls, might occasionally have reached the canoe. Deerslayer felt the tremor that passed through the frame of his friend, when the latter first caught the sweet sounds that issued from the plump, pretty lips of Hist. He even laid a hand on the shoulder of the Indian, as a sort of admonition to command himself. As the conversation grew more earnest each leaned forward to listen.

"The Hurons have more curious beasts than that!" said one of the girls, contemptuously, for, like the men, they conversed of the elephant and his qualities. "The Delawares will think this creature wonderful, but to-morrow, no Huron tongue will talk of it. Our young men will find him, if the animal dares to come near our wigwams!"

This was in fact addressed to Wah-ta!-Wah, though she who spoke uttered her words with an assumed diffidence and humility, that prevented her looking at the other.

"The Delawares are so far from letting such creatures come into their country," returned Hist, "that no one has even seen their images there! *Their* young men would frighten away the *images*, as well as the *beasts*."

"The Delaware young men! — the nation is women; even the deer walk when they hear their hunters coming! Who has ever heard the name of a young Delaware warrior?"

This was said in good humour, and with a laugh; but it was

also said, bitingly. That Hist so felt it, was apparent by the spirit betrayed in her answer.

"Who has ever heard the name of a young Delaware!" she repeated earnestly. "Tamenund, himself, though now as old as the pines on the hill, or as the eagles in the air, was once young; his name was heard from the great salt lake, to the sweet waters of the west. What is the family of Uncas? Where is another as great, though the pale faces have ploughed up its graves, and trodden on its bones? Do the eagles fly as high, is the deer as swift, or the panther as brave? Is there no young warrior of that race? Let the Huron maidens open their eyes wider, and they may see one called Chingachgook, who is as stately as a young ash, and as tough as the hickory."

As the girl used her figurative language, and told her companions to "open their eyes, and they would see" the Delaware, Deerslayer thrust his fingers into the side of his friend, and indulged in a fit of his hearty, but silent laughter. The other smiled, but the language of the speaker was so flattering, and the tones of her voice too sweet for him to be led away, by any accidental coincidence, however ludicrous. The speech of Hist produced a retort, and the dispute, though conducted in good humour, and without any of the coarse violence of tone and gesture that often impairs the charms of the sex, in what is called civilized life, grew warm and slightly clamorous. In the midst of this scene, the Delaware caused his friend to stoop, so as completely to conceal himself, and then he made a noise so closely resembling the little chirrup of the smallest species of the American squirrel, that, Deerslayer himself, though he had heard the imitation a hundred times, actually thought it came from one of the little animals, skipping about, over his head. The sound is so familiar in the woods, that none of the Hurons paid it the least attention. Hist, however, instantly ceased talking, and sate motionless. Still, she had sufficient self-command to abstain from turning her head. She had heard the signal, by which her lover so often called her from the wigwam, to a stolen interview, and it came over her senses and her heart, as the serenade affects the maiden in the land of song.

From that moment, Chingachgook felt certain that his presence was known. This was effecting much, and he could now hope for a bolder line of conduct on the part of his mistress, than she might dare to adopt under an uncertainty of his situation. It left no doubt of her endeavoring to aid him in his effort to release her. Deerslayer arose, as soon as the signal was given, and though he had never held that sweet communion which is known only to lovers, he was not slow to detect the great change that had come over the manner of the girl. She still affected to dispute, though it was no longer with spirit and ingenuity, but what she said was uttered more as a lure to draw her antagonists on to an easy conquest, than with any hopes of succeeding herself. Once or twice, it is true, her native readiness suggested a retort, or an argument that raised a laugh, and gave her a momentary advantage; but these little rallies, the offspring of mother wit, served the better to conceal her real feelings, and to give to the triumph of the other party, a more natural air than it might have possessed without them. At length the disputants became wearied, and they rose in a body, as if about to separate. It was now that Hist, for the first time, ventured to turn her face in the direction whence the signal had come. In doing this, her movements were natural but guarded, and she stretched her arms and yawned, as if overcome with a desire to sleep. The chirrup was again heard, and the girl felt satisfied as to the position of her lover, though the strong light in which she herself was placed, and the comparative darkness in which the adventurers stood, prevented her from seeing their heads, the only portions of their forms that appeared above the ridge at all. The tree against which they were posted, had a dark shadow cast upon it, by the intervention of an enormous pine that grew between it and the fire, a circumstance which alone would have rendered objects within its cloud invisible at any distance. This Deerslayer well knew, and it was one of the reasons why he had selected this particular tree.

The moment was near when it became necessary for Hist to act. She was to sleep in a small hut, or bower, that had been built near the spot where she stood, and her companion was the aged hag, already mentioned. Once within the hut, with this sleepless old woman stretched across the entrance, as was her nightly practice, the hope of escape was nearly destroyed, and she might, at any moment, be summoned to her bed. Luckily, at this instant, one of the warriors called to the old woman by name, and bade her bring him water to drink. There was a delicious spring on the northern side of the point, and the hag took a gourd from a branch, and, summoning Hist to her side, she moved towards the summit of the ridge, intending to descend and cross the point to the natural fountain. All this was seen and understood by the adventurers, and they fell back into the obscurity, concealing their persons by trees, until the two females had passed them. In walking, Hist was held tightly by the hand. As she moved by the tree, that hid Chingachgook and his friend, the former felt for his tomahawk, with the intention to bury it in the brain of the woman. But the other saw the hazard of such a measure, since a single scream might bring all the warriors upon them, and he was averse to the act on the considerations of humanity. His hand, therefore, prevented the blow. Still as the two moved past, the chirrup was repeated, and the Huron woman stopped and faced the tree whence the sounds seemed to proceed, standing at the moment, within six feet of her enemies. She expressed her surprise that a squirrel should be in motion at so late an hour, and said it boded evil. Hist answered that she had heard the same squirrel three times, within the last twenty minutes, and that she supposed it was waiting to obtain some of the crumbs left from the late supper. This explanation appeared satisfactory, and they moved towards the spring, the men following stealthily and closely. The gourd was filled, and the old woman was hurrying back, her hand still grasping the wrist of the girl, when she was suddenly seized so violently by the throat, as to cause her to release her captive, and to prevent her making any other sound than a sort of gurgling, suffocating noise. The Serpent passed his arm round the waist of his mistress and darted through the bushes with her, on the north side of the point. Here he immediately turned along the beach, and ran towards the canoe. A more direct course could have been taken, but it might have led to a discovery of the place of embarking.

Deerslayer kept playing on the throat of the old woman like the keys of an organ, occasionally allowing her to breathe, and then compressing his fingers again, nearly to strangling. The brief intervals for breath, however, were well improved, and the hag succeeded in getting out a screech or two that served to alarm the camp. The tramp of the warriors, as they sprung from the fire, was plainly audible, and, at the next moment three or four of them appeared on the top of the ridge, drawn against the back ground of light, resembling the dense shadows of the phantasmagoria. It was now quite time for the hunter to retreat. Tripping up the heels of his captive, and giving her throat a parting squeeze, quite as much in resentment at her indomitable efforts to sound the alarm, as from any policy, he left her on her back, and moved towards the bushes, his rifle at a poise, and his head over his shoulders, like a lion at bay.

Chapter XVII.

"There, ye wise saints, behold your light, your star,
Ye *would* be dupes and victims and ye *are*.
Is it enough? or, must I, while a thrill
Lives in your sapient bosoms, cheat you still?"
Thomas Moore, *Lalla Rookh*, "The Veiled Prophet
of Khorassan, " ll.1954–57.

T H E fire, the canoe, and the spring, near which Deer-slayer commenced his retreat, would have stood in the angles of a triangle of tolerably equal sides. The distance from the fire to the boat was a little less than the distance from the fire to the spring, while the distance from the spring to the boat, was about equal to that between the two points first named. This, however, was in straight lines, a means of escape to which the fugitives could not resort. They were obliged to have recourse to a *détour* in order to get the cover of the bushes, and to follow the curvature of the beach. Under these disadvantages, then, the hunter commenced his retreat, disadvantages that he felt to be so much the greater from his knowledge of the habits of all Indians, who rarely fail in cases of sudden alarms, more especially when in the midst of cover, immediately to throw out flankers, with a view to meet their foes at all points, and if possible to turn their rear. That some such course was now adopted he believed from the tramp of feet, which not only came up the ascent, as related, but were also heard, under the first impulse, diverging not only towards the hill in the rear, but towards the extremity of the point, in a direction opposite to that he was about to take himself. Promptitude, consequently became a matter of the last importance, as the parties might meet on the strand, before the fugitive could reach the canoe.

Notwithstanding the pressing nature of the emergency, Deerslayer hesitated a single instant, ere he plunged into the bushes that lined the shore. His feelings had been awakened by the whole scene, and a sternness of purpose had come over him, to which he was ordinarily a stranger. Four dark figures loomed on the ridge, drawn against the brightness of the fire, and an enemy might have been sacrificed at a glance. The Indians had paused to gaze into the gloom, in search of the screeching hag, and with many a man less given to reflection than the hunter, the death of one of them would have been certain. Luckily he was more prudent. Although the rifle dropped a little towards the foremost of his pursuers, he did not aim or fire, but disappeared in the cover. To gain the beach, and to follow it round to the place where Chingachgook was already in the canoe, with Hist, anxiously waiting his appearance, occupied but a moment. Laying his rifle in the bottom of the canoe, Deerslayer stooped to give the latter a vigorous shove from the shore, when a powerful Indian leaped through the bushes, alighting like a panther on his back. Every thing was now suspended by a hair; a false step ruining all. With a generosity that would have rendered a Roman illustrious throughout all time, but which, in the career of one so simple and humble, would have been forever lost to the world but for this unpretending legend, Deerslayer threw all his force into a desperate effort, shoved the canoe off with a power that sent it a hundred feet from the shore, as it might be in an instant, and fell forward into the lake, himself, face downward; his assailant necessarily following him.

Although the water was deep within a few yards of the beach, it was not more than breast high, as close in, as the spot where the two combatants fell. Still this was quite sufficient to destroy one who had sunk, under the great disadvantages in which Deerslayer was placed. His hands were free, however, and the savage was compelled to relinquish his hug, to keep his own face above the surface. For half a minute there was a desperate struggle, like the floundering of an alligator that has just seized some powerful prey, and then both stood erect, grasping each other's arms, in order to prevent the use of the deadly knife, in the darkness. What might have been the issue of this severe personal struggle cannot be known, for half a dozen savages came leaping into the water to the aid of their friend, and, Deerslayer yielded himself a prisoner, with a dignity that was as remarkable as his self-devotion.

To quit the lake and lead their new captive to the fire, occupied the Indians but another minute. So much engaged were they all with the struggle and its consequences, that the canoe was unseen, though it still lay so near the shore as to render every syllable that was uttered, perfectly intelligible to the Delaware and his betrothed; and the whole party left the spot, some continuing the pursuit after Hist, along the beach, though most proceeded to the light. Here Deerslayer's antagonist so far recovered his breath and his recollection, for he had been throttled nearly to strangulation, as to relate the manner in which the girl had got off. It was now too late to assail the other fugitives, for no sooner was his friend led into the bushes, than the Delaware placed his paddle into the water, and the light canoe glided noiselessly away, holding its course towards the centre of the lake, until safe from shot, after which it sought the Ark.

When Deerslayer reached the fire, he found himself surrounded by no less than eight grim savages, among whom was his old acquaintance Rivenoak. As soon as the latter caught a glimpse of the captive's countenance, he spoke apart to his companions, and a low, but general exclamation of pleasure and surprise escaped them. They knew that the conqueror of their late friend, he who had fallen on the opposite side of the lake, was in their hands, and subject to their mercy, or vengeance. There was no little admiration mingled in the ferocious looks that were thrown on the prisoner; an admiration that was as much excited by his present composure, as by his past deeds. This scene may be said to have been the commencement of the great and terrible reputation that Deerslayer, or Hawkeye, as he was afterwards called, enjoyed among all the tribes of New York and Canada; a reputation that was certainly more limited in its territorial and numerical extent, than those which are possessed in civilized life, but which was compensated for what it wanted in these particulars, perhaps, by its greater justice, and the total absence of mystification and management.

The arms of Deerslayer were not pinioned, and he was left the free use of his hands, his knife having been first removed. The only precaution that was taken to secure his person was untiring watchfulness, and a strong rope of bark that passed from ancle to ancle, not so much to prevent his walking, as to place an obstacle in the way of his attempting to escape by any sudden leap. Even this extra provision against flight was not made, until the captive had been brought to the light, and his character ascertained. It was, in fact, a compliment to his prowess, and he felt proud of the distinction. That he might be bound when the warriors slept he thought probable, but to be bound in the moment of capture, showed that he was already, and thus early, attaining a name. While the young Indians were fastening the rope, he wondered if Chingachgook would have been treated in the same manner, had he too fallen into the hands of the enemy. Nor did the reputation of the young pale face rest altogether on his success in the previous combat, or in his discriminating and cool manner of managing the late negotiation, for it had received a great accession by the occurrences of the night. Ignorant of the movements of the Ark, and of the accident that had brought their fire into view, the Iroquois attributed the discovery of their new camp to the vigilance of so shrewd a foe. The manner in which he ventured upon the point, the abstraction or escape of Hist, and most of all the self-devotion of the prisoner, united to the readiness with which he had sent the canoe adrift, were so many important links in the chain of facts, on which his growing fame was founded. Many of these circumstances had been seen, some had been explained, and all were understood.

While this admiration, and these honors were so unreservedly bestowed on Deerslayer, he did not escape some of the penalties of his situation. He was permitted to seat himself on the end of a log, near the fire, in order to dry his clothes, his late adversary standing opposite, now holding articles of his own scanty vestments to the heat, and now feeling his throat, on which the marks of his enemy's fingers were still quite visible. The rest of the warriors consulted together, near at hand, all those who had been out having returned to report that no signs of any other prowlers near the camp were to be found. In this state of things, the old woman, whose name was Shebear, in plain English, approached Deerslayer, with her fists clenched and her eyes flashing fire. Hitherto, she had been occupied with screaming, an employment at which she had played her part with no small degree of success, but having succeeded in effectually alarming all within reach of a pair of lungs that had been strengthened by long practice, she next turned her attention to the injuries her own person had sustained in the struggle. These were in no manner material, though they were of a nature to arouse all the fury of a woman who had long ceased to attract by means of the gentler qualities, and who was much disposed to revenge the hardships she had so long endured, as the neglected wife and mother of savages, on all who came within her power. If Deerslayer had not permanently injured her, he had temporarily caused her to suffer, and she was not a person to overlook a wrong of this nature, on account of its motive.

"Skunk of the pale-faces—" commenced this exasperated and semi-poetic fury, shaking her fist under the nose of the impassable hunter, "you are not even a woman. Your friends the Delawares are only women, and you are their sheep. Your own people will not own you, and no tribe of red *men* would have you in their wigwams; you skulk among petticoated warriors. *You* slay our brave friend who has left us?—No—his great soul scorned to fight you, and left his body rather than have the shame of slaying *you!* But the blood that you spilt when the spirit was not looking on, has not sunk into the ground. It must be buried in your groans. What music do I hear? Those are not the wailings of a red man!—no red warrior groans so much like a hog. They come from a pale face throat—a Yengeese bosom, and sound as pleasant as girls singing—Dog—skunk—wood-chuck—mink—hedge-hog—pig—toad—spider—yengee—"

Here the old woman having expended her breath, and exhausted her epithets, was fain to pause a moment, though both her fists were shook in the prisoner's face, and the whole of her wrinkled countenance was filled with fierce resentment. Deerslayer looked upon these impotent attempts to arouse him, as indifferently as a gentleman in our own state of society, regards the vituperative terms of a blackguard: the one party feeling that the tongue of an old woman could never injure a warrior, and the other knowing that mendacity and vulgarity can only permanently affect those who resort to their use; but he was spared any further attack at present, by the interposition of Rivenoak, who shoved aside the hag, bidding her quit the spot, and prepared to take his seat at the side of his prisoner. The old woman withdrew, but the hunter well understood that he was to be the subject of all her means of annoyance, if not of positive injury, so long as he remained in the power of his enemies, for nothing rankles so deeply as the consciousness that an attempt to irritate has been met by contempt, a feeling that is usually the most passive of any that is harbored in the human breast. Rivenoak quietly took the seat we have mentioned, and, after a short pause, he commenced a dialogue, which we translate as usual, for the benefit of those readers who have not studied the North American languages.

"My paleface friend is very welcome," said the Indian, with a familiar nod, and a smile so covert that it required all Deerslayer's vigilance to detect, and not a little of his philosophy to detect unmoved—"he is welcome. The Hurons keep a hot fire to dry the white man's clothes by."

"I thank you, Huron—or Mingo, as I most like to call you—" returned the other—"I thank you for the welcome, and I thank you for the fire. Each is good in its way, and the last is very good, when one has been in a spring as cold as the Glimmerglass. Even Huron warmth may be pleasant, at such a time, to a man with a Delaware heart."

"The paleface—but my brother has a name? So great a warrior would not have lived without a name?"

"Mingo," said the hunter, a little of the weakness of human nature exhibiting itself in the glance of his eye, and the colour on his cheek—"Mingo, *your* brave, called me Hawkeye, I suppose on account of a quick and sartain aim, when he was lying with his head in my lap, afore his spirit started for the Happy Hunting Grounds."

"'Tis a good name! The hawk is sure of his blow. Hawkeye is not a woman; why does he live with the Delawares?"

"I understand you, Mingo, but we look on all that as a sarcumvention of some of your subtle devils, and deny the charge. Providence placed me among the Delawares young, and, 'bating what christian usages demand of my colour and gifts, I hope to live and die in their tribe. Still I do not mean to throw away altogether, my natyve rights, and shall strive to do a pale face's duty, in red skin society."

"Good; a Huron is a red skin, as well as a Delaware. Hawkeye is more of a Huron than of a woman."

"I suppose you know, Mingo, your own meaning; if you do'n't I make no question t'is well known to Satan. But if you wish to get any thing out of me, speak plainer, for bargains can not be made blindfolded, or tongue tied."

"Good; Hawkeye has not a forked tongue, and he likes to say what he thinks. He is an acquaintance of the Muskrat;" this was the name by which all the Indians designated Hutter—"and has lived in his wigwam. But he is not a friend. He wants no scalps, like a miserable Indian, but fights like a stout-hearted pale face. The Muskrat is neither white, nor red. Neither a beast nor a fish. He is a water snake; sometimes in the spring and sometimes on the land. He looks for scalps, like an out-cast. Hawkeye can go back and tell him how he has out-witted the Hurons, how he has escaped, and when his eyes are in a fog, when he ca'n't see as far as from his cabin to the shore, then Hawkeye can open the door for the Hurons. And how will the plunder be divided? Why, Hawkeye, will carry away the most, and the Hurons will take what he may choose to leave behind him. The scalps can go to Canada, for a pale-face has no satisfaction in *them*."

"Well, well, Rivenoak—for so I hear 'em tarm you—This is plain English, enough, though spoken in Iroquois. I understand all you mean, now, and must say it out-devils even Mingo deviltry! No doubt, twould be easy enough to go back and tell the Muskrat, that I had got away from you, and gain some credit, too, by the expl'ite."

"Good. That is what I want the paleface to do."

"Yes—yes—That's plain enough. I know what you want me to do, without more words. When inside the house, and eating the Muskrat's bread, and laughing and talking with his pretty darters, I might put his eyes into so thick a fog, that he could'n't even see the door, much less the land."

"Good! Hawkeye should have been born a Huron! His blood is not more than half white!"

"There you're out, Huron; yes, there you're as much out, as if you mistook a wolf for a catamount. I'm white in blood, heart, natur' and gifts, though a little red skin in feelin's and habits. But when old Hutter's eyes are well be-fogged, and his pretty darters perhaps in a deep sleep, and Hurry Harry, the Great Pine as you Indians tarm him, is dreaming of any thing but mischief, and all suppose Hawkeye is acting as a faithful sentinel, all I have to do is to set a torch somewhere in sight for a signal, open the door, and let in the Hurons, to knock 'em all on the head."

"Surely my brother is mistaken; he *cannot* be white! He is worthy to be a great chief among the Hurons!"

"That is true enough, I dares to say, if he could do all this. Now, harkee, Huron, and for once hear a few honest words from the mouth of a plain man. I am christian born, and them that come of such a stock, and that listen to the words that were spoken to their fathers, and will be spoken to their children, until 'arth, and all it holds perishes, can never lend themselves to such wickedness. Sarcumventions in war, may be, and *are*, lawful; but sarcumventions, and deceit, and treachery, among fri'nds are fit only for the pale-face devils. I know that there are white men enough, to give you this wrong idee of our natur', but such are ontrue to their blood and gifts, and ought to be, if they are not, out casts and vagabonds. No upright pale-face could do what you wish, and to be as plain with you as I wish to be, in my judgment, no upright Delaware either. With a Mingo it may be different."

The Huron listened to this rebuke with obvious disgust, but he had his ends in view, and was too wily to lose all chance of effecting them, by a precipitate avowal of resentment. Affecting to smile, he seemed to listen eagerly, and he then pondered on what he had heard.

"Does Hawkeye love the Muskrat," he abruptly demanded. "Or does he love his daughters?"

"Neither, Mingo. Old Tom is not a man to gain my love, and, as for the darters, they are comely enough to gain the liking of any young man, but there's reason ag'in any very great love for either. Hetty is a good soul, but natur' has laid a heavy hand on her mind, poor thing!"

"And the Wild Rose!" exclaimed the Huron—for the fame of Judith's beauty had spread among those who could travel the wilderness, as well as the highway, by means of old eagles' nests, rocks, and riven trees, known to them by report and tradition, as well as among the white borderers, "And the Wild Rose; is she not sweet enough to be put in the bosom of my brother?"

Deerslayer had far too much of the innate gentleman to insinuate aught against the fair fame of one who, by nature and position was so helpless, and as he did not choose to utter an untruth, he preferred being silent. The Huron mistook the motive, and supposed that disappointed affection lay at the bottom of his reserve. Still bent on corrupting, or bribing his captive, in order to obtain possession of the treasures with which his imagination filled the Castle, he persevered in his attack.

"Hawkeye is talking with a friend," he continued. "He knows that Rivenoak is a man of his word, for they have traded together, and trade opens the soul. My friend has come here, on account of a little string held by a girl, that can pull the whole body of the sternest warrior?"

"You are nearer the truth, now, Huron, than you've been afore, since we began to talk. This is true. But one end of that string was not fast to my heart, nor did the Wild Rose hold the other."

"This is wonderful! Does my brother love in his head, and not in his heart? And can the Feeble Mind pull so hard against so stout a warrior?"

"There it is ag'in; sometimes right, and sometimes wrong! The string you mean, is fast to the heart of a great Delaware; one of Mohican stock in fact, living among the Delawares since the disparsion of his own people, and of the family of Uncas—Chingachgook by name, or Great Sarpent. He has come here, led by the string, and I've followed, or rather come afore, for I got here first, pulled by nothing stronger than fri'ndship; which is strong enough for such as are not niggardly of their feelin's, and are willing to live a little for their fellow creatur's, as well as for themselves."

"But a string has two ends—one is fast to the mind of a Mohican; and the other?"—

"Why the other was here close to the fire, half an hour since. Wah-ta!-Wah held it in her hand, if she did'n't hold it to her heart."

"I understand what you mean, my brother," returned the

Indian gravely, for the first time catching a direct clue to the adventures of the evening. "The Great Serpent, being strongest, pulled the hardest, and Hist was forced to leave us."

"I do'n't think there was much pulling about it," answered the other, laughing, always in his silent manner, with as much heartiness as if he were not a captive, and in danger of torture or death — "I do'n't think there was much pulling about it; no I do'n't. Lord help you, Huron! He likes the gal, and the gal likes him, and it surpassed Huron sarcumventions to keep two young people apart, where there was so strong a feelin' to bring 'em together."

"And Hawkeye and Chingachgook came into our camp on this errand, only?"

"That's a question that'll answer itself, Mingo! Yes, if a question could talk it would answer itself, to your parfect satisfaction. For what else should we come? And yet, it is'n't exactly so, neither; for we did'n't come into your camp at all, but only as far as that pine, there, that you see on the other side of the ridge, where we stood watching your movements, and conduct, as long as we liked. When we were ready, the Sarpent gave his signal, and then all went just as it should, down to the moment when yonder vagabond leaped upon my back. Sartain; we come for that, and for no other purpose, and we got what we come for; there's no use in pretending otherwise. Hist is off with a man who's the next thing to her husband, and come what will to me, *that's* one good thing detarmined."

"What sign, or signal, told the young maiden that her lover was nigh?" asked the Huron with more curiosity than it was usual for him to betray.

Deerslayer laughed again, and seem'd to enjoy the success of the exploit, with as much glee, as if he had not been its victim.

"Your squirrels are great gadabouts, Mingo," he cried still laughing — "yes, they're sartainly, great gadabouts! When other folk's squirrels are at home and asleep, yourn keep in motion among the trees, and chirrup and sing, in a way that even a Delaware gal can understand their musick! Well, there's four legged squirrels, and there's two legged squirrels, and give me the last, when there's a good tight string atween two hearts. If one brings 'em together, t'other tells when to pull hardest!"

The Huron look'd vexed, though he succeeded in suppressing any violent exhibition of resentment. He now quitted his prisoner, and joining the rest of the warriors, he communicated the substance of what he had learned. As in his own case, admiration was mingled with anger, at the boldness and success of their enemies. Three or four of them ascended the little acclivity and gazed at the tree where it was understood the adventurers had posted themselves, and one even descended to it, and examined for foot prints around its roots, in order to make sure that the statement was true. The result confirmed the story of the captive, and they all returned to the fire, with increased wonder and respect. The messenger who had arrived with some communication from the party above, while the two adventurers were watching the camp, was now despatched with some answer, and doubtless bore with him the intelligence of all that had happened.

Down to this moment, the young Indian who had been seen walking in company with Hist and another female, had made no advances to any communication with Deerslayer. He had held himself aloof from his friends even, passing near the bevy of younger women, who were clustering together, apart as usual, and conversed in low tones on the subject of the escape of their late companion. Perhaps it would be true to say, that these last were pleased as well as vexed at what had just occurred. Their female sympathies were with the lovers, while their pride was bound up in the success of their own tribe. It is possible too, that the superior personal advantages of Hist, rendered her dangerous to some of the younger part of the group, and they were not sorry to find she was no longer in the way of their own ascendency. On the whole, however, the better feeling was most prevalent, for neither the wild condition in which they lived, the clannish prejudices of tribes, nor their hard fortunes as Indian women, could entirely conquer the inextinguishable leaning of their sex to the affections. One of the girls even laughed at the disconsolate look of the swain who might fancy himself deserted, a circumstance that seemed suddenly to arouse his energies, and induce him to move towards the log, on which the prisoner was still seated, drying his clothes.

"This is Catamount!" said the Indian, striking his hand boastfully on his naked breast, as he uttered the words in a manner to show how much weight he expected them to carry.

"This is Hawkeye—" quietly returned Deerslayer, adopting the name by which he knew he would be known in future, among all the tribes of the Iroquois. "My sight is keen—is my brother's leap long?"

"From here to the Delaware villages. Hawkeye has stolen my wife—he must bring her back, or his scalp will hang on a pole, and dry in my wigwam."

"Hawkeye has stolen nothing, Huron. He does'n't come of a thieving breed, nor has he thieving gifts. Your wife, as you call Wah-ta!-Wah, will never be the wife of any red skin of the Canadas; her mind is in the cabin of a Delaware, and her body has gone to find it. The catamount is act*y*ve I know, but its legs can't keep pace with a woman's wishes."

"The Serpent of the Delawares is a dog—he is a poor bull-pout, that keeps in the water; he is afraid to stand on the hard earth, like a brave Indian!"

"Well, well, Huron, that's pretty impudent, considering it's not an hour since the Sarpent stood within a hundred feet of you, and would have tried the toughness of your skin with a rifle bullet, when I pointed you out to him, had'n't I laid the weight of a little judgment on his hand. You may take in timersome gals in the settlements, with your catamount whine, but the ears of a man can tell truth from ontruth."

"Hist laughs at him! She sees he is lame, and a poor hunter, and he has never been on a war path. She will take a man for a husband, and not a fish."

"How do you know that, Catamount; how do you know that," returned Deerslayer laughing. "She has gone into the lake, you see, and may be she prefars a trout to a mongrel cat. As for war paths, neither the Sarpent nor I, have much exper'ence, we are ready to own, but if you do n't call this one, you must tarm it, what the gals in the settlements tarm it, the high road to matrimony. Take my advice Catamount, and s'arch for a wife among the Huron women; you'll never get one, with a willing mind, from among the Delawares."

Catamount's hand felt for his tomahawk, and when the fingers reached the handle, they worked convulsively, as if their owner hesitated between policy and resentment. At this critical moment Rivenoak approached, and by a gesture of authority, induced the young man to retire, assuming his former position, himself, on the log, at the side of Deerslayer. Here he continued silent for a little time, maintaining the grave reserve of an Indian chief.

"Hawkeye is right—" the Iroquois at length began; "his sight is so strong that he can see truth in a dark night, and our eyes have been blinded. He is an owl, darkness hiding nothing from him. He ought not to strike his friends. He is right."

"I'm glad you think so, Mingo," returned the other, "for a traitor, in my judgment, is worse than a coward. I care as little for the Muskrat, as one pale face ought to care for another, but I care too much for him, to ambush him in the way you wished. In short, according to my idees, any sarcumventions, except open-war sarcumventions, are ag'in both law, and what we whites call 'gospel', too."

"My pale-face brother is right; he is no Indian, to forget his Manitou and his colour. The Hurons know that they have a great warrior for their prisoner, and they will treat him as one. If he is to be tortured, his torments shall be such as no common man can bear; if he is to be treated as a friend, it will be the friendship of chiefs."

As the Huron uttered this extraordinary assurance of consideration, his eye furtively glanced at the countenance of his listener, in order to discover how he stood the compliment, though his gravity and apparent sincerity would have prevented any man but one practised in artifices, from detecting his motives. Deerslayer belonged to the class of the unsuspicious, and acquainted with the Indian notions of what constitutes respect, in matters connected with the treatment of captives, he felt his blood chill at the announcement, even while he maintained an aspect so steeled that his quick sighted enemy could discover in it, no signs of weakness.

"God has put me in your hands, Huron," the captive at

length answered, "and I suppose you will act your will on me. I shall not boast of what I can do, under torment, for I've never been tried, and no man can say 'till he has been; but I'll do my endivours not to disgrace the people among whom I got my training. Howsever, I wish you now to bear witness that I'm altogether of white blood, and, in a nat'ral way of white gifts too; so, should I be overcome and forget myself, I hope you'll lay the fault where it properly belongs, and, in no manner put it on the Delawares, or their allies and friends the Mohicans. We're all created with more or less weakness, and I'm afeard it's a pale face's to give in, under great bodily torment, when a red skin will sing his songs, and boast of his deeds in the very teeth of his foes."

"We shall see. Hawkeye has a good countenance, and he is tough—But why should he be tormented, when the Hurons love him?—He is not born their enemy, and the death of one warrior will not cast a cloud between them forever."

"So much the better, Huron; so much the better. Still I do'n't wish to owe any thing to a mistake about each other's meaning. It is so much the better that you bear no malice for the loss of a warrior who fell in war, and yet it is ontrue that there is no inmity—lawful inmity I mean—atween us. So far as I have red skin feelin's at all, I've Delaware feelin's, and I leave you to judge for yourself how far they are likely to be fri'ndly to the Mingos"—

Deerslayer ceased, for a sort of spectre stood before him, that put a stop to his words, and, indeed, caused him for a moment to doubt the fidelity of his boasted vision. Hetty Hutter was standing at the side of the fire as quietly as if she belonged to the tribe.

As the hunter and the Indian sat watching the emotions that were betrayed in each other's countenance, the girl had approached unnoticed, doubtless ascending from the beach on the southern side of the point, or that next to the spot where the Ark had anchored, and had advanced to the fire with the fearlessness that belonged to her simplicity, and which was certainly justified by the treatment formerly received from the Indians. As soon as Rivenoak perceived the girl, she was recognised, and calling to two or three of the younger warriors, the chief sent them out to reconnoitre, lest her appearance should be the forerunner of another attack. He then motioned to Hetty to draw near.

"I hope your visit is a sign that the Sarpent and Hist are in safety, Hetty," said Deerslayer, as soon as the girl had complied with the Huron's request. "I do'n't think you'd come ashore ag'in, on the ar'n'd that brought you here afore."

"Judith told me to come this time, Deerslayer," Hetty replied, "she paddled me ashore herself, in a canoe as soon as the Serpent had shown her Hist, and told his story. How handsome Hist is to-night, Deerslayer, and how much happier she looks than when she was with the Hurons!"

"That's natur' gal; yes, that may be set down as human natur'. She's with her betrothed, and no longer fears a Mingo husband. In my judgment, Judith, herself, would lose most of her beauty if she thought she was to bestow it all on a Mingo! Content is a great fortifier of good looks, and I'll warrant you, Hist is contented enough, now she is out of the hands of these miscreants, and with her chosen warrior! Did you say that Judith told you to come ashore — why should your sister do that?"

"She bid me come to see you, and to try and persuade the savages to take more elephants to let you off, but I've brought the bible with me — *that* will do more than all the elephants in father's chest!"

"And your father, good little Hetty — and Hurry; did they know of your ar'n'd?"

"Not they. Both are asleep, and Judith and the Serpent thought it best they should not be woke, lest they might want to come again after scalps, when Hist had told them how few warriors, and how many women and children there were in the camp. Judith would give me no peace, 'till I had come ashore to see what had happened to *you*."

"Well, that's remarkable as consarns Judith! Why should she feel so much unsartainty about me? — Ah — I see how it is, now; yes, I see into the whole matter, now. You must understand, Hetty, that your sister is oneasy lest Harry March should wake, and come blundering here into the hands of the inimy ag'in, under some idee that, being a travelling comrade, he ought to help me in this matter! Hurry is a blunderer, I will allow, but I do n't think he'd risk as much for my sake, as he would for his own."

"Judith do n't care for Hurry, though Hurry cares for her," replied Hetty innocently, but quite positively.

"I've heard you say as much as that afore; yes, I've heard that from you, afore, gal, and yet it is'n't true. One don't live in a tribe, not to see something of the way in which liking works in a woman's heart. Though no way given to marrying myself, I've been a looker on among the Delawares, and this is a matter in which pale-face and red skin gifts are all as one as the same. When the feelin' begins, the young woman is thoughtful, and has no eyes or ears onless for the warrior that has taken her fancy; then follows melancholy and sighing, and such sort of actions; after which, especially if matters don't come to plain discourse, she often flies round to back biting and fault finding, blaming the youth for the very things she likes best in him. Some young creatur's are forward in this way of showing their love, and I'm of opinion, Judith is one of 'em. Now, I've heard her as much as deny that Hurry was good-looking, and the young woman who could do *that*, must be far gone indeed!"

"The young woman who liked Hurry would own that he is handsome. *I* think Hurry *very* handsome, Deerslayer, and I'm sure every body must think so, that has eyes. Judith do n't like Harry March, and that's the reason she finds fault with him."

"Well—well—my good little Hetty, have it your own way. If we should talk from now 'till winter, each would think as at present, and there's no use in words. I must believe that Judith is much wrapped up in Hurry, and that, sooner or later, she'll have him; and this, too, all the more from the manner in which she abuses him; and I dare to say, you think just the contrary. But mind what I now tell you, gal, and pretend not to know it—" continued this being, who was so obtuse on a point on which men are usually quick enough to make discoveries, and so acute in matters that would baffle the observation of much the greater portion of mankind, "I see how it is, with them vagabonds. Rivenoak has left us, you see, and is talking yonder with his young men, and though too far to be *heard*, I can *see* what he is telling them. Their orders is to watch your movements, and to find where the canoe is to meet you, to take you back to the Ark, and then to seize all and what they can. I'm sorry Judith sent you, for I suppose she wants you to go back ag'in."

"All that's settled, Deerslayer," returned the girl, in a low, confidential and meaning manner, "and you may trust me to out-wit the best Indian of them all. I know I am feeble minded, but I've got *some* sense, and you'll see how I'll use it, in getting back, when my errand is done!"

"Ahs! me, poor girl; I'm afeard all that's easier said than done. They're a venomous set of riptyles and their p'ison's none the milder, for the loss of Hist. Well, I'm glad the Sarpent was the one to get off with the gal, for now there'll be two happy at least, whereas had *he* fallen into the hands of the Mingos, there'd been two miserable, and another far from feelin' as a man likes to feel."

"Now you put me in mind of a part of my errand, that I had almost forgotten, Deerslayer. Judith told me to ask you, what you thought the Hurons would do with you, if you could'n't be bought off, and what *she* had best do to serve you. Yes, this was the most important part of the errand — what *she* had best do, in order to serve you?"

"That's as *you* think, Hetty; but it's no matter. Young women are apt to lay most stress on what most touches their feelin's; but no matter; have it your own way, so you be but careful not to let the vagabonds get the mastery of a canoe. When you get back to the Ark, tell 'em to keep close, and to keep moving too, most especially at night. Many hours can't go by, without the troops on the river hearing of this party, and then your fri'nds may look for relief. 'Tis but a day's march from the nearest garrison, and true soldiers will never lie idle with the foe in their neighborhood. This is my advice, and you may say to your father and Hurry, that scalp-hunting will be a poor business now, as 'the Mingos are up and awake, and nothing can save 'em, 'till the troops come, except keeping a good belt of water atween 'em and the savages."

"What shall I tell Judith about you, Deerslayer; I know she will send me back again, if I don't bring her the truth about *you*."

"Then tell her the *truth*. I see no reason Judith Hutter

should n't hear the *truth* about me, as well as a *lie*. I'm a captyve in Indian hands, and Providence only knows what will come of it! Harkee, Hetty—" dropping his voice and speaking still more confidentially, "you *are* a little weak minded, it must be allowed, but you know something of Injins. Here I am in their hands, after having slain one of their stoutest warriors, and they've been endivouring to work upon me through fear of consequences, to betray your father, and all in the Ark. I understand the blackguards as well as if they'd told it all out plainly, with their tongues. They hold up avarice afore me, on one side, and fear on t'other, and think honesty will give way, atween 'em both. But let your father and Hurry know, 'tis all useless; as for the Sarpent, *he* knows it already."

"But what shall I tell *Judith?*—She will certainly send me back, if I don't satisfy her mind."

"Well, tell Judith the same. No doubt the savages will try the torments, to make me give in, and to revenge the loss of their warrior, but I must hold out ag'in nat'ral weakness in the best manner I can. You may tell Judith to feel no consarn on my account—it will come hard I know, seeing that a white man's gifts don't run to boasting and singing under torment, for he generally feels smallest when he suffers most—but you may tell her not to have any consarn. I think I shall make out to stand it, and she may rely on this, let me give in, as much as I may, and prove completely that I am white, by wailings, and howlings, and even tears, yet I'll never fall so far as to betray my fri'nds. When it gets to burning holes in the flesh, with heated ramrods, and to hacking the body, and tearing the hair out by the roots, natur' may get the upperhand, so far as groans, and complaints are consarned, but there the triumph of the vagabonds will ind; nothing short of god's abandoning him to the devils, can make an honest man ontrue to his colour and duty."

Hetty listened with great attention, and her mild but speaking countenance manifested a strong sympathy in the anticipated agony of the supposititious sufferer. At first she seemed at a loss how to act; then, taking a hand of Deerslayer's she affectionately recommended to him to borrow her bible, and to read it, while the savages were inflicting their torments. When the other honestly admitted that it exceeded his power to read, she even volunteered to remain with him, and to perform this holy office in person. The offer was gently declined, and Rivenoak being about to join them, Deerslayer requested the girl to leave him, first enjoining her again, to tell those in the Ark to have full confidence in his fidelity. Hetty now walked away, and approached the group of females, with as much confidence and self-possession, as if she were a native of the tribe. On the other hand the Huron resumed his seat by the side of his prisoner, the one continuing to ask questions with all the wily ingenuity of a practised Indian counsellor, and the other baffling him by the very means that are known to be the most efficacious in defeating the finesse of the more pretending diplomacy of civilisation, or by confining his answers to the truth, and the truth only.

Chapter XVIII.

"Thus died she; never more on her
Shall sorrow light, or shame. She was not made
Through years or moons the inner weight to bear,
Which colder hearts endure till they are laid
By age in earth; her days and pleasures were
Brief but delightful—such as had not stayed
Long with her destiny; but she sleeps well
By the sea shore whereon she loved to dwell."
                              Byron, *Don Juan*, IV.lxxi.

T H E young men who had been sent out to reconnoitre, on the sudden appearance of Hetty, soon returned to report their want of success in making any discovery. One of them had even been along the beach as far as the spot opposite to the Ark, but the darkness completely concealed that vessel from his notice. Others had examined in different directions, and every where the stillness of night was added to the silence and solitude of the woods. It was consequently believed that the girl had come alone, as on her former visit, and on some similar errand. The Iroquois were ignorant that the Ark had left the Castle, and there were movements projected, if not in the course of actual execution by this time, which also greatly added to the sense of security. A watch was set therefore, and all but the sentinels disposed themselves to sleep.

Sufficient care was had to the safe keeping of the captive, without inflicting on him any unnecessary suffering, and, as for Hetty, she was permitted to find a place among the Indian girls, in the best manner she could. She did not find the friendly offices of Hist, though her character not only bestowed impunity from pain and captivity, but it procured for her a consideration and an attention that placed her, on the score of comfort quite on a level with the wild but gentle beings around her. She was supplied with a skin, and made her own bed on a pile of boughs a little apart from the huts. Here she was soon in a profound sleep, like all around her.

There were now thirteen men in the party, and three kept watch at a time. One remained in shadow, not far from the fire, however. His duty was to guard the captive, to take care that the fire neither blazed up so as to illuminate the spot, nor yet became wholly extinguished, and to keep an eye generally on the state of the camp. Another passed from one beach to the other, crossing the base of the point, while the third kept moving slowly around the strand on its outer extremity, to prevent a repetition of the surprise that had already taken place that night. This arrangement was far from being usual among savages, who ordinarily rely more on the secrecy of their movements, than on vigilance of this nature, but it had been called for by the peculiarity of the circumstances in which the Hurons were now placed. Their position was known to their foes, and it could not easily be changed at an hour, which demanded rest. Perhaps, too, they placed most of their confidence on the knowledge of what they believed to be passing higher up the lake, and which, it was thought, would fully occupy the whole of the pale-faces, who were at liberty, with their solitary Indian ally. It was also probable Rivenoak was aware, that, in holding his captive, he had in his own hands the most dangerous of all his enemies.

The precision with which those, accustomed to watchfulness, or lives of disturbed rest, sleep, is not the least of the phenomena of our mysterious being. The head is no sooner on the pillow, than consciousness is lost, and yet, at a necessary hour, the mind appears to arouse the body, as promptly as if it had stood sentinel over it the while. There can be no doubt that they who are thus roused, awake by the influence of thought over matter, though the mode in which this influence is exercised must remain hidden from our curiosity, until it shall be explained, should that hour ever arrive, by the entire enlightenment of the soul, on the subject of all human mysteries. Thus it was with Hetty Hutter. Feeble as the immaterial portion of her existence was thought to be, it was sufficiently active to cause her to open her eyes at midnight. At that hour she awoke, and leaving her bed of skin and boughs, she walked innocently and openly to the embers of the fire, stirring the latter, as the coolness of the night and the woods, in connection with an exceedingly unsophisticated bed, had a little chilled her. As the flame shot up, it lighted the swarthy countenance of the Huron on watch, whose dark eyes glistened under its light, like the balls of the panther that is pursued to his den with burning brands. But Hetty felt no fear, and she approached the spot where the Indian stood. Her movements were so natural, and so perfectly devoid of any of the stealthiness of cunning, or deception, that he imagined she had merely arisen on account of the coolness of the night, a common occurrence in a bivouac, and the one of all others, perhaps, the least likely to excite suspicion. Hetty spoke to him, but he understood no English. She then gazed near a minute at the sleeping captive, and moved slowly away, in a sad and melancholy manner.

The girl took no pains to conceal her movements. Any ingenious expedient of this nature quite likely exceeded her powers; still her step was habitually light, and scarcely audible. As she took the direction of the extremity of the point, or the place where she had landed in her first adventure, and where Hist had embarked, the sentinel saw her light form gradually disappear in the gloom without uneasiness, or changing his own position. He knew that others were on the look-out, and he did not believe that one who had twice come into the camp voluntarily, and had already left it openly, would take refuge in flight. In short, the conduct of the girl excited no more attention than that of any person of feeble intellect would excite in civilized society, while her person met with more consideration and respect.

Hetty certainly had no very distinct notions of the localities, but she found her way to the beach, which she reached on the same side of the point as that on which the camp had been made. By following the margin of the water, taking a northern direction, she soon encountered the Indian, who paced the strand as sentinel. This was a young warrior, and when he heard her light tread coming along the gravel, he approached swiftly, though with any thing but menace in his manner. The darkness was so intense that it was not easy to discover forms, within the shadows of the woods, at the distance of twenty feet, and quite impossible to distinguish persons until near enough to touch them. The young Huron manifested disappointment when he found whom he had met, for truth to say, he was expecting his favorite, who had promised to relieve the *ennui* of a midnight watch with her presence. This man was also ignorant of English, but he was at no loss to understand why the girl should be up at that hour. Such things were usual in an Indian village and camp, where sleep is as irregular as the meals. Then poor Hetty's known imbecility, as in most things connected with the savages, stood her friend on this occasion. Vexed at his disappointment, and impatient of the presence of one he thought an intruder, the young warrior signed for the girl to move forward, holding the direction of the beach. Hetty complied, but as she walked away, she spoke aloud in English, in her usual, soft, tones, which the stillness of the night made audible at some little distance.

"If you took me for a Huron girl, warrior," she said, "I do n't wonder you are so little pleased. I am Hetty Hutter, Thomas Hutter's daughter, and have never met any man at night, for mother always said it was wrong, and modest young women should never do it—modest young women of the pale-faces, I mean, for customs are different in different parts of the world, I know. No—no—I'm Hetty Hutter, and would n't meet even Hurry Harry, though he should fall down on his knees and ask me! Mother said it was wrong."

By the time Hetty had said this, she reached the place where the canoes had come ashore, and owing to the curvature of the land and the bushes, would have been completely hid from the sight of the sentinel, had it been broad day. But another footstep had caught the lover's ear, and he was already nearly beyond the sound of the girl's silvery voice. Still Hetty, bent only on her own thoughts and purposes, continued to speak, though the gentleness of her tones prevented the sounds from penetrating far into the woods. On the water they were more widely diffused.

"Here I am, Judith," she added, "and there is no one near me. The Huron on watch has gone to meet his sweetheart, who is an Indian girl, you know, and never had a christian mother to tell her how wrong it is to meet a man at night.—"

Hetty's voice was hushed by a "hist!," that came from the water, and then she caught a dim view of the canoe, which approached noiselessly, and soon grated on the shingle with its bow. The moment the weight of Hetty was felt in the light craft, the canoe withdrew stern foremost, as if possessed of life and volition, until it was a hundred yards from the shore. Then it turned, and making a wide sweep, as much to prolong the passage as to get beyond the sound of voices, it held its way towards the Ark. For several minutes nothing was uttered, but believing herself to be in a favorable position to confer with her sister, Judith, who alone sat in the stern, managing the canoe with a skill little short of that of a man, began a discourse, which she had been burning to commence ever since they quitted the point.

"Here we are safe, Hetty," she said, "and may talk without the fear of being overheard. You must speak low, however, for sounds are heard far on the water, in a still night. I was so close to the point, some of the time, while you were on it that I heard the voices of the warriors, and I heard your shoes on the gravel of the beach, even before you spoke."

"I do n't believe, Judith, the Hurons know I have left them!"

"Quite likely they do not, for a lover makes a poor sentry, unless it be to watch for his sweetheart! — But, tell me, Hetty, did you see, and speak with Deerslayer?"

"Oh! yes — There he was seated near the fire, with his legs tied, though they left his arms free, to move them as he pleased."

"Well, what did he tell you, child? Speak, quick; I am dying to know what message he sent me."

"What did he tell me? — Why, what do you think, Judith; he told me that he could n't read! Only think of that; a white man, and not know how to read his bible, even! He never could have had a mother, sister!"

"Never mind *that*, Hetty. All men can't read; though mother knew so much, and taught us so much, father knows very little about books, and he can barely read the bible, you know."

"Oh! I never thought fathers *could* read much, but *mothers* ought all to read, else how can they teach their children. Depend on it, Judith, Deerslayer could never have had a mother, else he would know how to read."

"Did you tell him *I* sent you ashore, Hetty, and how much concern I felt for his misfortune?" asked the other, impatiently.

"I believe I did, Judith; but you know I am feeble-minded, and I may have forgotten. I *did* tell him you brought me ashore. And he told me a great deal that I was to say to you, which I remember well, for it made my blood run cold to hear him. He told me to say that his friends—I suppose you are one of them, sister?"

"How can you torment me thus, Hetty! Certainly, I am one of the truest friends he has on earth."

"Torment you! yes, now I remember all about it. I am glad you used that word, Judith, for it brings it all back to my mind. Well he said he might be *tormented* by the savages, but he would try to bear it as becomes a christian white-man, and that no one need be afeard—why does Deerslayer call it afeard, when mother always taught us to say afraid?"

"Never mind, dear Hetty, never mind *that*, now," cried the other, almost gasping for breath. "Did Deerslayer really tell you that he thought the savages would put him to the torture? Recollect now well, Hetty, for this is a most awful and serious thing."

"Yes he did, and I remembered it, by your speaking about my tormenting you. Oh! I felt very sorry for him, and Deerslayer took all so quietly and without noise! Deerslayer is not as handsome as Hurry Harry, Judith, but he is more quiet."

"He's worth a million Hurry's! Yes, he's worth all the young men who ever came upon the lake put together," said Judith, with an energy and positiveness that caused her sister to wonder. "He is *true*. There is no lie about Deerslayer. *You*, Hetty, may not know what a merit it is in a man to have truth, but when you get—no—I hope you will never know it. Why should one like you, be ever made to learn the hard lesson to distrust and hate!"

Judith bowed her face, dark as it was, and unseen as she must have been, by any eye but that of omniscience, between her hands, and groaned. This sudden paroxysm of feeling, however, lasted but for a moment, and she continued more calmly, still speaking frankly to her sister, whose intelligence, and whose discretion in any thing that related to herself, she did not in the least distrust. Her voice, however, was low and husky, instead of having its former clearness and animation.

"It is a hard thing to fear truth, Hetty," she said, "and yet do I more dread Deerslayer's truth, than any enemy! One cannot tamper with such truth—so much honesty—such obstinate uprightness! But we are not altogether unequal, sister — Deer-slayer and I? He is not altogether my superior?"

It was not usual for Judith so far to demean herself, as to appeal to Hetty's judgment. Nor did she often address her by the title of sister, a distinction that is commonly given by the junior to the senior, even where there is perfect equality in all other respects. As trifling departures from habitual deportment oftener strike the imagination than more important changes, Hetty perceived the circumstances, and wondered at them in her own simple way.

Her ambition was a little quickened, and the answer was as much out of the usual course of things, as the question, the poor girl attempting to refine beyond her strength.

"Superior, Judith!" she repeated with pride. "In what *can* Deerslayer be *your* superior? — Are you not mother's child, and does he know how to read, and was n't mother before any woman in all this part of the world? I should think so far from supposing himself *your* superior, he would hardly believe himself *mine*. You are handsome and he is ugly" —

"No, not ugly, Hetty —" interrupted Judith — "Only plain. But his honest face has a look in it, that is far better than beauty. In my eyes Deerslayer is handsomer than Hurry Harry."

"Judith Hutter! You frighten me. Hurry is the handsomest mortal in the world — even handsomer than you are yourself, because a man's good looks, you know, are always better than a woman's good looks."

This little innocent touch of natural taste did not please the elder sister at the moment, and she did not scruple to betray it.

"Hetty, you now speak foolishly, and had better say no more, on this subject," she answered. "Hurry is not the handsomest mortal in the world, by many, and there are officers in the garrisons —" Judith stammered at the words — "there are officers in the garrisons, near us, far comelier than he. But, why do you think me the equal of Deerslayer — speak of *that*, for I do not like to hear you show so much admiration of a man like Hurry Harry, who has neither feelings, manners, nor conscience. *You* are too good for *him*, and he ought to be told it, at once."

"*I!* Judith how you forget! Why *I* am not beautiful, and am feeble minded."

"You are *good*, Hetty, and that is more than can be said of Henry March. He may have a *face*, and a *body*, but he has no *heart*. But enough of this for the present. Tell me what raises me to an equality with Deerslayer."

"To think of you asking me this, Judith! He can n't read, and you can. He do n't know how to talk, but speaks worse than Hurry even;—for, sister, Harry does n't always pronounce his words right! Did you ever notice *that?*"

"Certainly. He is as coarse in speech, as in every thing else. But, I fear you flatter me, Hetty, when you think I can be justly called the equal of a man like Deerslayer. It is true, I have been better taught; in one sense am more comely; and perhaps might look higher, but then his truth—his truth—makes a fearful difference between us! Well, I will talk no more of this, and we will bethink us of the means of getting him out of the hands of the Hurons. We have father's chest in the Ark, Hetty, and might try the temptation of more elephants; though I fear such baubles will not buy the liberty of a man like Deerslayer. I am afraid Father and Hurry will not be as willing to ransom Deerslayer, as Deerslayer was to ransom them!"

"Why not, Judith? Hurry and Deerslayer are friends, and friends should always help one another."

"Alas! poor Hetty, you little know mankind! Seeming friends are often more to be dreaded than open enemies, particularly by females. But you'll have to land in the morning, and try again what can be done for Deerslayer. Tortured he *shall* not be, while Judith Hutter lives, and can find means to prevent it."

The conversation now grew desultory, and was drawn out, until the elder sister had extracted from the younger, every fact that the feeble faculties of the latter permitted her to retain, and to communicate. When Judith was satisfied—though, she could never be said to be satisfied whose feelings seemed to be so interwoven with all that related to the subject as to have excited a nearly inappeasable curiosity—but, when Judith could think of no more questions to ask, without resorting to repetition, the canoe was paddled towards the scow. The intense darkness of the night, and the deep shadows which the hills and forest cast upon the water, rendered it difficult to find the vessel, anchored, as it had been, as close to the shore as a regard to safety rendered prudent. Judith was expert in the management of a bark canoe, the lightness of which demanded skill rather than strength, and she forced her own little vessel swiftly over the water, the moment she had ended her conference with Hetty, and had come to the determination to return. Still no Ark was seen. Several times the sisters fancied they saw it, looming up in the obscurity, like a low black rock, but on each occasion it was found to be either an optical illusion, or some swell of the foliage on the shore. After a search that lasted half an hour, the girls were forced to the unwelcome conviction that the Ark had departed.

Most young women would have felt the awkwardness of their situation, in a physical sense, under the circumstances in which the sisters were left, more than any apprehensions of a different nature. Not so with Judith, however; and even Hetty felt more concern about the motives that might have influenced her father and Hurry, than any fears for her own safety.

"It cannot be, Hetty," said Judith, when a thorough search had satisfied them both that no Ark was to be found, "it cannot be that the Indians have rafted, or swam off, and surprised our friends as they slept?"

"I do n't believe that Hist and Chingachgook would sleep, until they had told each other all they had to say, after so long a separation, do you sister?"

"Perhaps not, child. There was much to keep them awake, but one Indian may have been surprised even when not asleep, especially as his thoughts may have been on other things. Still we should have heard a noise, for in a night like this, an oath of Hurry Harry's would have echoed in the eastern hills like a clap of thunder."

"Hurry *is* sinful and thoughtless about his words, Judith," Hetty meekly and sorrowfully answered.

"No—no; 'tis impossible the Ark could be taken and I not hear the noise. It is not an hour since I left it, and the whole time I have been attentive to the smallest sound. And, yet, it is not easy to believe a father would willingly abandon his children!"

"Perhaps Father has thought us in our cabin, asleep, Judith, and has moved away to go home. You know, we often move the Ark in the night."

"This is true, Hetty, and it must be as you suppose. There is a little more southern air than there was, and they have gone up the lake. — "

Judith stopped, for, as the last word was on her tongue, the scene was suddenly lighted, though only for a single instant, by a flash. The crack of a rifle succeeded, and then followed the roll of the echo along the eastern mountains. Almost at the same moment, a piercing female cry arose in the air in a prolonged shriek. The awful stillness that succeeded was, if possible, more appalling than the fierce and sudden interruption of the deep silence of midnight. Resolute as she was both by nature and habit, Judith scarce breathed, while poor Hetty hid her face and trembled.

"That was a woman's cry, Hetty," said the former solemnly, "and it was a cry of anguish! If the Ark has moved from this spot, it can only have gone north with this air, and the gun and shriek came from the point. Can any thing have befallen Hist!"

"Let us go and see, Judith; she may want our assistance, for besides herself, there are none but men in the Ark."

It was not a moment for hesitation, and ere Judith had ceased speaking her paddle was in the water. The distance to the point, in a direct line was not great, and the impulses under which the girls worked were too exciting to allow them to waste the precious moments in useless precautions. They paddled incautiously for them, but the same excitement kept others from noting their movements. Presently a glare of light caught the eye of Judith through an opening in the bushes, and steering by it she so directed the canoe as to keep it visible, while she got as near the land as was either prudent or necessary.

The scene that was now presented to the observation of the girls, was within the woods, on the side of the acclivity, so often mentioned, and in plain view from the boat. Here all in the camp were collected, some six or eight carrying torches of fat-pine, which cast a strong but funereal light on all beneath the arches of the forest. With her back supported against a tree, and sustained on one side by the young sentinel whose remissness had suffered Hetty to escape, sate the female whose expected visit had produced his delinquency. By the glare of the torch that was held near her face, it was evident that she was in the agonies of death, while the blood that trickled from her bared bosom betrayed the nature of the injury she had received. The pungent, peculiar smell of gunpowder, too, was still quite perceptible in the heavy, damp, night air. There could be no question that she had been shot. Judith understood it all, at a glance. The streak of light had appeared on the water, a short distance from the point, and either the rifle had been discharged from a canoe hovering near the land, or it had been fired from the Ark, in passing. An incautious exclamation, or laugh, may have produced the assault, for it was barely possible that the aim had been assisted by any other agent than sound. As to the effect, that was soon still more apparent, the head of the victim dropping, and the body sinking in death. Then all the torches but one were extinguished, a measure of prudence, and the melancholy train that bore the body to the camp, was just to be distinguished by the glimmering light that remained.

Judith sighed heavily and shuddered, as her paddle again dipped, and the canoe moved cautiously around the point. A sight had afflicted her senses, and now haunted her imagination, that was still harder to be borne, than even the untimely fate, and passing agony of the deceased girl. She had seen, under the strong glare of all the torches, the erect form of Deerslayer, standing, with commiseration, and as she thought with shame, depicted on his countenance, near the dying female. He betrayed neither fear, nor backwardness, *himself*, but it was apparent by the glances cast at him by the warriors, that fierce passions were struggling in *their* bosoms. All this seemed to be unheeded by the captive, but it remained impressed on the memory of Judith throughout the night.

No canoe was met hovering near the point. A stillness and darkness, as complete as if the silence of the forest had never been disturbed, or the sun had never shone on that retired region, now reigned on the point, and on the gloomy water, the slumbering woods, and even the murky sky. No more could be done, therefore, than to seek a place of safety, and this was only to be found in the centre of the lake. Paddling, in silence to that spot, the canoe was suffered to drift northerly, while the girls sought such repose as their situation and feelings would permit.

Chapter XIX.

"Stand to your arms, and guard the door—all's lost
Unless that fearful bell be silenced soon.
The officer hath miss'd his path, or purpose,
Or met some unforeseen and hideous obstacle.
Anselmo, with thy company proceed
Straight to the tower; the rest remain with me."
                    Byron, *Marino Faliero*, IV.ii.230–35.

T H E conjecture of Judith Hutter, concerning the manner in which the Indian girl had met her death, was accurate in the main. After sleeping several hours, her father and March awoke. This occurred a few minutes after she had left the Ark to go in quest of her sister, and when of course Chingachgook and his betrothed were on board. From the Delaware the old man learned the position of the camp, and the recent events, as well as the absence of his daughters. The latter gave him no concern, for he relied greatly on the sagacity of the elder, and the known impunity with which the younger passed among the savages. Long familiarity with danger, too, had blunted his sensibilities. Nor did he seem much to regret the captivity of Deerslayer, for, while he knew how material his aid might be in a defence, the difference in their views on the morality of the woods, had not left much sympathy between them. He would have rejoiced to know the position of the camp before it had been alarmed by the escape of Hist, but it would be too hazardous now to venture to land, and he reluctantly relinquished for the night, the ruthless designs that cupidity and revenge had excited him to entertain. In this mood Hutter took a seat in the head of the scow, where he was quickly joined by Hurry, leaving the Serpent and Hist in quiet possession of the other extremity of the vessel.

"Deerslayer has shown himself a boy, in going among the savages at this hour, and letting himself fall into their hands like a deer that tumbles into a pit," growled the old man, perceiving as usual the mote in his neighbor's eyes, while he overlooked the beam in his own; "if he is left to pay for his stupidity with his own flesh, he can blame no one but himself."

"That's the way of the world, old Tom," returned Hurry. "Every man must meet his own debts, and answer for his own sins. I'm amazed, howsever, that a lad as skilful and watchful as Deerslayer, should have been caught in such a trap! Did n't he know any better than to go prowling about a Huron camp, at midnight, with no place to retreat to, but a lake; or did he think himself a buck, that by taking to the water could throw off the scent and swim himself out of difficulty. I had a better opinion of the boy's judgment, I'll own; but we must overlook a little ignorance in a raw hand. I say, Master Hutter, do you happen to know what has become of the gals — I see no signs of Judith, or Hetty, though I've been through the Ark, and looked into all its living creatur's."

Hutter briefly explained the manner in which his daughters had taken to the canoe, as it had been related by the Delaware, as well as the return of Judith after landing her sister, and her second departure.

"This comes of a smooth tongue, Floating Tom," exclaimed Hurry, grating his teeth in pure resentment — "This comes of a smooth tongue, and a silly gal's inclinations, and you had best look into the matter! You and I were both prisoners — " Hurry could recal that circumstance *now* — "you and I were both prisoners and yet Judith never stirred an inch to do us any sarvice! She is bewitched with this lank-looking Deerslayer, and he, and she, and you, and all of us, had best look to it. I am not a man to put up with such a wrong quietly, and I say, all the parties had best look to it! Let's up kedge, old fellow, and move nearer to this p'int, and see how matters are getting on."

Hutter had no objections to this movement, and the Ark was got under way, in the usual manner; care being taken to make no noise. The wind was passing northward, and the sail soon swept the scow so far up the lake, as to render the dark outlines of the trees that clothed the point, dimly visible. Floating Tom steered, and he sailed along as near the land, as the depth of the water, and the overhanging branches would allow. It was impossible to distinguish any thing that stood within the shadows of the shore, but the forms of the sail and of the hut, were discerned by the young sentinel on the beach, who has already been mentioned. In the moment of sudden surprise, a deep Indian exclamation escaped him. In that spirit of recklessness and ferocity that formed the essence of Hurry's character, this man dropped his rifle and fired. The ball was sped by accident, or by that overruling providence which decides the fates of all, and the girl fell. Then followed the scene with the torches, which has just been described.

At the precise moment when Hurry committed this act of unthinking cruelty, the canoe of Judith was within a hundred feet of the spot from which the Ark had so lately moved. Her own course has been described, and it has now become our office to follow that of her father and his companions. The shriek announced the effects of the random shot of March, and it also proclaimed that the victim was a woman. Hurry himself was startled at these unlooked for consequences, and for a moment he was sorely disturbed by conflicting sensations. At first he laughed, in reckless and rude-minded exultation; and then conscience, that monitor planted in our breasts by God, and which receives its more general growth from the training bestowed in the tillage of childhood, shot a pang to his heart. For a minute, the mind of this creature equally of civilization and of barbarism, was a sort of chaos as to feeling, not knowing what to think of its own act; and then the obstinacy and pride of one of his habits, interposed to assert their usual ascendency. He struck the butt of his rifle on the bottom of the scow, with a species of defiance, and began to whistle a low air with an affectation of indifference. All this time the Ark was in motion, and it was already opening the bay above the point, and was consequently quitting the land.

Hurry's companions did not view his conduct with the same indulgence, as that with which he appeared disposed to regard it himself. Hutter growled out his dissatisfaction, for the act led to no advantage, while it threatened to render the warfare more vindictive than ever, and none censure motiveless departures from the right, more severely than the mercenary and unprincipled. Still he commanded himself, the captivity of Deerslayer rendering the arm of the offender of double consequence to him at that moment. Chingachgook arose, and for a single instant the ancient animosity of tribes was forgotten, in a feeling of colour; but he recollected himself in season to prevent any of the fierce consequences that, for a passing moment, he certainly meditated. Not so with Hist. Rushing through the hut, or cabin, the girl stood at the side of Hurry, almost as soon as his rifle touched the bottom of the scow, and with a fearlessness that did credit to her heart, she poured out her reproaches with the generous warmth of a woman.

"What for you shoot?" she said. "What Huron gal do, dat you kill him? What you t'ink Manitou *say?* What you t'ink Manitou, *feel?* What Iroquois *do?* No get honour—no get camp—no get prisoner—no get battle—no get scalp—no get not'ing at all! Blood come after blood! How you feel, your wife killed? Who pity you, when tear come for moder, or sister? You big as great pine—Huron gal little slender birch—why you fall on her and crush her! You t'ink Huron forget it? No; red skin never forget! Never forget friend; never forget enemy. Red man Manitou in *dat.* Why you so wicked, great pale-face?"

Hurry had never been so daunted as by this close and warm attack of the Indian girl. It is true that she had a powerful ally in his conscience, and while she spoke earnestly, it was in tones so feminine as to deprive him of any pretext for unmanly anger. The softness of her voice added to the weight of her remonstrance, by lending to the latter an air of purity and truth. Like most vulgar minded men, he had only regarded the Indians through the medium of their coarser and fiercer characteristics. It had never struck him that the affections are human, that even high principles—modified by habits and prejudices, but not the less elevated within their circle—can exist in the savage state, and that the warrior who is most ruthless in the field, can submit to the softest and gentlest influences, in the moments of domestic quiet. In a word, it was the habit of his mind to regard all Indians as being only a slight degree removed from the wild beasts that roamed the woods, and to feel disposed to treat them accordingly, whenever interest or caprice supplied a motive, or an impulse. Still, though daunted by these reproaches, the handsome barbarian could hardly be said to be penitent. He was too much rebuked by conscience to suffer an outbreak of temper to escape him, and perhaps he felt that he had already committed an act that might justly bring his manhood in question. Instead of resenting, or answering the simple but natural appeal of Hist, he walked away, like one who disdained entering into a controversy with a woman.

In the mean while, the Ark swept onward, and by the time the scene with the torches, was enacting beneath the trees, it had reached the open lake, Floating Tom causing it to sheer further from the land, with a sort of instinctive dread of retaliation. An hour now passed in gloomy silence, no one appearing disposed to break it. Hist had retired to her pallet, and Chingachgook lay sleeping in the forward part of the scow. Hutter and Hurry alone remained awake, the former at the steering oar, while the latter brooded over his own conduct, with the stubbornness of one little given to a confession of his errors, and the secret goadings of the worm that never dies. This was at the moment when Judith and Hetty reached the centre of the lake, and had lain down to endeavor to sleep, in their drifting canoe.

The night was calm, though so much obscured by clouds. The season was not one of storms, and those which did occur in the month of June, on that embedded water, though frequently violent were always of short continuance. Nevertheless, there was the usual current of heavy, damp night air, which, passing over the summits of the trees, scarcely appeared to descend as low as the surface of the glassy lake, but kept moving a short distance above it, saturated with the humidity that constantly arose from the woods, and apparently never proceeding far in any one direction. The currents were influenced by the formation of the hills, as a matter of course, a circumstance that rendered even fresh breezes baffling, and which reduced the feebler efforts of the night air to be a sort of capricious and fickle sighings of the woods. Several times the head of the Ark pointed east, and once it was actually turned towards the south, again; but, on the whole, it worked its way north; Hutter making always a fair wind, if wind it could be called, his principal motive appearing to be a wish to keep in motion, in order to defeat any treacherous design of his enemies. He, now, felt some little concern about his daughters, and perhaps as much about the canoe; but, on the whole, this uncertainty did not much disturb him, as he had the reliance already mentioned on the intelligence of Judith.

It was the season of the shortest nights, and it was not long before the deep obscurity which precedes the day began to yield to the returning light. If any earthly scene could be presented to the senses of man that might soothe his passions and temper his ferocity, it was that which grew upon the eyes of Hutter and Hurry, as the hours advanced, changing night to morning. There were the usual soft tints of the sky, in which neither the gloom of darkness nor the brilliancy of the sun prevails, and under which objects appear more unearthly and we might add holy, than at any other portion of the twenty four hours. The beautiful and soothing calm of even tide has been extolled by a thousand poets, and yet it does not bring with it, the far-reaching and sublime thoughts of the half hour that precedes the rising of a summer sun. In the one case the panorama is gradually hid from the sight, while in the other, its objects start out from the unfolding picture, first dim and misty; then marked in, in solemn back ground; next seen in the witchery of an *increasing*, a thing as different as possible from the *decreasing* twilight, and finally mellow, distinct and luminous, as the rays of the great centre of light diffuse themselves in the atmosphere. The hymns of birds, too, have no moral counterpart in the retreat to the roost, or the flight to the nest, and these invariably accompany the advent of the day, until the appearance of the sun itself —

"Bathes in deep joy, the land and sea."

All this, however, Hutter and Hurry witnessed without experiencing any of that calm delight, which the spectacle is wont to bring, when the thoughts are just, and the aspirations pure. They not only witnessed it, but they witnessed it under circumstances that had a tendency to increase its power, and to heighten its charms. Only one solitary object became visible in the returning light, that had received its form or uses from human taste, or human desires which as often deform as beautify a landscape. This was the castle, all the rest being native, and fresh from the hand of God. That singular residence, too, was in keeping with the natural objects of the view, starting out from the gloom, quaint, picturesque, and ornamental. Nevertheless the whole was lost on the observers, who knew no feeling of poetry, had lost their sense of natural devotion in lives of obdurate and narrow selfishness, and had little other sympathy with nature, than that which originated with her lowest wants.

As soon as the light was sufficiently strong to allow of a distinct view of the lake, and more particularly of its shores, Hutter turned the head of the Ark directly towards the castle, with the avowed intention of taking possession, for the day at least, as the place most favorable for meeting his daughters, and for carrying on his operations against the Indians. By this time, Chingachgook was up, and Hist was heard stirring among the furniture of the kitchen. The place for which they steered was distant only a mile, and the air was sufficiently favorable to permit it to be reached by means of the sail. At this moment, too, to render the appearances generally auspicious, the canoe of Judith was seen floating northward in the broadest part of the lake; having actually passed the scow in the darkness, in obedience to no other power than that of the elements. Hutter got his glass, and took a long and anxious survey, to ascertain if his daughters were in the light craft, or not, and a slight exclamation like that of joy escaped him, as he caught a glimpse of what he rightly conceived to be a part of Judith's dress above the top of the canoe. At the next instant the girl arose, and was seen gazing about her, like one assuring herself of her situation. A minute later, Hetty was seen on her knees, in the other end of the canoe, repeating the prayers that had been taught her, in childhood, by a misguided but repentant mother. As Hutter laid down the glass, still drawn to its focus, the Serpent raised it to his eye, and turned it towards the canoe. It was the first time he had ever used such an instrument, and Hist understood by his "hugh!," the expression of his face, and his entire mien, that something wonderful had excited his admiration. It is well known that the American Indians, more particularly those of superior characters and stations, singularly maintain their self-possession and stoicism, in the midst of the flood of marvels that present themselves in their occasional visits to the abodes of civilization, and Chingachgook had imbibed enough of this impassibility to suppress any very undignified manifestation of surprise. With Hist, however, no such law was binding, and when her lover managed to bring the glass in a line with a canoe, and her eye was applied to the smaller end, the girl started back in alarm;

then she clapped her hands with delight, and a laugh, the usual attendant of untutored admiration, followed. A few minutes sufficed to enable this quick witted girl to manage the instrument for herself, and she directed it at every prominent object that struck her fancy. Finding a rest in one of the windows, she and the Delaware first surveyed the lake; then the shores, the hills, and, finally, the castle attracted their attention. After a long steady gaze at the latter, Hist took away her eye, and spoke to her lover in a low earnest manner. Chingachgook immediately placed his eye to the glass, and his look even exceeded that of his betrothed in length and intensity. Again they spoke together, confidentially, appearing to compare opinions, after which the glass was laid aside, and the young warrior quitted the cabin to join Hutter and Hurry.

The Ark was slowly but steadily advancing, and the castle was materially within half a mile, when Chingachgook joined the two white men in the stern of the scow. His manner was calm, but it was evident to the others, who were familiar with the habits of the Indians, that he had something to communicate. Hurry was generally prompt to speak and, according to custom, he took the lead on this occasion.

"Out with it, red-skin," he cried, in his usual rough manner. "Have you discovered a chip-munk in a tree, or is there a salmon-trout swimming under the bottom of the scow? You find what a pale-face can do in the way of eyes, now, Sarpent, and must n't wonder that they can see the land of the Indians from afar off."

"No good to go to Castle," put in Chingachgook with emphasis, the moment the other gave him an opportunity of speaking. "Huron there."

"The devil he is! — If this should turn out to be true, Floating Tom, a pretty trap were we about to pull down on our heads! Huron, there! — Well, this may be so; but no signs can I see of any thing, near or about the old hut, but logs, water, and bark — bating two or three windows, and one door."

Hutter called for the glass, and took a careful survey of the spot, before he ventured an opinion, at all; then he somewhat cavalierly expressed his dissent from that given by the Indian.

"You've got this glass wrong end foremost, Delaware," continued Hurry. "Neither the old man, nor I can see any trail in the lake."

"No trail—water make no trail," said Hist, eagerly. "Stop boat—no go too near. Huron there!"

"Ay, that's it!—Stick to the same tale, and more people will believe you. I hope Sarpent, you and your gal will agree in telling the same story arter marriage, as well as you do now. 'Huron, there!'—Whereabouts is he to be seen—in the padlock, or the chains, or the logs. There is n't a gaol in the colony that has a more lock up look about it, than old Tom's *chientè*, and, I know something about gaols from exper'ence."

"No see moccasin—" said Hist, impatiently—"why no *look*— and see him."

"Give me the glass, Harry," interrupted Hutter, "and lower the sail. It is seldom that an Indian woman meddles, and when she does, there is generally a cause for it. There *is*, truly, a moccasin floating against one of the piles, and it may, or may not be a sign that the castle has n't escaped visitors, in our absence. Moccasins are no rarities, however, for I wear 'em myself; and Deerslayer wears 'em, and you wear 'em, March, and, for that matter so does Hetty, quite as often as she wears shoes, though I never yet saw Judith trust her pretty foot in a moccasin."

Hurry had lowered the sail, and by this time the Ark was within two hundred yards of the castle, setting in, nearer and nearer, each moment, but at a rate too slow to excite any uneasiness. Each now took the glass in turn, and the castle, and every thing near it, was subjected to a scrutiny still more rigid than ever. There the moccasin lay, beyond a question, floating so lightly, and preserving its form so well, that it was scarcely wet. It had caught by a piece of the rough bark of one of the piles, on the exterior of the water-palisade that formed the dock already mentioned, which circumstance alone prevented it from drifting away before the air. There were many modes, however, of accounting for the presence of the moccasin, without supposing it to have been dropped by an enemy. It might have fallen from the platform, even while Hutter was in possession of the place, and drifted to the spot where it was now seen, remaining unnoticed until detected by the acute vision of Hist. It might have drifted from a distance, up or down the lake, and accidentally become attached to the pile, or palisade. It might have been thrown from a window, and alighted in that particular place; or it might certainly have fallen from a scout, or an assailant, during the past night, who was obliged to abandon it, to the lake, in the deep obscurity which then prevailed.

All these conjectures passed from Hutter to Hurry, the former appearing disposed to regard the omen as a little sinister, while the latter treated it with his usual reckless disdain. As for the Indian, he was of opinion that the moccasin should be viewed as one would regard a trail in the woods, which might, or might not, equally, prove to be threatening. Hist, however, had something available to propose. She declared her readiness to take a canoe, to proceed to the palisade and bring away the moccasin, when its ornaments would show whether it came from the Canadas or not. Both the white men were disposed to accept this offer, but the Delaware interfered to prevent the risk. If such a service was to be undertaken, it best became a warrior to expose himself in its execution, and he gave his refusal to let his betrothed proceed, much in the quiet but brief manner in which an Indian husband issues his commands.

"Well then, Delaware, go yourself if you're so tender of your squaw," put in the unceremonious Hurry. "That moccasin must be had, or Floating Tom will keep off, here, at arm's length, till the hearth cools in his cabin. It's but a little deer-skin, a'ter all, and cut this-a-way or that-a-way, it's not a skear-crow to frighten true hunters from their game. What say you, Sarpent, shall you or I canoe it?"

"Let red man go. — Better eyes than pale-face — know Huron trick better, too."

"That I'll gainsay, to the hour of my death! A white man's eyes, and a white man's nose, and for that matter his sight and ears are all better than an Injin's when fairly tried. Time and ag'in have I put that to the proof, and what is proved is sartain. Still I suppose the poorest vagabond going, whether Delaware or Huron, can find his way to yonder hut and back ag'in, and so, Sarpent, use your paddle and welcome."

Chingachgook was already in the canoe, and he dipped the implement the other named into the water, just as Hurry's limber tongue ceased. Wah-ta!-Wah saw the departure of her warrior on this occasion, with the submissive silence of an Indian girl, but with most of the misgivings and apprehensions of her sex. Throughout the whole of the past night, and down to the moment, when they used the glass together in the hut, Chingachgook had manifested as much manly tenderness towards his betrothed, as one of the most refined sentiment could have shown under similar circumstances, but now every sign of weakness was lost in an appearance of stern resolution. Although Hist timidly endeavored to catch his eye, as the canoe left the side of the Ark, the pride of a warrior would not permit him to meet her fond and anxious looks. The canoe departed and not a wandering glance rewarded her solicitude.

Nor were the Delaware's care and gravity misplaced, under the impressions with which he proceeded on this enterprise. If the enemy had really gained possession of the building, he was obliged to put himself under the very muzzles of their rifles, as it were, and this too without the protection of any of that cover, which forms so essential an ally in Indian warfare. It is scarcely possible to conceive of a service more dangerous, and had the Serpent been fortified by the experience of ten more years, or had his friend the Deerslayer been present, it would never have been attempted; the advantages in no degree compensating for the risk. But the pride of an Indian chief was acted on by the rivalry of colour, and it is not unlikely that the presence of the very creature from whom his ideas of manhood prevented his receiving a single glance, overflowing as he was with the love she so well merited, had no small influence on his determination.

Chingachgook paddled steadily towards the palisades, keeping his eyes on the different loops of the building. Each instant he expected to see the muzzle of a rifle protruded, or to hear its sharp crack; but he succeeded in reaching the piles in safety. Here he was, in a measure, protected, having the heads of the palisades between him and the hut, and the chances of any attempt on his life while thus covered, were greatly diminished. The canoe had reached the piles with its head inclining northward, and at a short distance from the moccasin. Instead of turning to pick up the latter, the Delaware slowly made the circuit of the whole building, deliberately examining every object that should betray the presence of enemies, or the commission of violence. Not a single sign could he discover, however, to confirm the suspicions that had been awakened. The stillness of desertion pervaded the building; not a fastening was displaced, not a window had been broken. The door looked as secure as at the hour when it was closed by Hutter, and even the gate of the dock had all the customary fastenings. In short, the most wary and jealous eye could detect no other evidence of the visit of enemies, than that which was connected with the appearance of the floating moccasin.

The Delaware was now greatly at a loss how to proceed. At one moment, as he came round in front of the castle, he was on the point of stepping up on the platform, and of applying his eye to one of the loops, with a view of taking a direct personal inspection of the state of things within; but he hesitated. Though of little experience in such matters, himself, he had heard so much of Indian artifices through traditions, had listened with such breathless interest to the narration of the escapes of the elder warriors, and, in short, was so well schooled in the theory of his calling, that it was almost as impossible for him to make any gross blunder on such an occasion, as it was for a well grounded scholar, who had commenced correctly, to fail in solving his problem in mathematics. Relinquishing the momentary intention to land, the chief slowly pursued his course round the palisades. As he approached the moccasin, having now nearly completed the circuit of the building, he threw the ominous article into the canoe, by a dexterous and almost imperceptible movement of his paddle. He was now ready to depart, but retreat was even more dangerous than the approach, as the eye could no longer be riveted on the loops. If there was really any one in the castle, the motive of the Delaware in reconnoitring must be understood, and it was the wisest way, however perilous it might be, to retire with an air of confidence, as if all distrust were terminated by the examination. Such, accordingly, was the course adopted by the Indian, who paddled deliberately away, taking the direction of the Ark, suffering no nervous impulse to quicken the motions of his arms, or to induce him to turn even a furtive glance behind him.

No tender wife, reared in the refinements of the highest civilization, ever met a husband on his return from the field, with more of sensibility in her countenance, than Hist discovered, as she saw the Great Serpent of the Delawares, step, unharmed, into the Ark. Still she repressed her emotion, though the joy that sparkled in her dark eyes, and the smile that lighted her pretty mouth, spoke a language that her betrothed could understand.

"Well, Sarpent," cried Hurry, always the first to speak, "what news from the muskrats? Did they shew their teeth, as you surrounded their dwelling?"

"I no like him—" sententiously returned the Delaware. "Too still. So still, can see silence!"

"That's downright Injin—as if any thing could make less noise than nothing! If you've no better reason than this to give, old Tom had better hoist his sail, and go and get his breakfast under his own roof. What has become of the moccasin?"

"Here," returned Chingachgook, holding up his prize for the general inspection.

The moccasin was examined, and Hist confidently pronounced it to be Huron, by the manner in which the porcupine's quills were arranged on its front. Hutter and the Delaware, too, were decidedly of the same opinion. Admitting all this, however, it did not necessarily follow that its owners were in the castle. The moccasin might have drifted from a distance, or it might have fallen from the foot of some scout, who had quitted the place when his errand was accomplished. In short it explained nothing, while it awakened so much distrust.

Under the circumstances, Hutter and Hurry were not men to be long deterred from proceeding by proofs as slight as that of the moccasin. They hoisted the sail again, and the Ark was soon in motion, heading towards the castle. The wind, or air continued light, and the movement was sufficiently slow, to allow of a deliberate survey of the building, as the scow approached. The same death-like silence reigned, and it was difficult to fancy that any thing possessing animal life could be in or around the place. Unlike the Serpent, whose imagination had acted through his traditions, until he was ready to perceive an artificial, in a natural stillness, the others saw nothing to apprehend in a tranquility that, in truth, merely denoted the repose of inanimate objects. The accessories of the scene, too, were soothing and calm, rather than exciting. The day had not yet advanced so far as to bring the sun above the horizon, but the heavens, the atmosphere, and the woods and lake were all seen under that softened light which immediately precedes his appearance, and which perhaps is the most witching period of the four and twenty hours. It is the moment, when every thing is distinct, even the atmosphere seeming to possess a liquid lucidity, the hues appearing gray and softened, with the outlines of objects defined, and the perspective just as moral truths, that are presented in their simplicity, without the meretricious aids of ornament, or glitter. In a word, it is the moment when the senses seem to recover their powers, in the simplest and most accurate forms, like the mind emerging from the obscurity of doubts, into the tranquility and peace of demonstration. Most of the influence that such a scene is apt to produce on those who are properly constituted in a moral sense, was lost on Hutter and Hurry; but both the Delawares, though too much accustomed to witness the loveliness of morning-tide, to stop to analyze their feelings, were equally sensible of the beauties of the hour, though it was probably in a way unknown to themselves. It disposed the young warrior to peace, and never had he felt less longings for the glory of the combat, than when he joined Hist in the cabin, the instant the scow rubbed against the side of the platform. From the indulgence of such gentle emotions, however, he was aroused by a rude summons from Hurry, who called on him to come forth, and help to take in the sail, and to secure the Ark.

Chingachgook obeyed, and by the time he had reached the head of the scow, Hurry was on the platform, stamping his feet, like one glad to touch what, by comparison, might be called *terra firma*, and proclaiming his indifference to the whole Huron tribe, in his customary noisy, dogmatical, manner. Hutter had hauled a canoe up to the head of the scow, and was already about to undo the fastenings of the gate, in order to enter within the 'dock.' March had no other motive in landing than a senseless bravado, and having shaken the door, in a manner to put its solidity to the proof, he joined Hutter in the canoe, and began to aid him in opening the gate. The reader will remember that this mode of entrance was rendered necessary by the manner in which the owner of this singular residence habitually secured it, whenever it was left empty; more particularly at moments when danger was apprehended. Hutter had placed a line in the Delaware's hand, on entering the canoe, intimating that the other was to fasten the Ark to the platform and to lower the sail. Instead of following these directions, however, Chingachgook left the sail standing, and throwing the bight of the rope over the head of a pile, he permitted the Ark to drift round, until it lay against the defences, in a position where it could be entered only by means of a boat, or by passing along the summits of the palisades; the latter being an exploit that required some command of the feet, and which was not to be attempted in the face of a resolute enemy.

In consequence of this change in the position of the scow, which was effected before Hutter had succeeded in opening the gate of his dock, the Ark and the Castle, lay, as sailors would express it, yard-arm and yard-arm, kept asunder some ten or twelve feet, by means of the piles. As the scow pressed close against the latter, their tops formed a species of breast work, that rose to the height of a man's head, covering in a certain degree, the parts of the scow that were not protected by the cabin. The Delaware surveyed this arrangement with great satisfaction, and, as the canoe of Hutter passed through the gate, into the dock, he thought that he might defend his position against any garrison in the castle, for a sufficient time, could he but have had the helping arm of his friend Deerslayer. As it was, he felt comparatively secure, and no longer suffered the keen apprehensions he had lately experienced in behalf of Hist.

A single shove sent the canoe from the gate, to the trap beneath the castle. Here Hutter found all fast, neither pad lock nor chain, nor bar, having been molested. The key was produced, the locks removed, the chain loosened, and the trap pushed upward. Hurry now thrust his head in at the opening; the arms followed, and the colossal legs rose without any apparent effort. At the next instant, his heavy foot was heard stamping in the passage above; that which separated the chambers of the father and daughters, and into which the trap opened. He then gave a shout of triumph.

"Come on, old Tom," the reckless woodsman called out from within the building—"here's your tenement, safe and sound; ay, and as empty as a nut that has passed half an hour in the paws of a squirrel! The Delaware brags of being able to *see* silence; let him come here, and he may *feel* it, in the bargain."

"Any silence where you are, Hurry Harry," returned Hutter, thrusting his head in at the hole, as he uttered the last word, which instantly caused his voice to sound smothered to those without—"Any silence where you are, ought to be both seen and felt, for it's unlike any other silence."

"Come—come—old fellow; hoist yourself up, and we'll open doors and windows and let in the fresh air to brighten up matters. Few words in troublesome times, make men the best fri'nds. Your darter Judith, is what I call a misbehaving young woman, and the hold of the whole family on me is so much weakened by her late conduct, that it would n't take a speech as long as the ten commandments to send me off to the river, leaving you and your traps, your Ark and your children, your man servants and your maid servants, your oxen and your asses, to fight this battle with the Iroquois, by yourselves. Open that window, Floating Tom, and I'll blunder through and do the same job to the front door."

A moment of silence succeeded, and a noise like that produced by the fall of a heavy body followed. A deep execration from Hurry succeeded, and then the whole interior of the building seemed alive. The noises that now so suddenly, and we may add so unexpectedly even to the Delaware, broke the stillness within, could not be mistaken. They resembled those that would be produced by a struggle between tigers in a cage. Once or twice the Indian yell was given, but it seemed smothered, and as if it proceeded from exhausted or compressed throats, and, in a single instance, a deep and another shockingly revolting execration came from the throat of Hurry. It appeared as if bodies were constantly thrown upon the floor with violence, as often rising to renew the struggle. Chingachgook felt greatly at a loss what to do. He had all the arms in the

Ark, Hutter and Hurry having proceeded without their rifles, but there was no means of using them, or of passing them to the hands of their owners. The combatants, were literally caged, rendering it almost as impossible under the circumstances to get out, as to get into the building. Then there was Hist to embarrass his movements, and to cripple his efforts. With a view to relieve himself from this disadvantage, he told the girl to take the remaining canoe, and to join Hutter's daughters, who were incautiously but deliberately approaching, in order to save herself, and to warn the others of their danger. But the girl positively and firmly refused to comply. At that moment, no human power, short of an exercise of superior physical force, could have induced her to quit the Ark. The exigency of the moment did not admit of delay, and the Delaware seeing no possibility of serving his friends, cut the line and by a strong shove forced the scow some twenty feet clear of the piles. Here he took the sweeps and succeeded in getting a short distance to windward, if any direction could be thus termed in so light an air, but neither the time, nor his skill at the oars, allowed the distance to be great. When he ceased rowing, the Ark might have been a hundred yards from the platform, and half that distance to the southward of it, the sail being lowered. Judith and Hetty had now discovered that something was wrong, and were stationary a thousand feet farther north.

All this while the furious struggle continued within the house. In scenes like these, events thicken in less time than they can be related. From the moment when the first fall was heard within the building to that when the Delaware ceased his awkward attempts to row, it might have been three or four minutes, but it had evidently served to weaken the combatants. The oaths and execrations of Hurry were no longer heard, and even the struggles had lost some of their force and fury. Nevertheless they still continued with unabated perseverance. At this instant the door flew open, and the fight was transferred to the platform, the light and the open air.

A Huron had undone the fastenings of the door, and three or four of his tribe rushed after him upon the narrow space, as if glad to escape from some terrible scene within. The body of another followed, pitched headlong through the door, with terrific violence. Then March appeared, raging like a lion at bay, and for an instant free'd from his numerous enemies. Hutter was already a captive and bound. There was now a pause in the struggle, which resembled a lull in a tempest. The necessity of breathing was common to all, and the combatants stood watching each other, like mastiffs that have been driven from their holds, and are waiting for a favorable opportunity of renewing them. We shall profit by this pause to relate the manner in which the Indians had obtained possession of the castle, and this the more willingly because it may be necessary to explain to the reader why a conflict which had been so close and fierce, should have also been so comparatively bloodless.

Rivenoak and his companion, particularly the latter who had appeared to be a subordinate and occupied solely with his raft, had made the closest observations in their visits to the castle. Even the boy had brought away minute and valuable information. By these means the Hurons obtained a general idea of the manner in which the place was constructed and secured, as well as of details that enabled them to act intelligently in the dark. Notwithstanding the care that Hutter had taken to drop the Ark on the east side of the building when he was in the act of transferring the furniture from the former to the latter, he had been watched in a way to render the precaution useless. Scouts were on the look-out on the eastern, as well as on the western, shore of the lake, and the whole proceeding had been noted. As soon as it was dark, rafts like that already described, approached from both shores to reconnoitre, and the Ark had passed within fifty feet of one of them, without its being discovered; the men it held lying at their length on the logs, so as to blend themselves and their slow moving machine with the water. When these two sets of adventurers drew near the castle they encountered each other, and after communicating their respective observations, they unhesitatingly approached the building. As had been expected, it was found empty. The rafts were immediately sent for a reinforcement to the shore, and two of the savages remained to profit by their situation. These men succeeded in getting on the roof, and by removing some of the bark, in entering what might be termed the garret. Here they were found by their companions. Hatchets now opened a hole through the squared logs of the upper floor, through which no less than eight of the most athletic of the Indians

dropped into the rooms beneath. Here they were left, well supplied with arms and provisions, either to stand a siege, or to
make a sortie, as the case might require. The night was passed
in sleep, as is usual with Indians in a state of inactivity. The
returning day brought them a view of the approach of the Ark
through the loops, the only manner in which light and air were
now admitted, the windows being closed most effectually with
plank, rudely fashioned to fit. As soon as it was ascertained
that the two white men were about to enter by the trap, the
chief who directed the proceedings of the Hurons took his
measures accordingly. He removed all the arms from his own
people, even to the knives, in distrust of savage ferocity when
awakened by personal injuries, and he hid them where they
could not be found, without a search. Ropes of bark were then
prepared, and taking their stations in the three different
rooms, they all waited for the signal to fall upon their intended
captives. As soon as the party had entered the building, men
without replaced the bark of the roof, removed every sign of
their visit, with care, and then departed for the shore. It was
one of these who had dropped his moccasin, which he had not
been able to find, again, in the dark. Had the death of the girl
been known, it is probable nothing could have saved the lives
of Hurry and Hutter, but that event occurred after the ambush
was laid, and at a distance of several miles from the encampment near the castle. Such were the means that had been
employed to produce the state of things we shall continue to
describe.

Chapter XX.

"Now all is done that man can do,
 And all is done in vain!
My love! my native land, adieu
 For I must cross the main,
  My dear,
For I must cross the main."
 James Johnson, "It Was a' for our Rightfu King," ll.7–12.

I n the last chapter we left the combatants breathing in
their narrow lists. Accustomed to the rude sports of wrestling,
and jumping, then so common in America, more especially on
the frontiers, Hurry possessed an advantage, in addition to his
prodigious strength, that had rendered the struggle less unequal than it might otherwise appear to be. This alone had
enabled him to hold out so long, against so many enemies, for
the Indian is by no means remarkable for his skill, or force, in
athletic exercises. As yet, no one had been seriously hurt,
though several of the savages had received severe falls, and he,
in particular, who had been thrown bodily upon the platform,
might be said to be temporarily *hors de combat*. Some of the rest
were limping, and March himself had not entirely escaped
from bruises, though want of breath was the principal loss that
both sides wished to repair.

Under circumstances like those in which the parties were
placed, a truce, let it come from what cause it might, could not
well be of long continuance. The arena was too confined, and
the distrust of treachery, too great, to admit of this. Contrary
to what might be expected, in his situation, Hurry was the first
to recommence hostilities. Whether this proceeded from
policy, an idea that he might gain some advantage by making
a sudden and unexpected assault or was the fruit of irritation
and his undying hatred of an Indian, it is impossible to say.
His onset was furious, however, and at first it carried all before
it. He seized the nearest Huron by the waist, raised him entirely from the platform, and hurled him into the water, as if
he had been a child. In half a minute, two more were at his

side, one of whom received a grave injury by falling on the friend who had just preceded him. But four enemies remained, and, in a hand to hand conflict, in which no arms were used but those which nature had furnished, Hurry believed himself fully able to cope with that number of red-skins.

"Hurrah! Old Tom," he shouted—"The rascals are taking to the lake, and I'll soon have 'em all swimming!" As these words were uttered a violent kick in the face sent back the injured Indian, who had caught at the edge of the platform and was endeavoring to raise himself to its level, helplessly and hopelessly into the water. When the affray was over, his dark body was seen, through the limpid element of the Glimmer-glass, lying, with outstretched arms, extended on the bottom of the shoal on which the Castle stood, clinging to the sands and weeds, as if life were to be retained by this frenzied grasp of death. A blow sent into the pit of another's stomach doubled him up like a worm that had been trodden on, and but two able bodied foes remained to be dealt with. One of these, however, was not only the largest and strongest, of the Hurons, but he was also the most experienced of their warriors present, and that one whose sinews were the best strung in fights, and by marches on the warpath. This man fully appreciated the gigantic strength of his opponent, and had carefully husbanded his own. He was also equipped in the best manner for such a conflict, standing in nothing but his breech-cloth, the model of a naked and beautiful statue of agility and strength. To grasp him required additional dexterity and unusual force. Still Hurry did not hesitate, but the kick that had actually destroyed one fellow creature was no sooner given, than he closed in with this formidable antagonist, endeavoring to force him into the water, also. The struggle that succeeded was truly frightful. So fierce did it immediately become, and so quick and changeful were the evolutions of the athletæ, that the remaining savage had no chance for interfering, had he possessed the desire; but wonder and apprehension held him spell bound. He was an inexperienced youth, and his blood curdled as he witnessed the fell strife of human passions, exhibited too, in an unaccustomed form.

Hurry first attempted to throw his antagonist. With this view he seized him by the throat, and an arm, and tripped with the quickness and force of an American borderer. The effect was frustrated by the agile movements of the Huron, who had clothes to grasp by, and whose feet avoided the attempt with a nimbleness equal to that with which it was made. Then followed a sort of *mêlée*, if such a term can be applied to a struggle between two, in which no efforts were distinctly visible, the limbs and bodies of the combatants assuming so many attitudes and contortions, as to defeat observation. This confused but fierce rally lasted less than a minute, however; when, Hurry, furious at having his strength baffled by the agility and nakedness of his foe, made a desperate effort, which sent the Huron from him, hurling his body violently against the logs of the hut. The concussion was so great as momentarily to confuse the latter's faculties. The pain, too, extorted a deep groan; an unusual concession to agony, to escape a red man in the heat of battle. Still he rushed forward again, to meet his enemy, conscious that his safety rested on his resolution. Hurry now seized the other by the waist, raised him bodily from the platform, and fell with his own great weight on the form beneath. This additional shock so far stunned the sufferer, that his gigantic white opponent now had him completely at his mercy. Passing his hands round the throat of his victim, he compressed them with the strength of a vice, fairly doubling the head of the Huron over the edge of the platform, until the chin was uppermost, with the infernal strength he expended. An instant sufficed to show the consequences. The eyes of the sufferer seemed to start forward, his tongue protruded, and his nostrils dilated nearly to splitting. At this instant a rope of bark, having an eye, was passed dexterously within the two arms of Hurry, the end threaded the eye, forming a noose, and his elbows were drawn together behind his back, with a power that all his gigantic strength could not resist. Reluctantly, even under such circumstances, did the exasperated borderer see his hands drawn from their deadly grasp, for all the evil passions were then in the ascendant. Almost at the same instant, a similar fastening secured his ancles, and his body was rolled to the centre of the platform as helplessly, and as cavalierly, as if it were a log of wood. His rescued antagonist, however, did not rise, for while he began again to breathe, his head still hung helplessly over the edge of the logs, and it was thought at first that his neck was dislocated. He recovered gradually only, and it was hours before he could walk. Some fancied that neither his body, nor his mind, ever totally recovered from this near approach to death.

Hurry owed his defeat and capture to the intensity with which he had concentrated all his powers, on his fallen foe. While thus occupied, the two Indians he had hurled into the water mounted to the heads of the piles, along which they passed, and joined their companion on the platform. The latter had so far rallied his faculties as to have gotten the ropes, which were in readiness for use as the others appeared, and they were applied in the manner related, as Hurry lay pressing his enemy down with his whole weight, intent only on the horrible office of strangling him. Thus were the tables turned, in a single moment; he who had been so near achieving a victory that would have been renowned for ages, by means of traditions, throughout all that region, lying, helpless, bound and a captive. So fearful had been the efforts of the pale face, and so prodigious the strength he exhibited, that even as he lay, tethered like a sheep before them, they regarded him with respect, and not without dread. The helpless body of their stoutest warrior was still stretched on the platform, and, as they cast their eyes towards the lake, in quest of the comrade that had been hurled into it so unceremoniously, and of whom they had lost sight in the confusion of the fray, they perceived his lifeless form clinging to the grass on the bottom, as already described. These several circumstances contributed to render the victory of the Hurons almost as astounding to themselves, as a defeat.

Chingachgook, and his betrothed, witnessed the whole of this struggle from the Ark. When the three Hurons were about to pass the cords around the arms of the prostrate Hurry, the Delaware sought his rifle, but, before he could use it, the white man was bound, and the mischief was done. He might still bring down an enemy, but to obtain the scalp was impossible, and the young chief, who would so freely risk his own life, to obtain such a trophy, hesitated about taking that of a foe, without such an object in view. A glance at Hist, and the recollection of what might follow, checked any transient wish for revenge. The reader has been told that Chingachgook could scarcely be said to know how to manage the oars of the Ark at all, however expert he might be in the use of the paddle. Perhaps there is no manual labor, at which men are so bungling and awkward, as in their first attempts to pull an oar, even the experienced mariner, or boat man, breaking down in his efforts to figure with the celebrated rullock of the gondolier. In short it is, temporarily, an impracticable thing for a new beginner to succeed with a single oar, but, in this case, it was necesary to handle two, at the same time, and those of great size. Sweeps, or large oars, however, are sooner rendered of use by the raw hand, than lighter implements, and this was the reason that the Delaware had succeeded in moving the Ark as well as he did, in a first trial. That trial, notwithstanding, sufficed to produce distrust, and he was fully aware of the critical situation in which Hist and himself were now placed, should the Hurons take to the canoe that was still lying beneath the trap, and come against them. At one moment he thought of putting Hist into the canoe in his own possession, and of taking to the eastern mountain, in the hope of reaching the Delaware villages by direct flight. But many considerations suggested themselves to put a stop to this indiscreet step. It was almost certain that scouts watched the lake on both sides, and no canoe could possibly approach the shore without being seen from the hills. Then a trail could not be concealed from Indian eyes, and the strength of Hist was unequal to a flight sufficiently sustained, to outstrip the pursuit of trained warriors. This was a part of America in which the Indians did not know the use of horses, and every thing would depend on the physical energies of the fugitives. Last, but far from being least, were the thoughts connected with the situation of Deerslayer, a friend who was not to be deserted in his extremity.

Hist, in some particulars, reasoned, and even felt, differently, though she arrived at the same conclusions. Her own danger disturbed her less than her concern for the two sisters, in whose behalf her womanly sympathies were now strongly enlisted. The canoe of the girls, by the time the struggle on the platform had ceased, was within three hundred yards of the castle, and here Judith ceased paddling, the evidences of strife first becoming apparent to the eyes. She and Hetty were standing erect, anxiously endeavoring to ascertain what had occurred, but unable to satisfy their doubts from the circumstance that the building, in a great measure, concealed the scene of action.

The parties in the Ark, and in the canoe, were indebted to the ferocity of Hurry's attack for their momentary security. In any ordinary case, the girls would have been immediately captured, a measure easy of execution now the savages had a canoe, were it not for the rude check the audacity of the Hurons had received, in the recent struggle. It required some little time to recover from the effects of this violent scene, and this so much the more, because the principal man of the party, in the way of personal prowess at least, had been so great a sufferer. Still it was of the last importance that Judith and her sister should seek immediate refuge in the Ark, where the defences offered a temporary shelter at least, and the first step was to devise the means of inducing them to do so. Hist showed herself in the stern of the scow, and made many gestures and signs, in vain, in order to induce the girls to make a circuit to avoid the Castle, and to approach the Ark from the eastward. But these signs were distrusted or misunderstood. It is probable Judith was not yet sufficiently aware of the real state of things to put full confidence in either party. Instead of doing as desired, she rather kept more aloof, paddling slowly back to the north, or into the broadest part of the lake, where she could command the widest view, and had the fairest field for flight before her. At this instant the sun appeared above the pines of the eastern range of mountains and a light southerly breeze arose, as was usual enough, at that season and hour.

Chingachgook lost no time in hoisting the sail. Whatever might be in reserve for him, there could be no question that it was every way desirable to get the Ark at such a distance from the castle, as to reduce his enemies to the necessity of approaching the former in the canoe, which the chances of war had so inopportunely for his wishes and security, thrown into their hands. The appearance of the opening duck seemed first to arouse the Hurons from their apathy, and by the time the head of the scow had fallen off before the wind, which it did unfortunately in the wrong direction, bringing it within a few yards of the platform, Hist found it necessary to warn her lover of the importance of covering his person against the rifles of his foes. This was a danger to be avoided under all circumstances, and so much the more, because the Delaware found that Hist would not take to the cover herself, so long as he remained exposed. Accordingly, Chingachgook abandoned the scow to its own movements, forced Hist into the cabin, the doors of which he immediately secured, and then he looked about him for the rifles.

The situation of the parties was now so singular as to merit a particular description. The Ark was within sixty yards of the castle, a little to the southward, or to windward of it, with its sail full, and the steering oar abandoned. The latter, fortunately, was loose, so that it produced no great influence on the crab like movements of the unwieldy craft. The sail being set, as sailors term it, flying, or having no braces, the air forced the yard forward, though both sheets were fast. The effect was threefold on a boat with a bottom that was perfectly flat, and which drew merely some three or four inches of water. It pressed the head slowly round to leeward, it forced the whole fabric bodily in the same direction at the same time, and the water that unavoidably gathered under the lee, gave the scow also a forward movement. All these changes were exceedingly slow, however, for the wind was not only light, but it was baffling as usual, and twice or thrice the sail shook. Once it was absolutely taken aback.

Had there been any keel to the Ark, it would inevitably have run foul of the platform, bows on, when it is probable nothing could have prevented the Hurons from carrying it; more particularly as the sail would have enabled them to approach under cover. As it was, the scow wore slowly round, barely clearing that part of the building. The piles projecting several feet, *they* were not cleared, but the head of the slow moving craft caught between two of them, by one of its square corners, and hung. At this moment the Delaware was vigilantly watching through a loop, for an opportunity to fire, while the Hurons kept within the building, similarly occupied. The exhausted warrior reclined against the hut, there having been no time to remove him, and Hurry lay, almost as helpless as a log, tethered like a sheep on its way to the slaughter, near the middle of the platform. Chingachgook could have slain the first, at any moment, but his scalp would have been safe, and the young chief disdained to strike a blow that could lead to neither honor nor advantage.

"Run out one of the poles, Sarpent, if Sarpent you be," said Hurry, amid the groans that the tightness of the ligatures was beginning to extort from him—"run out one of the poles, and shove the head of the scow off, and you'll drift clear of us—and, when you've done that good turn for *yourself*, just finish this gagging blackguard for *me*."

The appeal of Hurry, however, had no other effect, than to draw the attention of Hist to his situation. This quick witted creature comprehended it at a glance. His ancles were bound with several turns of stout bark rope, and his arms, above the elbows, were similarly secured behind his back; barely leaving him a little play of the hands and wrists. Putting her mouth near a loop she said in a low but distinct voice—

"Why you do n't roll here, and fall in scow? Chingachgook shoot Huron, if he chace!"

"By the Lord, gal, that's a judgematical thought, and it shall be tried, if the starn of your scow will come a little nearer. Put a bed at the bottom, for me to fall on."

This was said at a happy moment, for, tired of waiting, all the Indians made a rapid discharge of their rifles, almost simultaneously, injuring no one; though several bullets passed through the loops. Hist had heard part of Hurry's words, but most of what he said was lost in the sharp reports of the fire arms. She undid the bar of the door that led to the stern of the scow, but did not dare to expose her person. All this time, the head of the Ark hung, but by a gradually decreasing hold as the other end swung slowly round, nearer and nearer to the platform. Hurry, who now lay with his face towards the Ark, occasionally writhing and turning over like one in pain, evolutions he had performed ever since he was secured, watched every change, and, at last, he saw that the whole vessel was free, and was beginning to grate slowly along the sides of the piles. The attempt was desperate, but it seemed to be the only chance for escaping torture and death, and it suited the reckless daring of the man's character. Waiting to the last moment, in order that the stern of the scow might fairly rub against the platform, he began to writhe again, as if in intolerable suffering, execrating all Indians in general, and the Hurons in particular, and then he suddenly and rapidly rolled over and over, taking the direction of the stern of the scow.

Unfortunately, Hurry's shoulders required more space to revolve in than his feet, and, by the time he reached the edge of the platform his direction had so far changed as to carry him clear of the Ark altogether, and the rapidity of his revolutions and the emergency admitting of no delay, he fell into the water. At this instant, Chingachgook, by an understanding with his betrothed drew the fire of the Hurons, again, not a man of whom saw the manner in which one, whom they knew to be effectually tethered, had disappeared. But Hist's feelings were strongly interested in the success of so bold a scheme, and she watched the movements of Hurry, as the cat watches the mouse. The moment he was in motion she foresaw the consequences, and this the more readily, as the scow was now beginning to move with some steadiness, and she bethought her of the means of saving him. With a sort of instinctive readiness, she opened the door, at the very moment the rifles were ringing in her ears, and, protected by the intervening cabin, she stepped into the stern of the scow, in time to witness the fall of Hurry into the lake. Her foot was unconsciously placed on the end of one of the sheets of the sail, which was fastened aft, and catching up all the spare rope, with the awkwardness, but also with the generous resolution, of a woman, she threw it in the direction of the helpless Hurry. The line fell on the head and body of the sinking man, and he not only succeeded in grasping separate parts of it with his hands, but he actually got a portion of it between his teeth. Hurry was an expert swimmer, and, tethered as he was, he resorted to the very expedient that philosophy and reflection would have suggested. He had fallen on his back, and instead of floundering and drowning himself by desperate efforts to walk on the water, he permitted his body to sink as low as possible, and was already submerged, with the exception of his face, when the line reached him. In this situation he might possibly have remained until rescued by the Hurons, using his hands as fishes use their fins, had he received no other succour, but the movement of Ark soon tightened the rope, and of course he was dragged gently ahead, holding even pace with the scow. The motion aided in keeping his face above the surface of the water, and it would have been possible for one accustomed to endurance, to have been towed a mile in this singular but simple manner.

It has been said that the Hurons did not observe the sudden disappearance of Hurry. In his present situation, he was not only hid from view, by the platform, but, as the Ark drew slowly ahead, impelled by a sail that was now filled, he received the same friendly service from the piles. The Hurons, indeed, were too intent on endeavoring to slay their Delaware foe, by sending a bullet through some one of the loops or crevices of the cabin, to bethink them at all, of one whom they fancied so thoroughly tied. Their great concern was the manner in which the Ark rubbed past the piles, although its motion was lessened at least one half by the friction, and they passed into the northern end of the castle, in order to catch opportunities of firing through the loops of that part of the building. Chingachgook was similarly occupied, and remained as ignorant as his enemies, of the situation of Hurry. As the Ark grated along, the rifles sent their little clouds of smoke from one cover to the other, but the eyes and movements of the opposing parties were too quick to permit any injury to be done. At length one side had the mortification, and the other the pleasure of seeing the scow swing clear of the piles altogether, when it immediately moved away, with a materially accelerated motion, towards the north.

Chingachgook now first learned from Hist, the critical condition of Hurry. To have exposed either of their persons in the stern of the scow, would have been certain death, but, fortunately, the sheet to which the man clung, led forward to the foot of the sail. The Delaware found means to unloosen it from the cleet aft, and Hist, who was already forward for that purpose, immediately began to pull upon the line. At this moment Hurry was towing fifty or sixty feet astern, with nothing but his face above water. As he was dragged out clear of the castle and the piles, he was first perceived by the Hurons, who raised a hideous yell, and commenced a fire on, what may very well be termed, the floating mass. It was at the same instant, that Hist began to pull upon the line forward, a circumstance that probably saved Hurry's life, aided by his own self-possession and border readiness. The first bullet struck the water directly on the spot, where the broad chest of the young giant was visible through the pure element, and might have pierced his heart, had the angle at which it was fired, been less acute. Instead of penetrating the lake, however, it glanced from its smooth surface, rose, and actually buried itself in the logs of the cabin, near the spot at which Chingachgook had shown himself the minute before, while clearing the line from the cleet. A second, and a third, and a fourth bullet followed, all meeting with the same resistance from the surface of the water; though Hurry sensibly felt the violence of the blows they struck upon the lake so immediately above, and so near his breast. Discovering their mistake, the Hurons now changed their plan, and aimed at the uncovered face, but, by this time Hist was pulling on the line, the target advanced, and the deadly missiles still fell upon the water. In another moment the body was dragged past the end of the scow, and became concealed. As for the Delaware and Hist they worked perfectly covered by the cabin, and in less time than it requires to tell it, they had hauled the huge frame of Hurry to the place they occupied. Chingachgook stood in readiness with his keen knife, and bending over the side of the scow, he soon severed the bark that bound the limbs of the borderer. To raise him high enough to reach the edge of the boat, and to aid him in entering were less easy tasks, as Hurry's arms were still nearly useless, but both were done in time, when the liberated man staggered forward, and fell exhausted and helpless, into the bottom of the scow. Here we shall leave him to recover his strength and the due circulation of his blood, while we proceed with the narrative of events that crowd upon us too fast to admit of any postponement.

The moment the Hurons lost sight of the body of Hurry, they gave a common yell of disappointment, and three of the most active of their number ran to the trap and entered the canoe. It required some little delay, however, to embark with their weapons, to find the paddles and, if we may use a phrase so purely technical, "to get out of dock." By this time Hurry was in the scow, and the Delaware had his rifles, again, in readiness. As the Ark necessarily sailed before the wind, it had got by this time quite two hundred yards from the castle, and was sliding away each instant, farther and farther, though with a motion so easy as scarcely to stir the water. The canoe of the girls was quite a quarter of a mile distant from the Ark, obviously keeping aloof, in ignorance of what had occurred, and in apprehension of the consequences of venturing too near. They had taken the direction of the eastern shore, endeavoring at the same time to get to windward of the Ark, and in a manner between the two parties, as if distrusting which was to be considered a friend, and which an enemy. The girls, from long habit, used the paddles with great dexterity, and Judith, in particular, had often sportively gained races, in trials of speed with the youths that occasionally visited the lake.

When the three Hurons emerged from behind the palisades, and found themselves on the open lake, and under the necessity of advancing unprotected on the Ark, if they persevered in the original design, their ardor sensibly cooled. In a bark canoe, they were totally without cover, and Indian discretion was entirely opposed to such a sacrifice of life as would most probably follow any attempt to assault an enemy, entrenched as effectually as the Delaware. Instead of following the Ark therefore, these three warriors inclined towards the eastern shore, keeping at a safe distance from the rifles of Chingachgook. But this manœuvre rendered the position of the girls exceedingly critical. It threatened to place them if not between two fires, at least between two dangers, or what they conceived to be dangers, and, instead of permitting the Hurons to enclose her, in what she fancied a sort of net, Judith immediately commenced her retreat, in a southern direction, at no very great distance from the shore. She did not dare to land; if such an expedient were to be resorted to at all, she could only venture on it, in the last extremity. At first the Indians paid little or no attention to the other canoe, for, fully apprised of its contents, they deemed its capture of comparatively little moment, while the Ark, with its imaginary treasures, the persons of the Delaware and of Hurry, and its means of movement on a large scale, was before them. But this Ark had its dangers as well as its temptations, and after wasting near an hour, in vacillating evolutions, always at a safe distance from the rifle, the Hurons seemed suddenly to take their resolution, and began to display it by giving eager chase to the girls.

When this last design was adopted, the circumstances of all parties, as connected with their relative positions, were materially changed. The Ark had sailed and drifted quite half a mile, and was nearly that distance due north of the castle. As soon as the Delaware perceived that the girls avoided him, unable to manage his unwieldy craft, and knowing that flight from a bark canoe, in the event of pursuit, would be a useless expedient if attempted, he had lowered his sail, in the hope it might induce the sisters to change their plan, and to seek refuge in the scow. This demonstration produced no other effect than to keep the Ark nearer to the scene of action, and to enable those in her to become witnesses of the chase. The canoe of Judith was about a quarter of a mile south of that of the Hurons, a little nearer to the east shore, and about the same distance to the southward of the castle, as it was from the hostile canoe, a circumstance which necessarily put the last nearly abreast of Hutter's fortress. With the several parties thus situated the chase commenced.

At the moment when the Hurons so suddenly changed their mode of attack their canoe was not in the best, possible, racing trim. There were but two paddles, and the third man was so much extra and useless cargo. Then the difference in weight, between the sisters and the other two men, more especially in vessels so extremely light, almost neutralized any difference that might proceed from the greater strength of the Hurons, and rendered the trial of speed far from being as unequal, as it might seem. Judith did not commence her exertions, until the near approach of the other canoe, rendered the object of the movement certain, and then she exhorted Hetty to aid her with her utmost skill and strength.

"Why should we run, Judith?" asked the simple minded girl. "The Hurons have never harmed *me*, nor do I think they ever will."

"That may be true as to you, Hetty, but it will prove very different with me. Kneel down and say your prayer, and then rise, and do your utmost to help escape. Think of me, dear girl, too, as you pray."

Judith gave these directions from a mixed feeling; first because she knew that her sister ever sought the support of her great ally in trouble, and next because a sensation of feebleness and dependance suddenly came over her own proud spirit, in that moment of apparent desertion and trial. The prayer was quickly said, however, and the canoe was soon in rapid motion. Still, neither party resorted to their greatest exertions from the outset, both knowing that the chase was likely to be arduous and long. Like two vessels of war that are preparing for an encounter, they seemed desirous of first ascertaining their respective rates of speed, in order that they might know how to graduate their exertions, previously to the great effort. A few minutes sufficed to show the Hurons that the girls were expert, and that it would require all their skill and energies to overtake them.

Judith had inclined towards the eastern shore, at the commencement of the chase, with a vague determination of landing and flying to the woods, as a last resort, but as she approached the land, the certainty that scouts must be watching her movements, made her reluctance to adopt such an expedient unconquerable. Then she was still fresh, and had sanguine hopes of being able to tire out her pursuers. With such feelings she gave a sweep with her paddle, and sheered off from the fringe of dark hemlocks beneath the shades of which she was so near entering, and held her way, again, more towards the centre of the lake. This seemed the instant favorable for the Hurons to make their push, as it gave them the entire breadth of the sheet to do it in; and this too in the widest part, as soon as they had got between the fugitives and the land. The canoes now flew, Judith making up for what she wanted in strength, by her great dexterity and self command. For half a mile the Indians gained no material advantage, but the continuance of so great exertions for so many minutes sensibly affected all concerned. Here the Indians resorted to an expedient that enabled them to give one of their party time to breathe, by shifting their paddles from hand to hand, and this too without sensibly relaxing their efforts. Judith occasionally looked behind her, and she saw this expedient practised. It caused her immediately to distrust the result, since her powers of endurance were not likely to hold out against those of men who had the means of relieving each other. Still she persevered, allowing no very visible consequences immediately to follow the change.

As yet the Indians had not been able to get nearer to the girls, than two hundred yards, though they were what seamen would term 'in their wake'; or in a direct line behind them, passing over the same track of water. This made the pursuit what is technically called a "stern chase", which is proverbially a "long chase": the meaning of which is that, in consequence of the relative positions of the parties, no change becomes apparent except that which is a direct gain in the nearest possible approach. "Long" as this species of chase is admitted to be, however, Judith was enabled to perceive that the Hurons were sensibly drawing nearer and nearer, before she had gained the centre of the lake. She was not a girl to despair, but there was an instant when she thought of yielding, with the wish of being carried to the camp where she knew the Deerslayer to be a captive; but the considerations connected with the means she hoped to be able to employ, in order to procure his release, immediately interposed, in order to stimulate her to renewed exertions. Had there been any one there to note the progress of the two canoes, he would have seen that of Judith flying swiftly away from its pursuers, as the girl gave it freshly impelled speed, while her mind was thus dwelling on her own ardent and generous schemes. So material, indeed, was the difference in the rate of going between the two canoes, for the next five minutes, that the Hurons began to be convinced all their powers must be exerted, or they would suffer the disgrace of being baffled by women. Making a furious effort, under the mortification of such a conviction, one of the strongest of their party broke his paddle at the very moment when he had taken it from the hand of a comrade, to relieve him. This at once decided the matter, a canoe containing three men and having but one paddle, being utterly unable to overtake fugitives like the daughters of Thomas Hutter.

"There, Judith!" exclaimed Hetty, who saw the accident — "I hope, now, you will own, that praying is useful! The Hurons have broke a paddle, and they never *can* overtake us."

"I never denied it, poor Hetty, and sometimes wish, in bitterness of spirit, that I had prayed more myself, and thought less of my beauty! As you say, we are now safe and need only go a little south, and take breath."

This was done; the enemy giving up the pursuit, as suddenly as a ship that has lost an important spar, the instant the accident occurred. Instead of following Judith's canoe, which was now lightly skimming over the water towards the south, the Hurons turned their bows towards the castle, where they soon arrived and landed. The girls, fearful that some spare paddles might be found in, or about the buildings, continued on, nor did they stop, until so distant from their enemies as to give them every chance of escape, should the chase be renewed. It would seem that the savages meditated no such design, but at the end of an hour their canoe, filled with men, was seen quitting the castle, and steering towards the shore. The girls were without food, and they now drew nearer to the buildings and the Ark, having finally made up their minds, from its manoeuvres, that the latter contained friends.

Nothwithstanding the seeming desertion of the castle, Judith approached it with extreme caution. The Ark was now quite a mile to the northward, but sweeping up towards the buildings, and this, too, with a regularity of motion that satisfied Judith a white man was at the oars. When within a hundred yards of the building, the girls began to encircle it, in order to make sure that it was empty. No canoe was nigh, and this emboldened them, to draw nearer and nearer, until they had gone round the piles, and reached the platform.

"Do you go into the house, Hetty," said Judith, "and see that the savages are gone. They will not harm you, and if any of them are still here, you can give me the alarm. I do not think they will fire on a poor defenceless girl, and I at least may escape, until I shall be ready to go among them of my own accord."

Hetty did as desired, Judith retiring a few yards from the platform, the instant her sister landed, in readiness for flight. But the last was unnecessary, not a minute elapsing before Hetty returned to communicate that all was safe.

"I've been in all the rooms, Judith," said the latter earnestly, "and they are empty, except father's; he is in his own chamber, sleeping, though not as quietly as we could wish."

"Has any thing happened to father?" demanded Judith, as her foot touched the platform; speaking quick, for her nerves were in a state to be easily alarmed.

Hetty seemed concerned, and she looked furtively about her, as if unwilling any one but a child should hear what she had to communicate, and even that *she* should learn it abruptly.

"You know how it is with father, sometimes, Judith," she said, "When overtaken with liquor he does n't always know what he says, or does, and he seems to be overtaken with liquor, now."

"That is strange! — Would the savages have drunk with him, and then leave him behind? But tis a grievous sight to a child, Hetty, to witness such a failing in a parent, and we will not go near him 'till he wakes."

A groan from the inner room, however, changed this resolution, and the girls ventured near a parent, whom it was no unusual thing for them to find in a condition that lowers a man to the level of brutes. He was seated, reclining in a corner of the narrow room, with his shoulders supported by the angle, and his head fallen heavily on his chest. Judith moved forward, with a sudden impulse, and removed a canvass cap that was forced so low on his head as to conceal his face, and indeed all but his shoulders. The instant this obstacle was taken away, the quivering and raw flesh, the bared veins and muscles, and all the other disgusting signs of mortality, as they are revealed by tearing away the skin, showed he had been scalped, though still living.

Chapter XXI.

"Lightly they'll talk of the spirit that's gone,
And o'er his cold ashes upbraid him;
But nothing he'll reck, if they'll let him sleep on,
In the grave where a Briton has laid him."
    Charles Wolfe, "The Burial of Sir John Moore," vi.

THE reader must imagine the horror that daughters would experience, at unexpectedly beholding the shocking spectacle that was placed before the eyes of Judith and Esther, as related in the close of the last chapter. We shall pass over the first emotions, the first acts of filial piety, and proceed with the narrative, by imagining rather than relating most of the revolting features of the scene. The mutilated and ragged head was bound up, the unseemly blood was wiped from the face of the sufferer, the other appliances required by appearances and care were resorted to, and there was time to enquire into the more serious circumstances of the case. The facts were never known until years later, in all their details, simple as they were, but they may as well be related here, as it can be done in a few words. In the struggle with the Hurons, Hutter had been stabbed by the knife of the old warrior, who had used the discretion to remove the arms of every one but himself. Being hard pushed by his sturdy foe, his knife had settled the matter. This occurred just as the door was opened, and Hurry burst out upon the platform, as has been previously related. This was the secret of neither party's having appeared in the subsequent struggle; Hutter having been literally disabled, and his conqueror being ashamed to be seen with the traces of blood about him, after having used so many injunctions to convince his young warriors of the necessity of taking their prisoners alive. When the three Hurons returned from the chase, and it was determined to abandon the castle, and join the party on the land, Hutter was simply scalped, to secure the usual trophy, and was left to die by inches, as has been done in a thousand similar instances, by the ruthless warriors of this part of the American continent. Had the injury of Hutter been confined to his head, he might have recovered, however, for it was the blow of the knife that proved mortal.

There are moments of vivid consciousness, when the stern justice of God stands forth in colours so prominent, as to defy any attempts to veil them from the sight, however unpleasant they may appear, or however anxious we may be to avoid recognising it. Such was now the fact with Judith and Hetty, who both perceived the decrees of a retributive Providence, in the manner of their father's suffering, as a punishment for his own recent attempts on the Iroquois. This was seen and felt by Judith with the keenness of perception and sensibility that were suited to her character, while the impression made on the simpler mind of her sister was perhaps less lively, though it might well have proved more lasting.

"Oh! Judith—" exclaimed the weak minded girl, as soon as their first care had been bestowed on the sufferer—"Father went for scalps, himself, and now where is his own? The bible might have foretold this dreadful punishment!"

"Hush—Hetty—hush, poor sister—He opens his eyes; he may hear and understand you. 'Tis as you say and think, but 'tis too dreadful to speak of!"

"Water—" ejaculated Hutter, as it might be by a desperate effort, that rendered his voice frightfully deep and strong, for one as near death as he evidently was—"Water—foolish girls—will you let me die of thirst."

Water was brought and administered to the sufferer; the first he had tasted in hours of physical anguish. It had the double effect of clearing his throat, and of momentarily reviving his sinking system. His eyes opened with that anxious, distended gaze, which is apt to accompany the passage of a soul surprised by death, and he seemed disposed to speak.

"Father—" said Judith, inexpressibly pained by his deplorable situation, and this so much the more from her ignorance of what remedies ought to be applied—"Father, can we do any thing for you?—Can Hetty and I relieve your pain?"

"Father!"—slowly repeated the old man. "No—Judith—no—Hetty—I'm no father. *She* was your mother, but I'm no father. Look in the chest—Tis all there—give me more water."

The girls complied, and Judith, whose early recollections extended farther back than her sister's, and who, on every account, had more distinct impressions of the past, felt an uncontrollable impulse of joy, as she heard these words. There had never been much sympathy between her reputed father and herself, and suspicions of this very truth had often glanced across her mind, in consequence of dialogues she had overheard between Hutter and her mother. It might be going too far to say she had never loved him, but it is not so to add, that she rejoiced it was no longer a duty. With Hetty the feeling was different. Incapable of making all the distinctions of her sister, her very nature was full of affection, and she *had* loved her reputed parent, though far less tenderly than the real parent, and it grieved her, now, to hear him declare he was not naturally entitled to that love. She felt a double grief, as if his death and his words together, were twice depriving her of parents. Yielding to her feelings, the poor girl went aside and wept.

The very opposite emotions of the two girls, kept both silent for a long time. Judith gave water to the sufferer frequently, but she forbore to urge him with questions, in some measure out of consideration for his condition, but, if truth must be said, quite as much, lest something he should add, in the way of explanation, might disturb her pleasing belief that she was not Thomas Hutter's child. At length Hetty dried her tears, and came and seated herself on a stool by the side of the dying man, who had been placed at his length on the floor, with his head supported by some coarse vestments that had been left in the house.

"Father—" she said—"you will let me *call* you father, though you say you are not one—Father shall I read the bible to you—mother always said the bible was good for people in trouble. She was often in trouble herself, and then she made me read the bible to her—for Judith was n't as fond of the bible as I am—and it always did her good. Many is the time I've known mother begin to listen with the tears streaming from her eyes, and end with smiles and gladness. Oh! father, you do n't know how much good the bible can do, for you've never tried it—Now, I'll read a chapter, and it will soften your heart, as it softened the hearts of the Hurons."

While poor Hetty had so much reverence for, and faith in, the virtues of the bible, her intellect was too shallow to enable her fully to appreciate its beauties, or to fathom its profound, and sometimes mysterious wisdom. That instinctive sense of right, which appeared to shield her from the commission of wrong, and even cast a mantle of moral loveliness and truth around her character, could not penetrate abstrusities, or trace the nice affinities between cause and effect, beyond their more obvious and indisputable connection, though she seldom failed to see all the latter, and to defer to all their just consequences. In a word, she was one of those who feel and act correctly, without being able to give a logical reason for it, even admitting revelation as her authority. Her selections from the bible, therefore, were commonly distinguished by the simplicity of her own mind, and were oftener marked for containing images of known and palpable things, than for any of the higher cast of moral truths with which the pages of that wonderful book abound—wonderful, and unequalled, even without referring to its divine origin, as a work replete with the profoundest philosophy, expressed in the noblest language. Her mother, with a connection that will probably strike the reader, had been fond of the book of Job, and Hetty had, in a great measure, learned to read by the frequent lessons she had received from the different chapters of this venerable and sublime poem—now believed to be the oldest book in the world. On this occasion the poor girl was submissive to her training, and she turned to that well known part of the sacred volume, with the readiness with which the practised counsel would cite his authorities from the stores of legal wisdom. In selecting the particular chapter, she was influenced by the caption, and she chose that which stands in our English version as *"Job excuseth his desire of death."* This she read steadily, from beginning to end, in a sweet, low and plaintive voice; hoping devoutly that the allegorical and abstruse sentences might convey to the heart of the sufferer the consolation he needed. It is another peculiarity of the comprehensive wisdom of the bible, that scarce a chapter, unless it be strictly narration, can be turned to, that does not contain some searching truth that is applicable to the condition of every human heart, as well as to the temporal state of its owner, either through the workings of that heart, or even in a still more direct form. In this instance, the very opening sentence — *"Is there not an appointed time to man on earth?"* was startling, and as Hetty proceeded, Hutter applied, or fancied he could apply many aphorisms and figures to his own worldly and mental condition. As life is ebbing fast, the mind clings eagerly to hope when it is not absolutely crushed by despair. The solemn words *"I have sinned; what shall I do unto thee, O thou preserver of men? Why hast thou set me as a mark against thee, so that I am a burden to myself,"* struck Hutter more perceptibly than the others, and, though too obscure for one of his blunted feelings and obtuse mind either to feel or to comprehend in their fullest extent, they had a directness of application to his own state that caused him to wince under them.

"Do n't you feel better now, father?" asked Hetty, closing the volume. "Mother was always better when she had read the bible."

"Water —" returned Hutter —"give me water, Judith. I wonder if my tongue will always be so hot! Hetty, is n't there something in the bible about cooling the tongue of a man who was burning in Hell fire?"

Judith turned away shocked, but Hetty eagerly sought the passage, which she read aloud to the conscience stricken victim of his own avaricious longings.

"That's it — poor Hetty — yes — that's it. My tongue wants cooling, *now* — what will it be *here after!*"

This appeal silenced even the confiding Hetty, for she had no answer ready for a confession so fraught with despair. Water, so long as it could relieve the sufferer, it was in the power of the sisters to give, and, from time to time, it was offered to the lips of the sufferer, as he asked for it. Even Judith prayed. As for Hetty, as soon as she found that her efforts to make her father listen to her texts were no longer rewarded with success, she knelt at his side, and devoutly repeated the words which the Saviour has left behind him, as a model for human petitions. This she continued to do, at intervals, as long as it seemed to her that the act could benefit the dying man. Hutter, however, lingered longer than the girls had believed possible, when they first found him. At times he spoke intelligibly, though his lips oftener moved in utterance of sounds that carried no distinct impressions to the mind. Judith listened intently, and she heard the words—"husband"—"death"—"pirate"—"law"—"scalps"—and several others of similar import, though there was no sentence to tell the precise connection in which they were used. Still they were sufficiently expressive to be understood by one whose ears had not escaped all the rumours that had been circulated to her reputed father's discredit, and whose comprehension was as quick, as her faculties were attentive.

During the whole of the painful hour that succeeded, neither of the sisters bethought her sufficiently of the Hurons, to dread their return. It seemed as if their desolation and grief placed them above the danger of such an interruption, and when the sound of oars was at length heard, even Judith, who alone had any reason to apprehend the enemy, did not start, but at once understood that the Ark was near. She went upon the platform fearlessly, for should it turn out that Hurry was not there, and that the Hurons were masters of the scow also, escape was impossible. Then she had the sort of confidence that is inspired by extreme misery. But there was no cause for any new alarm, Chingachgook, Hist, and Hurry all standing in the open part of the scow, cautiously examining the building to make certain of the absence of the enemy. They, too, had seen the departure of the Hurons, as well as the approach of the canoe of the girls to the castle, and presuming on the latter fact, March had swept the scow up to the platform. A word sufficed to explain that there was nothing to be apprehended, and the Ark was soon moored in her old berth.

Judith said not a word concerning the condition of her father, but Hurry knew her too well, not to understand that something was more than usually wrong. He led the way, though with less of his confident bold manner than usual, into the house, and penetrating to the inner room, found Hutter lying on his back, with Hetty sitting at his side, fanning him with pious care. The events of the morning had sensibly changed the manner of Hurry. Notwithstanding his skill as a swimmer, and the readiness with which he had adopted the only expedient that could possibly save him, the helplessness of being in the water, bound hand and foot, had produced some such effect on him, as the near approach of punishment is known to produce on most criminals, leaving a vivid impression of the horrors of death upon his mind, and this too in connection with a picture of bodily helplessness; the daring of this man being far more the offspring of vast physical powers, than of the energy of the will, or even of natural spirit. Such heroes invariably lose a large portion of their courage with the failure of their strength, and, though Hurry was now unfettered and as vigorous as ever events were too recent to permit the recollection of his late deplorable condition to be at all weakened. Had he lived a century, the occurrences of the few momentous minutes during which he was in the lake, would have produced a chastening effect on his character, if not always on his manner.

Hurry was not only shocked when he found his late associate in this desperate situation, but he was greatly surprised. During the struggle in the building, he had been far too much occupied himself, to learn what had befallen his comrade, and, as no deadly weapon had been used in his particular case, but every effort had been made to capture him without injury, he naturally believed that Hutter had been overcome, while he owed his own escape to his great bodily strength, and to a fortunate concurrence of extraordinary circumstances. Death, in the silence and solemnity of a chamber, was a novelty to him. Though accustomed to scenes of violence, he had been unused to sit by the bedside, and watch the slow beating of the pulse, as it gradually grew weaker and weaker. Notwithstanding the change in his feelings, the manners of a life could not be altogether cast aside in a moment, and the unexpected scene extorted a characteristic speech from the borderer.

"How now! old Tom," he said, "have the vagabonds got you at an advantage, where you're not only down, but are likely to be kept down! I thought you a cap*t*yve it's true, but never supposed you so hard run as this!"

Hutter opened his glassy eyes, and stared wildly at the speaker. A flood of confused recollections rushed on his wavering mind, at the sight of his late comrade. It was evident that he struggled with his own images, and knew not the real from the unreal.

"Who are you?" he asked in a husky whisper, his failing strength refusing to aid him in a louder effort of his voice.

"Who are you? — You look like the mate of 'The Snow' — he was a giant, too, and near overcoming us."

"I'm your mate, Floating Tom, and your comrade, but have nothing to do with any snow. It's summer now, and Harry March always quits the hills, as soon after the frosts set in, as is convenient."

"I know you — Hurry Skurry — I'll sell you a scalp! — a sound one, and of a full grown man — What'll you give?"

"Poor Tom! That scalp business has n't turned out at all profitable, and I've pretty much concluded to give it up; and to follow a less bloody calling."

"Have you got any scalp? Mine's gone — How does it feel to have a scalp? — I know how it feels to lose one — Fire and flames about the brain — and, a wrenching at the heart — no — no — kill *first*, Hurry, and scalp, *afterwards*."

"What does the old fellow mean, Judith? He talks like one that is getting tired of the business as well as myself. Why have you bound up his head; or, have the savages tomahawked him about the brains."

"They have done that for *him*, which you and he, Harry March, would have so gladly done for *them*. His skin and hair have been torn from his head to gain money from the governor of Canada, as you would have torn theirs from the heads of the Hurons, to gain money from the governor of York."

Judith spoke with a strong effort to appear composed, but it was neither in her nature, nor in the feeling of the moment to speak altogether without bitterness. The strength of her emphasis, indeed, as well as her manner caused Hetty to look up reproachfully.

"These are high words to come from Thomas Hutter's darter, as Thomas Hutter lies dying before her eyes," retorted Hurry.

"God be praised for that! — whatever reproach it may bring on my poor mother, I am *not* Thomas Hutter's daughter."

"Not Thomas Hutter's darter! — Don't disown the old fellow in his last moments, Judith, for *that's* a sin the Lord will never overlook. If you're not Thomas Hutter's darter, whose darter be you?"

This question rebuked the rebellious spirit of Judith, for, in getting rid of a parent, whom she felt it was a relief to find she might own she had never loved, she overlooked the important circumstance that no substitute was ready to supply his place.

"I cannot tell you, Harry, who my father was," she answered more mildly; "I hope he was an honest man, at least."

"Which is more than you think was the case, with old Hutter? Well, Judith, I'll not deny that hard stories were in circulation consarning Floating Tom, but who is there that does n't get a scratch, when an inimy holds the rake? There's them that say hard things of *me*, and even *you*, beauty as you be, do n't always escape."

This was said with a view to set up a species of community of character between the parties, and, as the politicians are wont to express it, with ulterior intentions. What might have been the consequences with one of Judith's known spirit, as well as her assured antipathy to the speaker, it is not easy to say, for, just then, Hutter gave unequivocal signs that his last moment was nigh. Judith and Hetty had stood by the dying bed of their mother, and neither needed a monitor to warn them of the crisis, and every sign of resentment vanished from the face of the first. Hutter opened his eyes, and even tried to feel about him with his hands, a sign that sight was failing. A minute later, his breathing grew ghastly; a pause totally without respiration followed; and, then, succeeded the last, long drawn sigh, on which the spirit is supposed to quit the body. This sudden termination of the life of one who had hitherto filled so important a place in the narrow scene on which he had been an actor, put an end to all discussion.

The day passed by without further interruption, the Hurons, though possessed of a canoe, appearing so far satisfied with their success as to have relinquished all immediate designs on the castle. It would not have been a safe undertaking, indeed, to approach it under the rifles of those it was now known to contain, and it is probable that the truce was more owing to this circumstance than to any other. In the mean while the preparations were made for the interment of Hutter. To bury him on the land was impracticable, and it was Hetty's wish that his body should lie by the side of that of her mother, in the lake. She had it in her power to quote one of his speeches, in which he himself had called the lake the "family burying ground," and luckily this was done without the knowledge of her sister, who would have opposed the plan, had she known it, with unconquerable disgust. But Judith had not meddled with the arrangement, and every necessary disposition was made without her privity or advice.

The hour chosen for the rude ceremony, was just as the sun was setting, and a moment and a scene more suited to paying the last offices to one of calm and pure spirit could not have been chosen. There are a mystery and a solemn dignity in death, that dispose the living to regard the remains of even a malefactor with a certain degree of reverence. All worldly distinctions have ceased; it is thought that the veil has been removed, and that the character and destiny of the departed are now as much beyond human opinions, as they are beyond human ken. In nothing is death more truly a leveller than in this, since, while it may be impossible absolutely to confound the great with the low, the worthy with the unworthy, the mind feels it to be arrogant to assume a right to judge of those who are believed to be standing at the judgment seat of God. When Judith was told that all was ready, she went upon the platform, passive to the request of her sister, and then she first took heed of the arrangement. The body was in the scow, enveloped in a sheet, and quite a hundred weight of stones, that had been taken from the fire place, were enclosed with it, in order that it might sink. No other preparation seemed to be thought necessary, though Hetty carried her bible beneath her arm.

When all were on board the Ark, the singular habitation of the man whose body it now bore to its final abode, was set in motion. Hurry was at the oars. In his powerful hands, indeed, they seemed little more than a pair of sculls, which were wielded without effort, and, as he was expert in their use, the Delaware remained a passive spectator of the proceedings. The progress of the Ark had something of the stately solemnity of a funeral procession, the dip of the oars being measured, and the movement slow and steady. The wash of the water, as the blades rose and fell, kept time with the efforts of Hurry, and might have been likened to the measured tread of mourners. Then the tranquil scene was in beautiful accordance with a rite that ever associates with itself the idea of God. At that instant, the lake had not even a single ripple, on its glassy surface, and the broad panorama of woods seemed to look down on the holy tranquillity of the hour and ceremony in melancholy stillness. Judith was affected to tears, and even Hurry, though he hardly knew why, was troubled. Hetty preserved the outward signs of tranquillity, but her inward grief greatly surpassed that of her sister, since her affectionate heart loved more from habit and long association, than from the usual connections of sentiment and taste. She was sustained by religious hope, however, which in her simple mind usually occupied the space that worldly feelings filled in that of Judith, and she was not without an expectation of witnessing some open manifestation of divine power, on an occasion so solemn. Still she was neither mystical nor exaggerated; her mental imbecility denying both. Nevertheless her thoughts had generally so much of the purity of a better world about them that it was easy for her to forget earth altogether, and to think only of heaven. Hist was serious, attentive and interested, for she had often seen the interments of the pale-faces, though never one that promised to be as peculiar as this; while the Delaware, though grave, and also observant, in his demeanor was stoical and calm.

Hetty acted as pilot, directing Hurry how to proceed, to find that spot in the lake, which she was in the habit of terming "mother's grave." The reader will remember that the castle stood near the southern extremity of a shoal that extended near half a mile northerly, and it was at the farthest end of this shallow water that Floating Tom had seen fit to deposit the remains of his wife and child. His own were now in the course of being placed at their side. Hetty had marks on the land by which she usually found the spot, although the position of the buildings, the general direction of the shoal, and the beautiful transparency of the water all aided her, the latter even allowing the bottom to be seen. By these means the girl was enabled to note their progress, and at the proper time, she approached March, whispering—

"Now, Hurry you can stop rowing. We have passed the stone on the bottom, and mother's grave is near."

March ceased his efforts, immediately dropping the kedge, and taking the warp in his hand, in order to check the scow. The Ark turned slowly round, under this restraint, and when it was quite stationary, Hetty was seen at its stern, pointing into the water, the tears streaming from her eyes, in ungovernable natural feeling. Judith had been present at the interment of her mother, but she had never visited the spot since. This neglect proceeded from no indifference to the memory of the deceased, for she had loved her *mother*, and, bitterly, bitterly had she found occasion to mourn her loss, but she was averse to the contemplation of death, and there had been passages in her own life since the day of that interment, which increased this feeling, and rendered her if possible still more reluctant to approach the spot that contained the remains of one whose severe lessons of female morality and propriety had been deepened and rendered doubly impressive by remorse for her own failings. With Hetty, the case had been very different. To her simple and innocent mind the remembrance of her mother, brought no other feeling than one of gentle sorrow; a grief that is so often termed luxurious, even, because it associates with itself the images of excellence, and the purity of a better state of existence. For an entire summer, she had been in the habit of repairing to the place after night-fall, and carefully anchoring her canoe so as not to disturb the body, she would sit and hold fancied conversations with the deceased, sing sweet hymns to the evening air, and repeat the orisons that the being who now slumbered below, had taught her in infancy. Hetty had passed her happiest hours in this indirect communion with the spirit of her mother, the wildness of Indian traditions, and Indian opinions, unconsciously to herself, mingling with the christian lore received in childhood. Once she had even been so far influenced by the former, as to have bethought her of performing some of those physical rites at her mother's grave, which the red men are known to observe, but the passing feeling had been obscured by the steady, though mild, light of christianity, which never ceased to burn in her gentle bosom. Now, her emotions were merely the natural outpourings of a daughter that wept for a mother whose love was indelibly impressed on the heart, and whose lessons had been too earnestly taught to be easily forgotten by one who had so little temptation to err.

There was no other priest than nature, at that wild and singular funeral rite. March cast his eyes below, and through the transparent medium of the clear water, which was almost as pure as air, he saw what Hetty was accustomed to call "mother's grave." It was a low straggling mound of earth, fashioned by no spade, out of a corner of which gleamed a bit of the white cloth, that formed the shroud of the dead. The body had been lowered to the bottom, and Hutter brought earth from the shore and let it fall upon it, until all was concealed. In this state the place had remained, until the movement of the waters revealed the solitary sign of the uses of the spot, that has just been mentioned. Even the most rude and brawling are chastened by the ceremonies of a funeral. March felt no desire to indulge his voice in any of its coarse outbreakings, and was disposed to complete the office he had undertaken in decent sobriety. Perhaps he reflected on the retribution that had alighted on his late comrade, and bethought him of the frightful jeopardy in which his own life had so lately been placed. He signified to Judith that all was ready, received her directions to proceed, and with no other assistant than his own vast strength, raised the body and bore it to the end of the scow. Two parts of a rope were passed beneath the legs and shoulders, as they are placed beneath coffins, and then the corpse was slowly lowered beneath the surface of the lake.

"Not *there*—Harry March—no, not *there*," said Judith, shuddering involuntarily—"do not lower it, quite so near the spot where mother lies!"

"Why, not, Judith?" asked Hetty, earnestly—"They lived together in life, and should lie together in death."

"No—no—Harry March; further off—further off—Poor Hetty, you know not what you say.—Leave me to order this."

"I know I am weak minded, Judith, and that you are clever—but, surely a husband should be placed near a wife. Mother always said that this was the way they bury in christian church yards!"

This little controversy was conducted earnestly, but in smothered voices, as if the speakers feared that the dead might overhear them. Judith could not contend with her sister, at such a moment, but a significant gesture from her, induced March to lower the body, at a little distance from that of his wife, when he withdrew the cords, and the act was performed.

"There's an end of Floating Tom!" exclaimed Hurry, bending over the scow, and gazing through the water at the body. "He was a brave companion on a scout, and a notable hand with traps. Do n't weep, Judith, do n't be overcome Hetty, for the righteousest of us all must die; and when the time comes, lamentations and tears can't bring the dead to life. Your father will be a loss to you, no doubt; most fathers are a loss, especially to onmarried darters; but there's a way to cure that evil, and you're both too young and handsome to live long without finding it out. When it's agreeable to hear what an honest and onpretending man has to say, Judith, I should like to talk a little with you, apart."

Judith had scarce attended to this rude attempt of Hurry's at consolation, although she necessarily understood its general drift, and had a tolerably accurate notion of its manner. She was weeping at the recollection of her mother's early tenderness, and painful images of long forgotten lessons and neglected precepts were crowding her mind. The words of Hurry, however, recalled her to the present time, and abrupt and unseasonable as was their import, they did not produce those signs of distaste that one might have expected from the girl's character. On the contrary, she appeared to be struck with some sudden idea, gazed intently for a moment at the young man, dried her eyes, and led the way to the other end of the scow, signifying her wish for him to follow. Here she took a seat and motioned for March to place himself at her side. The decision and earnestness with which all this was done, a little intimidated her companion, and Judith found it necessary to open the subject herself.

"You wish to speak to me of marriage, Harry March," she said, "and I have come here, over the grave of my parents, as it might be — no — no — over the grave of my poor, dear — dear, mother, to hear what you have to say."

"This is oncommon, and you have a skearful way with you, this evening, Judith," answered Hurry, more disturbed than he would have cared to own, "but truth is truth, and it shall come out, let what will follow. You well know, gal, that I've long thought you the comeliest young woman my eyes ever beheld, and that I've made no secret of that fact, either here on the lake, out among the hunters and trappers, or in the settlements."

"Yes—yes, I've heard this before, and I suppose it to be true," answered Judith with a sort of feverish impatience.

"When a young man holds such language of any particular young woman, it's reasonable to calculate he sets store by her."

"True—true, Hurry—all this you've told me, again and again."

"Well, if it's agreeable, I should think a woman coul'n't hear it too often. They all tell me this is the way with your sex, that nothing pleases them more than to repeat over and over, for the hundredth time, how much you like 'em, unless it be to talk to 'em of their good looks!"

"No doubt—we like both, on most occasions, but this is an uncommon moment, Hurry, and vain words should not be too freely used. I would rather hear you speak plainly."

"You shall have your own way, Judith, and I some suspect you always will. I've often told you that I not only like you better than any other young woman going, or, for that matter, better than *all* the young women going, but you must have observed, Judith, that I've never asked you, in up and down tarms, to marry me."

"I have observed both," returned the girl, a smile struggling about her beautiful mouth, in spite of the singular and engrossing intentness which caused her cheeks to flush and lighted her eyes with a brilliancy that was almost dazzling—"I have observed both, and have thought the last remarkable for a man of Harry March's decision and fearlessness."

"There's been a reason, gal, and it's one that troubles me even now—nay, do n't flush up so, and look fiery like, for there are thoughts which will stick long in any man's mind, as there be words that will stick in his throat—but, then, ag'in, there's feelin's that will get the better of 'em all, and to these feelin's I find I must submit. You've no longer a father, or a mother, Judith, and it's morally unpossible that you and Hetty could live here, alone, allowing it was peace and the Iroquois was quiet; but, as matters stand, not only would you starve, but you'd both be prisoners, or scalped, afore a week was out. It's time to think of a change and a husband, and, if you'll accept of me, all that's past shall be forgotten, and there's an end on't."

Judith had difficulty in repressing her impatience until this rude declaration and offer were made, which she evidently wished to hear, and which she now listened to with a willingness that might well have excited hope. She hardly allowed the young man to conclude, so eager was she to bring him to the point, and so ready to answer.

"There—Hurry—that's enough—" she said, raising a hand as if to stop him—"I understand you as well, as if you were to talk a month. You prefer me to other girls, and you wish me to become your wife."

"You put it in better words than I can do, Judith, and I wish you to fancy them said, just as you most like to hear 'em."

"They're plain enough, Harry, and 'tis fitting they should be so. This is no place to trifle or deceive in. Now, listen to my answer, which shall be, in every tittle, as sincere as your offer. There is a reason, March, why I should never—"

"I suppose I understand you, Judith, but if I'm willing to overlook that reason, it's no one's consarn but mine—Now, do n't brighten up like the sky at sundown, for no offence is meant, and none should be taken."

"I do not brighten up, and will *not* take offence," said Judith, struggling to repress her indignation, in a way she had never found it necessary to exert before. "There is a reason why I should not, *cannot*, ever be your wife, Hurry, that you seem to overlook, and which it is my duty now to tell you, as plainly as you have asked me to consent to become so. I do not, and I am certain that I never shall, love you well enough to marry you. No man can wish for a wife who does not prefer him to all other men, and when I tell you this frankly, I suppose you yourself will thank me for my sincerity."

"Ah! Judith, them flaunting, gay, scarlet-coated officers of the garrisons, have done all this mischief!"

"Hush, March; do not calumniate a daughter over her mother's grave! Do not, when I only wish to treat you fairly, give me reason to call for evil on your head in bitterness of heart! Do not forget that I am a woman, and that you are a man; and that I have neither father, nor brother, to revenge your words!"

"Well, there is something in the last, and I'll say no more. Take time, Judith, and think better on this."

"I want no time—my mind has long been made up, and I have only waited for you to speak plainly, to answer plainly. We now understand each other, and there is no use in saying any more."

The impetuous earnestness of the girl awed the young man, for never before had he seen her so serious and determined. In most of their previous interviews she had met his advances with evasion, or sarcasm, but these Hurry had mistaken for female coquetry, and had supposed might easily be converted into consent. The struggle had been with himself, about offering, nor had he ever seriously believed it possible that Judith would refuse to become the wife of the handsomest man on all that frontier. Now that the refusal came, and that in terms so decided, as to put all cavilling out of the question, if not absolutely dumbfounded, he was so much mortified and surprised, as to feel no wish to attempt to change her resolution.

"The Glimmerglass has now no great call for me," he exclaimed, after a minute's silence. "Old Tom is gone, the Hurons are as plenty on the shore, as pigeons in the woods, and altogether it is getting to be an onsuitable place."

"Then leave it. You see it is surrounded by dangers, and there is no reason why you should risk your life for others. Nor do I know that you can be of any service to us. Go, tonight; we'll never accuse you of having done any thing forgetful, or unmanly."

"If I do go, 'twill be with a heavy heart on your account, Judith; I would rather take you with me."

"That is not to be spoken of any longer, March; but, I will land you in one of the canoes, as soon as it is dark and you can strike a trail for the nearest garrison. When you reach the fort, if you send a party—"

Judith smothered the words, for she felt that it was humiliating to be thus exposing herself to the comments and reflections of one who was not disposed to view her conduct in connection with all in those garrisons, with an eye of favor. Hurry however, caught the idea, and, without perverting it, as the girl dreaded, he answered to the purpose.

"I understand *what* you would say, and *why* you do n't say it," he replied. "If I get safe to the fort, a party shall start on the trail of these vagabonds, and I'll come with it, myself, for I should like to see you, and Hetty, in a place of safety, before we part forever."

"Ah, Harry March, had you always spoken thus, felt thus, my feelings towards you might have been different!"

"Is it too late, now, Judith? I'm rough and a woodsman, but we all change under different treatment from what we have been used to."

"It *is* too late, March. I can never feel towards you, or any other man but *one*, as you would wish to have me. There, I've said enough, surely, and you will question me no further. As soon as it is dark, I, or the Delaware will put you on the shore. You will make the best of your way to the Mohawk, and the nearest garrison, and send all you can to our assistance. And, Hurry, we are now friends, and I may trust in you, may I not?"

"Sartain, Judith; though our fri'ndship would have been all the warmer, could you look upon me, as I look upon you."

Judith hesitated, and some powerful emotion was struggling within her. Then, as if determined to look down all weaknesses, and accomplish her purposes, at every hazard, she spoke more plainly.

"You will find a captain of the name of Warley at the nearest post," she said, pale as death, and even trembling as she spoke; "I think it likely he will wish to head the party, but I would greatly prefer it should be another. If Captain Warley *can* be kept back, 't would make me very happy!"

"That's easier said than done, Judith, for these officers do pretty much as they please. The Major will order, and captains, and lieutenants, and ensigns must obey. I know the officer you mean, a red faced, gay, oh! be joyful sort of a gentleman, who swallows madeira enough to drown the Mohawk, and yet a pleasant talker. All the gals in the valley admire him, and they say he admires all the gals. I do n't wonder he is your dislike, Judith, for he's a very gin'ral lover, if he is n't a gin'ral officer."

Judith did not answer, though her frame shook, and her colour changed from pale to crimson, and from crimson back again to the hue of death.

"Alas! my poor mother!" she ejaculated mentally instead of uttering it aloud, "we are over thy grave, but little dost thou know how much thy lessons have been forgotten; thy care neglected; thy love defeated!"

As this goading of the worm that never dies was felt, she arose and signified to Hurry, that she had no more to communicate.

Chapter XXII.

"—That point
In misery, which makes the oppressed man
Regardless of his own life, makes him too
Lord of the oppressor's.—"
                                    Coleridge, *Remorse*, V.i.201-04.

A L L this time Hetty had remained seated in the head of the scow, looking sorrowfully into the water which held the body of her mother, as well as that of the man whom she had been taught to consider her father. Hist stood near her in gentle quiet, but had no consolation to offer in words. The habits of her people taught her reserve in this respect, and the habits of her sex induced her to wait patiently for a moment when she might manifest some soothing sympathy by means of acts, rather than of speech. Chingachgook held himself a little aloof, in grave reserve, looking like a warrior, but feeling like a man.

Judith joined her sister with an air of dignity and solemnity it was not her practice to show, and, though the gleamings of anguish were still visible on her beautiful face, when she spoke it was firmly and without tremor. At that instant Hist and the Delaware withdrew, moving towards Hurry, in the other end of the boat.

"Sister," said Judith kindly, "I have much to say to you; we will get into this canoe, and paddle off to a distance from the Ark—The secrets of two orphans ought not to be heard by every ear."

"Certainly, Judith, by the ears of their parents? Let Hurry lift the grapnel and move away with the Ark, and leave us here, near the graves of father and mother, to say what we may have to say."

"Father!" repeated Judith slowly, the blood for the first time since her parting with March mounting to her cheeks—"He was no father of ours, Hetty! *That* we had from his own mouth, and in his dying moments."

"Are you glad, Judith, to find you had no father! He took care of us, and fed us, and clothed us, and loved us; a father could have done no more. I do'n't understand why he was'n't a father."

"Never mind, dear child, but let us do as you have said. It may be well to remain here, and let the Ark move a little away. Do you prepare the canoe, and I will tell Hurry and the Indians our wishes."

This was soon and simply done, the Ark moving, with measured strokes of the sweeps a hundred yards from the spot, leaving the girls floating, seemingly in air, above the place of the dead; so buoyant was the light vessel that held them, and so limpid the element by which it was sustained.

"The death of Thomas Hutter," Judith commenced, after a short pause had prepared her sister to receive her communications, "has altered all our prospects, Hetty. If he was *not* our father, we are *sisters*, and must feel alike and live together."

"How do I know, Judith, that you would n't be as glad to find I am not your sister, as you are in finding that Thomas Hutter, as you call him, was not your father. I am only half witted, and few people like to have half-witted relations; and then I'm not handsome—at least, not as handsome as you—and you may wish a handsomer sister."

"No—no—Hetty. *You* and you only are my sister—my heart, and my love for you tell me that—and mother was my mother—of that too am I glad, and proud; for she was a mother to be proud of—but father was not father!"

"Hush, Judith! His spirit may be near; it would grieve it to hear his children talking so, and that, too, over his very grave. Children should never grieve parents, mother often told me, and especially when they are dead!"

"Poor Hetty! They are happily removed beyond all cares on our account. Nothing that *I* can do or say, will cause mother any sorrow *now*—there is some consolation in that, at least!—and nothing *you* can say or do will make her smile, as she used to smile on your good conduct when living."

"You do n't know that, Judith. Spirits can see, and mother may see as well as any spirit. She always told us that God saw all we did, and that we should do nothing to offend *him*; and now *she* has left us, I strive to do nothing that can displease *her*. Think how her spirit would mourn and feel sorrow, Judith, did it see either of us doing what is not right; and spirits *may* see, after all; especially the spirits of parents that feel anxious about their children."

"Hetty—Hetty—you know not what you say!" murmured Judith, almost livid with emotion—"The dead *cannot* see, and know nothing of what passes, here! But, we will not talk of this any longer. The bodies of Mother and Thomas Hutter lie together in the lake, and we will hope that the spirits of both are with God. That we, the children of one of them, remain on earth is certain; it is now proper to know what we are to do in future."

"If we are not Thomas Hutter's children, Judith, no one will dispute our right to his property. We have the castle and the Ark, and the canoes, and the woods, and the lakes, the same as when he was living, and what can prevent us from staying here, and passing our lives just as we ever have done."

"No—no—poor sister—this can no longer be. Two girls would not be safe here, even should these Hurons fail in getting us into their power. Even father had as much as he could sometimes do, to keep peace upon the lake, and we should fail altogether. We must quit this spot, Hetty, and remove into the settlements."

"I am sorry you think so, Judith," returned Hetty, dropping her head on her bosom, and looking thoughtfully down at the spot where the funeral pile of her mother could just be seen. "I am *very* sorry to hear it. I would rather stay here, where, if I was n't born, I've passed my life. I do n't like the settlements—they are full of wickedness and heart burnings, while God dwells unoffended in these hills! I love the trees, and the mountains, and the lake, and the springs; all that his bounty has given us, and it would grieve me sorely, Judith, to be forced to quit them. You are handsome, and not at all half-witted, and one day you will marry, and then you will have a husband, and I a brother to take care of us, if women can't really take care of themselves in such a place as this."

"Ah! if this *could* be so, Hetty, then, indeed, I could *now* be a thousand times happier in these woods, than in the settlements. *Once*, I did not feel thus, but *now* I do. Yet where is the man to turn this beautiful place into such a garden of Eden, for us?"

"Harry March loves you, sister," returned poor Hetty, unconsciously picking the bark off the canoe as she spoke. "He would be glad to be your husband, I'm sure, and a stouter and a braver youth is not to be met with the whole country round."

"Harry March and I understand each other, and no more need be said about *him*. There is one—but no matter. It is all in the hands of providence, and we must shortly come to some conclusion about our future manner of living. Remain here—that is, remain here, alone, we cannot—and perhaps no occasion will ever offer for remaining in the manner you think of. It is time, too, Hetty, we should learn all we can concerning our relations and family. It is not probable we are altogether without relations, and they may be glad to see us. The old chest is now our property, and we have a right to look into it, and learn all we can by what it holds. Mother was so very different from Thomas Hutter, that, now I know we are not his children, I burn with a desire to know whose children we can be. There are papers in that chest, I am certain, and those papers may tell us all about our parents and natural friends."

"Well, Judith, you know best, for you are cleverer than common, mother always said, and I am only half-witted. Now father and mother are dead, I do n't much care for any relation but you, and do n't think I could love them I never saw, as well as I ought. If you do n't like to marry Hurry, I do n't see who you can choose for a husband, and then I fear we shall have to quit the lake, after all."

"What do you think of Deerslayer, Hetty?" asked Judith, bending forward like her unsophisticated sister, and endeavoring to conceal her embarrassment in a similar manner.—"Would he not make a brother-in-law to your liking?"

"Deerslayer!" repeated the other, looking up in unfeigned surprise. "Why, Judith, Deerslayer is n't, in the least, comely, and is altogether unfit for one like you!"

"He is not ill-looking, Hetty, and beauty in a man is not of much matter."

"Do you think so, Judith?—I know that beauty is of no great matter, in man or woman, in the eyes of God, for mother has often told me so, when she thought I might have been sorry I was not as handsome as you, though she need n't have been uneasy on that account, for I never coveted any thing that is yours, sister; — but, tell me so she did — still, beauty is very pleasant to the eye, in both! I think, if I were a man, I should pine more for good looks, than I do as a girl. A handsome man is a more pleasing sight, than a handsome woman."

"Poor child! — You scarce know what you say, or what you mean! Beauty in our sex *is* something, but in men, it passes for little. To be sure, a man ought to be tall, but others are tall, as well as Hurry; and active — and I think I know those that are more active; — and strong; well, he has n't all the strength in the world — and brave — I am certain I can name a youth who is braver!"

"This is strange, Judith! — I did n't think the earth held a handsomer, or a stronger, or a more active or a braver man than Hurry Harry! I'm sure, *I* never met his equal, in either of these things."

"Well — well — Hetty — say no more of this. I dislike to hear *you* talking in this manner. Tis not suitable to your innocence, and truth, and warm-hearted sincerity — . Let Harry March go. He quits us to-night, and no regret of mine will follow him, unless it be that he has staid so long, and to so little purpose."

"Ah! Judith; that is what I've long feared — and I did *so* hope he might be my brother-in-law!"

"Never mind it now. Let us talk of our poor mother — and of Thomas Hutter."

"Speak kindly then, sister, for you can't be quite certain that spirits do n't both hear and see. If father was n't father, he was good to us, and gave us food and shelter. We can't put any stones over their graves, here in the water, to tell people all this, and so we ought to say it with our tongues."

"They will care little for that, girl. 'Tis a great consolation to know, Hetty, that if mother ever did commit any heavy fault when young, she lived sincerely to repent of it; no doubt her sins were forgiven her."

"Tis n't right, Judith, for children to talk of their parents' sins. We had better talk of our own."

"Talk of your sins, Hetty! — If there ever was a creature on earth without sin, it is you! I wish I could say, or think the same of myself; but we shall see. No one knows what changes affection for a good husband, can make in a woman's heart. I do n't think, child, I have even now the same love for finery I once had."

"It would be a pity, Judith, if you did think of clothes, over your parents' graves! We will never quit this spot, if you say so, and will let Hurry go where he pleases."

"I am willing enough to consent to the last, but cannot answer for the first, Hetty. We must live, in future, as becomes respectable young women, and cannot remain here, to be the talk and jest of all the rude and foul tongu'd trappers and hunters that may come upon the lake. Let Hurry go by himself, and then I'll find the means to see Deerslayer, when the future shall be soon settled. Come, girl, the sun has set, and the Ark is drifting away from us; let us paddle up to the scow, and consult with our friends. This night I shall look into the chest, and to-morrow shall determine what we are to do. As for the Hurons, now we can use our stores without fear of Thomas Hutter, they will be easily bought off. Let me get Deerslayer once out of their hands, and a single hour shall bring things to an understanding."

Judith spoke with decision, and she spoke with authority, a habit she had long practised towards her feeble-minded sister. But, while thus accustomed to have her way, by the aid of manner and a readier command of words, Hetty occasionally checked her impetuous feelings and hasty acts by the aid of those simple moral truths, that were so deeply engrafted in all her own thoughts and feelings; shining through both, with a mild and beautiful lustre, that threw a sort of holy halo around so much of what she both said and did. On the present occasion, this healthful ascendancy of the girl of weak intellect, over her of a capacity that, in other situations, might have become brilliant and admired, was exhibited in the usual simple and earnest manner.

"You forget, Judith, what has brought us here," she said reproachfully. "This is mother's grave, and we have just laid the body of father by her side. We have done wrong to talk so much of ourselves at such a spot, and ought now to pray God to forgive us, and ask *him* to teach us where we are to go, and what we are to do."

Judith involuntarily laid aside her paddle, while Hetty dropped on her knees, and was soon lost in her devout but simple petitions. Her sister did not pray. This she had long ceased to do directly, though anguish of spirit frequently wrung from her mental and hasty appeals to the great source of benevolence for support, if not for a change of spirit. Still she never beheld Hetty on her knees, that a feeling of tender recollection, as well as of profound regret at the deadness of her own heart, did not come over her. Thus had she herself done in childhood, and even down to the hour of her ill fated visits to the garrisons, and she would willingly have given worlds, at such moments, to be able to exchange her present sensations, for the confiding faith, those pure aspirations, and the gentle hope that shone through every lineament and movement of her, otherwise, less favored sister. All she could do, however, was to drop her head to her bosom, and assume in her attitude some of that devotion in which her stubborn spirit refused to unite.

When Hetty rose from her knees, her countenance had a glow and serenity that rendered a face that was always agreeable, positively handsome. Her mind was at peace, and her conscience acquitted her, of a neglect of duty.

"Now, you may go, if you want to, Judith," she said, "for God has been kind to me, and lifted a burden off my heart. Mother had many such burdens, she used to tell me, and she always took them off in this way. Tis the only way, sister, such things can be done. You may raise a stone, or a log, with your hands; but the heart *must* be lightened by prayer. I do n't think you pray as often as you used to do, when younger, Judith!"

"Never mind — never mind, child —" answered the other huskily — "'tis no matter, now. Mother is gone, and Thomas Hutter is gone, and the time has come when we must think and act for ourselves."

As the canoe moved slowly away from the place, under the gentle impulsion of the elder sister's paddle, the younger sat musing, as was her wont, whenever her mind was perplexed by any idea more abstract and difficult of comprehension than common.

"I do n't know what you mean by 'future', Judith," she at length, suddenly observed. "Mother used to call Heaven the future, but you seem to think it means next week, or to-morrow!"

"It means both, dear sister—every thing that is yet to come, whether in this world or another. It is a solemn word, Hetty, and most so, I fear, to them that think the least about it. Mother's future is eternity; ours may yet mean what will happen while we live in this world—Is not that a canoe just passing behind the castle—here, more in the direction of the point, I mean; it is hid, now; but certainly I saw a canoe stealing behind the logs!"

"I've seen it some time," Hetty quietly answered, for the Indians had few terrors for her, "but I did n't think it right to talk about such things over mother's grave! The canoe came from the camp, Judith, and was paddled by a single man. He seemed to be Deerslayer, and no Iroquois."

"Deerslayer!" returned the other, with much of her native impetuosity—"That cannot be! Deerslayer is a prisoner, and I have been thinking of the means of setting him free. Why did you fancy it Deerslayer, child?"

"You can look for yourself, sister, for there comes the canoe in sight, again, on this side of the hut."

Sure enough, the light boat had passed the building, and was now steadily advancing towards the Ark; the persons on board of which were already collecting in the head of the scow, to receive their visiter. A single glance sufficed to assure Judith that her sister was right, and that Deerslayer was alone in the canoe. His approach was so calm and leisurely, however, as to fill her with wonder, since a man who had effected his escape from enemies, by either artifice or violence, would not be apt to move with the steadiness and deliberation with which his paddle swept the water. By this time the day was fairly departing, and objects were already seen dimly under the shores. In the broad lake, however, the light still lingered, and around the immediate scene of the present incidents, which was less shaded than most of the sheet, being in its broadest part, it cast a glow that bore some faint resemblance to the warm tints of an Italian or Grecian sunset. The logs of the hut and Ark had a sort of purple hue, blended with the growing obscurity, and the bark of the hunter's boat was losing its distinctness in colours richer, but more mellowed, than those it showed under a bright sun. As the two canoes approached each other—for Judith and her sister had plied their paddles so as to intercept the unexpected visiter ere he reached the Ark—even Deerslayer's sun-burned countenance wore a brighter aspect than common, under the pleasing tints that seemed to dance in the atmosphere. Judith fancied that delight at meeting her had some share in this unusual and agreeable expression. She was not aware that her own beauty appeared to more advantage than common, from the same natural cause, nor did she understand, what it would have given her so much pleasure to know, that the young man actually thought her, as she drew nearer, the loveliest creature of her sex, his eyes had ever dwelt on.

"Welcome—welcome, Deerslayer!" exclaimed the girl, as the canoes floated at each other's side; "we have had a melancholy—a frightful day—but your return is, at least, one misfortune the less! Have the Hurons become more human, and let you go; or have you escaped from the wretches, by your own courage and skill?"

"Neither, Judith—neither one nor t'other. The Mingos are Mingos still, and will live and die Mingos; it is not likely their natur's will ever undergo much improvement. Well! They've *their* gifts, and we've our'n, Judith, and it does'n't much become either to speak ill of what the Lord has created; though, if the truth must be said, I find it a sore trial to think kindly, or to talk kindly of them vagabonds. As for outwitting them, that might have been done, and it *was* done, too, atween the Sarpent, yonder, and me, when we were on the trail of Hist—" here the hunter stopped to laugh in his own silent fashion—"but it's no easy matter to sarcumvent the sarcumvented. Even the fa'ans get to know the tricks of the hunters afore a single season is over, and an Indian whose eyes have once been opened by a sarcumvention never shuts them ag'in in precisely the same spot. I've known whites to do that, but never a red skin. What they l'arn comes by practice, and not by books, and of all schoolmasters exper'ence gives lessons that are the longest remembered."

"All this is true, Deerslayer, but if you have not escaped from the savages, how came you here?"

"That's a nat'ral question, and charmingly put. You *are* wonderful handsome this evening, Judith, or, Wild Rose, as the Sarpent calls you, and I may as well say it, since I honestly think it! You may well call them Mingos, savages too, for savage enough do they feel, and savage enough will they act, if you once give them an opportunity. They feel their loss here, in the late skrimmage, to their hearts' cores, and are ready to revenge it on any creatur' of English blood that may fall in their way. Nor, for that matter do I much think they would stand at taking their satisfaction out of a Dutch man."

"They have killed father; that ought to satisfy their wicked cravings for blood," observed Hetty reproachfully.

"I know it, gal—I know the whole story—partly from what I've seen from the shore, since they brought me up from the point, and partly from their threats ag'in myself, and their other discourse. Well, life is unsartain at the best, and we all depend on the breath of our nostrils for it, from day to day. If you've lost a staunch fri'nd, as I make no doubt you have, Providence will raise up new ones in his stead, and since our acquaintance has begun in this oncommon manner, I shall take it as a hint that it will be a part of my duty in futur', should the occasion offer, to see you do n't suffer for want of food in the wigwam. I can't bring the dead to life, but as to feeding the living, there's few on all this frontier can outdo me, though I say it in the way of pity and consolation, like, and in no particular, in the way of boasting."

"We understand you, Deerslayer," returned Judith, hastily, "and take all that falls from your lips, as it is meant, in kindness and friendship. Would to Heaven all men had tongues as true, and hearts as honest!"

"In that respect men *do* differ, of a sartainty, Judith. I've known them that was n't to be trusted any farther than you can see them; and others ag'in whose messages, sent with a small piece of wampum, perhaps, might just as much be depended on, as if the whole business was finished afore your face. Yes, Judith, you never said truer word, than when you said some men might be depended on, and other some might not."

"You are an unaccountable being, Deerslayer," returned the girl, not a little puzzled with the childish simplicity of character that the hunter so often betrayed—a simplicity so striking that it frequently appeared to place him nearly on a level with the fatuity of poor Hetty, though always relieved by the beautiful moral truth that shone through all that this unfortunate girl both said and did—"You are a most unaccountable man, and I often do not know how to understand you. But never mind, just now; you have forgotten to tell us by what means you are here."

"I!—Oh! That's not very onaccountable, if I am myself, Judith. I'm out on furlough."

"Furlough!—That word has a meaning among the soldiers that I understand; but I cannot tell what it signifies when used by a prisoner."

"It means just the same. You're right enough; the soldiers do use it, and just in the same way as I use it. A furlough is when a man has leave to quit a camp, or a garrison for a sartain specified time; at the end of which he is to come back and shoulder his musket, or submit to his torments, just as he may happen to be a soldier, or a captyve. Being the last, I must take the chances of a prisoner."

"Have the Hurons suffered you to quit them in this manner, without watch or guard."

"Sartain—I woul'n't have come in any other manner, unless indeed it had been by a bold rising, or a sarcumvention."

"What pledge have they that you will ever return?"

"My word," answered the hunter simply. "Yes, I own I gave 'em *that*, and big fools would they have been to let me come without it! Why in that case, I should n't have been obliged to go back and ondergo any deviltries their fury may invent, but might have shouldered my rifle, and made the best of my way to the Delaware villages. But, Lord! Judith, they know'd this, just as well as you and I do, and would no more let me come away, without a promise to go back, than they would let the wolves dig up the bones of their fathers!"

"Is it possible you mean to do this act of extraordinary self-destruction and recklessness?"

"Anan!"

"I ask if it can be possible that you expect to be able to put yourself again in the power of such ruthless enemies, by keeping your word."

Deerslayer looked at his fair questioner for a moment, with stern displeasure. Then the expression of his honest and guileless face suddenly changed, lighting as by a quick illumination of thought, after which he laughed in his ordinary manner.

"I did n't understand you, at first, Judith; no, I did n't! You believe that Chingachgook and Hurry Harry won't suffer it; but you do n't know mankind thoroughly yet, I see. The Delaware would be the last man on 'arth to offer any objections to what he knows is a duty, and, as for March, he does n't care enough about any creatur' but himself to spend many words on such a subject. If he did, 'twould make no great difference howsever; but not he, for he thinks more of his gains than of even his own word. As for my promises, or your'n, Judith, or any body else's, they give him no consarn. Don't be under any oneasiness, therefore, gal; I shall be allowed to go back according to the furlough; and if difficulties was made, I've not been brought up, and edicated as one may say, in the woods, without knowing how to look 'em down."

Judith made no answer for some little time. All her feelings as a woman, and as a woman who, for the first time in her life was beginning to submit to that sentiment which has so much influence on the happiness or misery of her sex, revolted at the cruel fate that she fancied Deerslayer was drawing down upon himself, while the sense of right, which God has implanted in every human breast, told her to admire an integrity as indomitable and as unpretending as that which the other so unconsciously displayed. Argument, she felt would be useless, nor was she, at that moment, disposed to lessen the dignity and high principle that were so striking in the intentions of the hunter, by any attempt to turn him from his purpose. That something might yet occur to supersede the necessity for this self immolation she tried to hope, and then she proceeded to ascertain the facts in order that her own conduct might be regulated by her knowledge of circumstances.

"When is your furlough out, Deerslayer," she asked, after both canoes were heading towards the Ark, and moving, with scarcely a perceptible effort of the paddles, through the water.

"To-morrow noon; not a minute afore; and you may depend

on it, Judith, I shan't quit what I call christian company, to go and give myself up to them vagabonds, an instant sooner than is downright necessary. They begin to fear a visit from the garrisons, and would n't lengthen the time a moment, and it's pretty well understood atween us, that, should I fail in my ar'n'd, the torments are to take place when the sun begins to fall, that they may strike upon their home trail as soon as it is dark."

This was said solemnly, as if the thought of what was believed to be in reserve duly weighed on the prisoner's mind, and yet so simply, and without a parade of suffering, as rather to repel than to invite any open manifestations of sympathy.

"Are they bent on revenging their losses?" Judith asked faintly, her own high spirit yielding to the influence of the other's quiet but dignified integrity of purpose.

"Downright, if I can judge of Indian inclinations, by the symptoms. They think howsever I do n't suspect their designs, I do believe, but one that has lived so long among men of red skin gifts, is no more likely to be misled in Injin feelin's, than a true hunter is like to lose his trail, or a stanch hound his scent. My own judgment is greatly ag'in my own escape, for I see the women are a good deal enraged on behalf of Hist, though I say it, perhaps, that should n't say it, seein' that I had a considerable hand myself in getting the gal off. Then there was a cruel murder in their camp last night, and that shot might just as well have been fired into my breast. Howsever, come what will, the Sarpent and his wife will be safe, and that is some happiness in any case."

"Oh! Deerslayer, they will think better of this, since they have given you until to-morrow noon to make up your mind!"

"I judge not, Judith; yes, I judge not. An Injin is an Injin, gal, and it's pretty much hopeless to think of swarving him, when he's got the scent and follows it with his nose in the air. The Delawares, now, are a half christianized tribe — not that I think such sort of christians much better than your whole blooded onbelievers — but, nevertheless, what good half christianizing can do to a man, some among 'em have got, and yet revenge clings to their hearts like the wild creepers here to the tree! Then, I slew one of the best and boldest of their warriors, they say, and it *is* too much to expect that they should captivate the man who did this deed, in the very same scouting on which it was performed, and they take no account of the matter. Had a month, or so, gone by, their feelin's would have been softened down, and we might have met in a more friendly way, but it is, as it is, Judith, this is talking of nothing but myself, and my own consarns, when you have had trouble enough, and may want to consult a fri'nd a little about your own matters. Is the old man laid in the water, where I should think his body would like to rest?"

"It is, Deerslayer," answered Judith, almost inaudibly. "That duty has just been performed. You are right in thinking that I wish to consult a friend; and that friend is yourself. Hurry Harry is about to leave us; when he is gone, and we have got a little over the feelings of this solemn office, I hope you will give me an hour alone. Hetty and I are at a loss what to do."

"That's quite nat'ral, coming as things have, suddenly and fearfully. But here's the Ark, and we'll say more of this, when there is a better opportunity."

Chapter XXIII.

"The winde is great upon the highest hilles;
The quiet life is in the dale below;
Who tread on ice shall slide against their willes;
They want not cares, that curious arts should know.
Who lives at ease and can content him so,
Is perfect wise, and sets us all to schoole:
Who hates this lore may well be called a foole."
                    Thomas Churchyard, "Shore's Wife," xlvii.

T H E meeting between Deerslayer and his friends in the Ark was grave and anxious. The two Indians, in particular, read in his manner that he was not a successful fugitive, and a few sententious words sufficed to let them comprehend the nature of what their friend had termed his 'furlough.' Chingachgook immediately became thoughtful, while Hist, as usual, had no better mode of expressing her sympathy than by those little attentions which mark the affectionate manner of woman.

In a few minutes, however, something like a general plan for the proceedings of the night was adopted, and to the eye of an uninstructed observer things would be thought to move in their ordinary train. It was now getting to be dark, and it was decided to sweep the Ark up to the castle, and secure it in its ordinary berth. This decision was come to, in some measure on account of the fact that all the canoes were again in the possession of their proper owners, but principally, from the security that was created by the representations of Deerslayer. He had examined the state of things among the Hurons, and felt satisfied that they meditated no further hostilities during the night, the loss they had met having indisposed them to further exertions for the moment. Then, he had a proposition to make; the object of his visit; and, if this were accepted, the war would at once terminate between the parties; and it was improbable that the Hurons would anticipate the failure of a project on which their chiefs had apparently set their hearts, by having recourse to violence previously to the return of their messenger.

As soon as the Ark was properly secured, the different members of the party occupied themselves in their several peculiar manners, haste in council, or in decision, no more characterizing the proceedings of these border whites, than it did those of their red neighbors. The women busied themselves in preparations for the evening meal, sad and silent, but ever attentive to the first wants of nature. Hurry set about repairing his moccasins, by the light of a blazing knot; Chingachgook seated himself in gloomy thought, while Deerslayer proceeded, in a manner equally free from affectation and concern, to examine 'Killdeer', the rifle of Hutter that has been already mentioned, and which subsequently became so celebrated, in the hands of the individual who was now making a survey of its merits. The piece was a little longer than usual, and had evidently been turned out from the work shops of some manufacturer of a superior order. It had a few silver ornaments, though, on the whole, it would have been deemed a plain piece by most frontier men, its great merit consisting in the accuracy of its bore, the perfection of the details, and the excellence of the metal. Again and again did the hunter apply the breech to his shoulder, and glance his eye along the sights, and as often did he poise his body and raise the weapon slowly, as if about to catch an aim at a deer, in order to try the weight, and to ascertain its fitness for quick and accurate firing. All this was done, by the aid of Hurry's torch, simply, but with an earnestness and abstraction that would have been found touching by any spectator who happened to know the real situation of the man.

" 'Tis a glorious we'pon, Hurry!" Deerslayer at length exclaimed, "and it may be thought a pity that it has fallen into the hands of women. The hunters have told me of its expl'ites, and by all I have heard, I should set it down as sartain death in exper'enced hands. Hearken to the tick of this lock — a wolf trap has'n't a livelier spring; pan and cock speak together, like two singing masters undertaking a psalm in meetin'. I never *did* see so true a bore, Hurry, that's sartain!"

"Ay, Old Tom used to give the piece a character, though he

was n't the man to particularize the ra'al natur' of any sort of fire arms, in practise," returned March, passing the deer's thongs through the moccasin with the coolness of a cobbler. "He was no marksman, that we must all allow; but he had his good p'ints, as well as his bad ones. I have had hopes that Judith might consait the idee of giving Killdeer to me."

"There's no saying what young women may do, that's a truth, Hurry, and I suppose you're as likely to own the rifle as another. Still, when things are so very near perfection, it's a pity not to reach it entirely."

"What do you mean by that? — Would not that piece look as well on my shoulder, as on any man's?"

"As for looks, I say nothing. You are both good-looking, and might make what is called a good-looking couple. But the true p'int is as to conduct. More deer would fall in one day, by that piece, in some man's hands, than would fall in a week in your'n, Hurry! I've seen you try; yes, remember the buck t'other day."

"That buck was out of season, and who wishes to kill venison out of season. I was merely trying to frighten the creatur', and I think you will own that he was pretty well skeared, at any rate."

"Well, well, have it as you say. But this is a lordly piece, and would make a steady hand and quick eye the King of the Woods!"

"Then keep it, Deerslayer, and become King of the Woods," said Judith, earnestly, who had heard the conversation, and whose eye was never long averted from the honest countenance of the hunter. "It can never be in better hands than it is, at this moment, and there I hope it will remain these fifty years."

"Judith you can't be in 'arnest!" exclaimed Deerslayer, taken so much by surprise, as to betray more emotion than it was usual for him to manifest on ordinary occasions. "Such a gift would be fit for a ra'al King to make; yes, and for a ra'al King to receive."

"I never was more in earnest, in my life, Deerslayer, and I am as much in earnest in the wish as in the gift."

"Well, gal, well; we'll find time to talk of this ag'in. You must n't be down hearted, Hurry, for Judith is a sprightly young woman, and she has a quick reason; she knows that the credit of her father's rifle is safer in my hands, than it can possibly be in yourn; and, therefore, you must n't be down hearted. In other matters, more to your liking, too, you'll find she'll give you the preference."

Hurry growled out his dissatisfaction, but he was too intent on quitting the lake, and in making his preparations, to waste his breath on a subject of this nature. Shortly after, the supper was ready, and it was eaten in silence, as is so much the habit of those who consider the table as merely a place of animal refreshment. On this occasion, however, sadness and thought contributed their share to the general desire not to converse, for Deerslayer was so far an exception to the usages of men of his cast, as not only to wish to hold discourse on such occasions, but as often to create a similar desire in his companions.

The meal ended, and the humble preparations removed, the whole party assembled on the platform to hear the expected intelligence from Deerslayer on the subject of his visit. It had been evident he was in no haste to make his communication, but the feelings of Judith would no longer admit of delay. Stools were brought from the Ark and the hut, and the whole six placed themselves in a circle, near the door, watching each other's countenances, as best they could, by the scanty means that were furnished by a lovely star-light night. Along the shores, beneath the mountains, lay the usual body of gloom, but in the broad lake no shadow was cast, and a thousand mimic stars were dancing in the limpid element, that was just stirred enough by the evening air to set them all in motion.

"Now, Deerslayer," commenced Judith, whose impatience resisted further restraint—"now, Deerslayer, tell us all the Hurons have to say, and the reason why they have sent you on parole, to make us some offer."

"Furlough, Judith; furlough is the word; and it carries the same meaning with a captyve at large, as it does with a soldier who has leave to quit his colors. In both cases the word is past to come back, and now I remember to have heard that's the ra'al signification; 'furlough' meaning a 'word' passed for the doing of any thing of the like. Parole I rather think is Dutch, and has something to do with the tattoos of the garrisons. But this makes no great difference, since the vartue of a pledge lies in the idee, and not in the word. Well, then, if the message must be given, it must; and perhaps there is no use in putting it off. Hurry will soon be wanting to set out on his journey to the river, and the stars rise and set, just as if they cared for neither Injin nor message. Ah's! me; 'Tis n't a pleasant, and I know it's a useless ar'n'd, but it must be told."

"Harkee, Deerslayer," put in Hurry, a little authoritatively — "You're a sensible man in a hunt, and as good a fellow on a march, as a sixty-miler-a-day could wish to meet with, but you're oncommon slow about messages; especially them that you think won't be likely to be well received. When a thing is to be told, why tell it; and do n't hang back like a Yankee lawyer pretending he can't understand a Dutchman's English, just to get a double fee out of him."

"I understand you, Hurry, and well are you named to-night, seeing you've no time to lose. But let us come at once to the p'int, seeing that's the object of this council — for council it may be called, though women have seats among us. The simple fact is this. When the party came back from the castle, the Mingos held a council, and bitter thoughts were uppermost, as was plain to be seen by their gloomy faces. No one likes to be beaten, and a red skin, as little as a pale face. Well, when they had smoked upon it, and made their speeches, and their council fire had burnt low, the matter came out. It seems the elders among 'em consaited I was a man to be trusted on a furlough — They're wonderful obsarvant, them Mingos; *that* their worst inimies must allow — but they consaited I was such a man; and it is n't often —" added the hunter, with a pleasing consciousness that his previous life justified this implicit reliance on his good faith — "it is'n't often they consait any thing so good of a pale face; but so they did with me, and, therefore, they did n't hesitate to speak their minds, which is just this: — You see the state of things. The lake, and all on it, they fancy, lie at their marcy. Thomas Hutter is deceased, and, as for Hurry, they've got the idee he has been near enough to death to-day, not to wish to take another look at him, this summer. Therefore, they account all your forces as reduced to Chingach-gook and the two young women, and, while they know the Delaware to be of a high race, and a born warrior, they know he's now on his first war path. As for the gals, of course they set them down much as they do women in gin'ral."

"You mean that they despise us!" interrupted Judith, with eyes that flashed so brightly as to be observed by all present.

"That will be seen in the ind. They hold that all on the lake lies at their marcy, and, therefore, they send by me this belt of wampum," showing the article in question to the Delaware, as he spoke, "with these words. 'Tell the Sarpent, they say, that he has done well for a beginner; he may now strike across the mountains, for his own villages, and no one shall look for his trail. If he has found a scalp, let him take it with him, for the Huron braves have hearts, and can feel for a young warrior who does n't wish to go home empty-handed. If he is nimble, he is welcome to lead out a party in pursuit. Hist, howsever, must go back to the Hurons, for, when she left them in the night, she carried away, by mistake, that which does n't belong to her—"

"That *can't* be true!" said Hetty earnestly. "Hist is no such girl, but one that gives every body his due—"

How much more she would have said, in remonstrance, cannot be known, inasmuch as Hist, partly laughing, and partly hiding her face in shame, past her own hand across the speaker's mouth, in a way to check the words.

"You do n't understand Mingo messages, poor Hetty—" resumed Deerslayer, "which seldom mean what lies exactly uppermost. Hist has brought away with her the inclinations of a young Huron, and they want her back again, that the poor young man may find them where he last saw them! The Sarpent they say is too promising a young warrior not to find as many wives as he wants, but this one he cannot have. That's their meaning, and nothing else, as I understand it."

"They are very obliging and thoughtful, in supposing a young woman can forget all her own inclinations in order to let this unhappy youth find his!" said Judith, ironically; though her manner became more bitter as she proceeded. "I suppose a woman is a woman, let her colour be white, or red, and your chiefs know little of a woman's heart, Deerslayer, if they think it can ever forgive when wronged, or ever forget when it fairly loves."

"I suppose that's pretty much the truth, with some women, Judith, though I've known them that could do both. The next message is to you. They say the Muskrat, as they called your father, has dove to the bottom of the lake; that he will never come up again, and that his young will soon be in want of wigwams if not of food. The Huron huts they think, are better than the huts of York, and they wish you to come and try them. Your colour is white, they own, but they think young women who've lived so long in the woods, would lose their way in the clearin's. A great warrior among them, has lately lost his wife, and he would be glad to put the Wild Rose on her bench at his fireside. As for the Feeble Mind, she will always be honored and taken care of by red warriors. Your father's goods they think ought to go to enrich the tribe, but your own property, which is to include every thing of a female natur', will go like that of all wives, into the wigwam of the husband. Moreover, they've lost a young maiden by violence, lately, and 'twill take two pale faces to fill her seat."

"And do *you* bring such a message to *me!*" exclaimed Judith, though the tone in which the words were uttered, had more in it of sorrow than of anger. "Am I a girl to be an Indian's slave?"

"If you wish my honest thoughts on this p'int, Judith, I shall answer that I do n't think you'll, willingly, ever become any man's slave; red-skin or white. You're not to think hard, howsever, of my bringing the message, as near as I could, in the very words in which it was given to me. Them was the conditions on which I got my furlough, and a bargain is a bargain, though it is made with a vagabond. I've told you what *they've* said, but I've not yet told you what I think you ought, one and all, to answer."

"Ay; let's hear that, Deerslayer," put in Hurry. "My cur'osity is up on that consideration, and I should like, right well, to hear your ideas of the reasonableness of the reply. For my part, though, my own mind is pretty much settled, on the p'int of my own answer, which shall be made known as soon as necessary."

"And so is mine, Hurry, on all the different heads, and on no one is it more sartainly settled that on yourn. If I was you, I should say — 'Deerslayer, tell them scamps, they don't know Harry March! He is human; and having a white skin, he has also a white natur', which natur' won't let him desart females of his own race and gifts, in their greatest need. So set me down as one that will refuse to come into your treaty, though you should smoke a hogshead of tobacco over it.' "

March was a little embarrassed at this rebuke, which was uttered with sufficient warmth of manner, and with a point that left no doubt of the meaning. Had Judith encouraged him, he would not have hesitated about remaining to defend her and her sister, but under the circumstances, a feeling of resentment rather urged him to abandon them. At all events, there was not a sufficiency of chivalry in Hurry Harry to induce him to hazard the safety of his own person, unless he could see a direct connection between the probable consequences and his own interests. It is no wonder, therefore, that his answer partook equally of his intention, and of the reliance he so boastingly placed on his gigantic strength, which if it did not always make him courageous, usually made him impudent, as respects those with whom he conversed.

"Fair words make long friendships, Master Deerslayer," he said a little menacingly. "You're but a stripling and, you know by exper'ence, what you are in the hands of a man. As you're not me, but only a go between, sent by the savages to us christians, you may tell your emply'ers that they do know Harry March, which is a proof of their sense, as well as his. He's human enough to follow human natur', and that tells him to see the folly of one man's fighting a whole tribe. If females desart him, they must expect to be desarted *by* him, whether they're of his own gifts, or another man's gifts. Should Judith see fit to change her mind, she's welcome to my company to the river, and Hetty with her; but should n't she come to this conclusion, I start as soon as I think the enemy's scouts are beginning to nestle themselves in among the brush and leaves, for the night."

"Judith will *not* change her mind, and she does not ask your company, Master March," returned the girl, with spirit.

"That p'int's settled, then," resumed Deerslayer, unmoved by the other's warmth. "Hurry Harry must act for himself, and do that which will be most likely to suit his own fancy. The course he means to take will give him an easy race, if it don't give him an easy conscience. Next comes the question with

Hist—what say you gal?—Will you desart your duty, too, and go back to the Mingos and take a Huron husband, and all not for the love of the man you're to marry, but for the love of your own scalp?"

"Why you talk so to Hist!" demanded the girl half-offended. "You t'ink a red-skin girl made like captain's lady, to laugh and joke with any officer that come."

"What I think, Hist, is neither here nor there, in this matter. I must carry back your answer, and in order to do so it is necessary that you should send it. A faithful messenger gives his ar'n'd, word for word."

Hist no longer hesitated to speak her mind fully. In the excitement she rose from her bench, and naturally recurring to that language in which she expressed herself the most readily, she delivered her thoughts and intentions, beautifully and with dignity, in the tongue of her own people.

"Tell the Hurons, Deerslayer," she said, "that they are as ignorant as moles; they do n't know the wolf from the dog. Among my people, the rose dies on the stem where it budded, the tears of the child fall on the graves of its parents; the corn grows where the seed has been planted. The Delaware girls are not messengers to be sent, like belts of wampum, from tribe to tribe. They are honeysuckles, that are sweetest in their own woods; their own young men carry them away in their bosoms, because they are fragrant; they are sweetest when plucked from their native stems. Even the robin and the martin come back, year after year, to their old nests; shall a woman be less true hearted than a bird? Set the pine in the clay and it will turn yellow; the willow will not flourish on the hill; the tamarack is healthiest in the swamp; the tribes of the sea love best to hear the winds that blow over the salt water. As for a Huron youth, what is he to a maiden of the Lenni Lenape. He may be fleet, but her eyes to not follow him in the race; they look back towards the lodges of the Delawares. He may sing a sweet song for the girls of Canada, but there is no music for Wah, but in the tongue she has listened to from childhood. Were the Huron born of the people that once owned the shores of the salt lake, it would be in vain, unless he were of the family of Uncas. The young pine will rise to be as high as any of its fathers. Wah-ta!-Wah has but one heart, and it can love but one husband."

Deerslayer listened to this characteristic message, which was given with an earnestness suited to the feelings from which it sprung, with undisguised delight, meeting the ardent eloquence of the girl, as she concluded, with one of his own heart-felt, silent, and peculiar fits of laughter.

"That's worth all the wampum in the woods!" he exclaimed. "You don't understand it, I suppose, Judith, but if you'll look into your feelin's, and fancy that an inimy had sent to tell you to give up the man of your ch'ice, and to take up with another that was n't the man of your ch'ice, you'll get the substance of it, I'll warrant! Give me a woman for ra'al eloquence, if they'll only make up their minds to speak what they *feel*. By speakin', I do n't mean chatterin', howsever; for most of them will do *that* by the hour; but comin' out with their honest, deepest, feelin's in proper words. And now, Judith, having got the answer of a red skin girl, it is fit I should get that of a pale face, if, indeed, a countenance that is as blooming as your'n can in any wise, so be tarmed. You are well named the Wild Rose, and so far as colour goes, Hetty ought to be called the Honeysuckle."

"Did this language come from one of the garrison gallants, I should deride it, Deerslayer, but coming from *you*, I know it can be depended on," returned Judith, deeply gratified by his unmeditated and characteristic compliments. "It is too soon, however, to ask my answer; the Great Serpent has not yet spoken."

"The Sarpent! Lord; I could carry back his speech without hearing a word of it! I did n't think of putting the question to him at all, I will allow; though 'twould be hardly right either, seeing that truth is truth, and I'm bound to tell these Mingos the fact and nothing else. So, Chingachgook, let us hear *your* mind on this matter—are you inclined to strike across the hills towards your village, to give up Hist to a Huron, and to tell the chiefs at home, that, if they're act*y*ve and successful, they may possibly get *on* the end of the Iroquois trail some two or three days a'ter the inimy has got *off* of it?"

Like his betrothed, the young chief arose, that his answer might be given with due distinctness and dignity. Hist had

spoken with her hands crossed upon her bosom, as if to suppress the emotions within, but the warrior stretched an arm
before him with a calm energy that aided in giving emphasis to
his expressions.

"Wampum should be sent for wampum," he said; "a
message must be answered by a message. Hear what the Great
Serpent of the Delawares has to say to the pretended wolves
from the great lakes, that are howling through our woods.
They are no wolves; they are dogs that have come to get their
tails and ears cropped by the hands of the Delawares. They are
good at stealing young women; bad at keeping them. Chingachgook takes his own where he finds it; he asks leave of no
cur from the Canadas. If he has a tender feeling in his heart, it
is no business of the Hurons. He tells it to her who most likes
to know it; he will not bellow it in the forest, for the ears of
those that only understand yells of terror. What passes in his
lodge is not for the chiefs of his own people to know; still less
for Mingo rogues —"

"Call 'em vagabonds, Sarpent —" interrupted Deerslayer,
unable to restrain his delight — "yes, just call 'em up-and-down
vagabonds, which is a word easily intarpreted, and the most
hateful of all to their ears, it's so true. Never fear me; I'll give
'em your message, syllable for syllable, sneer for sneer, idee for
idee, scorn for scorn, and they desarve no better at your
hands — only call 'em vagabonds, once or twice, and that will set
the sap mounting in 'em, from their lowest roots to the uppermost branches!"

"Still less for Mingo vagabonds," resumed Chingachgook,
quite willingly complying with his friend's request. "Tell the
Huron dogs to howl louder, if they wish a Delaware to find
them in the woods, where they burrow like foxes, instead of
hunting like warriors. When they had a Delaware maiden in
their camp, there was a reason for hunting them up; now they
will be forgotten unless they make a noise. Chingachgook do
n't like the trouble of going to his villages for more warriors; he
can strike their run-a-way trail; unless they hide it under
ground, he will follow it to Canada alone. He will keep Wah-
ta!-Wah with him to cook his game; they two will be
Delawares enough to scare all the Hurons back to their own
country."

"That's a grand despatch, as the officers call them things!" cried Deerslayer; "twill set all the Huron blood in motion; most particularily that part where he tells 'em Hist, too, will keep on their heels, 'till they're fairly driven out of the country. Ahs! me; big words arn't always big deeds, notwithstanding! The Lord send that we be able to be only one half as good as we promise to be! And now, Judith, it's your turn to speak, for them miscreants will expect an answer from each person, poor Hetty, perhaps, excepted."

"And why not Hetty, Deerslayer? She often speaks to the purpose; the Indians may respect her words, for they feel for people in her condition."

"That is true, Judith, and quick-thoughted in you. The red-skins *do* respect misfortunes of all kinds, and Hetty's in particular. So, Hetty, if you have any thing to say, I'll carry it to the Hurons as faithfully as if it was spoken by a schoolmaster, or a missionary."

The girl hesitated a moment, and then she answered in her own gentle, soft, tones, as earnestly as any who had preceded her.

"The Hurons can't understand the difference between white people and themselves," she said, "or they would n't ask Judith and me to go and live in their villages. God has given one country to the red men and another to us. He meant us to live apart. Then mother always said that we should never dwell with any but christians, if possible, and *that* is a reason why we can't go. This lake is ours, and we wo'n't leave it. Father and mother's graves are in it, and even the worst Indians love to stay near the graves of their fathers. I will come and see them, again, if they wish me to, and read more out of the bible to them, but I can't quit father's and mother's graves."

"That will do—that will do, Hetty, just as well as if you sent them a message twice as long," interrupted the hunter. "I'll tell 'em all you've said, and all you mean, and I'll answer for it, that they'll be easily satisfied. Now, Judith, your turn comes next, and then this part of my ar'n'd will be tarminated, for the night."

Judith manifested a reluctance to give her reply, that had awakened a little curiosity in the messenger. Judging from her known spirit, he had never supposed the girl would be less true to her feelings and principles than Hist, or Hetty, and yet there was a visible wavering of purpose that rendered him slightly uneasy. Even now when directly required to speak, she seemed to hesitate, nor did she open her lips, until the profound silence told her how anxiously her words were expected. Then, indeed, she spoke, but it was doubtingly and with reluctance.

"Tell me, first — tell *us*, first, Deerslayer," she commenced, repeating the words merely to change the emphasis — "what effect will our answers have on *your* fate? If you are to be the sacrifice of our spirit, it would have been better had we all been more wary as to the language we use. What, then, are likely to be the consequences to yourself?"

"Lord, Judith, you might as well ask me which way the wind will blow next week, or what will be the age of the next deer that will be shot! I can only say that their faces look a little dark upon me, but it does n't thunder every time a black cloud rises, nor does every puff of wind blow up rain. That's a question, therefore, much more easily put than answered."

"So is this message of the Iroquois to me," answered Judith rising, as if she had determined on her own course for the present. "My answer shall be given, Deerslayer, after you and I have talked together alone, when the others have laid themselves down for the night."

There was a decision in the manner of the girl, that disposed Deerslayer to comply, and this he did the more readily as the delay could produce no material consequences, one way or the other. The meeting now broke up, Hurry announcing his resolution to leave them speedily. During the hour that was suffered to intervene, in order that the darkness might deepen, before the frontier-man took his departure, the different individuals occupied themselves in their customary modes, the hunter, in particular, passing most of the time in making further enquiries into the perfection of the rifle already mentioned.

The hour of nine soon arrived, however, and then it had been determined that Hurry should commence his journey. Instead of making his adieus frankly, and in a generous spirit, the little he thought it necessary to say was uttered sullenly and in coldness. Resentment at what he considered Judith's obstinacy, was blended with mortification at the career he had run, since reaching the lake, and, as is usual with the vulgar and narrow-minded, he was more disposed to reproach others with his failures, than to censure himself. Judith gave him her hand, but it was quite as much in gladness, as with regret, while the two Delawares were not sorry to find he was leaving them. Of the whole party, Hetty alone betrayed any real feeling. Bashfulness, and the timidity of her sex and character, kept even her aloof, so that Hurry entered the canoe, where Deerslayer was already waiting for him, before she ventured near enough to be observed. Then, indeed, the girl came into the Ark, and approached its end, just as the little bark was turning from it, with a movement so light and steady as to be almost imperceptible. An impulse of feeling now overcame her timidity, and Hetty spoke.

"Good bye, Hurry—" she called out, in her sweet voice— "good bye, dear Hurry. Take care of yourself in the woods, and do n't stop once, 'till you reach the garrison. The leaves on the trees are scarcely plentier than the Hurons round the lake, and they'll not treat a strong man like you, as kindly as they treat me."

The ascendency which March had obtained over this feeble-minded, but right-thinking, and right-feeling girl, arose from a law of nature. Her senses had been captivated by his personal advantages, and her moral communications with him had never been sufficiently intimate to counteract an effect that must have been otherwise lessened, even with one whose mind was as obtuse as her own. Hetty's instinct of right, if such a term can be applied to one who seemed taught by some kind spirit how to steer her course with unerring accuracy, between good and evil, would have revolted at Hurry's character, on a thousand points, had there been opportunities to enlighten her, but while he conversed and trifled with her sister, at a distance from herself, his perfection of form and feature had been left to produce their influence on her simple imagination, and naturally tender feelings, without suffering by the alloy of his opinions and coarseness. It is true, she found him rough and rude; but her father was that, and most of the other men she had seen, and that which she believed to belong to all of the sex, struck her less unfavorably in Hurry's character, than it might otherwise have done. Still, it was not absolutely love that Hetty felt for Hurry, nor do we wish so to portray it, but merely that awakening sensibility and admiration, which, under more propitious circumstances, and always supposing no untoward revelations of character on the part of the young man, had supervened to prevent it, might soon have ripened into that engrossing feeling. She felt for him an incipient tenderness, but scarcely any passion. Perhaps the nearest approach to the latter, that Hetty had manifested, was to be seen in the sensitiveness which had caused her to detect March's predilection for her sister, for, among Judith's many admirers, this was the only instance in which the dull mind of the girl had been quickened into an observation of the circumstances.

Hurry received so little sympathy at his departure, that the gentle tones of Hetty, as she thus called after him, sounded soothingly. He checked the canoe, and with one sweep of his powerful arm brought it back to the side of the Ark. This was more than Hetty, whose courage had risen with the departure of her hero, expected, and she now shrunk timidly back at this unexpected return.

"You're a good gal, Hetty, and I can't quit you without shaking hands," said March kindly. "Judith, a'ter all, is n't worth as much as you, though she may be a trifle better looking. As to wits, if honesty and fair dealing with a young man is a sign of sense in a young woman, you're worth a dozen Judiths; ay, and for that matter, most young women of my acquaintance."

"Don't say any thing against Judith, Harry," returned Hetty imploringly. "Father's gone, and mother's gone, and nobody's left but Judith and me, and it is n't right for sisters to speak evil, or to hear evil of each other. Father's in the lake, and so is mother, and we should all fear God, for we do n't know when we may be in the lake, too."

"That sounds reasonable, child, as does most you say. Well, if we ever meet ag'in, Hetty, you'll find a fri'nd in me, let your sister do what she may. I was no great fri'nd of your mother I'll allow, for we did n't think alike on most p'ints, but then your father, Old Tom, and I, fitted each other as remarkably as a buckskin garment will fit any reasonable-built man. I've always been unanimous of opinion that Old Floating Tom Hutter, at the bottom, was a good fellow, and will maintain that ag'in all inimies for his sake, as well as for your'n."

"Good bye, Hurry," said Hetty, who now wanted to hasten the young man off, as ardently as she had wished to keep him only the moment before, though she could give no clearer account of the latter than of the former feeling; "good bye, Hurry; take care of yourself in the woods; do n't halt 'till you reach the garrison. I'll read a chapter in the bible for you, before I go to bed, and think of you in my prayers."

This was touching a point on which March had no sympathies, and without more words, he shook the girl cordially by the hand, and re-entered the canoe. In another minute the two adventurers were a hundred feet from the Ark, and half a dozen had not elapsed before they were completely lost to view. Hetty sighed deeply, and rejoined her sister and Hist.

For some time Deerslayer and his companion paddled ahead in silence. It had been determined to land Hurry at the precise point where he is represented, in the commencement of our tale, as having embarked, not only as a place little likely to be watched by the Hurons, but because he was sufficiently familiar with the signs of the woods, at that spot, to thread his way through them in the dark. Thither, then, the light craft proceeded, being urged as diligently, and as swiftly, as two vigorous and skilful canoe-men could force their little vessel through, or rather *over*, the water. Less than a quarter of an hour sufficed for the object, and, at the end of that time, being within the shadows of the shore, and quite near the point they sought, each ceased his efforts in order to make their parting communications out of ear shot of any straggler who might happen to be in the neighborhood.

"You will do well to persuade the officers at the garrison to lead out a party ag'in these vagabonds, as soon as you git in, Hurry," Deerslayer commenced; "and you'll do better if you volunteer to guide it up yourself. You know the paths, and the shape of the lake, and the natur' of the land, and can do it better than a common, gin'ralizing scout. Strike at the Huron camp first, and follow the signs that will then show themselves. A few looks at the hut and the Ark will satisfy you, as to the state of the Delaware and the women, and, at any rate, there'll be a fine opportunity to fall on the Mingo trail, and to make a mark on the memories of the blackguards that they'll be apt to carry with 'em a long time. It won't be likely to make much difference with me, since *that* matter will be detarmined afore to-morrow's sun has set, but it may make a great change in Judith and Hetty's hopes and prospects!"

"And as for yourself, Nathaniel," Hurry enquired with more interest than he was accustomed to betray in the welfare of others — "And, as for yourself, what do you think is likely to turn up?"

"The Lord, in his wisdom, only can tell, Henry March! The clouds look black and threatening, and I keep my mind in a state to meet the worst. Vengeful feelin's are uppermost in the hearts of the Mingos, and any little disapp'intment about the plunder, or the prisoners, or Hist, may make the torments sartain. The Lord, in his wisdom, can only detarmine my fate, or yourn!"

"This is a black business, and ought to be put a stop to in some way or other — " answered Hurry, confounding the distinctions between right and wrong, as is usual with selfish and vulgar men. "I heartily wish old Hutter and I had scalped every creatur' in their camp, the night we first landed with that capital object! Had you not held back, Deerslayer, it might have been done, and then you would n't have found yourself, at the last moment, in the desperate condition you mention."

"'Twould have been better had you said, you wished you had never attempted to do what it little becomes any white man's gifts to undertake; in which case, not only might we have kept from coming to blows, but Thomas Hutter would now have been living, and the hearts of the savages would be less given to vengeance. The death of that young woman, too, was on-called for, Henry March, and leaves a heavy load on our names if not on our consciences!"

This was so apparent, and it seemed so obvious to Hurry himself, at the moment, that he dashed his paddle into the water, and began to urge the canoe towards the shore, as if bent only on running away from his own lively remorse. His companion humoured this feverish desire for change, and, in a minute or two, the bows of the boat grated lightly on the shingle of the beach. To land, shoulder his pack and rifle, and to get ready for his march occupied Hurry but an instant, and with a growling adieu, he had already commenced his march, when a sudden twinge of feeling brought him to a dead stop, and immediately after to the other's side.

"You cannot mean to give yourself up ag'in to them murdering savages, Deerslayer!" he said, quite as much in angry remonstrance, as with generous feeling. "Twould be the act of a madman or a fool!"

"There's them that thinks it madness to keep their words, and there's them that don't, Hurry Harry. You may be one of the first, but I'm one of the last. No red skin breathing shall have it in his power to say, that a Mingo minds his word more than a man of white blood and white gifts, in any thing that consarns me. I'm out on a furlough, and if I've strength and reason, I'll go in on a furlough afore noon to-morrow!"

"What's an Injin, or a word passed, or a furlough taken from creatur's like them, that have neither souls, nor reason!"

"If they've got neither souls nor reason, you and I have both, Henry March, and one is accountable for the other. This furlough is not, as you seem to think, a matter altogether atween me and the Mingos, seeing it is a solemn bargain made atween me and God. He who thinks that he can say what he pleases, in his distress, and that twill all pass for nothing, because 'tis uttered in the forest, and into red men's ears, knows little of his situation, and hopes, and wants. The woods are but the ears of the Almighty, the air is his breath, and the light of the sun is little more than a glance of his eye. Farewell, Harry; we may not meet ag'in, but I would wish you never to treat a furlough, or any other solemn thing, that your christian God has been called on to witness, as a duty so light that it may be forgotten according to the wants of the body, or even accordin' to the cravings of the spirit."

March was now glad again to escape. It was quite impossible that he could enter into the sentiments that ennobled his companion, and he broke away from both with an impatience that caused him secretly to curse the folly that could induce a man to rush, as it were, on his own destruction. Deerslayer, on the contrary, manifested no such excitement. Sustained by his principles, inflexible in the purpose of acting up to them, and superior to any unmanly apprehension, he regarded all before him, as a matter of course, and no more thought of making any unworthy attempt to avoid it, than a Mussulman thinks of counteracting the decrees of Providence. He stood calmly on the shore, listening to the reckless tread with which Hurry betrayed his progress through the bushes, shook his head in dissatisfaction at the want of caution, and then stepped quietly into his canoe. Before he dropped the paddle again into the water, the young man gazed about him, at the scene presented by the star-lit night. This was the spot where he had first laid his eyes on the beautiful sheet of water on which he floated. If it was then glorious in the bright light of a summer's noon-tide, it was now sad and melancholy under the shadows of night. The mountains rose around it like black barriers to exclude the outer world, and the gleams of pale light that rested on the broader parts of the basin, were no bad symbols of the faintness of the hopes that were so dimly visible in his own future. Sighing heavily, he pushed the canoe from the land, and took his way, back, with steady diligence towards the Ark and the castle.

Chapter XXIV.

"Thy secret pleasure turns to open shame;
Thy private feasting to a public fast;
Thy smoothing titles to a ragged name;
Thy sugar'd tongue to bitter worm wood taste:
Thy violent vanities can never last."
                    Shakespeare, *Rape of Lucrece*, 11.890-94.

JUDITH was waiting the return of Deerslayer on the platform, with stifled impatience, when the latter reached the hut. Hist and Hetty were both in a deep sleep, on the bed usually occupied by the two daughters of the house, and the Delaware was stretched on the floor of the adjoining room, his rifle at his side, and a blanket over him, already dreaming of the events of the last few days. There was a lamp burning in the Ark, for the family was accustomed to indulge in this luxury on extraordinary occasions, and possessed the means, the vessel being of a form and material to render it probable it had once been an occupant of the chest.

As soon as the girl got a glimpse of the canoe, she ceased her hurried walk up and down the platform, and stood ready to receive the young man, whose return she had now been anxiously expecting for some time. She helped him to fasten the canoe, and by aiding in the other little similar employments, manifested her desire to reach a moment of liberty as soon as possible. When this was done, in answer to an inquiry of his, she informed him of the manner in which their companions had disposed of themselves. He listened attentively, for the manner of the girl was so earnest and impressive as to apprise him that she had something on her mind of more than common concern.

"And now, Deerslayer," Judith continued, "you see I have lighted the lamp, and put it in the cabin of the Ark. That is never done with us, unless on great occasions, and I consider this night as the most important of my life. Will you follow me and see what I have to show you — hear what I have to say."

The hunter was a little surprised, but, making no objections, both were soon in the scow, and in the room that contained the light. Here two stools were placed at the side of the chest, with the lamp on another, and a table near by to receive the different articles as they might be brought to view. This arrangement had its rise in the feverish impatience of the girl, which could brook no delay that it was in her power to obviate. Even all the padlocks were removed, and it only remained to raise the heavy lid, again, to expose all the treasures of this long secreted hoard.

"I see, in part, what all this means," observed Deerslayer—"yes, I see through it, in part. But why is not Hetty present; now, Thomas Hutter is gone, she is one of the owners of these cur'osities, and ought to see them opened and handled."

"Hetty sleeps—" answered Judith, huskily. "Happily for her, fine clothes and riches have no charms. Besides she has this night given her share of all that the chest may hold, to me, that I may do with it as I please."

"Is poor Hetty composs enough for that, Judith?" demanded the just-minded young man. "It's a good rule, and a righteous one, never to take when them that give don't know the valie of their gifts; and such as god has visited heavily in their wits, ought to be dealt with as carefully as children that have n't yet come to their understandings."

Judith was hurt at this rebuke, coming from the person it did, but she would have felt it far more keenly had not her conscience fully acquitted her of any unjust intentions towards her feeble-minded but confiding sister. It was not a moment, however, to betray any of her usual mountings of the spirit, and she smothered the passing sensation in the desire to come to the great object she had in view.

"Hetty will not be wronged," she mildly answered; "she even knows not only what I am about to do, Deerslayer, but *why* I do it. So take your seat, raise the lid of the chest, and this time we will go to the bottom. I shall be disappointed if something is not found to tell us more of the history of Thomas Hutter and my mother."

"Why Thomas Hutter, Judith, and not your father? The dead ought to meet with as much reverence as the living!"

"I have long suspected that Thomas Hutter was not *my* father, though I did think he might have been Hetty's, but now we know he was the father of neither. He acknowledged that much in his dying moments. I am old enough to remember better things than we have seen on this lake, though they are so faintly impressed on my memory, that the earlier part of my life seems like a dream."

"Dreams are but miserable guides when one has to detarmine about realities, Judith," returned the other, admonishingly. "Fancy nothing, and hope nothing on their account, though I've known chiefs that thought 'em useful."

"I expect nothing for the future, from them, my good friend, but cannot help remembering what has been. This is idle, however, when half an hour of examination may tell us all, or even more than I want to know."

Deerslayer, who comprehended the girl's impatience, now took his seat, and proceeded once more to bring to light the different articles that the chest contained. As a matter of course, all that had been previously examined were found where they had been last deposited, and they excited much less interest, or comment, than when formerly exposed to view. Even Judith laid aside the rich brocade with an air of indifference, for she had a far higher aim before her than the indulgence of vanity, and was impatient to come at the still hidden, or rather unknown, treasures.

"All these we have seen before," she said, "and will not stop to open. The bundle under your hand, Deerslayer, is a fresh one; that we will look into. God send it may contain something to tell poor Hetty and myself, who we really are!"

"Ay, if some bundles could speak, they might tell wonderful secrets," returned the young man deliberately undoing the folds of another piece of coarse canvass, in order to come at the contents of the roll that lay on his knees: "though this doesn't seem to be one of that family, seeing 'tis neither more nor less than a sort of flag, though of what nation, it passes my l'arnin' to say."

"That flag must have some meaning to it—" Judith hurriedly interposed. "Open it wider, Deerslayer, that we may see the colours."

"Well, I pity the ensign that has to shoulder this cloth, and to parade it about on the field. Why 'tis large enough, Judith, to make a dozen of them colours the King's officers set so much store by. These can be no ensign's colours, but a gin'ral's!"

"A ship might carry it, Deerslayer, and ships I know do use such things. Have you never heard any fearful stories about Thomas Hutter's having once been concerned with the people they call buccaneers?"

"*Buck-ah-near*! Not I — not I — I never heard him mentioned as good at a buck far off, or near by. Hurry Harry did till me something about its being supposed that he had formerly, in some way or other, dealings with sartain sea robbers, but, Lord, Judith, it can't surely give you any satisfaction to make out that ag'in your mother's own husband, though he isn't your father."

"Any thing will give me satisfaction that tells me who I am, and helps to explain the dreams of childhood. My mother's husband! Yes, he must have been that, though why a woman like *her*, should have chosen a man like *him*, is more than mortal reason can explain. You never saw mother, Deerslayer, and can't feel the vast, vast difference there was between them!"

"Such things *do* happen, howsever; — yes, they *do* happen; though why providence lets them come to pass, is more than I understand. I've knew the f'ercest warriors with the gentlest wives of any in the tribe, and awful scolds fall to the lot of Injins fit to be missionaries."

"That was not it, Deerslayer; that was not it. Oh! if it should prove that — no; I can not wish she should not have been his wife at all. *That* no daughter can wish for her own mother! Go on, now, and let us see what the square looking bundle holds."

Deerslayer complied, and he found that it contained a small trunk of pretty workmanship, but fastened. The next point was to find a key; but, search proving ineffectual, it was determined to force the lock. This Deerslayer soon effected by the aid of an iron instrument, and it was found that the interior was nearly filled with papers. Many were letters; some fragments of manuscripts, memorandums, accounts, and other similar documents. The hawk does not pounce upon the chicken with a more sudden swoop, than Judith sprang forward to seize this mine of hitherto concealed knowledge. Her education, as the reader will have perceived, was far superior to her situation in life, and her eye glanced over page after page of the letters, with a readiness that her schooling supplied, and with an avidity that found its origin in her feelings. At first, it was evident that the girl was gratified; and we may add with reason, for the letters written by females, in innocence and affection, were of a character to cause her to feel proud of those with whom she had every reason to think she was closely connected by the ties of blood. It does not come within the scope of our plan to give more of these epistles, however, than a general idea of their contents, and this will best be done by describing the effect they produced on the manner, appearance, and feeling of her who was so eagerly perusing them.

It has been said, already, that Judith was much gratified with the letters that first met her eye. They contained the correspondence of an affectionate and intelligent mother, to an absent daughter, with such allusions to the answers, as served, in a great measure, to fill up the vacuum left by the replies. They were not without admonitions and warnings, however, and Judith felt the blood mounting to her temples, and a cold shudder succeeding, as she read one in which the propriety of the daughter's indulging in as much intimacy, as had evidently been described in one of the daughter's own letters, with an officer "who came from Europe, and who could hardly be supposed to wish to form an honorable connection in America," was rather coldly commented on by the mother. What rendered it singular, was the fact that the signatures had been carefully cut from every one of these letters, and wherever a name occurred in the body of the epistles, it had been erased with so much diligence as to render it impossible to read it. They had all been enclosed in envelopes, according to the fashion of the age, and not an address either was to be found. Still the letters themselves had been religiously preserved, and Judith thought she could discover traces of tears remaining on several. She now remembered to have seen the little trunk in her mother's keeping, previously to her death, and she supposed it had first been deposited in the chest, along with the other forgotten, or concealed objects, when the letters could no longer contribute to that parent's grief or happiness.

Next came another bundle, and these were filled with the

protestations of love, written with passion certainly, but also with that deceit which men so often think it justifiable to use to the other sex. Judith had shed tears abundantly over the first packet, but now she felt a sentiment of indignation and pride better sustaining her. Her hand shook, however, and cold shivers again passed through her frame, as she discovered a few points of strong resemblance between these letters and some it had been her own fate to receive. Once, indeed, she laid the packet down, bowed her head to her knees, and seemed nearly convulsed. All this time Deerslayer sat a silent, but attentive observer of every thing that passed. As Judith read a letter, she put it into his hands to hold, until she could peruse the next; but this served in no degree to enlighten her companion, as he was totally unable to read. Nevertheless he was not entirely at fault, in discovering the passions that were contending in the bosom of the fair creature by his side, and, as occasional sentences escaped her in murmurs, he was nearer the truth, in his divinations, or conjectures, than the girl would have been pleased at discovering.

Judith had commenced with the earliest letters, luckily for a ready comprehension of the tale they told, for they were carefully arranged in chronological order, and to any one who would take the trouble to peruse them, would have revealed a sad history of gratified passion, coldness, and finally of aversion. As she obtained the clue to their import, her impatience would not admit of delay, and she soon got to glancing her eyes over a page, by way of coming at the truth, in the briefest manner possible. By adopting this expedient, one to which all who are eager to arrive at results, without encumbering themselves with details, are so apt to resort, Judith made a rapid progress in these melancholy revelations of her mother's failing and punishment. She saw that the period of her own birth was distinctly referred to, and even learned that the homely name she bore, was given her by the father, of whose person she retained so faint an impression as to resemble a dream. This name was not obliterated from the text of the letters, but stood as if nothing was to be gained by erasing it. Hetty's birth was mentioned once, and in that instance the name was the mother's, but ere this period was reached came the signs of coldness, shadowing forth the desertion that was so soon to follow. It was in this stage of the correspondence that her mother had recourse to the plan of copying her own epistles. They were but few, but were eloquent with the feelings of blighted affection, and contrition. Judith sobbed over them, until again and again she felt compelled to lay them aside from sheer physical inability to see; her eyes being literally obscured with tears. Still she returned to the task, with increasing interest, and finally succeeded in reaching the end of the latest communication that had probably ever passed between her parents.

All this occupied fully an hour, for near a hundred letters were glanced at, and some twenty had been closely read. The truth now shone clear upon the acute mind of Judith, so far as her own birth and that of Hetty, were concerned. She sickened at the conviction, and for the moment the rest of the world seemed to be cut off from her, and she had now additional reasons for wishing to pass the remainder of her life on the lake, where she had already seen so many bright and so many sorrowing days.

There yet remained more letters to examine. Judith found these were a correspondence between her mother and Thomas Hovey. The originals of both parties were carefully arranged, letter and answer, side by side; and they told the early history of the connection between the ill-assorted pair far more plainly than Judith wished to learn it. Her mother made the advances towards a marriage, to the surprise, not to say horror of her daughter, and she actually found a relief when she discovered traces of what struck her as insanity – or a morbid desperation, bordering on that dire calamity — in the earlier letters of that ill-fated woman. The answers of Hovey were coarse and illiterate, though they manifested a sufficient desire to obtain the hand of a woman of singular personal attractions, and whose great error he was willing to overlook for the advantage of possessing one, every way so much his superior, and, who, it also appeared was not altogether destitute of money. The remainder of this part of the correspondence was brief, and it was soon confined to a few communications on business, in which the miserable wife hastened the absent husband in his preparations to abandon a world, which there was a sufficient reason to think was as dangerous to one of the parties, as it was disagreeable to the other. But a single expression had escaped her mother, by which Judith could get a clue to the motives that had induced her to marry Hovey, or Hutter, and this she found was that feeling of resentment which so often tempts the injured to inflict wrongs on themselves, by way of heaping coals on the heads of those through whom they have suffered. Judith had enough of the spirit of that mother, to comprehend this sentiment, and for a moment did she see the exceeding folly which permitted such revengeful feelings to get the ascendancy.

There, what may be called the historical part of the papers ceased. Among the loose fragments, however, was an old newspaper that contained a proclamation offering a reward for the apprehension of certain free-booters by name, among which was that of Thomas Hovey. The attention of the girl was drawn to the proclamation and to this particular name, by the circumstance that black lines had been drawn under both, in ink. Nothing else was found among the papers that could lead to a discovery of either the name or the place of residence of the wife of Hutter. All the dates, signatures, and addresses, had been cut from the letters, and wherever a word occurred in the body of the communications, that might furnish a clue, it was scrupulously erased. Thus Judith found all her hopes of ascertaining who her parents were, defeated, and she was obliged to fall back on her own resources and habits for every thing connected with the future. Her recollection of her mother's manners, conversation, and sufferings filled up many a gap in the historical facts she had now discovered, and the truth, in its outlines, stood sufficiently distinct before her, to take away all desire, indeed, to possess any more details. Throwing herself back in her seat, she simply desired her companion to finish the examination of the other articles in the chest, as it might yet contain something of importance.

"I'll do it, Judith; I'll do it," returned the patient Deerslayer, "but if there's many more letters to read, we shall see the sun ag'in, afore you've got through with the reading of them! Two good hours have you been looking at them bits of papers!"

"They tell me of my parents, Deerslayer, and have settled my plans for life. A girl may be excused who reads about her *own* father and mother, and that too for the first time in her life. I am sorry to have kept you waiting."

"Never mind me, gal, never mind me. It matters little

whether I sleep or watch; but, though you be pleasant to look at, and are so handsome, Judith, it is not altogether agreeable to sit so long to behold you shedding tears. I know that tears do n't kill, and that some people are better for shedding a few, now and then, especially women, but I'd rather see you smile, any time, Judith, than see you weep."

This gallant speech was rewarded with a sweet, though a melancholy smile, and then the girl again desired her companion to finish the examination of the chest. The search necessarily continued some time, during which Judith collected her thoughts, and regained her composure. She took no part in the search, leaving every thing to the young man, looking listlessly, herself, at the different articles that came uppermost. Nothing further of much interest, or value, however, was found. A sword or two, such as were then worn by gentlemen, some buckles of silver, or so richly plated as to appear silver, and a few handsome articles of female dress composed the principal discoveries. It struck both Judith and the Deerslayer notwithstanding, that some of these things might be made useful in effecting a negotiation with the Iroquois, though the latter saw a difficulty in the way that was not so apparent to the former. The conversation was first renewed in connection with this point.

"And now, Deerslayer," said Judith, "we may talk of yourself, and of the means of getting you out of the hands of the Hurons. Any part, or all of what you have seen in the chest will be cheerfully given by me and Hetty, to set you at liberty."

"Well, that's ginerous—yes, 'tis downright free-hearted, and free-handed, and ginerous. This is the way with women; when they take up a fri'ndship, they do nothing by halves, but are as willing to part with their property, as if it had no valie in their eyes. Howsever, while I thank you both, just as much as if the bargain was made, and Rivenoak, or any of the other vagabonds, was here to accept and close the treaty, there's two principal reasons why it can never come to pass, which may be as well told at once, in order no onlikely expectations may be raised in you, or any onjustifiable hopes in me."

"What reason *can* there be, if Hetty and I are willing to part with the trifles for your sake, and the savages are willing to receive them?"

"That's it, Judith—you've got the idees, but they're a little out of their places, as if a hound should take the back'ard instead of the leading scent. That the Mingos will be willing to receive them things, or any more like 'em, you may have to offer is probable enough, but whether they'll pay valie for 'em, is quite another matter. Ask yourself, Judith, if any one should send you a message to say that, for such or such a price, you and Hetty might have that chist and all it holds, whether you'd think it worth your while to waste many words on the bargain?"

"But this chest and all it holds, are already ours; there is no reason why we should purchase what is already our own."

"Just so the Mingos caculate! They say the chist is theirn, already; or, as good as theirn, and they'll not thank anybody for the key."

"I understand you, Deerslayer; surely we are yet in possession of the lake, and we can keep possession of it, until Hurry sends troops to drive off the enemy. This we may certainly do, provided you will stay with us, instead of going back and giving yourself up a prisoner, again, as you now seem determined on".

"That Hurry Harry should talk in thisaway, is nat'ral, and according to the gifts of the man. He knows no better, and, therefore, he is little likely to feel, or to act any better; but, Judith, I put it to your heart and conscience—would you, *could* you think of me as favorably, as I hope and believe you now do, was I to forget my furlough and not go back to the camp?"

"To think *more* favorably of you than I now do, Deerslayer, would not be easy; but I might continue to think *as* favorably—at least it seems so—I hope I could, for, a world would n't tempt me to let you do any thing that might change my real opinion of you."

"Then do n't try to entice me to overlook my furlough, gal!— A furlough is a sacred thing among warriors and men that carry their lives in their hands, as we of the forests do, and what a grievous disapp'intment would it be to old Tamenund, and to Uncas, the father of the Sarpent, and to my other fri'nds in the tribe, if I was so to disgrace myself, on my very first warpath? This you will pairceive, moreover, Judith, is without laying any stress on nat'ral gifts, and a white man's duties, to say nothing of conscience. The last is king with me, and I try never to dispute his orders."

"I believe you are right, Deerslayer," returned the girl, after a little reflection and in a saddened voice: "a man like *you*, ought not to act, as the selfish and dishonest would be apt to act; *you* must, indeed, go back. We will talk no more of this, then. Should I persuade you to any thing for which you would be sorry hereafter, my own regret would not be less than yours. You shall not have it to say, Judith—I scarce know by what name to call myself, now!"

"And why not?—Why not, gal? Children take the names of their parents, nat'rally, and by a sort of gift, like, and why should n't you and Hetty do, as others have done afore ye? Hutter was the old man's name, and Hutter should be the name of his darters;—at least until you are given away in lawful and holy wedlock."

"I am Judith, and Judith only," returned the girl positively—"until the law gives me a right to another name. Never will I use that of Thomas Hutter again; nor, with my consent, shall Hetty! Hutter was not even his own name, I find, but had he a thousand rights to it, it would give none to me. *He* was not my father, thank heaven; though I may have no reason to be proud of him that *was!*"

"This is strange!" said Deerslayer, looking steadily at the excited girl, anxious to know more, but unwilling to inquire into matters that did not properly concern him; "yes, this is very strange and oncommon! Thomas Hutter was n't Thomas Hutter, and his darters were n't his darters! Who, then, could Thomas Hutter be, and who are his darters?"

"Did you never hear any thing whispered against the former life of this person, Deerslayer?" demanded Judith—"Passing, as I did, for his child, such reports reached even me."

"I'll not deny it, Judith; no, I'll not deny it. Sartain things have been said, as I've told you, but I'm not very credible as to reports. Young as I am, I've lived long enough to l'arn there's two sorts of characters in the world—them that is 'arned by deeds, and them that is 'arned by tongues, and so I prefar to see and judge for myself, instead of letting every jaw that chooses to wag become my judgment. Hurry Harry spoke pretty plainly of the whole family, as we journeyed this-a-way, and he did hint something consarning Thomas Hutter's having been a free-liver on the water, in his younger days. By free-liver, I mean that he made free to live on other men's goods."

"He told you he was a pirate — there is no need of mincing matters between friends. Read that, Deerslayer, and you will see that he told you no more than the truth. This Thomas Hovey was the Thomas Hutter you knew, as is seen by these letters."

As Judith spoke, with a flushed cheek and eyes dazzling with the brilliancy of excitement, she held the newspaper towards her companion, pointing to the proclamation of a Colonial Governor, already mentioned.

"Bless you, Judith!" answered the other laughing, "you might as well ask me to print that — or, for that matter to write it. My edication has been altogether in the woods; the only book I read, or care about reading, is the one which God has opened afore all his creatur's in the noble forests, broad lakes, rolling rivers, blue skies, and the winds and tempests, and sunshine, and other glorious marvels of the land! This book I can read, and I find it full of wisdom and knowledge."

"I crave your pardon, Deerslayer," said Judith, earnestly, more abashed than was her wont, in finding that she had inadvertently made an appeal that might wound her companion's pride. "I had forgotten your manner of life, and least of all did I wish to hurt your feelings."

"Hurt my feelin's? — Why should it hurt my feelin's to ask me to read, when I can't read. I'm a hunter — and I may now begin to say a warrior, and no missionary, and therefore books and papers are of no account with such as I — No, no — - Judith," and here the young man laughed cordially, "not even for wads, seeing that your true deerkiller always uses the hide of a fa'a'n, if he's got one, or some other bit of leather suitably prepared. There's some that *do* say, all that stands in print is true, in which case I'll own an unl'arned man must be somewhat of a loser; nevertheless, it can't be truer than that which God has printed with his own hand, in the sky, and the woods, and the rivers, and the springs."

"Well, then, Hutter, or Hovey, was a pirate, and being no

father of mine, I cannot wish to call him one. His name shall no longer be my name."

"If you dislike the name of that man, there's the name of your mother, Judith. Hern may sarve you just as good a turn."

"I do not know it. I've look'd through those papers, Deerslayer, in the hope of finding some hint, by which I might discover who my mother was, but there is no more trace of the past, in that respect, than the bird leaves in the air."

"That's both oncommon, and onreasonable. Parents are bound to give their offspring a name, even though they give 'em nothing else. Now I come of a humble stock, though we have white gifts and a white natur', but we are not so poorly off, as to have no name. Bumppo we are called, and I've heard it said —" a touch of human vanity glowing on his cheek, "that the time has been when the Bumppos had more standing and note among mankind, than they have just now."

"They never deserved them more, Deerslayer, and the name is a good one; either Hetty, or myself, would a thousand times rather be called Hetty Bumppo, or Judith Bumppo, than to be called Hetty or Judith Hutter."

"That's a moral impossible," returned the hunter, good-humouredly, "onless one of you should so far demean herself as to marry me."

Judith could not refrain from smiling, when she found how simply and naturally the conversation had come round to the very point at which she had aimed to bring it. Although far from unfeminine or forward, either in her feelings, or her habits, the girl was goaded by a sense of wrongs not altogether merited, incited by the hopelessness of a future that seemed to contain no resting place, and still more influenced by feelings that were as novel to her, as they proved to be active and engrossing. The opening was too good, therefore, to be neglected, though she came to the subject with much of the indirectness and perhaps, justifiable, address of a woman.

"I do not think Hetty will ever marry, Deerslayer," she said, "and if your name is to be borne by either of us, it must be borne by me."

"There's been handsome women too, they tell me, among the Bumppos, Judith, afore now, and should you take up with the name, oncommon as you be, in this particular, them that knows the family won't be altogether surprised."

"This is not talking as becomes either of us, Deerslayer, for whatever is said on such a subject, between man and woman, should be said seriously, and in sincerity of heart. Forgetting the shame that ought to keep girls silent, until spoken to, in most cases, I will deal with you as frankly as I know one of your generous nature will most like to be dealt by. Can you — do you think, Deerslayer, that you could be happy with such a wife as a woman like myself would make?"

"A woman like you, Judith! But where's the sense in trifling about such a thing? — A woman like you, that is handsome enough to be a captain's lady, and fine enough, and so far as I know edicated enough, would be little apt to think of becoming my wife. I suppose young gals that feel themselves to be smart, and know themselves to be handsome, find a sartain satisfaction in passing their jokes ag'in them that's neither, like a poor Delaware hunter."

This was said good naturedly, but not without a betrayal of feeling which showed that some thing like mortified sensibility was blended with the reply. Nothing could have occurred more likely to awaken all Judith's generous regrets, or to aid her in her purpose, by adding the stimulant of a disinterested desire to atone, to her other impulses, and cloaking all under a guise so winning and natural, as greatly to lessen the unpleasant feature of a forwardness unbecoming the sex.

"You do me injustice if you suppose I have any such thought, or wish," she answered, earnestly. "Never was I more serious in my life, or more willing to abide by any agreement, that we may make to-night. I have had many suitors, Deerslayer — nay, scarce an unmarried trapper or hunter has been in at the Lake these four years, who has not offered to take me away with him, and I fear some that were married, too —"

"Ay, I'll warrant that!" interrupted the other — "I'll warrant all that! Take 'em as a body, Judith, 'arth don't hold a set of men more given to theirselves, and less given to God and the law."

"Not one of them would I — could I listen to; happily for myself perhaps, has it been that such was the case. There have

been well looking youths among them too, as you may have
seen in your acquaintance, Henry March."

"Yes, Harry is sightly to the eye, though, to my idees, less so
to the judgment. I thought, at first, you meant to have him,
Judith, I did; but afore he went, it was easy enough to verify
that the same lodge would n't be big enough for you both."

"You have done me justice in that at least, Deerslayer.
Hurry is a man I could never marry, though he were ten times
more comely to the eye, and a hundred times more stout of
heart, than he really is."

"Why not, Judith, why not? I own I'm cur'ous to know why
a youth like Hurry should n't find favor with a maiden like
you?"

"Then you shall know, Deerslayer," returned the girl, gladly
availing herself of the opportunity of indirectly extolling the
qualities which had so strongly interested her in her listener;
hoping by these means covertly to approach the subject nearest
her heart. "In the first place, looks in a man are of no importance with a woman, provided he is manly, and not disfigured,
or deformed."

"There I can't altogether agree with you," returned the other
thoughtfully, for he had a very humble opinion of his own personal appearance; "I have noticed that the comeliest warriors
commonly get the best-looking maidens of the tribe, for wives,
and the Sarpent, yonder, who is sometimes wonderful in his
paint, is a gineral favorite with all the Delaware young
women, though he takes to Hist, himself, as if she was the only
beauty on 'arth!"

"It may be so with Indians; but it is different with white
girls. So long as a young man has a straight and manly frame,
that promises to make him able to protect a woman, and to
keep want from the door, it is all they ask of the figure. Giants
like Hurry may do for grenadiers, but are of little account as
lovers. Then as to the face, an honest look, one that answers
for the heart within, is of more value than any shape or colour,
or eyes, or teeth, or trifles like them. The last may do for girls,
but who thinks of them at all, in a hunter, or a warrior, or a
husband? — If there are women so silly, Judith is not among
them."

"Well, this is wonderful! I always thought that handsome liked handsome, as riches love riches!"

"It may be so with you men, Deerslayer, but it is not always so with us women. We like stout-hearted men, but we wish to see them modest; sure on a hunt, or the war-path, ready to die for the right, and unwilling to yield to the wrong. Above all we wish for honesty—tongues that are not used to say what the mind does not mean, and hearts that feel a little for others, as well as for themselves. A true-hearted girl could die for such a husband! while the boaster, and the double-tongued suitor gets to be as hateful to the sight, as he is to the mind."

Judith spoke bitterly, and with her usual force, but her listener was too much struck with the novelty of the sensations he experienced to advert to her manner. There was something so soothing to the humility of a man of his temperament, to hear qualities that he could not but know he possessed himself, thus highly extolled by the loveliest female he had ever beheld, that, for the moment, his faculties seemed suspended in a natural and excusable pride. Then it was that the idea of the possibility of such a creature as Judith becoming his companion for life, first crossed his mind. The image was so pleasant, and so novel, that he continued completely absorbed by it, for more than a minute, totally regardless of the beautiful reality that was seated before him, watching the expression of his upright and truth-telling countenance with a keenness that gave her a very fair, if not an absolutely accurate clue to his thoughts. Never before had so pleasing a vision floated before the mind's eye of the young hunter, but, accustomed most to practical things, and little addicted to submitting to the power of his imagination, even while possessed of so much true poetical feeling in connection with natural objects in particular, he soon recovered his reason, and smiled at his own weakness, as the fancied picture faded from his mental sight, and left him the simple, untaught, but highly moral being he was, seated in the Ark of Thomas Hutter, at midnight, with the lovely countenance of its late owner's reputed daughter, beaming on him with anxious scrutiny, by the light of the solitary lamp.

"You're wonderful handsome, and enticing, and pleasing to look on, Judith!" he exclaimed, in his simplicity, as fact resumed its ascendency over fancy. "Wonderful! I do n't remember ever to have seen so beautiful a gal, even among the Delawares; and I'm not astonished that Hurry Harry went away soured as well as disapp'inted!"

"Would you have had me, Deerslayer, become the wife of such a man as Henry March?"

"There's that which is in his favor, and there's that which is ag'in him. To my taste, Hurry would n't make the best of husbands, but I fear that the tastes of most young women, hereaway, would n't be so hard upon him."

"No — no — Judith without a name, would never consent to be called Judith March! Any thing would be better than *that*."

"Judith Bumppo would n't sound as well, gal; and there's many names that would fall short of March, in pleasing the ear."

"Ah! Deerslayer, the pleasantness of the sound, in such cases, does n't come through the ear, but through the heart. Every thing is agreeable, when the heart is satisfied. Were Natty Bumppo, Henry March, and Henry March, Natty Bumppo, I might think the name of March better than it is; or were he, you, I should fancy the name of Bumppo, horrible!"

"That's just it — yes, that's the reason of the matter. Now, I'm nat'rally avarse to sarpents, and I hate even the word, which, the missionaries tell me, comes from human natur', on account of a sartain sarpent at the creation of the 'arth, that outwitted the first woman; yet, ever since Chingachgook has 'arned the title he bears, why the sound is as pleasant to my ears as the whistle of the whip-poor-will, of a calm evening, it is. The feelin's make all the difference in the world, Judith, in the natur' of sounds; ay, even in that of looks, too."

"This is so true, Deerslayer, that I am surprised you should think it remarkable a girl, who may have some comeliness herself, should not think it necessary that her husband should have the same advantage; or, what you fancy an advantage. To me, looks in a man are nothing, provided his countenance be as honest as his heart."

"Yes, honesty is a great advantage, in the long run; and they that are the most apt to forget it, in the beginning, are the most apt to l'arn it in the ind. Nevertheless, there's more, Judith, that look to present profit, than to the benefit that is to come after a time. One they think a sartainty, and the other an on-sartainty. I'm glad, howsever, that *you* look at the thing in its true light, and not in the way in which so many is apt to deceive themselves."

"I do thus look at it, Deerslayer," returned the girl with emphasis, still shrinking, with a woman's sensitiveness, from a direct offer of her hand, "and can say, from the bottom of my heart, that I would rather trust my happiness to a man whose truth and feelings may be depended on, than to a false-tongued and false hearted wretch, that had chests of gold, and houses and lands—yes though he were even seated on a throne!"

"These are brave words, Judith; yes, they're downright brave words, but do you think that the feelin's would keep 'em company, did the ch'ice actually lie afore you? If a gay gallant in a scarlet coat stood on one side, with his head smelling like a deer's foot, his face smooth and blooming as your own, his hands as white and soft as if god had n't bestowed 'em that man might live by the sweat of his brow, and his step as lofty as dancing teachers and a light heart could make it; and on the other side, stood one that has passed his days in the open air, 'till his forehead is as red as his cheek; had cut his way through swamps and bushes till his hand was as rugged as the oaks he slept under; had trodden on the scent of game 'till his step was as stealthy as the catamount's, and had no other pleasant odour about him, than such as natur' gives in the free air, and the forest—now, if both these men stood here, as suitors for your feelin's, which do you think would win your favor?"

Judith's fine face flushed, for the picture that her companion had so simply drawn of a gay officer of the garrisons had once been particularly grateful to her imagination, though experience and disappointment had not only chilled all her affections, but given them a backward current, and the passing image had a momentary influence on her feelings; but the mounting colour was succeeded by a paleness so deadly, as to make her appear ghastly.

"As God is my judge," the girl solemnly answered, "did both these men stand before me, as I may say one of them does, my choice, if I know my own heart, would be the latter. I have no wish for a husband who is any way better than myself."

"This is pleasant to listen to, and might lead a young man in time, to forget his own onworthiness, Judith! Howsever, you hardly think all that you say. A man like me is too rude and ignorant for one that has had such a mother to teach her. Vanity is nat'ral, I do believe, but vanity like that, would surpass reason."

"Then you do not know of what a woman's heart is capable! Rude *you* are not, Deerslayer, nor can one be called ignorant that has studied what is before his eyes as closely as you have done. When the affections are concerned, all things appear in their pleasantest colors, and trifles are overlooked, or are forgotten. When the heart feels sunshine, nothing is gloomy, even dull looking objects, seeming gay and bright, and so it would be between you and the woman who should love you, even though your wife might happen, in some matters, to possess what the world calls the advantage over you."

"Judith, you come of people altogether above mine, in the world, and onequal matches, like onequal fri'ndships can't often tarminate kindly. I speak of this matter altogether as a fanciful thing, since it's not very likely that *you*, at least, would be apt to treat it as a matter that can ever come to pass."

Judith fastened her deep blue eyes on the open, frank countenance of her companion, as if she would read his soul. Nothing there betrayed any covert meaning, and she was obliged to admit to herself, that he regarded the conversation as argumentative, rather than positive, and that he was still without any active suspicion that her feelings were seriously involved in the issue. At first, she felt offended; then she saw the injustice of making the self-abasement and modesty of the hunter a charge against him, and this novel difficulty gave a piquancy to the state of affairs that rather increased her interest in the young man. At that critical instant, a change of plan flashed on her mind, and with a readiness of invention that is peculiar to the quick-witted and ingenious, she adopted a scheme by which she hoped effectually to bind him to her person. This scheme partook equally of her fertility of invention, and of the decision and boldness of her character. That the conversation might not terminate too abruptly, however, or any suspicion of her design exist, she answered the last remark of Deerslayer, as earnestly and as truly, as if her original intention remained unaltered.

"I, certainly, have no reason to boast of parentage, after

what I have seen this night," said the girl, in a saddened voice. "I had a mother, it is true; but of her name even, I am ignorant—and, as for my father, it is better, perhaps, that I should never know who he was, lest I speak too bitterly of him!"

"Judith," said Deerslayer, taking her hand kindly, and with a manly sincerity that went directly to the girl's heart, "'tis better to say no more to-night. Sleep on what you've seen and felt; in the morning things that now look gloomy, may look more che'rful. Above all, never do any thing in bitterness, or because you feel as if you'd like to take revenge on yourself, for other people's backslidings. All that has been said, or done, atween us, this night, is your secret, and shall never be talked of by me, even with the Sarpent, and you may be sartain if he can't get it out of me no man can. If your parents have been faulty, let the darter be less so; remember that you're young, and the youthful may always hope for better times; that you're more quick-witted than usual, and such gin'rally get the better of difficulties, and that, as for beauty, you're oncommon, which is an advantage with all. It is time to get a little rest, for to-morrow is like to prove a trying day to some of us."

Deerslayer arose as he spoke, and Judith had no choice but to comply. The chest was closed and secured, and they parted in silence, she to take her place by the side of Hist and Hetty, and he to seek a blanket on the floor of the cabin he was in. It was not five minutes ere the young man was in a deep sleep, but the girl continued awake for a long time. She scarce knew whether to lament, or to rejoice, at having failed in making herself understood. On the one hand, were her womanly sensibilities spared; on the other was the disappointment of defeated, or at least of delayed expectations, and the uncertainty of a future that looked so dark. Then came the new resolution, and the bold project for the morrow, and when drowsiness finally shut her eyes, they closed on a scene of success and happiness, that was pictured by the fancy, under the influence of a sanguine temperament, and a happy invention.

Chapter XXV.

"But, mother, now a shade has past,
    Athwart my brightest visions here,
A cloud of darkest gloom has wrapt,
    The remnant of my brief career!
No song, no echo can I win,
The sparkling fount has died within."
            Margaret Davidson, "To my Mother," ll. 7–12.

HIST and Hetty arose with the return of light, leaving Judith still buried in sleep. It took but a minute for the first to complete her toilet. Her long coal-black hair was soon adjusted in a simple knot, the calico dress belted tight to her slender waist, and her little feet concealed in their gaudily ornamented moccasins. When attired, she left her companion employed in household affairs, and went herself on the platform to breathe the pure air of the morning. Here she found Chingachgook studying the shores of the lake, the mountains and the heavens, with the sagacity of a man of the woods, and the gravity of an Indian.

The meeting between the two lovers was simple, but affectionate. The chief showed a manly kindness, equally removed from boyish weakness and haste, while the girl betrayed, in her smile and half averted looks, the bashful tenderness of her sex. Neither spoke, unless it were with the eyes, though each understood the other as fully as if a vocabulary of words and protestations had been poured out. Hist seldom appeared to more advantage, than at that moment, for just from her rest and ablutions, there was a freshness about her youthful form and face, that the toils of the wood do not always permit to be exhibited, by even the juvenile and pretty. Then Judith had not only imparted some of her own skill in the toilet, during their short intercourse, but she had actually bestowed a few well selected ornaments from her own stores, that contributed not a little to set off the natural graces of the Indian maid. All this the lover saw and felt, and for a moment his countenance was illuminated with a look of pleasure, but it soon grew grave, again, and became saddened and anxious. The stools used the previous night were still standing on the platform; placing two against the walls of the hut, he seated himself on one, making a gesture to his companion to take the other. This done, he continued thoughtful and silent, for quite a minute, maintaining the reflecting dignity of one born to take his seat at the Council Fire, while Hist was furtively watching the expression of his face, patient and submissive as became a woman of her people. Then the young warrior stretched his arm before him, as if to point out the glories of the scene at that witching hour, when the whole panorama, as usual, was adorned by the mellow distinctness of early morning, sweeping with his hand slowly over lake, hills and heavens. The girl followed the movement with pleased wonder, smiling as each new beauty met her gaze.

"Hugh!" exclaimed the chief, in admiration of a scene so unusual even to him, for this was the first lake he had ever beheld — "this is the country of the Manitou! It is too good for Mingos, Hist; but the curs of that tribe are howling in packs through the woods. They think that the Delawares are asleep, over the mountains."

"All but one of them is, Chingachgook. There is one here; and he is of the blood of Uncas!"

"What is one warrior against a tribe? — The path to our villages is very long and crooked, and we shall travel it under a cloudy sky. I am afraid, too, Honeysuckle of the Hills, that we shall travel it alone!"

Hist understood the allusion, and it made her sad; though it sounded sweet to her ears to be compared, by the warrior she so loved, to the most fragrant, and the pleasantest of all the wild-flowers of her native woods. Still she continued silent, as became her when the allusion was to a grave interest that men could best control, though it exceeded the power of education to conceal the smile that gratified feeling brought to her pretty mouth.

"When the sun is thus," continued the Delaware, pointing to the zenith, by simply casting upward a hand and finger, by a play of the wrist, "the great hunter of our tribe, will go back to the Hurons, to be treated like a bear, that they roast and skin, even on full stomachs."

"The Great Spirit may soften their hearts, and not suffer them to be so bloody minded. I have lived among the Hurons, and know them. They have hearts, and will not forget their own children, should they fall into the hands of the Delawares."

"A wolf is forever howling; a hog will always eat. They have lost warriors; even their women will call out for vengeance. The pale face has the eyes of an eagle, and can see into a Mingo's heart; he looks for no mercy. There is a cloud over his spirit, though it is not before his face."

A long, thoughtful pause succeeded, during which Hist stealthily took the hand of the chief, as if seeking his support, though she scarce ventured to raise her eyes to a countenance that was now literally becoming terrible, under the conflicting passions, and stern resolution that were struggling in the breast of its owner.

"What will the Son of Uncas do?" the girl at length timidly asked. "He is a chief, and is already celebrated in council, though so young; what does his heart tell him is wisest; does the head, too, speak the same words as the heart?"

"What does Wah-ta!-Wah say, at a moment when my dearest friend is in such danger. The smallest birds sing the sweetest; it is always pleasant, to hearken to their songs. I wish I could hear the Wren of the Woods in my difficulty; its note would reach deeper than the ear."

Again Hist experienced the profound gratification that the language of praise can always awaken, when uttered by those we love. The 'Honeysuckle of the Hills' was a term often applied to the girl, by the young men of the Delawares, though it never sounded so sweet in her ears, as from the lips of Chingachgook; but the latter alone had ever styled her the Wren of the Woods. With him, however, it had got to be a familiar phrase, and it was past expression pleasant to the listener, since it conveyed to her mind the idea that her advice and sentiments were as acceptable to her future husband, as the tones of her voice and modes of conveying them were agreeable; uniting the two things most prized by an Indian girl, as coming from her betrothed, admiration for a valued physical advantage, with respect for her opinion. She pressed the hand she held, between both her own, and answered —

"Wah-ta!-Wah says that neither she nor the Great Serpent could ever laugh, again, or ever sleep without dreaming of the Hurons, should the Deerslayer die under a Mingo tomahawk, and they do nothing to save him. She would rather go back, and start on her long path alone, than let such a dark cloud pass before her happiness."

"Good! The husband and the wife will have but one heart; they will see with the same eyes, and feel with the same feelings."

What further was said, need not be related here. That the conversation was of Deerslayer, and his hopes, has been seen already, but the decision that was come to, will better appear in the course of the narrative. The youthful pair were yet conversing when the sun appeared above the tops of the pines, and the light of a brilliant American day streamed down into the valley, bathing "in deep joy" the lake, the forests and the mountain sides. Just at this instant Deerslayer came out of the cabin of the Ark, and stepped upon the platform. His first look was at the cloudless heavens, then his rapid glance took in the entire panorama of land and water, when he had leisure for a friendly nod at his friends, and a cheerful smile for Hist.

"Well," he said, in his usual, composed manner, and pleasant voice, "he that sees the sun set in the west, and wakes 'arly enough in the morning will be sartain to find him coming back ag'in in the east, like a buck that is hunted round his ha'nt. I dare say, now, Hist, you've beheld this, time and ag'in, and yet it never entered into your galish mind to ask the reason?"

Both Chingachgook and his betrothed looked up at the luminary, with an air that betokened sudden wonder, and then they gazed at each other, as if to seek the solution of the difficulty. Familiarity deadens the sensibilities, even as connected with the gravest natural phenomena, and never before had these simple beings thought of enquiring into a movement that was of daily occurrence, however puzzling it might appear on investigation. When the subject was thus suddenly started, it struck both alike, and at the same instant, with some such force, as any new and brilliant proposition in the natural sciences would strike the scholar. Chingachgook alone saw fit to answer.

"The pale-faces know every thing," he said; "can they tell us why the sun hides his face, when he goes back, at night."

"Ay, that is downright red-skin l'arnin'," returned the other, laughing, though he was not altogether insensible to the pleasure of proving the superiority of his race, by solving the difficulty, which he set about doing, in his own peculiar manner. "Harkee, Sarpent," he continued more gravely, though too simply for affectation; "this is easierly explained than an Indian brain may fancy. The sun, while he seems to keep travelling in the heavens, never budges, but it is the 'arth that turns round, and any one can understand, if he is placed on the side of a mill-wheel, for instance, when it's in motion, that he must some times see the heavens, while he is at other times under water. There's no great secret in that; but plain natur'; the difficulty being in setting the 'arth in motion."

"How does my brother know that the earth turns round?" demanded the Indian. "Can he see it?"

"Well, that's been a puzzler, I will own, Delaware, for I've often tried, but never could fairly make it out. Sometimes I've consaited that I could; and then ag'in, I've been obliged to own it an onpossibility. Howsever, turn it does, as all my people say, and you ought to believe 'em, since they can foretel eclipses, and other prodigies, that used to fill the tribes with terror, according to your own traditions of such things."

"Good. This is true; no red-man will deny it. When a wheel turns, my eyes can see it — they do not see the earth turn."

"Ay, that's what I call sense obstinacy! Seeing is believing, they say, and what they can't see, some men won't in the least give credit to. Nevertheless, chief, that is n't quite as good reason as it may at first seem. You believe in the Great Spirit, I know, and yet, I conclude, it would puzzle you to show where you see him!"

"Chingachgook can see Him every where — every where in *good* things — the Evil Spirit in *bad*. Here, in the lake; there, in the forest; yonder, in the clouds; in Hist, in the Son of Uncas, in Tamenund, in Deerslayer. The Evil Spirit is in the Mingos. That I see; I do not see the earth turn round."

"I do n't wonder they call you the Sarpent, Delaware; no, I do n't! There's always a meaning in your words, and there's often a meaning in your countenance, too! Notwithstanding, your answers does n't quite meet my idee. That God is obsarvable in all nat'ral objects is allowable, but then he is not parceptible in the way I mean. *You* know there is a Great Spirit by his works, and the pale faces know that the 'arth turns round by its works. This is the reason of the matter, though how it is to be explained, is more than I can exactly tell you. This I know; all my people consait that fact, and what all the pale-faces consait, is very likely to be true."

"When the sun is in the top of that pine to-morrow, where will my brother Deerslayer be?"

The hunter started, and he looked intently, though totally without alarm, at his friend. Then he signed for him to follow, and led the way into the Ark, where he might pursue the subject unheard by those, whose feelings he feared might get the mastery over their reason. Here he stopped, and pursued the conversation in a more confidential tone.

"'Twas a little onreasonable in you, Sarpent," he said, "to bring up such a subject afore Hist, and when the young women of my own colour might overhear what was said. Yes, 'twas a little more onreasonable than most things that you do. No matter; Hist did n't comprehind, and the other did n't hear. Howsever, the question is easier put than answered. No mortal can say where he will be when the sun rises to-morrow. I will ask you the same question, Sarpent, and should like to hear what answer you can give."

"Chingachgook will be with his friend Deerslayer — If he be in the land of spirits, the Great Serpent will crawl at his side; if beneath yonder sun, its warmth and light shall fall on both."

"I understand you Delaware," returned the other, touched with the simple self-devotion of his friend. "Such language is as plain in one tongue as in another. It comes from the heart, and goes to the heart, too. 'Tis well to think so, and it may be well to *say* so, for that matter, but it would not be well to *do* so, Sarpent. You are no longer alone in life, for though you have the lodges to change, and other ceremonies to go through, afore Hist becomes your lawful wife, yet are you as good as married, in all that bears on the feelin's, and joy, and misery. No — no — Hist must not be desarted, because a cloud is passing atween you and me, a little onexpectedly and a little darker than we may have looked for."

"Hist is a daughter of the Mohicans. She knows how to obey her husband. Where he goes, she will follow. *Both* will be with the Great Hunter of the Delawares, when the sun shall be in the pine to-morrow."

"The Lord bless and protect you! — Chief; this is downright madness. Can either, or both of you, alter a Mingo natur'. Will your grand looks, or Hist's tears and beauty, change a wolf into a squirrel, or make a catamount as innocent as a fa'an? No — Sarpent, you will think better of this matter, and leave me in the hands of God. A'ter all, it's by no means sartain that the scamps design the torments, for they may yet be pitiful, and bethink them of the wickedness of such a course — though it *is* but a hopeless expectation to look forward to a Mingo's turning aside from evil, and letting marcy get uppermost in his heart — Nevertheless, no one knows to a sartainty what will happen, and young creatur's, like Hist, an't to be risked on onsartainties. This marrying is altogether a different undertaking from what some young men fancy. Now, if you was single, or as good as single, Delaware, I should expect you to be act*y*ve and stirring about the camp of the vagabonds, from sunrise to sunset, sarcumventing and contriving, as restless as a hound off the scent, and doing all manner of things to help me, and to distract the inimy, but two are oftener feebler than one, and we must take things as they are, and not as we want 'em to be."

"Listen, Deerslayer," returned the Indian with an emphasis so decided as to show how much he was in earnest. "If Chingachgook was in the hands of the Hurons, what would my pale-face brother do? Sneak off to the Delaware villages, and say to the chiefs, and old men, and young warriors — 'see, here is Wah-ta!-Wah; she is safe, but a little tired; and here is the Son of Uncas, not as tired as the Honeysuckle, being stronger, but just as safe.' Would he do this?"

"Well, that's oncommon ingen'ous; it's cunning enough for a Mingo, himself! The Lord only knows what put it into your head to ask such a question. What would I do? — Why, in the first place, Hist would n't be likely to be in my company at all, for she would stay as near you as possible, and therefore all that part about *her* could n't be said, without talking nonsense. As for her being tired, that would fall through, too, if she did n't go, and no part of your speech would be likely to come from me; so, you see, Sarpent, reason is ag'in you, and you may as well give it up, since to hold out ag'in reason, is no way becoming a chief of your character and repitation."

"My brother is not himself; he forgets that he is talking to one who has sat at the Council Fire of his nation," returned the other kindly. "When men speak, they should say that which does not go in at one side of the head and out at the other. Their words should n't be feathers, so light that a wind which does not ruffle the water, can blow them away. He has not answered my question; when a chief puts a question, his friend should not talk of other things."

"I understand you, Delaware; I understand well enough what you mean, and truth won't allow me to say otherwise. Still it's not as easy to answer as you seem to think, for this plain reason. You wish me to say what I would do if I had a betrothed as you have, here, on the lake, and a fri'nd yonder in the Huron camp, in danger of the torments. That's it, is n't it?"

The Indian bowed his head silently, and always with un-moved gravity, though his eye twinkled at the sight of the other's embarrassment.

"Well, I never had a betrothed—never had the kind of feelin's toward any young woman, that you have towards Hist, though the Lord knows my feelin's are kind enough towards 'em all!—still my heart, as they call it, in such matters, is n't touched, and therefore I can't say what I would do. A fri'nd pulls strong, that I know by exper'ence, Sarpent, but, by all that I've seen and heard consarning love, I'm led to think that a betrothed pulls stronger."

"True; but the betrothed of Chingachgook does not pull towards the lodges of the Delawares; she pulls towards the camp of the Hurons."

"She's a noble gal, for all her little feet, and hands that an't bigger than a child's, and a voice that is as pleasant as a mocker's; she's a noble gal, and like the stock of her sires! Well, what is it, Sarpent; for I conclude she has n't changed her mind, and means to give herself up, and turn Huron wife. What is it you want?"

"Wah-ta!-Wah will never live in the wigwam of an Iroquois," answered the Delaware drily. "She has little feet, but they can carry her to the villages of her people; she has small hands, too, but her mind is large. My brother will see what we can do, when the time shall come, rather than let him die under Mingo torments."

"Attempt nothing heedlessly, Delaware," said the other earnestly; "I suppose you must and will have your way; and, on the whole it's right you should, for you'd neither be happy, unless something was undertaken. But attempt nothing heedlessly — I did n't expect you'd quit the lake, while my matter remained in unsartainty, but remember, Sarpent, that no torments that Mingo ingenuity can invent, no ta'ntings, and revilings; no burnings, and roastings, and nail-tearings, nor any other onhuman contrivances can so soon break down my spirit, as to find that you and Hist, have fallen into the power of the inimy, in striving to do something for my good."

"The Delawares are prudent. The Deerslayer will not find them running into a strange camp, with their eyes shut."

Here the dialogue terminated. Hetty announced that the breakfast was ready, and the whole party was soon seated around the simple board, in the usual primitive manner of borderers. Judith was the last to take her seat, pale, silent, and betraying in her countenance that she had passed a painful, if not a sleepless, night. At this meal scarce a syllable was exchanged, all the females manifesting want of appetites, though the two men were unchanged in this particular. It was early when the party arose, and there still remained several hours before it would be necessary for the prisoner to leave his friends. The knowledge of this circumstance, and the interest all felt in his welfare, induced the whole to assemble on the platform again, in the desire to be near the expected victim, to listen to his discourse, and if possible to show their interest in him, by anticipating his wishes. Deerslayer, himself, so far as human eyes could penetrate, was wholly unmoved, conversing cheerfully and naturally, though he avoided any direct allusions to the expected and great event of the day. If any evidence could be discovered of his thought's reverting to that painful subject at all, it was in the manner in which he spoke of death and the last great change.

"Grieve not, Hetty," he said, for it was while consoling this simple-minded girl for the loss of her parents that he thus betrayed his feelings, "since God has app'inted that all must die. Your parents, or them you fancied your parents, which is the same thing, have gone afore you; this is only in the order of natur', my good gal, for the aged go first, and the young follow. But one that had a mother like your'n, Hetty, can be at no loss to hope the best, as to how matters will turn out in another world. The Delaware, here, and Hist, believe in happy hunting grounds, and have idees befitting their notions and gifts, as red skins, but we who are of white blood hold altogether to a different doctrine. Still, I rather conclude our heaven is their land of spirits, and that the path which leads to it will be travelled by all colours alike. 'Tis onpossible for the wicked to enter on it, I will allow, but fri'nds can scarce be separated, though they are not of the same race on 'arth. Keep up your spirits, poor Hetty, and look forward to the day when you will meet your mother ag'in, and that without pain, or sorrowing."

"I do expect to see mother," returned the truth-telling and simple girl, "but what will become of father?"

"That's a non-plusser, Delaware," said the hunter, in the Indian dialect—"yes, that is a down-right non-plusser! The Muskrat was not a saint on 'arth, and it's fair to guess he'll not be much of one, here after! Howsever, Hetty," dropping into the English by an easy transition, "howsever, Hetty, we must all hope for the best. That is wisest, and it is much the easiest to the mind, if one can only do it. I ricommend to you, trusting to God, and putting down all misgivings and faint-hearted feelin's. It's wonderful, Judith, how different people have different notions about the futur', some fancying one change, and some fancying another. I've known white teachers that have thought all was spirit, hereafter, and them, ag'in, that believed the body will be transported to another world, much as the red-skins themselves imagine, and that we shall walk about, in the flesh, and know each other, and talk together, and be fri'nds there, as we've been fri'nds here."

"Which of these opinions is most pleasing to *you*, Deerslayer?" asked the girl, willing to indulge his melancholy mood, and far from being free from its influence herself. "Would it be disagreeable to think that you should meet all who are now on this platform in another world? Or have you known enough of us here, to be glad to see us no more."

"The last would make death a bitter portion; yes it would. It's eight good years since the Sarpent and I began to hunt together, and the thought that we were never to meet ag'in, would be a hard thought to me. He looks forward to the time when he shall chase a sort of spirit-deer, in company, on plains where there's no thorns, or brambles, or marshes, or other hardships to overcome, whereas I can't fall into all these notions, seeing that they appear to be ag'in reason. Spirits can't eat, nor have they any use for clothes, and deer can only rightfully be chased to be slain, or slain, unless it be for the venison, or the hides. Now, I find it hard to suppose that blessed spirits can be put to chasing game, without an object, tormenting the dumb animals just for the pleasure and agreeableness of their own amusements. I never, yet, pulled a trigger on buck or doe, Judith, unless when food or clothes was wanting."

"The recollection of which, Deerslayer, must now be a great consolation to you."

"It is the thought of such things, my fri'nds, that enables a man to keep his furlough. It might be done without it, I own; for the worst red skins, sometimes do their duty in this matter; but it makes that which might otherwise be hard, easy, if not altogether to our liking. Nothing truly makes a bolder heart, than a light conscience."

Judith turned paler than ever, but she struggled for self-command, and succeeded in obtaining it. The conflict had been severe, however, and it left her so little disposed to speak, that Hetty pursued the subject. This was done in the simple manner natural to the girl.

"It would be cruel to kill the poor deer," she said, "in this world, or any other, when you do n't want their venison, or their skins. No good white-man, and no good red man would do it. But it's wicked for a christian to talk about chasing any thing in heaven. Such things are not done before the face of God, and the missionary that teaches these doctrines, can't be a true missionary. He must be a wolf in sheep's clothing. I suppose you know what a sheep is, Deerslayer."

"That I do, gal, and a useful creatur' it is, to such as like cloths better than skins, for winter garments. I understand the natur' of sheep, though I've had but little to do with 'em, and the natur' of wolves too, and can take the idee of a wolf in the fleece of a sheep, though I think it would be like to prove a hot jacket for such a beast, in the warm months!"

"And sin, and hypocrisy are hot jackets, as *they* will find, who put them on," returned Hetty, positively, "so the wolf would be no worse off than the sinner. Spirits do n't hunt, nor trap, nor fish, nor do any thing that vain men undertake, since they've none of the longings of this world to feed. Oh! Mother told me all that, years ago, and I don't wish to hear it denied."

"Well, my good Hetty, in that case you'd better not broach your doctrine to Hist, when she and you are alone, and the young Delaware maiden is inclined to talk religion. It's her fix-ed idee, I know, that the good warriors do nothing but hunt, and fish in the other world, though I do n't believe that she fancies any of them are brought down to trapping, which is no empl'yment for a brave. But of hunting and fishing, accordin' to her notion, they've their fill, and that, too, over the most agreeablest hunting grounds, and among game that is never out of season, and which is just actyve and instinctyve enough to give a pleasure to death. So I would n't ricommend it to you to start Hist on that idee."

"Hist can't be so wicked as to believe any such thing," returned the other, earnestly. "No Indian hunts after he is dead."

"No wicked Indian, I grant you; no wicked Indian, sartainly. He is obliged to carry the ammunition, and to look on without sharing in the sport, and to cook, and to light the fires, and to do every thing that is n't manful. Now, mind; I do n't tell you these are my idees, but they are Hist's idees, and, therefore, for the sake of peace the less you say to her ag'in 'em, the bet-ter."

"And what are your ideas of the fate of an Indian, in the other world?" demanded Judith, who had just found her voice.

"Ah! gal, any thing but that! I am too christianized to expect any thing so fanciful, as hunting and fishing after death, nor do I believe there is one Manitou for the red skin and another for a pale face. You find different colours on 'arth, as any one may see, but you do n't find different natur's. Different gifts, but only one natur'."

"In what is a gift different from a nature? Is not nature itself a gift from God?"

"Sartain; that's quick-thoughted, and creditable, Judith, though the main idee is wrong. A natur' is the creatur' itself; its wishes, wants, idees and feelin's, as all are born in him. This natur' never can be changed, in the main, though it may undergo some increase, or lessening. Now, gifts come of sar-cumstances. Thus, if you put a man in a town, he gets town gifts; in a settlement, settlement gifts; in a forest, gifts of the woods. A soldier has soldierly gifts, and a missionary preaching gifts. All these increase and strengthen, until they get to fortify natur', as it might be, and excuse a thousand acts and idees. Still the creatur' is the same at the bottom; just as a man who is clad in regimentals is the same as the man that is clad in skins. The garments make a change to the eye, and some change in the conduct, perhaps; but none in the man. Herein lies the apology for gifts; seein' that you expect dif-ferent conduct from one in silks and satins, from one in homespun; though the Lord, who did n't make the dresses, but who made the creatur's themselves, looks only at his own work. This is n't ra'al missionary doctrine, but it's as near it, as a man of white colour need be. Ah's! me; little did I think to be talking of such matters, to-day, but it's one of our weaknesses never to know what will come to pass. Step into the Ark with me, Judith, for a minute; I wish to converse with you."

Judith complied with a willingness she could scarce conceal. Following the hunter into the cabin, she took a seat on a stool, while the young man brought Killdeer, the rifle she had given him, out of a corner, and placed himself on another, with the weapon laid upon his knees. After turning the piece round and round, and examining its lock and its breech with a sort of af-fectionate assiduity, he laid it down and proceeded to the sub-ject which had induced him to desire the interview.

"I understand you, Judith, to say that you gave me this rifle," he said. "I agreed to take it, because a young woman can have no particular use for fire-arms. The we'pon has a great name, and it desarves it, and ought of right to be carried by some known and sure hand, for the best repitation may be lost by careless and thoughtless handling."

"Can it be in better hands than those in which it is now, Deerslayer. Thomas Hutter seldom missed with it; with you it must turn out to be—"

"Sartain death!" interrupted the hunter, laughing. "I once know'd a beaver-man that had a piece he called by that very name, but 'twas all boastfulness, for I've seen Delawares that were as true with arrows, at a short range. Howsever, I'll not deny my gifts—for *this* is a gift, Judith, and not natur'—but, I'll not deny my gifts, and therefore allow that the rifle could n't well be in better hands than it is at present. But, how long will it be likely to remain there? Atween us, the truth may be said, though I should n't like to have it known to the Sarpent and Hist; but, to *you* the truth may be spoken, since *your* feelin's will not be as likely to be tormented by it, as those of them that have known me longer and better. How long am I like to own this rifle or any other? That is a serious question for our thoughts to rest on, and should that happen which is so likely to happen, Killdeer would be without an owner."

Judith listened with apparent composure, though the conflict within came near overpowering her. Appreciating the singular character of her companion, however, she succeeded in appearing calm, though, had not his attention been drawn exclusively to the rifle, a man of his keenness of observation could scarce have failed to detect the agony of mind with which the girl had hearkened to his words. Her great self-command, notwithstanding, enabled her to pursue the subject in a way still to deceive him.

"What would you have me do with the weapon," she asked— "should that which you seem to expect, take place?"

"That's just what I wanted to speak to you about, Judith; that's just it. There's Chingachgook, now, though far from being parfect sartainty, with a rifle—for few red skins ever get to be *that*—though far from being parfect sartainty, he is respectable, and is coming on. Nevertheless, he is my fri'nd, and all the better fri'nd, perhaps, because there never can be any hard feelin's atween us, touchin' our gifts, his'n bein' red, and mine bein' altogether white. Now, I should like to leave Killdeer to the Sarpent, should any thing happen to keep me from doing credit and honor to your precious gift, Judith."

"Leave it to whom you please, Deerslayer. The rifle is your own, to do with as you please. Chingachgook shall have it, should you never return to claim it, if that be your wish."

"Has Hetty been consulted in this matter? — Property goes from the parent to the children, and not to one child, in partic'lar!"

"If you place your right on that of the law, Deerslayer, I fear none of us can claim to be the owner. Thomas Hutter was no more the father of Esther, than he was the father of Judith. Judith and Esther we are truly, having no other name!"

"There may be law in that, but there's no great reason, gal. Accordin' to the custom of families, the goods are your'n, and there's no one here to gainsay it. If Hetty would only say that she is willing, my mind would be quite at ease in the matter. It's true, Judith, that your sister has neither your beauty, nor your wit; but we should be the tenderest of the rights and welfare of the most weak-minded."

The girl made no answer but placing herself at a window, she summoned her sister to her side. When the question was put to Hetty, that simple-minded and affectionate creature cheerfully assented to the proposal to confer on Deerslayer a full right of ownership to the much-coveted rifle. The latter now seemed perfectly happy, for the time being at least, and after again examining and re-examining his prize, he expressed a determination to put its merits to a practical test, before he left the spot. No boy could have been more eager to exhibit the qualities of his trumpet, or his cross-bow, than this simple forester was to prove those of his rifle. Returning to the plat-form, he first took the Delaware aside, and informed him that this celebrated piece was to become his property, in the event of any thing serious befalling himself.

"This is a new reason why you should be wary, Sarpent, and not run into any oncalculated danger," the hunter added, "for, it will be a victory of itself, to a tribe to own such a piece as this! The Mingos will turn green with envy, and, what is more, they will not ventur' heedlessly near a village where it is known to be kept. So, look well to it, Delaware, and remember that you've now to watch over a thing that has all the valie of a creatur', without its failin's. Hist may be, and should be precious to you, but Killdeer will have the love and veneration of your whole people."

"One rifle like another, Deerslayer," returned the Indian, in English, the language used by the other, a little hurt at his friend's lowering his betrothed to the level of a gun. "All kill; all wood and iron. Wife dear to heart; rifle good to shoot."

"And what is a man in the woods without something to shoot with? — a miserable trapper, or a forlorn broom and basket maker, at the best. Such a man may hoe corn, and keep soul and body together, but he can never know the savory morsels of venison, or tell a bear's ham from a hog's. Come, my fri'nd, such another occasion may never offer ag'in, and I feel a strong craving for a trial with this celebrated piece. You shall bring out your own rifle, and I will just sight Killdeer in a careless way, in order that we may know a few of its secret vartues."

As this proposition served to relieve the thoughts of the whole party, by giving them a new direction, while it was likely to produce no unpleasant results, every one was willing to enter into it; the girls bringing forth the fire-arms with an alacrity, bordering on cheerfulness. Hutter's armory was well supplied, possessing several rifles, all of which were habitually kept loaded, in readiness to meet any sudden demand for their use. On the present occasion, it only remained to freshen the primings, and each piece was in a state for service. This was soon done, as all assisted in it, the females being as expert in this part of the system of defence, as their male companions.

"Now, Sarpent, we'll begin in a humble way, using Old Tom's commoners first, and coming to your we'pon and Killdeer as the winding up observations," said Deerslayer, delighted to be again, weapon in hand, ready to display his skill. "Here's birds in abundance, some in, and some over the lake, and they keep at just a good range, hovering round the hut. Speak your mind, Delaware, and p'int out the creatur' you wish to alarm. Here's a diver nearest in, off to the eastward, and that's a creatur' that buries itself at the flash, and will be like enough to try both piece and powder."

Chingachgook was a man of few words. No sooner was the bird pointed out to him, than he took his aim and fired. The duck dove at the flash, as had been expected, and the bullet skipped harmlessly along the surface of the lake, first striking the water within a few inches of the spot where the bird had so lately swam. Deerslayer laughed, cordially and naturally, but, at the same time, he threw himself into an attitude of preparation, and stood keenly watching the sheet of placid water. Presently a dark spot appeared, and then the duck arose to breathe, and shook its wings. While in this act, a bullet passed directly through its breast, actually turning it over lifeless, on its back. At the next moment, Deerslayer stood with the breech of his rifle on the platform, as tranquil as if nothing had happened, though laughing in his own peculiar manner.

"There's no great trial of the pieces in that!" he said, as if anxious to prevent a false impression of his own merit. "No, that proof's neither for, nor ag'in the rifles, seeing it was all quickness of hand and eye. I took the bird at a disadvantage, or he might have got under, again, afore the bullet reached him. But the Sarpent is too wise to mind such tricks, having long been used to them. Do you remember the time, chief, when you thought yourself sartain of the wild-goose, and I took him out of your very eyes, as it might be with a little smoke! Howsever, such things pass for nothing, atween fri'nds, and young folk will have their fun, Judith. Ay; here's just the bird we want, for it's as good for the fire, as it is for the aim, and nothing should be lost that can be turned to just account. There, further north, Delaware."

The latter looked in the required direction, and he soon saw a large black duck floating in stately repose on the water. At that distant day, when so few men were present to derange the harmony of the wilderness, all the smaller lakes with which the interior of New York so abounds, were places of resort for the migratory aquatic birds, and this sheet like the others had once been much frequented by all the varieties of the duck, by the goose, the gull, and the loon. On the appearance of Hutter, the spot was comparatively deserted for other sheets, more retired and remote, though some of each species continued to resort thither, as indeed they do to the present hour. At that instant, a hundred birds were visible from the castle, sleeping on the water, or laving their feathers in the limpid element, though no other offered so favorable a mark as that Deerslayer had just pointed out to his friend. Chingachgook as usual, spared his words, and proceeded to execution. This time his aim was more careful than before, and his success in proportion. The bird had a wing crippled, and fluttered along the water screaming, materially increasing its distance from its enemies.

"That bird must be put out of pain," exclaimed Deerslayer, the moment the animal endeavored to rise on the wing, "and this is the rifle and the eye to do it."

The duck was still floundering along, when the fatal bullet overtook it, severing the head from the neck as neatly as if it had been done with an axe. Hist had indulged in a low cry of delight at the success of the young Indian, but now she affected to frown and resent the greater skill of his friend. The chief, on the contrary, uttered the usual exclamation of pleasure, and his smile proved how much he admired, and how little he envied.

"Never mind the gal, Sarpent, never mind Hist's feelin's, which will neither choke, nor drown, slay nor beautify," said Deerslayer, laughing. "'Tis nat'ral for women to enter into their husband's victories and defeats, and you are as good as man and wife, so far as prejudyce and fri'ndship go. Here is a bird over head that will put the pieces, to the proof. I challenge you to an upward aim, with a flying target. That's a ra'al proof, and one that needs sartain rifles, as well as sartain eyes."

The species of eagle that frequents the water, and lives on fish, was also present, and one was hovering at a considerable height above the hut, greedily watching for an opportunity to make a swoop; its hungry young elevating their heads from a nest that was in sight, in the naked summit of a dead pine. Chingachgook silently turned a new piece against this bird, and after carefully watching his time, fired. A wider circuit than common, denoted that the messenger had passed through the air, at no great distance from the bird though it missed its object. Deerslayer, whose aim was not more true than it was quick, fired as soon as it was certain his friend had missed, and the deep swoop that followed left it momentarily doubtful whether the eagle was hit or not. The marksman himself, however, proclaimed his own want of success, calling on his friend to seize another rifle, for he saw signs on the part of the bird of an intention to quit the spot.

"I made him wink, Sarpent, I do think his feathers were ruffled, but no blood has yet been drawn, nor is that old piece fit for so nice and quick a sight. Quick, Delaware, you've now a better rifle, and, Judith, bring out Killdeer, for this is the occasion to try his merits, if he has 'em."

A general movement followed, each of the competitors got ready, and the girls stood in eager expectation of the result. The eagle had made a wide circuit after his low swoop, and fanning his way upward, once more hovered nearly over the hut, at a distance even greater than before. Chingachgook gazed at him, and then expressed his opinion of the impossibility of striking a bird at that great height, and while he was so nearly perpendicular, as to the range. But a low murmur from Hist, produced a sudden impulse and he fired. The result showed how well he had calculated, the eagle not even varying his flight, sailing round and round in his airy circle, and looking down, as if in contempt, at his foes.

"Now, Judith," cried Deerslayer, laughing, with glistening and delighted eyes, "we'll see if Killdeer is n't Killeagle, too! Give me room Sarpent, and watch the reason of the aim, for by reason any thing may be l'arned."

A careful sight followed, and was repeated again and again, the bird continuing to rise higher and higher. Then followed the flash and the report. The swift messenger sped upward, and, at the next instant, the bird turned on its side, and came swooping down, now struggling with one wing and then with the other, sometimes whirling in a circuit, next fanning desperately as if conscious of its injury, until, having described several complete circles around the spot, it fell heavily into the end of the Ark. On examining the body, it was found that the bullet had pierced it about half way between one of its wings and the breast-bone.

Chapter XXVI.

"Upon two stony tables, spread before her,
She lean'd her bosom, more than stony hard,
There slept th' impartial judge, and strict restorer
Of wrong, or right, with pain or with reward;
There hung the score of all our debts, the card
Where good, and bad, and life, and death, were painted;
Was never heart of mortal so untainted,
But when the roll was read, with thousand terrors fainted."
Giles Fletcher, *Christ's Victory in Heaven*, I.xv.

"WE'VE done an unthoughtful thing, Sarpent—yes, Judith, we've done an unthoughtful thing in taking life with an object no better than vanity!" exclaimed Deerslayer, when the Delaware held up the enormous bird, by its wings, and exhibited the dying eyes riveted on its enemies with the gaze that the helpless ever fasten on their destroyers. "Twas more becomin' two boys to gratify their feelin's, in this onthoughtful manner, than two warriors on a war path, even though it be their first. Ah's! me; well, as a punishment I'll quit you at once, and when I find myself alone with them bloody-minded Mingos, it's more than like I'll have occasion to remember that life is sweet, even to the beasts of the woods and the fowls of the air. There, Judith; there's Killdeer; take him back, ag'in, and keep him for some hand that's more desarving to own such a piece."

"I know of none as deserving as your own, Deerslayer," answered the girl in haste; "none but yours shall keep the rifle."

"If it depended on skill, you might be right enough, gal, but we should know *when* to use fire-arms, as well as *how* to use 'em. I have n't l'arnt the first duty yet, it seems; so keep the piece till I have. The sight of a dyin' and distressed creatur', even though it be only a bird, brings wholesome thoughts to a man who don't know how soon his own time may come, and who *is* pretty sartain that it will come afore the sun sets; I'd give back all my vain feelin's, and rej'icin's in hand and eye, if that poor eagle was only on its nest ag'in, with its young, praisin' the Lord, for any thing that we can know about the matter, for health and strength!"

The listeners were confounded with this proof of sudden repentance in the hunter, and that too for an indulgence so very common, that men seldom stop to weigh its consequences, or the physical suffering it may bring on the unoffending and helpless. The Delaware understood what was said, though he scarce understood the feelings which had prompted the words, and by way of disposing of the difficulty, he drew his keen knife, and severed the head of the sufferer from its body.

"What a thing is power!" continued the hunter, "and what a thing it is, to have it, and not to know how to use it. It's no wonder, Judith, that the great so often fail of their duties, when even the little and the humble find it so hard to do what's right, and not to do what's wrong. Then, how one evil act brings others a'ter it! Now, wasn't it for this furlough of mine, which must soon take me back to the Mingos, I'd find this creatur's nest, if I travelled the woods a forthnight—though an eagle's nest is soon found by them that understands the bird's natur',—but I'd travel a forthnight rather than not find it, just to put the young, too, out of their pain."

"I'm glad to hear you say this, Deerslayer," observed Hetty, "and God will be more apt to remember your sorrow for what you've done, than the wickedness itself. I thought how wicked it was to kill harmless birds, while you were shooting, and meant to tell you so; but, I do n't know how it happened,—I was so curious to see if you *could* hit an eagle at so great a height, that I forgot altogether to speak, 'till the mischief was done."

"That's it; that's just it, my good Hetty. We can all see our faults and mistakes when it's too late to help them! Howsever, I'm glad you did n't speak, for I do n't think a word or two would have stopped me, just at that moment, and so the sin stands in its nakedness, and not aggravated by any unheeded calls to forbear. Well, well, bitter thoughts are hard to be borne at all times, but there's times when they're harder than at others."

Little did Deerslayer know, while thus indulging in feelings that were natural to the man, and so strictly in accordance with his own unsophisticated and just principles, that, in the course of the inscrutable providence, which so uniformly and yet so mysteriously covers all events with its mantle, the very fault he was disposed so severely to censure, was to be made the means of determining his own earthly fate. The mode and the moment in which he was to feel the influence of this interference, it would be premature to relate, but both will appear in the course of the succeeding chapters. As for the young man, he now slowly left the Ark, like one sorrowing for his misdeeds, and seated himself in silence on the platform. By this time the sun had ascended to some height, and its appearance, taken in connection with his present feelings, induced him to prepare to depart. The Delaware got the canoe ready for his friend, as soon as apprised of his intention, while Hist busied herself in making the few arrangements that were thought necessary to his comfort. All this was done without ostentation, but in a way that left Deerslayer fully acquainted with, and equally disposed to appreciate, the motive. When all was ready, both returned to the side of Judith and Hetty, neither of whom had moved from the spot where the young hunter sat.

"The best fri'nds must often part," the last began, when he saw the whole party grouped around him—"yes, fri'ndship can't alter the ways of Providence, and let our feelin's be as they may, we must part. I've often thought there's moments when our words dwell longer on the mind than common, and when advice is remembered, just because the mouth that gives it, is n't likely to give it ag'in. No one knows what will happen in this world, and therefore it may be well, when fri'nds separate under a likelihood that the parting may be long, to say a few words in kindness, as a sort of keepsakes. If all but one will go into the Ark, I'll talk to each in turn, and what is more, I'll listen to what you may have to say back ag'in, for it's a poor counsellor that won't take as well as give."

As the meaning of the speaker was understood, the two Indians immediately withdrew as desired, leaving the sisters, however, still standing at the young man's side. A look of Deerslayer's induced Judith to explain.

"You can advise Hetty as you land," she said hastily, "for I intend that she shall accompany you to the shore."

"Is this wise, Judith? It's true, that under common sar-cumstances a feeble-mind is a great protection among red-skins, but when their feelin's are up, and they're bent on revenge, it's hard to say what may come to pass. Besides—"

"What were you about to say, Deerslayer?" asked Judith, whose gentleness of voice and manner amounted nearly to tenderness, though she struggled hard to keep her emotions and apprehensions in subjection.

"Why, simply that there are sights and doin's that one even as little gifted with reason and memory as Hetty here, might better not witness. So, Judith, you would do well to let me land alone, and to keep your sister back."

"Never fear for me, Deerslayer," put in Hetty, who com-prehended enough of the discourse to know its general drift, "I'm feeble minded, and that they say is an excuse for going any where; and what that won't excuse, will be overlooked on account of the bible I always carry. It is wonderful, Judith, how all sorts of men; the trappers as well as the hunters; red-men as well as white; Mingos as well as Delawares do reverence and fear the bible!"

"I think you have not the least ground to fear any injury, Hetty," answered the sister, "and therefore I shall insist on your going to the Huron camp with our friend. Your being there can do no harm, not even to yourself, and may do great good to Deerslayer."

"This is not a moment, Judith, to dispute, and so have the matter your own way," returned the young man. "Get yourself ready, Hetty, and go into the canoe, for I've a few parting words to say to your sister, which can do you no good."

Judith, and her companion, continued silent, until Hetty had so far complied, as to leave them alone, when Deerslayer took up the subject, as if it had been interrupted by some or-dinary occurrence, and in a very matter of fact way.

"Words spoken at parting, and which may be the last we ever hear from a fri'nd are not soon forgotten," he repeated, "and so Judith, I intend to speak to you like a brother, seein' I'm not old enough to be your father. In the first place, I wish to caution you ag'in your inimies, of which two may be said to ha'nt your very footsteps, and to beset your ways. The first is oncommon good-looks, which is as dangerous a foe to some young women, as a whole tribe of Mingos could prove, and which calls for great watchfulness — not to admire and praise — but to distrust and sarcumvent. Yes, good looks may be sarcumvented, and fairly outwitted, too. In order to do this you've only to remember that they melt like the snows, and, when once gone, they never come back ag'in. The seasons come and go, Judith, and if we have winter, with storms and frosts, and spring with chills and leafless trees, we have summer with its sun and glorious skies, and fall with its fruits, and a garment thrown over the forest, that no beauty of the town could rummage out of all the shops in America. 'Arth is in an etarnal round, the goodness of God, bringing back the pleasant when we've had enough of the onpleasant. But it's not so with good looks. *They* are lent for a short time in youth, to be used and not abused, and, as I never met with a young woman to whom providence has been as bountiful, as it has to you, Judith, in this partic'lar, I warn you, as it might be with my dyin' breath, to beware of the inimy — fri'nd, or inimy, as we deal with the gift."

It was so grateful to Judith to hear these unequivocal admissions of her personal charms, that much would have been forgiven to the man, who made them, let him be who he might. But, at that moment, and from a far better feeling, it would not have been easy for Deerslayer seriously to offend her, and she listened with a patience, which, had it been foretold only a week earlier, it would have excited her indignation to hear.

"I understand your meaning, Deerslayer," returned the girl, with a meekness and humility that a little surprised her listener, "and hope to be able to profit by it. But, you have mentioned only one of the enemies I have to fear; who, or what is the other."

"The other is givin' way afore your own good sense and judgment, I find, Judith; yes, he's not as dangerous as I supposed. Howsever, havin' opened the subject, it will be as well to end it honestly. The first inimy you have to be watchful of, as I've already told you, Judith, is oncommon good-looks, and the next is an oncommon knowledge of the sarcumstance. If the first is bad, the last does n't, in any way, mend the matter, so far as safety and peace of mind are consarned."

How much longer the young man would have gone on in his

simple and unsuspecting, but well intentioned manner, it might not be easy to say, had he not been interrupted by his listener's bursting into tears, and giving way to an outbreak of feeling, which was so much the more violent from the fact that it had been with so much difficulty suppressed. At first her sobs were so violent and uncontrollable that Deerslayer was a little appalled, and he was abundantly repentant from the instant that he discovered how much greater was the effect produced by his words, than he had anticipated. Even the austere and exacting are usually appeased by the signs of contrition, but the nature of Deerslayer did not require proofs of intense feelings so strong in order to bring him down to a level with the regrets felt by the girl herself. He arose, as if an adder had stung him, and the accents of the mother that soothes her child were scarcely more gentle and winning than the tones of his voice, as he now expressed his contrition at having gone so far.

"It was well meant, Judith," he said, "but it was not intended to hurt your feelin's so much. I have overdone the advice, I see; yes, I've overdone it, and I crave your pardon for the same. Fri'ndship's an awful thing! Sometimes it chides us for not having done enough; and then, ag'in it speaks in strong words for havin' done too much. Howsever, I acknowledge I've overdone the matter, and as I've a ra'al and strong regard for you, I rej'ice to say it, inasmuch as it proves how much better you are, than my own vanity and consaits had made you out to be."

Judith now removed her hands from her face, her tears had ceased, and she unveiled a countenance so winning with the smile which rendered it even radiant, that the young man gazed at her, for a moment, with speechless delight.

"Say no more, Deerslayer," she hastily interposed; "it pains me to hear you find fault with yourself. I know my own weakness, all the better, now I see that you have discovered it; the lesson, bitter as I have found it for a moment, shall not be forgotten. We will not talk any longer, of these things, for I do not feel myself brave enough for the undertaking, and I should not like the Delaware, or Hist, or even Hetty, to notice my weakness. Farewell, Deerslayer; may God bless and protect you as your honest heart deserves blessings and protection, and as I must think he will."

Judith had so far regained the superiority that properly

belonged to her better education, high spirit, and surpassing personal advantages, as to preserve the ascendancy she had thus accidentally obtained, and effectually prevented any return to the subject that was as singularly interrupted, as it had been singularly introduced. The young man permitted her to have every thing her own way, and when she pressed his hard hand in both her own, he made no resistance, but submitted to the homage as quietly, and with quite as matter of course a manner, as a sovereign would have received a similar tribute from a subject, or the mistress from her suitor. Feeling had flushed the face and illuminated the whole countenance of the girl, and her beauty was never more resplendant than when she cast a parting glance at the youth. That glance was filled with anxiety, interest and gentle pity. At the next instant, she darted into the hut and was seen no more, though she spoke to Hist from a window, to inform her that their friend expected her appearance.

"You know enough of red skin natur', and red skin usages, Wah-ta!-Wah, to see the condition I am in on account of this furlough," commenced the hunter in Delaware, as soon as the patient and submissive girl of that people had moved quietly to his side; "you will therefore best onderstand how onlikely I am ever to talk with you ag'in. I've but little to say; but that little comes from long livin' among your people, and from havin' obsarved and noted their usages. The life of a woman is hard at the best, but I must own, though I'm not opinionated in favor of my own colour, that it is harder among the red men than it is among the pale faces. This is a p'int on which christians may well boast, if boasting can be set down for christianity in any manner or form, which I rather think it cannot. Howsever, all women have their trials. Red women have their'n in what I should call the nat'ral way, while white women take 'em innoculated like. Bear your burthen, Hist, becomingly, and remember if it be a little toilsome, how much lighter it is than that of most Indian women. I know the Sarpent well — what I call cordially — and he will never be a tyrant to any thing he loves, though he will expect to be treated himself like a Mohican Chief. There will be cloudy days in your lodge I suppose, for they happen under all usages, and among all people, but, by keepin' the windows of the heart open there will always be room for the sun-shine to enter. You come of a great stock yourself, and so does Chingachgook. It's not very likely that either will ever forget the sarcumstance, and do any thing to disgrace your forefathers. Nevertheless, likin' is a tender plant, and never thrives long when watered with tears. Let the 'arth around your married happiness be moistened by the dews of kindness."

"My pale brother is very wise; Wah will keep in her mind all that his wisdom tells her."

"That's judicious and womanly, Hist. Care in listening, and stout-heartedness in holding to good counsel, is a wife's great protection. And, now, ask the Sarpent to come and speak with me, for a moment, and carry away with you all my best wishes and prayers. I shall think of you Hist, and of your intended husband, let what may come to pass, and always wish you well, here and hereafter, whether the last is to be according to Indian idees, or christian doctrines."

Hist shed no tear at parting. She was sustained by the high resolution of one who had decided on her course, but her dark eyes were luminous with the feelings that glowed within, and her pretty countenance beamed with an expression of determination that was in marked and singular contrast to its ordinary gentleness. It was but a minute ere the Delaware advanced to the side of his friend with the light, noiseless tread of an Indian.

"Come, this-a-way, Sarpent, here more out of sight of the women," commenced the Deerslayer, "for I've several things to say that must n't so much as be suspected, much less overheard. *You* know too well the natur' of furloughs and Mingos to have any doubts or misgivin's consarnin' what is like to happen, when I get back to the camp. On them two p'ints therefore, a few words will go a great way. In the first place, chief, I wish to say a little about Hist, and the manner in which you red men treat your wives. I suppose it's accordin' to the gifts of your people that the women should work, and the men hunt; but there's such a thing as moderation in all matters. As for huntin', I see no good reason why any limits need be set to *that*, but Hist comes of too good a stock to toil like a common drudge. One of your means and standin' need never want for corn, or potatoes, or any thing that the fields yield;

therefore, I hope the hoe will never be put into the hands of any wife of yourn. You know I am not quite a beggar, and all I own, whether in ammunition, skins, arms, or calicoes, I give to Hist, should I not come back to claim them by the end of the season. This will set the maiden up, and will buy labor for her, for a long time to come. I suppose I need n't tell you to love the young woman, for that you do already, and whomsoever the man ra'ally loves, he'll be likely enough to cherish. Nevertheless, it can do no harm to say that kind words never rankle, while bitter words do. I know you're a man, Sarpent, that is less apt to talk in his own lodge, than to speak at the Council Fire; but forgetful moments may overtake us all, and the practyse of kind doin', and kind talkin', is a wonderful advantage in keepin' peace in a cabin, as well as on a hunt."

"My ears are open," returned the Delaware gravely; "the words of my brother have entered so far that they never can fall out again. They are like rings, that have no end, and cannot drop. Let him speak on; the song of the wren and the voice of a friend never tire."

"I will speak a little longer, chief, but you will excuse it for the sake of old companionship, should I now talk about myself. If the worst comes to the worst, it's not likely there'll be much left of me but ashes, so a grave would be useless, and a sort of vanity. On that score I'm no way partic'lar, though it might be well enough to take a look at the remains of the pile, and should any bones, or pieces be found, 'twould be more decent to gather them together, and bury them, than to let them lie for the wolves to gnaw at, and howl over. These matters can make no great difference in the ind, but men of white blood and christian feelin's have rather a gift for graves."

"It shall be done as my brother says," returned the Indian, gravely. "If his mind is full, let him empty it in the bosom of a friend."

"I thank you, Sarpent; my mind's easy enough; yes, it's tolerable easy. Idees will come uppermost that I'm not apt to think about in common, it's true, but by striving ag'in some, and lettin' other some out, all will come right, in the long run. There's one thing, howsever,chief, that *does* seem to me to be *on*reasonable, and ag'in natur', though the missionaries say it's true, and bein' of my religion and colour I feel bound to believe them. They say an Injin may torment and tortur' the body to his heart's content, and scalp, and cut, and tear, and burn, and consume all his inventions and deviltries, until nothin' is left but ashes, and they shall be scattered to the four winds of heaven, yet when the trumpet of God shall sound, all will come together ag'in, and the man will stand forth in his flesh, the same creatur' as to looks, if not as to feelin's, that he was afore he was harmed!"

"The missionaries are good men — mean well," returned the Delaware courteously; "they are not great medicines. They think all they say, Deerslayer; that is no reason why warriors and orators should be all ears. When Chingachgook shall see the father of Tamenund standing in his scalp, and paint, and war lock, then will he believe the missionaries."

"Seein' *is* believin', of a sartainty; ahs! me — and some of us may see these things sooner than we thought. I comprehind your meanin' about Tamenund's father, Sarpent, and the idee's a close idee. Tamenund is now an elderly man, say eighty every day of it, and his father was scalped, and tormented, and burnt, when the present prophet was a youngster. Yes, if one could see *that* come to pass, there would n't be much difficulty in yieldin' faith to all that the missionaries say. Howsever, I am not ag'in the opinion now, for you must know, Sarpent, that the great principle of christianity is to believe *without* seeing, and a man should always act up to his religion and principles, let them be what they may."

"That is strange for a wise nation!" said the Delaware with emphasis. "The red man looks hard, that he may *see* and understand."

"Yes, that's plauserble, and is agreeable to mortal pride, but it's not as deep as it seems. If we could understand *all* we see, Sarpent, there might be not only sense, but safety, in refusin' to give faith to any *one* thing that we might find oncomperhensible; but when there's so many things, about which, it may be said, we know nothin' at all, why, there's little use, and no reason, in bein' difficult touchin' any one in partic'lar. For my part, Delaware, all my thoughts have n't been on the game, when outlyin' in the hunts and scoutin's, of our youth. Many's the hour I've passed, pleasantly enough too, in what is tarmed conterplation by my people. On such occasions the mind is actyve, though the body seems lazy and listless. An open spot on a mountain side, where a wide look can be had at the heavens and the 'arth, is a most judicious place for a man to get a just idee of the power of the Manitou, and of his own littleness. At such times, there is n't any great disposition to find fault with little difficulties, in the way of comperhension, as there are so many big ones to hide them. Believin' comes easy enough to me, at such times, and, if the Lord made man first out of 'arth, as they tell me it is written in the bible; then turns him into dust, at death; I see no great difficulty in the way to bringin' him back in the body, though ashes be the only substance left. These things lie beyond our understandin', though they may and do lie so close to our feelin's. But, of all the doctrines, Sarpent, that which disturbs me, and disconsarts my mind the most, is the one which teaches us to think that a pale face goes to one heaven, and a red skin to another; it may separate in death, them which lived much together, and loved each other well, in life!"

"Do the missionaries teach their white brethren to think it is so?" demanded the Indian, with serious earnestness. "The Delawares believe that good men and brave warriors will hunt together in the same pleasant woods, let them belong to whatever tribe they may; that all the unjust Indians and cowards, will have to sneak in with the dogs and the wolves, to get venison for their lodges."

"Tis wonderful how many consaits mankind have consarnin' happiness and misery, here after!" exclaimed the hunter, borne away by the power of his own thoughts. "Some believe in burnin's and flames, and some think punishment is to eat with the wolves and dogs. Then, ag'in, some fancy heaven to be only the carryin' out of their own 'arthly longin's, while others fancy it all gold and shinin' lights! Well, I've an idee of my own, in that matter, which is just this, Sarpent. Whenever I've done wrong, I've ginirally found 'twas owin' to some blindness of the mind, which hid the right from view, and when sight has returned, then has come sorrow and repentance. Now, I consait that, after death, when the body is laid aside, or, if used at all, is purified and without its longin's, the spirit sees all things in their ra'al lights and never becomes blind to truth and justice. Such bein' the case, all that has been done in life, is beheld as plainly as the sun is seen at noon; the good brings joy, while the evil brings sorrow. There's nothin' onreasonable in that, but it's agreeable to every man's exper'ence."

"I thought the pale faces believed *all* men were wicked; who then could ever find the white man's heaven?"

"That's ingen'ous, but it falls short of the missionary teachin's. You'll be christianized one day, I make no doubt, and then 'twill all come plain enough. You must know, Sarpent, that there's been a great deed of salvation done, that, by God's help, enables all men to find a pardon for their wickednesses, and *that* is the essence of the white man's religion. I can't stop to talk this matter over with you any longer, for Hetty's in the canoe, and the furlough takes me away, but the time will come I hope, when you'll *feel* these things; for, after all, they must be *felt* rather than reasoned about. Ah's! me; well, Delaware, there's my hand; you know it's that of a fri'nd, and will shake it as such, though it never has done you one half the good its owner wishes it had."

The Indian took the offered hand, and returned its pressure warmly. Then falling back on his acquired stoicism of manner, which so many mistake for constitutional indifference, he drew up in reserve, and prepared to part from his friend with dignity. Deerslayer, however, was more natural, nor would he have at all cared about giving way to his feelings, had not the recent conduct and language of Judith given him some secret, though ill defined apprehensions of a scene. He was too humble to imagine the truth concerning the actual feelings of that beautiful girl, while he was too observant not to have noted the struggle she had maintained with herself, and which had so often led her to the very verge of discovery. That something extraordinary was concealed in her breast, he thought obvious enough, and, through a sentiment of manly delicacy that would have done credit to the highest human refinement, he shrunk from any exposure of her secret that might subsequently cause regret to the girl, herself. He, therefore, determined to depart, now, and that without any further manifestations of feeling either from himself, or from others.

"God bless you! Sarpent — God bless you!" cried the hunter, as the canoe left the side of the platform. "Your Manitou and my God, only know when and where we shall meet agin; I shall count it a great blessing, and a full reward for any little good I may have done on 'arth, if we shall be permitted to know each other, and to consort together, hereafter, as we have so long done in these pleasant woods afore us!"

Chingachgook waved his hand. Drawing the light blanket he wore over his head, as a Roman would conceal his grief in his robes, he slowly withdrew into the Ark, in order to indulge his sorrow and his musings, alone. Deerslayer did not speak again, until the canoe was half-way to the shore. Then he suddenly ceased paddling, at an interruption that came from the mild, musical voice of Hetty.

"Why do *you* go back to the Hurons, Deerslayer?" demanded the girl. "They say *I* am feeble-minded, and such they never harm, but you have as much sense as Hurry Harry; and more too, Judith thinks, though I don't see how that can well be."

"Ah! Hetty, afore we land I must converse a little with you child, and that too on matters touching your own welfare, principally. Stop paddling—or, rather, that the Mingos need n't think we are plotting and contriving, and so treat us accordingly, just dip your paddle lightly, and give the canoe a little motion and no more. That's just the idee and the movement; I see you're ready enough at an appearance, and might be made useful at a sarcumvention if it was lawful now to use one—that's just the idee and the movement! Ah's! me. Desait and a false tongue are evil things, and altogether onbecoming our colour, Hetty, but it *is* a pleasure and a satisfaction to outdo the contrivances of a red-skin in the strife of lawful warfare. My path has been short, and is like soon to have an end, but I can see that the wanderings of a warrior ar n't altogether among brambles and difficulties. There's a bright side to a war-path, as well as to most other things, if we'll only have the wisdom to see it, and the ginerosity to own it."

"And why should your war path, as you call it, come so near to an end, Deerslayer?"

"Because, my good girl, my furlough comes so near to an end. They're likely to have pretty much the same tarmination, as regards time, one following on the heels of the other, as a matter of course."

"I don't understand your meaning, Deerslayer—" returned the girl, looking a little bewildered. "Mother always said people ought to speak more plainly to me than to most other persons, because I'm feeble-minded. Those that are feeble minded, don't understand as easily, as those that have sense."

"Well then, Hetty, the simple truth is this. You know that I'm now a capt*y*ve to the Hurons, and capt*y*ves can't do, in all things, as they please —"

"But how can you be a captive," eagerly interrupted the girl — "when you are out here on the lake, in father's best canoe, and the Indians are in the woods with no canoe at all? *That* can't be true, Deerslayer!"

"I wish with all my heart and soul, Hetty, that you was right, and that I was wrong, instead of your bein' all wrong, and I bein' only too near the truth. Free as I seem to your eyes, gal, I'm bound hand and foot in ra'ality."

"Well it *is* a great misfortune not to have sense! Now, I can't see, or understand that you are a captive, or bound in any manner. If you are bound, with what are your hands and feet fastened?"

"With a furlough, gal; that's a thong that binds tighter than any chain. One *may* be broken, but the other can't. Ropes and chains allow of knives, and desait, and contrivances; but a furlough can be neither cut, slipped nor sarcumvented."

"What sort of a thing is a furlough, then, if it be stronger than hemp or iron? I never saw a furlough."

"I hope you may never feel one, gal; the tie is altogether in the feelin's, in these matters, and therefore is to be felt and not seen. You can understand what is is to give a promise, I dare to say, good little Hetty?"

"Certainly. A promise is to say you will do a thing, and that binds you to be as good as your word. Mother always kept her promises to me, and then she said it would be wicked if I did n't keep my promises to her, and to every body else."

"You have had a good mother, in some matters, child, whatever she may have been in other some. That is a promise, and as you say it must be kept. Now, I fell into the hands of the Mingos last night, and they let me come off to see my fri'nds and send messages in to my own colour, if any such feel consarn on my account, on condition that I shall be back, when the sun is up to-day, and take whatever their revenge and hatred can contrive, in the way of torments, in satisfaction for the life of a warrior that fell by my rifle, as well as for that of the young woman shot by Hurry, and other disapp'intments met with on and about this lake. What is called a promise atween mother and darter, or even atween strangers in the settlements is called a furlough when given by one soldier to another, on a warpath. And now I suppose you understand my situation, Hetty."

The girl made no answer for some time, but she ceased paddling altogether, as if the novel idea distracted her mind too much to admit of other employment. Then she resumed the dialogue earnestly and with solicitude.

"Do you think the Hurons will have the heart to do what you say, Deerslayer?" she asked. "I have found them kind and harmless."

"That's true enough as consarns one like you, Hetty, but it's a very different affair, when it comes to an open inimy, and he too the owner of a pretty sartain rifle. I don't say that they bear me special malice on account of any expl'ites already performed, for that would be bragging, as it might be, on the varge of the grave, but it's no vanity to believe that they know one of their bravest and cunnin'est chiefs fell by my hands. Such bein' the case, the tribe would reproach them if they failed to send the spirit of a pale face to keep the company of the spirit of their red brother; always supposin' that he can catch it. I look for no marcy, Hetty, at their hands; and my principal sorrow is that such a calamity should befal me on my first war-path: that it would come sooner or later, every soldier counts on and expects."

"The Hurons shall *not* harm you, Deerslayer," cried the girl, much excited—"'Tis wicked as well as cruel; I have the bible, here, to tell them so. Do you think I would stand by and see you tormented?"

"I hope not, my good Hetty, I hope not; and, therefore, when the moment comes, I expect you will move off, and not be a witness of what you can't help, while it would grieve you. But, I have n't stopped the paddles to talk of my own afflictions and difficulties, but to speak a little plainly to you, gal, consarnin' your own matters."

"What can you have to say to me, Deerslayer! Since mother died, few talk to me of such things."

"So much the worse, poor gal; yes, 'tis so much the worse, for one of your state of mind needs frequent talking to, in order to escape the snares and desaits of this wicked world. You have n't forgotten Hurry Harry, gal, so soon, I calculate?"

"I!—I forget Henry March!" exclaimed Hetty, starting. "Why should I forget him, Deerslayer, when he is our friend, and only left us last night. Then, the large bright star that mother loved so much to gaze at, was just over the top of yonder tall pine on the mountain, as Hurry got into the canoe; and when you landed him on the point, near the east bay, it was n't more than the length of Judith's handsomest ribbon above it."

"And how can you know how long I was gone, or how far I went to land Hurry, seein' you were not with us, and the distance was so great, to say nothing of the night?"

"Oh! I know when it was, well enough," returned Hetty positively—"There's more ways than one for counting time and distance. When the mind is engaged, it is better than any clock. Mine is feeble, I know, but it goes true enough, in all that touches poor Hurry Harry. Judith will never marry March, Deerslayer."

"That's the p'int, Hetty; that's the very p'int I want to come to. I suppose you know, that it's nat'ral for young people to have kind feelin's for one another, more especially when one happens to be a youth and t'other a maiden. Now, one of your years and mind, gal, that has neither father nor mother, and who lives in a wilderness frequented by hunters and trappers, needs be on her guard against evils she little dreams of."

"What harm can it be to think well of a fellow creature," returned Hetty simply, though the conscious blood was stealing to her cheeks in spite of a spirit so pure that it scarce knew why it prompted the blush, "the bible tells us to 'love them who despitefully use' us, and why should n't we like them that do not."

"Ah! Hetty, the love of the missionaries is n't the sort of likin' I mean. Answer me one thing, child; do you believe yourself to have mind enough to become a wife, and a mother?"

"That's not a proper question to ask a young woman, Deerslayer, and I'll not answer it," returned the girl, in a reproving manner—much as a parent rebukes a child for an act of indiscretion. "If you have any thing to say about Hurry, I'll hear *that*—but you must not speak evil of him; he is absent, and 'tis unkind to talk evil of the absent."

"Your mother has given you so many good lessons, Hetty, that my fears for you, are not as great as they were. Nevertheless, a young woman without parents, in your state of mind, and who is not without beauty, must always be in danger in such a lawless region as this. I would say nothin' amiss of Hurry, who, in the main, is not a bad man for one of his callin', but you ought to know one thing, which it may not be altogether pleasant to tell you, but which must be said. March has a desperate likin' for your sister Judith."

"Well, what of that? Every body admires Judith, she's so handsome, and Hurry has told me, again and again, how much he wishes to marry her. But that will never come to pass, for Judith don't like Hurry. She likes another, and talks about him in her sleep; though you need not ask me who he is, for all the gold in King George's crown, and all the jewels too, would n't tempt me to tell you his name. If sisters can't keep each other's secrets, who can?"

"Sartainly, I do not wish you to tell me, Hetty, nor would it be any advantage to a dyin' man to know. What the tongue says when the mind's asleep, neither head nor heart is answerable for."

"I wish I knew why Judith talks so much in her sleep, about officers, and honest hearts, and false tongues, but I suppose she don't like to tell me, as I'm feeble minded. Is n't it odd, Deerslayer, that Judith don't like Hurry—he, who is the bravest looking youth that ever comes upon the lake, and is as handsome as she is herself. Father always said they would be the comeliest couple in the country, though mother did n't fancy March any more than Judith. There's no telling what will happen, they say, until things actually come to pass."

"Ahs! me—well, poor Hetty, 'tis of no great use to talk to them that can't understand you, and so I'll say no more about what I did wish to speak of, though it lay heavy on my mind. Put the paddle in motion, ag'in, gal, and we'll push for the shore, for the sun is nearly up, and my furlough is almost out."

The canoe now glided ahead, holding its way towards the point where Deerslayer well knew that his enemies expected him, and where he now began to be afraid he might not arrive in season to redeem his plighted faith. Hetty perceiving his impatience, without very clearly comprehending its cause, however, seconded his efforts, in a way that soon rendered their timely return no longer a matter of doubt. Then, and then only, did the young man suffer his exertions to flag, and Hetty began, again, to prattle in her simple confiding manner, though nothing farther was uttered that it may be thought necessary to relate.

Chapter XXVII.

"Thou hast been busy, Death, this day, and yet
But half thy work is done! The gates of hell
Are thronged, yet twice ten thousand spirits more
Who from their warm and healthful tenements
Fear no divorce, must, ere the sun go down,
Enter the world of woe!"—
　　　Southey, *Roderick, the Last of the Goths*, XXIV, 1-6.

O N E experienced in the signs of the heavens, would have seen that the sun wanted but two or three minutes of the zenith, when Deerslayer landed on the point, where the Hurons were now encamped, nearly abreast of the castle. This spot was similar to the one already described, with the exception that the surface of the land was less broken, and less crowded with trees. Owing to these two circumstances, it was all the better suited to the purpose for which it had been selected, the space beneath the branches bearing some resemblance to a densely wooded lawn. Favoured by its position and its spring, it had been much resorted to by savages and hunters, and the natural grasses had succeeded their fires, leaving an appearance of sward in places, a very unusual accompaniment of the virgin forest. Nor was the margin of water fringed with bushes, as on so much of its shore, but the eye penetrated the woods immediately on reaching the strand, commanding nearly the whole area of the projection.

If it was a point of honor with the Indian warrior to redeem his word, when pledged to return and meet his death at a given hour, so was it a point of characteristic pride to show no womanish impatience, but to reappear as nearly as possible at the appointed moment. It was well not to exceed the grace accorded by the generosity of the enemy, but it was better to meet it to a minute. Something of this dramatic effect mingles with most of the graver usages of the American aborigines, and no doubt, like the prevalence of a similar feeling among people more sophisticated and refined, may be referred to a principle of nature. We all love the wonderful, and when it

comes attended by chivalrous self-devotion and a rigid regard
to honor, it presents itself to our admiration in a shape doubly
attractive. As respects Deerslayer, though he took a pride in
showing his white blood, by often deviating from the usages of
the red-men, he frequently dropped into their customs, and
oftener into their feelings, unconsciously to himself, in consequence of having no other arbiters to appeal to, than their
judgments and tastes. On the present occasion, he would have
abstained from betraying a feverish haste by a too speedy
return, since it would have contained a tacit admission that
the time asked for, was more than had been wanted; but, on
the other hand, had the idea occurred to him, he would have
quickened his movements a little, in order to avoid the
dramatic appearance of returning at the precise instant set as
the utmost limit of his absence. Still, accident had interfered to
defeat the last intention, for when the young man put his foot
on the point, and advanced with a steady tread towards the
group of chiefs that was seated in grave array on a fallen tree,
the oldest of their number cast his eye upward, at an opening
in the trees, and pointed out to his companions the startling
fact that the sun was just entering a space that was known to
mark the zenith. A common, but low exclamation of surprise
and admiration, escaped every mouth, and the grim warriors
looked at each other, some with envy and disappointment,
some with astonishment at the precise accuracy of their victim,
and others with a more generous and liberal feeling. The
American Indian always deemed his moral victories the
noblest, prizing the groans and yielding of his victim under
torture, more than the trophy of his scalp; and the trophy itself
more than his life. To slay, and not to bring off the proof of
victory, indeed, was scarcely deemed honorable, even these
rude and fierce tenants of the forest, like their more nurtured
brethren of the court and the camp, having set up for
themselves imaginary and arbitrary points of honor, to sup-
plant the conclusions of the right, and the decisions of reason.

The Hurons had been divided in their opinions concerning
the probability of their captive's return. Most among them, indeed, had not expected it possible for a pale-face to come back
voluntarily, and meet the known penalties of an Indian torture; but a few of the seniors expected better things from one

who had already shown himself so singularly cool, brave and upright. The party had come to its decision, however, less in the expectation of finding the pledge redeemed, than in the hope of disgracing the Delawares by casting into their teeth the delinquency of one bred in their villages. They would have greatly preferred that Chingachgook should be their prisoner, and prove the traitor, but the pale-face scion of the hated stock was no bad substitute, for their purposes, failing in their designs against the ancient stem. With a view to render their triumph as signal as possible, in the event of the hour's passing without the reappearance of the hunter, all the warriors and scouts of the party had been called in, and the whole band, men, women and children, was now assembled at this single point, to be a witness of the expected scene. As the castle was in plain view, and by no means distant, it was easily watched by day-light, and, it being thought that its inmates were now limited to Hurry, the Delaware and the two girls, no apprehensions were felt, of their being able to escape unseen. A large raft having a breast-work of logs, had been prepared, and was in actual readiness to be used against either Ark or Castle, as occasion might require, so soon as the fate of Deerslayer was determined, the seniors of the party having come to the opinion that it was getting to be hazardous to delay their departure for Canada, beyond the coming night. In short, the band waited merely to dispose of this single affair, ere it brought matters with those in the Castle to a crisis, and prepared to commence its retreat towards the distant waters of Ontario.

It was an imposing scene, into which Deerslayer now found himself advancing. All the older warriors were seated on the trunk of the fallen tree, waiting his approach with grave decorum. On the right, stood the young men, armed, while the left was occupied by the women and children. In the centre was an open space of considerable extent, always canopied by leaves, but from which the underbrush, dead wood, and other obstacles had been carefully removed. The more open area had probably been much used by former parties, for this was the place where the appearance of a sward was the most decided. The arches of the woods, even at high noon, cast their sombre shadows on the spot, which the brilliant rays of the sun that struggled through the leaves contributed to mellow, and, if such an expression can be used, to illuminate. It was probably from a similar scene that the mind of man first got its idea of the effects of gothic tracery and churchly hues, this temple of nature producing some such effect, so far as light and shadow were concerned, as the well known offspring of human invention.

As was not unusual among the tribes and wandering bands of the Aborigines, two chiefs shared, in nearly equal degrees, the principal and primitive authority that was wielded over these children of the forest. There were several who might claim the distinction of being chief men, but the two in question were so much superior to all the rest in influence, that, when they agreed, no one disputed their mandates, and when they were divided the band hesitated, like men who had lost their governing principle of action. It was also in conformity with practice, perhaps we might add in conformity with nature, that one of the chiefs was indebted to his mind for his influence, whereas the other owed his distinction altogether to qualities that were physical. One was a senior, well known for eloquence in debate, wisdom in council, and prudence in measures; while his great competitor, if not his rival, was a brave distinguished in war, notorious for ferocity, and remarkable, in the way of intellect, for nothing but the cunning and expedients of the war path. The first was Rivenoak, who has already been introduced to the reader, while the last was called le Panthère, in the language of the Canadas, or the Panther, to resort to the vernacular of the English colonies. The appellation of the fighting chief was supposed to indicate the qualities of the warrior, agreeably to a practice of the red man's nomenclature, ferocity, cunning and treachery being, perhaps, the distinctive features of his character. The title had been received from the French, and was prized so much the more from that circumstance, the Indian submitting profoundly to the greater intelligence of his pale face allies, in most things of this nature. How well the *sobriquet* was merited, will be seen in the sequel.

Rivenoak and the Panther sat side by side awaiting the approach of their prisoner, as Deerslayer put his moccasined foot on the strand, nor did either move, or utter a syllable, until the young man had advanced into the centre of the area, and proclaimed his presence with his voice. This was done firmly, though in the simple manner that marked the character of the individual.

"Here I am, Mingos," he said, in the dialect of the Delawares, a language that most present understood; "here I am, and there is the sun. One is not more true to the laws of natur', than the other has proved true to his word. I am your prisoner; do with me what you please. My business with man and 'arth is settled; nothing remains now but to meet the white man's God, accordin' to a white man's duties and gifts."

A murmur of approbation escaped even the women at this address, and, for an instant there was a strong and pretty general desire to adopt into the tribe, one who owned so brave a spirit. Still there were dissenters from this wish, among the principal of whom might be classed the Panther, and his sister, le Sumach, so called from the number of her children, who was the widow of le Loup Cervier, now known to have fallen by the hand of the captive. Native ferocity held one in subjection, while the corroding passion of revenge prevented the other from admitting any gentler feeling at the moment. Not so with Rivenoak. This chief arose, stretched his arm before him, in a gesture of courtesy, and paid his compliments with an ease and dignity that a prince might have envied. As, in that band, his wisdom and eloquence were confessedly without rivals, he knew that on himself would properly fall the duty of first replying to the speech of the pale-face.

"Pale-face, you are honest," said the Huron orator. "My people are happy in having captured a man, and not a skulking fox. We now know you; we shall treat you like a brave. If you have slain one of our warriors, and helped to kill others, you have a life of your own ready to give away in return. Some of my young men thought that the blood of a pale face was too thin; that it would refuse to run under the Huron knife. You will show them it is not so; your heart is stout, as well as your body. It is a pleasure to make such a prisoner; should my warriors say that the death of le Loup Cervier ought not to be forgotten, and that he cannot travel towards the land of spirits alone, that his enemy must be sent to overtake him, they will remember that he fell by the hand of a brave, and send you after him with such signs of our friendship as shall not make him ashamed to keep your company. I have spoken; you know what I have said."

"True enough, Mingo, all true as the gospel," returned the simple minded hunter, "you *have* spoken, and I *do* know not only what you have *said*, but, what is still more important, what you *mean*. I dare to say your warrior the Lynx, was a stout-hearted brave, and worthy of your fri'ndship and respect, but I do not feel unworthy to keep his company, without any passport from your hands. Nevertheless, here I am, ready to receive judgment from your council, if, indeed, the matter was not detarmined among you, afore I got back."

"My old men would not sit in council over a pale face until they saw him among them," answered Rivenoak, looking around him a little ironically; "they said it would be like sitting in council over the winds; they go where they will, and come back as they see fit, and not otherwise. There was one voice that spoke in your favor, Deerslayer, but it was alone, like the song of the wren whose mate has been struck by the hawk."

"I thank that voice whosever it may have been, Mingo, and will say it was as true a voice, as the rest were lying voices. A furlough is as binding on a pale-face, if he be honest, as it is on a red skin, and was it not so, I would never bring disgrace on the Delawares, among whom I may be said to have received my edication. But words are useless, and lead to braggin' feelin's; here I am; act your will on me."

Rivenoak made a sign of acquiescence, and then a short conference was privately held among the chiefs. As soon as the latter ended, three or four young men fell back from among the armed group, and disappeared. Then it was signified to the prisoner that he was at liberty to go at large on the point, until a council was held concerning his fate. There was more of seeming, than of real confidence, however, in this apparent liberality, inasmuch as the young men mentioned, already formed a line of sentinels across the breadth of the point, in-land, and escape from any other part was out of the question. Even the canoe was removed beyond this line of sentinels, to a spot where it was considered safe from any sudden attempt. These precautions did not proceed from a failure of con-fidence, but from the circumstance that the prisoner had now complied with all the required conditions of his parole, and it would have been considered a commendable and honorable exploit to escape from his foes. So nice, indeed, were the distinctions drawn by the savages, in cases of this nature, that they often gave their victims a chance to evade the torture, deeming it as creditable to the captors to overtake, or to out wit a fugitive, when his exertions were supposed to be quickened by the extreme jeopardy of his situation, as it was for him to get clear from so much extraordinary vigilance.

Nor was Deerslayer unconscious of, or forgetful, of his rights, and of his opportunities. Could he now have seen any probable opening for an escape, the attempt would not have been delayed a minute. But the case seem'd desperate. He was aware of the line of sentinels, and felt the difficulty of breaking through it, unharmed. The lake offered no advantages, as the canoe would have given his foes the greatest facilities for over-taking him; else would he have found it no difficult task to swim as far as the castle. As he walked about the point, he even examined the spot to ascertain if it offered no place of conceal-ment, but its openness, its size, and the hundred watchful glances that were turned towards him, even while those who made them affected not to see him, prevented any such expe-dient from succeeding. The dread and disgrace of failure had no influence on Deerslayer, who deemed it even a point of honor to reason and feel like a white man, rather than as an In-dian, and who felt it a sort of duty, to do all he could, that did not involve a dereliction from principle, in order to save his life. Still he hesitated about making the effort, for he also felt that he ought to see the chance of success before he committed himself.

In the mean time the business of the camp appeared to pro-ceed in its regular train. The chiefs consulted apart, admitting no one but the Sumach to their councils, for she, the widow of the fallen warrior, had an exclusive right to be heard on such an occasion. The young men strolled about in indolent listlessness, awaiting the result with Indian patience, while the females prepared the feast that was to celebrate the termina-tion of the affair, whether it proved fortunate, or otherwise, for our hero. No one betrayed feeling, and an indifferent observer, beyond the extreme watchfulness of the sentinels, would have detected no extraordinary movement or sensation to denote the real state of things. Two or three old women put their heads together, and it appeared unfavorably to the prospects of Deerslayer, by their scowling looks, and angry gestures; but a group of Indian girls were evidently animated by a different impulse, as was apparent by stolen glances that expressed pity and regret. In this condition of the camp, an hour soon glided away.

Suspense is perhaps the feeling of all others that is most difficult to be supported. When Deerslayer landed, he fully expected in the course of a few minutes to undergo the tortures of an Indian revenge, and he was prepared to meet his fate, manfully; but, the delay proved far more trying than the nearer approach of suffering, and the intended victim began seriously to meditate some desperate effort at escape, as it might be from sheer anxiety to terminate the scene, when he was suddenly summoned, to appear once more in front of his judges, who had already arranged the band in its former order, in readiness to receive him.

"Killer of the Deer," commenced Rivenoak, as soon as his captive stood before him, "my aged men have listened to wise words; they are ready to speak. You are a man whose fathers came from beyond the rising sun; we are children of the setting sun; we turn our faces towards the Great Sweet Lakes, when we look towards our villages. It may be a wide country and full of riches towards the morning, but it is very pleasant towards the evening. We love most to look in that direction. When we gaze at the east, we feel afraid, canoe after canoe bringing more and more of your people in the track of the sun, as if their land was so full as to run over. The red men are few already; they have need of help. One of our best lodges has lately been emptied, by the death of its master; it will be a long time before his son can grow big enough to sit in his place. There is his widow; she will want venison to feed her and her children, for her sons are yet like the young of the robin, before they quit the nest. By your hand has this great calamity befallen her. She has two duties; one to le Loup Cervier, and one to his children. Scalp for scalp, life for life, blood for blood, is one law; to feed her young, another. We know you, Killer of the Deer. You are honest; when you say a thing, it is so. You have but one tongue, and that is not forked, like a snake's. Your head is never hid in the grass; all can see it. What you say, that will you do. You are just. When you have done wrong, it is your wish to do right, again, as soon as you can. Here is the Sumach; she is alone in her wigwam, with children crying around her for food—yonder is a rifle; it is loaded and ready to be fired. Take the gun, go forth and shoot a deer; bring the venison and lay it before the widow of Le Loup Cervier, feed her children; call yourself her husband. After which, your heart will no longer be Delaware, but Huron; le Sumach's ears will not hear the cries of her children; my people will count the proper number of warriors."

"I fear'd this, Rivenoak," answered Deerslayer, when the other had ceased speaking—"yes, I did dread that it would come to this. Howsever, the truth is soon told, and that will put an end to all expectations on this head. Mingo, I'm white and christian born; 't would ill become me to take a wife, under red-skin forms, from among heathen. That which I wouln't do, in peaceable times, and under a bright sun, still less would I do behind clouds, in order to save my life. I may never marry; most likely Providence in putting me, up here, in the woods, has intended I should live single, and without a lodge of my own; but should such a thing come to pass, none but a woman of my own colour and gifts shall darken the door of my wigwam. As for feeding the young of your dead warrior, I would do that cheerfully, could it be done without discredit; but it cannot, seeing that I can never live in a Huron village. Your own young men must find the Sumach in venison, and the next time she marries, let her take a husband whose legs are not long enough to overrun territory that do n't belong to him. We fou't a fair battle, and he fell; in this, there is nothin' but what a brave expects, and should be ready to meet. As for getting a Mingo heart, as well might you expect to see gray hairs on a boy, or the blackberry growing on the pine. No— no—Huron; my gifts are white so far as wives are consarned; it is Delaware, in all things touchin' Injins."

These words were scarcely out of the mouth of Deerslayer, before a common murmur betrayed the dissatisfaction with which they had been heard. The aged women, in particular, were loud in their expressions of disgust, and the gentle

Sumach, herself, a woman quite old enough to be our hero's mother, was not the least pacific in her denunciations. But all the other manifestations of disappointment and discontent were thrown into the back-ground, by the fierce resentment of the Panther. This grim chief had thought it a degradation to permit his sister to become the wife of a pale face of the Yengeese, at all, and had only given a reluctant consent to the arrangement — one by no means unusual among the Indians, however — at the earnest solicitations of the bereaved widow; and it goaded him to the quick to find his condescension slighted, the honor he had with so much regret been persuaded to accord, contemned. The animal from which he got his name, does not glare on his intended prey, with more frightful ferocity, than his eyes gleamed on the captive, nor was his arm backward in seconding the fierce resentment that almost consumed his breast.

"Dog of the pale faces!" he exclaimed in Iroquois, "go yell among the curs of your own evil hunting grounds!"

The denunciation was accompanied by an appropriate action. Even while speaking his arm was lifted, and the tomahawk hurled. Luckily the loud tones of the speaker had drawn the eye of Deerslayer towards him, else would that moment have probably closed his career. So great was the dexterity with which this dangerous weapon was thrown, and so deadly the intent, that it would have riven the scull of the prisoner, had he not stretched forth an arm, and caught the handle in one of its turns, with a readiness quite as remarkable, as the skill with which the missile had been hurled. The projectile force was so great, notwithstanding, that when Deerslayer's arm was arrested, his hand was raised above and behind his own head, and in the very attitude necessary to return the attack. It is not certain whether the circumstance of finding himself unexpectedly in this menacing posture and armed, tempted the young man to retaliate, or whether sudden resentment overcame his forbearance and prudence. His eye kindled, however, and a small red spot appeared on each cheek, while he cast all his energy into the effort of his arm, and threw back the weapon at his assailant. The unexpectedness of this blow contributed to its success, the Panther neither raising an arm, nor bending his head to avoid it. The keen little axe struck the victim in a perpendicular line with the nose, directly between the eyes, literally braining him on the spot. Sallying forward, as the serpent darts at its enemy even while receiving its own death wound, this man of powerful frame, fell his length into the open area formed by the circle, quivering in death. A common rush to his relief left the captive, for a single instant, quite without the crowd, and, willing to make one desperate effort for life, he bounded off, with the activity of a deer. There was but a breathless instant, when the whole band, old and young, women and children, abandoning the lifeless body of the Panther, where it lay, raised the yell of alarm and followed in pursuit.

Sudden as had been the event which induced Deerslayer to make this desperate trial of speed, his mind was not wholly unprepared for the fearful emergency. In the course of the past hour, he had pondered well on the chances of such an experiment, and had shrewdly calculated all the details of success and failure. At the first leap, therefore, his body was completely under the direction of an intelligence that turned all its efforts to the best account, and prevented every thing like hesitation or indecision at the important instant of the start. To this alone was he indebted for the first great advantage, that of getting through the line of sentinels unharmed. The manner in which this was done, though sufficiently simple, merits a description.

Although the shores of the point were not fringed with bushes, as was the case with most of the others on the lake, it was owing altogether to the circumstance that the spot had been so much used by hunters and fishermen. This fringe commenced on what might be termed the main land, and was as dense as usual, extending in long lines both north and south. In the latter direction, then, Deerslayer held his way, and, as the sentinels were a little without the commencement of this thicket, before the alarm was clearly communicated to them, the fugitive had gained its cover. To run among the bushes, however, was out of the question, and Deerslayer held his way, for some forty or fifty yards, in the water, which was barely knee deep, offering as great an obstacle to the speed of his pursuers, as it did to his own. As soon as a favorable spot presented, he darted through the line of bushes, and issued into the open woods.

Several rifles were discharged at Deerslayer while in the water, and more followed as he came out into the comparative exposure of the clear forest. But the direction of his line of flight, which partially crossed that of the fire, the haste with which the weapons had been aimed, and the general confusion that prevailed in the camp prevented any harm from being done. Bullets whistled past him, and many cut twigs from the branches at his side, but not one touched even his dress. The delay caused by these fruitless attempts was of great service to the fugitive, who had gained more than a hundred yards on even the leading men of the Hurons, ere something like concert and order had entered into the chase. To think of following with rifles in hand, was out of the question, and after emptying their pieces in vague hopes of wounding their captive, the best runners of the Indians threw them aside, calling out to the women and boys to recover and load them, again, as soon as possible.

Deerslayer knew too well the desperate nature of the struggle in which he was engaged to lose one of the precious moments. He also knew that his only hope was to run in a straight line, for as soon as he began to turn, or double, the greater number of his pursuers would put escape out of the question. He held his way therefore, in a diagonal direction up the acclivity, which was neither very high nor very steep, in this part of the mountain, but which was sufficiently toilsome for one contending for life, to render it painfully oppressive. There, however, he slackened his speed, to recover breath, proceeding even at a quick walk, or a slow trot, along the more difficult parts of the way. The Hurons were whooping and leaping behind him, but this he disregarded, well knowing they must overcome the difficulties he had surmounted, ere they could reach the elevation to which he had attained. The summit of the first hill was now quite near him, and he saw, by the formation of the land, that a deep glen intervened, before the base of a second hill could be reached. Walking deliberately to the summit, he glanced eagerly about him, in every direction, in quest of a cover. None offered in the ground, but a fallen tree lay near him, and desperate circumstances required desperate remedies. This tree lay in a line parallel to the glen, at the brow of the hill. To leap on it, and then to force his person as close as possible, under its lower side, took but a moment. Previously to disappearing from his pursuers, however, Deerslayer stood on the height, and gave a cry of triumph, as if exulting at the sight of the descent that lay before him. In the next instant he was stretched beneath the tree.

No sooner was this expedient adopted, than the young man ascertained how desperate had been his own efforts, by the violence of the pulsations in his frame. He could hear his heart beat, and his breathing was like the action of a bellows, in quick motion. Breath was gained, however, and the heart soon ceased to throb, as if about to break through its confinement. The footsteps of those who toiled up the opposite side of the acclivity were now audible, and presently voices and treads announced the arrival of the pursuers. The foremost shouted as they reached the height; then, fearful that their enemy would escape under favor of the descent, each leaped upon the fallen tree, and plunged into the ravine, trusting to get a sight of the pursued, ere he reached the bottom. In this manner, Huron followed Huron, until Natty began to hope the whole had passed. Others succeeded, however, until quite forty had leaped over the tree, and then he counted them, as the surest mode of ascertaining how many could be behind. Presently all were in the bottom of the glen, quite a hundred feet below him, and some had even ascended part of the opposite hill, when it became evident an inquiry was making, as to the direction he had taken. This was the critical moment, and one of nerves less steady, or of a training that had been neglected, would have seized it to rise, and fly. Not so with Deerslayer. He still lay quiet, watching with jealous vigilance every movement below, and fast regaining his breath.

The Hurons now resembled a pack of hounds, at fault. Little was said, but each man ran about, examining the dead leaves, as the hound hunts for the lost scent. The great number of moccasins that had passed made the examination difficult, though the in-toe of an Indian was easily to be distinguished from the freer and wider step of a white man. Believing that no more pursuers remained behind, and hoping to steal away unseen, Deerslayer suddenly threw himself over the tree, and fell on the upper side. This achievement appeared to be effected successfully, and hope beat high in the bosom of the fugitive.

Rising to his hands and feet, after a moment lost in listening to the sounds in the glen, in order to ascertain if he had been seen, the young man next scrambled to the top of the hill, a distance of only ten yards, in the expectation of getting its brow between him and his pursuers, and himself so far under cover. Even this was effected, and he rose to his feet, walking swiftly but steadily along the summit, in a direction opposite to that in which he had first fled. The nature of the calls in the glen, however, soon made him uneasy, and he sprang upon the summit, again, in order to reconnoitre. No sooner did he reach the height than he was seen, and the chase renewed. As it was better footing, on the level ground, Deerslayer now avoided the side hill, holding his flight along the ridge; while the Hurons, judging from the general formation of the land, saw that the ridge would soon melt into the hollow, and kept to the latter, as the easiest mode of heading the fugitive. A few, at the same time, turned south, with a view to prevent his escaping in that direction, while some crossed his trail towards the water, in order to prevent his retreat by the lake, running southerly.

The situation of Deerslayer was now more critical than it ever had been. He was virtually surrounded on three sides, having the lake on the fourth. But he had pondered well on all the chances, and took his measures with coolness, even while at the top of his speed. As is generally the case, with the vigorous border men, he could outrun any single Indian among his pursuers, who were principally formidable to him, on account of their numbers, and the advantages they possessed in position, and he would not have hesitated to break off, in a straight line, at any spot, could he have got the whole band again, fairly behind him. But no such chance did, or indeed could now offer, and when he found that he was descending towards the glen, by the melting away of the ridge, he turned short, at right angles to his previous course, and went down the declivity with tremendous velocity, holding his way towards the shore. Some of his pursuers, came panting up the hill, in direct chase, while most still kept on, in the ravine, intending to head him at its termination.

Deerslayer had now a different, though a desperate project in view. Abandoning all thoughts of escape by the woods, he made the best of his way towards the canoe. He knew where it lay; could it be reached, he had only to run the gauntlet of a few rifles, and success would be certain. None of the warriors had kept their weapons, which would have retarded their speed, and the risk would come either from the uncertain hands of the women, or from those of some well grown boy; though most of the latter were already out in hot pursuit. Every thing seemed propitious to the execution of this plan, and the course being a continued descent, the young man went over the ground at a rate that promised a speedy termination to his toil.

As Deerslayer approached the point, several women, and children were passed, but, though the former endeavoured to cast dried branches between his legs, the terror inspired by his bold retaliation on the redoubted Panther, was so great, that none dared come near enough seriously to molest him. He went by all triumphantly, and reached the fringe of bushes. Plunging through these, our hero found himself once more in the lake, and within fifty feet of the canoe. Here he ceased to run, for he well understood that his breath was now all important to him. He even stooped, as he advanced, and cooled his parched mouth, by scooping water up in his hand, to drink. Still the moments pressed, and he soon stood at the side of the canoe. The first glance told him that the paddles had been removed! This was a sore disappointment, after all his efforts, and, for a single moment, he thought of turning, and of facing his foes by walking with dignity into the centre of the camp, again. But an infernal yell, such as the American savage alone can raise, proclaimed the quick approach of the nearest of his pursuers, and the instinct of life triumphed. Preparing himself duly, and giving a right direction to its bows, he ran off into the water bearing the canoe before him, threw all his strength and skill into a last effort, and cast himself forward so as to fall into the bottom of the light craft, without materially impeding its way. Here he remained on his back, both to regain his breath, and to cover his person from the deadly rifle. The lightness, which was such an advantage in paddling the canoe, now operated unfavorably. The material was so like a feather, that the boat had no momentum, else would the impulse in that smooth and placid sheet have impelled it to a distance from the shore, that would have rendered paddling with the hands safe. Could such a point once be reached, Deerslayer thought he might get far enough out to attract the attention of Chingachgook and Judith, who would not fail to come to his relief, with other canoes, a circumstance that promised every thing. As the young man lay in the bottom of the canoe, he watched its movements, by studying the tops of the trees on the mountainside, and judged of his distance by the time and the motions. Voices on the shore were now numerous, and he heard something said about manning the raft, which, fortunately for the fugitive, lay at a considerable distance, on the other side of the point.

Perhaps the situation of Deerslayer had not been more critical that day, than it was at this moment. It certainly had not been one half as tantalizing. He lay perfectly quiet, for two or three minutes, trusting to the single sense of hearing, confident that the noise in the lake would reach his ears, did any one venture to approach by swimming. Once or twice, he fancied that the element was stirred by the cautious movement of an arm, and then he perceived it was the wash of the water on the pebbles of the strand; for, in mimicry of the ocean, it is seldom that those little lakes are so totally tranquil, as not to possess a slight heaving and setting on their shores. Suddenly all the voices ceased, and a death like stillness pervaded the spot: A quietness as profound as if all lay in the repose of inanimate life. By this time, the canoe had drifted so far as to render nothing visible to Deerslayer, as he lay on his back, except the blue void of space, and a few of those brighter rays, that proceed from the effulgence of the sun, marking his proximity. It was not possible to endure this uncertainty long. The young man well knew that the profound stillness foreboded evil, the savages never being so silent, as when about to strike a blow; resembling the stealthy foot of the panther ere he takes his leap. He took out a knife, and was about to cut a hole through the bark, in order to get a view of the shore, when he paused from a dread of being seen, in the operation, which would direct the enemy where to aim their bullets. At this instant a rifle *was* fired, and the ball pierced both sides of the canoe, within eighteen inches of the spot where his head lay. This was close work, but our hero had too lately gone through that which was closer to be appalled. He lay still half a minute longer, and then he saw the summit of an oak coming slowly within his narrow horizon.

Unable to account for this change, Deerslayer could restrain his impatience no longer. Hitching his body along, with the utmost caution, he got his eye at the bullet hole, and fortunately commanded a very tolerable view of the point. The canoe, by one of those imperceptible impulses that so often decide the fate of men as well as the course of things, had inclined southerly, and was slowly drifting down the lake. It was lucky that Deerslayer had given it a shove sufficiently vigorous to send it past the end of the point, ere it took this inclination, or it must have gone ashore again. As it was, it drifted so near it, as to bring the tops of two or three trees within the range of the young man's view, as has been mentioned, and, indeed, to come in quite as close proximity with the extremity of the point, as was at all safe. The distance could not much have exceeded a hundred feet, though fortunately a light current of air, from the south west, began to set it slowly off shore.

Deerslayer now felt the urgent necessity of resorting to some expedient to get farther from his foes, and if possible to apprise his friends of his situation. The distance rendered the last difficult, while the proximity to the point rendered the first indispensable. As was usual in such craft, a large, round, smooth stone, was in each end of the canoe, for the double purpose of seats and ballast; one of these was within reach of his feet. This stone he contrived to get so far between his legs, as to reach it with his hands, and then he managed to roll it to the side of its fellow in the bows, where the two served to keep the trim of the light boat, while he worked his own body as far aft as possible. Before quitting the shore, and as soon as he perceived that the paddles were gone, Deerslayer had thrown a bit of dead branch into the canoe, and this was within reach of his arm. Removing the cap he wore, he put it on the end of this stick, and just let it appear over the edge of the canoe, as far as possible from his own person. This *ruse* was scarcely adopted, before the young man had a proof how much he had underrated the intelligence of his enemies. In contempt of an artifice so shallow and common place, a bullet was fired directly through another part of the canoe, which actually rased his skin. He dropped the cap, and instantly raised it immediately over his head, as a safeguard. It would seem that this second artifice was unseen, or what was more probable, the Hurons feeling certain of recovering their captive, wished to take him alive.

Deerslayer lay passive a few minutes longer, his eye at the bullet hole, however, and much did he rejoice at seeing that he was drifting, gradually, farther and farther, from the shore. When he looked upward, the tree-tops had disappeared, but he soon found that the canoe was slowly turning, so as to prevent his getting a view of any thing at his peep-hole, but of the two extremities of the lake. He now bethought him of the stick, which was crooked, and offered some facilities for rowing, without the necessity of rising. The experiment succeeded on trial, better even than he had hoped, though his great embarrassment was to keep the canoe straight. That his present manoeuvre was seen, soon became apparent by the clamor on the shore, and a bullet entering the stern of the canoe, traversed its length whistling between the arms of our hero, and passed out at the head. This satisfied the fugitive that he was getting away with tolerable speed, and induced him to increase his efforts. He was making a stronger push than common, when another messenger from the point, broke the stick out-board, and at once deprived him of his oar. As the sound of voices seemed to grow more and more distant, however, Deerslayer determined to leave all to the drift, until he believed himself beyond the reach of bullets. This was nervous work, but it was the wisest of all the expedients that offered, and the young man was encouraged to persevere in it, by the circumstance that he felt his face fanned by the air, a proof that there was a little more wind.

Chapter XXVIII.

"Nor widows' tears, nor tender orphans' cries
Can stop th' invader's force;
Nor swelling seas, nor threatening skies,
Prevent the pirate's course:
Their lives to selfish ends decreed
Through blood and rapine they proceed;
No anxious thoughts of ill repute,
Suspend the impetuous and unjust pursuit;
But power and wealth obtain'd, guilty and great,
Their fellow creatures' fears they raise, or urge their hate."
Congreve, "Pindaric Ode," ii.

By this time, Deerslayer had been twenty minutes in the
the canoe, and he began to grow a little impatient for some
signs of relief from his friends. The position of the boat still
prevented his seeing in any direction, unless it were up or
down the lake, and, though he knew that his line of sight must
pass within a hundred yards of the castle, it, in fact, passed
that distance to the westward of the buildings. The profound
stillness troubled him also, for he knew not whether to ascribe
it to the increasing space between him and the Indians, or to
some new artifice. At length, wearied with fruitless watchfulness, the young man turned himself on his back, closed his
eyes, and awaited the result in determined acquiescence. If the
savages could so completely control their thirst for revenge, he
was resolved to be as calm as themselves, and to trust his fate
to the interpositon of the currents and air.

Some additonal ten minutes may have passed in this quies-
cent manner, on both sides, when Deerslayer thought he heard
a slight noise, like a low rubbing against the bottom of his
canoe. He opened his eyes of course, in expectation of seeing
the face or arm of an Indian rising from the water, and found
that a canopy of leaves was impending directly over his head.
Starting to his feet, the first object that met his eye was
Rivenoak, who had so far aided the slow progress of the boat,
as to draw it on the point, the grating on the strand being the

sound that had first given our hero the alarm. The change in the drift of the canoe, had been altogether owing to the baffling nature of the light currents of the air, aided by some eddies in the water.

"Come," said the Huron with a quiet gesture of authority, to order his prisoner to land, "my young friend has sailed about till he is tired; he will forget how to run again, unless he uses his legs."

"You've the best of it, Huron," returned Deerslayer, stepping steadily from the canoe, and passively following his leader to the open area of the point; "Providence has helped you in an onexpected manner. I'm your prisoner ag'in, and I hope you'll allow that I'm as good at breaking gaol, as I am at keeping furloughs."

"My young friend is a Moose!" exclaimed the Huron. "His legs are very long; they have given my young men trouble. But he is not a fish; he cannot find his way in the lake. We did not shoot him; fish are taken in nets, and not killed by bullets. When he turns Moose, again, he will be treated like a Moose."

"Ay, have your talk, Rivenoak; make the most of your advantage. 'Tis your right, I suppose, and I know it is your gift. On that p'int there'll be no words atween us, for all men must and ought to follow their gifts. Howsever, when your women begin to ta'nt and abuse me, as I suppose will soon happen, let 'em remember that if a pale face struggles for life so long as it's lawful and manful, he knows how to loosen his hold on it, decently, when he feels that the time has come. I'm your captyve; work your will on me."

"My brother has had a long run on the hills, and a pleasant sail on the water," returned Rivenoak, more mildly, smiling, at the same time, in a way that his listener knew denoted pacific intentions. "He has seen the woods; he has seen the water. Which does he like best? Perhaps, he has seen enough, to change his mind, and make him hear reason."

"Speak out, Huron. Something is in your thoughts, and the sooner it is said, the sooner you'll get my answer."

"That is straight! There is no turning in the talk of my pale face friend, though he is a fox in running. I will speak to him; his ears are now open wider than before, and his eyes are not shut. The Sumach is poorer than ever. Once she had a brother and a husband. She had children, too. The time came and the husband started for the Happy Hunting Grounds, without saying farewell; he left her alone with his children. This he could not help, or he would not have done it; le Loup Cervier was a good husband. It was pleasant to see the venison, and wild ducks, and geese, and bear's meat, that hung in his lodge, in winter. It is now gone; it will not keep in warm weather. Who shall bring it back again? Some thought the brother would not forget his sister, and that, next winter, he would see that the lodge should not be empty. We thought this; but the Panther yelled, and followed the husband on the path of death. They are now trying which shall first reach the Happy Hunting Grounds. Some think the Lynx can run fastest, and some think the Panther can jump the farthest. The Sumach thinks both will travel so fast and so far that neither will ever come back. Who shall feed her and her young? The man who told her husband and her brother to quit her lodge, that there might be room for him to come into it. He is a great hunter, and we know that the woman will never want."

"Ay, Huron this is soon settled, accordin' to your notions, but it goes sorely ag'in the grain of a white man's feelin's. I've heard of men's saving their lives this-a-way, and I've know'd them that would prefar death to such a sort of captivity. For my part, I do not seek my end, nor do I seek matrimony."

"The pale face will think of this, while my people get ready for the council. He will be told what will happen. Let him remember how hard it is to lose a husband and a brother. Go; when we want him, the name of Deerslayer will be called."

This conversation had been held with no one near but the speakers. Of all the band that had so lately thronged the place, Rivenoak alone was visible. The rest seemed to have totally abandoned the spot. Even the furniture, clothes, arms, and other property of the camp had entirely disappeared, and the place bore no other proofs of the crowd that had so lately occupied it, than the traces of their fires and resting places, and the trodden earth, that still showed the marks of their feet. So sudden and unexpected a change caused Deerslayer a good deal of surprise and some uneasiness, for he had never known it to occur, in the course of his experience among the Delawares. He suspected, however, and rightly, that a change of encampment was intended, and that the mystery of the movement was resorted to, in order to work on his apprehensions.

Rivenoak walked up the vista of trees, as soon as he ceased speaking, leaving Deerslayer by himself. The chief disappeared behind the covers of the forest, and one unpractised in such scenes might have believed the prisoner left to the dictates of his own judgment. But the young man, while he felt a little amazement at the dramatic aspect of things, knew his enemies too well to fancy himself at liberty, or a free agent. Still, he was ignorant how far the Hurons meant to carry their artifices, and he determined to bring the question, as soon as practicable, to the proof. Affecting an indifference he was far from feeling, he strolled about the area, gradually getting nearer and nearer to the spot where he had landed, when he suddenly quickened his pace, though carefully avoiding all appearance of flight, and pushing aside the bushes, he stepped upon the beach. The canoe was gone, nor could he see any traces of it, after walking to the northern and southern verges of the point, and examining the shores in both directions. It was evidently removed beyond his reach and knowledge, and under circumstances to show that such had been the intention of the savages.

Deerslayer now better understood his actual situation. He was a prisoner on the narrow tongue of land, vigilantly watched beyond a question, and with no other means of escape than that of swimming. He, again, thought of this last expedient, but the certainty that the canoe would be sent in chase, and the desperate nature of the chances of success deterred him from the undertaking. While on the strand, he came to a spot where the bushes had been cut, and thrust into a small pile. Removing a few of the upper branches, he found beneath them the dead body of the Panther. He knew that it was kept until the savages might find a place to inter it, where it would be beyond the reach of the scalping knife. He gazed wistfully towards the castle, but there all seemed to be silent and desolate, and a feeling of loneliness and desertion came over him to increase the gloom of the moment.

"God's will be done!" murmured the young man, as he walked sorrowfully away from the beach, entering again beneath the arches of the wood. "God's will be done, on 'arth as it is in heaven! I did hope that my days would not be numbered so soon, but it matters little a'ter all. A few more winters, and a few more summers, and 'twould have been over, accordin' to natur'. Ah's! me, the young and actyve seldom think death possible, till he grins in their faces, and tells 'em the hour is come!"

While this soliloquy was being pronounced, the hunter advanced into the area, where to his surprise he saw Hetty alone, evidently awaiting his return. The girl carried the bible under her arm, and her face, over which a shadow of gentle melancholy was usually thrown, now seemed sad, and downcast. Moving nearer, Deerslayer spoke.

"Poor Hetty," he said, "times have been so troublesome, of late, that I'd altogether forgotten you; we meet, as it might be to mourn over what is to happen. I wonder what has become of Chingachgook and Wah!"

"Why did you kill the Huron, Deerslayer? — " returned the girl reproachfully. "Don't you know your commandments, which say 'Thou shalt not kill!' They tell me you have now slain the woman's husband and brother!"

"It's true, my good Hetty — 'tis gospel truth, and I'll not deny what has come to pass. But, you must remember, gal, that many things are lawful in war, which would be onlawful in peace. The husband was shot in open fight — or, open so far as I was consarned, while he had a better cover than common — and the brother brought his end on himself, by casting his tomahawk at an unarmed prisoner. Did you witness that deed, gal?"

"I saw it, and was sorry it happened, Deerslayer, for I hoped you would n't have returned blow for blow, but good for evil."

"Ah, Hetty, that may do among the Missionaries, but 'twould make an onsartain life in the woods! The Panther craved my blood, and he was foolish enough to throw arms into my hands, at the very moment he was striving a'ter it. 'Twould have been ag'in natur' not to raise a hand in such a trial, and 'twould have done discredit to my training and gifts. No — no — I'm as willing to give every man his own, as another, and so I hope you'll testify to them that will be likely to question you as to what you've seen this day."

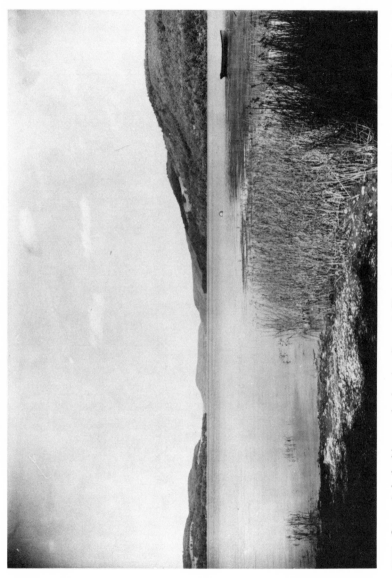

XIII. Otsego Lake looking north, showing Cooper's Chalet Farm in the cleared hillside area to the right of center.

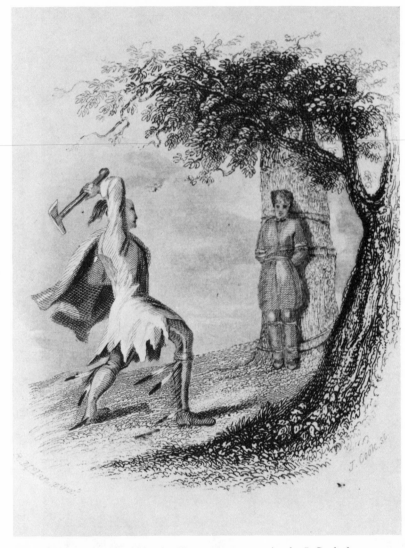

XIV. "Deerslayer tortured by the Hurons," an engraving by J. Cook, from a drawing by R. McIan

XV. "The Burial of Hetty Hutter," an engraving by J. McGoffin from a drawing by James Hamilton

XVI. "Salvator Rosa Sketching Banditti," by Thomas Cole (see p. 279)

"Deerslayer, do you mean to marry Sumach, now she has neither husband nor brother to feed her?"

"Are such your idees of matrimony, Hetty! Ought the young to wive with the old—the pale face with the red skin—the christian with the heathen? It's ag'in reason and natur', and so you'll see, if you think of it a moment."

"I've always heard mother say," returned Hetty, averting her face more from a feminine instinct, than from any consciousness of wrong, "that people should never marry, until they loved each other better than brothers and sisters, and I suppose that is what you mean. Sumach *is* old, and you *are* young!"

"Ay and she's red, and I'm white. Beside, Hetty, suppose you was a wife, now, having married some young man of your own years, and state, and colour—Hurry Harry, for instance—" Deerslayer selected this example, simply from the circumstance that he was the only young man known to both—"and that he had fallen on a war path, would you wish to take to your bosom, for a husband, the man that slew him?"

"Oh! no, no, no—" returned the girl shuddering—"*That* would be wicked as well as heartless! No christian girl could, or would do *that*! I never shall be the wife of Hurry, I know, but were he my husband no man should ever be it, again, after his death!"

"I thought it would get to this, Hetty, when you come to understand sarcumstances. 'Tis a moral impossibility that I should ever marry Sumach, and, though Injin weddin's have no priests and not much religion, a white man who knows his gifts and duties can't profit by that, and so make his escape at the fitting time. I do think, death would be more nat'ral like, and welcome, than wedlock with this woman."

"Don't say it too loud," interrupted Hetty impatiently; "I suppose she will not like to hear it. I'm sure Hurry would rather marry even me than suffer torments, though I *am* feeble minded; and I am sure it would kill me to think he'd prefer death to being my husband."

"Ay, gal, you an't Sumach, but a comely young Christian, with a good heart, pleasant smile, and kind eye. Hurry might be proud to get you, and that, too, not in misery and sorrow, but in his best and happiest days. Howsever, take my advice, and never talk to Hurry about these things; he's only a borderer, at the best."

"I would n't tell him, for the world!" exclaimed the girl, looking about her, like one affrighted, and blushing, she knew not why. "Mother always said young women should n't be forward, and speak their minds before they're asked; Oh! I never forget what mother told me. Tis a pity Hurry is so handsome, Deerslayer; I do think fewer girls would like him then, and he would sooner know his own mind."

"Poor gal, poor gal, it's plain enough how it is, but the Lord will bear in mind one of your simple heart, and kind feelin's! We'll talk no more of these things; if you had reason, you'd be sorrowful at having let others so much into your secret. Tell me, Hetty, what has become of all the Hurons, and why they let you roam about the p'int, as if you, too, was a prisoner?"

"I'm no prisoner, Deerslayer, but a free girl, and go when and where I please. Nobody dare hurt *me!* If they did, God would be angry, as I can show them in the bible. No—no— Hetty Hutter is not afraid; *she's* in good hands. The Hurons are up yonder in the woods, and keep a good watch on us both, I'll answer for it, since all the women and children are on the look-out. Some are burying the body of the poor girl who was shot, so that the enemy and the wild beasts can't find it. I told 'em that father and mother lay in the lake, but I would n't let them know, in what part of it, for Judith and I don't want any of their heathenish company, in our burying ground."

"Ahs! me;—Well, it *is* an awful despatch to be standing here, alive and angry, and with the feelin's up and ferocious, one hour, and then to be carried away at the next, and put out of sight of mankind in a hole in the 'arth! No one knows what will happen to him on a warpath, that's sartain."

Here the stirring of leaves and the cracking of dried twigs interrupted the discourse, and apprised Deerslayer of the approach of his enemies. The Hurons closed around the spot that had been prepared for the coming scene, and in the centre of which the intended victim now stood, in a circle, the armed men being so distributed, among the feebler members of the band, that there was no safe opening through which the prisoner could break. But the latter no longer contemplated flight, the recent trial having satisfied him of his inability to escape when pursued so closely by numbers. On the contrary, all his energies were aroused, in order to meet his expected fate, with a calmness that should do credit to his colour and his manhood; one equally removed from recreant alarm, and savage boasting.

When Rivenoak re-appeared in the circle, he occupied his old place at the head of the area. Several of the elder warriors stood near him, but, now that the brother of Sumach had fallen, there was no longer any recognised chief present, whose influence and authority offered a dangerous rivalry to his own. Nevertheless, it is well known that little which could be called monarchical, or despotic entered into the politics of the North American tribes, although the first colonists, bringing with them to this hemisphere, the notions and opinions of their own countries, often dignified the chief men of those primitive nations, with the titles of kings and princes. Hereditary influence did certainly exist, but there is much reason to believe it existed rather as a consequence of hereditary merit and acquired qualifications, than as a birth-right. Rivenoak, however, had not even this claim, having risen to consideration purely by the force of talents, sagacity, and, as Bacon expresses it, in relation to all distinguished statesmen, "by a union of great and mean qualities;" a truth of which the career of the profound Englishman himself furnishes so apt an illustration. Next to arms, eloquence offers the great avenue to popular favor, whether it be in civilized or savage life, and Rivenoak had succeeded, as so many have succeeded, before him, quite as much by rendering fallacies acceptable to his listeners, as by any profound or learned expositions of truth, or the accuracy of his logic. Nevertheless, he had influence; and was far from being altogether without just claims to its possession. Like most men who reason more than they feel, the Huron was not addicted to the indulgence of the more ferocious passions of his people: he had been commonly found on the side of mercy, in all the scenes of vindictive torture and revenge that had occurred in his tribe, since his own attainment to power. On the present occasion, he was reluctant to proceed to extremities, although the provocation was so great. Still it exceeded his ingenuity to see how that alternative could well be avoided. Sumach

resented her rejection more than she did the deaths of her husband and brother, and there was little probability that the
woman would pardon a man who had so unequivocally preferred death to her embraces. Without her forgiveness, there was
scarce a hope that the tribe could be induced to overlook its
loss, and even to Rivenoak, himself, much as he was disposed
to pardon, the fate of our hero now appeared to be almost
hopelessly sealed.

When the whole band was arrayed around the captive, a
grave silence, so much the more threatening from its profound
quiet, pervaded the place. Deerslayer perceived that the
women and boys had been preparing splinters of the fat pine
roots, which he well knew were to be stuck into his flesh, and set
in flames, while two or three of the young men held the thongs of
bark with which he was to be bound. The smoke of a distant
fire announced that the burning brands were in preparation,
and several of the elder warriors passed their fingers over the
edges of their tomahawks, as if to prove their keenness and
temper. Even the knives seemed loosened in their sheathes,
impatient for the bloody and merciless work to begin.

"Killer of the Deer," recommenced Rivenoak, certainly
without any signs of sympathy or pity in his manner, though
with calmness and dignity, "Killer of the Deer, it is time that
my people knew their minds. The sun is no longer over our
heads; tired of waiting on the Hurons, he has begun to fall
near the pines on this side of the valley. He is travelling fast
towards the country of our French fathers; it is to warn his
children that their lodges are empty, and that they ought to be
at home. The roaming wolf has his den, and he goes to it,
when he wishes to see his young. The Iroquois are not poorer
than the wolves. They have villages, and wigwams, and fields
of corn; the Good Spirits will be tired of watching them alone.
My people must go back, and see to their own business. There
will be joy in the lodges when they hear our whoop from the
forest! It will be a sorrowful whoop; when it is understood,
grief will come after it. There will be one scalp-whoop, but
there will be only one. We have the fur of the Muskrat; his
body is among the fishes. Deerslayer must say whether
another scalp shall be on our pole. Two lodges are empty; a
scalp, living or dead, is wanted at each door."

"Then take 'em dead, Huron," firmly, but altogether without dramatic boasting, returned the captive. "My hour is come, I do suppose, and what must be, must. If you are bent on the tortur', I'll do my indivours to bear up ag'in it, though no man can say how far his natur' will stand pain, until he's been tried."

"The pale face cur begins to put his tail between his legs!" cried a young and garrulous savage, who bore the appropriate title of the Corbeau Rouge; a *sobriquet* he had gained from the French, by his facility in making unseasonable noises, and an undue tendency to hear his own voice; "he is no warrior; he has killed the Loup Cervier when looking behind him not to see the flash of his own rifle. He grunts like a hog, already; when the Huron women begin to torment him, he will cry like the young of the catamount. He is a Delaware woman, dressed in the skin of a Yengeese!"

"Have your say, young man; have your say," returned Deerslayer, unmoved; "you know no better, and I can overlook it. Talking may aggravate women, but can hardly make knives sharper, fire hotter, or rifles more sartain."

Rivenoak now interposed, reproving the Red Crow for his premature interference, and then directing the proper persons to bind the captive. This expedient was adopted, not from any apprehensions that he would escape, or from any necessity, that was yet apparent, of his being unable to endure the torture with his limbs free, but from an ingenious design of making him feel his helplessness, and of gradually sapping his resolution, by undermining it, as it might be, little by little. Deerslayer offered no resistance. He submitted his arms and legs, freely if not cheerfully, to the ligaments of bark, which were bound around them, by order of the chief, in a way to produce as little pain as possible. These directions were secret, and given in the hope that the captive would finally save himself from any serious bodily suffering, by consenting to take the Sumach for a wife. As soon as the body of Deerslayer was withed in bark sufficiently to create a lively sense of helplessness, he was literally carried to a young tree, and bound against it, in a way that effectually prevented him from moving, as well as from falling. The hands were laid flat against the legs, and thongs were passed over all, in a way nearly to incorporate the prisoner with the tree. His cap was then removed, and he was left half-standing, half-sustained by his bonds, to face the coming scene, in the best manner he could.

Previously to proceeding to any thing like extremities, it was the wish of Rivenoak to put his captive's resolution to the proof, by renewing the attempt at a compromise. This could be effected only in one manner, the acquiescence of the Sumach being indispensably necessary to a compromise of her right to be revenged. With this view, then, the woman was next desired to advance, and to look to her own interests; no agent being considered as efficient as the principal, herself, in this negotiation. The Indian females, when girls, are usually mild, and submissive, with musical tones, pleasant voices, and merry laughs, but toil and suffering generally deprive them of most of these advantages, by the time they have reached an age which the Sumach had long before passed. To render their voices harsh, it would seem to require active, malignant, passions, though, when excited, their screams can rise to a sufficiently conspicuous degree of discordancy, to assert their claim to possess this distinctive peculiarity of the sex. The Sumach was not altogether without feminine attraction, however, and had so recently been deemed handsome in her tribe, as not to have yet learned the full influence that time and exposure produce on man, as well as on woman. By an arrangement of Rivenoak's, some of the women around her, had been employing the time in endeavoring to persuade the bereaved widow, that there was still a hope Deerslayer might be prevailed on to enter her wigwam, in preference to entering the world of spirits, and this, too, with a success that previous symptoms scarcely justified. All this was the result of a resolution on the part of the chief to leave no proper means unemployed, in order to get transferred to his own nation the greatest hunter that was then thought to exist in all that region, as well as a husband for a woman who he felt would be likely to be troublesome, were any of her claims to the attention and care of the tribe overlooked.

In conformity with this scheme, the Sumach had been secretly advised to advance into the circle, and to make her appeal to the prisoner's sense of justice, before the band had recourse to the last experiment. The woman, nothing loth, consented, for there was some such attraction in becoming the wife of a noted hunter, among the females of the tribes, as is experienced by the sex, in more refined life, when they bestow their hands on the affluent. As the duties of a mother were thought to be paramount to all other considerations, the widow felt none of that embarrassment, in preferring her claims, to which even a female fortune hunter among ourselves, might be liable. When she stood forth, before the whole party, therefore, the children that she led by the hands, fully justified all she did.

"You see me before you, cruel pale face," the woman commenced; "your spirit must tell you my errand. I have found *you*; I cannot find le Loup Cervier, nor the Panther; I have looked for them, in the lake, in the woods, in the clouds. I cannot say where they have gone."

"No man knows, good Sumach, no man knows," interposed the captive. "When the spirit leaves the body, it passes into a world beyond our knowledge, and the wisest way, for them that are left behind, is to hope for the best. No doubt both your warriors, have gone to the Happy Hunting Grounds, and at the proper time you will see 'em ag'in, in their improved state. The wife and sister of braves, must have looked forward to some such tarmination of their 'arthly careers."

"Cruel pale-face, what had my warriors done that you should slay them! They were the best hunters, and the boldest young men of their tribe; the Great Spirit intended that they should live until they withered like the branches of the hemlock, and fell of their own weight—"

"Nay—nay—good Sumach," interrupted Deerslayer, whose love of truth was too indomitable to listen to such hyperbole, with patience, even though it came from the torn breast of a widow—"Nay—nay, good Sumach, this is a little out-doing red skin privileges. Young man was neither, any more than you can be called a young woman, and as to the Great Spirit's intending that they should fall otherwise than they did, that's a grievous mistake, inasmuch as what the Great Spirit intends, is sartain to come to pass. Then, ag'in, it's plain enough neither of your fri'nds did me any harm; I raised my hand ag'in 'em on account of what they were *striving* to do, rather than what they did. This is nat'ral law, 'to do lest you should be done by.' "

"It is so. Sumach has but one tongue; she can tell but one story. The Pale face struck the Hurons lest the Hurons should strike him. The Hurons are a just nation; they will forget it. The chiefs will shut their eyes and pretend not to have seen it; the young men will believe the Panther and the Lynx have gone to far off hunts, and the Sumach, will take her children by the hand, and go into the lodge of the pale face and say — 'See; these are *your* children; they are also mine — feed us, and we will live with you.' "

"The tarms are onadmissable, woman, and though I feel for your losses, which must be hard to bear, the tarms cannot be accepted. As to givin' you ven'son, in case we lived near enough together, that would be no great expl'ite; but as for becomin' your husband, and the father of your children, to be honest with you, I feel no callin' that-a-way."

"Look at this boy, cruel pale face; he has no father to teach him to kill the deer, or to take scalps. See this girl; what young man will come to look for a wife in a lodge that has no head? There are more among my people in the Canadas, and the Killer of Deer will find as many mouths to feed, as his heart can wish for."

"I tell you, woman," exclaimed Deerslayer, whose imagination was far from seconding the appeal of the widow, and who began to grow restive under the vivid pictures she was drawing, "all this is nothing to me. People and kindred must take care of their own fatherless, leaving them that have no children to their own loneliness. As for me, I have no offspring, and I want no wife. Now, go away Sumach; leave me in the hands of your chiefs, for my colour, and gifts, and natur' itself cry out ag'in the idee of taking you for a wife."

It is unnecessary to expatiate on the effect of this downright refusal of the woman's proposals. If there was any thing like tenderness in her bosom — and no woman was probably ever entirely without that feminine quality — it all disappeared at this plain announcement. Fury, rage, mortified pride, and a volcano of wrath burst out, at one explosion, converting her into a sort of maniac, as it might be at the touch of a magician's wand. Without deigning a reply in words, she made the arches of the forest ring with screams, and then flew forward at her victim, seizing him by the hair, which she appeared resolute to draw out by the roots. It was some time before her grasp could be loosened. Fortunately for the prisoner her rage was blind, since his total helplessness left him entirely at her mercy. Had it been better directed it might have proved fatal before any relief could have been offered. As it was, she did succeed in wrenching out two or three handsful of hair, before the young men could tear her away from her victim.

The insult that had been offered to the Sumach was deemed an insult to the whole tribe; not so much, however, on account of any respect that was felt for the woman, as on account of the honor of the Huron nation. Sumach, herself, was generally considered to be as acid as the berry from which she derived her name, and now that her great supporters, her husband and brother, were both gone, few cared about concealing their aversion. Nevertheless, it had become a point of honor to punish the pale face who disdained a Huron woman, and more particularly one who coolly preferred death to relieving the tribe from the support of a widow and her children. The young men showed an impatience to begin to torture, that Rivenoak understood, and, as his older associates manifested no disposition to permit any longer delay, he was compelled to give the signal, for the infernal work to proceed.

Chapter XXIX.

"The ugly bear now minded not the stake,
Nor how the cruel mastiffs do him tear,
The stag lay still unroused from the brake,
The foamy boar feared not the hunter's spear:
All thing was still in desert, bush, and briar:"
Thomas Sackville, "The Complaint of Henry Duke
of Buckingham," lxxxi.

I T was one of the common expedients of the savages, on such occasions, to put the nerves of their victims to the severest proofs. On the other hand, it was a matter of Indian pride to betray no yielding to terror, or pain, but for the prisoner to provoke his enemies to such acts of violence as would soonest produce death. Many a warrior had been known to bring his own sufferings to a more speedy termination, by taunting reproaches and reviling language, when he found that his physical system was giving way under the agony of sufferings produced by a hellish ingenuity that might well eclipse all that has been said of the infernal devices of religious persecution. This happy expedient of taking refuge from the ferocity of his foes, in their passions, was denied Deerslayer however, by his peculiar notions of the duty of a white man, and he had stoutly made up his mind to endure every thing, in preference to disgracing his colour.

No sooner did the young men understand that they were at liberty to commence, than some of the boldest and most forward among them sprang into the arena, tomahawk in hand. Here they prepared to throw that dangerous weapon, the object being to strike the tree as near as possible to the victim's head, without absolutely hitting him. This was so hazardous an experiment, that none but those who were known to be exceedingly expert with the weapon, were allowed to enter the lists, at all, lest an early death might interfere with the expected entertainment. In the truest hands it was seldom that the captive escaped injury in these trials, and it often happened that death followed, even when the blow was not premeditated. In the particular case of our hero, Rivenoak and the older warriors were apprehensive that the example of the Panther's fate might prove a motive with some fiery spirit suddenly to sacrifice his conqueror, when the temptation of effecting it in precisely the same manner, and possibly with the identical weapon with which the warrior had fallen, offered. This circumstance of itself, rendered the ordeal of the tomahawk doubly critical for the Deerslayer.

It would seem, however, that all who now entered, what we shall call the lists, were more disposed to exhibit their own dexterity, than to resent the deaths of their comrades. Each prepared himself for the trial, with the feelings of rivalry, rather than with the desire for vengeance, and, for the first few minutes, the prisoner had little more connection with the result, than grew out of the interest that necessarily attached itself to a living target. The young men were eager, instead of being fierce, and Rivenoak thought he still saw signs of being able to save the life of the captive, when the vanity of the young men had been gratified; always admitting, that it was not sacrificed to the delicate experiments that were about to be made.

The first youth who presented himself, for the trial, was called The Raven, having as yet had no opportunity of obtaining a more warlike *sobriquet*. He was remarkable for high pretension, rather than for skill, or exploits, and those who knew his character thought the captive in imminent danger, when he took his stand, and poised the tomahawk. Nevertheless, the young man was good natured, and no thought was uppermost in his mind, other than the desire to make a better cast, than any of his fellows. Deerslayer got an inkling of this warrior's want of reputation, by the injunctions that he had received from the seniors, who, indeed, would have objected to his appearing in the arena, at all, but for an influence derived from his father; an aged warrior of great merit, who was then in the lodges of the tribe. Still, our hero maintained an appearance of self-possession. He had made up his mind that his hour was come, and it would have been a mercy, instead of a calamity, to fall by the unsteadiness of the first hand that was raised against him. After a suitable number of flourishes, and gesticulations that promised much more than he could perform, the Raven let the tomahawk quit his hand. The weapon whirled through the air, with the usual evolutions, cut a chip from the sapling to which the prisoner was bound, within a few inches of his cheek, and stuck in a large oak that grew several yards behind him. This was decidedly a bad effort, and a common sneer proclaimed as much, to the great mortification of the young man. On the other hand, there was a general but suppressed murmur of admiration, at the steadiness with which the captive stood the trial. The head was the only part he could move, and this had been purposely left free, that the tormentors might have the amusement, and the tormented endure the shame, of his dodging, and otherwise attempting to avoid the blows. Deerslayer disappointed these hopes, by a command of nerve that rendered his whole body as immovable as the tree to which he was bound. Nor did he even adopt the natural and usual expedient of shutting his eyes, the firmest and oldest warrior of the red-men never having more disdainfully denied himself this advantage, under similar circumstances.

The Raven had no sooner made his unsuccessful and puerile effort, than he was succeeded by le Daim-Mose, or the Moose; a middle aged warrior, who was particularly skilful in the use of the tomahawk, and from whose attempt the spectators confidently looked for gratification. This man had none of the good nature of the Raven, but he would gladly have sacrificed the captive to his hatred of the pale faces generally, were it not for the greater interest he felt in his own success as one particularly skilled in the use of this weapon. He took his stand quietly, but with an air of confidence, poised his little axe but a single instant, advanced a foot with a quick motion, and threw. Deerslayer saw the keen instrument whirling towards him, and believed all was over; still, he was not touched. The tomahawk had actually bound the head of the captive to the tree, by carrying before it some of his hair, having buried itself deep beneath the soft bark. A general yell expressed the delight of the spectators, and the Moose felt his heart soften a little towards the prisoner, whose steadiness of nerve alone, enabled him to give this evidence of his consummate skill.

Le Daim-Mose was succeeded by the Bounding Boy, or *le Garçon qui Bondi* who came leaping into the circle, like a hound, or a goat, at play. This was one of those elastic youths, whose muscles seemed always in motion, and who either affected, or who from habit was actually unable, to move in any other manner, than by showing the antics just mentioned. Nevertheless, he was both brave and skilful, and had gained the respect of his people, by deeds in war, as well as success in the hunts. A far nobler name would long since have fallen to his share, had not a French-man of rank inadvertently given him this *sobriquet*, which he religiously preserved as coming from his Great Father, who lived beyond the Wide Salt Lake. The Bounding Boy skipped about in front of the captive, menacing him with his tomahawk, now on one side and now on another, and then again in front, in the vain hope of being able to extort some sign of fear by this parade of danger. At length Deerslayer's patience became exhausted by all this mummery, and he spoke for the first time, since the trial had actually commenced.

"Throw away, Huron," he cried, "or your tomahawk will forget its ar'n'd. Why do you keep loping about like a fa'a'n that's showing its dam how well it can skip, when you're a warrior grown, yourself, and a warrior grown defies you and all your silly antiks. Throw, or the Huron gals will laugh in your face."

Although not intended to produce such an effect, the last words aroused the "Bounding" warrior to fury. The same nervous excitability which rendered him so active in his person, made it difficult to repress his feelings, and the words were scarcely past the lips of the speaker, than the tomahawk left the hand of the Indian. Nor was it cast without ill-will, and a fierce determination to slay. Had the intention been less deadly, the danger might have been greater. The aim was uncertain, and the weapon glanced near the cheek of the captive, slightly cutting the shoulder in its evolutions. This was the first instance in which any other object, than that of terrifying the prisoner, and of displaying skill had been manifested, and the Bounding Boy was immediately led from the arena, and was warmly rebuked for his intemperate haste, which had come so near defeating all the hopes of the band.

To this irritable person succeeded several other young warriors, who not only hurled the tomahawk, but who cast the knife, a far more dangerous experiment, with reckless indifference; yet they always manifested a skill that prevented any injury to the captive. Several times Deerslayer was grazed, but in no instance did he receive what might be termed a wound. The unflinching firmness with which he faced his assailants, more especially in the sort of rally with which this trial terminated, excited a profound respect in the spectators, and when the chiefs announced that the prisoner had well withstood the trials of the knife and the tomahawk, there was not a single individual in the band who really felt any hostility towards him, with the exception of Sumach and the Bounding Boy. These two discontented spirits got together, it is true, feeding each other's ire, but, as yet, their malignant feelings were confined very much to themselves, though there existed the danger that the others, ere long, could not fail to be excited by their own efforts, into that demoniacal state which usually accompanied all similar scenes among the red men.

Rivenoak now told his people that the pale face had proved himself to be a man. He might live with the Delawares, but he had not been made woman, with that tribe. He wished to know whether it was the desire of the Hurons to proceed any further. Even the gentlest of the females, however, had received too much satisfaction in the late trials, to forego their expectations of a gratifying exhibition, and there was but one voice, in the request to proceed. The politic chief, who had some such desire to receive so celebrated a hunter into his tribe, as a European Minister has to devise a new and available means of taxation, sought every plausible means of arresting the trial in season, for, he well knew, if permitted to go far enough to arouse the more ferocious passions of the tormentors, it would be as easy to dam the waters of the great lakes of his own region, as to attempt to arrest them in their bloody career. He therefore called four or five of the best marksmen to him, and bid them put the captive to the proof of the rifle, while, at the same time he cautioned them touching the necessity of their maintaining their own credit, by the closest attention to the manner of exhibiting their skill.

When Deerslayer saw the chosen warriors step into the circle, with their arms prepared for service, he felt some such relief, as the miserable sufferer, who has long endured the agonies of disease, feels at the certain approach of death. Any trifling variance in the aim of this formidable weapon, would prove fatal; since, the head being the target, or rather the point it was desired to graze without injuring, an inch or two of difference in the line of projection, must at once determine the question of life or death.

In the torture by the rifle there was none of the latitude permitted that appeared in the case of even Gessler's apple, a hair's breadth being, in fact, the utmost limits that an expert marksman would allow himself on an occasion like this. Victims were frequently shot through the head by too eager, or unskilful hands, and it often occurred that, exasperated by the fortitude and taunts of the prisoner, death was dealt intentionally, in a moment of ungovernable irritation. All this Deerslayer well knew, for it was in relating the traditions of such scenes, as well as of the battles and victories of their people, that the old men beguiled the long winter evenings, in their cabins. He now fully expected the end of his career, and experienced a sort of melancholy pleasure in the idea that he was to fall by a weapon as much beloved as the rifle. A slight interruption, however, took place before the business was allowed to proceed.

Hetty Hutter witnessed all that passed, and the scene at first had pressed upon her feeble mind in a way to paralyze it entirely; but, by this time, she had rallied, and was growing indignant at the unmerited suffering the Indians were inflicting on her friend. Though timid, and shy as the young of the deer, on so many occasions, this right-feeling girl was always intrepid in the cause of humanity; the lessons of her mother, and the impulses of her own heart, — perhaps we might say the promptings of that unseen and pure spirit that seemed ever to watch over and direct her actions — uniting to keep down the apprehensions of woman, and to impel her to be bold and resolute. She now appeared in the circle, gentle, feminine, even bashful in mien, as usual, but earnest in her words and countenance, speaking like one who knew herself to be sustained by the high authority of God.

"Why do you torment Deerslayer, red-men?" she asked — "What has he done that you trifle with his life; who has given you the right to be his judges? Suppose one of your knives, or tomahawks had hit him; what Indian among you all could cure the wound you would make. Besides, in harming Deerslayer, you injure your own friend; when father and Hurry Harry came after your scalps, he refused to be of the party, and staid in the canoe by himself. You are tormenting a good friend, in tormenting this young man!"

The Hurons listened with grave attention, and one among them, who understood English, translated what had been said into their native tongue. As soon as Rivenoak was made acquainted with the purport of her address he answered it in his own dialect; the interpreter conveying it to the girl in English.

"My daughter is very welcome to speak," said the stern old orator, using gentle intonations and smiling as kindly as if addressing a child — "The Hurons are glad to hear her voice; they listen to what she says. The Great Spirit often speaks to men with such tongues. This time, her eyes have not been open wide enough, to see all that has happened. Deerslayer did not come for our scalps; that is true; why did he not come? Here they are; on our heads; the war-locks are ready to be taken hold of; a bold enemy ought to stretch out his hand to seize them. The Iroquois are too great a nation to punish men that take scalps. What they do themselves, they like to see others do. Let my daughter look around her and count my warriors. Had I as many hands as four warriors, their fingers would be fewer than my people, when they came into your hunting grounds. Now, a whole hand is missing. Where are the fingers? Two have been cut off by this pale face; my Hurons wish to see if he did this by means of a stout heart, or by treachery. Like a skulking fox, or like a leaping panther."

"You know yourself, Huron, how one of them fell. I saw it, and you all saw it, too. 'Twas too bloody to look at; but it was not Deerslayer's fault. Your warrior sought his life, and he defended himself. I do n't know whether this good book says that it was right, but all men will do that. Come, if you want to know which of you, can shoot best, give Deerslayer a rifle, and then you will find how much more expert he is, than any of your warriors; yes, than *all* of them together!"

Could one have looked upon such a scene with indifference, he would have been amused at the gravity with which the savages listened to the translation of this unusual request. No taunt, no smile mingled with their surprise, for Hetty had a character and a manner too saintly to subject her infirmity to the mockings of the rude and ferocious. On the contrary, she was answered with respectful attention.

"My daughter does not always talk, like a chief at a Council Fire," returned Rivenoak, "or she would not have said this. Two of my warriors have fallen by the blows of our prisoner; their grave is too small to hold a third. The Hurons do not like to crowd their dead. If there is another spirit about to set out for the far off world, it must not be the spirit of a Huron; it must be the spirit of a pale face. Go, daughter, and sit by Sumach, who is in grief; let the Huron warriors show how well they can shoot; let the pale face show how little he cares for their bullets."

Hetty's mind was unequal to a sustained discussion, and accustomed to defer to the directions of her seniors she did as told, seating herself passively on a log, by the side of the Sumach, and averting her face from the painful scene that was occurring within the circle.

The warriors, as soon as this interruption had ceased, resumed their places, and again prepared to exhibit their skill. As there was a double object in view, that of putting the constancy of the captive to the proof, and that of showing how steady were the hands of the marksmen, under circumstances of excitement, the distance was small, and, in one sense, safe. But in diminishing the distance taken by the tormentors, the trial to the nerves of the captive was essentially increased. The face of Deerslayer, indeed, was just removed sufficiently from the ends of the guns to escape the effects of the flash, and his steady eye was enabled to look directly into their muzzles, as it might be, in anticipation of the fatal messenger that was to issue from each. The cunning Hurons well knew this fact, and scarce one levelled his piece without first causing it to point as near as possible at the forehead of the prisoner, in the hope that his fortitude would fail him, and that the band would enjoy the triumph of seeing a victim quail under their ingenious cruelty. Nevertheless each of the competitors was still careful not to injure, the disgrace of striking prematurely, being second only to that of failing altogether in attaining the object. Shot after shot was made; all the bullets coming in close proximity to the Deerslayer's head, without touching it. Still no one could detect even the twitching of a muscle on the part of the captive, or the slightest winking of an eye. This indomitable resolution, which so much exceeded every thing of its kind that any present had before witnessed, might be referred to three distinct causes. The first was resignation to his fate, blended with natural steadiness of deportment; for our hero had calmly made up his mind that he must die, and preferred this mode to any other; the second was his great familiarity with this particular weapon, which deprived it of all the terror that is usually connected with the mere form of the danger; and the third was this familiarity carried out in practice, to a degree so nice as to enable the intended victim to tell, within an inch, the precise spot where each bullet must strike, for he calculated its range by looking in at the bore of the piece. So exact was Deerslayer's estimation of the line of fire, that his pride of feeling finally got the better of his resignation, and when five or six had discharged their bullets into the tree, he could not refrain from expressing his contempt at their want of hand and eye.

"You may call this shooting, Mingos!" he exclaimed, "but we've squaws among the Delawares, and I have known Dutch gals on the Mohawk, that could outdo your greatest indivours. Ondo these arms of mine, put a rifle into my hands, and I'll pin the thinnest warlock in your party, to any tree you can show me, and this at a hundred yards — ay, or at two hundred if the objects can be seen, nineteen shots in twenty; or, for that matter twenty in twenty, if the piece is creditable and trusty!"

A low menacing murmur followed this cool taunt. The ire of the warriors kindled at listening to such a reproach from one, who so far disdained their efforts as to refuse even to wink, when a rifle was discharged as near his face as could be done without burning it. Rivenoak perceived that the moment was critical, and, still retaining his hope of adopting so noted a hunter into his tribe, the politic old chief interposed in time, probably to prevent an immediate resort to that portion of the torture, which must necessarily have produced death through extreme bodily suffering, if in no other manner. Moving into the centre of the irritated groupe, he addressed them with his usual wily logic, and plausible manner, at once suppressing the fierce movement that had commenced.

"I see how it is," he said. "We have been like the pale faces when they fasten their doors at night, out of fear of the red men. They use so many bars that the fire comes and burns them, before they can get out. We have bound the Deerslayer too tight: the thongs keep his limbs from shaking and his eyes from shutting. Loosen him; let us see what his own body is really made of."

It is often the case when we are thwarted in a cherished scheme, that any expedient, however unlikely to succeed, is gladly resorted to in preference to a total abandonment of the project. So it was with the Hurons. The proposal of the chief found instant favor, and several hands were immediately at work, cutting and tearing the ropes of bark from the body of our hero. In half a minute Deerslayer stood as free from bonds, as when, an hour before he had commenced his flight on the side of the mountain. Some little time was necessary that he should recover the use of his limbs, the circulation of the blood having been checked by the tightness of the ligatures, and this was accorded to him by the politic Rivenoak, under the pretence that his body would be more likely to submit to apprehension, if its true tone were restored; though really with a view to give time to the fierce passions which had been awakened in the bosoms of his young men, to subside. This *ruse* succeeded, and Deerslayer by rubbing his limbs, stamping his feet, and moving about, soon regained the circulation, recovering all his physical powers, as effectually as if nothing had occurred to disturb them.

It is seldom men think of death in the pride of their health and strength. So it was with Deerslayer. Having been helplessly bound and, as he had every reason to suppose, so lately on the very verge of the other world, to find himself so unexpectedly liberated, in possession of his strength and with a full command of limb, acted on him like a sudden restoration to life, reanimating hopes that he had once absolutely abandoned. From that instant all his plans changed. In this, he simply obeyed a law of nature; for while we have wished to represent our hero as being resigned to his fate, it has been far from our intention to represent him as anxious to die. From the instant that his buoyancy of feeling revived, his thoughts were keenly bent on the various projects that presented themselves as modes of evading the designs of his enemies, and he again became, the quick witted, ingenious and determined woodsman, alive to all his own powers and resources. The change was so great, that his mind resumed its elasticity, and no longer thinking of submission, it dwelt only on the devices of the sort of warfare in which he was engaged.

As soon as Deerslayer was released, the band divided itself in a circle around him, in order to hedge him in, and the desire to break down his spirit grew in them, precisely as they saw proofs of the difficulty there would be in subduing it. The honor of the band was now involved in the issue, and even the sex lost all its sympathy with suffering, in the desire to save the reputation of the tribe. The voices of the girls, soft and melodious as nature had made them, were heard mingling with the menaces of the men, and the wrongs of Sumach suddenly assumed the character of injuries inflicted on every Huron female. Yielding to this rising tumult, the men drew back a little, signifying to the females, that they left the captive, for a time, in their hands, it being a common practice on such occasions, for the women to endeavor to throw the victim into a rage, by their taunts and revilings, and then to turn him suddenly over to the men, in a state of mind that was little favorable to resisting the agony of bodily suffering. Nor was this party without the proper instruments for effecting such a purpose. Sumach had a notoriety as a scold, and one or two crones, like the She Bear, had come out with the party, most probably as the conservators of its decency and moral discipline; such things occurring in savage as well as in civilized life. It is unnecessary to repeat all that ferocity and ignorance could invent for such a purpose, the only difference between this outbreaking of feminine anger, and a similar scene among ourselves, consisting in the figures of speech and the epithets, the Huron women calling their prisoner by the names of the lower and least respected animals that were known to themselves.

But Deerslayer's mind was too much occupied, to permit him to be disturbed by the abuse of excited hags, and their rage necessarily increasing with his indifference, as his indifference increased with their rage, the furies soon rendered themselves impotent by their own excesses. Perceiving that the attempt was a complete failure, the warriors interfered to put a stop to this scene, and this so much the more, because preparations were now seriously making for the commencement of the real tortures, or that which would put the fortitude of the sufferer to the test of severe bodily pain. A sudden and unlooked for announcement, that proceeded from one of the look-outs, a boy ten or twelve years old, however, put a momentary check to the whole proceedings. As this interruption has a close connection with the *dénouement* of our story, it shall be given in a separate chapter.

Chapter XXX.

"So deem'st thou — so each mortal deems
Of that which is from that which seems;
        But other harvest here
Than that which peasant's scythe demands,
Was gather'd in by sterner hands,
        With bayonet, blade, and spear."
                    Scott, "The Field of Waterloo," V.1-6.

I T exceeded Deerslayer's power to ascertain what had produced the sudden pause in the movements of his enemies, until the fact was revealed in the due course of events. He perceived that much agitation prevailed among the women in particular, while the warriors rested on their arms, in a sort of dignified expectation. It was plain no alarm was excited, though it was not equally apparent that a friendly occurrence produced the delay. Rivenoak was evidently apprised of all, and by a gesture of his arm he appeared to direct the circle to remain unbroken, and for each person to await the issue in the situation he, or she, then occupied. It required but a minute or two, to bring an explanation of this singular and mysterious pause, which was soon terminated by the appearance of Judith on the exterior of the line of bodies, and her ready admission within its circle.

If Deerslayer was startled by this unexpected arrival, well knowing that the quick witted girl could claim none of that exemption from the penalties of captivity, that was so cheerfully accorded to her feebler minded sister, he was equally astonished at the guise in which she came. All her ordinary forest attire, neat and becoming as this usually was, had been laid aside for the brocade that has been already mentioned, and which had once before wrought so great and magical an effect in her appearance. Nor was this all. Accustomed to see the ladies of the garrison, in the formal, gala attire of the day, and familiar with the more critical niceties of these matters, the girl had managed to complete her dress, in a way to leave nothing strikingly defective in its details, or even to betray an incongruity that would have been detected by one practised in the mysteries of the toilet. Head, feet, arms, hands, bust, and drapery, were all in harmony, as female attire was then deemed attractive and harmonious, and the end she aimed at, that of imposing on the uninstructed senses of the savages, by causing them to believe their guest was a woman of rank and importance, might well have succeeded with those whose habits had taught them to discriminate between persons. Judith, in addition to her rare native beauty, had a singular grace of person, and her mother had imparted enough of her own deportment, to prevent any striking or offensive vulgarity of manner; so that, sooth to say, the gorgeous dress might have been worse bestowed in nearly every particular. Had it been displayed in a capital, a thousand might have worn it, before one could have been found to do more credit to its gay colours, glossy satins, and rich laces, than the beautiful creature whose person it now aided to adorn.

The effect of such an apparition had not been miscalculated. The instant Judith found herself within the circle, she was, in a degree, compensated for the fearful personal risk she ran, by the unequivocal sensation of surprise and admiration produced by her appearance. The grim old warriors uttered their favorite exclamation "hugh!" The younger men were still more sensibly overcome, and even the women were not backward in letting open manifestations of pleasure escape them. It was seldom that these untutored children of the forest had ever seen any white female above the commonest sort, and, as to dress, never before had so much splendor shone before their eyes. The gayest uniforms of both French and English seemed dull compared with the lustre of the brocade, and while the rare personal beauty of the wearer added to the effect produced by its hues, the attire did not fail to adorn that beauty in a way which surpassed even the hopes of its wearer. Deerslayer himself was astounded, and this quite as much by the brilliant picture the girl presented, as at the indifference to consequences with which she had braved the danger of the step she had taken. Under such circumstances, all waited for the visiter to explain her object, which to most of the spectators seemed as inexplicable as her appearance.

"Which of these warriors is the principal chief?" demanded

Judith of Deerslayer, as soon as she found it was expected that she should open the communications; "my errand is too important to be delivered to any of inferior rank. First explain to the Hurons, what I say; then give an answer to the question I have put."

Deerslayer quietly complied, his auditors greedily listening to the interpretation of the first words that fell from so extraordinary a vision. The demand seemed perfectly in character for one who had every appearance of an exalted rank, herself. Rivenoak gave an appropriate reply, by presenting himself before his fair visiter in a way to leave no doubt that he was entitled to all the consideration he claimed.

"I can believe this, Huron," resumed Judith, enacting her assumed part, with a steadiness and dignity that did credit to her powers of imitation, for she strove to impart to her manner the condescending courtesy she had once observed in the wife of a general officer, at a similar though a more amicable scene: "I can believe you to be the principal person of this party; I see in your countenance the marks of thought and reflection. To you, then, I must make my communication."

"Let the Flower of the Woods speak," returned the old chief courteously, as soon as her address had been translated so that all might understand it — "If her words are as pleasant as her looks, they will never quit my ears; I shall hear them long after the winter of Canada has killed all the flowers, and frozen all the speeches of summer."

This admiration was grateful to one constituted like Judith, and contributed to aid her self-possession, quite as much as it fed her vanity. Smiling involuntarily, or in spite of her wish to seem reserved, she proceeded in her plot.

"Now, Huron," she continued, "listen to my words. Your eyes tell you that I am no common woman. I will not say I am queen of this country; *she* is afar off, in a distant land; but under our gracious monarchs, there are many degrees of rank; one of these I fill. What that rank is precisely, it is unnecessary for me to say, since you would not understand it. For that information you must trust your eyes. You *see* what I am; you must *feel* that in listening to my words, you listen to one who can be your friend, or your enemy, as you treat her."

This was well uttered, with a due attention to manner, and a steadiness of tone, that was really surprising, considering all the circumstances of the case. It was well, though simply rendered into the Indian dialect too, and it was received with a respect and gravity that augured favourably for the girl's success. But Indian thought is not easily traced to its sources. Judith waited with anxiety to hear the answer, filled with hope even while she doubted. Rivenoak was a ready speaker, and he answered as promptly as comported with the notions of Indian decorum; that peculiar people seeming to think a short delay respectful, inasmuch as it manifests that the words already heard, have been duly weighed.

"My daughter is handsomer than the wild roses of Ontario; her voice is pleasant to the ear as the song of the wren," answered the cautious and wily chief, who of all the band, stood alone in not being fully imposed on by the magnificent and unusual appearance of Judith; but who distrusted even while he wondered: "the humming bird is not much larger than the bee; yet its feathers are as gay as the tail of the peacock. The Great Spirit sometimes puts very bright clothes on very little animals. Still He covers the Moose with coarse hair. These things are beyond the understanding of poor Indians, who can only comprehend what they see and hear. No doubt my daughter has a very large wigwam, somewhere about the lake; the Hurons have not found it, on account of their ignorance?"

"I have told you, chief, that it would be useless to state my rank and residence, in as much as you would not comprehend them. You must trust to your eyes for this knowledge; what red man is there who cannot see? This blanket that I wear, is not the blanket of a common squaw; these ornaments are such as the wives and daughters of chiefs only appear in. Now, listen and hear why I have come alone, among your people, and hearken to the errand that has brought me here. The Yengeese have young men, as well as the Hurons; and plenty of them, too; this you well know."

"The Yengeese are as plenty as the leaves on the trees! This every Huron knows, and feels."

"I understand you, chief. Had I brought a party with me, it

might have caused trouble. My young men and your young men, would have looked angrily at each other; especially had my young men seen that pale face bound for the torture. He is a great hunter, and is much loved by all the garrisons, far and near. There would have been blows about him, and the trail of the Iroquois back to the Canadas would have been marked with blood."

"There is so much blood on it, now," returned the chief, gloomily, "that it blinds our eyes. My young men see that it is all Huron."

"No doubt; and more Huron blood would be spilt had I come surrounded with pale faces. I have heard of Rivenoak, and have thought it would be better to send him back in peace to his village, that he might leave his women and children behind him; if he then wished to come for our scalps, we would meet him. He loves animals made of ivory, and little rifles. See; I have brought some with me to show him. I am his friend. When he has packed up these things among his goods, he will start for his village, before any of my young men can overtake him, and then he will show his people in Canada what riches they can come to seek, now that our great fathers, across the Salt Lake, have sent each other the war hatchet. I will lead back with me, this great hunter, of whom I have need to keep my house in venison."

Judith, who was sufficiently familiar with Indian phraseology, endeavored to express her ideas in the sententious manner common to those people, and she succeeded even beyond her own expectations. Deerslayer did her full justice in the translation, and this so much the more readily, since the girl carefully abstained from uttering any direct untruth; a homage she paid to the young man's known aversion to falsehood, which he deemed a meanness altogether unworthy of a white man's gifts. The offering of the two remaining elephants, and of the pistols already mentioned, one of which was all the worse for the recent accident, produced a lively sensation among the Hurons, generally, though Rivenoak received it coldly, notwithstanding the delight with which he had first discovered the probable existence of a creature with two tails. In a word, this cool and sagacious savage was not so easily imposed on, as his followers, and with a sentiment of honor, that half the civilized world would have deemed supererogatory, he declined the acceptance of a bribe that he felt no disposition to earn by a compliance with the donor's wishes.

"Let my daughter keep her two-tailed hog, to eat, when venison is scarce," he drily answered, "and the little gun, which has two muzzles. The Hurons will kill deer when they are hungry, and they have long rifles to fight with. This hunter cannot quit my young men now; they wish to know if he is as stout hearted, as he boasts himself to be."

"That I deny, Huron—" interrupted Deerslayer, with warmth—"Yes, that I down right deny, as ag'in truth and reason. No man has heard me *boast*, and no man shall, though ye flay me alive, and then roast the quivering flesh, with your own infarnal devices and cruelties! I may be humble, and misfortunate, and your prisoner; but I'm no boaster, by my very gifts."

"My young pale-face *boasts* he is *no* boaster," returned the crafty chief: "he *must* be right. I hear a strange bird singing. It has very rich feathers. No Huron ever before saw such feathers! They will be ashamed to go back to their village, and tell their people that they let their prisoner go on account of the song of this strange bird and not be able to give the *name* of the bird. They do not know how to say whether it is a wren, or a cat bird. This would be a great disgrace; my young men would not be allowed to travel in the woods, without taking their mothers with them, to tell them the names of the birds!"

"You can ask my name of your prisoner," returned the girl. "It is Judith; and there is a great deal of the history of Judith in the Pale face's best book, the bible. If I am a bird of fine feathers, I have also my name."

"No," answered the wily Huron, betraying the artifice he had so long practised, by speaking in English, with tolerable accuracy, "I not ask prisoner. He tired; he want rest. I ask my daughter, with feeble mind. She speak truth. Come here, daughter; you answer. *Your* name, Hetty?"

"Yes, that's what they call me," returned the girl, "though it's written Esther in the bible."

"He write *him* in bible, too! All write in bible. No matter— what *her* name?"

"That's Judith, and it's so written in the bible, though father sometimes called her Jude. That's my sister Judith, Thomas Hutter's daughter—Thomas Hutter, whom you called the Muskrat; though he was *no* muskrat, but a man like yourselves—he lived in a house on the water, and that was enough for *you!*"

A smile of triumph gleamed on the hard wrinkled countenance of the chief, when he found how completely his appeal to the truth-loving Hetty had succeeded. As for Judith, herself, the moment her sister was questioned, she saw that all was lost; for no sign, or even intreaty could have induced the right feeling girl to utter a falsehood. To attempt to impose a daughter of the Muskrat on the savages, as a princess, or a great lady, she knew would be idle, and she saw her bold and ingenious expedient for liberating the captive fail, through one of the simplest and most natural causes that could be imagined. She turned her eye on Deerslayer, therefore, as if imploring him to interfere, to save them both.

"It will not do, Judith," said the young man, in answer to this appeal, which he understood, though he saw its uselessness; "it will not do. Twas a bold idee, and fit for a general's lady, but yonder Mingo—" Rivenoak had withdrawn to a little distance, and was out of ear-shot—"but yonder Mingo, is an oncommon man, and not to be deceived by any unnat'ral sarcumvention. Things must come afore him, in their right order, to draw a cloud afore *his* eyes! Twas too much to attempt making him fancy that a queen, or a great lady, lived in these mountains, and no doubt he thinks the fine clothes you wear, is some of the plunder of your own father—or, at least, of him who once passed for your father; as quite likely it was, if all they say is true."

"At all events, Deerslayer, my presence here, will save you for a time. They will hardly attempt torturing you before my face!"

"Why not, Judith? Do you think they will treat a woman of the pale faces, more tenderly than they treat their own? It's true that your sex will most likely save you from the torments, but it will not save your liberty, and may not save your scalp. I wish you had n't come, my good Judith; it can do no good to me, while it may do great harm to yourself."

"I can share your fate," the girl answered with generous enthusiasm. "They shall not injure you, while I stand by, if in my power to prevent it—besides—"

"Besides, what, Judith? What means have you to stop Injin cruelties, or to avart Injin deviltries?"

"None, perhaps, Deerslayer," answered the girl, with firmness, "but I can suffer with my friends—die with them if necessary."

"Ah! Judith—suffer you may; but die you will not, until the Lord's time shall come. It's little likely that one of your sex and beauty will meet with a harder fate than to become the wife of a chief, if, indeed your white inclinations can stoop to match with an Injin. 'Twould have been better had you staid in the Ark, or the castle, but what has been done, is done. You was about to say something, when you stopped at 'besides'?"

"It might not be safe to mention it here, Deerslayer," the girl hurriedly answered, moving past him carelessly, that she might speak in a lower tone; "half an hour, is all in all to us. None of your friends are idle."

The hunter replied merely by a grateful look. Then he turned towards his enemies, as if ready again to face their torments. A short consultation had passed among the elders of the band, and by this time they also were prepared with their decision. The merciful purpose of Rivenoak had been much weakened by the artifice of Judith, which, failing of its real object, was likely to produce results the very opposite of those she had anticipated. This was natural; the feeling being aided by the resentment of an Indian, who found how near he had been to becoming the dupe of an inexperienced girl. By this time, Judith's real character was fully understood, the wide spread reputation of her beauty contributing to the exposure. As for the unusual attire, it was confounded with the profound mystery of the animals with two tails, and, for the moment lost its influence.

When Rivenoak, therefore, faced the captive again, it was with an altered countenance. He had abandoned the wish of saving him, and was no longer disposed to retard the more serious part of the torture. This change of sentiment was, in effect, communicated to the young men, who were already eagerly engaged in making their preparations for the contemplated scene. Fragments of dried wood were rapidly collected, near the sapling, the splinters which it was intended to thrust into the flesh of the victim, previously to lighting, were all collected, and the thongs were already produced that were again to bind him to the tree. All this was done in profound silence, Judith watching every movement with breathless expectation, while Deerslayer himself, stood seemingly as unmoved, as one of the pines of the hills. When the warriors advanced to bind him, however, the young man glanced at Judith, as if to enquire whether resistance or submission were most advisable. By a significant gesture she counselled the last, and, in a minute, he was once more fastened to the tree, a helpless object of any insult, or wrong, that might be offered. So eagerly did every one now act, that nothing was said. The fire was immediately lighted in the pile, and the end of all was anxiously expected.

It was not the intention of the Hurons absolutely to destroy the life of their victim by means of fire. They designed merely to put his physical fortitude to the severest proofs it could endure, short of that extremity. In the end, they fully intended to carry his scalp with them into their village, but it was their wish first to break down his resolution, and to reduce him to the level of a complaining sufferer. With this view, the pile of brush and branches had been placed at a proper distance, or, one at which it was thought the heat would soon become intolerable, though it might not be immediately dangerous. As often happened, however, on these occasions, this distance had been miscalculated, and the flames began to wave their forked tongues in a proximity to the face of the victim, that would have proved fatal, in another instant, had not Hetty rushed through the crowd, armed with a stick, and scattered the blazing pile, in a dozen directions. More than one hand was raised to strike this presumptuous intruder to the earth, but the chiefs prevented the blows, by reminding their irritated followers of the state of her mind. Hetty, herself, was insensible to the risk she ran, but, as soon as she had performed this bold act, she stood looking about her, in frowning resentment, as if to rebuke the crowd of attentive savages, for their cruelty.

"God bless you, dearest sister, for that brave and ready act!" murmured Judith, herself unnerved so much as to be incapable of exertion—"Heaven, itself, has sent you on its holy errand."

"Twas well meant, Judith—" rejoined the victim—"twas excellently meant, and 'twas timely; though it may prove ontimely in the ind! What is to come to pass, must come to pass soon, or 'twill quickly be too late. Had I drawn in one mouthful of that flame in breathing, the power of man could not save my life, and you see that, this time, they've so bound my forehead, as not to leave my head the smallest chance. Twas well meant, but it might have been more marciful to let the flames act their part."

"Cruel, heartless Hurons!" exclaimed the still indignant Hetty—"Would you burn a man and a christian, as you would burn a log of wood! Do you never read your bibles?—Or do you think God will forget such things?"

A gesture from Rivenoak caused the scattered brands to be collected. Fresh wood was brought, even the women and children busying themselves eagerly, in the gathering of dried sticks. The flame was just kindling a second time, when an *Indian* female pushed through the circle, advanced to the heap, and with her foot dashed aside the lighted twigs, in time to prevent the conflagration. A yell followed this second disappointment, but when the offender turned, towards the circle, and presented the countenance of Hist, it was succeeded by a common exclamation of pleasure and surprise. For a minute, all thought of pursuing the business in hand was forgotten. Young and old crowded around the girl, in haste to demand an explanation of her sudden and unlooked-for return. It was at this critical instant that Hist spoke to Judith in a low voice, placed some small object unseen in her hand, and then turned to meet the salutations of the Huron girls, with whom she was personally a great favorite. Judith recovered her self-possession, and acted promptly. The small, keen edged knife, that Hist had given to the other, was passed by the latter into the hands of Hetty, as the safest and least suspected medium of transferring it to Deerslayer. But the feeble intellect of the last, defeated the well-grounded hopes of all three. Instead of first cutting loose the hands of the victim, and then concealing the knife in his clothes, in readiness for action, at the most available instant, she went to work herself, with earnestness and simplicity, to cut the thongs that bound his head, that he might not again be in danger of inhaling flames. Of course this deliberate procedure was seen, and the hands of Hetty were arrested, ere she had more than liberated the upper portion of the captive's body, not including his arms, below the elbows. This discovery at once pointed distrust towards Hist, and to Judith's surprise, when questioned on the subject, that spirited girl was not disposed to deny her agency in what had passed.

"Why should I not help the Deerslayer?" the girl demanded, in the tones of a firm minded woman. "He is the brother of a Delaware chief; my heart is all Delaware. Come forth, miserable Briarthorn, and wash the Iroquois paint from your face; stand before the Hurons, the crow that you are. You would eat the carrion of your own dead, rather than starve. Put him face to face with Deerslayer, chiefs and warriors; I will show you how great a knave you have been keeping in your tribe."

This bold language, uttered in their own dialect, and with a manner full of confidence, produced a deep sensation among the Hurons. Treachery is always liable to distrust, and though the recreant Briarthorn had endeavoured to serve the enemy well, his exertions and assiduities had gained for him little more than toleration. His wish to obtain Hist for a wife, had first induced him to betray her, and his own people, but serious rivals to his first project had risen up among his new friends, weakening still more their sympathies with treason. In a word, Briarthorn had been barely permitted to remain in the Huron encampment, where he was as closely and as jealously watched as Hist, herself, seldom appearing before the chiefs, and sedulously keeping out of view of Deerslayer, who, until this moment, was ignorant even of his presence. Thus summoned, however, it was impossible to remain in the back ground. "Wash the Iroquois paint from his face," he did not, for when he stood in the centre of the circle, he was so disguised in these new colours, that at first, the hunter did not recognise him. He assumed an air of defiance, notwithstanding, and haughtily demanded what any could say against "Briarthorn."

"Ask yourself that," continued Hist with spirit, though her manner grew less concentrated, and there was a slight air of abstraction that became observable to Deerslayer and Judith, if to no others—"Ask that of your own heart, sneaking wood-chuck of the Delawares; come not here with the face of an innocent man. Go look into the spring; see the colours of your enemies on your lying skin; then come back and boast how you run from your tribe and took the blanket of the French for your covering! Paint yourself as bright as the humming bird, you will still be black as the crow!"

Hist had been so uniformly gentle, while living with the Hurons, that they now listened to her language with surprise. As for the delinquent, his blood boiled in his veins, and it was well for the pretty speaker that it was not in his power to execute the revenge he burned to inflict on her, in spite of his pretended love.

"Who wishes Briarthorn?" he sternly asked—"If this pale face is tired of life, if afraid of Indian torments, speak, Rivenoak; I will send him after the warriors we have lost."

"No, chiefs—no, Rivenoak—" eagerly interrupted Hist—"Deerslayer fears nothing; least of all a crow! Unbind him—cut his withes, place him face to face with this cawing bird; then let us see which is tired of life!"

Hist made a forward movement, as if to take a knife from a young man, and perform the office she had mentioned in person, but an aged warrior interposed, at a sign from Rivenoak. This chief watched all the girl did with distrust, for, even while speaking in her most boastful language, and in the steadiest manner, there was an air of uncertainty and expectation about her, that could not escape so close an observer. She acted well; but two or three of the old men were equally satisfied that it was merely acting. Her proposal to release Deerslayer, therefore, was rejected, and the disappointed Hist found herself driven back from the sapling, at the very moment she fancied herself about to be successful. At the same time, the circle, which had got to be crowded and confused, was enlarged, and brought once more into order. Rivenoak now announced the intention of the old men again to proceed, the delay having continued long enough, and leading to no result.

"Stop Huron—stay chiefs! —" exclaimed Judith, scarce knowing what she said, or why she interposed, unless to obtain time. "For God's sake, a single minute longer—"

The words were cut short, by another and a still more extraordinary interruption. A young Indian came bounding through the Huron ranks, leaping into the very centre of the circle, in a way to denote the utmost confidence, or a temerity bordering on fool-hardiness. Five or six sentinels were still watching the lake at different and distant points, and it was the first impression of Rivenoak that one of these had come in, with tidings of import. Still the movements of the stranger were so rapid, and his war dress, which scarcely left him more drapery than an antique statue, had so little distinguishing about it, that, at the first moment, it was impossible to ascertain whether he were friend or foe. Three leaps carried this warrior to the side of Deerslayer, whose withes were cut, in the twinkling of an eye, with a quickness and precision that left the prisoner perfect master of his limbs. Not till this was effected, did the stranger bestow a glance on any other object; then he turned and showed the astonished Hurons, the noble brow, fine person, and eagle-eye, of a young warrior, in the paint and panoply of a Delaware. He held a rifle in each hand, the butts of both, resting on the earth, while from one dangled its proper pouch and horn. This was Killdeer which, even as he looked boldly and in defiance at the crowd around him, he suffered to fall back into the hands of its proper owner. The presence of two armed men, though it was in their midst, startled the Hurons. Their rifles were scattered about against the different trees, and their only weapons were their knives and tomahawks. Still they had too much self-possession to betray fear. It was little likely that so small a force would assail so strong a band, and each man expected some extraordinary proposition to succeed so decisive a step. The stranger did not seem disposed to disappoint them; he prepared to speak.

"Hurons," he said, "this earth is very big. The Great Lakes are big, too; there is room beyond them for the Iroquois; there is room for the Delawares on this side. I am Chingachgook the Son of Uncas; the kinsman of Tamenund. This is my betrothed;

that pale face is my friend. My heart was heavy, when I missed him; I followed him to your camp, to see that no harm happened to him. All the Delaware girls are waiting for Wah; they wonder that she stays away so long. Come, let us say farewell, and go on our path."

"Hurons, this is your mortal enemy, the Great Serpent of them you hate!" cried Briarthorn. "If he escape, blood will be in your moccasin prints, from this spot to the Canadas. *I* am *all* Huron!"

As the last words were uttered, the traitor cast his knife at the naked breast of the Delaware. A quick movement of the arm, on the part of Hist, who stood near, turned aside the blow, the dangerous weapon burying its point in a pine. At the next instant, a similar weapon glanced from the hand of the Serpent, and quivered in the recreant's heart. A minute had scarcely elapsed from the moment in which Chingachgook bounded into the circle, and that in which Briarthorn fell, like a log, dead in his tracks. The rapidity of events had prevented the Hurons from acting; but this catastrophe permitted no farther delay. A common exclamation followed, and the whole party was in motion. At this instant a sound unusual to the woods was heard, and every Huron, male and female, paused to listen, with ears erect and faces filled with expectation. The sound was regular and heavy, as if the earth were struck with beetles. Objects became visible among the trees of the back ground, and a body of troops, was seen advancing with measured tread. They came upon the charge, the scarlet of the King's livery shining among the bright green foliage of the forest.

The scene that followed is not easily described. It was one in which wild confusion, despair, and frenzied efforts, were so blended, as to destroy the unity and distinctness of the action. A general yell burst from the enclosed Hurons; it was succeeded by the hearty cheers of England. Still not a musket or rifle was fired, though that steady, measured, tramp continued, and the bayonet was seen gleaming in advance of a line that counted nearly sixty men. The Hurons were taken at a fearful disadvantage. On three sides was the water, while their formidable and trained foes, cut them off from flight, on the fourth. Each warrior rushed for his arms, and then all on the point, man, woman and child, eagerly sought the covers. In this scene of confusion and dismay, however, nothing could surpass the discretion and coolness of Deerslayer. His first care was to place Judith and Hist, behind trees, and he looked for Hetty; but she had been hurried away in the crowd of Huron women. This effected, he threw himself on a flank of the retiring Hurons, who were inclining off towards the southern margin of the point, in the hope of escaping through the water. Deerslayer watched his opportunity, and finding two of his recent tormentors in a range, his rifle first broke the silence of the terrific scene. The bullet brought down both at one discharge. This drew a general fire from the Hurons, and the rifle and war cry of the Serpent were heard in the clamor. Still the trained men returned no answering volley, the whoop and piece of Hurry alone being heard on their side, if we except, the short, prompt word of authority, and that heavy, measured and menacing tread. Presently, however, the shrieks, groans, and denunciations that usually accompany the use of the bayonet followed. That terrible and deadly weapon was glutted in vengeance. The scene that succeeded was one of those, of which so many have occurred in our own times, in which neither age nor sex forms an exemption to the lot of a savage warfare.

Chapter XXXI.

"The flower that smiles to-day
　To-morrow dies;
All that we wish to stay,
　Tempts and then flies:
What is this world's delight? —
Lightning that mocks the night,
Brief even as bright."

Shelley, "Mutability," ll. 1–7.

T HE picture next presented, by the point of land that the unfortunate Hurons had selected for their last place of encampment, need scarcely be laid before the eyes of the reader. Happily for the more tender-minded and the more timid, the trunks of the trees, the leaves, and the smoke had concealed much of that which passed, and night shortly after drew its veil over the lake, and the whole of that seemingly interminable wilderness; which may be said to have then stretched, with few and immaterial interruptions, from the banks of the Hudson to the shores of the Pacific Ocean. Our business carries us into the following day, when light returned upon the earth, as sunny and as smiling, as if nothing extraordinary had occurred.

When the sun rose on the following morning, every sign of hostility and alarm had vanished from the basin of the Glimmerglass. The frightful event of the preceding evening had left no impression on the placid sheet, and the untiring hours pursued their course in the placid order prescribed by the powerful hand that set them in motion. The birds were again skimming the water, or were seen poised on the wing, high above the tops of the tallest pines of the mountains, ready to make their swoops, in obedience to the irresistable law of their natures. In a word, nothing was changed, but the air of movement and life that prevailed in and around the castle. Here, indeed, was an alteration that must have struck the least observant eye. A sentinel, who wore the light infantry uniform of a royal regiment, paced the platform with measured tread, and some twenty more of the same corps, lounged about the place, or were seated in the ark. Their arms were stacked under the eye of their comrade on post. Two officers stood examining the shore, with the ship's glass so often mentioned. Their looks were directed to that fatal point, where scarlet coats were still to be seen gliding among the trees, and where the magnifying power of the instrument also showed spades at work, and the sad duty of interment going on. Several of the common men bore proofs on their persons, that their enemies had not been overcome entirely without resistance, and the youngest of the two officers on the platform, wore an arm in a sling. His companion, who commanded the party, had been more fortunate. He it was who used the glass, in making the reconnoissances in which the two were engaged.

A serjeant approached to make a report. He addressed the senior of these officers, as Capt. Warley, while the other was alluded to as Mr. —— which was equivalent to Ensign —— Thornton. The former it will at once be seen was the officer who had been named with so much feeling, in the parting dialogue between Judith and Hurry. He was, in truth, the very individual with whom the scandal of the garrisons, had most freely connected the name of this beautiful but indiscreet girl. He was a hard featured, red faced, man, of about five and thirty; but of a military carriage, and with an air of fashion that might easily impose on the imagination of one as ignorant of the world, as Judith.

"Craig is covering us with benedictions," observed this person to his young ensign, with an air of indifference as he shut the glass, and handed it to his servant; "to say the truth, not without reason; it is certainly more agreeable to be here in attendance on Miss Judith Hutter, than to be burying Indians, on a point of the lake, however romantic the position, or brilliant the victory. By the way, Wright—is Davis still living?"

"He died about ten minutes since, your honor," returned the sergeant to whom this question was addressed. "I knew how it would be, as soon as I found the bullet had touched the stomach. I never knew a man who could hold out long, if he had a hole in his stomach."

"No; it is rather inconvenient for carrying away any thing very nourishing," observed Warley gaping. "This being up two nights *de suite*, Arthur, plays the devil with a man's faculties! I'm as stupid, as one of those Dutch parsons on the Mohawk — I hope your arm is not painful, my dear boy?"

"It draws a few grimaces from me, sir, as I suppose you see," answered the youth, laughing at the very moment, his countenance was a little awry with pain. "But it may be borne. I suppose Graham can spare a few minutes, soon, to look at my hurt."

"She is a lovely creature, this Judith Hutter, after all, Thornton; and it shall not be my fault if she is not seen and admired in the Parks!" resumed Warley, who thought little of his companion's wound—"your arm, eh! Quite true—Go into the ark, serjeant, and tell Dr. Graham I desire he would look at Mr. Thornton's injury, as soon as he has done with the poor fellow with the broken leg. A lovely creature! and she looked like a queen in that brocade dress in which we met her. I find all changed here; father and mother both gone, the sister dying, if not dead, and none of the family left, but the beauty! This has been a lucky expedition all round, and promises to terminate better than Indian skirmishes in general."

"Am I to suppose, sir, that you are about to desert your colours, in the great corps of bachelors, and close the campaign with matrimony?"

"I, Tom Warley, turn Benedict! Faith, my dear boy, you little know the corps you speak of, if you fancy any such thing. I do suppose there *are* women in the colonies, that a captain of Light Infantry need not disdain; but they are not to be found up here, on a mountain lake; or even down on the Dutch river where we are posted. It is true, my uncle, the general, once did me the favor to choose a wife for me in Yorkshire; but she had no beauty, and I would not marry a princess, unless she were handsome."

"If handsome, you would marry a beggar?"

"Ay, these are the notions of an ensign! Love in a cottage — doors—and windows—the old story, for the hundredth time. The twenty —th do n't *marry*. We are not a marrying corps, my dear boy. There's the Colonel, Old Sir Edwin—, now;

though a full General he has never thought of a wife; and when a man gets as high as a Lieutenant General, without matrimony, he is pretty safe. Then the Lieutenant Colonel is *confirmed*, as I tell my cousin the Bishop. The Major is a widower, having tried matrimony, for twelve months in his youth, and we look upon him, now, as one of our most certain men. Out of ten captains, but one is in the dilemma, and he, poor devil, is always kept at regimental head quarters, as a sort of *memento mori*, to the young men as they join. As for the subalterns, not one has ever yet had the audacity to speak of introducing a wife into the regiment. But your arm is troublesome, and we'll go ourselves and see what has become of Graham."

The Surgeon who had accompanied the party, was employed very differently from what the captain supposed. When the assault was over, and the dead and wounded were collected, poor Hetty had been found among the latter. A rifle bullet had passed through her body, inflicting an injury that was known at a glance, to be mortal. How this wound was received, no one knew; it was probably one of those casualties that ever accompany scenes like that related in the previous chapter.

The Sumach, all the elderly women, and some of the Huron girls, had fallen by the bayonet, either in the confusion of the *mêlée*, or from the difficulty of distinguishing the sexes, when the dress was so simple. Much the greater portion of the warriors suffered on the spot. A few had escaped, however, and two or three had been taken unharmed. As for the wounded, the bayonet saved the surgeon much trouble. Rivenoak had escaped with life and limb, but was injured and a prisoner. As Captain Warley, and his ensign, went into the Ark, they passed him, seated, in dignified silence, in one end of the scow, his head and leg bound, but betraying no visible sign of despondency or despair. That he mourned the loss of his tribe, is certain; still he did it in a manner that best became a warrior and a chief.

The two soldiers found their surgeon in the principal room of the Ark. He was just quitting the pallet of Hetty, with an expression of sorrowful regret, on his hard, pock-marked Scottish features, that it was not usual to see there. All his assiduity had been useless, and he was compelled, reluctantly to abandon the expectation of seeing the girl survive many hours. Dr. Graham was accustomed to death-bed scenes, and ordinarily they produced but little impression on him. In all that relates to religion, his was one of those minds which, in consequence of reasoning much on material things, logically and consecutively, and overlooking the total want of premises which such a theory must ever possess, through its want of a primary agent, had become sceptical; leaving a vague opinion concerning the origin of things, that, with high pretentions to philosophy, failed in the first of all philosophical principles, a cause. To him religious dependence appeared a weakness, but when he found one gentle and young like Hetty, with a mind beneath the level of her race, sustained at such a moment by these pious sentiments, and that, too, in a way that many a sturdy warrior, and reputed hero might have looked upon with envy, he found himself affected by the sight, to a degree that he would have been ashamed to confess. Edinburgh and Aberdeen, then as now, supplied no small portion of the medical men of the British service, and Dr. Graham, as indeed his name and countenance equally indicated, was, by birth, a North Briton.

"Here is an extraordinary exhibition for a forest, and one but half-gifted with reason," he observed with a decided Scotch accent, as Warley and the ensign entered; "I just hope, gentlemen, that when we three shall be called on to quit the twenty — th, we may be found as resigned to go on the half pay of another existence, as this poor demented chiel!"

"Is there no hope that she can survive the hurt?" demanded Warley, turning his eyes towards the pallid Judith, on whose cheeks, however, two large spots of red had settled, as soon as he came into the cabin.

"No more than there is for Chairlie Stuart! Approach and judge for yourselves, gentlemen; ye'll see faith exemplified in an exceeding and wonderful manner. There is a sort of *arbitrium* between life and death, in actual conflict in the poor girl's mind, that renders her an interesting study to a philosopher. Mr. Thornton, I'm at your service, now; we can just look at the arm, in the next room, while we speculate as much as we please on the operations and sinuosities of the human mind."

The surgeon and ensign retired, and Warley had an opportunity of looking about him, more at leisure, and with a better understanding of the nature and feelings of the group collected in the cabin. Poor Hetty had been placed on her own simple bed, and was reclining in a half seated attitude, with the approaches of death on her countenance, though they were singularly dimmed by the lustre of an expression, in which all the intelligence of her entire being appeared to be concentrated. Judith and Hist were near her, the former seated in deep grief; the latter standing, in readiness to offer any of the gentle attentions of feminine care. Deerslayer stood at the end of the pallet, leaning on Killdeer, unharmed in person, all the fine martial ardor that had so lately glowed in his countenance, having given place to the usual look of honesty and benevolence, qualities of which the expression was now softened by manly regret and pity. The Serpent was in the back-ground of the picture, erect, and motionless as a statue; but so observant that not a look of the eye, escaped his own keen glances. Hurry completed the group, being seated on a stool near the door, like one who felt himself out of place in such a scene, but who was ashamed to quit it, unbidden.

"Who is that, in scarlet?" asked Hetty, as soon as the Captain's uniform caught her eye. "Tell me, Judith, is it the friend of Hurry?"

" 'Tis the officer who commands the troops, that have rescued us all from the hands of the Hurons," was the low answer of the sister.

"Am I rescued, too!—I thought they said I was shot, and about to die. Mother is dead; and so is father; but you are living, Judith, and so is Hurry. I was afraid Hurry would be killed, when I heard him shouting among the soldiers."

"Never mind—never mind, dear Hetty—" interrupted Judith, sensitively alive to the preservation of her sister's secret, more, perhaps, at such a moment, than at any other. "Hurry is well, and Deerslayer is well, and the Delaware is well, too."

"How came they to shoot a poor girl like me, and let so many men go unharmed? I did n't know that the Hurons were so wicked, Judith!"

" 'Twas an accident, poor Hetty; a sad—sad—accident it has been! No one would willingly have injured *you*."

"I'm glad of that!—I thought it strange; I am feeble minded, and the red men have never harmed me before. I should be sorry to think that they had changed their minds. I am glad too, Judith, that they haven't hurt Hurry. Deerslayer, I don't think God will suffer any one to harm. It was very fortunate the soldiers came as they did though, for fire *will* burn!"

"It was, indeed fortunate, my sister; God's holy name be forever blessed for the mercy!"

"I dare say, Judith, you know some of the officers; you used to know so many!"

Judith made no reply; she hid her face in her hands and groaned. Hetty gazed at her in wonder; but naturally supposing her own situation was the cause of this grief, she kindly offered to console her sister.

"Don't mind me, dear Judith," said the affectionate and pure-hearted creature—"I don't suffer; if I do die, why father and mother are both dead, and what happens to *them*, may well happen to *me*. You know I am of less account than any of the family; therefore few will think of me after I'm in the lake."

"No—no—no—poor, dear, dear Hetty!" exclaimed Judith, in an uncontrollable burst of sorrow, "I, at least, will ever think of you; and gladly, oh! how gladly would I exchange places with you, to be the pure, excellent, sinless creature you are!"

Until now, Captain Warley had stood leaning against the door of the cabin; when this outbreak of feeling, and perchance of penitence, however, escaped the beautiful girl, he walked slowly and thoughtfully away; even passing the ensign, then suffering under the surgeon's care, without noticing him.

"I have got my bible here, Judith," returned her sister, in a voice of triumph. "It's true, I can't read any longer, there's something the matter with my eyes—*you* look dim and distant—and so does Hurry, now I look at him—well, I never could have believed that Henry March would have so dull a look!—What can be the reason, Judith, that I see so badly, to-day? I, who mother always said, had the best eyes in the whole family. Yes, that was it: my mind was feeble—what people call half-witted—but my eyes were *so* good!"

Again Judith groaned; this time no feeling of self, no retrospect of the past caused the pain. It was the pure, heart-felt sorrow of sisterly love, heightened by a sense of the meek humility and perfect truth of the being before her. At that moment, she would gladly have given up her own life to save that of Hetty. As the last, however, was beyond the reach of human power, she felt there was nothing left her but sorrow. At this moment Warley returned to the cabin, drawn by a secret impulse he could not withstand, though he felt, just then, as if he would gladly abandon the American continent for ever, were it practicable. Instead of pausing at the door, he now advanced so near the pallet of the sufferer as to come more plainly within her gaze. Hetty could still distinguish large objects, and her look soon fastened on him.

"Are you the officer that came with Hurry?" she asked— "If you are, we ought all to thank you, for, though I am hurt, the rest have saved their lives. Did Harry March tell you, where to find us, and how much need there was for your services?"

"The news of the party reached us by means of a friendly runner," returned the Captain, glad to relieve his feelings by this appearance of a friendly communication, "and I was immediately sent out to cut it off. It was fortunate, certainly, that we met Hurry Harry, as you call him, for he acted as a guide, and it was not less fortunate, that we heard a firing, which I now understand was merely a shooting at the mark, for it not only quickened our march, but called us to the right side of the lake. The Delaware saw us on the shore, with the glass it would seem, and he and Hist, as I find his squaw is named, did us excellent service. It was really altogether, a fortunate concurrence of circumstances, Judith?"

"Talk not to me of any thing fortunate, sir," returned the girl huskily, again concealing her face. "To me the world is full of misery. I wish never to hear of marks, or rifles, or soldiers, or *men*, again!"

"Do you know my sister?" asked Hetty, ere the rebuked soldier had time to rally for an answer. "How came you to know that her name is Judith? You are right, for that *is* her name; and I am Hetty, Thomas Hutter's daughters."

"For heaven's sake, dearest sister,—for *my* sake, beloved Hetty," interposed Judith, imploringly, "say no more of this!"

Hetty looked surprised, but accustomed to comply, she ceased her awkward and painful interrogations of Warley, bending her eyes towards the bible which she still held between her hands, as one would cling to a casket of precious stones, in a shipwreck, or a conflagration. Her mind now adverted to the future, losing sight, in a great measure, of the scenes of the past.

"We shall not long be parted, Judith," she said; "when *you* die, you must be brought and be buried in the lake, by the side of mother too."

"Would to God, Hetty, that I lay there, at this moment!"

"No, that cannot be, Judith; people must die before they have any right to be buried. 'Twould be wicked to bury you, or for you to bury yourself, while living. Once I thought of burying myself; God kept me from that sin."

"You! — You, Hetty Hutter, think of such an act!" exclaimed Judith, looking up in uncontrollable surprise, for she well knew nothing passed the lips of her conscientious sister, that was not religiously true.

"Yes, I did, Judith, but God has forgotten — no he *forgets* nothing — but he has *forgiven* it," returned the dying girl, with the subdued manner of a repentant child. " 'Twas after mother's death; I felt I had lost the best friend I had on earth, if not the *only* friend. 'Tis true, you and father were kind to me, Judith, but I was so feeble-minded, I knew I should only give you trouble; and then you were so often ashamed of such a sister and daughter, and 'tis hard to live in a world where all look upon you as below them. I thought then, if I could bury myself by the side of mother, I should be happier in the lake, than in the hut."

"Forgive me — pardon me, dearest Hetty — on my bended knees, I beg you to pardon me, sweet sister, if any word, or act of mine drove you to so maddening and cruel a thought!"

"Get up, Judith — kneel to God; do n't kneel to me. Just so I felt when mother was dying! I remembered every thing I had said and done to vex her, and could have kissed her feet for forgiveness. I think it must be so with all dying people; though, now I think of it, I don't remember to have had such feelings on account of father."

Judith arose, hid her face in her apron, and wept. A long pause — one of more than two hours succeeded, during which Warley entered and left the cabin several times; apparently uneasy when absent, and yet unable to remain. He issued various orders, which his men proceeded to execute, and there was an air of movement in the party, more especially as Mr. Craig, the lieutenant, had got through the unpleasant duty of burying the dead, and had sent for instructions from the shore, desiring to know what he was to do with his detachment. During this interval Hetty slept a little, and Deerslayer and Chingachgook left the Ark to confer together. But, at the end of the time mentioned, the Surgeon passed upon the platform, and with a degree of feeling his comrades had never before observed in one of his habits, he announced that the patient was rapidly drawing near her end. On receiving this intelligence the group collected again, curiosity to witness such a death — or a better feeling — drawing to the spot, men who had so lately been actors in a scene seemingly of so much greater interest and moment. By this time, Judith had got to be inactive through grief, and Hist alone was performing the little offices of feminine attention that are so appropriate to the sick bed. Hetty herself, had undergone no other apparent change, than the general failing that indicated the near approach of dissolution. All that she possessed of mind was as clear as ever, and, in some respects, her intellect perhaps was more than usually active.

"Don't grieve for me so much, Judith," said the gentle sufferer, after a pause in her remarks — "I shall soon see mother — I think I see her *now*; her face is just as sweet and smiling as it used to be! Perhaps when I'm dead, God will give me all my mind, and I shall become a more fitting companion for mother, than I ever was before."

"You will be an angel in heaven, Hetty," sobbed the sister; "no spirit there will be more worthy of its holy residence!"

"I don't understand it quite; still, I know it must be all true; I've read it in the bible. How dark it's becoming! Can it be night so soon? I can hardly see you at all — where is Hist?"

"I here, poor girl — Why you no see me."

"I do see you; but I could n't tell whether 'twas you, or Judith. I believe I shan't see you much longer, Hist."

"Sorry for that, poor Hetty. Never mind — pale face got a heaven for girls as well as for warrior."

"Where's the Serpent — let me speak to him — Give me his

hand—so—I feel it. Delaware you will love and cherish this young Indian woman—I know how fond she is of *you*; you must be fond of *her*. Don't treat her as some of your people treat their wives; be a real husband to her. Now, bring Deerslayer near me; give me *his* hand."

This request was complied with, and the hunter stood by the side of the pallet, submitting to the wishes of the girl, with the docility of a child.

"I feel, Deerslayer," she resumed—"though I could n't tell why—but I feel that you and I are not going to part for ever. 'Tis a strange feeling!—I never had it before—I wonder what it comes from!"

" 'Tis God encouraging you in extremity, Hetty; as such it ought to be harbored and respected. Yes, we *shall* meet ag'in, though it may be a long time, first, and in a far distant land."

"Do you mean to be buried in the lake, too? If so, that may account for the feeling."

" 'Tis little likely, gal; 'tis little likely—but there's a region for christian souls, where there's no lakes, nor woods, they say; though why there should be none of the *last*, is more than I can account for; seeing that pleasantness and peace is the object in view. My grave will be found in the forest, most likely, but I hope my spirit will not be far from yourn."

"So it must be, then. I am too weak-minded to understand these things, but I *feel* that you and I will meet again.—Sister, where are you?—I can't see, now, any thing but darkness—it must be night, surely!"

"Oh! Hetty, I am here—at your side—these are my arms that are around you," sobbed Judith. "Speak, dearest; is there any thing you wish to say, or have done, in this awful moment."

By this time Hetty's sight had entirely failed her. Nevertheless death approached with less than usual of its horrors, as if in tenderness to one of her half endowed faculties. She was pale as a corpse, but her breathing was easy and unbroken, while her voice, though lowered almost to a whisper, remained clear and distinct. When her sister put this question, however, a blush diffused itself over the features of the dying girl, so faint however as to be nearly imperceptible; resembling that hue of the rose which is thought to portray the tint of modesty, rather than the dye of the flower in its richer bloom. No one but Judith detected this exposure of feeling, one of the gentle expressions of womanly sensibility even in death. On her however, it was not lost, nor did she conceal from herself the cause.

"Hurry is here, dearest Hetty—" whispered the sister, with her face so near the sufferer, as to keep the words from other ears. "Shall I tell him to come and receive your good wishes?"

A gentle pressure of the hand answered in the affirmative. Then Hurry was brought to the side of the pallet. It is probable that this handsome, but rude woodsman had never before found himself so awkwardly placed, though the inclination which Hetty felt for him—a sort of secret yielding to the instincts of nature, rather than any unbecoming impulse of an ill regulated imagination—was too pure and unobtrusive to have created the slightest suspicion of the circumstance in his mind. He allowed Judith to put his hard colossal hand between those of Hetty, and stood waiting the result in awkward silence.

"This is Hurry, dearest," whispered Judith, bending over her sister, ashamed to utter the words so as to be audible to herself. "Speak to him, and let him go."

"What shall I say, Judith?"

"Nay, whatever your own pure spirit teaches, my love. Trust to that, and you need fear nothing."

"Good bye, Hurry—" murmured the girl, with a gentle pressure of his hand—"I wish you would try and be more like Deerslayer."

These words were uttered with difficulty; a faint flush succeeded them for a single instant. Then the hand was relinquished, and Hetty turned her face aside, as if done with the world. The mysterious feeling that bound her to the young man, a sentiment so gentle as to be almost imperceptible to herself, and which could never have existed at all, had her reason possessed more command over her senses, was forever lost in thoughts of a more elevated, though scarcely of a purer character.

"Of what are you thinking, my sweet sister?" whispered Judith—"Tell me, that I may aid you, at this moment."

"Mother—I see Mother, now, and bright beings around her

in the lake. Why is n't father there? — It's odd, that I can see mother, when I can't see *you!* — Farewell, Judith."

The last words were uttered after a pause, and her sister had hung over her some time, in anxious watchfulness, before she perceived that the gentle spirit had departed. Thus died Hetty Hutter, one of those mysterious links between the material and immaterial world, which, while they appear to be deprived of so much that is esteemed and necessary for this state of being, draw so near to, and offer so beautiful an illustration of the truth, purity, and simplicity of another.

Chapter XXXII.

"A baron's chylde to be begylde! it were a cursed dede:
To be felàwe with an outlàwe! Almighty God forbede!
Yea, better were, the pore squyère alone to forest yede,
Then ye sholde say another day, that by my cursed dede
Ye were betrayed: wherefore, good mayde, the best rede that I can,
Is, that I to the grene wode go, alone, a banyshed man."
    Thomas Percy, "Notbrowne Mayde," ll. 265-76 from *Reliques
        of Ancient English Poetry*, Vol. II.

T H E day that followed, proved to be melancholy, though one of much activity. The soldiers, who had so lately been employed in interring their victims, were now called on to bury their own dead. The scene of the morning had left a saddened feeling on all the gentlemen of the party, and the rest felt the influence of a similar sensation, in a variety of ways, and from many causes. Hour dragged on after hour, until evening arrived, and then came the last melancholy offices in honor of poor Hetty Hutter. Her body was laid in the lake, by the side of that of the mother she had so loved and reverenced, the surgeon, though actually an unbeliever, so far complying with the received decencies of life, as to read the funeral service over her grave, as he had previously done over those of the other *christian* slain! It mattered not; — that all seeing eye which reads the heart, could not fail to discriminate between the living and the dead, and the gentle soul of the unfortunate girl, was already far removed beyond the errors, or deceptions, of any human ritual. These simple rites, however, were not wholly wanting in suitable accompaniments. The tears of Judith and Hist were shed freely, and Deerslayer gazed upon the limpid water, that now flowed over one whose spirit was even purer than its own mountain springs, with glistening eyes. Even the Delaware turned aside to conceal his weakness, while the common men gazed on the ceremony with wondering eyes and chastened feelings.

The business of the day closed with this pious office. By order of the commanding officer, all retired early to rest, for it was intended to begin the march homeward, with the return of light. One party, indeed, bearing the wounded, the prisoners, and the trophies, had left the castle in the middle of the day, under the guidance of Hurry, intending to reach the fort by shorter marches. It had been landed on the point, so often mentioned, or that described in our opening pages, and, when the sun set, was already encamped on the brow of the long, broken, and ridgy hills, that fell away towards the valley of the Mohawk. The departure of this detachment had greatly simplified the duty of the succeeding day, disencumbering its march of its baggage and wounded, and otherwise leaving him who had issued the order greater liberty of action.

Judith held no communications with any but Hist, after the death of her sister, until she retired for the night. Her sorrow had been respected, and both the females had been left with the body, unintruded on, to the last moment. The rattling of the drum broke the silence of that tranquil water, and the echoes of the tattoo were heard among the mountains, so soon after the ceremony was over, as to preclude the danger of interruption. That star which had been the guide of Hist, rose on a scene as silent as if the quiet of nature had never yet been disturbed, by the labors or passions of man. One solitary sentinel, with his relief, paced the platform throughout the night, and morning was ushered in, as usual, by the martial beat of the reveillé.

Military precision succeeded to the desultory proceedings of border men, and when a hasty and frugal breakfast was taken, the party began its movement towards the shore, with a regularity and order, that prevented noise or confusion. Of all the officers, Warley alone remained. Craig headed the detachment in advance, Thornton was with the wounded, and Graham accompanied his patients as a matter of course. Even the chest of Hutter, with all the more valuable of his effects, was borne away, leaving nothing behind that was worth the labor of a removal. Judith was not sorry to see that the captain respected her feelings, and that he occupied himself entirely with the duty of his command, leaving her to her own discretion and feelings. It was understood by all, that the place was to be totally abandoned; but beyond this no explanations were asked or given.

The soldiers embarked in the Ark, with the captain at their head. He had enquired of Judith in what way she chose to proceed, and understanding her wish to remain with Hist to the last moment, he neither molested her with requests, nor offended her with advice. There was but one safe and familiar trail to the Mohawk, and on that, at the proper hour, he doubted not that they should meet in amity, if not in renewed intercourse.

When all were on board, the sweeps were manned, and the Ark moved in its sluggish manner towards the distant point. Deerslayer and Chingachgook, now lifted two of the canoes from the water, and placed them in the castle. The windows and door were then barred, and the house was left by means of the trap, in the manner already described. On quitting the palisades, Hist was seen in the remaining canoe, where the Delaware immediately joined her, and paddled away, leaving Judith standing alone on the platform. Owing to this prompt proceeding, Deerslayer found himself alone with the beautiful and still weeping mourner. Too simple to suspect any thing, the young man swept the light boat round, and received its mistress in it, when he followed the course already taken by his friend.

The direction to the point, led diagonally past, and at no great distance from, the graves of the dead. As the canoe glided by, Judith, for the first time that morning spoke to her companion. She said but little; merely uttering a simple request to stop, for a minute or two, ere she left the place.

"I may never see this spot again, Deerslayer," she said, "and it contains the bodies of my mother and sister! Is it not possible, think you, that the innocence of one of these beings, may answer in the eyes of God, for the salvation of both?"

"I do n't understand it so, Judith, though I'm no missionary, and am but poorly taught. Each spirit answers for its own backslidings, though a hearty repentance will satisfy God's laws."

"Then *must* my poor poor mother be in heaven! — Bitterly — bitterly — has she repented of her sins, and surely her sufferings in this life, ought to count as something against her sufferings in the next!"

"All this goes beyond me, Judith—I strive to do right, here, as the surest means of keeping all right, hereafter. Hetty was oncommon, as all that know'd her must allow, and her soul was as fit to consart with angels the hour it left its body, as that of any saint in the bible!"

"I do believe you only do her justice! Alas!—Alas!—that there should be so great differences between those who were nursed at the same breast, slept in the same bed, and dwelt under the same roof! But, no matter—move the canoe, a little farther east, Deerslayer—the sun so dazzles my eyes that I cannot see the graves. This is Hetty's, on the right of mother's?"

"Sartain—you ask'd that of us, and all are glad to do as you wish, Judith, when you do that which is right."

The girl gazed at him near a minute, in silent attention; then she turned her eyes backward, at the castle.

"This lake will soon be entirely deserted," she said—"and this, too, at a moment when it will be a more secure dwelling place than ever. What has so lately happened will prevent the Iroquois from venturing again to visit it, for a long time to come."

"That it will!—yes, that may be set down as sartain. I do not mean to pass this-a-way, ag'in, so long as the war lasts, for, to my mind no Huron moccasin will leave its print on the leaves of this forest, until their traditions have forgotten to tell their young men of their disgrace and rout."

"And do you so delight in violence and bloodshed?—I had thought better of *you*, Deerslayer—believed you one, who could find his happiness in a quiet domestic home, with an attached and loving wife, ready to study your wishes, and healthy and dutiful children, anxious to follow in your footsteps, and to become as honest and just as yourself."

"Lord, Judith, what a tongue you're mistress of! Speech and looks go hand in hand, like, and what one can't do, the other is pretty sartain to perform! Such a gal, in a month, might spoil the stoutest warrior in the colony."

"And am I then so mistaken?—Do you really love war, Deerslayer, better than the hearth, and the affections?"

"I understand your meaning, gal; yes, I do understand what

you mean, I believe, though I do n't think you altogether understand *me*. Warrior I may now call myself, I suppose, for I've both fou't and conquered, which is sufficient for the name; neither will I deny that I've feelin's for the callin', which is both manful and honorable, when carried on accordin' to nat'ral gifts, but I've no relish for blood. Youth is youth, howsever, and a Mingo is a Mingo. If the young men of this region stood by, and suffered the vagabonds to overrun the land, why, we might as well all turn Frenchers at once, and give up country and kin. I'm no fire eater, Judith, or one that likes fightin' for fightin's sake, but I can see no great difference atween *givin' up territory afore a war, out of a dread of war, and givin' it up a'ter a war, because we can't help it, onless it be that the last is the most manful and honorable.*"

"No woman would ever wish to see her husband, or brother, stand by, and submit to insult and wrong, Deerslayer, however she might mourn the necessity of his running into the dangers of battle. But, you've done enough already, in clearing this region of the Hurons; since to you is principally owing the credit of our late victory. Now, listen to me patiently, and answer me with that native honesty, which it is as pleasant to regard in one of your sex, as it is unusual to meet with."

Judith paused, for now that she was on the very point of explaining herself, native modesty asserted its power, notwithstanding the encouragement and confidence she derived from the great simplicity of her companion's character. Her cheeks, which had so lately been pale, flushed, and her eyes lighted with some of their former brilliancy. Feeling gave expression to her countenance and softness to her voice, rendering her who was always beautiful, trebly seductive and winning.

"Deerslayer," she said, after a considerable pause, "this is not a moment for affectation, deception, or a want of frankness of any sort. Here, over my mother's grave, and over the grave of truth-loving, truth-telling Hetty, every thing like unfair dealing seems to be out of place. I will, therefore, speak to you without any reserve, and without any dread of being misunderstood. You are not an acquaintance of a week, but it appears to me as if I had known you for years. So much, and so much that is important has taken place, within that short time, that the sorrows, and dangers, and escapes of a whole life have been crowded into a few days, and they who have suffered and acted together in such scenes, ought not to feel like strangers. I know that what I am about to say might be misunderstood by most men, but I hope for a generous construction of my course from you. We are not here, dwelling among the arts and deceptions of the settlements, but young people who have no occasion to deceive each other, in any manner or form. — I hope I make myself understood?"

"Sartain, Judith; few convarse better than yourself, and none more agreeable, like. Your words are as pleasant as your looks."

"It is the manner in which you have so often praised those looks, that gives me courage to proceed — Still, Deerslayer, it is not easy, for one of my sex and years to forget all her lessons of infancy, all her habits, and her natural diffidence, and say openly what her heart feels!"

"Why not, Judith? Why should n't women as well as men deal fairly and honestly by their fellow creatur's? I see no reason why you should not speak as plainly as myself, when there is any thing ra'ally important to be said."

This indomitable diffidence, which still prevented the young man from suspecting the truth, would have completely discouraged the girl, had not her whole soul, as well as her whole heart, been set upon making a desperate effort to rescue herself from a future that she dreaded with a horror as vivid, as the distinctness with which she fancied she foresaw it. This motive, however, raised her above all common considerations, and she persevered even to her own surprise, if not to her great confusion.

"I will — I *must* deal as plainly with you, as I would with poor, dear Hetty, were that sweet child living!" she continued, turning pale, instead of blushing, the high resolution by which she was prompted reversing the effect that such a procedure would ordinarily produce on one of her sex; "yes, I will smother all other feelings, in the one that is now uppermost! You love the woods and the life that we pass, here, in the wilderness, away from the dwellings and towns of the whites."

"As I loved my parents, Judith, when they was living! This very spot, would be all creation to me, could this war be fairly over, once; and the settlers kept at a distance."

"Why quit it then? — It has no owner — at least none who can claim a better right than mine, and *that* I freely give to you. Were it a kingdom, Deerslayer, I think I should delight to say the same. Let us then return to it, after we have seen the priest at the fort, and never quit it again, until God calls us away to that world where we shall find the spirits of my poor mother and sister."

A long, thoughtful pause succeeded; Judith here covered her face with both her hands, after forcing herself to utter so plain a proposal, and Deerslayer musing equally in sorrow and surprise, on the meaning of the language he had just heard. At length the hunter broke the silence, speaking in a tone that was softened to gentleness by his desire not to offend.

"You have n't thought well of this, Judith — " he said — "no, your feelin's are awakened by all that has lately happened, and believin' yourself to be without kindred in the world, you are in too great haste to find some to fill the places of them that's lost."

"Were I living in a crowd of friends, Deerslayer, I should still think, as I now think — say as I now say," returned Judith, speaking with her hands still shading her lovely face.

"Thank you, gal — thank you, from the bottom of my heart. Howsever, I am not one to take advantage of a weak moment, when you're forgetful of your own great advantages, and fancy 'arth and all it holds, is in this little canoe. No — no — Judith 'twould be onginerous in me; what you've offered can never come to pass!"

"It all may be, and that without leaving cause of repentance to any — " answered Judith, with an impetuosity of feeling and manner, that at once unveiled her eyes. "We can cause the soldiers to leave our goods on the road, till we return, when they can easily be brought back to the house; the lake will be no more visited by the enemy, this war at least; all your skins may be readily sold at the garrison; there *you* can buy the few necessaries we shall want, for I wish never to see the spot, again; and Deerslayer," added the girl smiling with a sweetness and nature that the young man found it hard to resist — "as a proof how wholly I am and wish to be yours, — how completely I desire to be nothing but your wife, the very first fire that we kindle, after our return, shall be lighted with the brocade dress, and fed by every article I have that you may think unfit for the woman you wish to live with!"

"Ah's! me—you're a winning and a lovely creatur', Judith; yes, you *are* all that, and no one can deny it, and speak truth. These pictur's are pleasant to the thoughts, but they mightn't prove so happy as you now think 'em. Forget it all, therefore, and let us paddle after the Sarpent and Hist, as if nothing had been said on the subject."

Judith was deeply mortified, and, what is more, she was profoundly grieved. Still there was a steadiness and quiet in the manner of Deerslayer that completely smothered her hopes, and told her that for once, her exceeding beauty had failed to excite the admiration and homage it was wont to receive. Women are said seldom to forgive those who slight their advances, but this high spirited and impetuous girl entertained no shadow of resentment, then or ever, against the fair dealing and ingenuous hunter. At the moment, the prevailing feeling was the wish to be certain that there was no misunderstanding. After another painful pause, therefore, she brought the matter to an issue by a question too direct to admit of equivocation.

"God forbid, that we lay up regrets, in after life, through any want of sincerity now," she said. "I hope we understand each other, at least. You will not accept me for a wife, Deerslayer?"

" 'Tis better for both that I should n't take advantage of your own forgetfulness, Judith. We can never marry."

"You do not love me,—cannot find it in your heart, perhaps, to esteem me, Deerslayer!"

"Every thing in the way of fri'ndship, Judith—every thing, even to sarvices and life itself. Yes, I'd risk as much for you, at this moment, as I would risk in behalf of Hist, and that is sayin' as much as I can say of any darter of woman. I do not think I feel towards either—mind I say *either*, Judith—as if I wished to quit father and mother—if father and mother was livin', which, howsever, neither is—but if both was livin', I do not feel towards any woman as if I wish'd to quit 'em in order to cleave unto *her*."

"This is enough!" answered Judith, in a rebuked and smothered voice—"I understand all that you mean. Marry you cannot without loving, and that love you do not feel for me. Make no answer, if I am right, for I shall understand your silence— *That* will be painful enough of itself."

Deerslayer obeyed her, and he made no reply. For more than a minute, the girl riveted her bright eyes on him, as if to read his soul, while he sat playing with the water, like a corrected school boy. Then Judith, herself, dropped the end of her paddle, and urged the canoe away from the spot, with a movement as reluctant as the feelings which controlled it. Deerslayer quietly aided the effort, however, and they were soon on the trackless line taken by the Delaware.

In their way to the point, not another syllable was exchanged between Deerslayer and his fair companion. As Judith sat in the bow of the canoe, her back was turned towards him, else it is probable the expression of her countenance might have induced him to venture some soothing terms of friendship and regard. Contrary to what would have been expected, resentment was still absent, though the colour frequently changed, from the deep flush of mortification to the paleness of disappointment. Sorrow, deep, heart-felt sorrow, however, was the predominant emotion, and this was betrayed in a manner not to be mistaken.

As neither labored hard at the paddle, the ark had already arrived and the soldiers had disembarked, before the canoe of the two loiterers reached the point. Chingachgook had preceded it, and was already some distance in the wood, at a spot, where the two trails, that to the garrison, and that to the villages of the Delawares separated. The soldiers, too, had taken up their line of march, first setting the Ark adrift again, with a reckless disregard of its fate. All this Judith saw, but she heeded it not. The Glimmerglass had no longer any charms for her, and when she put her foot on the strand, she immediately proceeded on the trail of the soldiers, without casting a single glance behind her. Even Hist was passed unnoticed, that modest young creature shrinking from the averted face of Judith, as if guilty herself of some wrong doing.

"Wait you here, Sarpent," said Deerslayer as he followed in the footsteps of the dejected beauty, while passing his friend—"I will just see Judith among her party, and come and j'ine you."

A hundred yards had hid the couple from those in front, as well as those in their rear, when Judith turned, and spoke.

"This will do, Deerslayer," she said sadly—"I understand your kindness but shall not need it. In a few minutes I shall reach the soldiers. As you cannot go with me on the journey of life, I do not wish you to go further on this. But, stop—before we part, I would ask you a single question. And I require of you, as you fear God, and reverence the truth, not to deceive me in your answer. I know you do not love another and I can see but one reason why you cannot, *will* not love me. Tell me then, Deerslayer,—" The girl paused, the words she was about to utter seeming to choke her. Then rallying all her resolution, with a face that flushed and paled at every breath she drew, she continued.

"Tell me then, Deerslayer, if any thing light of me, that Henry March has said may not have influenced your feelings?"

Truth was the Deerslayer's polar star. He ever kept it in view, and it was nearly impossible for him to avoid uttering it, even when prudence demanded silence. Judith read his answer in his countenance, and with a heart nearly broken by the consciousness of undue erring, she signed to him an adieu, and buried herself in the woods. For some time Deerslayer was irresolute as to his course; but, in the end, he retraced his steps, and joined the Delaware. That night the three 'camped on the head waters of their own river, and the succeeding evening they entered the village of the tribe, Chingachgook and his betrothed in triumph; their companion honored and admired, but in a sorrow that it required months of activity to remove.

The war that then had its rise was stirring and bloody. The Delaware chief rose among his people, until his name was never mentioned without eulogiums, while another Uncas, the last of his race, was added to the long line of warriors who bore that distinguishing appellation. As for the Deerslayer, under the *sobriquet* of Hawkeye, he made his fame spread far and near, until the crack of his rifle became as terrible to the ears of the Mingos, as the thunders of the Manitou. His services were soon required by the officers of the crown, and he especially attached himself, in the field, to one in particular, with whose after life, he had a close and important connection.

Fifteen years had passed away, ere it was in the power of the

Deerslayer to revisit the Glimmerglass. A peace had intervened, and it was on the eve of another and still more important war, when he and his constant friend, Chingachgook, were hastening to the forts to join their allies. A stripling accompanied them, for Hist already slumbered beneath the pines of the Delawares, and the three survivors had now become inseparable. They reached the lake just as the sun was setting. Here all was unchanged. The river still rushed through its bower of trees; the little rock was washing away, by the slow action of the waves, in the course of centuries, the mountains stood in their native dress, dark, rich and mysterious, while the sheet glistened in its solitude, a beautiful gem of the forest.

The following morning, the youth discovered one of the canoes drifted on the shore, in a state of decay. A little labor put it in a state for service, and they all embarked, with a desire to examine the place. All the points were passed, and Chingachgook pointed out to his son, the spot where the Hurons had first encamped, and the point whence he had succeeded in stealing his bride. Here they even landed, but all traces of the former visit had disappeared. Next they proceeded to the scene of the battle, and there they found a few of the signs that linger around such localities. Wild beasts had disinterred many of the bodies, and human bones were bleaching in the rains of summer. Uncas regarded all with reverence and pity, though traditions were already rousing his young mind to the ambition and sternness of a warrior.

From the point, the canoe took its way toward the shoal, where the remains of the castle were still visible, a picturesque ruin. The storms of winter had long since unroofed the house, and decay had eaten into the logs. All the fastenings were untouched, but the seasons rioted in the place, as if in mockery at the attempt to exclude them. The palisades were rotting, as were the piles, and it was evident that a few more recurrences of winter, a few more gales and tempests, would sweep all into the lake, and blot the building from the face of that magnificent solitude. The graves could not be found. Either the elements had obliterated their traces, or time had caused those who looked for them, to forget their position.

The Ark was discovered stranded on the eastern shore,

where it had long before been driven with the prevalent north-west winds. It lay on the sandy extremity of a long low point, that is situated about two miles from the outlet, and which is itself fast disappearing before the action of the elements. The scow was filled with water, the cabin unroofed, and the logs were decaying. Some of its coarser furniture still remained, and the heart of Deerslayer beat quick, as he found a ribband of Judith's fluttering from a log. It recalled all her beauty, and we may add all her failings. Although the girl had never touched his heart, the Hawkeye, for so we ought now to call him, still retained a kind and sincere interest in her welfare. He tore away the ribband, and knotted it to the stock of Killdeer, which had been the gift of the girl herself.

A few miles farther up the lake, another of the canoes was discovered, and on the point where the party finally landed, were found those which had been left there upon the shore. That in which the present navigation was made, and the one discovered on the eastern shore, had dropped through the decayed floor of the castle, drifted past the falling palisades, and had been thrown as waifs upon the beach.

From all these signs, it was probable the lake had not been visited, since the occurrence of the final scene of our tale. Accident, or tradition, had rendered it again, a spot sacred to nature, the frequent wars, and the feeble population of the colonies, still confining the settlements within narrow boundaries. Chingachgook and his friend left the spot with melancholy feelings. It had been the region of their First War Path, and it carried back the minds of both to scenes of tenderness, as well as to hours of triumph. They held their way towards the Mohawk in silence, however, to rush into new adventures, as stirring and as remarkable as those which had attended their opening careers, on this lovely lake. At a later day, they returned to the place, where the Indian found a grave.

Time and circumstances have drawn an impenetrable mystery around all else connected with the Hutters. They lived, erred, died, and are forgotten. None connected have felt sufficient interest in the disgraced and disgracing to withdraw the veil, and a century is about to erase even the recollection of their names. The history of crime is ever revolting, and it is fortunate that few love to dwell on its incidents. The sins of the family have long since been arraigned at the judgment seat of God, or are registered for the terrible settlement of the last great day.

The same fate attended Judith. When Hawkeye reached the garrison on the Mohawk he enquired anxiously after that lovely but misguided creature. None knew her — even her person was no longer remembered. Other officers had, again and again, succeeded the Warleys and Craigs and Grahams, though an old sergeant of the garrison, who had lately come from England, was enabled to tell our hero, that Sir Robert Warley lived on his paternal estates, and that there was a lady of rare beauty in the Lodge, who had great influence over him, though she did not bear his name. Whether this was Judith relapsed into her early failing, or some other victim of the soldier's, Hawkeye never knew, nor would it be pleasant or profitable to inquire. We live in a world of transgressions and selfishness, and no pictures that represent us otherwise can be true, though, happily, for human nature, gleamings of that pure spirit in whose likeness man has been fashioned, are to be seen relieving its deformities, and mitigating if not excusing its crimes.

Explanatory Notes

4.37   Cooper's efforts to indicate the sense or senses in which *The Deerslayer* contains "faithful transcripts from nature" are essentially successful. His geographic fidelity, with one self-confessed exception (his relocation of the "Sunken Islands"), is the most obvious. In this sense, as the novelist indicates, most of "the descriptions" can be "easily recognized by all who are familiar with the scenery." See the Map on p. 19.

As for the book's historicity, Cooper apparently intended to achieve a generalized fidelity, incorporating situations and details indigenous to the period. His own understanding was undoubtedly derived from word of mouth and published sources, few of which are identifiable; but a reading of appropriate portions of the monumental series *Documents Relating to the Colonial History of the State of New York*, ed. with translations from the French and the Dutch by E.B. O'Callaghan (Albany: Weed, Parsons & Co., 1853–87), especially the letters to the British Lords of Trade, suggests an imaginative fidelity on Cooper's part that is well within the limits he set for himself: "that the annals of America do not contain a syllable, in opposition to what has been now laid before the world."

In a few instances, specific sources do suggest themselves. In addition to Heckewelder's *History, Manners, and Customs of the Indian Nations* (Philadelphia: Abraham Small, 1819), a book which Cooper thoroughly digested and valued far more highly than its critics (many of whom, unlike Cooper, were not well disposed towards Indians), he almost certainly read and studied James Adair's *The History of the American Indians* (London: Edward and Charles Dilly, 1775), a book addressed to Col. George Craghan (or Croghan), from whose original Patent the lands acquired by Judge William Cooper indirectly derived. Scalpings and tortures visited by Indians upon their captives are here vividly described. In *The Oak Openings* (1848), Cooper employed Adair's theory that the American Indians were descended from the Lost Tribes of Israel; and he seems to have employed in *The Deerslayer* suggestions about their social (or unsocial) behavior.

Professor Richard Vanderbeets' "Cooper and the 'Semblance of Reality,'" (*American Literature*, 42 [1971], 544–46) has suggested that the ambush in Chapter IV derives from a similar incident in a captivity narrative by Charles Johnston, *A Narrative of the Incidents Attending the Capture, Detention, and Ransom of Charles Johnston, of Botetourt County, Virginia, Who Was Made Prisoner by the Indians, on the River Ohio, in the Year 1790; Together with an Interesting Account of the Fate of His Companions, Five in Number, One of Whom Suffered at the Stake* (New York: 1827). While there would seem to be no doubt that Cooper used this incident and others in Johnston's *Narrative*, it is not clear whether they derived from the 1827 publication or from the account of Johnston's adventure contained in *Travels Through the United States* (1795) by François Alexandre Frederick Rochfoucald-Liancourt D'Estissac, a work Cooper certainly had read and probably owned.

14.11   Otsego Rock: "There is a small rock near the outlet of the lake, called the Otsego rock, at which precise point the savages, according to an early tradition of the country, were accustomed to rendezvous." Cooper, *Chronicles of Cooperstown*, reprinted in *A History of Cooperstown*, James Fenimore Cooper, Samuel M. Shaw, Walter R. Littell, Harold H. Hollis (Cooperstown: New York State Historical Association, 1976), 1.

18.5–8   A residence of a younger branch of the Van Rensselaers . . . loopholes constructed for defence . . . although it dates from a period scarcely so distant: On 4 December 1841, Dr. Jeremiah Van Rensselaer, a boyhood friend and fellow student at Albany in 1800–02, wrote Cooper from Rome, Italy, to express "much pleasure derived" from his reading of *The Deerslayer* and to correct Cooper's impression as to the age of his house. According to Van Rensselaer, the Greenbush Mansion was built in the mid-1680s or 1690s at the direction of the head of the family to avoid the flooding that had severely damaged the Patroon's house on "Westerlo' or the patroon's island." Of the house and the "loopholes," Van Rensselaer wrote:

"The loopholes you mention were used as a protection against attacks of the indians, and did good service during what is familiarly called the french war, between 1755 and 1763, when Canada was taken. At that time Fort Orange was crowded with men, and the women and children came over to the mansion, the strongest house in that region, where they sought and found protection. Col. John Van Rensselaer-Hansurn as he was called at that time — had a sufficient body of slaves and retainers successfully to resist the savages, who frequently surrounded and attacked his house, and who were always on the alert, in hopes of killing or capturing some unfortunate individual, who might perchance venture out alone. I well remember <an enormous> a fine old oak tree, just east of the old coach-house, under whose enormous branches an Albanian was shot and scalped by the indians within sight, almost within shot, of his companions at the house. These hostile bands belonged to the Senecas and Cayugas, who had joined the French, while the Mohawks and Oneidas were with Sir W[illia]m Johnson, at the north.

The memory of the oldest inhabitants of Albany can furnish many anecdotes of events occurring at that period, when the house in question was the sure refuge of the distressed, and the stronghold of the feeble and destitute. Major Nich^S Van Rensselaer, and his brother K.K. Van Rensselaer, and Mrs. L. Gansevort [sic] of Albany are familiar with many of these details, which are now almost forgotten, and will scarcely be credited by the next generation.

It is singular, as you justly remark, how soon (these and) similar circumstances are forgotten among us, who have scarcely any history, while in older countries such events are carefully recorded." Jeremiah Van Rensselaer Miscellaneous Papers, Courtesy, Manuscript Division, The New York Public Library.

37.9   a vessel called an Ark: Vessels called "arks," some said to have been seventy-five feet long and sixteen feet wide, were actually used to carry cargoes down the Susquehanna River in the late eighteenth and early nineteenth centuries. They were, in fact, large scows guided by long pine sweeps and difficult to manage, useless for navigating upstream. (Harry Sinclair Drago, *Canal Days in America: The History and Romance of Old Towpaths and Waterways* (New York: Bramhall House, 1972). *In The Chronicles of Cooperstown* (Cooperstown: H. & E. Phinney, 1838), Cooper stated: "In 1794, there was a large flat boat on the lake, called the ship Jay, on board of which Admiral Hassy first hoisted his flag. His sails were boards, and his speed more than doubtful."

43.   The sight brought back to his mind a rush of childish recollections: In her 1876 Introduction, Susan Fenimore Cooper described the childhood of Deerslayer in a manner that may have emanated from her father's own storytelling. The pertinent passage (pp. xxiv-xxix) is worth recalling:

Natty and Hurry Harry are supposed to have approached this secluded lake from the little colony on the Schoharie, founded thirty years earlier by the "Palatines," as they were called.

There was a village of the Mohegans on the Schoharie, at the foot of a hill called by them "Mohegonter," or "the falling away of the Mohegan Hill." These Mohegans came, it is said, originally from the eastward, beyond the Hudson. The clan is reported to have numbered some three hundred warriors when the Germans arrived among them. A tortoise and a serpent were the tokens of this clan. Documents, chiefly sales of land to the Germans, still exist bearing their signatures in this shape.

But this village on the Schoharie was not the region of Natty's early forest training. It was not on the Onistagrawa, the "Hill of Maize," that he had learned to chase the elk and the deer. It was among the mountains farther south on the banks of the Susquehanna and the Upper Delaware, that the young pale-face hunter had received from the "Lenni Lennapi" the name of the Deerslayer. Here in some rude frontier home, in a log-cabin, under a bark roof, the boy had grown up to a simple, hardy, brave, and kindly manhood. Here he had learned from the dark-skinned lads his comrades to tread lightly on the summer moss, to track the game over the winter snow. Here he had played with the fawn, tamed the beaver, and the cub of the bear. Here, by the broad uncouth chimney, the brilliant flame of the hickory log, or the torch of a pine knot lighting his honest face, he had listened to the wild legends of prowess and adventure of the Lenni Lennapi until his spirit kindled at the recital. Here, stretched at night on feathers of the wild fowl, covered with skins torn as trophies from panther and wolf, he dreamed stirring dreams of daring deed, hair-breadth escape, manly endurance. Here he dreamed of showing his red-skinned friends what a white brave could do and suffer. Here, in short, he became a hero at heart, although the word would have carried no meaning for his ear.

And, waking with the morning sun, he saw a Christian mother moving about the cabin, busy with homely household errands, — a woman ignorant in the ways of the world, of kindly nature, simple, true, and warm-hearted. He rose to do her bidding. Unlike the young Indian lad, he scorned no errand in behalf of the mother who bore him: he brought the water from the spring, he hewed the wood for the fire, he planted the potato and the maize. Homely tasks these, which he did not disdain, although, forsooth, the young Panther and the young Serpent looked on with cold disapprobation, in the idle dignity of their savage manhood. The father — a pale-face hunter and trapper of note — died of some dire forest mischance, trampled to death, it was said, by an enraged moose at bay. Then it was that the lad took upon him to provide food for his mother's lodge. He shouldered his father's rifle, and before two days had passed he brought home an elk and laid it at the cabin door, at his mother's feet. From that hour game was never wanting in the forest home. Skins for the dainty moccasins worn by his young sister, for the rude leather leggings worn by himself, were plenty in the cabin. Nay, more than once did some poor Indian widow, some ailing or wounded hunter, find a supply of venison laid secretly at their door by a kindly hand, suspected to be his own. Among all the lads of the region there was no eye so sure, no hand so steady, as that of the young pale-face, "Straight-tongue," as they first called him from his love of truth.

"After a while they found out I was quick of foot, and then they called me 'the Pigeon,' which you know has a swift wing, and flies in a direct line."

"From carrying messages and striking blind trails, I got at last to following the hunters, when it was thought I was quicker and surer at finding the game than most lads, and then they called me 'Lap-Ear,' as they said I partook of the sagacity of a hound."

"Then it was seen I could keep a wigwam in ven'son; and in time I got the name of 'Deerslayer,' which is that I now bear."

And now it was that after joining a hunting-party of the Delawares, among the mountains which overhang the Susquehanna, he returned laden with choice venison, and at a great feast solemnly received the name of the "Deerslayer," in a speech by the father of Chingachgook.

The Christian mother was growing old. Her head had turned gray since her husband was killed by the moose. When the lad returned to the cabin he would often hear her singing some pious song, psalm, or hymn, learned in her girlhood. Morning and night he saw her kneel, he heard her simple, short, but earnest prayer. She could not read, never a horn-book or primer had she held in her hand. But she knew by heart a few verses from the Holy Book. The red-skinned warriors no longer came with their tales of war and their wild traditions to the cabin fireside, as they had done when the hunter was living. But the mother now told her children more than one sacred history learned in her youth; she told them of Noah and the Ark; she told them of David and Goliah. And above all she told them the glad tidings of the Gospel. Here and there some verses of the Sermon on the Mount she could say by heart. These she taught her young daughter; and the lad listening at her elbow received into his guileless, kindly heart, many a word which gave coloring to his later life.

Ever and anon some missionary would come to preach to the tribe. It was at the widow's cabin that he always stayed. And in this way also the lad learned important truths.

The mother fell sick. Her heart yearned for her kindred and the Lowlands where she was born. The Indian women were kind to her; she took their medicines, but when the mystery-man came she shuddered, and would have naught to say to him. She longed to see a Christian minister of the gospel. With his rifle on his shoulder, and his comrade Chingachgook at his side, the young Deerslayer set out in the morning, walked a hundred miles over mountain and fell, and when the third sun was setting he came to his mother's bed-side with a Moravian Brother. Solemn words were spoken. The good woman was near her end. She bade her son remember through life that he came of a Christian stock; she bade him keep a Christian heart and a straight tongue and a clean hand, to his last hour. And solemnly she charged him to take his young sister without loss of time into the Lowlands, among their own kindred, and to leave her there. She would have been glad if he would promise to turn farmer, and live among his own race. But she told him that she knew he loved the woods, [as] his father had loved the life in the wilderness. Let him only be a good man, good and true, and her blessing would be with him whether in forest or field.

She died. Her son closed her eyes. The Moravian Brother stayed to give her Christian burial. They carried her body in a canoe across the stream into the forest, and laid her under the moss beside her hunter husband. The Delawares and Mohegans living with them followed, making a great wailing and mourning.

The next day, with the rising sun, the Deerslayer and his young sister with the Moravian Brother, and Chingachgook as an escort, went on their way through the forest towards the low country. Here there was an aunt who was glad to fill a mother's place to the young girl. Here, also, kindred gathered about the young Natty and urged him to stay among his own people. His sister hung about him. Chingachgook looked cold and stoical, but his heart beat as he listened. Natty wavered. Had not his mother bade him try a farmer's life? The trial he thought ought to be made. He went into the woods with the young Serpent. He told him his heart was heavy, but his mother's spirit bade him try the life in the fields; he could not leave his young sister yet awhile. It was now planting-time. He would stay with his kindred until the maize was in the tassel, and then if the life of spade and plough did not suit him, he could return to the Delaware village with a clear conscience; and when he passed his mother's grave his heart would not smite him with having forgotten her words. Chingachgook listened coldly. "It is well," he said, with something of scorn and something of bitterness in his tone. Drawing the girdle tight about his waist, the young brave turned on his heel and walked off straight as an arrow in the direction of his father's wigwam. Natty stood rooted to the spot, leaning on his rifle, and his eyes fixed upon his comrade so long as the lithe figure could be seen. Then he sat down in a clump of bushes and a tear came into his eye and fell upon the down of his boyish beard.

The next day's sun saw Natty behind a plough; but shallow and crooked was the furrow he made. They tried him at gardening, but maize, beans, and squashes were the only plants he knew by sight in their seedling state. They put a goad in his hand and sent him a-field with a yoke of oxen. Small was his success as a teamster. Brindle and Dobbin did as well without him as with him. He was kindly with all the brute creatures, but pitied their tame, dull life. They put him on horseback and sent him to the mill for a sack of flour; the horse was old, the sack heavy ; Natty considered it unmanly to ride the poor creature, especially as Providence had given him long sound legs of his own. He dismounted and led his steed, to the merriment of miller and man. The farm people laughed at his forest ways and forest talk. Long before the maize was in the tassel his uncle had told him he never would make a farmer. The lad himself was sick at heart with longing for his old free life. One morning he took his rifle, told his kindred with one of his silent laughs that he could bear the life in the thickly peopled country no longer ; he parted kindly with all, and then with an eager heart and a light step turned his face toward the Delaware country.

In a few hours he reached the first belt of forest. He threw himself down to drink from a mossy spring, and then leaning against an old tree sat in silent happiness looking upward toward the blue sky through the shady canopy of leaves he loved so well. Squirrels gamboled about him. A wood-thrush sang him a song of greeting. A twig cracked beside him. He looked up, and there stood young Chingachgook. Great was Natty's delight.

"I knew my brother would come!" were the only words of welcome spoken by the young Mohegan brave. He had lingered for weeks on the border of the forest, awaiting his comrade. They went on their way with eager steps. Before a week had passed Natty had received a wild but most hospitable welcome in the Indian village. He was formally adopted as a son by the father of the young Serpent. He was regularly engrafted into the tribe with full and solemn cermony.

279.22–23   the foreground of a picture that Salvator Rosa would have delighted to draw: A remarkably versatile artist, Rosa (1615–1673) captured in his landscapes and battle scenes a roughness and wildness that anticipated Romantic tastes and recommended him to Cooper and his generation. Horace Walpole characterized Rosa as "Precipices, mountains, torrents, wolves, rumblings."

TEXTUAL APPARATUS

Textual Commentary

The present edition of *The Deerslayer* takes as its copy-text Cooper's corrected holograph manuscript, from which the first edition was set. By eliminating scores of first-edition compositorial errors affecting substantives and thousands of non-authorial pointings, the present eclectic text protects Cooper's original intentions for the last of the Leather-Stocking Tales against the corruption of the printing shop. At the same time, careful and repeated collation of the manuscript with the two printed texts over which Cooper exercised control—the 1841 American first edition of Lea and Blanchard (A hereafter) and the 1850 Putnam "Author's Revised Edition" (B hereafter)—permits the adoption of those revisions which the present editors believe to be the author's final intentions.

Following contemporary practices in textual editing first stated by W. W. Greg and later developed by Fredson Bowers and others,[1] in producing the eclectic text the editors have adhered to Cooper's corrected manuscript rigorously, both in readings affecting meaning (substantives) and pointing (accidentals). The generic problems of reading the manuscript accurately will be addressed below; succeeding sections will examine the grounds of authority for the A and B texts and will present the textual policies employed in emending the manuscript accordingly. Finally, non-authoritative editions in Cooper's lifetime will be surveyed in terms of their derivation from these three authorial sources for the text.

Cooper's Corrected Manuscript (AMS)

In preparing the present edition, Cooper's manuscript was twice collated against A, enlarged positive copies of the microfilm of the manuscript were similarly collated twice, and the printer's copy for the present edition was finally inspected against the original manuscript. (A full description of the physical properties of the manuscript is offered in "Note on the Manuscript," pp. 580 to 583). Although Cooper's interlineated and crossed-over emendations were crowded onto sheets already extraordinarily parsimonious with blank space, the Lea and Blanchard compositors set the text, where substantives were concerned, with considerable fidelity to the manuscript. Nevertheless, in the inevitable rush of setting the text commercially, significant compositorial misreadings occurred which were plausible enough to evade Cooper's proofing and thus to pass down in time through both authoritative and non-authoritative lines of textual descent.

The generic problems of reading and setting the manuscript accurately may be conveniently grouped under three heads:

1. misreading the actual words Cooper wrote, most often because of his cramped lines of script (especially at the edges of the sheets) but also occasionally from lapses in the clarity of his hand;
2. overlooking or misreading his interpolations and transpositions, or failing to observe his use of underlined dots or dashes to indicate "stet";
3. failing to follow his punctuation, either from misreading or ignoring his actual marks.

Taken individually, the compositorial misreadings of words provide the most signal examples of corruptions in setting the manuscript. Cooper's irregular spacing of words or separate syllables occasionally led the compositors to set as one word what Cooper clearly meant as two; the results are sometimes bizarre. (In the following examples, the compositorial error is italicized for emphasis.)

For example, at 285.16–17 A states that Deerslayer "indulged in a fit of his hearty, *benevolent* laughter"; but what Cooper wrote was "hearty, but silent laughter" — a trait of Deerslayer since his introduction in *The Pioneers*. When at 545.20–22 Judith in deep regret acknowledges Deerslayer's rejection of her, A records that "with a heart nearly broken by the consciousness of *undeserving*, she signed to him an adieu, and buried herself in the woods." The word taken as "undeserving" by A is cramped indeed in the manuscript, but a close look at the separate strokes discloses that Cooper wrote "undue [that is, 'excessive'] erring" — a reading, hitherto unknown, which reveals that at novel's end Cooper intended Judith to recognize how her errant conduct led Deerslayer to reject her. Combining two prepositions into a compound preposition also at least once corrupts Cooper's meaning. At 221.14, where Judith is frightened by the bursting gun, A causes Deerslayer to offer improbably to "lead her *into* a seat"; Cooper had written "in [referring to the cabin] to a seat."

Not scrutinizing Cooper's hand closely led A to perpetrate some other egregious blunders. At 186.23 A causes the pious Hetty to praise Hutter for failing in his scalping mission against the Hurons: "Thank *you* for that, father!" But what Cooper had written was "Thank god . . . !" In a passage at 324.20–24 where Hutter's and Harry's savagery is figured by their insensitivity to the solemn beauty of daybreak, an elaborate contrast between morning and evening twilight is sabotaged by A printing "novel" for Cooper's "moral" in the following:

> The hymns of birds, too, have no *novel* counterpart in the retreat to the roost, or the flight to the nest, and these invariably accompany the advent of the day, until the appearance of the sun itself —
> > "Bathes in deep joy, the land and sea."

Cooper's landscape painting is again perverted at 91.15–18, where in A the men rowing the ark pause temporarily to enjoy Hetty's simple song: "nor did their oars again dip until the last of the sweet sounds had actually died among the remarkable *shores*, which, at that witching hour would waft, even the lowest modulations of the human voice, more than a mile." "Shores," no matter how remarkable, do not "waft" sounds, but "echoes"—which is what Cooper wrote—do.

Cooper frequently elided the final syllable of words ending in "ing" or "ary," or of common prepositions like "among," especially if the word occurred at the sheet edge. Close inspection of the manuscript occasionally discloses a compositorial misreading of such an elision, like "flary" for Cooper's "flaring" at 69.8 or "motives" for Cooper's "motions" at 116.11.

Like most people's, Cooper's handwriting often failed to distinguish vowels clearly; consequently in revising he took pains to clarify certain vowels. Small "e's" are made more prominent by an extra loop added on top—a characteristic the A compositor overlooked when he set "persons" for Cooper's "parsons" at 23.37. Extra strokes added in revision also help to distinguish among "a," "o," and "u" though on occasion compositorial error could lead to mistakes like setting "lost prize" for "last prize" at 113.1, where Deerslayer picks up the last canoe intentionally set adrift. Misreading of vowels is especially common in dialect words, the compositors tending to normalize such dialect forms as "parfect" (33.28), "git" (38.33), "suppersition" (59.10), "congergate" (59.21–22), "rumernates" (96.37), "ingenuerty" (101.12), "interprise" (101.18), "proclomation" (186.37), "onseemly" (207.39), "wownded" (221.12), and others.

Terminal vowel/consonant constructions are at times difficult to distinguish in Cooper's script, especially when the chance is great of misreading a near substitute for Cooper's actual relative pronoun or article. For example, A sets "where" for Cooper's "when" at 107.16 and elsewhere, "the" for Cooper's "this" at 85.4. Several other patterns of compositorial corruption emerge from the difficulties of distinguishing between Cooper's upper and lower case script for certain letters, especially "A/a," "C/c," "G/g," "S/s," and "T/t." For example, Cooper usually writes "Ark" and "castle," though counterinstances ("ark" at 37.13 and "Castle" at 239.33–34) do occur. A regularizes both words to the lower case. On the other hand, A always sets "God" for Cooper's lower case form (though the upper case form in A may well have been house styling.) Cooper also often begins articles with upper case "T" in sentence fragments; A sets these forms as lower case. (Upper and lower case "T's" are unusually hard to discriminate and many forms in the manuscript remain indeterminate. The present edition has read many of these indeterminate forms as upper case "T's" in incomplete sentence constructions. In the other instances of mis-set lower or upper case forms, the present edition follows Cooper's clear intent.)

The last category of difficulty in reading Cooper's hand is the observation of Cooper's often miniscule terminal "s." As an examination of the Rejected

Readings list shows, A frequently missed the small stroke which Cooper used to designate a plural construction, as at 23.27; restoring the plural forms often makes Cooper's intention more clear.

The second category of problematic manuscript readings results from the various modes of authorial revision of the first draft. Cooper's emendations affecting substantives are clear and straightforward; only rarely did the compositor miss added material, as he did for example at 466.26 where Cooper clarified the phrase "matters to a crisis" by interpolating "with those in the Castle" after the first noun in the phrase.

At times, however, the carets adding new material, new matter replacing something cancelled, or wavy lines and balloons repositioning words or phrases reflect Cooper's intent, but errors in execution obscure perfect or correct readings, especially for accidentals. A few examples will suffice. At 59.6 Cooper revised "that's" to "that it's" but the apostrophe after "that" remains. At 17.35 Cooper eliminated a sentence fragment by joining it to the previous sentence; this juncture was effected by adding "and" after "feel." and converting the period after "feel" to a comma. However, the first word of the unrevised fragment remained capitalized. In both instances the compositor correctly interpreted Cooper's intent, by ignoring the superfluous apostrophe in the former instance and emending to the lower case in the latter.

Occasionally simple logic and grammar resolve possible ambiguities of a revised reading. For example, at 61.22 Cooper altered "a bit of level" to "a small bit of low land," by placing "small" directly over "bit" (which was at the left edge of the sheet.) Over the cancelled "level" Cooper wrote "low land," with no carets or lines to clarify the passage. The A compositor correctly read the passage as "a small bit of low land," though he ignored the terminal comma (here restored).

A special difficulty arises with Cooper's use of the caret, which he habitually constructed from two separate strokes; at times the caret is constructed from an earlier comma and the resultant figure may still have the force of the comma. For example, at 439.7-9, Cooper originally wrote "This natur' never can be changed, though it may undergo some increase . . . ." In revision he interpolated "in the main," over "changed," adding a short penstroke to the comma to convert it to a caret while still preserving the unambiguous comma stroke. A read the passage as "changed in the main,"; the present edition corrects A to follow Cooper's intent: "changed, in the main,".

In instances such as 17.35 and 59.6-7 where Cooper's manuscript revisions are faulty in execution but his intentions are unambiguous, the present edition has followed A in silently emending such slips of the pen. In instances such as 49.25 where Cooper's intent is ambiguous, whether the present edition has followed A or not, a Textual Note discusses the reading here adopted.

The final category of difficulty in reading the manuscript which arises from Cooper's revisions is the correct interpretation of passages underlined by a broken or dotted line. Following older usage Cooper employed such underlinings to indicate "stet"; again generally the A compositor follows Cooper's intention, but in at least one instance misses the significance of the dotted underlining. At 421.14-16, Cooper originally wrote of Judith's attempt to win favor with Deerslayer that the girl was "gladly availing herself of the opportunity of indirectly extolling the qualities which had so strongly interested her" in Deerslayer. Cooper cancelled "indirectly" but later restored it by a broken underlining; A ignored the dotted underline and failed to set the restored adverb, which by suggesting Judith's roundabout approach, clarifies Cooper's meaning.

The last category of problematic readings in the manuscript affects Cooper's intention for punctuation. In revision, occasionally two punctuation marks are superimposed, as at 378.9-13, where Cooper wrote:

"To be sure, a man ought to be tall, but others are tall, as well as Hurry; and active-;-and I think I know those that are most active — and strong; well, he has n't all the strength in the world — and brave — I am certain I can name a youth who is braver!"

In setting the passage the A compositor assumed that the heavy dash over the bottom of the semi-colon after the first "active" signified that Cooper wanted a dash, not a semi-colon. The present edition agrees with this reading, though it should be noted that in the rest of the passage Cooper's characteristic double punctuation (like the second "active; — ") is simplified and thus distorted in A.

At times in the manuscript the sequence of Cooper's punctuation is not clear. Normally Cooper followed modern practice in placing quotes after commas and periods, though at times — as at 374.26 (ear.") — the quote comes directly *over* the other punctuation marks. In such instances the present edition has followed Cooper's usual sequencing; however, in instances where Cooper clearly placed the quote *before* commas, periods, dashes, or other marks, Cooper's clear intention has been followed here.

The First Edition, Lea and Blanchard, Philadelphia, 1841 (A)

Though no page proofs of the text containing revisions in the author's hand are known to be extant, his correspondence with Richard Bentley concerning the British edition, and later with Mrs. Cooper concerning the progress of the first edition in Philadelphia, establishes Cooper's authorial control over the Lea and Blanchard printing. Writing from Cooperstown on 14 May 1841, Cooper indicated to Bentley that his reading of the novel was well under way:

Messrs Lea & Blanchard are now printing "The Deerslayer, or The First War Path," at Philadelphia. I have seen near a hundred pages, and the first half will be sent to you at the close of this month — The rest will follow quite soon afterwards, as I shall go down and attend to the printing in person. At present, the proofs are sent 300 miles to be read.[2]

On 10 June Cooper wrote his wife that he had arrived in Philadelphia, had already seen his printers, and expected to move on to New York by 23 June. However, the printing schedule kept him in Philadelphia longer than he planned, for on 22 June he wrote Mrs. Cooper that

> Here I am still, contrary to my expectations. I shall leave P—this week . . . I am detained by a new bargain [an abridgement of his *Naval History*] and a desire to get rid of Deerslayer entirely . . . . About 80 pages of Deerslayer remain to be printed. Of these some 30 will be disposed of to day.[3]

The Deerslayer finally appeared on 27 August 1841.[4]

That Cooper paid close attention to seeing the manuscript through the press is demonstrated by a note on the verso of folio 108 of the manuscript, probably written by an A compositor:

> I send the Ms., that Mr. Cooper may see the doubtful word. I can make nothing of it but association.
>
> G.T. [?]

The word in question on recto 108 is in fact "association," in the following context: "Hetty did not answer at first, but, with that indescribable feeling that awakens sympathy and association among the youthful and unpractised of her sex, she hung her head, and the blood suffused her cheek ere she found her tongue" (232.35–38). In response to the query Cooper altered the word to "intelligence," the A reading.

This evidence of Cooper's close involvement in the printing process makes it extremely probable that those other variants between manuscript and A which correct substantive errors, improve style or sense, or execute the typical improvements or regularizations discussed below, are Cooper's work. Furthermore, since Cooper's letters demonstrate his concern to oversee the printing in Philadelphia through to completion, it is reasonable to expect—given that the manuscript was a corrected first draft—that Cooper treated the A proofs as a modern writer would treat a professional typescript: as a fair copy upon which necessary substantive and accidental corrections could be made to prepare the text for its first public appearance.

Over 2000 variants affecting substantive readings occur between the manuscript and A. Few of these variants initiate lengthy new readings; instead brief variants of one or a few words commonly emend obvious faults in the manuscript or introduce clarifications distinctively authorial. Only in four instances does Cooper add a whole sentence, as, for example at 194.37 where he identifies Rivenoak by name, or 42.25 where he augments his initial description of the Castle by a reference to the chest holding Hutter's treasures. In both these cases, early in the text Cooper distinguishes more clearly some plot element subsequently developed (see 5.3–5 and 89.36 for the other additions of sentences).

Variants affecting phrases constitute about a tenth of the total of substantive variants. These phrase-length variants significantly improve the text, by eliminating verbiage (eg, 114.27, A expected distance; AMS distance he had expected); enhancing dialect (eg, 22.30–31, A hold it to be onlawful; AMS do not hold it to be lawful); clarifying meaning (eg, 268.23, A Judith would not willingly; AMS Judith certainly would never); making descriptions more accurate (eg, 74.11, A narrow and sinuous stream; AMS narrow stream); correcting faulty information (eg, 175.29–30, A Iroquois, or Hurons, as it would be better to call them; AMS Iroquois); or rephrasing awkward constructions (eg, 349.25–26, A She did not dare to land, if such an expedient; AMS Land she did not dare to do, or, if it).

Numerous single word variants also demonstrate Cooper's concern in proofing to revise the text with care. In the examples following, Cooper corrects faulty information and grammatical errors as above, and also substitutes synonyms for contiguously-repeated words (variants italicized for emphasis):

A	AMS
27.37–39 The Redskins honor and respect them [the feeble minded] who are so *gifted*, knowing that the Evil Spirit delights more to dwell in an artful body	The Redskins honor and respect them who are so *situated*, knowing that the Evil Spirit delights more to dwell in an artful body
82.17–18 *find* our friends food; a long march gives a sharp appetite	*give* our friends food; a long march gives a sharp appetite
282.35–283.1 since the knoll behind the huts and the fire, offered a cover for those who were now *stealthily* approaching, rather than any protection to the Indians. Deerslayer did not break through the *fringe* of bushes immediately abreast of the canoe, which might have brought him too suddenly within the influence of the light, since the *hillock* did not extend to the water	since the knoll behind the huts and the fire, offered a cover for those who were now *covertly* approaching, rather than any protection to the Indians. Deerslayer did not break through the *cover* of bushes immediately abreast of the canoe, which might have brought him too suddenly within the influence of the light, since the *rise* did not extend to the water . . . .
155.4–5 The manner of his appearance, and of his entrance into the craft, *is* known.	The manner of his appearance, and of his entrance into the craft *are* known.
188.20 before the *Delaware* girl [Wah-ta!-Wah]	before the *Iroquois* girl

At eight places in the manuscript, Cooper by accident omits a grammatically-necessary word. The repairing of such slips of the pen might well be Cooper's work, since the compositors were known to consult him concerning problematic readings. But the readings could equally likely be the result of silent emendations by the compositor. For example, at 55.38, A supplies the missing verb (here italicized) in the following passage:

> The placid water swept round in a graceful curve, the rushes bent
> gently towards its surface, and the trees over-hung it as usual, but
> all *lay* in the soothing and sublime solitude of a wilderness.

Again, at 67.12 the manuscript reads "Judith I stay at home"; A supplies
the missing "and." Similar omissions are repaired by A at 391.28, 441.34,
442.21, 451.4, 483.34 and 514.23. In all these cases the choice of words
corrects the oversight in an acceptable and logical way, and may be
authorial. Consequently the present edition follows A in these readings;
authority for the reading is attributed to A because of the reasonable
possibility that Cooper may have supplied these readings himself, or en-
dorsed the compositorial emendation of these obvious deficiencies in the
manuscript.

Not every substantive variant in A can be accepted as an improvement
certain or likely to have originated with Cooper. If compositorial
misreading is suspected as the source of the A variant, and if the new
reading offers no improvement of text, the A variant is rejected. For example, at 161.3–4 the compositors misread "turn" for Cooper's "tone" in the
following from the manuscript: "Hurry's fine face and manly form had
never compensated for his boisterous and vulgar *tone* . . . ." Where no
likelihood of compositorial eye-slip nor clear improvement exists, the new
reading is also rejected. For example, at 398.21–22 Cooper originally wrote
"a word easily intarpreted, and the most *hateful of all to their ears*, it's so true."
A modified the passage to "hateful to all their ears," a reduction of the
original passage here rejected as a suspected compositorial misreading.
Again, at 50.17–18, A prints " 'Tis *cruel* work I'll allow but for them it's
lawful work, while for *us* it would be *grievous* work." [first three italicized
words authorial]. However, the manuscript reads ". . . would be a grievous
sin," a reading superior to the printed text. The present edition believes the
A reading likely to be a compositorial slip, given the previous appearance of
"work," and rejects the A variant in favor of the manuscript. Finally all A
normalizations of dialect for Deerslayer and Hurry Harry are rejected
because Cooper's own manuscript revisions always enhance and never
diminish the rustic talk of these characters.

Countless variants affecting accidentals, especially in spelling and punctuation, occur between A and the manuscript. A conservative textual policy
for emending manuscript spelling retains Cooper's scribal forms except in
instances for which no evidence of other contemporary usage may be
found, or in which the authorial form causes confusion to the reader by
violating elementary usage. The authority for determining contemporary
usage for Cooper has been the 1828 *Webster's Dictionary* and the historical examples of the *Oxford English Dictionary*. When A corrects an obvious
authorial misspelling (eg, Cooper's "labarynth" at 19.16, "Schorarie" at
18.20 and elsewhere, "cooly" at 43.39 and elsewhere, "particularily" at
21.15 and elsewhere), the present edition accepts the emendation, with A
cited as authority for historical record. The present edition also follows A
readings where, as explained in "Note on the Manuscript," blots or sheet-

edge damage now obscure words or parts of words in the manuscript, and for the missing folio 6 (25.29 to 27.18 in the present text).

The present edition has not attempted to impose consistency upon variant but acceptable spelling or typographical forms of words. Variants like red skin/red-skin/redskin, towards/toward, further/farther, Ahs/Ah's have been left in whichever form is found in the manuscript. Cooper's characteristic use of the form now restricted to the past participle for the past tense, a permissable option in the early nineteenth century, has been retained, as at 114.24. For contractions, the present edition follows Cooper's manuscript forms, which are often inconsistent in spelling, spacing and use of apostrophes, as long as such holograph forms do not result in misleading or incomprehensible readings. For example, such forms as *can't*, *can'n't*, *can n't*, and *cannot* are followed, but not *cant* which could be misread as the noun. The author's inconsistent use of apostrophes and spacing in other manuscript forms like *t'other* or *t' other*, or *'Twould*, *'T would*, *T'would*, *T would* or *'T'would* are also followed, but holograph readings where the apostrophe does not represent a possible elision (*'tother*, *your'e*) are regarded as errors of inscription, and are treated like other spelling errors by emending to the form in A.

In two instances of inconsistent manuscript spelling for proper names — Hurry Harry and Wah-ta!-Wah — the present edition has followed A in consistently using the form most clearly established as Cooper's initial preference. An elaborate derivation of Henry March's sobriquet beginning at 20.14 establishes that the boisterous muscle man is commonly known as "Hurry Harry," or, occasionally "Hurry Skurry." "Hurry Harry" remains his most frequent designation until 56.1 where Cooper slips into the habit of reversing the vowels: "Harry Hurry." Only at the end of the manuscript does the "Hurry Harry" form return, and numerically "Harry Hurry" preponderates. However, given that Cooper was at pains in introducing the name to establish the *Hurry* Harry/*Hurry* Skurry parallel, and that others commonly refer to him as "Hurry," the present edition has followed A in using Cooper's first version of the name throughout. All instances of the vowel-reversed form are reported in the Emendations.[5]

In establishing a consistent form for the name of Chingachgook's betrothed, the present edition like A has also followed Cooper's first intention: "Wah-ta!-Wah." Beginning at 138.33 Wah-ta!-Wah's name is explained in its Delaware and English forms, "Wah-ta!-Wah" and "Hist-oh!-Hist."[6] Given the difficult form of the name, Cooper understandably forgot in later scenes to follow precisely the "Wah-ta!-Wah" form established in the paragraph introducing her: a hyphen, the exclamation point, or the second capital "W" is often dropped. (Indeed, in initial stages of the manuscript, Cooper several times forgot her name altogether but in revising restored it to something close to "Wah-ta!-Wah.") As with "Hurry Harry," while in Philadelphia Cooper presumably could have altered the A form of "Wah-ta!-Wah" but did not, and as with "Hurry Harry," the present edition has followed Cooper's first clear preference for spelling the Indian maiden's name. All instances of Cooper's manuscript variants from the accepted form are reported in the Emendations.

The present edition makes no silent emendation of manuscript punctuation. In the instances where A remedies obvious oversights in elementary punctuation — supplying apostrophes for plurals, adding terminal punctuation for sentences, or correcting Cooper's inconsistent use of double and/or single quotation marks — the present edition follows A, citing it for historical record as the source of the emendation.

In certain passages the present edition also follows A in altering Cooper's manuscript use of commas and semi-colons; again A is cited in Emendations as the first occurrence of the variant. To clarify Cooper's obvious meaning, the present edition follows A in adding commas in 72 instances, and deleting them in 30.[7] Commas are added (examples in italics) most frequently to separate parallel constructions (eg, 141.28–29, indifference to danger, manly devotion to herself and *sister*, guilelessness of manner) or to avoid confusion by distinguishing a noun or pronoun of address from the rest of the clause (e.g., 193.1 You *forget*, Hist, these are the words . . .). Commas are deleted (examples in italics) from the manuscript most commonly because they cause temporary ambiguity by separating closely related grammatical elements, like subject and verb (eg, 113.20–21, *Deerslayer*, adjusted his hard pillow,) or create a meaning clearly not Cooper's intent (eg, 83.19–20, If you've *understood*, Hurry, here, to mean that he intends to desart you).

Cooper's manuscript revisions disclose that in a number of long passages he substituted semi-colons for "comma + conjunction" constructions (eg, twice in Deerslayer's dialogue at 426.8 and 16). Though A on its own frequently makes such alterations, the present edition, given the evidence of Cooper's manuscript revisions, has accepted as authorial revisions in proofing those semi-colon variants which eliminate verbal conjunctions in long passages containing several other conjunctions. Cooper's manuscript substitution of semi-colons is especially noticeable in Indian dialect, no doubt to produce what Cooper calls at 175.40–176.1 "the usual, abbreviated manner of an Indian" speaking English. Consequently the present edition follows A variants which replace verbal conjunctions with semi-colons in all passages where Indian dialogue is rendered.

For every instance where the A emendation of punctuation remedies glaring oversights, dozens of A punctuation variants occur which neither clarify Cooper's text nor serve the reader's interests. The A compositor imposed upon Cooper's manuscript a system of pointing modern-seeming and bookish, but at the expense of the author's original narrative style and pacing.

The following passage illustrates how the extensive A repointing of Cooper's prose altered the flow of the original dialogue, making a marked change in effect even though no substantive variants occur. The first version is the repunctuated A text, upon which the compositor has imposed a coordination of clauses not authorial; the second, with Cooper's characteristic semi-colons serving to set off a parenthetical phrase, is the manuscript text which the present edition follows at 449.13–20.

(A text)
"Never fear for me, Deerslayer," put in Hetty, who comprehended enough of the discourse to know its general drift; "I'm feeble-minded, and that, they say, is an excuse for going anywhere; and what that won't excuse will be overlooked, on account of the bible I always carry. It is wonderful, Judith, how all sorts of men, the trappers as well as the hunters, red men as well as white, Mingos as well as Delawares, do reverence and fear the bible!"

(AMS text)
"Never fear for me, Deerslayer," put in Hetty, who comprehended enough of the discourse to know its general drift, "I'm feeble minded, and that they say is an excuse for going any where; and what that won't excuse, will be overlooked on account of the bible I always carry. It is wonderful, Judith, how all sorts of men; the trappers as well as the hunters; red-men as well as white; Mingos as well as Delawares do reverence and fear the bible!"

More serious corruptions of Cooper's meaning occur when the misreading or misunderstanding of Cooper's punctuation led the A compositors to set readings substantively different from the author's intention. The alteration of even a comma, as every teacher of composition knows, can significantly change the meaning of a sentence, as at 262.6–10 where the addition in A of the second comma (here italicized) produced a possible syntactical structure but a meaning decidedly less subtle than Cooper's original intent:

As for the old man, the father of two young *women*, who might ripen better feelin's in his heart, and Harry March, here, who, pine as he is, might better bear the fruit of a more christianized tree, as for *them* two, I leave 'em in the hands of the white man's god.

More drastic repointing in A quite reverses Cooper's meaning at 87.28–29, where Hurry is defending the proposed scalping expedition against the Huron camp:

(AMS and present edition)
"The savages scalp—your fr'inds the Delawares, or Mohicans, whichever they may be, among the rest—and why should'n't we scalp?"

(A)
"The savages scalp your fri'nds, the Delawares, or Mohicans, whichever they may be, among the rest; and why shouldn't we scalp?"

In the final example, the A compositor at 503.20–25 failed to observe Cooper's coordination between the following two sentences:

(AMS and the present edition)

The warriors, as soon as this interruption had ceased, resumed their places, and again prepared to exhibit their skill. As there was a double object in view, that of putting the constancy of the captive to the proof, and that of showing how steady were the hands of the marksmen, under circumstances of excitement, the distance was small, and, in one sense, safe.

Unfortunately the compositor misread "the distance" as "The distance," and resolved the ensuing sentence fragment beginning with "As there" by attaching it to the first sentence in the passage, producing:

The warriors, as soon as this interruption had ceased, resumed their places, and again prepared to exhibit their skill, as there was a double object in view, that of putting the constancy of the captive to the proof, and that of showing how steady were the hands of the marksmen under circumstances of excitement. The distance was small, and, in one sense, safe.

Passages corrupted by non-authorial changes in punctuation like those above often produced plausible misreadings, which easily escaped the notice of authors proofing or revising without close reference to what they originally wrote. In such passages the present edition follows Cooper's original intention as disclosed by the manuscript. These examples of major compositorial corruptions resulting from apparently minor repointing illustrate, perhaps better than any other category of variants, the importance of following the text closest to the author's hand in matters involving accidentals.

The Second American Edition, Putnam, New York, 1850 (B)

The Deerslayer, the first of the Leather-Stocking Tales to appear in Putnam's "Author's Revised Edition," was published on 13 September 1850. For the $500 Putnam offered for the revised text, Cooper provided several hundred emendations, three new footnotes, and a general "Preface to the Leather-Stocking Tales."[8]

Cooper's textual revisions are limited primarily to heightening dialect, correcting a few remaining grammatical errors, and occasionally clarifying meanings or compressing verbose constructions. For example in the dialogue of dialect speakers, "Indian" is frequently altered to "Injin," "after" to "a'ter" or "arter," and for the Indians, "other" to "udder." At 200.10–14 the plural pronouns and nouns (here italicized) are changed to singular forms to accord with the "or" conjunction of the subject: "Once, or twice, in the course of the night, it is true, Deerslayer, or the Delaware, arose and looked out upon the tranquil lake; when, finding all safe, *they* returned to *their pallets*, and slept like *men* who *were* not easily deprived of *their* natural rest." At 164.5–7 in the interests of brevity, Cooper revised "The rifles were now laid aside, as useless, and then the two men seized the oars, and began to sweep the head of the scow round, in the direction of the canoe" to "The rifles were now laid aside, as useless, the two men seizing the oars, and sweeping the head of the scow round, in the direction of the canoe." At 544.15, Cooper eliminated a glaring solecism by altering "its expression" to "the expression of her countenance" in the following: "As Judith sat in the bow of the canoe, her back was turned towards him, else it is probable *its expression* might have induced him to venture some soothing terms of friendship and regard." Other emendations eliminate superfluous words like "now" or "then," or drop "had" in verbal constructions where the perfect tense is unneeded or illogical (as at 160.33). Occasional B corrections of self-evident A typos (as "did" for "die" at 126.35) also occur.

Only if the B variant contributes to textual clarity or concision is it accepted by the present edition; variants for which compositorial error or sophistication is the suspected cause are rejected. The following comparisons illustrate the kinds of B variants rejected because they are at least equally likely to be compositorial as authorial.

A	B
52.23 a long low point, that had *gotten* the name	a long, low point, that had *got* the name
62.3 Hurry laughed at *this* suggestion	Hurry laughed at *the* suggestion
75.21–22 raise my voice in *council*	raise my voice in *counsel*
110.9 *I'm* withed like a saw-log	*I am* withed like a saw-log
127.21–24 The yell was the customary lamentation . . . without which a victory *was* never considered complete.	The yell was the customary lamentation . . . without which a victory *is* never considered complete.
179.39–180.1 I sometimes think wickedness will get the better of me	I sometimes think *that* wickedness will get the better of me
192.33 they are the *very* words of the Great Spirit	they are the words of the Great Spirit

Obvious errors in B ("he" for "he'll" at 70.26, "tract" for "track" at 161.32) are of course also rejected.

House-styling accounts for hundreds of non-authorial changes in accidentals in the Putnam edition. For example, the punctuation of hyphenated words in the Lea and Blanchard edition is virtually ignored; prefixes of words such as "enclosed" are changed to "inclosed"; "connection" is spelled "connexion"; expressions like "any thing" become one word; most occurrences of "farther" and "farthest" are changed to "further" and "furthest" respectively; and "upward" is restyled as "upwards."

European Editions

Two European editions of *The Deerslayer* appeared during Cooper's lifetime: Richard Bentley published the novel on 7 September 1841 to coincide with the 1841 Lea and Blanchard publication, and a French edition (in English) was issued as part of the Baudry's European Library, under the auspices of Galignani. Sample sight collations indicate that the Baudry edition was set from the first Bentley edition in view of its identical system of punctuation as well as duplication of Bentley's errors.

Because Cooper supplied Bentley with the manuscript of *The Deerslayer*, the possibility exists that the Bentley edition contained authoritative readings or revisions overlooked in Lea and Blanchard's setting of the holograph. However, two sight collations of the Bentley text against both the manuscript and the Lea and Blanchard edition indicate that Bentley took the incompletely-revised Lea and Blanchard proof sheets as copy-text. Though the manuscript was available, no evidence exists that Bentley's staff consulted it in setting the text; all variants between Bentley and its copy-text may be attributed to compositorial intervention. Cooper's reason for supplying the manuscript was apparently only to aid Bentley in securing the British copyright.[9]

Among the most common kinds of non-authorial variants from copy-text are changes from plural to singular (or vice versa) in noun forms; reversal of word order in phrases like "to either," "of but," and "be neither"; and regularization of dialect to forms uncharacteristic of Cooper. Numerous obvious corruptions of the text appear, such as "the scene at first had *passed* upon her feeble mind . . ." for the A ". . . had pressed . . ." at 501.23–24. The occasional Bentley correction of A errors results from commonsense emendation: "knee deep" for the A "knee keep" at 474.37 or "pack of hungry wolves" for the A "back of hungry wolves" at 186.39. Bentley's use of incompletely-revised Lea and Blanchard proof sheets as copy-text is demonstrated by variants where the London text follows Cooper's manuscript, as, for example, eight references to "Harry Hurry" and ten unapostrophized "ing" forms between 451.18 and 454.37. In these instances Bentley apparently is relying upon early Lea and Blanchard proof sheets containing original manuscript readings in passages Cooper subsequently revised after the sheets were sent to London in early July 1841. The Lea and Blanchard edition, published in August, therefore contains some late authorial emendations not found in the London edition.

In sum, the internal evidence of sight collation of the Bentley text fails to indicate persuasively that Cooper intervened in any way to provide revisions unique to the Bentley printing. Where the Bentley edition does vary from Lea and Blanchard, the variant may be ascribed to compositorial misreading or restyling, or to reliance upon proof sheets mailed to London before Cooper in Philadelphia completed his revisions for the text Lea and Blanchard ultimately issued.

Bentley reissued *The Deerslayer* again in 1841, and in 1843, 1850, and 1854(?) as No. 91 in the "Bentley Standard Novels" series. Sample collation reveals that the "Bentley Standard Novels" text compresses and freely rearranges passages in Cooper's text. Since no evidence suggests that Cooper had any involvement in the text for any of Bentley's issues, these editions (and those like the Baudry deriving from them) are not considered relevant to the establishment of the present text.

Other American Editions

About a fortnight before the Lea and Blanchard edition was issued, an "Extract from 'The Deerslayer,' " consisting of Chapter VI, appeared in the 14 August 1841 edition of *Brother Jonathan*, p. 2. Sight collation of this text with the Lea and Blanchard equivalent readily discloses that the Philadelphia proof sheets were taken as copy-text. No substantive or accidental variants between the two texts appear to be authorial. Consequently this text, and a similarly-titled extract consisting of the same chapter, published in the September issue of *The Dollar Magazine* (Volume I, pp. 270–73), are not considered as relevant to establishing the present text.

Subsequent to 1841, Lea and Blanchard reissued *The Deerslayer* from its stereotyped plates in 1845, 1846 and 1849. Stringer and Townsend purchased the copyrights and plates for all the Leather-Stocking Tales on 6 September 1850,[10] and published the novel under its imprint in 1850 and 1851.[11] In 1852 Stringer and Townsend issued the "New Edition" of *The Deerslayer* in a one-volume format with lined margins (but retaining the original two-volume separate pagination); this "New Edition"—new only in cosmetics—was reissued in 1854, 1855, and 1857. Hinman collation of the first edition against copies of the 1845, 1846 and 1849 Lea and Blanchard issues, and against copies of the 1850, 1852 and 1857 Stringer and Townsend issues discloses only successive deterioration of the plates accompanied by occasional repairs.[12]

The Putnam "Author's Revised Edition" of 1850 was reissued by Putnam in 1853, and by Stringer and Townsend in its "Choice" edition in 1856. The first illustrated edition of *The Deerslayer* appeared in 1861 as part of W. A. Townsend's edition "Illustrated from Drawings by F.O.C. Darley." However, since all these reprints of the Putnam text occurred posthumously, the editors have not considered them relevant to the establishment of the present text.[13]

Conclusion

Except where reported, the present edition follows Cooper's clear and unambiguous initial intentions for *The Deerslayer*, as disclosed in the almost-complete authorially-revised holograph. Where possible ambiguities occur in this manuscript, the transcriptions of those passages presented here are described in the Textual Notes—whether or not the present edition follows the A reading in question. Where the manuscript copy-text is missing (for AMS folio 6, for blotted or damaged portions in AMS) the present edition follows A.

Stemma

The following chart or *stemma* summarizes the lines of descent from the
1841 Lea and Blanchard edition to the Townsend editions of the 1850's:

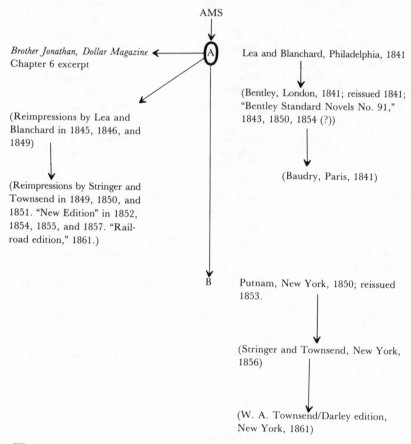

The present edition has emended Cooper's manuscript on the grounds of
one of three reasons:

1. The post-copy-text variant alters a substantive meaning in the
    manuscript in a way which strongly suggests Cooper's authority for
    the variant. Authority for these presumed authorial emendations is
    assigned to either of the two texts — Lea and Blanchard, 1841 (A) or
    Putnam, 1850 (B) — which Cooper is known to have revised.
2. The post-copy-text variant emends an obvious oversight in a
    manuscript accidental such as correcting spelling (eg, 19.16) or
    capitalization (eg, 27.31), or adding or normalizing punctuation
    (eg, 22.7 and 27.27, respectively). Authority for these variants rests
    with the Cooper Edition, since such obvious emendations are more
    likely compositorial than authorial. However, for historical interest
    the listed source of the correction is the edition which initiates it.

3. The post-copy-text variant is necessary to actualize a meaning which the present edition believes is Cooper's intention, but which through oversight he failed to present clearly in the manuscript. The present edition has followed A in eight instances (see p. 582) in supplying omitted words; in eight other instances the present edition has been the first text of the novel to emend the substantives or accidentals required to actualize the meaning Cooper apparently had in mind.[14] Authority for these emendations rests with the Cooper Edition (CE).

The present edition has made varying verbal forms consistent only when the evidence of Cooper's work on the manuscript discloses the author's clear preference. For example, at 257.13 and elsewhere Cooper revises "a'r'n'd" to "ar'n'd"; consequently the present edition has printed every instance of this dialect form of "errand" as "ar'n'd," and has listed these variants as CE emendations. Since the manuscript also discloses that the novelist at times forgot later in the text what forms he had earlier used for "Hurry Harry" and "Wah-ta!-Wah," and occasionally caught these slips in revision, the present edition has followed A in printing these names consistently in the form Cooper's early practice most clearly established. The manuscript also shows Cooper frequently revising standard verbal forms to dialect for the two dialect speakers, Hurry Harry and Leather-Stocking; consequently the present edition has accepted as authorial those A and B variants which enhance dialect. In all these instances, the emendations are indicated on the Emendations list.

However, consistency for its own sake has been avoided. Where varying but equally comprehensible verbal forms occur in Cooper's text (Ahs/Ah's, Tis/'Tis, can't/can'n't/ca'nt, further/farther), and no pattern of manuscript revision establishes an authorial preference, whichever form was found in the holograph at each instance has been followed. Manuscript form has also been followed for idiosyncrasies which do not violate elementary usage, such as the consistent upper case "Ark" and lower case "castle."[15] Though Hurry Harry and Deerslayer frequently employ dialect, many times they also use the standard form of the same word. Only when A or B alters such standard forms to their dialect equivalents has the present edition emended to dialect; the present edition has not attempted on its own authority to impose a consistency of dialect usage in the absence of specific evidence of authorial revision.

Noah Webster's *An American Dictionary of the English Language* (2 vols., New York, 1828) has been employed as a guide to spelling and meanings of standard words current in the period in which *Deerslayer* was written. However, if the historical examples of the *Oxford English Dictionary* indicate that a form in the holograph unsanctioned by Webster was current in the eighteenth or nineteenth centuries (eg, "tennons" at 40.17 and 40.20), the holograph form has been retained and subsequent variants (if any) listed in Rejected Readings.

To aid the reader in appreciating the significance of Cooper's contextual use of epigraphs, the present edition has emended the often-sketchy holograph citations of sources to include the surname of the author, and the title and location of the quoted passage. Since Cooper's usual holograph practice was to place all such "mottos" in double quotation marks, the present edition has supplied such marks where they are lacking or inconsistent in the holograph. Such additions of punctuation and expansions of sources are treated as CE emendations and listed fully in the Emendations list. Texts of the epigraphs follow the holograph; substantive variants with respect to contemporaneous editions (possibly Cooper's sources) are listed in the notes.[16] For the convenience of the reader, the epigraphs are keyed when possible to standard modern texts (for example, *The Riverside Shakespeare*, ed. G. Blakemore Evans [Boston: Houghton Mifflin, 1974]); where such standard editions are lacking, the line reference derives from an American edition contemporaneous with *The Deerslayer*.

The present edition follows Cooper's revised holograph for the Preface and text of *The Deerslayer*, emending that copy-text only to supply emendations regarded as authorial or occasionally required to clarify ambiguities or oversights in the manuscript. The present edition also includes the 1850 "Preface to the Leather-Stocking Tales," written to accompany the Putnam *Deerslayer*, and supplies appropriate expansions of the epigraphs and dates for the notes. By referring to the Emendations and Rejected Readings, readers may reconstruct all the substantive variants between the manuscript and the two authoritative post-copy-texts, the 1841 Lea and Blanchard first edition (A) and the 1850 Putnam "Author's Revised Edition" (B). The Cooper Edition text thus presents the last of the Leather-Stocking Tales in the form which most fully follows Cooper's original intentions, but which also reflects the labor which Cooper, as a professional writer, expended revising his original text for the two printings over which he exerted his control.

NOTES

1. Greg's seminal 1949 essay "The Rationale of Copy-Text" is reprinted, along with essays by Bowers and others, in both Ronald Gottesman and Scott Bennett, eds., *Art and Error: Modern Textual Editing* (Bloomington: Indiana Univ. Press, 1970) and O.M. Brack, Jr., and Warner Barnes, eds., *Bibliography and Textual Criticism* (Chicago: Univ. of Chicago Press, 1969).

2. James Franklin Beard, ed., *The Letters and Journals of James Fenimore Cooper* (Cambridge, MA: Belknap Press of Harvard Univ. Press, 1964), 4, 153. Hereafter cited as *Letters and Journals*.

3. Ibid, 158–59. Cooper's wish "to get rid of Deerslayer entirely" probably refers to his earlier intent, mentioned in his letter to his wife of 13 June, of finishing work on the novel in New York. Instead of completing his labors through the mail, he now planned to finish with the text before leaving Philadelphia.

4. The 27 August 1841 date of publication is established by a notice headed "Mr Cooper's New Novel" in the 28 August (Saturday) issue of the tri-weekly (Tuesday, Thursday, Saturday) Philadelphia newspaper *National Gazette and Literary Register* (Vol. 21, No. 3122, p. 1): " 'The Deerslayer or the First War Path' is the title of Mr. Cooper's new novel just issued in two volumes, by Messrs Lea & Blanchard . . . ." Three advertisements in the same issue offer the new book for sale, noting the date of publication as 27 August. Cooper also wrote to his wife on Sunday, 29 August, that "Deerslayer is just out — no opinions yet of its standing. Of course nothing is yet known of its sale." (*Letters and Journals*, 4, 167).

The plates of the text were stereotyped by J. Fagan, and printed in two different Philadelphia shops: I. Ashmead, and T.K. and P.G. Collins. Hinman collation of four copies of these 1841 issues — three printed by Ashmead and one by the Collinses — discloses significant plate deterioration in the Collins copy. This record of plate wear indicates that the Collins printing occurred subsequent to the Ashmead, on plates worn by earlier machining. Copies of both printings have been found in two formats: two separate volumes and two volumes bound as one. (The four copies examined on the Hinman Collator were Lilly Library, Indiana University, PS 1406.A1 1841, 2 vols.; American Antiquarian Society, First Editions, 2 vols. in 1; and two sets owned by James Franklin Beard, 2 vols. each.)

5. At 244.16 (twice), 251.34 and 378.16 the present edition emends to "Hurry Harry" the "Harry Hurry" readings found in the manuscript and in the two authoritative editions.

6. The initial form in the paragraph may well be "Wah-Ta!-Wah," but the subsequent instances in the paragraph clearly establish the lower case "ta!" form. Frequently the capitalization of initial syllables in the girl's name, in both the English and Indian forms, is difficult to discern in the manuscript.

7. Commas added for clarity (49 instances): 22.7 (twice), 23.32, 29.36, 36.5, 36.39, 52.23, 58.21, 62.17, 81.27, 83.29, 92.25, 104.11, 125.4, 128.10, 136.1-2, 136.38, 140.10, 141.29, 151.30, 177.23, 177.32, 202.25, 237.5, 241.6, 255.22, 260.37, 299.8, 310.2, 314.1, 335.26, 353.6, 363.29, 381.8, 383.7, 391.7, 415.12, 416.7, 431.10, 442.5, 448.35, 461.4, 485.26, 512.35, 516.13, 516.32, 522.1, 536.12 and 547.30.

Commas added before or after noun or pronoun of address (23 instances): 27.24, 93.38-39, 97.7, 105.33, 151.36, 168.36, 193.1, 211.20, 242.3, 242.12, 267.32, 274.15, 367.39, 375.35, 376.30, 397.9, 404.29, 410.11, 431.18, 437.21, 472.16, 531.6 and 541.17.

Commas deleted for clarity (30 instances): 34.40, 40.31, 50.37, 62.39, 83.19, 105.11, 112.19, 113.20, 126.28, 147.13, 156.39, 187.6, 199.5, 246.20, 254.26, 271.33, 275.32, 290.12, 329.12, 330.22, 389.39, 432.28, 443.10, 451.6, 461.4, 482.20, 484.4, 505.9, 543.3 and 546.37.

8. See *Letters and Journals*, 6, 3-6, for an account of the negotiations leading to the Putnam edition of Cooper's works.

On Wednesday, 11 September 1850, a Putnam advertisement in the New York *Evening Post* (Vol. XLVII, p. 2) indicated that *The Deerslayer*, in an edition newly-revised by the author, would be published the following

Friday. No notice of the publication of the Putnam *Deerslayer* on 13 September appeared in the *Evening Post* or in several other New York newspapers examined, but the Saturday, 14 September, issue of the *Post* listed *The Deerslayer* first among a number of Putnam's latest publications, and subsequent Putnam notices in various papers refer to *The Deerslayer* as recently published. Friday, 13 September, thus seems the likeliest date for the appearance of the Putnam edition of *The Deerslayer*.

Hinman collation of two copies of this edition discloses no variants in the text, though some slight plate wear was observed. However, the copy owned by James F. Beard apparently by error substitutes Cooper's new "Introduction" to *The Last of the Mohicans* for the general "Preface to the Leather-Stocking Tales," while the copy owned by the American Antiquarian Society (First Editions) contains the correct general "Preface."

9. See *Letters and Journals*, 4, 162–63, for Cooper's letters to Bentley of 28 June and 10 July 1841 concerning transmission of the manuscript and duplicate sets of proofsheets to London.

10. *Letters and Journals*, 6, 4.

11. Stringer and Townsend issues of *The Deerslayer* dated 1849 must have been issued before copyright purchase, perhaps through some contractual arrangement with Lea and Blanchard.

12. Copies used in these collations were as follows:
- Lea and Blanchard, 1841 (first edition)—— 4 copies as described in note 4.
- Lea and Blanchard, 1845 (American Antiquarian Society G526. C777.D845.deer).
- Lea and Blanchard, 1846 (American Antiquarian Society G526.C777. D846.deer—second volume dated 1845).
- Lea and Blanchard, 1849 (American Antiquarian Society G526.C777. D849.deer, 2 vols. in 1) and a copy owned by James Franklin Beard.
- Stringer and Townsend, 1850/51 (American Antiquarian Society G526.C777.D850.deer, vol. 1; G526.C777.D851.deer, vol.2).
- Stringer and Townsend, 1852 (American Antiquarian Society G526. C777.D852.deer).
- Stringer and Townsend, 1857 (copy owned by James F. Beard).

13. In addition to variants caused by plate wear and inking problems, Hinman collation of copies (both owned by James F. Beard) of the Putnam edition and the Darley edition disclosed the following variants which resulted from corrections made in the later edition:

Putnam (1850)	*Darley (1861)*
182.7 of dangerous serpents	of dangerous serpents
they were literally none	*there* were literally none
402.5–6 [two lines incorrectly transposed]	[two lines in proper order]

14. See Textual Notes at 46.39, 47.3, 125.17, 246.20, 254.12, 260.29, 343.24, and 425.11.

15. In only two cases has the present edition silently altered a holograph form: at 524.17, 525.16, and 532.3 "Mᴿ" is transcribed as "Mr." and at 525.15, 527.1, and 527.19, "Dᴿ" is transcribed as "Dr."

16. Comparison between Cooper's mottoes and roughly contemporaneous editions of their sources reveals the following substantive variants: at 114.10 "should ere" in CE reads "should e'er" in *The Poetical Works of Lord Byron* (Philadelphia: R.W. Pomeroy, 1839), III, 109; at 271.2 and 271.4 "I hear thee babbling" and "But unto me thou bring'st," respectively read "Though babbling only" and "Thou bringest unto me" in *The Poetical Works of William Wordsworth* (New Haven: Peck & Newton, 1836), p. 64; at 338.3, 338.4, and 338.5, "all is," "land, adieu," and "I must" read "a' is," "Land fareweel," and "I maun" in James Johnson, *The Scots Musical Museum* (Edinburgh: J. Johnson, 1803), V, 513; and at 388.4 and 388.5, "Who tread" and "should know," respectively read "Who treades" and "would knowe," in *Mirror for Magistrates*, ed. Joseph Haselwood (London: Lackington, Allen & Co., 1815), pp. 472–73. Whatever reasons for the variants—Cooper either quoted from memory or consulted texts containing the variants—CE retains the copy-text readings.

An extra motto appears with Chapter XXVII that is not used in the novel. The discarded epigraph and its source are as follows:

And with how free an eye doth he look down
Upon these lower regions of turmoil!
Where all the storms of passion manly beat
On flesh and blood: where honour, power, renown,
Are only gay afflictions, golden toil;
Where greatness stands upon as feeble feet
As frailty doth; and only great doth seem
To little minds, who do it so esteem.

> Samuel Daniel, "To the Ladie
> Margaret," 11. 9–16.

Cooper's "passion manly" reads "passions mainly" in *A Complete Edition of the Poets of Great Britain* (Worcester, MA: Isaiah Thomas, 1794), IV, 304.

Note On The Manuscript

The virtually complete manuscript for the Preface and text of *The Deerslayer*, written and corrected in Cooper's hand, is preserved at the Pierpont Morgan Library, New York, bound with the only other known prepublication material—the proofs of the Preface, lightly corrected by the author.[1] The Preface fills 1 and 7/8 leaves of unlined light tan paper 9⅞", which has been folded in half. The 261 following sheets of the manuscript preserve the complete text of the novel, except for an unlocated missing folio 6 (25.29 to 27.18 in the present edition). The text is written on closely-spaced (5/16") lightly-lined tan sheets 12" by 7½". Neither the sheets of the Preface nor of the text discloses evidence of watermarks or chainlines. The mottled surface indicates machine-made paper.

Numeration of the sheets is imperfect. The first folio of the Preface is marked "1" by Cooper, but the second folio is unnumbered. The text is numbered by Cooper, except for the first page where "page 1" is written at the upper right by someone other than the author. The following errors in pagination occur (although the order of the text is not disturbed):

1. Folio 26 is followed by folio 28, then folio 27, a second folio 28, folio 29, and so on;
2. Folio 89 is succeeded by folio 91 (though the last digit is partly obscured by a blot), then folio 90, folio 91½, folio 92, and so on;
3. Folio 151 is followed by a folio marked 152, with the last digit heavily inked over another number. Then follows a second folio 152, folio 153, and so on;
4. Folio 184 is followed by two folios 185, then 187.

The last folio is marked 259, but adding the three pages with duplicate numbers and subtracting the missing folio 6 results in 261 extant leaves of the text.[2]

Cooper wasted no space on these sheets: each of the 38 printed lines per page is crammed from edge to edge, and frequently extra lines of script are packed at the top or bottom of the page. New paragraphs are slightly indented, if at all; often they are introduced by Cooper's ¶ on the same line the previous paragraph ended. New chapters begin immediately after the previous, with the epigraphs (or "mottos" as Cooper called them) inscribed on the verso of the same sheet. At one point (folio 227) the verso is used for a three sentence interpolation (see textual note at 485.32).

Cooper's handwriting in brown ink, with revisions in darker ink and occasionally pencil, is neat and fairly legible despite its compression. Cooper's revisions are numerous though seldom long; their frequency and scope suggest that the manuscript was a first draft which, after copious light correcting, was deemed suitable for the printer. Letters, especially vowels, are sometimes made more clear, alternatives to repeated verbal forms are interpolated, phrases are transposed for greater clarity, and at times brief second thoughts concerning plot or characterization are introduced by appropriate additions or deletions. For example, on folio 73 Cooper revised a reference to Judith—"she had been compelled to stand on the defensive, in her intercourse with men, with what success was a matter of doubt with some" to " . . . with what success was best known to herself—an alteration clearly required in order not to compromise the girl's character too explicitly. On folio 135 two comparisons of the screeching of the old crone guarding Wah-ta!-Wah to the rude noises of the contemporary press are struck out, no doubt as irrelevant topical thrusts. The longest cancellation in the manuscript occurs on folio 42; after wrestling with a passage describing how Judith's "reason, taste and manners" failed to receive "due attention" in youth, Cooper simply deleted 3½ lines of multiply-revised material after 95.13. Possibly because the cancelled comparison between Judith and "established belles in all classes" was gratuitous here, Cooper did not replace it.

Except for the missing folio 6, the text of the novel is on the whole well-preserved. However, the shearing or crumbling away of the edges of the sheets at times obscures parts of words. It is conceivable that this damage occurred before the Philadelphia compositors set the text, but since very little time passed between Cooper's finishing the manuscript and the printing, it seems more likely that this deterioration of the manuscript occurred after the printing. Even if it did not, Cooper, who travelled to Philadelphia expressly to oversee work on the text, could conveniently have repaired the omissions. Consequently the present edition has relied upon the Lea and Blanchard first edition to restore occasional missing letters (or words like "a," "an," and "the") which presumably result from edge deterioration subsequent to the printing of the first edition. Blots on 6 sheets also obscure short words or parts of longer ones, and again the first printing is followed.[3] For the missing manuscript folio 6 (25.29 to 27.18 in the present text), the first edition also provides the copy-text. In all instances the first edition is cited in the Apparatus as the authority for the reading which cannot now be based on the manuscript.

On the verso of folio 1 the following note appears, indicating that the manuscript was setting copy for A:

> Long Primer Solid same Pages as
> The Pathfinder
> Running head-The Deerslayer.

Page numbers marking the pagination of the Lea and Blanchard first edition are frequently marked on the manuscript, along with occasional bars presumably estimating length of text. The names of seven different compositors appear in the manuscript. From folio 182 to 259, almost every sheet is signed at or near the top by one of these seven; from folio 1 to 181 only a dozen sheets are so marked. The closeness with which Cooper worked with the printers is disclosed by a note on the verso of folio 108, where a frustrated compositor sought the author's help in resolving an obscure reading. Finally, no evidence on the manuscript indicates that the British printers made use of it — all shop marks on the folios refer to the Lea and Blanchard edition.

Bound with the manuscript are the only known proofs of *The Deerslayer* — one page proof for each of the five pages of the Preface. Three of these proofs contain four minor corrections in ink — in Cooper's hand — which were incorporated into the Lea and Blanchard edition. The proofs are late, since they already contain all the readings accepted by the present edition as Cooper's revisions of the manuscript; these handwritten variants merely make two revisions affecting accidentals and two minor changes in substantives.[4]

NOTES

1. According to Herbert Cahoon, Curator of Autograph Manuscripts at the Pierpont Morgan Library, the *Deerslayer* manuscript was bought by Morgan's agents from the Chapman collection in September 1895. The manuscript was bound in red morocco in England, probably immediately after purchase for Morgan; the mounting on larger sheets was done with great care to avoid obscuring any of the text.

2. Another interruption to the continuity of the text occurs at folios 155 and 161. Short sections from the tops of each folio, containing the page numbers and five and seven lines of text respectively, were at some time severed from the body of the sheets. Probably in the mounting of folios the short and long sections were incorrectly paired, so that the top of folio 155 was joined with the body of folio 161, and the top of folio 161 with the body of folio 155. Pagination of the intervening folios is, however, correct.

3. These blots affect the following passages as located in the present edition; the obscured matter is italicized. In each case the first edition reading for the obscured text is accepted by the present edition.

folio 48 — *The* visible evidence (107.26)
folio 71 — forest [AMS reads "natur' "]. Were the men bound . . . . (155.31–32) [Period after "forest" missing]
folio 74 — I *hope we* may . . . . (162.7)
lake," returned the young man. (162.9)
folio 126 — men who were *on the*ir . . . . (274.31)
whose serv*ice they* were . . . . (274.33)
movement*s in the ste*rn. (274.35)

his *mistress.* The (274.37)
folio 139—and w*hat* we whites call . . . . (301.20–21)
folio 238—N*or* was this all. (508.32)
4. The variants in the Preface are as follows:

proofs as printed (PR)	proofs as corrected per first edition (CPR)
viii.6 that should	should
viii.14 labour	labours
x.10 novel readers	novel-readers
xi.5–6 fact: such	fact. Such

Textual Notes

The following comments refer to specific decisions to emend or not to emend requiring fuller explanation than could be provided in the Textual Commentary.

18.28 The printer's mark for page 15 possibly obliterates Cooper's comma after "sea," but a close look at the AMS discloses no comma.

20.14 AMS clearly reads "Harry," so the emendation to the more formal "Henry" presumably is authorial. Though Cooper does call the trapper "Harry March" at 31.6, in more formal passages — like Deerslayer's farewell when Hurry departs for the fort at 404.8 — "Henry March" is preferred.

21.23 Cooper interpolated "slovenly" after and above "careless" but failed to add the necessary comma, which A supplies.

35.15 Cooper wrote "of" over "its," then repeated "its" in AMS. The overwritten "of" apparently was mistaken for a deleted word by the compositor.

44.39 In this passage the present edition adopts an emendation in A required for correctness, while following Cooper's original form in respect to other variants in substantives or accidentals. Other CE emendations of this kind are at 52.20, 82.38, 111.19, 152.21, 202.10, 217.21, 250.30, 252.2, 265.3, 284.24, 317.17, 370.37, 382.31, 410.7, 433.32, 521.28, 526.2, and 526.3.

46.39 Neither the AMS nor the A version of lines 46.39–47.6 is satisfactory. The present edition attempts in this and the next emendation to carry through to completion the manuscript revision Cooper initiated by dividing the original sentence in two after "thoughts."

47.3 See Textual Note at 46.39.

49.25 The Cooper Edition takes the author's "is" for an incomplete "its," and supplies this reading to parallel the "its" at 49.23. Putnam makes the same revision.

52.20 See Textual Note at 44.39.

55.38 The present edition accepts the verb form supplied here by A to emend the obvious defect in AMS.

67.1 The present edition accepts the second pronoun supplied here by A to emend the obvious defect in AMS.

67.12 The conjunction is supplied here by A in order to remedy an obvious oversight in the manuscript.

82.31 The emendation away from dialect is accepted here because Hutter does not generally use dialect; Cooper himself in AMS occasionally normalizes dialect accidentally given to him. Similar emendations are accepted at 82.34, 83.31, and 85.28.

82.34 See Textual Note at 82.31.

82.38 See Textual Note at 44.39.

83.31 See Textual Note at 82.31.

85.28 See Textual Note at 82.31.

89.20 Cooper cancelled the "and" but before the inkstroke dried, the line was blurred. The present edition believes his intent was to eliminate the conjunction.

99.14 The adjective was deleted in AMS but then reinstated by Cooper's underlining it with a broken dotted line.

101.22 Cooper's revisions of this word in AMS at 257.13 and elsewhere indicate his preference for the "ar'n'd" form.

101.38 The interpolation of the adverb was probably overlooked by the compositor.

111.19 See Textual Note at 44.39.

117.24 The AMS "a" is taken by CE as Cooper's intending "as."

123.29 Here CE follows AMS conjunction but accepts B dialect spelling.

125.17 Cooper originally wrote "or a" in AMS, then cancelled the "or." To maintain the series of contrasts here, the present edition reinstates the cancelled "or."

126.28 AMS originally read "reflections, however,"; Cooper deleted the adverb and terminal comma but not the internal comma. CE executes his final intention by removing the other comma in the cancelled passage.

130.10 Cooper clearly interpolated "before the door, Hurry's door-yard" above "platform," but the resulting expression is awkward and obscure. Thus the present edition has deleted this cumbersome qualification.

133.21 The present edition, for the sake of clarity, here emends to Cooper's usual form for the word.

137.15 Cooper wrote "your father and Hutter," clearly intending "your father and Hurry" as at 137.32.

143.23 AMS first read "imaginations of the three in the castle," but all except "imaginations" was deleted by Cooper. The present edition therefore follows A in using the singular noun.

143.26 The verb is compressed into the right margin; "chance" is a possible reading, but "choose" is more likely given that the party is under Huron scrutiny.

147.37 Cooper wrote "the helmsman" over "Natty," but failed to delete "Natty," which is at the extreme bottom of the page. Though "The helmsman Natty" is a possible reading, in light of Cooper's rarely using "Natty" elsewhere to designate his hero, the present edition follows A in deleting the name.

149.16 Cooper apparently began the word "describing" but then altered it to what appears to be "writing," though the reshaping of the first three letters is imperfect.

149.29 In revising, Cooper began a new sentence here with "He," but the deletion of the previous "and" is ambiguous.

152.20 Cooper's preference for "Mingos" is established at 382.22 and elsewhere because here in revising he deleted the "e."

152.21 See Textual Note at 44.39.

152.28 The words "are all" are deleted in AMS, but not replaced; though they are not so marked by broken underlining, Cooper must have intended them to be restored.

162.35 See Textual Note at 101.22.

171.6 The present edition follows Cooper's apparent intention in this passage where in AMS the phrase "on one hand" and the preposition in the phrase "by the acclivity" are encircled to be moved to the beginning of the sentence. Cooper circled "by" accidentally; CE follows Cooper's A word order without accepting the non-authorial comma.

173.20 The sophistication in A of the comma to semi-colon probably led Cooper to delete the now-superfluous "but" in B. However, the present edition follows the clearer form of AMS.

174.37 In AMS "women" is written directly above "sex," probably with the intention of replacing it, but "sex" is not deleted.

177.36 Cooper apparently pluralized this form in the Putnam edition to make it parallel with the misreading "mountains" in A. Since CE follows the AMS singular "mountain," it rejects the spuriously pluralized "valleys."

179.22 CE here follows the A deletion of the AMS clause, but deletes the comma between subject and verb, which Cooper failed to delete in his revision of proof.

186.35 The word here is revised and smudged; "them" is the likeliest reading but "these" possible.

193.10 In AMS Cooper underlined the first three letters twice, probably intending by double italicization to stress Hetty's notion of goodness.

199.5 Originally Cooper wrote "sweeter, too," then deleted the adverb and interpolated "than old chest." The present edition deletes the unneeded comma to make this phrase parallel to the preceding one.

202.9 See Textual Note at 101.22.

202.10 See Textual Note at 44.39.

207.11 Cooper first wrote, "Yes, 'tis so," but then deleted "yes" and "so" when altering the construction. However, he did not cancel the " 'tis," but capitalized it to begin the sentence. The compositor mistakenly ignored "Tis," here restored.

208.8 In AMS "next" is partly deleted by a line drawn near its base. Cooper had deleted "next" five words earlier and replaced it with "adjoining"; probably in rereading the passage, he noticed the repetition and partly deleted the second "next" as well as replacing the first. The present edition therefore accepts "was next" as Cooper's intention for the passage.

210.35 AMS originally read "These," but Cooper wrote a terminal "y" over "se."

216.33 "So" clearly is capitalized in the AMS, and Cooper intended it to begin a new sentence. However, the previous sentence ends with a comma, not a full stop. Because the sentence beginning with "So" is long, the present edition has separated it by a full stop from the previous sentence.

217.21 See Textual Note at 44.39.

222.14 A printer's mark in AMS is superimposed after "had," obliterating a possible authorial comma.

241.6 The phrase "in any future collision between them" is interpolated without terminal punctuation; the present edition supplies a comma to clarify the construction.

246.20 The present edition here emends to the required passive form to clarify the passage.

250.30 See Textual Note at 44.39.

252.2 See Textual Note at 44.39.

254.12 In AMS the contrasting phrase "while its gathering gloom was in as singular unison with" is interpolated without terminal punctuation. The A compositor solved the resulting crux by ignoring Cooper's blotted "to" before "while" and placing a comma after "unison." The present edition, believing Cooper intended the contrasting phrases to be introduced by "contrast to" and "unison with," adds the comma after "with."

254.26 Cooper deleted a second adjective before "monitor" but failed to remove the comma after the first. See also Textual Note at 44.39.

258.16 In revision Cooper deleted "and" after "earth," replacing it with what appears to be a colon, and capitalized "one." For clarity, the present edition, however, here follows the more common grammatical form of A.

260.29 AMS clearly reads "winds," but the compositor set "wind," perhaps because Cooper's verb is singular. However, Cooper's intention throughout is to pluralize the noun forms referring to the wind, so the present edition has altered the AMS verb to agree with the AMS "winds."

262.1 The A compositor misread Cooper's interlineation, cramped as it was in the margin. The present edition supplies the comma after the last word of Deerslayer's speech.

265.3 See Textual Note at 44.39.

280.25 Cooper cancelled the first two letters of "and" and capitalized the following "the," but the resulting structure results in a sentence fragment. The present edition therefore follows the A compositor in restoring the "and."

283.37 In AMS Cooper first wrote "the original," then replaced the noun only with "an animal so extraordin[ay?]." The present edition follows A in deleting the superfluous article.

284.24 See Textual Note at 44.39.

285.18 Cooper here wrote "so" above an imperfectly-deleted "too"; the compositor failed to see the cancellation.

298.29 The compositor apparently overlooked Cooper's light cancellation of the adjective in AMS.

299.6 Cooper altered "his" to "the" in AMS, but the compositor apparently failed to observe the change.

305.17 Cooper here may have tried to alter "I had" to "I'd," but if so the alteration is indeterminate, for the "ad" is not stricken out. "I had" seems more appropriate to Hetty's usual formal language, and is thus retained.

306.9 In AMS Cooper originally wrote "They'd said" but altered "said" to "had told." CE follows Natty's colloquial usage as in A, and rejects the sophisticated form of B.

312.38 Cooper altered "feel" to "feet" in AMS, but the compositor apparently overlooked the alteration.

314.12 No punctuation is visible after the noun, which is written in the extreme right margin of the sheet. The present edition has thus supplied a comma, which seems consonant with the sense and grammar of the passage.

317.17 See Textual Note at 44.39.

329.12 Cooper originally began the sentence "Although Hist anxiously, but timidly," but cancelled "anxiously, but." He did not, however, delete the comma after "timidly" which the new construction rendered superfluous.

332.39 In AMS "dock" appears at the extreme right of the sheet; the only punctuation visible is the first single quote. The present edition thus executes Cooper's intention of placing the word in quotation marks, and adds the terminal punctuation.

338.30 Cooper originally wrote "or an" but struck out the "or," a deletion the compositor apparently ignored.

343.24 Cooper appears not to have deleted the relative pronoun here following the deletion of "It was" in B. The present edition thus makes the necessary deletion.

345.33 In AMS "to be" is interpolated after "seemed" but without a caret; the compositor appears to have overlooked the interpolation.

350.25 The A compositor either misread Cooper's "exerted" as "excited," or himself altered Cooper's text to avoid contiguous repetition after "commence her exertions." In either case, the A alteration of the verb prevented Cooper from making his own emendation to eliminate the repetition. The present edition has thus emended the A verb to a form which captures Cooper's meaning while eliminating the repetition.

362.1 Cooper clearly refers to a ship here; for clarity the present edition places its name in single quotation marks.

362.17 The AMS reading is indeterminate; either "timid" or "tired" is possible. But since timidity is not in Hurry's character, "tired," the A reading, seems more appropriate, and probably is Cooper's intention.

369.24 The adjective occurs at the extreme right side of the leaf, and no punctuation is visible after it. The present edition follows A in separating the word from the ensuing speech by a dash.

370.37 See Textual Note at 44.39.

376.11 A tear on the left side of the sheet destroyed the first letter of the word, probably "will."

377.4 The manuscript clearly says "county," but this usage would have been anachronistic for a wilderness area; the emendation is probably Cooper's.

381.8 A heavily-inked printer's mark obscures what punctuation, if any, followed "point" in AMS. For clarity the present edition follows B in punctuating the passage thus.

382.31 See Textual Note at 44.39.

390.16 The word here is very hard to make out—the singular is likely, but the plural is possible.

391.28 The missing noun is supplied here by A to remedy an obvious oversight in the manuscript.

405.23 Cooper first wrote: "The woods are but the ears of the Almighty, the air is his breath, and the light of the sun is little more than a glance of his eye." In manuscript alterations, Cooper apparently misread "woods" as "words," and thus altered "but" to "said to"; the A compositor furthered the sophistication by altering Cooper's comma after "Almighty" to a period. Since Cooper's original metaphoric meaning and syntax are superior to his misguided revision, the present edition has restored the original reading.

410.7 See Textual Note at 44.39.

412.31 Cooper replaced the phrase "sad history" with "melancholy revelations," but neglected to change "this" to the plural form. CE preserves Cooper's final intention for the phrase by rejecting A's alteration of the noun to the singular.

425.11 Cooper first wrote "a sunshiny," and then converted the adjective to noun by crossing out the stem of the "y" and placing an "e" over the upper part. In changing the construction, he and subsequent editions failed to drop the now-superfluous article.

428.7 Cooper first wrote "Hist sat," then added "was" above "sat" without deleting the first verb. The present edition follows A in accepting the revised verb as his final intention.

433.32 See Textual Note at 44.39.

434.40 What appears to have been "means" in AMS has been lightly traced over so that it appeared to the A compositor to read "mean." CE agrees with B that Cooper intended "means."

441.22 The A reading is a likely compositorial sophistication, based on the A misreading of "nature" for Cooper's "creature."

441.34 The missing pronoun is supplied by A to remedy the oversight in the manuscript.

442.21 The missing pronoun is supplied by A to remedy the oversight in the manuscript.

449.2 The sentence at 449.23–25 clarifies Judith's and Cooper's meaning: Hetty's presence at the camp may help Deerslayer. Deerslayer understands Judith's intent, and comments here upon the possible help the "feeble-mind" may be to him in the Huron camp.

451.4 The relative pronoun was supplied by A to remedy the oversight in the manuscript.

461.32 Here and in the next entry the present edition supplies single quotes where Cooper used double quotes.

483.34 The missing verb is supplied by A to remedy an oversight in the manuscript.

485.30 AMS looks like "thrust," but the last two letters are unclear; "thrown," however, is clearly not the reading.

485.32 The change from plural to singular pronoun in this and the next two emendations carries out Cooper's intention at 485.32 where in AMS the phrase "and the girl who had been killed the previous" is deleted after "Panther."

499.3 Cooper originally wrote "who either affected to—," indicating he intended to begin an infinitive construction parallel with "was actually unable to." However, the first "to" was cancelled in the manuscript. To restore the intended parallel construction and clarify the passage, the present edition adds the comma after "unable."

499.29 The sense of the passage here obviously calls for the opposite of what Cooper wrote, an error undetected in either A or B.

503.21 The period is questionable here in the manuscript, but A clearly misreads the passage and alters Cooper's meaning.

514.23 The present edition follows A in supplying the missing noun.

521.28 See Textual Note at 44.39.

526.2 See Textual Note at 44.39.

526.3 See Textual Note at 44.39.

540.19 The present edition follows A in supplying the verb missing here in the manuscript.

545.21 The manuscript reading is difficult, but the A version can be dismissed safely. The present reading accords with the configuration of strokes in the manuscript and with the sense of Judith's "undue [i.e., excessive] erring" expressed in the two concluding paragraphs of the novel.

Emendations

The following list records all changes introduced into the copy-text. The reading of the Cooper Edition appears to the left of the square bracket. The source for that reading appears to the right of the bracket, followed by a semicolon, the copy-text reading, and the copy-text symbol. If not listed, the readings of texts which fall between the copy-text and the source cited for the reading of the Cooper Edition may be presumed to agree substantively with the copy-text reading. If an intervening reading does not agree substantively with the copy-text, that intervening reading and its symbol are recorded after the copy-text reading and symbol.

Several conventions and sigla appear in the Emendations list of *The Deerslayer* for the reader's convenience and information. Within an entry, the curved dash ~ represents the exact word that appears before the square bracket and is used in recording punctuation and paragraphing variants. A caret ʌ to the right of the square bracket signals the absence of a mark of punctuation on the left. An asterisk * indicates that the reading is discussed in the Textual Notes. A dagger † preceding the entry indicates that the incorrect or anomalous reading in the manuscript copy-text was caused by Cooper's jamming his script closely against the left or right margin of the leaf; while the degree sign ° indicates those incorrect or anomalous readings in the manuscript copy-text caused by Cooper's alterations of it. The abbreviation CE identifies emendations initiated by the Cooper Edition. When identical emendations occur more than once, they are listed in a single entry located at the initial reading.

The following texts are referred to:

AMS Author's manuscript—used as printer's copy for the first American edition
PR Proof sheets of the 1841 "Preface"
CPR Cooper's holograph revisions of the "Preface" proof sheets
A Philadelphia: Lea & Blanchard, 1841
B New York: G. P. Putnam, 1850

Title Page Gray, *The Bard*, 11. 60–62.] CE; [*omitted*] A
1.5 works would] PR; works, would, on its face, AMS

1.7	may] PR; might AMS
1.7	it an act, of itself, that ought] PR; ought, of itself, AMS
1.12	has] PR; have AMS
1.13	necessity] PR; ncessity AMS
1.18	something like a] PR; a AMS
1.21	it.] PR; ∼ʌ AMS
1.22	should it decide] CPR; that should it come to the decision AMS; that should it decide PR
1.26	manuscript] PR; manscript AMS
1.27	labors] CE; labor AMS; labour PR; labours CPR
°2.6	it.] PR; ∼ʌ AMS
2.11	easily] PR; asily AMS
2.12	region] PR; spot AMS
2.21-22	the writer] PR; he AMS
2.25	been now] PR; here been AMS
2.29	novel-readers] CPR; human beings AMS; novel ʌ readers PR
2.35	persons] PR; readers AMS
2.38	than] PR; that AMS
3.3-5	works . . . . fiction] CPR; all works of the imagination backwards AMS; works . . . fact: such a plan . . . fiction PR
3.15	its author sincere gratification] PR; since gratification to the author AMS
5.10	"The Pioneers,"] CE; the Pioneers, B
5.17	"The Prairie,"] CE; the Prairie, B
6.2	1823] CE; 1822 B
6.3	eighteen] CE; nineteen B
11.4	"The Deerslayer"] CE; ∼∼ B
15.11	Byron, *Childe Harold's Pilgrimage*, IV.clxxviii] CE; Childe Harold AMS
15.35	otherwise] A; othewise AMS
15.35	a few] A; A few AMS
15.37	desire] A; esire AMS
16.6	branch* [*footnote*] *It is . . . family. [1850] B; branch ʌ AMS
16.6	Rensselaers] A; Rensselears AMS
16.20	Schoharie] A; Schorarie AMS. *Also emended at* 73.6 *and* 73.27.
16.26	Mississippi] A; Mississipi AMS
*16.28	sea,] A; ∼ʌ AMS
†16.30	solitude,] A; ∼ʌ AMS
16.30	design] A; wish AMS
17.1	harvest] A; harest AMS
†17.8	each] A; ch AMS
17.15	man of gigantic mould] B; man AMS
17.16	labyrinth] A; labarynth AMS
17.18	those] A; that AMS
20.6	hours'] A; hours AMS
20.10	men] A; two AMS
20.10	each] B; both AMS

20.10	is] B; are AMS
20.11	insignificant] A; insignifcant AMS
20.11	part] B; parts AMS
*20.14	Henry] A; Harry AMS
20.29	physique] A; phyique AMS
21.15	arrangements] A; arrangments AMS. *Also emended at* 140.19, 142.11, 200.15, *and* 448.15.
21.15	particularly] A; particularily AMS. *Also emended at* 45.21, 154.11, 234.27, 251.32, 260.26, 273.9, 315.24-25, 325.4, 325.32, 333.6, 336.12, 344.25-26, 424.31, 495.20, 498.22, *and* 498.27-28.
*21.23	careless,] A; ∼ₐ AMS
21.23	felt] A; manifested AMS
21.24	for] A; of AMS
21.24	accessories] A; accessaries AMS
21.38	comply] A; do as bid. AMS
†21.38	Delawares] A; Delaw[re?] AMS
22.7	vagabonds,] A; ∼ₐ AMS
22.7	Mingos,] A; ∼ₐ AMS
22.12	misconstruct] B; misconceive AMS
22.14	the proper time to strike comes] A; it is a proper time to strike AMS
†22.18	would] A; woul AMS
22.24	ingenuous] A; igenuous AMS
22.28-29	seeing that] A; for AMS
22.30-31	hold it to be onlawful] A; do not hold it to be lawful AMS
22.31	ginerous] A; lawful AMS
22.38	not] A; now, AMS
22.39	any] A; no AMS
23.1	them] A; that AMS
23.7	character] B; conscience AMS
23.29	Hurry] A; Hury AMS. *Also emended at* 29.18, 34.38, 41.40, 43.39, 53.14, 56.33, 61.35, 62.24, 84.6, 85.19, 163.35, 235.25, 251.27, 361.8, 371.36, 390.40, 394.37 *and* 404.38.
23.32	years'] A; years AMS
†23.32	possession,] A; ∼ₐ AMS/.
23.37	the land they own] B; 'em AMS
24.11	men's human natur'] A; men's human AMS
24.25	don't] A; dont AMS. *Also emended at* 54.22, 67.16, 256.39, 306.15, 385.15, *and* 487.32.
24.26-27	matters] A; consaits AMS
25.6	Judith] A; Hetty AMS
25.16	Judith] A; Hetty AMS
25.25	Judith] A; Jude AMS. *Also emended at* 27.22, 27.25, 28.3 *and* 28.14.
26.19	insartainty] B; unsartainty A
26.33	cussing] B; cursing A

27.10	not] B; never A
27.22-23	Hutter are in question] A͂; Hutter, are the parties AMS
27.24	thee,] A; ∼ʌ AMS
27.26	'compass] A; "∼ AMS. *Also emended at* 27.29 *and* 28.2.
27.27	us.' "] A; ∼." AMS
27.29	us, '] A; ∼," AMS
27.31	Compass] A; compass AMS
27.34	on one] A; one one AMS
27.38	gifted] A; situated AMS
28.2	us '] A; ∼" AMS
28.2-3	I have told you] A; the officers call it AMS
28.10	It's] A; Its AMS
28.13	if] A; of AMS
28.13	months!" A; ∼!ʌ AMS
28.19	hussy] A; huss[ey?] AMS
28.24	found] A; had found AMS
28.25	inimy] B; enemy AMS
28.34	enough] A; that which would AMS
28.34	to put] A; put AMS
28.39	you] A; thee AMS
†29.4	menaced] A; menced AMS
29.4	Nor] A; No[w?] AMS
29.5	jocularly] A; jocularily AMS
29.5	giant's] A; giants AMS
29.6	much more] A; more AMS
29.7	would] A; would really AMS
†29.17	resolution.] A; ∼ʌ AMS
29.23	gal] A; girl AMS
29.34	fri'nd] A; friend AMS. *Also emended at* 30.39, 34.5, 139.27, 139.27 *and* 434.29.
29.36	minded,] A; ∼ʌ AMS
†30.5	which] A; whi[c] AMS
†30.15	themselves.] A; ∼ʌ AMS
30.20	Judith] A; Judy AMS
30.22	cur'osity] A; curiosity AMS
30.29	be] B; are AMS
30.31	that] A; this AMS
30.32-33	trappers, and] A; ∼, & AMS
30.36	feelin's] A; feelings AMS
30.40	only justice] A; injustice AMS
31.1	being] A; being as AMS
31.3	but] A; and AMS
†31.3	turn] A; tu[rn?] AMS
31.3	a'ternoon's] B; afternoon's AMS
31.7	collected; then] A; collected, AMS
31.8	packs,] A; packs and AMS

32.6	Mrs. Hemans, "Edith. A Tale of the Woods," 11. 191–94] CE; Records of Woman AMS
32.16	usually] A; ever AMS
32.17	especially in] A; in AMS
32.24–25	exper'enced] A; experienced AMS
32.30	by forties] A; fortys AMS
32.30	fifties] A; fiftys AMS
32.36	are others] A; and more AMS
33.3	a'ter] B; after AMS. *Also emended at* 38.9, 54.20, 126.18, 138.26, 138.35, 144.3, 229.16, 328.28, 397.37, 402.21, 433.12, 447.17, 486.2, 486.34 *and* 540.12.
†33.3	all!"]A; ~!ʌ AMS
33.11	bend by its weight] A; bend, in that manner AMS
33.25	Uncas,* [*footnote*] *Last . . . Mohicans. [1850]] B; Uncas, ʌ AMS
33.36	obeyed] A; obyed AMS
33.36	some things] A; somethings AMS
34.14	this] A; here AMS
34.15	come] A; came AMS
†34.20	weight.] A; weigh[t?]ʌ AMS
34.21	brethren] A; bretheren AMS
34.25	destroys] A; destrys AMS
34.36	regularly] A; regularily AMS. *Also emended at* 183.9 *and* 189.33.
°34.40	attract] A; ~, AMS
35.11	men] A; two AMS. *Also emended at* 37.25 *and* 61.4.
35.13	or to] A; or AMS
†35.15	half] A; [h?] alf AMS
35.17	from] A; out of AMS
35.18	exclamation] A; exlamation AMS
†35.19	thoughtful] A; houghtful AMS
35.21	unexpectedly] A; unexpectedy AMS
35.23	broad sheet] A; sheet AMS
35.23	so] A; that was so AMS
†35.28	distance] A; distanc AMS
35.36	served] A; se[re?] d AMS
35.40	all sides] A; every side AMS
36.5	edge,] A; ~ʌ AMS
36.6	vegetation] A; vegitation AMS
36.6	were] A; was AMS
36.10	quivering] A; quivirg AMS
36.25	mention] A; have mentioned AMS
36.29	know'd] A; knowed AMS
36.35	ag'in] A; again AMS
36.37	the water] A; water AMS
36.39	himself,] A; ~ʌ AMS

36.40	character] A; charater AMS
37.9	was] B; were AMS
37.16	mine,] A; mine off AMS
†37.18	which] A; whic AMS
†37.23	paddles,] A; paddl[e?] AMS
37.26	looked] A; look AMS
37.29	changes] A; changs AMS
38.2	not being on] A; being on no AMS
38.3	I] B; but I AMS
38.18	raillery.] A; ∼∧ AMS
38.20	greatly] A; much AMS
38.22	pulls] A; pull AMS
†38.27	thought.] A; ∼∧ AMS
38.28	Why, they come and go] A; They come, and they go AMS
39.12	castle,"] A; ∼', AMS
39.12	familiarly] A; familiarily AMS. *Also emended at* 69.36 *and* 260.34.
39.23	northern] A; northen AMS
40.6	creature] A; creatures AMS
40.10	manifested] A; discovered AMS
40.23	contrivance] A; contrivances AMS
40.24	scarfing] A; halving AMS
40.25	similarly] A; similarily AMS. *Also emended at* 344.33, 345.11 *and* 347.14.
40.28	arrangement] A; arrangment AMS. *Also emended at* 64.26, 65.22, 207.6, 210.25–26, 251.4–5, 259.40, 270.13, 274.35–36, 283.13, 309.10, 333.26, 364.3, 364.21 *and* 473.8.
40.31	only] A; ∼, AMS
40.39–40	a stiff clay,] A; brick-clay ∧ AMS
41.3	had been] A; was AMS
41.4	was kindled] A; had been kindled AMS
41.12	"and] A; ∧∼ AMS
41.14	altogether] A; alltogether AMS
41.20–21	sweetheart's] A; sweethearts AMS
41.23	gang] A; party AMS
41.31	Hutter's] A; Hutters AMS
41.39	observed] A; obsered AMS
42.2	'castle court,'] A; "∼∼," AMS
42.5	v'y'ge] A; v'yge AMS
†42.10	trained] A; train[e] AMS
†42.15	kitchen.] A; ∼∧ AMS
42.25	day. There . . . chest.] A; day. AMS
42.36	nearly to] A; to nearly AMS
42.37	only] A; but AMS
43.8	those days] A; that day AMS
43.11	owner's arms] A; arms AMS
43.13	would] A; would would AMS

43.13	credit] A; cred[i]t AMS
43.24	spot] A; room AMS
43.39	coolly] A; cooly AMS. *Also emended at* 128.23, 195.18, 231.9, 257.19 *and* 495.20.
43.40	borderer's] A; border[ers] AMS
44.1	you're] A; your'e AMS. *Also emended at* 53.26, 89.25, 111.1, 118.14, 120.5 (twice) *and* 216.11.
44.17–18	out-of-the-way] A; oncommon AMS
44.19	out-of-the-way] A; oncommon AMS
44.19	not quarrelsome] A; onquarrelsome AMS
44.27	show the flint] A; be a man AMS
44.35	definition] A; accurate definition AMS
44.36	hunter] A; hunter, at the moment AMS
*44.39	governor's] CE; governors AMS; Governor's A-B
45.3	name.] A; ∼∧ AMS
45.9	know'd] A; knowed AMS
45.14	afore] A; before AMS. *Also emended at* 81.31, 126.13, 225.27, 297.19 *and* 455.8.
45.18	and] A; but AMS
45.25	were] CE; was AMS
45.25	moreover] A; more over AMS
46.7	Glimmerglass, '] A; ∼," AMS
46.16	nat'rally] A; natrally AMS
46.21	sound.] A; ∼∧ AMS
46.22	would be] A; would AMS
46.32	the points thrusting] A; whle the points thrust AMS
*46.39	He] CE; If he AMS
*47.3	either] CE; neither AMS
48.6	gored.]A; ∼∧ AMS
48.7	*As You Like It*, II.i.21–25] CE; Shakspeare AMS
48.15	indifferent] A; in different AMS
48.24	burrow] A; burow AMS
48.33	later] B; late AMS
48.35	them,] A; ∼; AMS
49.5	thorough] A; real AMS
49.10	pale-faces] A; pale-face AMS
49.19	singularly] A; singularily AMS. *Also emended at* 63.10, 66.39, 325.33, 452.4, 452.5, 466.1 *and* 528.7.
*49.25	its] CE; is AMS; his A
49.28	a fair] A; as fair a AMS
49.30	youth.] A; youth, as one may ever hope to meet." AMS
49.31	more than half] A; pretty near a AMS
50.11	feelin's] A; dispositon AMS
50.15	vartue] A; v[e?]rtue AMS
50.23	very Colony] A; Colony, itself, AMS
50.32	laws] A; situation AMS
°50.37	have] A; ∼, AMS

50.38	as] A; a AMS
51.33	enabling him to play] A; playing AMS
51.35	notwithstanding] A; not withstanding AMS
52.4	next to steer] A; he ought to steer next AMS
52.12	this outlet?] A; the outlet; AMS
52.13–14	a river like the] A; the AMS
52.17	atween] A; between AMS
*52.20	' 'Rat's Cove',] CE; ' 'rat's cove', AMS; 'Rat's Cove,' A-B
52.21	Cove] A; cove AMS
52.23	point,] A; ~ʌ AMS
52.24	Cove"] CE; cove' AMS; Cove," A-B
52.26–27	he found it convenient] A; it was convenient to him AMS
52.29	Hurry,] A; ~, " AMS
52.31–32	Canada man] B; Canadian AMS
52.33	Hutter] A; Hutter's AMS
52.34	scent] A; [sc?] ent AMS
53.12	ricommend] A; recommend AMS
53.21	reckless] A; reckless by nature AMS
53.21	manifest physical] A; physical AMS
53.25	cross his mind] A; be introduced AMS
54.5	though] A; while AMS
54.17	which I] A; as I AMS
54.29	frontier] A; man AMS
54.37	disapp'intment] A; disappointment AMS
54.38	*you*] A; you AMS
55.4	breathin'] A; breathing AMS
55.6	answered] A; returned AMS
55.7	turning] A; looking AMS
55.11	p'int] A; point AMS
55.16	a mile] A; mile AMS
55.17	valley] A; vally AMS
55.20	eyes] A; eyes, even AMS
55.30	minutes] A; minuts AMS
*55.38	all lay] A; all AMS
56.1	Hurry Harry] A; Harry Hurry AMS. *Also emended at* 67.1, 67.7, 69.20, 69.26, 72.13, 86.9, 125.20, 131.27, 131.30, 132.31, 155.29–30, 156.1, 156.32, 163.31–32, 168.30, 177.14, 204.23, 204.28, 232.29, 244.16 (*twice*), 267.22, 273.35–36, 296.2, 378.16, 387.13, 395.11, 395.37, 405.8, 410.8, 416.21, 417.39 *and* 423.3.
56.10	the bay] A; it AMS
56.16	but] A; and AMS
56.18	creatur's] A; creatur' AMS
56.27	point.] A; point, or in the same direction as himself ʌ AMS
56.30	after which] A; and then AMS
56.35	interruption of] A; breaking in upon AMS
56.36	weapon] A; rifle AMS

56.37	rifle] A; weapon AMS
56.38	the sudden crack] A; this sudden interruption AMS
57.5	echoes] A; echos AMS
57.9	one or two] A; three or four AMS
57.20	I'll own] A; it's true AMS
57.39	this calm summer weather] A; some times and seasons AMS
†58.2	when] A; whe AMS
58.3	r'ally] A; really AMS
58.5	can] A; can really AMS
58.5-6	hills yet] A; hills AMS
58.7	vartue] A; v[e?]rtue AMS
58.9	arrival] A; presence AMS
58.11	and let] A; by letting AMS
58.11	at hand] A; near by AMS
58.12	we will] A; let us AMS
58.14	spot] A; point AMS
58.15	turned] A; now turned AMS
58.16	sheet. In that direction, the] A; sheet in that direction. The AMS
†58.21	across,] A; ~⌃ AMS
58.22	nearest land] A; land nearest them AMS
58.29	feelin's] B; feelin' AMS; feelins' A
58.40	explite] A; exploit AMS
59.1	The] A; Your AMS
59.6	that it's] A; that 'it's AMS
59.10	Injin] B; Indian AMS. *Also emended at* 71.21, 89.6, 89.7, 89.17, 119.14, 120.9, 120.10, 120.28, 123.8, 123.29, 126.11, 126.19, 138.29, 139.8, 146.1, 192.1, 192.36, 195.17, 225.4, 225.9, 255.40, 256.33, 331.16, 386.19, 386.31 (*twice*), 392.5, 405.14, 455.1, 487.27, 515.4, 515.5, *and* 515.13.
59.13	such scruples] A; consideration AMS
59.13	nothing but] A; but AMS
59.15	to be quite as] A; as being as much AMS
59.30	Injins] B; Indians AMS. *Also emended at* 88.3, 182.7, 306.5, 410.24-25 *and* 472.36.
59.38	all well] A; well AMS
60.20	aquatic] A; acquatic AMS
†60.22	hearty] A; heaty AMS
60.24	undertake] B; attempt AMS
60.31	as a little singular] A; with some little surprise AMS
60.33	matter of doubt] A; question AMS
60.35	spot] A; spot where it occurred AMS
61.1	chin] A; nose AMS
61.5	rock] A; rock in question AMS
61.8	incessant washing] A; washing AMS
61.9	had so] A; had AMS
61.9	that] A; in such a way that AMS

61.11-12	past, that this rock] A; past it, that it AMS
61.18	Glimmerglass.] A; ∼ʌ AMS
61.19	described] A; describe AMS
61.35	and-bush,] A; ∼; AMS
62.1	appears] A; seems AMS
62.5	adventurers] A; adventures AMS. *Also emended at 275.26 and 403.11.*
62.17	however,] A; ∼ʌ AMS
62.31	spring] A; sping AMS
62.39	wherever] A; ∼, AMS
63.3	canoe] A; canoes AMS
63.7	society] A; company AMS
63.9	company] A; society AMS
63.12	Its] A; ∼' AMS
63.17	mirthful] A; laughing AMS
†63.18	indifference.] A; ∼ʌ AMS
63.19	surprise] A; surprise to both the men AMS
63.20	the men] A; they AMS
64.7	Bryant, "An Indian Story," 11. 11-15] CE; Bryant AMS
64.10	buoyant] A; bouyant AMS
64.10	vessel] A; abode AMS
64.18	though more rudely] A; rudely AMS
64.19	than] A; and of less length than AMS
64.23	cabin] A; interior AMS
64.33	fairly] A; usually AMS
65.15	discovery] A; effect of the discovery AMS
65.15	produced very different effects] A; was very different AMS
65.16-17	As . . . board] A; Hurry leaped on board, as soon as the canoe could be got round to the proper opening AMS
65.25	could] A; could not AMS
65.26	Hutter's contrivances] A; a forest artifice AMS
65.29	occur to] A; attract the attention of AMS
65.37	coarse] A; course AMS
66.4	intellect] A; reason AMS
66.7	tenderness] A; consideration AMS
66.14	discriminate] A; discrimiate AMS
66.27-28	a deep and lasting] A; an AMS
66.28	girl] A; girl that surprised themselves AMS
66.31	that it . . . unsuspecting] A; as almost to seem to share in the unsuspicious AMS
*67.1	her he] A; her AMS
67.4	nature, aided by some education,] A; nature more than education AMS
67.5	tone and] A; tone, or modes of AMS
*67.12	and I] A; I AMS
67.12	*your*] A; your AMS
67.21	has] A; had AMS
67.22	has] A; have AMS

67.24	councillings] A; consultations AMS
67.30	your] A; you AMS
68.16	bumped] A; thump'd AMS
69.3	'Deerslayer] A; "∼ AMS
69.12	last name] A; last AMS
69.23	little] A; little with excitement AMS
69.25	impulses] A; impulses that she proved AMS
70.11	gin'ral] A; gen'ral AMS
70.12	with having] A; with AMS
70.17	Deerslayer] A; Deerslayer, as he spoke AMS
70.30	count] A; 'count AMS
71.4	she] A; both AMS
71.4	her] B; their AMS
71.10	females, and −] A; females . AMS
71.14	very moment] A; moment AMS
71.36	man] A; feet AMS
72.2	place] A; spot AMS
72.5	other] A; ∼. AMS
72.15	has never been] A; was never seen AMS
72.17–18	hesitating . . . feelings] A; hesitating to betray their feelings on the score of delicacy AMS
†72.19	that] A; tha AMS
72.25	know] A; l'arn AMS
72.37	your way] A; you way AMS
73.28	ha'nts] B; h'ants AMS
†73.34	howsever] CE; howseve AMS; however A-B
74.1	foes,] A; ∼. AMS
74.11	on the opposite] A; in the woods of the opposite AMS
74.11	narrow and sinuous] A; narrow AMS
74.21	occasion."] A; ∼.ʌ AMS
74.23	can't] A; can AMS
74.24	square,] A; square, by all accounts AMS
74.30	could] A; would AMS
75.8	enemy] A; inimy AMS
75.28	*we*] B; we AMS
75.28	aim] A; fire AMS
76.7	into] A; into into AMS
76.13	through] A; Th[ou?]gh AMS
76.32	descended] A; desended AMS
†76.33	stones] A; stone[s?] AMS
†77.1	would] A; woul AMS
77.7	stream] A; steam AMS
77.10	sailor] A; sail[e?]r AMS
77.19	none] B; neither AMS
77.33	them] A; it AMS
77.33	won't] A; wont AMS. *Also emended at* 111.8, 179.7, 255.4, 385.7 *and* 403.40.
77.34	their] A; its AMS

78.12	rushing literally] A; literally rushing AMS
78.20	inexperienced] A; inxperienced AMS
78.26	each] A; all AMS
†78.30	branches] A; branche AMS
78.31	apprehended] A; apprehend AMS
78.36	belonged] A; belonging AMS
79.3	seemed] A; seem AMS
79.5	Perceiving] A; Percieving AMS
79.14	he was] A; it AMS
79.14	and] A; him, and AMS
79.21	sway; Judith looked] A; sway, Judith looking AMS
79.22	and the] A; the AMS
79.23	softened] A; softening AMS
80.2	from the shore] A; out AMS
80.3	any further] A; the AMS
81.6	*Hamlet*, III.ii. 271–74] CE; Shakspeare AMS
81.12	be sure] A; make certain AMS
†81.13	accomplishing] A; accomplising AMS
81.13	own destruction] A; object AMS
81.23	afloat,] A; ~. AMS
81.27	them,] A; ~ʌ AMS
82.3	pull.] A; ~, AMS
82.17	find]A; give AMS
82.19	We're] A; Wer'e AMS
82.26	girls] A; gals AMS
82.28	times] A; time AMS
*82.31	however] A; howsever AMS
82.32	peaceable] A; peacable AMS
82.33	woods] A; wods AMS
*82.34	serious] A; ser'ous AMS
*82.38	accordin'] CE; according AMS; Accordin' A
83.7	circumstances.] A; ~ʌ AMS
83.16	well; I]A; I AMS
83.19	understood] A; ~, AMS
83.21	its] A; his AMS
83.25	rende'vous] A; rendevous AMS
83.29	little,] A; ~ʌ AMS
83.29	its] A; it's AMS
*83.31	daughters] A; darters AMS
84.2	Neither 'old Tom, '] A; Neither, old Tom, AMS
84.22	Judith's] A; Judith' AMS
84.24	Jude] A; Judy AMS
85.9	restlessness] A; restlesness AMS
85.23	the one] B; one AMS
85.24	avarsion] A; aversion AMS

85.25	your] A; you AMS. *Also emended at* 118.36, 126.6, 139.39, 163.18, 289.5, 394.33, 430.27, 442.4, 459.17, *and* 545.4.
*85.28	however] A; howsever AMS
85.30	all his reserve] A; his reserve as respects the subject AMS
85.30–31	a renewed confidence] A; confidence AMS
†85.33	have bargained] CE; hav[e?] bargained AMS; bargained A-B
85.36	I,] A; ∼. AMS
85.39	the canoe] A; the the canoe AMS
86.8	strength."] A; ∼.ʌ AMS
86.23	girls] A; gals AMS
86.23	they're] A; they re AMS
87.6	fellow,] A; ∼ AMS
87.24	do] A; be AMS
87.24	so,] A; ∼; AMS
87.34	occasions] A; occasion AMS
88.9	he compelled] A; and compelling AMS
88.10	when he] A; he AMS
88.13	need] A; will AMS
88.21	Hurry] A; Hurrry AMS
89.2	way] A; lay AMS
89.2	savage] A; savage on AMS
89.8	you're] A; your AMS
89.11	shouted] A; Shouted AMS
89.18	forgiveness] A; forgivness AMS
89.23	put up with] A; submit to AMS
89.25	by] A; boy AMS
89.27	I've] A; Iv'e AMS
89.29	saying,] A; ∼. AMS
89.35–36	marcy. Who . . . muskrat!"] A; marcy. AMS
90.37	her mother] A; a missionary AMS
90.39	classes] A; clases AMS
91.3	through the] A; by that AMS
91.17–18	waft, . . . mile] A; would waft more than a mile, even the lowest modulations of the human voice AMS
91.18–19	Hutter was much] B; Hutter, himself, was AMS
91.30	manner] A; voice AMS
91.32	have] B; will have AMS
91.33	This is] A; You are AMS
92.10	understands] A; knows AMS
92.16–17	human blood] B; blood AMS
92.25	marries,] A; ∼ʌ AMS
92.38	mental] A; physical AMS
93.1	belong] A; be belong AMS
†93.15	these,] A; thes AMS
93.38–39	advantage, Hetty,] A; ∼ʌ∼ʌ AMS
†93.40	sought] A; sough AMS

†94.2	when] A; wh[e?] AMS
94.6	disposed] A; disposesed AMS
94.22	Hetty's] A; Hettys AMS
94.33	Hurry] A; Hutter AMS
95.12	on which] A; which AMS
95.13	dwell] A; dwell on AMS
†95.14	"I thought] A; ∧~~ AMS
95.16	when I]A; when AMS
95.35	created] A; created at once, AMS
95.36	them] A; the two AMS
96.28	associate's] A; assoiate's AMS
96.36	Judith] A; Judy AMS
97.7	Judith,] A; ~∧ AMS
97.31	officer] A; officers AMS
98.2	uncontrollable] A; unconquerable AMS
98.3	a] A; that of AMS
98.5	grasped] A; graped AMS
98.20	situation.] A; ~ — AMS
99.4	*Paradise Lost*, I.125–26] CE; Milton AMS
99.11	was spread] A; spread itself AMS
99.16	degrees] A; degress AMS
99.18	house] A; castle AMS
99.20	solitude] A; solitudes AMS
100.11	than] A; that AMS
†100.16	nothing] A; nothi[ng?] AMS
100.18	me] A; m AMS
100.21	companion's] A; companions AMS
100.21	vein] A; vien AMS
†100.21	and] A; an AMS
101.5	before now] A; myself AMS
101.7	it] A; its AMS
101.10	couldn't] A; did'n't AMS
101.10	*could*]A; *did* AMS
101.13	eye-sight. If] A; eye-sight, and if AMS
101.13–14	castle, therefore] A; castle AMS
*101.22	ar'n'd] CE; ar'r'n'd AMS. *Also emended at* 238.10, 241.33 *and* 242.5.
101.27	crack] A; angry crack AMS
101.27	an angry rifle] A; a rifle AMS
101.30	a Dutch housekeeper] A; one of your Dutch house-keepers AMS
101.37	concerning] A; of AMS
†102.15	which] A; whic AMS
†102.21	where] A; wher AMS
102.21	canoes] B; two canoes AMS
102.23	sound] B; sounds AMS

103.1-2	a gentle . . . audible] A; a sound barely audible, and a gentle motion AMS
103.2	Hurry] A; ~, AMS
103.3	friend's] A; friends AMS
103.13	boat] A; canoe AMS
103.24	great] A; material AMS
103.32	other.] A; ~, AMS
103.37	knowing] A; well knowing AMS
†103.38	southerly] A; southely AMS
103.38	and intending] A; intending AMS
104.2	it] A; this AMS
104.11	trees,] A; ~∧ AMS
104.11	only] A; but AMS
104.16	slip] A; s[1?]ipe AMS
†104.22	directly] A; direc AMS
104.23	hollow] A; fallen AMS
105.2	or] A; and AMS
105.11	that] A; ~, AMS
105.13	named.] A; ~, AMS
105.17-18	as "a] A; 'as' a AMS
105.20	Indians.] A; ~∧ AMS
105.23	used] A; taken AMS
105.33	canoe,] A; canoes AMS
106.1	sogering] B; soldiering AMS
106.10-11	great reluctance and] A; these directions with AMS
†106.15	former] A; for[me?] AMS
†106.17	float]A; floa AMS
†106.19	drift] A; drif AMS
106.19	could] A; would AMS
106.21	might] A; could AMS
106.30	land] A; shore AMS
106.36	suspense] A; a suspense AMS
106.38	would be difficult] A; is not easy AMS
†107.4	conceive] A; conceiv AMS
107.7	senses] A; powers AMS
107.8	at] A; to AMS
107.13	well] A; much AMS
107.19	with] A; to AMS
107.35	passed] A; rolled by AMS
108.6	sounds] A; waters AMS
108.13	they had been left] A; he had left them AMS
108.15	Deerslayer] A; him AMS
†108.20	call] A; cal AMS
108.24	mistaken.] A; ~, AMS
108.32	disregard] A; diregard AMS
108.35	profound] A; double AMS

108.38	female] A; gentler AMS
108.39	attained] A; [ob?]tained AMS
109.5	his] A; all AMS
109.7	were] B; were all AMS
109.18-19	back, as usual,] A; back AMS
109.19	echoes] A; echoes, as usual AMS
†110.8	is'n't] A; is'n AMS
110.13	when] A; and AMS
110.14	forced] A; drew AMS
110.19	*mêlée*] A; mélée AMS
110.25	bodily and] A; evident AMS
†110.27	former's] A; for[mer?] AMS
110.35	depend] A; you may depend AMS
111.5	be] A; be for you AMS
111.6	then] A; to AMS
111.13	same] A; same thing AMS
111.14	enemy] A; enimy AMS
*111.19	T'won't] CE; T'wont AMS; 'T won't A
†111.24	tongue.] A; tongu[e?] AMS
111.26	inimy] A; inemy AMS
111.28	part] A; parts AMS
111.33-34	torture by fire] A; torture AMS
111.35	knows] A; knews AMS
111.35	act] A; act, in common AMS
112.9	sounds] A; sound AMS
†112.13	Deerslayer's] A; Deerslaye' AMS
112.14	himself] A; himself to all appearances AMS
†112.17	woods.] A; wod AMS
112.19	Deerslayer] A; ~, AMS
113.5	hours'] A; hour's AMS
113.15	mild] A; accustomed AMS
113.20	Deerslayer] A; ~, AMS
114.9	Sounds] A; Sound AMS
114.11	Byron, *Childe Harold's Pilgrimage*, III.lxxxv] CE; Byron AMS
114.23	tribe.] A; ~, AMS
114.27	expected distance] A; distance he had expected AMS
114.28	more dangerous] A; worse AMS
114.33	unless] A; lest it were AMS
115.10-11	unnecessary] A; extraordinary AMS
115.17	shore.] A; ~, AMS
115.19	loose] A; lose AMS
115.20	be unencumbered] A; not be encumbered AMS
115.37	tell] A; tell it, AMS
116.3	encouragement] A; encouragment AMS
116.8	behaved] B; conducted AMS
116.15	name] A; has name AMS
116.23	buzz] A; buz AMS

†116.26	bottom of] A; botto f AMS
116.27	followed] A; arose AMS
116.35	swiftly] A; swifly AMS
117.10	irregularly] A; irregularily AMS
†117.12	penetrate] A; penetr AMS
*117.24	as yet] CE; a yet AMS; yet A-B
117.31	aim] A; aim aim AMS
119.4	Manitou] A; Manitow AMS. *Also emended at* 177.21, 225.19, 229.4, 262.17, 301.23, 322.8, 428.18 456.4, *and* 457.39.
119.21	fri'nds] A; friends AMS
119.22	scalp] A; scalps AMS
119.22	t'other] A; 't other AMS
119.24	his] A; with his AMS
120.9	know'd] A; knowed AMS
120.10	ole] B; old AMS
120.18–19	true current] A; current of air AMS
121.3	turn] A; turn with AMS
121.16	where] A; were AMS
121.18	visible.] A; ~; AMS
121.21	instant,] A; ~; AMS
121.21	report.] A; ~, AMS
121.31	charger.] A; ~; AMS
121.31	forty] A; twenty AMS
121.37	"I] A; ʌ I AMS
122.2	too] A; to AMS
122.3	riptyle's] A; reptyle's AMS
122.18	each] A; every AMS
†122.18	as] A; s AMS
†122.24	relieving] A; reieving AMS
†122.25	"No] A; ʌ~ AMS
122.25	red-skin,] A; ~; AMS
†122.26	is not] A; s not AMS
†122.33	found] A; [f?] ound AMS
†122.34	side] A; ide AMS
123.10	take] A; drink AMS
123.17	own lap] A; lap AMS
*123.29	Injin, and,] CE; Indian, and, AMS; Indian; A; Injin; B
123.29	onjust] B; unjust AMS
123.34	ole] B; old AMS
123.38	we] A; they AMS
124.25	for] A; of AMS
124.36	felt,] A; ~ʌ AMS
†125.4	attitude,] A; attitu AMS
125.7	it] A; that it AMS
†125.9	conduct] A; con[du?] AMS
125.10	so great] A; such AMS
*125.17	or a] CE; a AMS

126.4	atween] A; between AMS
126.6	You] A; Your AMS
126.19	know] A; knew AMS
126.21	onsartain] A; unsartain AMS
*126.28	reflections] CE; reflections, AMS; reflection A-B
126.29	sudden] A; suden AMS
127.6-7	so near] B; near AMS
127.12	the day] A; they day AMS
†127.14	time] A; tim AMS
127.28	unless] A; unlss AMS
127.29	may] A; may reasonably AMS
127.36	would have been] A; ought to be AMS
127.38	unseen] A; unseem AMS
128.10	certainly,] A; ∼∧ AMS
†128.36	quickened] A; quickene AMS
128.38	disappeared] B; had disappeared AMS
129.8-9	while steadily pursuing] A; as he steadily pursued AMS
†129.26	hands] A; han AMS
129.34	unchristened] A; unchistened AMS
130.8	might] A; may AMS
*130.10	platform] CE; platform, before the door, Hurry's door-yard AMS
131.6	*Two Gentlemen of Verona*, II.vii.75-78] CE; Shakspeare AMS
131.13	it," answered] A; it." Answered AMS
131.15	tarmination] A; ind on't AMS
131.17	come] A; get AMS
†131.18	manage] A; manag AMS
131.19	two] A; can two AMS
†131.26	defend] A; defe AMS
131.36	which would] A; that would AMS
†132.5-6	feeling.] A; ∼∧ AMS
†132.11	consequences.] A; consequen [ce?] AMS
132.16	ate] A; eat AMS
133.9	that it had encountered with] A; with AMS
133.9	itself] A; itself that it had encountered AMS
133.13	of] A; of articles of AMS
133.14	This] B; The AMS
133.14	quite large] B; large too AMS
133.16	the weight] A; its weight AMS
133.16	the external] A; its external AMS
133.20	on] A; of AMS
*133.21	to-day] A; to day AMS
134.13	call of the loons] A; loons AMS
134.17	another,] A; ∼. AMS
134.21	day dawned] A; dawned AMS
134.24	Deerslayer,] A; ∼; AMS
135.2	a female's] B; female AMS

135.2–3	sympathizing] A; sympathyzing AMS
135.3	heart] B; interest AMS
†135.28	as] A; a AMS
†135.33	war;] A; ~ʌ AMS
135.37	evening] A; eve[rr?]ing AMS
†136.1–2	warpath,] A; ~ʌ AMS
136.15	cloaks] A; coats AMS
136.19–20	extraordinary] A; extraordinay AMS
136.25	composedly] A; composodely AMS
136.29	ally] A; fiemd [?] AMS
†136.38	Still,] A; ~ʌ AMS
137.4	for] A; from AMS
137.13	accordin'] B; according AMS
137.14	ar'n'd] CE; 'ar'nd AMS
*137.15	Hurry] CE; Hutter AMS
137.22	affecting] A; effecting AMS
137.31 (*twice*) indivour] A; endivour AMS
137.39	*You*] A; *Yuo* AMS
138.22	title] A; name AMS
138.28	secret] A; s[ee?]nt AMS
138.30	the young] A; they young AMS
138.33	Wah-ta!-Wah] A; Wah-Ta!-Wah AMS
138.33	Hist-oh!-Hist] A; Hist-Oh!-Hist AMS
139.1	*her*] B; her AMS
139.2	*him*] B; him AMS
139.2	casting] B; after casting AMS
139.6	among] A; am[o?]g AMS
139.16	Wah-ta!-Wah] A; Wah-ta!Wah AMS
139.18	that she was] A; was AMS
140.3	partic'lars] B; particulars AMS
140.10	this,] A; ~ ʌ AMS
140.11	while] A; and AMS
140.12	derangement] A; derangment AMS
141.8	well knew] A; understood AMS
141.16	by] A; in AMS
141.24	anxiety.] A; ~ʌ AMS
141.29	sister,] A; ~ʌ AMS
141.29	guilelessness] A; guilessness AMS
141.30–31	affections] A; heart AMS
141.31	hours] A; day AMS
141.32	them] A; it AMS
142.2–3	Neither appeared] A; They did not appear AMS
142.4	intimated] A; suffered AMS
142.37	even allowing] A; allowing AMS
143.4	door] A; trap AMS
*143.23	imagination] A; imaginations AMS
143.25	must] A; could only AMS

*143.26	choose] CE; [ch?] AMS; chance A-B
143.30	seen; it's true, a] A; seen, as yet. A AMS
143.32	guess] A; know AMS
143.39	we] A; weve AMS
143.40	us] A; it AMS
144.36	offer] A; offer to him AMS
144.37	observed] A; remarked AMS
144.37	amidst] A; admidst AMS
144.40	her own] A; even her AMS
145.8-9	exceptions] A; exception AMS
145.15	proficiency] B; advantage AMS
145.16	an advantage] A; a grace AMS
145.17	drawback] A; draw back AMS
145.19	knew. She] A; knew; and she AMS
145.20	summers, and, as was] A; summers. As had been AMS
145.28	tenderly loved] A; loved AMS
146.2	dearly likes sarcumvention] A; likes sarcumventions in war AMS
146.10	Injin's] B; Indian's AMS
146.13	Mingos] A; Mingo's AMS
146.19	consciousness] A; feeling AMS
146.31	lengthened] A; lengthned AMS
°147.13	passed] A; ~, AMS
147.18	managed] B; had managed AMS
†147.28	get] A; g[e?] AMS
*147.37	helmsman] A; helmsman Natty AMS
148.8	Bryant, "The Firmament," 11.19-24] CE; The Skies AMS
148.12	irregularly] A; irregularily AMS
148.14	relieve] A; break AMS
148.25	feet beyond] A; out of AMS
148.33	limited] A; bounded AMS
148.36	lengthening] A; lenghtnening AMS
*149.16	writing] A; [dis?]ting AMS
*149.29	He]A; and He AMS
149.33-34	"paid out line,"] A; ʌ~~,ʌ AMS
149.34	"set down"] A; ʌ~~ʌ AMS
150.3	means of] A; means AMS
†150.5	as] A; [s?] AMS
†150.7	venture] A; [e?]nture AMS
†150.9	He]A; [H?]e AMS
†150.12	either] A; [either?] AMS
†150.20	any] A; [y?] AMS
150.23	twenty-four] A; twenty four AMS
150.26	withheld] A; witheld AMS
150.40	grieve] A; grive AMS
151.4	you!] A; ~ ? AMS
151.15	seen?"] A; ~?ʌ AMS

151.23	Mohican.'] A; ~.ʌ AMS
151.28	effected] A; affected AMS
151.30	warrior,] A; ~ʌ AMS
151.33	came leaping] A; cameleaping AMS
151.34-35	falling headlong] A; falling AMS
151.36	Pull,] A; ~ʌ AMS
152.7	for] A; of AMS
152.15	ahead] A; ahea AMS
*152.20	Mingos] A; Mingoes AMS. *Also emended at* 213.13, 241.32, 262.12, 271.32, 272.31, 302.25, 305.34, 396.2 *and* 404.11.
*152.21	present,"] CE; ~', AMS; ~?" A
152.26	has disappeared] A; disappears AMS
*152.28	are all safe] CE; safe AMS
152.29	another] A; an other AMS
152.35	bullets] A; bullets by means of its logs AMS
153.15	than] A; as AMS
153.19-20	was unwilling to communicate] A; disliked communicating AMS
153.22	courteous] A; corteous AMS
153.23	await] A; wait AMS
154.8	the facts] A; events AMS
†154.12	and] A; an AMS
154.19	and] A; and to AMS
154.24	Iroquois] A; Irroquois AMS
154.28	met another] A; had struck a AMS
154.32	kept] A; had kept AMS
154.37	the desired] A; a the desired AMS
155.5	is] A; are AMS
155.5	known.]A; ~ʌ AMS
155.19	which] A; which, always AMS
155.19	convenience only] A; convenience AMS
155.31	the human forest.] A; human natur' ʌ AMS
155.34	know."] A; ~.ʌ AMS
155.38	will] A; may AMS
156.2	well]A; well as AMS
156.26	comprehending] A; co[m?]prehending AMS
156.32	nought] CE; naught A; n[o?] ught AMS
156.38	feelin's] A; feelings AMS. *Also emended at* 302.23, 386.19 *and* 432.38.
156.39	sacrifice] A; ~, AMS
†157.1	I suppose] A; suppose AMS
†157.3	"Would] A; ʌ~ AMS
†157.6	"Their] A; ʌ~ AMS
157.19-20	pleasant] A; comely AMS
157.20	close] A; near AMS
157.28	Wah-ta!-Wah] A; Wah-ta!Wah AMS
157.37	gals] B; girls AMS

157.39	peltry] A; pelty AMS
158.1	thoughtless] A; thougtless AMS
158.8	a stream] A; water AMS
158.13	seein'] A; seeing AMS
158.28	courteously] A; corteously AMS
159.7	Uncas] A; Unca[s?] AMS
159.10	Christian] A; Christiain AMS
159.12	with the rifle] A; of aim AMS
159.17	stout-hearted] A; courageous AMS
159.27	shall] B; must AMS
159.31	tribe; it] A; tribe, and AMS
160.2	the hour] A; as hour AMS
160.6	clouded] A; clowded AMS
160.14	Chingachgook] A; Chincachgook AMS
160.21	occasionally] A; occasionly AMS
160.30	completely] A; complete AMS
160.32	our] A; the other AMS
160.33	excited] B; had excited AMS
160.33	created] A; awakened AMS
160.34	awakened] A; aroused AMS
160.39	her brother] A; a father AMS
161.12-13	impossible] A; not possible AMS
161.22	seemingly] A; seeming[ly?] AMS
161.25	it] A; her AMS
†162.7	hope we] A; h AMS
162.7	be able] A; able AMS
162.8	keep] A; keep in AMS
162.9	returned] A; [re?] turned AMS
162.16	land;] A; land, and AMS
*162.35	ar'n'd."] CE; a'r'n'd [."?] AMS
163.5	and] A; and then AMS
163.5	sprang instantly] A; sprang AMS
163.5	he]A; the he AMS
†163.9	human] A; humman AMS
163.16	which] A; of which AMS
163.29	poor] A; pooor AMS
164.5-6	the two men seizing] B; and then the two men seized AMS
164.6	sweeping] B; began to sweep AMS
164.29	Hetty] A; She AMS
164.40	their] A; the AMS
165.5	related] A; she had achieved AMS
165.7	the canoe] A; her canoe AMS
165.24	possession] A; in possession AMS
166.8	Joanna Baillie, *Rayner: A Tragedy*, II.i.3-4, 6-9] CE; Joanna Baillie AMS
†166.10	did] A; di AMS
†166.21	good] A; goo AMS

†166.23	harm.] A; ~∧ AMS
167.3	the wind] B; that the wind AMS
167.9	reasoning] A; reasons AMS
167.18	springing] A; spinging AMS
167.24	to pass] A; pass AMS
†167.27	on] A; [o?] n AMS
167.39	at the helm] A; steering AMS
†168.2	directions] A; directi AMS
168.10	Deerslayer's] A; Deerslayers' AMS
†168.15	it."] A; it ∧ AMS
†168.26	and] A; an AMS
168.30	am going] A; go AMS
168.36	than mine,] A; than mine ∧ AMS
169.6	her] A; its AMS
169.7	only;] A; only, and, AMS
†170.7	means] A; mean AMS
170.9	birth.] A; ~∧ AMS
170.9	Without] A; With out AMS
170.21 (*twice*)	its] A; her AMS
170.23	morrow] A; morrw AMS
170.24	quitted] A; left AMS
171.5-6	proceed.] A; ~, AMS
*171.6	hand it . . . bounded by the] CE; hand by it . . . bounded the AMS; hand, it . . . bounded by the A-B
171.10	brow] A; margin AMS
171.17	set] A; sat AMS
171.22	there] A; the[s?]e AMS
171.36	to children] A; with children AMS
172.4	necessary than is commonly the case] A; than is usually necessary, AMS
†172.10	forever] A; forev[r?] AMS
172.30	uttering] A; [au?]dibly murmuring AMS
172.30	Judith "] A; ~' AMS
172.37	doubtful] A; distrustful AMS
172.40	loud] A; lowd AMS. *Also emended at* 198.22, 235.26, 258.12, 277.13, 472.40, 473.21 *and* 487.32
†173.2	perceived] A; pereived AMS
173.2-3	watching her movements, with fiery eyes] A; with fiery eyes, watching her movements AMS
173.4	having] A; had AMS
173.4	fallen,] A; fallen, and AMS
173.18	clasped] A; clapsed AMS
173.23	girl] A; gril AMS
173.40	thrice the distance] A; about tenfold the progress AMS
174.1	period of time] A; time AMS
174.11	obliquely] A; southerly AMS
174.12	a plain] A; the plain AMS

174.12	hills] A; ranges of the hills AMS
174.18	own] A; soft AMS
†174.22	human] A; huma AMS
174.34	characterizes] A; characterize AMS
174.36	servitors] A; se[r?]iters AMS
*174.37	women] A; women sex AMS
174.37–39	Americans, before . . . . In] A; Americans is by no means uncommon, before they have become exposed to the hardships of wives and mothers. In AMS
175.2	but] A; and AMS
175.3	they are so early deprived;] A; *usage* so early deprives them, AMS
175.3	as much] A; equally AMS
175.4	life, as from any other cause] A; life AMS
175.8	knees,] A; ~; AMS
175.10	dark braids] A; braids of black AMS
175.20	herself] A; her herself AMS
175.21	Wah-ta!-Wah] A; Wah-ta-Wah! AMS
175.22	Hist-oh!-Hist] A; Hist-oh!-hist AMS
175.29–30	Iroquois, or Hurons, as it would be better to call them,] A; Iroquois AMS
175.31	indeed] A; in deed AMS
175.34	Wah-ta!-Wah] A; WahtaWah AMS *Also emended at* 176.3, 176.8, 176.11, 177.29, 178.27, 179.6, 179.9, 181.11, 182.20, 185.6 *and* 235.33.
175.35	readier] A; readiest AMS
176.9	cruel] B; very cruel AMS
176.16	Indian] B; Indian, then AMS; Indian then A
176.29	no] A; not AMS
176.30	t'ing] A; thing AMS
176.31	alway] A; always AMS
†176.38	deepened] A; deepeed AMS
177.17	"he] A; ∧~ AMS
†177.23	ten,] A; te AMS
177.25	chief] A; chiefs AMS
177.25	many scalp] A; many AMS
177.32	aspects,] A; ~∧ AMS
178.2	eaves-droppers] A; eves-droppers AMS
178.14	any of] A; any AMS
178.15	so frequently] A; sometimes AMS
178.17	the proofs] A; some signs AMS
178.20	by any] B; any AMS
178.27	friend] A; fri[nd?] AMS
178.35–36	except] A; but AMS
178.37	t'ink] A; think AMS
179.8	time;] A; time, and AMS
179.9	tongue;] A; tongue, and AMS

179.18	let] A; give AMS
179.18	party get] A; party AMS
179.21	interview] A; interviw AMS
*179.22	Hist] CE; Hist, as we prefer to call the Delaware maid, AMS; Hist, A
179.27	broder] A; brother AMS
179.27	fader] A; father AMS. *Also emended at* 179.28 *and* 182.19.
179.28	broder] A; brother AMS
180.9	privilege] A; priviliges AMS
180.20	almost,] A; ~. AMS
180.26	me,] A; ~. AMS
180.35	girl]A; speaker AMS
181.10	withheld] A; witheld AMS
181.25	soon as] A; soon AMS
181.28	*you*] B; you AMS
181.29	big] B; large AMS
181.38	not] B; not to AMS
181.39	*dat*] B; *that* AMS
181.40	*t'udder*] B; *'tother* AMS; *t'other* A
182.6	hear] B; overhear AMS; hear over A
182.12	gift] B; their gift AMS
182.12	t'udder] B; 't'other AMS; t'other A
182.13	tongue] B; their tongue AMS
182.13-14	Sarpent] B; Serpent AMS
182.14	so] B; so do AMS
182.14	Good] B; A good AMS
182.15	friend] B; a friend AMS
182.24	T'ink] B; Think AMS
182.24	dat,] B; that⌄ AMS
182.24	two, twenty] A; two AMS
182.25	Sarpent] B; Serpent AMS
183.7	*Richard III*, I.iv.195-97; 199-200] CE; Shakspeare AMS
183.8	That the] A; The AMS
183.8	compulsorily] A; compelsorily AMS
183.9	was] A; as was AMS
183.10	females. It] A; females; but it AMS
183.15	it] A; if AMS
184.5	the ingenious] A; those ingenious AMS
184.29	dark] B; concealed, dark AMS
184.34	men,] A; ~. AMS
†185.8	feelings.] A; ~⌄ AMS
185.11	without] A; with out AMS
†185.13	surprise] A; surpris AMS
185.18	surprise] B; emotion AMS
†185.22	ordinary] A; ordinay AMS
185.25-26	probable] A; probably AMS
185.29	attributed] A; attributed also AMS
185.34	slightest] A; slighest AMS

†185.34   those] A; th[os?] AMS
186.1   understood] A; undestood AMS
186.6   are as] B; as AMS
186.10   on which you came] A; you came here on AMS
186.17   creatur'] A; creature AMS
186.20   will] A; will you AMS
186.38   no] A; ho AMS
187.2   has] A; is has AMS
187.6   Not] A; ~, AMS
187.13   arter] B; after AMS
187.16   men] A; man AMS
187.17   next step] A; nexstep AMS
188.12   a Huron] A; an Iroquois AMS
188.16   furnished] A; furnished her with AMS
†188.18   Even] A; Ev AMS
188.20   Delaware] A; Iroquois AMS
188.22-23   companion] A; companions AMS
188.25   reason] A; intellect AMS
188.26   intellect] A; reason AMS
188.33-34   preparation] A; prepartions AMS
188.34   to be] B; that was to be AMS
188.39   affect] A; effect AMS
189.4   quiet] A; grave AMS
189.11   to forbear] A; forbear AMS
189.15   Hurons] A; Iroquois AMS. *Also emended at* 193.37, 243.10 *and* 282.13.
189.16   imperfectly.] A; ~ₐ AMS
189.17   Wah-ta!-Wah] A; Wahtawah AMS. *Also emended at* 190.11, 190.28, 191.11, 193.20, 199.6, 199.14, 199.17-18, 215.31 *and* 235.33.
189.20   deceive] A; decieve AMS
189.29   eyes] B; eye AMS
189.30   sunny] A; sensitive AMS
190.20   red men] A; savages AMS
190.28-29   as literally] A; a literally AMS
191.13   have] A; has AMS
191.20   pleasure] A; pleasures AMS
†191.28   slowly] A; slow[y?] AMS
191.33   miracle] A; effect AMS
192.1   Great] B; the Great AMS
192.2   was totally] A; was AMS
192.5-6   know how] A; how AMS
192.15   passions] A; passion AMS
192.22   to] A; to be AMS
192.22   great modern,] A; great AMS
192.23   things] A; all things AMS
†192.29   answer] A; anwer AMS

192.29	satisfied.] A; ∼ₐ AMS
192.37	Delaware] A; Delawarge AMS
193.1	forget,] A; ∼ₐ AMS
193.3	'*Whosoever*] A; "∼ AMS
193.6	lightning] A; lightening AMS
193.8	offender.] A; ∼ₐ AMS
193.9	" '*Love*] A; "∼ AMS
193.11	*persecute you.*' "] A; ∼∼." AMS
193.13	her checks] A; here checks AMS
193.24	opened] A; openend AMS
193.39–40	constituted] A; constructed AMS
194.10	this] A; the AMS
194.15	Huron] A; Iroquois AMS
194.21	face] A; face's AMS
194.23	horn,] A; ∼. AMS
194.31	ask] A; ask only AMS
194.37	war. My name is Rivenoak] A; war AMS
195.9	seem] B; seem to be AMS
195.12	though he] A; always AMS
195.12	t'other] A; 't'other AMS
195.16	be] A; be so AMS
195.18	faces,] B; ∼; AMS
195.19	Why] B; Why then AMS; Why, then, A
196.9	*evil*,'] A; ∼," AMS
196.11	such] B; such a AMS
196.12	answered] A; answed AMS
196.13	*dat*] B; *that* AMS
196.13	somet'ing] A; something AMS
196.28	understand] A; know AMS
196.29	or] A; and AMS
196.30	hesitating] A; hesitation AMS
196.38	confessed] A; admitted AMS
197.10	manhood.] A; ∼ₐ AMS
197.20	incessantly] A; incensantly AMS
†198.6	reckless] A; reckess AMS
198.15	friend] B; a friend AMS
199.3	enough] A; to all present AMS
*199.5	sweeter] A; ∼, AMS
†199.8	understand] A; undestand AMS
199.10	Hurry] A; Harry AMS
199.16	t'udder] B; t'other A; 'tother AMS
199.18–19	he do] A; do AMS
199.24	pale-faces] B; three pale-faces AMS
200.8	*Hamlet*, IV.v.4–9] CE; Shakspeare AMS
200.12	each] B; they AMS
200.12–13	his pallet] B; their pallets AMS
200.13	a man] B; men AMS

200.13	was] B; were AMS
200.13	his] B; their AMS
200.17	blanket] A; bed AMS
*202.9	ar'n'd] CE; 'ar'n'd AMS
*202.10	would'n't] CE; woul'd'n't AMS; wouldn't A-B
†202.25	Killdeer,] A; ∾ʌ AMS
202.37	then] A; and then AMS
203.9	with your own] A; wi[ll?] all your AMS
203.19	own finery] A; finery AMS
203.20	was] A; were AMS
203.26	bare] A; lay bare AMS
203.34-35	Deerslayer, if . . . . "But] A; Deerslayer," she said, affecting to laugh, "if you seriously think thus of those of your own colour! But AMS
203.35	me;] A; me, and AMS
204.1	wisest] A; wise AMS
†204.5	fri'nds.] A; friend ʌ AMS
204.10	very thing] B; thing AMS
204.16	valley] A; vallyy AMS
204.23	a prating] A; every AMS
204.24	goes] A; goes near AMS
205.20 (*twice*)	cur'osity] A; curiosity AMS
205.33	place] A; pla[e?] AMS
206.7	opened."] A; ∾.ʌ AMS
206.8	believe] A; belive AMS
206.11	foretell] A; foresee AMS
206.14	good;] A; good, and AMS
206.15	that even the] A; the AMS
206.40	deceased] A; dceased AMS
207.6	arrangement] A; arrangement AMS. *Also emended at* 210.25-26, 214.6, 259.40 *and* 270.13.
207.19	'Feeble-Mind'] A; "∾" AMS
207.19	chist] A; chest AMS
207.24	'Wild Rose'] A; "∾∾" AMS
207.39	s'arch] A; sarch AMS
*208.8	was next] A; was AMS
208.37	articles] A; things AMS
208.38	Deerslayer,] A; ∾. AMS
†209.17	enemies.] A; ene[mi?] AMS
†209.31	times] A; tim[e?] AMS
209.32	more especially] A; in particular AMS
210.13	bribe, answered] A; bribe.Answered AMS
210.20	temporary] A; temporay AMS
211.19	cheap,] A; ∾. AMS
†211.20	Sarpent,] A; ∾ʌ AMS
211.27	incongruities] A; incogruities AMS
211.28	this] A; th[is?] AMS

211.39	skins] B; skin AMS
212.2	comfort's] A; comforts' AMS
212.4	another,] A; ∼. AMS
213.32	"blessed] A; 'belessed AMS
213.34	one] A; on AMS
214.5	the part] A; thet part AMS
214.15	quickly.] A; ∼∧ AMS
214.22	them] B; these AMS
214.26	the wigwam] A; her wigwam AMS
215.5	glorious, in that dress,] A; glorious AMS
215.6	day] A; day, in that dress AMS
†215.11	pretensions.] A; ∼∧ AMS
215.18	character.] A; ∼, AMS
215.18	that] A; than AMS
215.29	enough] A; enogh AMS
215.30	Delaware!"] A; ∼!∧ AMS
215.35	'Wild] A; "∼ AMS
215.40	proves] B; prove AMS
216.1	*be*] A; *are* AMS
†216.1	melons.] A; me[lo?] AMS
216.2	stick] A; '∼ AMS
216.6	robes] A; robe AMS
†216.16	places."] A; ∼∧ AMS
216.30	possesses] A; posseses AMS
*216.33	Judith. So] CE; ∼,∼ AMS; Judith; so A-B
216.34	those] B; all AMS
216.37	as certain to rankle] B; certain to rankle AMS
*217.21	neighbor's] CE; neighbors AMS; neighbour's A-B
217.26	another] A; another' AMS
218.2	withhold] A; withold AMS
218.10	renewed] B; pushed further AMS
218.21	weapons] A; weapon's AMS
219.10	Thomas Sheridan, "A True and Faithful Inventory of the Goods belonging to Dr. Swift," 11.1-6, 13-14] CE; Dean Swift's Inventory AMS
219.17	satisfy] A; satify AMS
219.19	these] B; these we'pons AMS
220.12	Deerslayer,] A; ∼. AMS
221.13	foresee] A; have foreseen AMS
221.16	allowed] B; suffered AMS
221.21	am far] A; far AMS
221.25	Deerslayer] A; dear Deerslayer AMS
221.35	chief] A; Sarpent AMS
222.5	have burst] A; burst AMS
222.7	oncommon,] A; ∼; AMS
†222.10	pistol] A; pisol AMS
*222.14	Judith,] A; Judith had AMS

222.38	chist] A; chest AMS
223.23	condemnation] B; commendation AMS
223.33	replying] A; repling AMS
†224.1	laughed.] A; laugh[ed?] AMS
†224.11	country] A; cou[ty?] AMS
224.12	was] B; has been AMS
224.22	printed] A; pinted AMS
224.25	hastened] A; hasttened AMS
225.5	or] A; or and AMS
225.8	counterfeit] A; counterfiet AMS
†225.9	but] A; ut AMS
†225.12	"If] A; '∼ AMS
225.13	sin,] A; ∼. AMS
225.22	way] A; was AMS
225.31	something] A; somethig AMS
225.40	indirect] A; in direct AMS
226.1	mistake] A; mistak AMS
226.20	pressèd] A; packed AMS
226.28–29	admiration] A; admirat[io?] AMS
226.30	interview] A; inteview AMS
226.36	elephants] A; elephant's AMS
227.1	so] A; as AMS
227.2	one] A; being a AMS
227.13	and] A; & AMS *Also emended at* 284.13 *and* 474.28.
227.17	stealthy] A; startling AMS
227.23	contrivance] A; contivance AMS
227.28	surfaces] A; upper surfaces AMS
227.32	near,] A; ∼. AMS
228.31	Hurry,] A; ∼. AMS
†229.12	"I] A; ∧∼ AMS
†229.15	"First] A; '∼ AMS
†229.19	"Oh] A; ∧∼ AMS
†229.21	"Yes] A; ∧∼ AMS
229.26	had] A; they had AMS
229.31	but] B; and AMS
230.15	first] A; have first AMS
230.37	the men] A; men AMS
230.38	another?"] A; ∼?∧ AMS
†231.7	minds?"] A; ∼∧" AMS
231.14	human life] A; life AMS
231.16	Wigwam] A; Wigwams AMS
231.18	does explain] A; does explains AMS
231.25	sets."] A; ∼.∧ AMS
231.36	and] B; and then AMS
232.6	placing] A; musing with AMS
232.6	he remained a long time with] A; and AMS
232.16	her;] B; her, and AMS

†232.19	mind.] A; mi[nd?] AMS
232.36	intelligence] A; association AMS
†233.14	"Chin-] A; 'Chin- AMS
†233.	
15-16	Yengeese* tongue."] A; Yéngeese tong[ue?] (Note.*. AMS
233.20	Wah−ta!−Wah] A; Wah−ta−Wah AMS
233.21	Wah−ta!−Wah] A; Wah−ta−Wah AMS
233.29	*It] A; It AMS
233.35	Yengeese,] A; ∼. AMS
234.5	strange] A; queer AMS
234.16	Jupiter] A; Venus AMS
234.25	intercourse] A; intercouse AMS
°235.12	case.] A; ∼,." AMS
235.24	she loves] A; they love AMS
235.28	bird] A; birds AMS
237.2	'A stranger animal,'] A; "∼∼∼," AMS
237.3	'Sure] A; ∧∼ AMS
237.5	tongue,] A; ∼∧ AMS
237.6	foot] A; tooth [?] AMS
237.7	behind!'] A; ∼∧ AMS
237.8	James Merrick, "The Chameleon," 11.21-26] CE; Merrick AMS
237.17	truth] A; matter AMS
237.19	consented] A; assented AMS
237.30	lovers'] A; lovers's AMS
†238.5	interviews.] A; intervie[ws] ∧ AMS
238.8	friend's] A; friends AMS
238.16	shouldn't] A; should AMS
238.17	red skin] A; redskin AMS
238.18	s'arch] A; sarch AMS
238.22	"put] A; ∧∼ AMS
238.22	together] A; togethr AMS
238.31	sudden] A; sudeen AMS
238.31	idea.] A; ∼∧ AMS
239.5	till] A; t'ill AMS
239.26	serious] A; squally AMS
240.3	retain] A; retain all AMS
240.24	all] B; then all AMS
240.39-	
241.1	appearance] A; apparance AMS
*241.6	them,] CE; ∼∧ AMS; ∧; A
241.8	the dispositions] A; every disposition AMS
241.9	prepared] A; perpared AMS
241.13	Deerslayer] A; Deeslayer AMS
241.18	ascertain] A; discover AMS
241.38	keenness] A; keeness AMS
242.3	Rivenoak,] A; ∼∧ AMS

242.10	four] A; three AMS
242.10	only] A; not AMS
242.12	welcome,] A; ∼∧ AMS
†242.17	smiled] A; s[mil?] AMS
242.29	transaction] B; whole transaction AMS
243.10	Hurons] A; Iroquois AMS
243.20	raft] A; other AMS
243.22	ivory] A; ivoy AMS
243.32	lost the] B; lost all AMS
243.34	extraordinary.] A; extraordinay ∧ AMS
244.16	Hurry Harry] CE; Harry Hurry AMS *Also emended at* 251.34 *and* 378.16.
244.23	ricommend] B; recommend AMS
244.32	very bad] B; bad AMS
244.32	that] B; all that AMS
245.14	civilization] A; cvilization AMS
245.18	met.* [footnote] *The Otsego . . . . company.] B; met. AMS
245.26	would] A; would possess AMS
246.1	a toy like that] B; two toys like those AMS
246.4	being] A; beeing AMS
246.11	desire] B; savage desire AMS
246.15	and] A; tand AMS
*246.20	being done] CE; doing AMS
246.20	Rivenoak] A; ∼, AMS
246.35	glass] A; gla[sss?] AMS
246.38	employ] A; emply AMS
247.9	generous; they] A; generous, and AMS
†247.21	sun sets] A; sunsets AMS
247.22	number] A; numbers AMS
248.24	true,] A; ∼∧ AMS
248.26	they've] A; theyv'e AMS
248.31	let] A; letter AMS
†248.33	already.] A; ∼∧ AMS
249.1	valleys] A; vallies AMS
249.18	'twas] A; it 'twas AMS
†249.19	business.] A; ∼∧ AMS
250.11	or] A; and AMS
250.26	pinioned] A; pinnioned AMS
*250.30	labored] CE; larbored AMS; laboured A-B
250.37	compelled] A; compeled AMS
251.6	usual] A; a portion of their usual AMS
251.9	released to enable] A; released for the purpose, to help AMS
251.10	to ascend] A; ascend AMS
251.16	directed] A; des[ired?] AMS
251.19	remaining] A; remain[g?] AMS
251.20	back, to your old abode, Master Hutter] A; back, Master Hutter, to your old abode AMS

251.26   speaking] B; speaking of his own accord, AMS
251.31   picture] A; pictur AMS
251.37   "I'm] A; ∧∼ AMS
251.40   fiercely] A; feircely AMS
*252.2   christian] CE; chistian AMS; Christian A-B
†252.11   "You've] A; ∧∼ AMS
252.15   and] A; an AMS
252.15   a den] A; the den AMS
252.23   fully] A; quite AMS
253.3   no] A; No AMS
253.4   put his designs] A; carry his threats AMS
253.7   in regaining] A; of regaining AMS
253.8   reflections] A; reflection[s?] AMS
253.9   beginning] A; beginnig AMS
253.11   Before] A; Befor AMS
254.10   Chatterton, "Bristowe Tragedie," 11.357-64] CE; Chatterton AMS
*254.12   unison with,] CE; unison with AMS; unison, with A-B
254.14   ceased] B; had ceased AMS
254.17   but] A; though AMS
*254.26   keensighted] CE; keensighted, AMS; keen-sighted A
254.26   monitor] A; moniter AMS
255.17   fairly rained] A; rained AMS
255.22   trouble,] A; ∼∧ AMS
255.23   a low] A; low AMS
256.2   arter] A; after AMS
256.19   fri'nds] A; fri'ends AMS
256.24   come] A; comee AMS
256.30   ascertained] A; ascertaining by its aid, AMS
256.38   came] A; cam AMS
257.15   *you.*] A; ∼∧ AMS
257.29   carrying] A; carri[ng?] AMS
257.31   riptyle's] A; riptyles AMS
258.1   had] A; has AMS
*258.16   earth; one] A; earth: One AMS
259.17   helped.] A; ∼∧ AMS
259.24-25   opening] A; opening[ig?] AMS
259.27   occurred] A; had occurred AMS
259.34   secret] A; Secret AMS
260.5   their] A; theirr AMS
*260.29   are] CE; is AMS
260.34   baffling] A; baffing AMS
260.36   berth] A; birth AMS
260.37   platform,] A; ∼∧ AMS
†260.40   course] A; cou[rs?] AMS
261.4   these] A; the AMS
261.16   attention] A; watchfulness AMS

261.19	deceive] A; decive AMS
†261.27	announced] A; annou[n] AMS
261.31	belts,] A; ~. AMS
*262.1-2	it," returned Deerslayer. "Well] CE; it. "returned Deersly "Well AMS; it instead of Deerslayer; well A-B
†262.5	can] A; an AMS
262.35	much of] A; much AMS
263.7	desire] A; motive AMS
263.8	longing for] A; calculation of AMS
263.10	soon] B; had soon AMS
†263.24	Chingachgook] A; Chinga[ch?]gook AMS
263.32	effected] B; was effected AMS
263.36	of] A; of of AMS
264.2	encampment] B; position AMS
†264.15	clouded heaven.] A; clowded heav[en?] AMS
264.20	knees] A; knews AMS
264.25-26	hazardous] A; hazardous and bold AMS
264.28	proceeded] A; then proceded AMS
264.37	surprised] A; suprised AMS
*265.3	be honored] CE; meet with honor AMS; be honoured A-B
†265.15	minutes] A; minute AMS
265.16	find] A; meet AMS
265.24	Deerslayer] A; Deeslayer AMS
†265.27	wish] A; wis[h?] AMS
†265.30	churches] A; church [s?] AMS
265.35	can't] A; cant AMS
265.37	twould] CE; t would AMS
266.1	coloured] B; had coloured AMS
266.3	nearly] B; almost AMS
266.12	their] A; there AMS
266.23	concord] A; harmony AMS
267.32	despised,] A; ~ΛAMS
267.37	gone] A; go AMS
267.40	March.] A; ~Λ AMS
268.2-3	harm, means no great good] A; good, means no great harm AMS
268.23	would not willingly] A; certainly would never AMS
268.29	modesty.] A; ~Λ AMS
268.33	girl.] A; ~Λ AMS
269.19	ind] B; end AMS; *Also emended at* 306.31, 393.5, 423.39 *and* 454.29.
269.22	death have] B; death has AMS
269.24	*that's*] B; *that*'s AMS
269.39	truth] A; fact AMS
270.8	released] A; two released AMS
270.22	that] A; even that AMS
270.23	reference] A; reference now AMS

270.30	they might pass] A; that might offer AMS
270.31	doubled] B; had doubled AMS
270.38	of] A; of the AMS
270.39	them the rendezvous] A; her rendevous AMS
271.6	Wordsworth, "To the Cuckoo," 11. 9-12] CE; Wordsworth AMS
271.13	were] A; was AMS
271.16-17	rendezvous] A; rendevous AMS
271.23	forethought] A; fore thought AMS
271.24	wish] A; desire AMS
271.29	that object] A; it AMS
271.32	shows] A; shows that AMS
271.33	for] A; ~, AMS
272.9-10	further off] A; [more?] AMS
272.17	there] A; There AMS
272.37	Sarpent's] A; Sarpents' AMS
273.8	at the pinch] B; as the pinch come AMS; as the pinch came A
273.18	*you*] B; ~ AMS
273.20	yet] B; and yet AMS
273.24	satisfied."] A; ~.ᴀ AMS
273.31	inv*y*] B; envy AMS
273.34	her] B; her own AMS
274.15	him,] A; ~ᴀ AMS
274.31-32	twentieth] A; twentyeth AMS
274.33	fugitive] A; fugitve AMS
274.38	reflection] A; recollection AMS
275.2	instant] A; time AMS
275.4	soldiers] A; soldirs AMS
275.6	*debût*] A; *début* AMS
275.25	required] A; reguired AMS
†275.32	canoe] A; can[e?], AMS
†276.20	rendezvous.] A; rendezvou[s?] AMS
277.4	direction] A; derection AMS
277.7	selected] A; evening AMS
277.15	that there] A; there AMS
277.29	plausibly] B; reasonably AMS
277.34	understanding] A; undestanding AMS
†277.38	approached] A; appro[oached?] AMS
278.4	progress] A; movement AMS
278.10	noiseless] A; noisless AMS
278.15	light] A; brightness AMS
278.17	the illumination] A; light AMS
278.18	position] A; situation AMS
278.20-21	extraordinary] A; extraordinay AMS
278.27	rarely] B; seldom AMS
278.29	though seldom] A; without AMS
278.38	it] B; the scene AMS

278.39	canoe] A; Canoe AMS
279.24	while] A; as AMS
279.30	indolent] A; idolent AMS
279.30	arms] A; ams AMS
279.30	them] B; them all AMS
279.31	leaning] A; learning AMS
280.5	aged] A; elders AMS
280.16	walked] A; came AMS
280.18	view;] A; view, and AMS
†280.23 – 24	admiration.] A; ∼ʌ AMS
*280.25	and] CE; [an]d AMS
°281.7	proceedings.] A; ∼; AMS
281.10	indeed] A; in deed AMS
281.27	localities] A; localties AMS
281.29	necessary] A; necessary to escape AMS
281.30	also denoted] A; denoted AMS
281.33	any] A; their AMS
282.3	forests,] A; ∼. AMS
282.4	height] A; heighth AMS
282.37	stealthily] A; covertly AMS
282.38	fringe] A; cover AMS
283.1	hillock] A; rise AMS
283.13	in front] A; leading AMS
283.27	perceived] A; possessed AMS
283.28	which] A; that AMS
283.32	whom] A; that AMS
283.36	habits] B; the habits AMS
*283.37	so extraordinary an animal] A; the an animal so extraordinay AMS
284.5	adventurers] A; adenturers AMS
*284.24	that!"] CE; ∼!' AMS; ∼," A-B
284.30	in fact] A; infact AMS
284.30	Wah-ta!-Wah] A; Wah!ta-Wah! AMS
284.39	warrior?"] A; ∼?ʌ AMS
285.15	eyes,] A; ∼", AMS
†285.19	him] A; im AMS
285.23	impairs] A; impair AMS
285.35	so] A; had AMS
286.11	retort] A; returt AMS
286.11	argument] A; agument AMS
286.13	offspring] A; offsping AMS
286.30	its cloud] A; it AMS
286.35	companion] A; compaion AMS
287.1	bade] A; bid AMS
287.6	understood] A; undestood AMS
287.9	hand. As] A; hand, and as AMS
287.34	discovery] A; discovey AMS

288.1	warriors] A; warrior AMS
288.5	phantasmagoria] A; phantasmigoria AMS
289.6–7	Thomas Moore, *Lalla Rookh*, "The Veiled Prophet of Khorassan," 11. 1954–57] CE; Moore AMS
289.10	triangle] A; trangle AMS
289.12	spring] A; sping AMS
†289.15	obliged] A; oblige[d?] AMS
289.17	disadvantages] A; advantages AMS
289.30	strand] A; beach AMS
290.4	man] A; mind AMS
290.5	than the] B; than that of the AMS
†290.8	gain] A; gai AMS
290.12	Deerslayer] A; ~, AMS
290.19	into] A; in to AMS
291.6	proceeded] A; proceded AMS
291.13–14	after which] A; when AMS
291.32	compensated] A; compenstated AMS
291.36	first removed] A; taken from him AMS
291.40	attempting to] A; making his AMS
292.1	flight] A; a flight AMS
292.17	foe. The] A; foe, the AMS
292.18	or] A; and AMS
292.20	he had] A; had AMS
292.39	pair of] A; pair AMS
293.11	motive.] A; ~ʌ AMS
293.27	yengee] A; yengeese AMS
293.34	blackguard:] A; ~ʌ AMS
293.36	warrior] A; warrir AMS
294.5	for] A; for, editor or old woman, AMS
294.6–7	by contempt,] A; only by AMS
294.24	without] A; with out AMS
294.30	Hunting Grounds.] A; Hungting Grounds ʌ AMS
†294.32	Delawares?"] A; ~?ʌ AMS
295.18	Hurons. And] A; Hurons, and AMS
295.34	land."] A; ~.ʌ AMS
296.27	avowal] A; betrayal AMS
296.28	then] A; then he AMS
296.39	eagles'] B; eagle's AMS
297.2	be put in] A; lie on AMS
297.6–7	an untruth] B; untruth AMS
297.11	persevered] A; persev[ered?] AMS
297.11–12	attack.] A; ~." AMS
297.20	string] A; little string AMS
297.38	Wah-ta!-Wah] A; Wah!-ta-Wah! AMS *Also emended at* 300.16 *and* 329.3.
298.7	or] A; and AMS
298.11	together.] A; ~ʌ AMS

298.24	there's] A; so there's AMS
298.24–25	otherwise] A; othewise AMS
°298.29	more] A; a more AMS
†299.8	case,] A; ∼∧ AMS
299.23	passing] A; keeping AMS
299.36	their hard fortunes] A; the hard fortunes of their sex AMS
299.36	could entirely] A; could AMS
300.5	breast] A; chest AMS
300.21	water; he] A; water, and AMS
300.39	s'arch] A; sarch AMS
301.1	women] B; young women AMS
301.26	bear;] B; bear, and AMS; bear; and A
301.35	respect] A; consideration AMS
302.11	pale face's] A; pale faces AMS
302.27	stop] B; sudden stop AMS
302.37	received] A; recived AMS
303.9	she] A; and she AMS
303.10	his] A; her his AMS
303.13	human] A; ra'al AMS
303.26	Hurry;] A; ∼∧ AMS
303.33	*you*] B; you AMS
303.35	Ah] B; Ay AMS
304.1	ought to] B; ought AMS
304.15	actions] A; feelin's AMS
304.35	on which] A; in which AMS
304.38	them] B; these AMS
305.2	seize] A; sieze AMS
†305.4	ag'in.] A; ∼∧ AMS
305.6	trust] A; leave AMS
305.29	troops] A; troop's AMS
305.31	soldiers] A; soldirs AMS
*306.9	they'd] A; they'd had AMS
306.23	shall] A; may AMS
†306.26	even] A; [e?]ven AMS
306.35	manifested] A; discovered AMS
306.37	act;] A; act, and AMS
306.37–38	affectionately] A; affectionally AMS
306.39	it] B; in it AMS
307.4	tell] A; bid AMS
308.10	Byron, *Don Juan*, IV.lxxi] CE; Byron AMS
308.15	darkness] B; darkness had AMS
308.28	did not find] A; certainly missed AMS
308.31	an attention] A; attention AMS
308.35	profound] A; pround AMS
308.35	all] A; all the rest AMS
309.9	repetition] A; repitition AMS
309.28	it had] A; had AMS

309.28	over it the while] B; the while, over it AMS
309.32	arrive] A; arrived AMS
309.33	enlightenment] A; enlightment AMS
310.2	up,] A; ∼ₐ AMS
†310.22	position.] A; ∼ₐ AMS
310.37–38	forms . . . feet] A; forms, at AMS
310.38–39	feet, and] A; feet, within the shadows of the woods, and AMS
311.24	reached] A; had reached AMS
311.32	woods. On] A; woods; on AMS
312.10	burning] A; buring AMS
312.10	they] A; she AMS
312.10	quitted] B; had quitted AMS
313.12	to] A; so AMS
313.20	noise] A; fuss AMS
313.23	together,] A; ∼. AMS
313.26	in a] A; a AMS
313.26	truth] A; truth in a man AMS
313.33	but for] A; but AMS
313.34	whose] A; neither whose AMS
313.35	and] A; nor AMS
313.35–36	she did not] A; did she AMS
314.1	unequal,]A; ∼ₐ AMS
314.8	oftener] A; oftner AMS
314.11	ambition] A; own ambition AMS
*314.12	question,] CE; ∼ₐ AMS; ∼; A-B
314.22	eyes] A; eye AMS
314.30	subject,] A; ∼. AMS
314.33	comelier] A; comlier AMS
315.4	Deerslayer.] A; ∼ₐ AMS
315.27	lives] A; live AMS
315.36–37	repetition] A; repitition [s?] AMS
315.37	scow] A; Ark AMS
†316.1	expert] A; [e?]xpert AMS
†316.3	forced] A; [f?]orced AMS
†316.5	and] A; [a?] nd AMS
316.7	rock] A; mound AMS
316.11	conviction] A; conclusion AMS
316.12	awkwardness] A; frightfulness AMS
316.22	believe that] A; believe AMS
317.7	eastern mountains] A; range of eastern mountain AMS
317.8	arose] B; rose AMS
*317.17	Hist!"] CE; Hist! AMS; Hist?" A-B
317.18	Judith] A; sister AMS
317.24	precious] A; preious AMS
317.32	boat] A; canoe AMS
317.34	funereal] A; funerial AMS
317.39	evident that] A; evident AMS

318.1	betrayed] A; bespoke AMS
318.35	could] A; remained to AMS
319.4	purpose] A; purpoe AMS
319.5	unforeseen] A; unforseen AMS
319.8	Byron, *Marino Faliero*, IV.ii.230-35] CE; Marino Faliero AMS
319.28	revenge] A; revenged AMS
319.36	overlooked] A; overlooks AMS
†320.14	creatur's] A; creatur' AMS
320.32	wind] A; air AMS
320.35	sailed] A; swept AMS
320.36	of the] A; of AMS
320.39	discerned] A; discened AMS
321.4	overruling] A; overuling AMS
321.4	which] A; that AMS
321.8	unthinking] A; motiveless AMS
321.17	planted] A; plnted AMS
322.4	fearlessness] A; fearlesness AMS
322.10	not'ing] A; nothing AMS
322.18	true that] A; true AMS
322.18	powerful] A; powerfull AMS
322.24	fiercer] A; feircer AMS
322.25	affections] A; affectins AMS
322.31	being] B; beings AMS
322.31	only] A; but AMS
322.34	motive,] A; ~. AMS
323.1-2	controversy] A; controvery AMS
323.12	stubbornness] A; stubborness AMS
323.32	but,] A; ~; AMS
324.8	prevails] A; prevail AMS
324.8	unearthly] A; uneathly AMS
†324.13	precedes] A; prec[ds?] AMS
324.19	light] A; radiance AMS
324.31	Only one] A; But a AMS
324.32	uses] A; destination AMS
325.15	scow] A; Ark AMS
†325.26	mother.] A; ~∧ AMS
325.27	Serpent] A; Sarpent AMS
325.40	alarm] A; affright AMS
326.9	manner] A; manners AMS
326.22	usual rough] A; rough AMS
326.26	land] B; lands AMS
326.37	then] A; and then AMS
326.38	given by] A; of AMS
†327.15	meddles] A; medd[ls?] AMS
327.20	wears] A; weares AMS
328.1	have] A; had AMS

328.12	viewed] A; regarded AMS
328.15	proceed] A; paddle AMS
328.19	the risk] A; its execution AMS
328.35	an Injin's] B; Indians AMS; an Indian's A
329.9	betrothed] A; betrother AMS
*329.12	timidly] A; ~, AMS
329.29	his] A; him from AMS
°330.22	elder] A; ~, AMS
330.35	reconnoitring] A; reconnotreing AMS
331.6	discovered] A; discoverd AMS
331.13	dwelling?"] A; ~.ʌ AMS
331.21	general] A; genereral AMS
331.25	opinion.] A; ~ʌ AMS
331.39	that any] A; any AMS
332.3	merely denoted] B; denoted merely AMS
332.14	simplicity] A; simplicty AMS
332.15	meretricious] A; meritricious AMS
332.16	moment] A; hour AMS
332.22	loveliness] A; lovliness AMS
332.31	to take] A; take AMS
332.31	to secure] A; secure AMS
*332.39	'dock.'] CE; 'dock. ʌ' AMS; dock A-B
333.16	which was not] A; not AMS
333.16	attempted] A; attempted idly, AMS
333.24	a man's head] A; the head of a man AMS
333.24	covering] A; coveing AMS
333.25	degree] A; dregree AMS
333.40	instant,] A; ~. AMS
†334.3	triumph.] A; ~ʌ AMS
334.36–37	shockingly] A; shockinly AMS
334.38	floor] A; floors AMS
°335.5	building.] A; ~, AMS
335.7	relieve] A; releive AMS
†335.10	the others] A; [t?]he others AMS
†335.12	short] A; hort AMS
335.13	The] A; But the AMS
†335.15	by a] A; a AMS
†335.17	in] A; [in?] AMS
335.20	the distance] B; this distance AMS
335.26	scenes] A; moments AMS
335.26	these,] A; ~ʌ AMS
†335.28	building] A; build[in?] AMS
335.32	heard] A; head AMS
336.7	this] A; thise AMS
336.8	Indians] A; Indian's AMS
336.16	obtained] B; had obtained AMS
336.18	as well as of] B; no less than AMS; as well as A

336.24	proceeding] A; pr[e?]eding AMS
336.32	observations] A; obserations AMS
336.33	rafts] A; two rafts AMS
336.34	immediately] A; now AMS
337.2	either] A; eithe AMS
337.4	inactivity] B; activity AMS
337.26	shall] A; are now to AMS
338.8	Robert Burns, "It Was a' for our Rightfu King," 11. 7–12] CE; Scottish Ballad AMS
338.27	too] A; was too AMS
339.4	which nature] A; nature AMS
339.21	whose] A; who AMS
339.22	fully] B; had fully AMS
339.27	unusual] A; unsusual AMS
339.27	force] B; strength AMS
339.28	had actually] A; actually AMS
340.5	*mêlée]* A; *mélée* AMS
340.17	conscious] A; as if conscious AMS
340.20	form] B; body AMS
†340.26	consequences.] A; consequenc [es?] ʌ AMS
340.32	Reluctantly] A; Relcutantly AMS
341.29	witnessed] B; had witnessed AMS
342.8	size.] A; ~, AMS
342.12	sufficed] B; had sufficed AMS
342.28	physical] A; physial AMS
342.36	three] A; two AMS
343.5	savages] A; Huron's AMS
343.7	Hurons] A; Huron's AMS
343.18	were] A; were either AMS
343.20	full] A; her AMS
343.24	At] B; It was at AMS
*343.24	instant] CE; instant that AMS
343.25	mountains] B; moutain AMS
343.27	sail. Whatever] A; sail, for, whatever AMS
343.33	opening] A; unfolding AMS
344.1	cover] A; cver AMS
344.6	of the] A; of all the AMS
344.11	movements] B; movement AMS
344.11	The sail being] A; As the sail was AMS
344.12	having] A; had AMS
344.19	exceedingly] A; exceeding AMS
344.20	baffling] A; baffing AMS
344.38	his] B; still his AMS
345.2	was] B; were AMS
345.22	heard] A; heard of AMS
346.1	Hurry's] A; Hurry AMS
†346.6	water.] A; ~ʌ AMS

346.26	between] A; betwen AMS
346.40	a mile]A; miles AMS
†347.5	piles.] A; ∼ʌ AMS
347.26	the man] A; The man AMS
347.31	was dragged] A; dragged AMS
347.32	perceived] A; percieved AMS
348.4	the minute] A; [for?] minute AMS
†348.5	bullet] A; bulle AMS
348.27	postponement] A; postponment AMS
349.10	found] B; they found AMS
349.11	persevered] A; perservered AMS
349.19	manoeuvre] A; manoevere AMS
349.25–26	She . . . expedient] A; Land she did not dare to do, or, if it AMS
349.31	Delaware] A; Dealware AMS
349.35	and began] A; and AMS
349.39	drifted] A; difted AMS
350.19	other two] A; two other AMS
350.23	might] A; first might AMS
*350.25	exhorted] CE; exerted AMS; excited A-B
351.7	it] A; they AMS
351.13	adopt] A; resort to AMS
351.15	being] A; even being AMS
351.23	canoes] A; cannoes AMS
351.29	their] B; the AMS
352.13	in order to] A; to AMS
352.15	flying swiftly] A; flying AMS
352.16	its] A; that of her AMS
352.28	Hutter.] A; ∼ʌ AMS
352.31	*can*] A; can AMS
352.32	sometimes] A; I sometimes AMS
352.39	over the] B; the AMS
†353.5	would] A; w[ou?] AMS
353.6	men,] A; ∼ʌ AMS
353.7	and steering] A; steering AMS
353.7	towards] A; towarsds AMS
353.15	satisfied] A; satified AMS
353.16	encircle] B; circle AMS
353.17	sure] A; certain AMS
353.19	round] B; entirely round AMS
353.19	reached] A; had reached AMS
353.31	father's; he] A; father's, who AMS
353.38	*she*] A; she AMS
354.3	That] B; This AMS
354.4	behind] A; behind them AMS
354.12	heavily] A; forward AMS
354.16	quivering] A; quiving AMS

354.16	veins] A; viens AMS
354.18	he] A; that he AMS
355.6	Charles Wolfe, "The Burial of Sir John Moore," vi] CE; Disputed AMS
†355.11	emotions] A; [emo?]tions AMS
355.23	his] A; this AMS
356.10	father's] A; fathers AMS
356.12	keenness] A; keeness AMS
356.14	perhaps] A; perhabs AMS
356.23	ejaculated] A; ejactulated AMS
356.27	administered] A; adminstered AMS
†356.30	with] A; wit AMS
†356.32	disposed] A; diposed AMS
356.36	relieve] A; releive AMS
357.2	sister's] A; sisters AMS
357.6	suspicions] A; suspicons AMS
357.14	grieved] A; girived AMS
357.16-17	her of] A; of her AMS
357.22	for] A; of AMS
357.28	by] A; on AMS
357.39	read] A; try AMS
358.12	being] A; always being AMS
358.18	abound] A; abounds AMS
358.35	another] A; a another AMS
359.5	aphorisms] A; of aphorisms AMS
359.10	*myself,*] A; ~. AMS
359.11	the others] A; others AMS
†359.12	feel or] A; feel [or?] AMS
359.16-17	bible.] A; ~∧ AMS
359.22	sought] A; sought for AMS
†359.23	stricken] A; strick[e?] AMS
359.37	seemed to her that] A; struck her AMS
359.39	At times] A; Occasionally AMS
360.6	Still] A; Still they AMS
360.12	her] A; them AMS
360.15	was] A; were AMS
360.38	adopted] A; abopted AMS
361.3	upon] A; on AMS
361.18	particular] A; own AMS
361.23-24	him. Though] A; him, for, though AMS
†361.25	watch] A; [w?]atch AMS
361.32	captyve] A; captye AMS
361.33	so] B; as AMS
361.34	glassy] A; glasssy AMS
361.40	louder] A; lowder AMS
361.40	his] A; the AMS
*362.1	'The Snow'] CE; the snow AMS; the Snow A-B

362.3	your] A; you're AMS
*362.17	tired] A; ti[mid?] AMS
362.27	altogether] A; atogether AMS
363.12	politicians] B; politicians of the day, AMS
363.18	their] A; thier AMS
363.21	his hands] B; a hand AMS
363.22	a]A; [te?] AMS
363.28	by] A; away AMS
363.29	canoe,] A; ∼∧ AMS
363.29	so] A; So AMS
364.8	are] A; is AMS
364.8	solemn] A; mysterious AMS
364.9	dispose] A; disposes AMS
364.11	ceased; it] A; ceased, and it AMS
364.13	are] A; is AMS
364.13	they are] A; it is AMS
364.25	beneath] A; benath AMS
364.25	her] A; an AMS
364.28	its] B; his AMS
364.35	steady.] A; ∼∧ AMS
364.38	was] A; seemed AMS
365.2	ceremony] A; scene AMS
365.2	melancholy] A; mlancholy AMS
365.26	farthest] A; fartherest AMS
365.29	placed] A; deposited AMS
365.32	transparency] A; transparancy AMS
365.37	near] A; near by AMS
365.39	in his] A; into his AMS
366.22	sing] A; sing her AMS
366.34	outpourings] A; outporings AMS
367.6	brought] A; had brought AMS
†367.8	concealed.] A; ∼∧ AMS
367.9	revealed] B; had revealed AMS
367.39	minded,] A; ∼∧ AMS
367.40–	
368.1	bending] A; beending AMS
368.4	rightousest] A; righthouest AMS
368.13	necessarily] A; had unavoidably AMS
368.20	distaste] A; distate AMS
368.24	a] A; at AMS
369.1	I suppose] A; suppose AMS
369.4	it's] A; its' AMS
369.4	calculate] A; conclude AMS
369.7	it's] A; its' AMS
*369.24	dazzling—] CE; ∼∧ AMS
369.28	fiery] A; firy AMS
370.13	in. Now] A; in, and now AMS

370.23	*cannot*] B; *can* not AMS
370.31	mischief] A; mishief AMS
370.36	man; and that] B; man. That AMS; man; that A
*370.37	words!"] CE; words! AMS; words." A
370.39	on] B; of AMS
†371.7	most of] A; most [of?] AMS
371.34	reflections] A; refections AMS
371.39	replied] A; seplied AMS
372.4–5	my] A; and acted thus, my AMS
†372.5	different!"] A; diffent ʌ AMS
372.21	every] A; evey AMS
372.24–25	spoke; "I] A; ~ʌʌ~ AMS
372.35–36	(*twice*) gin'ral] B; gineral AMS
374.2	"—That] A; ʌ—~ AMS
374.5	oppressor's. —"] A; ~.—ʌ AMS
374.6	Coleridge, *Remorse*, V.i.201—04.] CE; Coleridge AMS
374.15	than of] B; than AMS
374.18	show] A; wear AMS
374.26	every] A; evey AMS
374.34	and in] A; in AMS
374.36	us;] A; us, and AMS
375.3	said.] A; ~ʌ AMS
375.23	mother] A; moth[er?] AMS
375.26	near;] A; near, and AMS
375.28	told me] A; said AMS
375.29	when] A; now AMS
375.35	that,] A; ~ʌ AMS
375.36	any spirit] A; another AMS
375.38	*her*] A; her AMS
†375.40	either] A; eith[er?] AMS
376.3	murmured] A; murmurmed AMS
†376.16	"No] A; ʌ No AMS
376.23	her] A; her own AMS
376.30	sorely,] A; ~ʌ AMS
†376.32	will marry] A; ill marry AMS
376.37	Yet] A; But yet AMS
*377.4	country] A; county AMS
377.10–11	think of] A; mean AMS
377.13	without] A; with out AMS
377.21	cleverer] A; cleeverer AMS
377.30	manner.—] CE; ~. [—?] AMS; ~. A-B
378.1	was] A; am AMS
378.2	coveted] A; covetted AMS
378.3	yours] A; your AMS
378.6	handsome] A; hadsome AMS
378.23	that] B; this AMS
378.27–28	that spirits] A; spirits AMS

378.30	water,] A; ~. AMS
378.33	heavy] A; great AMS
378.34	she] B; that she AMS
378.34	it;] A; it, and AMS
378.36	parents'] B; parent's AMS
379.5	parents'] A; parent's AMS
379.10	jest] A; gibes AMS
379.17	without] A; with out AMS
380.4–5	benevolence] A; benovelence AMS
380.10	would willingly] A; wuld AMS
°380.32	ourselves."] A; ~ʌ" AMS
*381.8	point,] B; ~ʌ AMS
381.37	had] A; were AMS
381.39	boat] A; canoe AMS
382.16	each other's] A; other's AMS
382.16	side] B; sides, the paddles having ceased their movements AMS
*382.31	fashion—] CE; ~ʌ AMS; ~;—A-B
382.35	to do] A; do AMS
383.7	skrimmage,] A; ~ʌ AMS
383.18	fri'nd] A; fri"[e?]nd AMS
384.1	place] A; leave AMS
384.3	that this] A; that AMS
384.9	furlough] A; furlogh AMS
384.10	Furlough] A; Furlogh AMS
384.10	soldiers] A; soldirs AMS
384.11	signifies] A; means AMS
384.12	prisoner] A; pisoner AMS
384.18	captyve] A; captyve AMS
†384.23	sarcumvention."] A; sarcumventi[on?] AMS
384.26	come] A; go AMS
384.34	extraordinary] A; extraordinay AMS
385.7	believe] A; belive AMS
385.15	else's] A; elses AMS
385.15	Don't] A; Dont AMS
385.21	and as] A; and AMS
385.27	that which] A; that AMS
385.28	Argument,] A; Contention, or argument AMS
386.4	lengthen] A; legthen AMS
386.6	ar'n'd] CE; ar-n'd AMS
386.6	when] A; as soon as AMS
†386.10	prisoner's] A; prisoner'[s?] AMS
386.17	symptoms] A; signs AMS
386.23	had a] B; had AMS
386.27	safe] A; happy AMS
386.29	they] A; you AMS
387.5	Judith] A; But, Judith AMS

387.19	better] A; good AMS
387.19	opportunity."] A; ~. AMS
388.2	"The] A; ʌ~ AMS
388.8	foole."] A; ~.ʌ AMS
388.9	Thomas Churchyard, "Shore's Wife," xlvii] CE; Churchyard AMS
389.13	concern] A; agitation AMS
389.15	individual] A; invidual AMS
389.15–16	making a survey of] B; inquiring into AMS; examining A
389.32	"and] A; and AMS
†389.34	should] A; shoul[d?] AMS
389.39	Tom] A; ~, AMS
390.17	Hurry] A; Harry AMS
390.33	surprise] A; surpise AMS
390.39	we'll] A; we'll talk of this; yes, we'll AMS
390.40	sprightly] A; spightly AMS
391.1	reason;] A; reason, and AMS
391.7	preparations,] A; ~ʌ AMS
391.20	no longer admit of] A; admit of no longer AMS
391.23	could] A; might AMS
*391.28	evening air] A; evening AMS
391.28	motion.] A; ~ʌ AMS
391.34	captyve] A; captyve AMS
392.7	authoritatively] A; authoratively AMS
392.15	to-night] A; to night AMS
392.28	pleasing] A; proud AMS
392.35	to-day] A; to day AMS
392.38	they] A; the AMS
393.2	gin'ral] B; gineral AMS
†393.10	villages] A; village AMS
†393.14	welcome] A; welco[m?] AMS
393.14	howsever] A; however AMS
393.19	his] A; their AMS
393.20	would have] A; would AMS
393.27–28	poor young] A; poor AMS
393.31	it.] A; ~ʌ AMS
394.4	lake;] A; lake, and AMS
394.10	clearin's] A; clearings AMS
394.39	'Deerslayer] A; "~ AMS
395.4	it.' "] A; ~.ʌ" AMS
395.12	safety] A; sacrifice AMS
395.29	company] A; escort AMS
395.35	company] A; escort AMS
395.35	March,] A; ~. AMS
396.6	captain's] A; captai[ns?] AMS
396.11	ar'n'd] CE; a'r'n'd AMS
396.17–18	ignorant as] A; ignorant AMS

396.18	moles; they] A; moles, and AMS
396.20	fall] A; falls AMS
396.20	parents;] A; parents, and AMS
396.22	messengers] A; belts of wampum AMS
396.22	belts of wampum] A; messages AMS
396.24	woods;] A; woods, and which AMS
396.24	carry them] A; carry AMS
396.24	their bosoms] A; branches AMS
396.25	fragrant; they are sweetest when] A; fragant, and most so when fresh AMS
396.27	nests;] A; nests, and AMS
396.30	swamp;] A; swamp, and AMS
396.31	best] A; at least AMS
396.31	water.] A; ∼∧ AMS
397.1	Wah-ta!-Wah] A; Wah-ta-Wah AMS
397.9	suppose,] A; ∼∧ AMS
397.11	ch'ice] B; choice AMS
397.12	ch'ice] B; choice AMS
397.14	*feel*] B; feel AMS
397.14	speakin'] A; speaking AMS
397.15	chatterin'] A; chattering AMS
397.16	comin'] A; coming AMS
†397.25	compliments.] A; compliment[s?] AMS
397.35	act*y*ve] A; actyve AMS
398.9	wolves; they are] A; wolves, but AMS
398.11	women;] A; women, but AMS
398.12	it;] A; it, and AMS
398.15	know] A; hear AMS
398.15	it;] A; it, but AMS
†398.16	understand] A; understa AMS
398.16	terror] A; fear AMS
398.31	burrow] A; burow AMS
398.31	like] A; like like AMS
398.32	hunting] A; hutting AMS
398.33	up; now] A; up, but now AMS
398.35–36	warriors; he can strike] A; warriors, before he strikes AMS
398.38	game;] A; game, and AMS
398.38	they two] A; they AMS
398.38–39	Wah-ta!-Wah] A; Wah-ta-wah AMS
†399.1	"That's] A; ∧∼ AMS
†399.2	in] A; [n?] AMS
†399.3	fairly] A; fair AMS
399.11	purpose;] A; purpose, and AMS
†399.14–15	particular.] A; ∼∧ AMS
399.33	long," interrupted] A; long." Interrupted AMS
399.34	'em] A; them AMS
399.36	ar'n'd] A; a'r'n'd AMS

400.10	*your*] B; your AMS
400.28	meeting] A; conference AMS
401.3	censure] A; reproach AMS
†401.10	observed] A; obs[erved?] AMS
†401.13	now overcame] A; overcame AMS
†401.14	timidity] A; timidity at this sight AMS
401.39	Hurry's] A; Hurry AMS
402.1	wish] A; wih AMS
402.5	prevent it] A; prevent AMS
402.7	passion.] A; passion ʌ AMS
402.8	had] A; had yet AMS
402.10	predilection] A; prediliction AMS
402.18	expected] B; had expected AMS
402.25	acquaintance."] A; ~ʌ" AMS
402.32	most] A; most that AMS
402.37	reasonable-built] A; reasonably built AMS
403.2-3	him only] A; him-only AMS
403.11	adventurers] A; adventures AMS
403.13	deeply] A; heavily AMS
403.17	place] A; spot AMS
403.30	git] A; ge[t?] AMS
403.33	can] A; can it AMS
403.34	gin'ralizing] A; gineralizing AMS
403.38	fall] A; strike AMS
403.39	apt] A; likely AMS
404.8	only can] A; can only AMS
404.10	Vengeful] A; Veangeful AMS
404.15	stop] A; shop AMS
404.18	vulgar] A; vicious AMS
†404.29	for,] A; ~ʌ AMS
404.31	so] A; to AMS
†404.34	lively remorse.] A; passing feeling ʌ AMS
404.36	boat] A; canoe AMS
405.6	or] A; and AMS
405.16	got neither] A; neither AMS
405.20	who] A; that AMS
*405.23	but] CE; said to AMS
405.26	not] A; never AMS
405.34	secretly] A; secretely AMS
406.5	quietly] A; quiety AMS
406.9	on which he floated] A; before him AMS
406.14	basin] A; water AMS
407.6	last."] A; ~ʌ AMS
407.7	Shakespeare, *Rape of Lucrece*, II. 890-94] CE; Rape of Lucrece AMS
407.10	both] A; already AMS
407.16	extraordinary] A; extrordinary AMS

407.21	receive] A; recieve AMS
407.25	in] A; in an AMS
408.9	hoard] A; horde AMS
408.11	But] A; By AMS
408.23	understandings.] A; ~∧ AMS
408.29	desire] A; desirre AMS
408.40	Hetty's] A; Hettys AMS
409.6–7	detarmine] A; detarnine AMS
409.15	bring to light] B; raise AMS
409.16	contained] B; contained from their places AMS
409.33	l'arnin'] A; l'arning AMS
409.38	cloth] A; thing AMS
†409.40	make a] A; make [a?] AMS
409.40	officers] A; offices AMS
410.2	gin'ral's] B; gineral's A; ginerals AMS
†410.3	"A] A; ∧ A AMS
†410.4	about] A; [ab?]out AMS
*410.7	"*Buck-ah-near*] CE; "Buck-and-near A; ["B?]*uck-ah-near* AMS
†410.7	Not] A; [No?]t AMS
†410.9	about] A; out AMS
410.9	its] A; its' AMS
410.11	Lord,] A; ~∧ AMS
410.24–25	Injins] B; Indians A; Indians' AMS
410.35	letters; some] A; letters, and others AMS
410.36	fragments] A; fraggments AMS
410.37	documents] A; documets AMS
410.38	chicken] A; hen AMS
411.22	much] A; much as AMS
411.28	wherever] A; whenever AMS
411.32	found.] A; ~∧ AMS
412.10	Deerslayer] A; ~, AMS
412.15	discovering] A; discoving AMS
*412.31	these melancholy revelations] CE; this melancholy revelations AMS; this melancholy revelation A-B
412.33	to] A; to her AMS
412.34	father] A; parent AMS
413.9	latest] A; last AMS
413.14	Hetty] A; Judith AMS
413.17	life] A; days AMS
413.25	learn] A; read AMS
413.30	Hovey] A; Hutter AMS
413.39	was a] B; was AMS
414.3	had induced] A; induced AMS
414.8	exceeding] A; exceding AMS
414.9	revengeful] A; vengeaful AMS
414.32	it] A; they AMS
415.6	any time] B; at any time AMS

415.12	search,] A; ∿ʌ AMS
415.19	notwithstanding] A; however AMS
416.1	back'ard] A; backward AMS
416.3	them] B; these AMS
416.7	holds,] A; ∿ʌ AMS
416.34	forests] A; forets AMS
416.35	grievous] A; grieous AMS
416.38	pairceive] A; paircieve AMS
417.20	his own] A; his AMS
417.22	proud] A; poud AMS
417.25	anxious] A; as if curious AMS
417.31	person] A; man AMS
418.14	"Bless] A; ʌ∿ AMS
418.16	woods;] A; woods, and AMS
418.23	in finding that] A; at finding AMS
418.30	No, no] A; no AMS
418.33	he's got] A; he get AMS
418.36	of a] A; of AMS
419.5	those] A; them AMS
419.8	air] B; air by its flight AMS
419.27	either in] B; in either AMS
419.32	too] A; to AMS
420.7	will] A; will then AMS
420.22–23	aid her] A; aid AMS
420.23	disinterested] A; disinterestd AMS
†420.30	to-night.] A; to-nigh[t?] AMS
420.32	years,] A; year[s?] AMS
421.17	means covertly] A; means AMS
421.18	heart] A; heart by covert means AMS
421.18	are] A; is AMS
421.23	comeliest] A; comliest AMS
421.28	'arth] A; "arth AMS
421.37	in a] A; in a a AMS
422.5	modest; sure] A; modest. Sure AMS
422.8	mind] A; heart AMS
422.8	hearts] A; feelings AMS
422.8	feel] A; think AMS
422.18–19	a natural] A; gratified AMS
422.20	Judith] A; Judith's AMS
422.25	keenness] A; keeness AMS
423.19	Bumppo, Henry] A; Bumppo, Heny AMS
423.28	evening] A; eving AMS
423.30	sounds] A; sound AMS
423.30	too.] A; ∿ʌ AMS
424.9	to] A; on AMS
424.13	are] A; arve AMS
424.15	company] A; Company AMS

425.1	onworthiness] A; unworthiness AMS
*425.11	sunshine] CE; a sunshine AMS
425.18	altogether] A; altogethe AMS
425.26	without] A; without a AMS
425.29	gave] A; gavve AMS
425.34	she hoped effectually] A; effectually AMS
425.35	person. This scheme] A; person, that AMS
425.37	conversation] A; convesation AMS
425.40	intention] A; purpose AMS
426.2	but of] A; of AMS
426.4	who he was] A; any more AMS
†426.14	be] A; [be?] AMS
†426.16	less] A; ss AMS
†426.18	witted] A; wit[te?]d AMS
426.18	gin'rally] B; ginerally AMS
426.21	to] A; among AMS
426.22	spoke] A; spok AMS
†426.23	parted] A; par[t?]ed AMS
427.3	Athwart] A; Atwhart AMS
427.7	within."] A; ~.ʌ AMS
427.8	Margaret Davidson, "To my Mother," 11. 7–12] CE; Margaret Davidson AMS
427.11	toilet] A; simple toilet AMS
427.13	the] A; her AMS
427.21	the two] B; the AMS
427.28–29	her rest and] A; rest and her AMS
428.2	platform;] A; platform, and AMS
*428.7	was] A; was sat AMS
428.19	Hist; but] A; Hist, and yet AMS
429.7	warriors;] A; warriors, and AMS
429.38	valued] A; great AMS
430.1	Wah-ta!-Wah] A; Wah-ta-Wah AMS
†430.8–9	feelings."] A; ~ʌ" AMS
†430.17	instant] A; insta AMS
430.27	entered into] A; entered AMS
431.3	l'arnin'] A; l'arning AMS
431.13	heavens,] A; ~ʌ AMS
431.13	at other times] A; sometimes AMS
431.18	own,] A; ~ʌ AMS
431.23	used] A; use AMS
431.28	can't] A; cant AMS
432.22	other] A; others AMS
432.27	be] A; is AMS
432.28	if] A; ~, AMS
432.29	yonder] A; younder AMS
433.27	be."] A; ~ʌ" AMS
*433.32	'see] CE; "see AMS; 'See A-B

434.11	in] A; into AMS
434.19	reason. You] A; reason; you AMS
434.24	other's] A; others' AMS
434.37	child's] A; childs AMS
*434.40	means] B; mean A; mean[s?] AMS
435.2	drily] A; proudly AMS
435.5	can] A; shall AMS
435.10	undertaken. But] A; undertaken, but AMS
435.19	running into a strange] A; coming into the AMS
435.20	Hetty] B; Hetty soon AMS
435.22	usual] A; unsusul AMS
435.36	naturally] A; naturall AMS
436.5	for] A; since AMS
436.7	hope] A; hope for AMS
436.16	spirits] A; heart AMS
436.27	ricommend] B; recommend AMS
436.33	believed] A; believe AMS
436.38	girl] A; gril AMS
437.7	he] B; we AMS
437.21	fri'nds,] A; ~ʌ AMS
437.24	otherwise] A; othewise AMS
437.28	The] A; The momentory AMS
437.37	these] A; such AMS
438.4	a hot] A; a a hot AMS
438.7	positively] A; earnestly AMS
438.18	accordin'] A; according AMS *Also emended at* 441.14 *and* 435.34.
438.25	earnestly] A; positively AMS
438.28	ammunition] A; amunition AMS
438.32	you] A; your AMS
439.2	natur'] B; natur AMS
439.6	creatur'] A; creatur AMS
439.23	ra'al missionary] A; ra'a'l missionary AMS
439.36	understand] B; understood AMS
439.38	particular] B; great AMS
440.3	those in which it is now] A; those it is now in AMS
440.34	parfect] B; perfect AMS
440.35	parfect] B; perfect AMS
†440.35–36	respectable] A; respec[t?]able AMS
440.38	touchin'] A; touching AMS
440.38	bein'] A; being AMS *Also emended at* 440.39, 454.40, 455.36, 456.40, 459.12, 459.13 *and* 460.21.
441.2	gift] A; present AMS
441.24	ownership] A; owernership AMS
441.24	to] A; in AMS
441.24	much] A; so much AMS

441.27	its] A; i'ts AMS
†441.27	before] A; befor AMS
441.28	eager] A; eaager AMS
*441.34	you should] A; should AMS
442.5	Indian,] A; ~ₐ AMS
442.8	shoot] A; shoot with AMS
442.10	forlorn] A; folorn AMS
*442.21	into it] A; into AMS
442.27	assisted] A; engaged AMS
442.31	observations,] A; ~. AMS
442.34	at just] A; just at AMS
442.34	hovering] A; hoverng AMS
443.7	to] A; to the AMS
443.10	Deerslayer] A; ~, AMS
443.26	There] A; Here AMS
443.27	he soon] A; there he AMS
443.28	water.] A; ~, AMS
443.32–33	once been] A; once AMS
444.8	the animal] A; it AMS
444.9	and the] A; and AMS
444.11	the head] A; its head AMS
444.19	beautify,] A; ~. AMS
†444.20	'Tis] A; 'Ti[s?] AMS
444.21	husband's] A; husbands AMS
444.24	ra'al] A; ra'a'l AMS *Also emended at* 451.23 *and* 456.39.
444.29–30	a nest] A; the nest AMS
444.34–35	missed its object] A; escaped unhurt AMS
445.13	impossibility] A; impossity AMS
445.19	down, as if] A; down AMS
445.29	the other] B; another AMS
445.33	wings] A; wing AMS
445.34	breast-bone] A; breat-bone AMS
446.2	"Upon] A; ₐ~ AMS
446.9	fainted."] A; ~.ₐ AMS
446.10	Giles Fletcher, *Christ's Victory in Heaven*, I.xv] CE; Giles Fletcher AMS
†446.14	its wings] A; wings AMS
†446.16	destroyers] A; [d?]estroyers AMS
446.17	becomin'] A; becoming AMS
446.17	onthoughtful] A; unthoughtful AMS
†446.18	warriors] A; war[r?]iors AMS
†446.20	and] A; [an?]d AMS
446.21	it's] A; its AMS
†446.21	remember] A; [re?]member AMS
†446.23	Killdeer] A; Kill[de?]er AMS
†446.26	"I know] A; know AMS
†446.27	shall] A; l AMS

†446.28	"If it] A; it AMS
†446.29	well] A; l AMS
446.30	seems;] A; seems, and AMS
†446.31	sight] A; t AMS
446.31	dyin'] A; dying AMS *Also emended at* 450.18 *and* 462.22.
†446.33	don't] A; [t?] AMS
446.34	sets;] A; sets, and AMS
446.35	rej'icin's] A; rej'icings AMS
447.1	praisin'] A; praising AMS
447.8	scarce] A; scare AMS
447.18	must] A; must so AMS
†447.19	travelled] A; travelle[d?] AMS
†447.21	but] A; bu[t?] AMS
448.11	height] A; heighth AMS
448.32	to each] A; with each AMS
448.35	understood,] A; ~ʌ AMS
448.36	sisters] A; sister[s?] AMS
449.9	doin's] A; doings AMS
450.13	not] A; no AMS
†450.21	that] A; tha[t?] AMS
450.33	givin'] A; giving AMS *Also emended at* 494.15, 540.11 *and* 540.12.
450.35	havin'] A; having AMS *Also emended at* 451.22 *and* 452.24.
451.3	bursting] A; busting AMS
451.3	into] A; int AMS
*451.4	feeling, which] A; feeling AMS
451.5	been] A; been long and AMS
451.6	uncontrollable] A; incontrollable AMS
451.6	Deerslayer] A; ~, AMS
451.8	discovered] A; discoverd AMS
451.33	it;] A; it, and AMS
451.34	have found] A; found AMS
451.37	notice] A; witness AMS
452.2	preserve] A; presever AMS
452.19	Wah-ta!-Wah] A; Wah-ta! wah AMS
452.22	side; "you will therefore] A; side, "and therefore will AMS
452.22	onderstand] B; understand AMS
452.22	onlikely] A; likely AMS
452.24	livin'] A; living AMS *Also emended at* 543.36 (*twice*).
452.38	cloudy] A; clowdy AMS
452.40	keepin'] A; keeping AMS
453.5	likin'] A; liking AMS
453.11	counsel] A; council AMS
†453.15	what] A; wha[t?] AMS
†453.25	Indian.] A; ~ʌ AMS
453.29	natur'] A; natur's AMS

453.30	misgivin's] A; misgivings AMS
453.30	consarnin'] A; consarning AMS *Also emended at* 456.26–27 *and* 460.37–38.
453.37	huntin'] A; hunting AMS
453.39	standin'] A; standing AMS
454.8	ra'ally] A; ra'a'lly AMS
454.13	doin'] A; doing AMS
454.13	talkin'] A; talking AMS
454.14	keepin'] A; keeping AMS
454.29	white blood] A; whiteblood AMS
454.37	lettin'] A; letting AMS
454.39	it's] A; its' AMS
455.4	nothin'] A; nothing AMS *Also emended at* 455.35, 457.2, 462.8 *and* 472.31.
455.10	courteously; "they] A; couteously, "but they AMS
†455.10	medicines.] A; medicines ʌ AMS
455.15	Seein'] A; Seeing AMS
455.15	believin'] A; believing AMS
455.17	meanin'] A; meaning AMS
455.22	yieldin'] A; yielding AMS
455.32	refusin'] A; refusing AMS
455.33–34	oncomperhensible] CE; oncomprehensible A; oncompherhensible AMS
455.34	there's] A; ther'e's AMS
455.36	touchin'] A; touching AMS
455.38	outlyin'] A; outlying AMS
†456.1	seems] A; sems AMS
456.7	ones] A; one AMS
456.10	bringin'] A; bringing AMS
456.12	understandin'] A; understanding AMS
456.16	another;] A; another, for AMS
456.20	so?"] A; ~?' AMS
456.23	may;] A; may, and AMS
456.25	lodges."] A; ~.ʌ AMS
456.28	borne] A; born AMS
456.29	burnin's] A; burnings AMS
456.31	longin's] A; longings AMS
456.32	others] A; other's AMS
456.34	owin'] A; owing AMS
456.38	longin's] A; longings AMS
457.4	*all*] A; all AMS
457.7	teachin's] A; teachings AMS
457.35	regret to the girl, herself] A; the girl, herself, regret AMS
457.39	platform.] A; ~, AMS
457.40	agin;] B; ag'in, but AMS; ag'n; A
458.7	slowly] A; next AMS

†458.21	more.] A; ~ₐ AMS
458.23	at] A; in AMS
458.29	arn't] B; are n't AMS
459.5	cap*ty*ves] A; captyves AMS
†459.5	can't] A; [c?]an't AMS
†459.12	your] A; you're AMS
†459.14	foot] A; foo[t?] AMS
459.32	and to] A; and AMS
459.37	in to] A; into AMS
460.2	disapp'intments] A; disap'intments AMS
†460.5	when] A; whe[n?] AMS
460.21	cunnin'est] A; cunningest AMS
460.24	supposin'] A; supposing AMS
460.24	he] A; they AMS
460.29	shall *not*] A; *shall* not AMS
†460.38	matters."] A; ~ₐ" AMS
461.4	forgotten] A; ~, AMS
461.4	soon,] A; ~ₐ AMS
461.7	Then] A; There AMS
461.14	seein'] A; seeing AMS
461.25	t'other] A; 'tother AMS
†461.25	a maiden] A; maiden AMS
*461.32	'love] CE; "~ AMS; ₐ~ A-B
461.33	use'] A; uses" AMS
461.35	likin'] A; liking AMS
†461.38	"That's] A; ["?] ~ AMS
462.10	callin'] A; calling AMS
462.12	has a desperate likin' for] A; is desperately in love with AMS
†462.18	crown] A; [c?]rown AMS
462.22	dyin'] A; dying AMS
462.23	is] A; can be made AMS
462.31	comeliest] A; comliest AMS
462.35	I'll] A; Ill AMS
464.2	"Thou] A; ₐ~ AMS
464.8	Southey, *Roderick, the Last of the Goths*, XXIV, 1–6] CE; Southey AMS
464.11	point,] A; ~. AMS
464.18	Favoured by] A; Owing to AMS
464.24	strand,] A; strand, and AMS
464.25	projection] A; point AMS
465.6	unconsciously] A; unconsiously AMS
465.9	too] A; two AMS
465.18	on a fallen tree] A; to receive him AMS
465.24	looked at] A; regarded AMS
465.35	conclusions] A; judgments AMS
466.9	ancient stem] A; young chief AMS
466.13	at] A; on AMS

466.21	so] A; as AMS
466.27	prepared to commence] A; commenced AMS
466.27–28	the distant waters of Ontario] A; its own region of country AMS
466.31	the fallen] A; a fallen AMS
466.36	more open area] A; precise place AMS
467.6–7	invention] A; hands AMS
467.27	le]A; the le AMS
†468.3	simple] A; [s?]imple AMS
468.9	you] A; your AMS
468.11	gifts] A; giftes AMS
468.15	from] A; to AMS
468.24–25	As . . . rivals] A; As his wisdom and eloquence were confessedly without rivals, in that band AMS
468.26	himself] A; him AMS
468.30	you; we] A; you, and AMS
468.34	thin;] A; thin, and AMS
468.35	your] A; that you AMS
468.39	that] A; but that AMS
469.6	important] A; convincing AMS
469.16	winds; they] A; winds, which AMS
469.24	received] A; recieved AMS
469.25	braggin'] A; bragging AMS
469.28	conference was privately] A; private conference was AMS
470.4	this] A; thi[s?] AMS
470.6	or to] A; or AMS
470.20	openness] A; openess AMS
470.27	dereliction] A; deriliction AMS
470.33	councils] A; counsels AMS
470.35	indolent] A; idolent AMS
471.10–11	fully expected in the course of a few minutes] B; fully, in the course of a few minutes, expected A; fully expected AMS
471.12	and he was] A; in the course of a few minutes, and was AMS
471.22	words; they] A; words, and AMS
471.22	fathers] A; father's AMS
471.24	sun; we] A; sun, and AMS
471.28	gaze] A; garze AMS
471.30	so full as to run] A; full to running AMS
471.31	already; they] A; already, and AMS
471.40	honest;] A; honest, and AMS
472.2	never] A; nev[e?] AMS
472.2	grass;] A; grass, but AMS
472.6	rifle; it] A; rifle, which AMS
†472.8	before] A; befo[re?] AMS
472.11	children;] A; children, and AMS
472.15	told] A; said AMS
472.16	Mingo,] A; ∼∧ AMS

472.20	life.] A; ∿∧ AMS
472.36	it is] A; and AMS
473.9	solicitations] A; solictations AMS
†473.	
15–16	consumed] A; consu[m?] ed AMS
473.20	lifted] A; uplifted AMS
473.20–21	hurled] A; was hurled AMS
473.25	prisoner] A; young man AMS
†473.26	stretched] A; strectc [h?] AMS
473.31	to] A; t AMS
473.37	into] B; to AMS
473.40	bending] A; beending AMS
474.5	circle] A; crowd AMS
474.7	crowd] A; circle AMS
474.11	raised] A; rais[ed?] AMS
474.12	pursuit] A; hot pursuit AMS
†474.24	simple] A; simp[le?] AMS
†474.27	the circumstance] A; [t?]he circumstance AMS
474.28	fishermen] A; fisherman AMS
474.29	termed] A; called AMS
475.13	hand] A; the hand AMS
475.13	the question] A; question AMS
†475.15	Indians] A; India[ns?] AMS
475.18	Deerslayer] A; The fugitive AMS
475.19	precious] A; precous AMS
†475.23	direction] A; [d?]irection AMS
475.27	There, however, he] A; Deerslayer now AMS
475.28	or a] A; or AMS
475.30	knowing] A; knowing that AMS
475.39	parallel] A; paralell AMS
476.2	disappearing] A; disappering AMS
476.7	his] A; [h?] is AMS
†476.3	Deerslayer] A; Deerslay AMS
†476.8	violence] A; ivolence AMS
476.15	height;] A; height, and AMS
476.18	reached] A; reached to AMS
476.19	whole] A; last AMS
476.36	a white] A; the white AMS
476.38	Deerslayer suddenly] A; Deerslayer, now suddenly AMS
476.39	achievement] A; achievment AMS
476.40	hope] A; hope now AMS
477.19	water] A; lake AMS
477.22	surrounded] A; surrouned AMS
477.36	shore] A; lake AMS
477.38	termination.] A; ∿∧ AMS
478.2	reached] A; ached AMS
478.2	gauntlet] A; guantlet AMS

†478.13	endeavoured] A; endeavour[ed?] AMS
478.37	canoe] B; canoes AMS
479.3	enough out] A; enough AMS
479.15	tantalizing] A; tantalyzing AMS
479.17	in the lake] A; of the water AMS
479.25	quietness] A; quiet AMS
479.25–26	inanimate] A; vegetable AMS
479.31	foreboded] A; forboded AMS
479.40	too lately] A; lately AMS
480.1	was] A; was so much AMS
480.11	a shove] A; such shove AMS
480.11	to] A; as to AMS
480.26	purpose] B; purposes AMS
480.26	seats] A; a seat AMS
480.37–38	underrated] A; underated AMS
480.38	In] A; As if in AMS
481.11	peep-hole] A; peep-holes AMS
481.18	entering] A; entered AMS
481.19	and passed] A; passing AMS
481.26	determined] A; determined now AMS
481.31	wind.] A; ~∧ AMS
482.2	orphans'] A; orphans AMS
482.8	repute,] A; ~; AMS
482.12	Congreve, "Pindaric Ode," ii] CE; Congreve AMS
482.14	began] A; beg[u?]n AMS
482.20	stillness] A; ~, AMS
483.16	trouble.] A; ~." AMS
†483.25	that if] A; [t?]hat [i?]f AMS
*483.34	hear reason] A; reason AMS
†483.35	"Speak] A; ["?] Speak AMS
†483.36	answer.] A; ~∧ AMS
484.3	farewell] A; good-bye AMS
484.4	Cervier] A; ~, AMS
484.9	that, next winter,] A; that AMS
484.9	see] A; see, next winter, AMS
484.32	clothes] A; lothes AMS
484.38	surprise] A; suprise AMS
485.5–6	disappeared] A; disappered AMS
†485.26	swimming.] A; ~∧ AMS
485.26	He,] A; ~∧ AMS
*485.30	thrust] CE; thru[st?] AMS; thrown A-B
*485.32	it was] A; they were AMS
485.33 (*twice*)	it] A; them AMS
485.38	murmured] A; mumured AMS
485.38	young] A; yong AMS
†486.1	that] A; [t?]hat AMS
†486.2	and a] A; [an?]d a AMS

486.4	natur'] A; natur', and I'll not repine AMS
486.19	'Thou] A; "~ AMS
486.19	kill!'] A; ~'!" AMS
486.23	which] A; that AMS
†487.19	him?] A; ~ʌ AMS
487.27	weddin's] A; weddings AMS
†487.30	fitting] A; [f?]itting AMS
487.35	prefer] A; perfer AMS
488.17-18	when and where] A; where and when AMS
488.24	shot] B; shot last night AMS
488.24	so that] A; so AMS
488.37	victim] A; victims AMS
489.13	of] A; of any of AMS
†489.15	hemisphere] A; hemisphe[re?] AMS
489.19	acquired] A; imparted AMS
†489.20	birth-right.] A; ~ʌ AMS
489.25	apt] A; clear AMS
489.29	fallacies] A; fallacies plausible in themselves, AMS
489.29-30	any profound or learned] A; his AMS
†489.30	his] A; [h?]is AMS
†489.34	of the] A; [f?] the AMS
489.34	people: he] A; people, The AMS
†489.36	scenes] A; [sc?]enes AMS
489.36	occurred] A; occured AMS
490.7-8	almost hopelessly] A; irretrievably AMS
491.2	is] A; has AMS
491.4	tortur'] A; torture AMS
491.9	*sobriquet*] A; sobriquet AMS
491.26	limbs] A; linds AMS
491.30	legs] B; his legs AMS
491.38	him] B; it AMS
492.10	advance] A; advanced AMS
492.18	sufficiently] A; sufficently AMS
492.21-22	had so recently] A; had AMS
492.22	tribe] A; tribe, so recently AMS
493.4	experienced] A; submitted to AMS
493.8-9	ourselves] A; ourselelves AMS
493.15	clouds] A; clowds AMS
493.34	privileges] A; priviliges AMS
494.1	ag'in] A; ag'in' AMS
494.2	'to] A; "~ AMS
494.3	by.' "] A; ~.ʌ" AMS
494.11	'See] A; "~ AMS
494.12	you.' "] A; ~ʌ." AMS
494.17	becomin'] A; becoming AMS
494.20	See] A; See at AMS
†495.1	wand] A; wan[d?] AMS

†495.4	before] A; befo[re?] AMS
495.17	concealing] A; betraying AMS
495.22	men] A; men now AMS
496.7-8	Thomas Sackville, "The Complaint of Henry Duke of Buckingham," lxxxi.] CE; Lord Dorset AMS
†496.14	death.] A; ~ʌ AMS
†496.26	boldest] A; boldes [t?] AMS
496.29	victim's] A; victims' AMS
497.24	remarkable] A; more remarkable AMS
497.24-25	pretension, rather than] A; pretension than AMS
497.28	no] A; no other AMS
497.29	other than] A; than AMS
497.31	had received] A; received AMS
498.15	he] B; it AMS
498.17	warrior] A; warriors AMS
498.37	nerve] A; nervve AMS
498.37	enabled] A; had enabled AMS
*499.3	unable,] CE; ~ʌ AMS
499.16	actually] A; actual AMS
*499.29	ill-will] CE; good-will AMS
499.34	object] A; objects AMS
500.1	far] A; still AMS
500.2	yet] A; still AMS
500.23	trials] A; exhibition AMS
501.12	it] A; if AMS
501.13	prisoner,] A; prisoner that AMS
501.14	ungovernable] A; ungoverable AMS
501.32	actions] A; feelings AMS
502.9	native] A; own AMS
502.9	Rivenoak] A; Renoak AMS
502.19	war-locks] A; war-lock AMS
502.21	men] A; them AMS
502.27	the fingers] A; their fingers AMS
503.2	a manner] B; manner AMS
503.5	talk] A; think AMS
†503.9	set] A; [s?]et AMS
†503.12	who is] A; who AMS
†503.16	seniors] A; senio[rs?] AMS
503.21	prepared] A; perpared AMS
*503.21	skill.] CE; skill[.?] AMS; skill, A-B
503.37	still] A; secretly AMS
503.40	made; all] A; made. All AMS
503.40	coming] A; came AMS
504.6	causes] A; cause AMS
504.9	other; the] A; other. The AMS
504.12	practice] A; prractice AMS
504.14	each] A; every AMS

504.15	piece] A; pieces AMS
†504.17	the better] A; [th?]e better AMS
†504.23	these] A; the[se?] AMS
504.34	into] B; in AMS
504.35	probably] A; as probably AMS
504.36	have produced] A; produced AMS
505.8	we] A; men AMS
505.9	however] A; ~, AMS
505.11	project] A; object AMS
505.22	fierce] A; firce AMS
505.33	to] A; of AMS
505.37	it] A; it is AMS
505.39	buoyancy] A; bouoyancy AMS
506.4	its] A; all its AMS
506.8	in order] A; as if AMS
506.11	was now] A; now seemed AMS
506.18	females] A; other sex AMS
506.26	She Bear] A; She bear AMS
506.40	Perceiving] A; Percieving AMS
507.1	attempt] A; object AMS
507.7	boy] B; boy of AMS
508.7	spear."] A; ~.ʌ AMS
508.8	Scott, "The Field of Waterloo," V.1-6.] CE; Scott AMS
†508.25	claim] A; cla[im?] AMS
508.31	magical] A; magial AMS
508.32	Nor] A; N[or?] AMS
509.1	detected] A; deteted AMS
509.5	imposing on] A; imposing AMS
509.13	Had] A; H[ad?] AMS
509.18	miscalculated. The] A; miscalculated, and the AMS
509.24	overcome] A; over come AMS
509.28	shone] A; shown AMS
509.29	uniforms] A; uniform AMS
509.30	with] A; to AMS
509.33	which] A; that AMS
509.35	the girl presented] A; presented by the girl AMS
509.37	visiter] A; girl AMS
†509.38	seemed] A; se[md?] AMS
510.1-2	found it was expected that she should] A; found, that she was expected to AMS
510.9	appearance] A; appearance herself AMS
510.23	it] A; them AMS
510.25	flowers] A; flows AMS
510.26	speeches] A; other speeches AMS
510.26	summer] A; the summer AMS
510.28	contributed] B; it contributed AMS
510.32-33	queen] B; the queen AMS

511.11	manifests] A; manifested AMS
511.11	have] A; had AMS
†511.20	sometimes] A; sometim[es?] AMS
511.36	well know] A; know as well as any one AMS
512.6	marked] A; markd AMS
512.12	surrounded] A; surounded AMS
512.21	now that] A; now AMS
512.35	accident,] A; ∼Λ AMS
512.39	so] A; as AMS
513.23	is] A; was AMS
513.26	names] B; name AMS
513.33	he want] B; want AMS
513.35	you answer] A; answer AMS
*514.23	oncommon man] A; oncommon AMS
514.39	yourself.] A; ∼? AMS
515.5	cruelties] B; cruelty AMS
515.12	match] A; that AMS
515.15	'besides"? A; "∼?" AMS
515.20	merely by] A; by merely AMS
515.26	those] A; those that AMS
515.33	lost] A; lost all AMS
515.39	communicated] A; made known AMS
516.4	into] A; in[o?] AMS
°516.13	tree,] A; ∼Λ AMS
516.18	intention] A; intentions AMS
†516.30	tongues] A; tongue[s?] AMS
516.32	stick,] A; ∼Λ AMS
517.1	dearest] A; dearet AMS
517.2	unnerved so much] A; so much unnerved AMS
517.12	more marciful] A; marciful AMS
517.20	busying] A; buysying AMS
†517.21	second] A; secon[d?] AMS
517.21–22	*Indian*] A; Indian AMS
517.29	crowded] A; crowed AMS
517.30	sudden and unlooked-for] A; unexpected and unhoped for AMS
†517.31	instant] A; instan AMS
517.32	in]A; into AMS
517.36	the other] A; Judith AMS
517.38	transferring] A; transfering AMS
518.21	their] A; thir AMS
†518.24	endeavoured] A; endeavoure[d?] AMS
518.25	assiduities] A; assidities AMS
518.28	to his] A; to the AMS
518.29	sympathies] A; sympathis AMS
†518.33	sedulously] A; sedulous[ly?] AMS
†518.36	paint] A; pain AMS

519.2	Briarthorn.] A; ∼? AMS
519.6	no] A; nos AMS
519.19	Briarthorn] A; Briar Thorn AMS
519.29	all] A; all that AMS
520.4	time.] A; ∼, AMS
520.14	which scarcely] A; which AMS
520.14	him] A; him little AMS
520.37	he] A; he now AMS
521.4	farewell] A; adieu AMS
521.19	permitted] A; admitted of AMS
521.27	tread. They] A; tread, they AMS
*521.28	King's] CE; Kings AMS; king's A
521.33	enclosed] A; cornered AMS
521.37	nearly] A; near AMS
522.1	child,] A; ∼∧ AMS
522.1	the covers] A; a cover AMS
522.5	in the] B; in a AMS
†522.6	retiring] A; [r?]etiring AMS
522.7	southern] A; sourthern AMS
522.8	water.] A; wat[or?] AMS
522.11	down both] B; both down AMS
522.20	vengeance] A; veageance AMS
†522.21	of which] A; [of?] which AMS
522.21	occurred] A; occurred even AMS
523.2	"The] A; ∧∼ AMS
523.8	bright."] A; ∼.∧ AMS
523.9	Shelley, "Mutability," 11.1−7.] CE; Shelley AMS
523.21	extraordinary] A; extraordinay AMS
523.32	in and around] A; at, and near, AMS
524.5–6	still to be] A; to be still AMS
524.11	platform] A; platform, too AMS
524.13	reconnoissances] A; reconoissances AMS
524.18–19	the officer] A; the very officer AMS
524.30	it] A; for it AMS
525.1–2	any thing very nourishing] A; a good substantial dinner AMS
525.2	gaping.] A; ∼∧ AMS
525.3	man's] A; mans AMS
525.13	Warley] A; Warly AMS
525.14	companion's] A; companions AMS
525.18	met] A; found AMS
°525.18	her.] A; ∼, AMS
525.19	father] A; fath[er?] AMS
525.22	better than Indian skirmishes in general] A; in true felicity AMS
525.25	with] A; in AMS
525.37	hundredth] A; hundreth AMS

*526.2	Lieutenant General] CE; Lt. General AMS; lieutenant-general A
*526.3	Lieutenant Colonel] CE; Lt. Colonel AMS; lieutenant-colonel A
526.22	some] B; several AMS
526.24	*mêlée*] A; *mélee* AMS
526.28	much] A; all AMS
526.29	was injured] A; he was wounded AMS
526.34	a manner] B; the manner AMS
†526.39	was] A; wa[s?] AMS
†527.4	those] A; tho[se?] AMS
527.17	Edinburgh] A; Edingburgh AMS
527.20-21	was, by birth, a North Briton] A; was a North Briton by birth AMS
527.32	Chairlie] B; Charlie AMS
°528.1	The] A; the AMS
528.26	Hurons] A; Huron AMS
†528.31	soldiers] A; soldie[rs?] AMS
528.32	interrupted] A; interupted AMS
528.34	secret, more, perhaps at such a moment] A; secret at such a moment, perhaps more AMS
528.34	any other] B; another AMS
529.7	indeed] A; in deed AMS
529.14	sister.] A; ~∧ AMS
529.25	Captain] A; Capt. AMS
529.28	even passing] A; passing AMS
529.28-29	then suffering] A; then AMS
529.29	without] A; even without AMS
529.32	*you*] A; you AMS
529.36	who] B; whom AMS
529.36	in] B; of AMS
529.36	whole] A; [w?]hole AMS
530.3	save] A; have saved AMS
530.5	her but] A; but her AMS
†530.26	and] A; [a?]nd AMS
†530.28	concurrence] A; con[cu?]rrence AMS
530.29	"Talk] A; ∧~ AMS
531.6	parted,] A; ~∧ AMS
531.15	uncontrollable] A; incontrollable AMS
531.19	it,] A; ~. AMS
531.21	felt] A; felt that AMS
531.23	but] A; but then AMS
531.23	feeble-minded,] A; feeble-minded that AMS
531.26	if] A; if if AMS
531.30	knees] A; knews AMS
531.33	remembered] A; remember AMS
531.36	though, now I think of it,] A; though AMS

532.4	through] B; through with AMS
532.6	do] A; do next AMS
532.9	time] A; period AMS
532.20	indicated] A; indicates AMS
532.22	was] A; was even AMS
532.23	active.] A; on active ʌ AMS
533.14	we *shall*] A; *we* shall AMS
533.23	but] A; and AMS
533.29	you," sobbed Judith.] A; you." returned Judith." AMS
533.38	over] A; on AMS
533.40	hue] A; tint AMS
533.40	portray] A; resemble AMS
534.12	so awkwardly placed] A; in so awkward a situation AMS
534.31	bound] B; had bound AMS
534.36	character] A; charater AMS
535.8	esteemed] A; valued AMS
535.9	draw] A; draws AMS
535.9	offer] A; offers AMS
536.2	baron's] A; barons AMS
536.6	mayde] A; mayd AMS
536.7	man."] A; ~.ʌ AMS
537.8-9	Thomas Percy, "Notbrowne Mayde," 11.265–76, from *Reliques of Ancient English Poetry*, Vol. II.] CE; Notbrwne Mayde AMS
536.9-10	though one of much activity] A; from a variety of causes AMS
536.12	victims,] A; ~ʌ AMS
536.15	sensation] A; sensation [n?] AMS
536.19	that of] A; that AMS
536.22	he had] A; he AMS
536.27	any] A; any of AMS
536.27	ritual] A; form AMS
536.29	were shed] B; flowed AMS
536.33-4	with wondering eyes and] A; with AMS
536.36	officer] A; [offic?]er AMS
537.10	duty of] A; duty AMS
537.17	broke the silence of] A; was heard on AMS
537.25	reveillé] A; drum AMS
537.26	succeeded] B; had now succeeded AMS
537.32	accompanied] B; had accompanied AMS
537.33	was] B; had been AMS
†537.34	borne] A; born[e?] AMS
537.38	understood by all]A; understood, as a matter of course AMS
537.39	be totally] A; be AMS
538.7	in renewed] A; renewed AMS
538.10	sluggish] A; stately AMS

538.23-24	past . . . dead] A; past the graves of the dead, and at no great distance from them AMS
538.33	answers for] A; meets AMS
538.34	though] A; but AMS
538.38	against her] A; in her AMS
539.10	sun so] A; sun AMS
539.10	eyes] A; eyes so AMS
539.15-16	attention; then] A; attention, and then AMS
539.27	so delight] A; delight only AMS
539.28	believed] A; belived AMS
†539.32	become] A; becom[e?] AMS
540.9	might as well] A; might AMS
540.17	mourn] A; mourn over AMS
*540.19	you is] A; you AMS
540.19	owing] A; due AMS
540.21	which it] A; which AMS
540.23	now that] A; now AMS
540.25	encouragement] A; encouragment AMS
540.28	their] A; the AMS
540.29	rendering] A; rending AMS
540.30	trebly seductive] A; seductive AMS
540.36	and] A; or AMS
540.38	for years] A; years AMS
†541.2	together] A; togethe[r?] AMS
541.10	agreeable] A; agreeably AMS
541.17	not,] A; ~ᴧ AMS
541.38	my] A; my own AMS
542.5	calls] A; call[s?] AMS
542.6	my poor mother] A; mother AMS
542.7	sister."] A; Hetty.ᴧ AMS
542.11	language] A; words AMS
542.19	living] A; lving AMS
542.20	now think] B; think AMS
542.26	me;] A; me, and AMS
543.3	lovely] A; ~, AMS
543.11	completely] A; at once AMS
543.16	shadow] A; feeling AMS
543.17	prevailing] A; prevalent AMS
543.26-27	your own] A; your AMS
543.28	me,] A; me, Deerslayer AMS
†543.29	Deerslayer!"] A; ~!ᴧ AMS
543.33	of] B; in favor of AMS
544.4	obeyed] A; obyed AMS
544.5	her] A; his AMS
544.7	boy.] A; ~ ᴧ AMS

544.10	quietly] A; soon AMS
544.14	bow] A; bows AMS
544.15	the expression of her countenance] B; its expression AMS
544.25	reached] A; reach AMS
544.25	preceded] A; preceeded AMS
544.26	was already] A; was AMS
545.25	succeeding] A; suceeding AMS
545.37	especially] A; particularily AMS
546.2	still] A; a still AMS
546.6	three survivors] A; three AMS
546.7	lake] A; lake in the evening, AMS
546.13	morning] A; day AMS
546.13	youth] A; three AMS
546.19	his bride] A; her person AMS
546.21	there they] A; here were AMS
546.24	summer] A; that region AMS
546.26	sternness] A; sterness AMS
546.32	the attempt] A; its attempt AMS
546.32	exclude them] A; exclude AMS
546.37	elements] A; element, AMS
547.4	elements] A; weather AMS
547.8	may add] A; add AMS
547.16	been left there] A; then been left AMS
547.18	dropped]A; fallen AMS
547.27	the region of their] A; their AMS
547.29	hours] A; scenes AMS
547.30	however,] A; hower ∧ AMS
547.30–31	as stirring] A; [a?]s stirring AMS
547.33	place, where the Indian found a grave] A; place to seek a grave for one of them AMS
547.38	names] A; name AMS
547.39	fortunate] A; well AMS
548.3	of] A; at AMS
548.4	attended] A; had attended AMS
548.6	her−] A; it, and AMS
548.8	succeeded] A; suceeded AMS
548.8	Craigs] A; Craigs' AMS
548.14	some other] A; another AMS
548.15–16	pleasant or profitable] A; pleasant AMS
548.17	otherwise] A; othewise AMS
548.21	crimes] A; sins AMS

Rejected Readings

The following list records all variant readings which appear in the texts subsequent to the accepted reading and which are rejected in the Cooper Edition. The reading accepted in the Cooper Edition appears to the left of the square bracket. The source for that reading appears to the right of the bracket, followed by a semicolon, the variant reading, and its source. All texts which contain rejected readings are cited to the right of the square bracket; texts which are subsequent to the source of the accepted reading and which are not cited may be presumed to agree with the accepted reading. An asterisk indicates that the reading is discussed in the Textual Notes.

Variant readings reported in this list include dialect spellings and obvious compositorial missettings. Variants in punctuation, preferred British spellings (color-colour), and other spellings which do not affect pronunciation are not cited on this list.

The following texts are referred to:

AMS   Author's Manuscript
PR   Proof sheets of the 1841 "Preface"
A   Philadelphia: Lea & Blanchard, 1841
B   New York: G. P. Putnam, 1850

1.18	form now] AMS; now form PR-A
1.21	Their] AMS; The PR-A
16.23	cover] AMS; covers A-B
17.27	lake, itself] AMS; lake A-B
20.5	wallet, lad] AMS; wallet A-B
21.11	deer skin] AMS; deer-skins A-B
21.12	passed] AMS; pass B
21.15–16	to the] AMS; in the A-B
22.31	ginerous] A; generous B
22.36	costs] AMS; cost B
23.14	consart] AMS; consort A-B
23.27	times] AMS; time A-B
23.37	parsons] AMS; persons A-B
24.9	human natur'] AMS; natur' A-B

24.20	There] AMS; Then A-B
25.27-28	to cast even] AMS; even to cast A-B
32.32	calcilate] AMS; calculate A-B
32.32	positions] AMS; position A-B
33.8	here] AMS; ∼, A-B
33.28	parfect] AMS; perfect A-B
*35.15	of its] AMS; its A-B
36.2	void] AMS; view A-B
36.2	wood] AMS; woods A-B
36.27	her] AMS; the A-B
38.7	does not] AMS; doesn't A-B
38.33	git] AMS; get A-B
38.38	fell] AMS; felled A-B
40.17	tennons] AMS; tenons A-B
40.20	tennons] AMS; tenons A-B
40.35	floors] AMS; floor A-B
41.30	in to] AMS; to A-B
43.31	him] AMS; himself A-B
43.34	lesser] AMS; less A-B
45.9	know'd] AMS; knowed B
45.32	times] AMS; time A
45.33	sufficient] AMS; a sufficient B
46.6	the others] AMS; others A-B
46.10	one outlet] AMS; an outlet, A-B
46.13	us. Having] AMS; us, having A-B
46.23	names] AMS; name A-B
46.30	limpid] AMS; as limpid A-B
47.2	thoughts. He] AMS; thoughts, he A-B
48.34	'em] AMS; them A-B
48.35	yet] AMS; as yet A-B
50.18	a grievous sin] AMS; grievous work A-B
51.8	other some] AMS; others come A-B
52.6	often] AMS; after A-B
52.23	gotten] AMS; got B
53.29	is not] AMS; isn't A
54.34	and so] AMS; and A-B
54.36	might be to] AMS; might A-B
56.5	frontier-men from habit] AMS; frontier-men, habitually, A-B
56.7	water,] AMS; ∼ₐ A-B
56.33	instant, and] AMS; instant; A-B
57.22	some sartainty] AMS; sartainty A-B
57.31	lament it, as] AMS; lament; A-B
58.30	true, or] AMS; truer—A-B
59.2	repitation] AMS; reputation B
59.4	miscaculation on] AMS; miscalculation of A-B
59.10	suppersition] AMS; supposition A-B

59.14	you] AMS; your A-B
59.21–22	congergate] AMS; congregate A-B
59.33	natur's] AMS; natur' A-B
60.7	mislead] AMS; misled A-B
60.27	near to] AMS; near A-B
61.14	their place] AMS; the place A-B
61.36–37	watchfulness, "and, depend] AMS; watchfulness; "depend A-B
62.1	other, "and it] AMS; other; "it A-B
62.3	this] AMS; the B
63.13	she then] AMS; she A
64.26	daughters] AMS; daughter B
65.37	at] AMS; on A-B
66.18	infrequent] AMS; unfrequent A-B
66.23	sister's] AMS; sister A-B
68.20	Hetty, again] AMS; Hetty A-B
68.32	appearances] AMS; appearance A
69.8	flaring] AMS; flary A-B
70.2	look'd] AMS; looked B
70.9	feelin'] AMS; feeling B
70.26	he'll] AMS; he B
70.35	exper'ence] AMS; experience B
71.19	misfortinate] AMS; misfortunate A-B
71.28	'lick'] AMS; ʌ~ʌ A-B
72.22–23	riccommend] AMS; ricommend A-B
73.2	was] AMS; were A-B
73.6	messages] AMS; moneys A-B
73.7	fri'ndly] AMS; friendly B
73.22	proceedin's] AMS; procedin's A
75.14	traditions] AMS; tradition A-B
75.15	these] AMS; them A-B
75.22	council] AMS; counsel B
76.5	covers] AMS; cover A-B
77.3–4	apprehensions] AMS; apprehension A-B
77.39	your life] AMS; life A-B
78.24	this tree] AMS; this B
79.16	her] AMS; the A-B *Also rejected at* 91.9, 214.26 *and* 310.19.
81.2	strucken] AMS; stricken A-B
82.37	j'iparday] AMS; jippardy A-B
84.4	as honest] AMS; honest A-B
84.23	garrisons] AMS; garrison A-B
85.4	this borderer] AMS; the borderer A
85.26	braggadocia] AMS; braggadocio A-B
85.31	dispositions] AMS; disposition A-B
85.31	companions] AMS; companion A-B
85.37	scalper's] AMS; scalpers' A-B
87.8	and if] AMS; if A-B

87.29	scalp—] AMS; ~∧ A-B
87.29	fr'inds] AMS; fri'nds, A-B
87.30	rest—] AMS; rest; A-B
87.31	I] AMS; me A-B
87.33	consarns] AMS; concerns B
88.2	can'n't] AMS; can't A-B
88.26	rights] AMS; right B
89.3	keepin'] AMS; keeping A-B
*89.20	Deerslayer's] AMS; and Deerslayer's A-B
89.25	even] AMS; ever A-B
89.26	parsons'] AMS; parson's A-B
89.39	conference] AMS; confidence B
90.12	companions] AMS; companion A-B
90.24	had permitted] AMS; permitted B
90.25	taken] AMS; took B
90.29	had brought] AMS; brought A-B
90.36	tune] AMS; time A-B
91.8	that] AMS; the A-B
91.16	echoes] AMS; shores A-B
92.3	one] AMS; man A-B
93.12	as comely] AMS; so comely A-B
94.10	made her] AMS; made A-B
94.39	cabins] AMS; cabin A-B
95.4	discern] AMS; discover A-B
95.21	for it] AMS; it A-B
96.14	uttered not] AMS; not uttered A-B
96.18	reason unexplained] AMS; unexplained reason A-B
96.21	where] AMS; when A-B
96.37	rumernates] AMS; ruminates A-B
96.38	riccommend] AMS; riccomend B
97.16	errors] AMS; errors of A
97.17	nothing about] AMS; nothing A
97.40	certain] AMS; certain that A-B
*99.14	black water] AMS; water A-B
99.27	reason] AMS; reasons A-B
99.33	'em] AMS; 'm B
100.16	on] AMS; of A-B
100.28	portions] AMS; portion A-B
101.12	ingenuerty] AMS; ingenuity A-B
101.18	interprise] AMS; enterprise A-B
101.20–21	oppertunity] AMS; opportunity A-B
101.33	howsever] AMS; however A-B *Also rejected at* 244.11, 248.13, 320.4, 425.1, *and* 543.36.
101.35	meekly, and] AMS; meekly; A-B
*101.38	uniformly sensitive] AMS; sensitive A-B
102.40	up on] AMS; upon A-B
103.5	lay at] AMS; lay A-B

103.31	as if expecting] AMS; expecting A-B
104.16	this] AMS; the A-B
104.27	down] AMS; round A-B
105.1	and if] AMS; if A-B
105.5	beavers] AMS; beaver A-B
105.5	'rats] AMS; rats A-B
105.9	signs] AMS; sign A-B
106.14	canoes] AMS; canoe A-B
107.16	when] AMS; where A-B
107.23	the shore] AMS; shore A-B
109.36	companions] AMS; companion B
110.9	I'm] AMS; I am B
110.27	all the] AMS; the A-B
111.4	a'nt] AMS; ar'n't A-B
111.31	incourage] AMS; encourage A-B
111.37	this] AMS; the A-B
112.4	hand's] AMS; hand A-B
112.6	understood English sufficiently,] AMS; sufficiently understood English A-B
112.16	after] AMS; when A-B
113.1	last] AMS; lost A-B
114.10	ere] AMS; e'er A-B
114.24	run] AMS; ran A-B *Also rejected at* 118.21, 150.27, 189.19 *and* 519.10.
114.36	drift] AMS; drifts A
116.11	motions] AMS; motives A-B
117.36	then God] AMS; God A-B
118.7	tree] AMS; trees A-B
119.3	brother,] AMS; ~ₐ A
119.13	sometime] AMS; sometimes A-B
119.30	my] AMS; I A-B
120.29	chief] AMS; chiefs A-B
120.33–34	his rifle] AMS; the rifle A-B
121.6	glaring] AMS; glancing A-B
121.29	shoulder] AMS; shoulders A-B
122.7	is not] AMS; isn't A-B
122.29	more] AMS; some A-B
122.30	devils] AMS; devils down A-B
123.20	You're] AMS; You've A-B
124.32	bear] AMS; have A-B
124.34	Get] AMS; He get A-B
124.37–38	lightening] AMS; lightning B
126.11	with] AMS; with the A-B
126.38	delay, and,] AMS; delay B
127.12	seemingly as] AMS; seemingly B
127.24	was] AMS; is B
128.12	swam] AMS; swum A-B

128.39	a distance] AMS; the distance A-B
129.27	another; and] AMS; another; A-B
130.18	pretending,] AMS; ~ₐ A-B
131.15	all the] AMS; the A-B
132.2	incidents] AMS; accidents A-B
132.12	their] AMS; the A-B *Also rejected at* 150.4, 275.13 *and* 339.20.
132.23	emotions] AMS; emotion A-B
132.31	tells] AMS; tells me B
135.15	nations and colours] AMS; nations A
136.28	friends] AMS; friend A-B
136.31	hopes] AMS; hope A-B
137.2	forest life] AMS; life A-B
137.13–14	practise] AMS; practice A-B
138.32	darter] AMS; daughter A-B
139.19	who wanted] AMS; wanted A-B
139.20	Mingo chief] AMS; Mingo A-B
139.23	scout] AMS; scent A-B
139.27	consarn a] AMS; consarns a A-B
139.30	I'd] AMS; I had A-B
140.27	apprehensions] AMS; apprehension A-B
142.1	their] AMS; her A-B
143.15	shade] AMS; shades A-B
143.17	to a] AMS; to A-B
143.18–19	every where] AMS; everywhere A-B
143.27	howsever] AMS; hows'ever A-B
144.1	hows'ever] AMS; how'sever A-B
144.3	well tired] AMS; tired A-B
145.36	as near] AMS; near A
146.10	he's fairly] AMS, he's A
146.24	aids] AMS; aid A-B
149.25	had existed] AMS; existed B
149.35	could] AMS; would A-B
150.11	rock] AMS; rocks A-B
150.35	trees] AMS; tree A-B
151.6	us all] AMS; all A-B
151.31	hughh] AMS; Hugh A-B
152.4	*inertia*] AMS; *inertiæ* A
152.10	but they reach] AMS; still they rush A-B
152.40	sure that] AMS; sure A-B
153.8	signifies] AMS; signifies the A-B
153.10	fri'nd] AMS; friend A-B
153.30	for] AMS; of A-B
153.34	idees] AMS; ideas B
154.14	two deserted] AMS; deserted A-B
154.16	grave] AMS; great A-B
154.36	his effecting] AMS; effecting A-B
154.37	junction] AMS; juncture A

154.39	soon led] AMS; led A-B
155.23	of another] AMS; another A-B
155.30	heighth] AMS; height A-B
155.30	comliness] AMS; comeliness A-B
156.10	great] AMS; good A-B
156.19	a novel] AMS; novel A-B
157.3	give] AMS; gave A-B
157.21	to hear] AMS; so well A
157.28	and] AMS; he A-B
157.35	the laugh] AMS; they laugh B
158.5	them] AMS; these A
158.9	forest] AMS; fresh A-B
159.7	your own] AMS; your A-B
159.31	glory] AMS; honour A-B
160.23	companions] AMS; companion A
161.4	tone] AMS; turn A-B
161.32	track] AMS; tract B
162.17	hard, back] AMS; back hard, A-B
162.37	ye] AMS; you A-B
163.30	see all] AMS; see A-B
163.30	rudeness] AMS; madness A-B
164.28	to make] AMS; make B
164.34	bent] AMS; leant A-B
165.2-3	last been] AMS; been A-B
165.20	released] AMS; relieved A-B
166.6	creaking] AMS; crackling A-B
168.3	companion aft] AMS; companion A-B
170.17	offered] AMS; afforded A-B
171.22	there] AMS; they B
173.15	hind] AMS; hinder A-B
*173.20	alarm, but] AMS; alarm; but A; alarm B
173.23	its feet] AMS; his feet B
175.28	easily followed] AMS; followed A-B
176.17	for] AMS; from A-B
176.21	fader] AMS; father B
177.22	pleased] AMS; please A-B
177.36	mountain] AMS; mountains A-B
*177.36	valley] AMS; valleys B
178.11	claims] AMS; claim A-B
178.17	observations] AMS; observation A-B
179.39	think] AMS; think that B
180.27	P'raps] AMS; P'r'haps A-B
180.36	speaking, and then] AMS; speaking; when A-B
181.1-2	precautions] AMS; precaution A-B
181.13	these] AMS; the A-B
182.25	friend] AMS; friends A-B
184.11	huts, or] AMS; huts— A-B

184.31	little of] AMS; little A-B
186.1	his] AMS; this A
186.23	god] AMS; you A-B
*186.35	them] AMS; these A-B
186.37	proclomation] AMS; proclamation A-B
186.39	pack] AMS; back A
187.15	vartues] AMS; vartue A-B
187.27	crimes] AMS; crime A-B
188.17–18	to whom] AMS; whom A-B
188.18	defer,] AMS; defer to A-B
188.22	person] AMS; presence A-B
188.38	Hetty's] AMS; Hetty A-B
188.38	smallest occurrence] AMS; smaller occurrences A-B
189.28	when] AMS; where A-B
190.8	brethren] AMS; brothers A-B
192.9	in a] AMS; in A-B
192.33	very words] AMS; words B
*193.10	good] AMS; *good* A-B
194.2	these] AMS; they A-B
194.5	hands] AMS; hand A-B
194.9	professes] AMS; profers A-B
194.22	and when] AMS; when B
194.31	Indian] AMS; Indians A-B
194.32	this] AMS; his A-B
195.12	he] AMS; he B
195.34	be] AMS; he be B
195.38	all its] AMS; its B
196.35	its proving] AMS; proving A-B
197.20	of] AMS; on B
199.17	fader] AMS; father A
200.3	breast] AMS; heart A-B
200.6	unshaped] AMS; unsuspected A-B
200.17	disturbances] AMS; disturbance A-B
200.35	it's] AMS; its A
202.7	p'inted] AMS; pointed B
204.9	wonderful] AMS; wonderfully B
204.14	half] AMS; half of A
204.25–26	opinion] AMS; opinions A-B
204.40	commands] AMS; command A-B
205.16	bass woods] AMS; bass-wood A-B
206.5	riprisentyve] AMS; riprisentatyve A-B
*207.11	Tis as] AMS; As A-B
207.15	say] AMS; ~, A-B
207.39	onseemly] AMS; unseemly A-B
207.40	Hetty's] AMS; Hetty A-B
208.11	Those] AMS; These A-B
209.27	had rendered] AMS; rendered B

209.28	began] AMS; begun A-B
*210.35	They] AMS; These A-B
211.6	with] AMS; with a B
211.8	ascendant] AMS; ascendancy A-B
211.32	avow] AMS; owe A-B
212.13	garrisons] AMS; garrison A-B
215.18	there's] AMS; ther's B
215.38	stoops] AMS; stops A-B
216.18	homely] AMS; humble A-B
216.30	offends] AMS; offend A-B
218.20	frontiers] AMS; frontier A-B
219.3	caudle-cup] AMS; candle-cup A
219.16	t'was] AMS; 'Tis A-B
221.3	rifle] AMS; trifle B
221.12	(*twice*) wownded] AMS; wounded A-B
221.14	in to] AMS; into A-B
221.17	her] AMS; to her B
222.14	gotten] AMS; got B
224.11	and like] AMS; like A-B
224.11	have] AMS; and have A-B
224.19	beast] AMS; head A-B
224.26	very deep] AMS; deep A-B
224.30	keenly] AMS; heavily A-B
224.33	those] AMS; these A-B
225.1	comperhends] AMS; comprehends A-B
225.4	'coon] AMS; coon A-B
225.26	iffigies] AMS; effigies A-B
225.27	afore] AMS; before A-B
226.13	all] AMS; and all A-B
226.29	eyes] AMS; eye A-B
228.15	related] AMS; stated A-B
228.20	these] AMS; the A-B
228.23	these] AMS; the A-B
229.30	comperhend] AMS; comprehend A-B
229.31	Canada] AMS; Canadian A-B
231.39–40	negotiations] AMS; negotiation A-B
232.24	way] AMS; ~, A-B
232.34	Iroquois] AMS; the Iroquois A-B
233.2	cheeks] AMS; cheek A-B
234.21	sing] AMS; sing to A-B
235.21	Alway] AMS; Always B
235.34	pale] AMS; pale-face A-B
237.14	maintaining] AMS; his maintaining A-B
239.4	oncommon] AMS; oncommon and A-B
239.15	idee] AMS; idea B
239.24	endivours] AMS; endivour A-B
239.30	sarve] AMS; serve A

240.29	and but] AMS; but B
241.34	them] AMS; the one A-B
243.2	bushes] AMS; the bushes A-B
243.8	tones] AMS; terms A-B
244.24	niver] AMS; never A-B
245.21	prevarication] AMS; prevarications A-B
246.12	he had] AMS; had B
246.24	tones] AMS; terms A-B
246.32	opportunely,] AMS; ~ₐ A-B
247.12	negotiations] AMS; negotiation A-B
248.7	two tail'd] AMS; two-tailed B
248.25	cur'ous] AMS; curious A-B
249.2	forests] AMS; forest, A
249.6-7	then think] AMS; think A-B
249.15	These] AMS; There A-B
249.39	watchfulness, of] AMS; watchfulness on A-B
250.27	two Indians] AMS; Indians A-B
252.7	be where] AMS; where A-B
254.5	blowde] AMS; bloode A-B
254.7	aduersitye] AMS; adversitye A-B
254.8	mee] AMS; me A-B
254.11	contrast to] AMS; contrast A-B
255.8	'em] AMS; them A-B
255.16	she] AMS; that she A-B
255.29	sarvice] AMS; service A
257.7	dicliration] AMS; declaration A
257.14-15	war post] AMS; war-pool A
257.24	lad] AMS; boy A-B
257.32	they'll] AMS; there'll A-B
258.1	spoken] AMS; spoke A
258.37	on] AMS; in A-B
259.20	Hurry] AMS; Harry A-B
260.28	winds] AMS; wind A-B
260.40	true currents] AMS; currents A-B
261.16	Hurry] AMS; Harry A-B
261.25	languages] AMS; language A-B
262.3	you] AMS; your A-B
262.7	women] AMS; ~, A-B
262.10	'em] AMS; them B
262.32	now sought] AMS; sought A-B
264.22	breathings] AMS; breathing A-B
264.25	at] AMS; on A-B
265.4	chiefly been] AMS; been chiefly A-B
266.21	Lord's] AMS; Lord A-B
266.21	minds] AMS; mind B
267.3	laughin'] AMS; laughing A-B
267.7	lovyer] AMS; lover A-B

267.21	act] AMS; are A-B
267.37	not as] AMS; not so A-B
268.33	all was] AMS; was all A-B
269.16	oncommon] AMS; uncommon A-B
269.30	had made] AMS; made B
269.30	reckless, and] AMS; reckless; and A; reckless. B
269.38	fires] AMS; fire's A-B
270.38	least to] AMS; least B
271.1	XVI] AMS; I A
271.15	position] AMS; positions A-B
273.15	sweetheart off] AMS; sweetheart A-B
275.40	little,] AMS; ∼∧ A-B
276.38	lake, but no] AMS; lake. No B
276.39	now] AMS; next A-B
277.1	But Deerslayer₁ AMS; Deerslayer B
277.1	more] AMS; was A-B
278.21	require] AMS; requires A-B
279.7	uses] AMS; use A-B
280.6	for no] AMS; no A-B
280.22	hers] AMS; her A-B
280.22	companion's] AMS; companion A-B
282.19–20	this spot] AMS; the spot B
283.38	peculiar] AMS; consonant A-B
285.16	side] AMS; sides A-B
285.17	but silent] AMS; benevolent A-B
*285.18	so] AMS; too A-B
285.35–36	a stolen] AMS; the stolen A-B
286.13	rallies] AMS; sallies A-B
286.20	arms] AMS; arm A-B
287.14	on the] AMS; on A-B
287.31	darted] AMS; dashed A-B
287.40	getting] AMS; letting A-B
288.1	sprung] AMS; sprang A-B
288.4	dense] AMS; dim A-B
289.1	XVII] AMS; II A
289.20	alarms] AMS; alarm A-B
289.26	first] AMS; faint A-B
293.30	shook] AMS; shaken B
294.13	that] AMS; which B
295.9	the name] AMS; a name A-B
295.10	has] AMS; he has A-B
295.17	shore] AMS; woods A-B
296.12	christian] AMS; a Christian A-B
297.17	sternest] AMS; stoutest A-B
297.28	disparsion] AMS; dispersion B
298.15	parfect] AMS; perfect B
298.23	come] AMS; came A-B

298.24	come] AMS; came A-B
*298.29	Huron] AMS; old Huron A-B
298.36	folk's] AMS; folks' A-B
299.5	now] AMS; soon A-B
*299.6	the warriors] AMS; his warriors A-B
299.11-12	descended to] AMS; descended B
300.1	induce] AMS; induced A-B
300.32	fish] AMS; fool A-B
300.35	prefars] AMS; prefers A-B
301.19	any sarcumventions] AMS; any sarcumvention B
301.35	constitutes] AMS; constituted A-B
303.20	Judith] AMS; your sister A-B
303.20	your sister] AMS; Judith A-B
303.28	Not they] AMS; Nothing A-B
304.11	one as the] AMS; one the A-B
305.15	been] AMS; be B
*305.17	I had] AMS; I'd A-B
306.9	they'd] AMS; they B
308.1	XVIII] AMS; III A
309.5	became] AMS; become A
310.19	her] AMS; the A-B
312.16	heard] AMS; have heard A-B
*312.38	feet] AMS; feel A-B
313.18	remembered] AMS; remember A-B
316.20	swam] AMS; swum A-B
317.31	acclivity] AMS; declivity A-B
319.1	XIX] AMS; IV A
319.17	elder] AMS; eldest A-B
319.28	cupidity] AMS; captivity A-B
320.27	I] AMS; do A-B
320.29	p'int] AMS; point A-B
321.21	of barbarism] AMS; barbarism A-B
323.23	as] AMS; so A-B
324.13	summer] AMS; summer's A-B
324.21	moral] AMS; novel A-B
325.12	reached] AMS; neared A-B
325.32	characters] AMS; character A-B
329.9	sentiment] AMS; sentiments A-B
329.33	eyes] AMS; eye A-B
330.5	he discover] AMS; be discovered A-B
331.7	emotion] AMS; emotions A-B
332.13	defined] AMS; diffused A-B
336.39	squared] AMS; square A-B
337.1	rooms] AMS; room A-B
338.1	XX] AMS; V A
*338.30	an] AMS; or an A
341.16	traditions] AMS; tradition A-B

345.16	judgematical] AMS; judgmatical A-B
*345.33	seemed to be] AMS; seemed A-B
352.3	positions] AMS; position A
352.23	strongest] AMS; stronger A-B
355.1	XXI] AMS; VI A
357.28	coarse] AMS; worn A-B
358.2	virtues] AMS; virtue A-B
358.10	the just] AMS; their just A-B
358.37	narration] AMS; narrative A-B
360.4	of] AMS; of a A
361.1	effect] AMS; an effect B
364.7	offices] AMS; office A-B
364.17	arrogant] AMS; arrogance A-B
365.20	observant,] AMS; ∼∧ A-B
365.20	demeanor] AMS; ∼, A-B
366.6	bitterly, bitterly] AMS; bitterly A-B
369.7	coul'n't] AMS; couldn't A
369.33	unpossible] AMS; impossible A-B
370.12	Harry] AMS; Hurry A
370.30	Ah!] AMS; O A
371.19	the shore] AMS; shore A-B
371.21	is surrounded] AMS; surrounded B
371.35	those] AMS; these A-B
372.15	in you] AMS; you A-B
372.25	party, but] AMS; party; A-B
374.1	XXII] AMS; VII A
375.31	account] AMS; accounts A-B
*376.11	will] AMS; can A-B
377.23	relation] AMS; relations A-B
378.8	men] AMS; man A-B
378.10	and I] AMS; I A-B
378.16	I'm] AMS; I am A-B
380.12	the confiding] AMS; that confiding A-B
380.22-23	said, "for God] AMS; said; "God A-B
381.12	n't] AMS; not A-B
381.17	cannot] AMS; can't A-B
381.20	sister, for] AMS; sister; A-B
381.36	glow] AMS; glare A-B
382.13	nearer] AMS; near A-B
382.18	human] AMS; humane A-B
383.4	savages] AMS; ∼, A-B
383.36	word] AMS; words A-B
383.37	other some] AMS; some others A
384.11	but I] AMS; I A-B
384.22	woul'n't] AMS; couldn't A-B
385.27	as unpretending] AMS; unpretending A-B
386.20	stanch] AMS; staunch A-B

386.36	onbelievers] AMS; disbelievers A-B
386.37	man,] AMS; man A-B
387.17	nat'ral] AMS; natural B
388.1	XXIII] AMS; VIII A
389.6	these] AMS; the A-B
389.17	shops] AMS; shop A
*390.16	man's] AMS; men's A-B
390.17	yes,] AMS; you A-B
390.30	moment, and] AMS; moment; A-B
391.9	ready, and] AMS; ready; A-B
391.19	communication] AMS; communications A-B
391.25	shores] AMS; shore A
391.38	thing of] AMS; thing, or A-B
392.21	plain] AMS; plainly A-B
393.11	him, for] AMS; him A-B
393.15	Hurons, for,] AMS; Hurons; A-B
393.22	past] AMS; put A-B
394.3	called] AMS; call A-B
394.7	York, and] AMS; York; A-B
396.26	martin] AMS; marten A-B
396.37	owned] AMS; roamed A-B
397.5	sprung] AMS; sprang B
397.28	Sarpent] AMS; Serpent A
398.22	of all to] AMS; to all A-B
401.19	they'll] AMS; they'd A
402.12	circumstances] AMS; circumstance A-B
402.18	shrunk] AMS; shrank B
402.18	this] AMS; his A-B
402.33	you'll] AMS; you'd A-B
403.30	gift] AMS; get B
404.21	done, and] AMS; done; A-B
405.15	reason] AMS; names A-B
405.16	reason] AMS; names A-B
405.17	Henry] AMS; Harry A-B
405.23	woods] AMS; words A-B
406.10	a summer's] AMS; summer's A-B
407.1	XXIV] AMS; IX A
407.2	pleasure turns] AMS; pleasures turned A-B
408.8	again,] AMS; and A-B
408.8	all the] AMS; the A-B
408.14	huskily] AMS; hastily A-B
408.20	them] AMS; those A-B
409.39	on] AMS; in A-B
410.8	till] AMS; tell A-B
412.13	served] AMS; seemed A-B
412.26	would] AMS; could A-B
412.32	failing] AMS; failings A-B

413.28	desperation] AMS; dispostion A-B
416.12	caculate] AMS; calculate A-B
416.12	theirn] AMS; theirs A-B
416.13	theirn] AMS; theirs A-B
416.21	thisaway] AMS; this way A-B
417.20	not even] AMS; not A-B
417.37	prefar] AMS; prefer A-B
417.39	judgment] AMS; judge A-B
419.4	Hern] AMS; Her name A-B
419.4	sarve] AMS; serve A
419.22	onless] AMS; unless A-B
419.29	hopelessness] AMS; helplessness A-B
419.35–36	said, "and if] AMS; said; "if A-B
420.14	edicated] AMS; edication A-B
420.20	some thing] AMS; something A-B
420.24	cloaking] AMS; clothing A-B
421.15	of indirectly] AMS; of A-B
421.38	Judith is] AMS; Judith's A-B
423.17	n't] AMS; not A-B
423.39	ind] AMS; end A
424.13	yes, they're] AMS; they're A-B
425.20	apt] AMS; able A-B
426.10	che'rful] AMS; cheerful A-B
426.20	which] AMS; this A-B
427.1	XXV] AMS; X A
427.7	died] AMS; dried A-B
429.22	in such] AMS; in B
430.25	ha'nt] AMS; ha'nts A-B
431.37	see] AMS; know A-B
432.19	women] AMS; woman A-B
432.22	comprehind] AMS; comprehend A-B
432.32	another. It] AMS; another; it A-B
433.18	an't] AMS; ar'n't A-B
433.26	oftener] AMS; often B
434.9	Fire] AMS; fires A-B
434.27	are kind] AMS; kind B
434.37	that is] AMS; that's A-B
435.15	contrivances] AMS; contrivance A-B
435.17	inimy] AMS; inemy A-B
435.21	was] AMS; were A-B
435.26	appetites] AMS; appetite A-B
436.36–37	allusions] AMS; allusion A-B
435.38	thought's] AMS; thoughts A-B
437.40	creatur'] AMS; creature B
438.4	like] AMS; likely A-B
438.11	don't] AMS; didn't A-B
438.22	ricommend] AMS; recommend A-B

439.8	changed,] AMS; ~ A-B
440.1	repitation] AMS; reputation A-B
*441.22	that] AMS; her A-B
441.22	creature] AMS; nature A-B
442.20	results] AMS; result A-B
442.29	a] AMS; an A-B
443.1	dove] AMS; dived B
443.4	swam] AMS; swum A-B
444.22	prejudyce] AMS; prejudice A-B
446.1	XXVI] AMS; XI A
446.23	There] AMS; Here A-B
446.31	piece] AMS; peace B
447.19	forthnight] AMS; fortnight A-B
447.21	forthnight] AMS; fortnight A-B
448.29	this] AMS; the A-B
448.39	hastily, "for I] AMS; hastily; "I A-B
*449.2	feeble-mind] AMS; feeble mind A-B
449.38	inimies] AMS; inemies A
450.11	is in] AMS; is B
450.12	etarnal] AMS; eternal A-B
451.37	Delaware] AMS; Delawares A-B
451.39	blessings] AMS; blessing A-B
452.33	innoculated] AMS; inoculated A-B
453.27	women] AMS; woman A
453.31	like] AMS; likely A-B
454.34	I thank] AMS; Thank A-B
454.37	other some] AMS; others come A-B
454.37	come] AMS; be A-B
454.38	seem to me] AMS; seem B
455.2	his] AMS; the A-B
455.9	mean] AMS; they mean A-B
455.16	comprehind] AMS; comprehend A-B
455.23	I am] AMS; I'm B
456.6	comperhension] AMS; comprehension B
456.39	lights] AMS; light A-B
457.3	exper'ence] AMS; experience B
457.11	wickednesses] AMS; wickedness B
457.34	shrunk] AMS; shrank B
459.8	best] AMS; bark A-B
459.13	I] AMS; my A-B
460.4	atween] AMS; atween a A-B
461.16	know] AMS; knew A-B
461.28	be] AMS; to be B
464.1	XXVII] AMS; XII A
464.4	more] AMS; move A
466.9	their] AMS; the A-B
466.26	matters with those in the Castle] AMS; matters A - B

467.5	shadow] AMS; shadows A-B
470.24	even] AMS; ever A-B
470.36	patience] AMS; impatience B
471.3–4	prospects] AMS; prospect A-B
471.25	wide] AMS; wise A-B
472.19	wouln't] AMS; wouldn't A
475.13	rifles] AMS; rifle A-B
475.38	required] AMS; require A
478.22	water up] AMS; up water A-B
479.9	motions] AMS; motion A-B
480.27	This] AMS; The B
482.1	XXVIII] AMS; XIII A
482.3	invader's] AMS; invaders' B
483.3	the air] AMS; air A-B
484.22	a-way] AMS; away A-B
484.23	prefar] AMS; prefer A-B
485.33	where] AMS; when A-B
486.14	be] AMS; ∼, A-B
487.13	Beside] AMS; Besides A-B
487.22	*that*] AMS; that A-B
488.29	ferocious] AMS; furious A-B
489.34	more] AMS; mere A-B
490.14	thongs] AMS; throngs B
491.4	indivours] AMS; indivors B
491.21	interposed] AMS; interfered A-B
491.33	the hope] AMS; a hope B
492.10	interests] AMS; interest A-B
492.31–32	get transferred to his own nation] AMS; get A-B
492.33	region,] AMS; region, transferred to his own nation A-B
493.10	hands] AMS; hand A-B
493.30	interrupted] AMS; interrupted the A-B
495.9	handsful] AMS; hands'-full A; handfuls B
495.23	older] AMS; elder A-B
496.1	XXIX] AMS; XIV A
496.4	still] AMS; ∼, A-B
498.12	his dodging] AMS; dodging A-B
498.28	skilled] AMS; skilfull A-B
501.4	injuring] AMS; injury A-B
501.8	Gessler's] AMS; Gesler's A-B
502.5	a good] AMS; your A-B
502.33	this] AMS; the A-B
503.25	excitement, the] AMS; excitement. The A-B
504.21	I have] AMS; I've A
504.26	objects] AMS; object A-B
505.3	red men] AMS; red-man A-B
506.28	well as in] AMS; well as A-B
508.1	XXX] AMS; XV A

508.27	feebler] AMS; feeble A-B
510.2	communications] AMS; communication A-B
510.25	of] AMS; in B
510.25	killed all] AMS; killed A-B
511.30	who] AMS; that B
512.3	torture] AMS; tortures A-B
514.23–24	sarcumvention] AMS; sarcumventions A-B
514.28	is] AMS; are A-B
515.18	lower] AMS; low A-B
515.21	their] AMS; the A-B
515.31	contributing] AMS; contributed B
516.34	this] AMS; the A-B
517.7	ind] AMS' end A
517.9	could not] AMS; couldn't A-B
517.28–29	forgotten. Young] AMS; forgotten, and young A-B
519.8	into] AMS; in A-B
519.9	then] AMS; and then B
519.22	chiefs] AMS; chief A-B
519.23	Deerslayer] AMS; The Deerslayer A-B
520.1	having] AMS; having been A-B
520.27	at] AMS; on A-B
521.18	had prevented] AMS; prevented B
523.1	XXXI] AMS; XVI A
523.17	few] AMS; far A-B
523.30	law] AMS; laws A-B
523.30	natures] AMS; nature A-B
524.1	more] AMS; men A-B
524.13	who] AMS; that A-B
526.25	when] AMS; where A-B
526.32	sign] AMS; signs A-B
528.18	glances] AMS; glance A-B
528.39	sad—sad—] AMS; sad A-B
529.16	suffer;] AMS; ~, A-B
529.16	die,] AMS; ~; A-B
529.27	penitence, however,] AMS; penitence A-B
530.40	interrogations] AMS; interrogatories A-B
531.4	adverted] AMS; reverted A-B
531.7	be buried] AMS; buried A-B
532.37	shan't] AMS; sha'n't A-B
532.39	girls] AMS; girl A-B
533.2	you] AMS; and you A-B
533.29	around] AMS; round A-B
534.2	exposure] AMS; expression A-B
534.9–10	affirmative. Then] AMS; affirmative, and then A-B
536.1	XXXII] AMS; XVII A-B
536.4	pore] AMS; poor A-B
537.13	communications] AMS; communication B

539.4	consart] AMS; consort A-B
539.22	sartain] AMS; settled A-B
542.8	here] AMS; having A-B
545.2	their] AMS; the B
*545.21	undue erring] AMS; undeserving A-B
545.33	distinguishing] AMS; distinguished A-B
546.9	washing] AMS; wasting A-B
547.32	careers] AMS; career A-B

Word-Division

List A records compounds or possible compounds which are hyphenated at the end of the line in the copy-text and which have been resolved editorially as hyphenated or unhyphenated. The resolution in the Cooper Edition is indicated by the form in which the compound appears in the List following the page and line numbers of its appearance in the CE text. Information for the preparation of this list was derived mainly from inspection of the treatment of these words and phrases in the manuscript.

List B records compounds or possible compounds which are hyphenated at the end of the line in the final printed text of the Cooper Edition. The editorial resolution, whether the word derives from copy-text or an emendation, is indicated by the form of the word listed.

LIST A

30.27	may-be
40.7	over-rate
46.2	something
48.32	blackguards
52.9	flood-wood
60.20	semi acquatic
68.36	Lap-ear
76.31	otherwise
78.10	over-head
107.24–25	self-possession
115.32	warfare
116.8	warfare
124.32	war-path
152.10	foremost
170.6	dumb-founded
189.38	pale-face
223.1	chess-men
251.31	somewhat
258.14	sledge-hammer
265.36	sometimes
266.13	head-stones

291.28	Hawkeye
306.28	ramrods
443.20	wild-goose
513.24	cat bird
520.23	eagle-eye
539.2	hereafter

LIST B

16.6	loop-holes
28.15	otherwise
29.38	plain-dealing
41.19	overcoming
41.20	sweetheart's
44.17	-the-way
44.24	onquarrelsome
53.6	yourself
54.16	onqualified
54.23	good-natured
61.17	and-bush
64.13	bulletproof
66.32	without
81.20	uppermost
81.29	red-skin
94.37	slow-moving
95.16	good-looking
97.8	good-name
98.16	steering-oar
107.24	self-possession
111.27	settlement-conscienced
117.15	re-loading
122.4	red-skin
135.39	this-a-
136.1	warpath
138.9	heart-felt
139.17	Briarthorn's
139.30	sweet-heart
144.2	-leg-weary
149.13	bee-hives
150.24	warpath
157.25	fierce-looking
168.11	quick-witted
175.32	self-possession
176.39	jet-black
177.38	half-offended
182.9	half-witted

185.16	self-command
208.25	pad-locks
213.28	frank-speaking
239.8	war-path
241.27	grim-looking
245.31	chess-men
249.33	bow-and-
256.27	deerskin
266.7	wind-rows
267.7	way-laying
281.11	back-ground
295.11	stout-hearted
295.15	outwitted
300.20	bull-pout
304.20	good-looking
322.15	paleface
328.27	deerskin
339.12	Glimmerglass
384.34	self-destruction
397.6	heart-felt
399.13	red-skins
401.21	feeble-minded
416.37	war-path
418.3	free-liver
418.19	sunshine
418.35	somewhat
419.21	good-humouredly
424.9	false-tongued
436.28	faint-hearted
437.27	self-command
442.30	Killdeer
449.2	redskins
449.18	red-men
454.17	cannot
470.16	overtaking
480.37	underrated
506.2	woodsman
514.3	yourselves
517.34	self-possession
519.6	wood-chuck
529.35	to-day
529.40	heart-felt